Social Psychology Through Literature

PN
6014
F4

Social Psychology
Through Literature

Edited by RONALD FERNANDEZ
Department of Sociology
Central Connecticut State College

JOHN WILEY & SONS, INC.   *New York · London · Sydney · Toronto*

To My Parents

Preface

This book is the product of both a sense of frustration and a sense of love. The sense of frustration stemmed from my feeling that a purely scientific rendering of social psychology was decidedly not enough. Although my students seemed to grasp the meaning of the material, I always felt that they did not really see the implications of social psychology in their actual lives, that is, outside of the classroom. I hoped that literature would solve this problem. I have used the materials in this book and they help significantly to bridge the gap between science and life. For it is easy to "dig" a Balzac, a Dostoyevsky, or a du Gard; and combining these with Mead and Sullivan and Lewin, one is able to at least partially transcend the severe constraints of the classroom.

The choice of articles is a compromise—a compromise that I reached after a thorough search of most of the textbooks on standard social psychology. Obviously, literature cannot help greatly in statistical analysis or research. The result is a selection of the topics that seem most essential. Naturally, the final choices are a reflection of my own frame of reference.

RONALD FERNANDEZ

Acknowledgments

Although I do not know Lewis A. Coser personally, his book, *Sociology Through Literature,* was the stimulus for this volume. I thank Deborah Offenbacher, who first interested me in social psychology. Chaim Waxman sat through a barrage of questions and provided replies that proved quite helpful. Serge Seminoff of Wiley also provided much necessary aid. But I owe the greatest debt of all to my wife.

R. F.

Contents

ix

Social Psychology Through Literature

Introduction

Social psychology is a fascinating discipline. Very few topics or vital life questions are foreign to it. Motivation, identity, anxiety, and socialization; culture, society, classes, castes, and roles; groups, conformity, power, competition, and conflict—all of these concepts are essential aspects of a social psychological approach. Moreover, a discussion of them raises questions of quite a profound nature. Their questions have led some to assert that man is socially determined, and others to assert that man is free; some to assert that an individual's class position is *the* vital life experience, and others to assert that class is but one of a number of influences which shape human beings; some to assert that man possesses aggressive instincts which make war inevitable, and others to assert that war is a cultural and not a biological phenomenon, and that war is, therefore, most certainly not inevitable.

Clearly, any discipline that raises such fundamental questions is worthy of the student's utmost attention. Usually, however, it is demanded that the study of these very vital processes be handled in a very scientific manner. "There can be no room for subjectivity in the social sciences," we are told; "there can be no room for motives and value judgments which will in any way impair the objectivity of the results. Our investigations must be methodical and rigorous, so that our results are precise and incontestable." Of course, such a view implies that the scientist qua scientist is some sort of controlled and quite rational creature who has somehow been purged of his own bias! Indeed, the attempt to achieve a sense of objectivity reflects the conviction that all other values are subordinate to that *value* which must be considered the most important—the pursuit of scientific truth.

There can be little doubt that this is the proper way for the scientist to approach his discipline. And we can also be certain that it is this method which has led to the insights which form the basis of the social sciences. I only add that it is *by no means* the whole story. For the classroom is representative of a constrained reality, and the laboratory is not indicative of life as it is actually lived. A belief in god, a love for another human being, a passionate affirmation of the state—these are phenomena which lose a great deal in the translation. I would go so far as to state that it is almost impossible to capture their essence in a classroom, a scientific situation. For in analyzing reality we are merely describing it; we are not living it. Unfortunately, the result is a qualitative loss for the student.

I believe that literature can serve us well here. The aim of literature is to depict reality as it is lived, or at least as it should or might be lived. Moreover, when we encounter good literature, when we are dealing with an artist who is really familiar with the essentials of his time, there is no doubt that in some manner we are able to participate with the characters in the interaction being described. And, in the case of a Kazantzakis or a Dostoyevsky, one would almost be correct in asserting that we are the characters in question—that we actually participate in their imagined humanity.

I see literature as a means to be used in the context of a course in the social sciences. It offers a possibility of transcending the severe limitations of the classroom, in order that we might be able to place the insights of the discipline in a light which more closely reflects the reality that is, or has been, or will be— LIVED.

Let me cite an example. Professor Festinger, in a discussion of the concept of cognitive dissonance, writes that "the maximum possible dissonance that can possibly exist between any two elements is equal to the total resistance to change of the less resisting element. The magnitude of dissonance cannot exceed this amount because, at the point of maximum possible dissonance, the less resistant element would change, thus eliminating the dissonance." Now this is a fine point and one that deserves our closest attention; but I suspect that, when it is broached in the classroom, even the most eager student will only have an inkling of what is being said. But if the student were to read of a situation in real life, where the phenomenon discussed was actually occurring, can we not assume that this would enhance the potentialities for his understanding of the concept in question?

This book, for example, contains a splendid example of just what Festinger is referring to. Consider the figure of Antoine Thibault, in du Gard's *The Thibaults*. Antoine, a doctor, is a consultant in a case involving one of his colleagues. The daughter is ill, and it is obvious that she will soon die. The hopelessness, the impossibility of ever relieving the suffering of this quite innocent child struck Antoine. "Confronted with the element of mystery and horror that attends a death agony, he found himself tonight as impotent to curb his anguish as if he were the veriest novice." He was stirred to the depths of his being; his self confidence was shaken, and with it, his confidence in science, in activity, in life itself. Indeed, Antoine (in debating the rights and wrongs of a mercy killing) goes on to say that life is meaningless, and that everything is permitted. In fact, he goes so far as to assert that "nothing is forbidden me! Nothing, provided I don't dupe myself; I know what I am doing and, as far as possible, why I am doing it."

"But, almost at once, a wry smile pursed Antoine's lips." For Antoine knew that all his life he had done just what the society had wanted him to do. Indeed, he is aware of the fact that he not only acts just like everybody else but, coincidentally enough, "in the very way which according to the present code of morals sets him among the best of men." The contradiction, of course, sets Antoine to thinking. For he must reconcile his beliefs about morality with the fact that he did not commit the mercy killing. His solution lies in the conclusion that there is a law of herd morality, "and that it is practically impossible for a man to act as if he were an isolated unit."

Still, such an assertion is not a solution. For Antoine recalls Nietzsche's dictum that a man should not be a problem but the solution of a problem. The difficulty, of course, is that Antoine sees that what he thinks and what he does are not the same. In fact, this insight leads Antoine to wonder: "Can I really be the man I think I am?" Here, however, the dissonance reaches its maximum. For this mere suspicion left Antoine "dazed and startled; it came like a lightning flash and slit the shadows, leaving them darker for its passing. But he was always quick to brush the thought aside and now again he flouted it." He settled instead on a compromise: the belief that conflict is the common rule and that it has always been this way and that it is just the same for everybody else. It is not, certainly, a "real" solution; but it is an efficient elimination of the very painful dissonance.

By concentrating on the concept of dissonance we have singled out but one meaning of this particular passage. In addition, Antoine lives at a specific time in history (the early twentieth century to be exact) and his problems are at least somewhat typical of others who lived at this time. He was socialized in a strongly Catholic home; he informs us, however, that science has undermined his beliefs in that religion and that he is today without a guiding principle. Can we then make the assertion that cognitive dissonance is characteristic of all who, because of their scientific frame of reference, have given up the traditional certitudes? Is being in the modern world really nothingness? Is modern man lost? Is anxiety that pervasive? Naturally, such questions can only be settled—if settled at all— after a thorough investigation of the matters in question. Suffice it here to bring to the reader's attention some of the complex factors that lurked behind Antoine's dissonance. For in fact, although separated analytically, these factors impinge on the actor in their *totality*. Literature helps to bring this out; science, separated from life, succeeds only in blurring it.

In concluding, I reiterate that this approach is intended as a complement to, and not a substitute for, scientific investigation. There is, in my opinion, no substitute for the painstaking analysis that is inevitably necessitated if we are to offer conclusive proof for our assertions. However, I believe that, just as literature can never be a substitute for empirical proof, so too science, in and of itself, can never truly compensate for the limitations that its methods necessitate. The literary artist is one of the few who can help us to do that.

Also, we should not forget that there are other, perhaps more important, advantages to be gained from the use of literature. For, in a period which can envision *Brave New World* and *Walden Two* as distinct possibilities, it is essential to recall that the origins of the social sciences are humanistic. They are rooted in a deep concern about the nature and the potentialities of man. Science serves to blur this concern. Our emphasis on objectivity has become, for all too many of us, an absolute. Literature forces us to come back to man, to remember in fact that the pursuit of scientific truth is primarily a means—a means to the betterment of the human condition. This concern is where the social sciences began; and we must never lose sight of it. For anybody can be a scientist. The real task is to be a truly *human* being.

PART 1

Socialization

Socialization is the process through which we learn the rules of the cultural game in question. Born free of any fixed action patterns, man, to a degree not closely approached by any other animal, depends almost entirely on others for the knowledge he will or will not possess. The family is, of course, the most important institution for the transmission of the cultural heritage, and social psychologists usually refer to family members as significant others. It must not be forgotten, however, that these significant others are also more or less typical representatives of the larger culture. These are my parents; I have no others; but they are also Americans. It is more than likely, then, that I too will be not only my mother and father's son but, in addition, a more or less typical representative of the larger American culture. Consider also that, besides my parents, there are numerous other people—teachers, church leaders, political and military figures—who also ask (and often demand) that I accept the standards which are considered proper. Indeed, socialization is a process which continues throughout the life cycle. The determinism inheres in the fact that the cultural leaders can assume that as an adult I *already* agree with them. They do not have to resocialize, so much as they have to call up the latencies that they assume exist.

The real key to the socialization process, then, is that, having no initial standard of comparison, I internalize (say yes to) these standards as if there were no other alternative. And once I have done this—once I now have an American or a French or a German conscience—we are justified in asserting that I have been "successfully" socialized. Of course, this does not imply any sort of absolute social determinism. The uniqueness of man is rooted in the fact that he can always say *no* to the significant and generalized others who were the vehicles of his association. However, this is an extremely difficult task. No one tells us about alternatives at birth, and a cultural conscience, once formed, is a thing which usually refuses to keep quiet. See *Portnoy's Complaint* for example.

Chapter 1

In this chapter we are concerned with motivation in general. In the first two selections, Kazantzakis presents use with a Saint Francis who is literally "possessed" by his love for God, while Balzac's portrait of Gobseck shows us a figure who is moved, indeed, jet-propelled by his desire for money. Witness Balzac's comment that Gobseck was "a bill of exchange incarnate." The two motives are, of course, universal ones in the history of civilization; in fact, that is precisely why these two readings were chosen. For they highlight the point that while both of these men *are* products of their respective cultures they are also, at the same time, unique personalities. In short, we could not answer the question of why

3

these men acted as they did—for it was *not* typical to be this motivated—unless we know more about the specific influences to which they were subjected.

The selection from Benjamin Constant's *Adolphe* is a brilliant description of self-deception. "For Adolphe uses his intelligence to get what he wants and to avoid or postpone the unpleasant consequences, using ingenious arguments to browbeat self-accusation into acquiescence, to dress up self-interest as prudence or common sense, to transform qualms of conscience into unworthy thoughts over which reason and farsightedness triumph." Adolphe demonstrates, then, the defenses which are necessitated if we cannot, or will not, come to terms with the forces which move us. It might also be interesting to ask whether Adolphe is a free man. For can a man who is so ruled by self-deception be considered free?

Chapter 2

Here we are concerned with the actual acquisition of motives and attitudes. The selection from Joyce describes something we have all been through. Whether Catholic, Protestant, or Jewish, religious, political, or social, we have all been subjected to formalized training. The Joyce passage offers a particularly fine depiction of what this implies for the individual. Stephen will internalize these standards, and he will discover that, try as he might later on in his life, this training, in some form, will *always* be with him.

The selection from *Walden Two,* although certainly not in the same literary class as the other pieces in this book, was included because it highlights what, I believe, is a very significant trend of modern civilization: to wit, the very real possibility that our ever increasing knowledge of man will be used not to free man but, on the contrary, to bind him. Can we accept Castle's contention that the "plan" for *Walden Two* is designed "to keep intelligence on the right track, for the good of society rather than of the intelligent individual—or for the eventual rather than the immediate good." Can any plan decide that? And is this not a reassertion, in "scientific" form, of Rousseau's dictum (in the Social Contract) that we will have "to force men to be free?" Indeed, Professor Skinner, in his *Science and Human Behavior,* wrote that "science implies prediction and, insofar as the relevant variables can be controlled, it implies control."

The selection from *Huckleberry Finn,* although it does not tell us very much about what Huck learned, symbolizes the rather helpless, tightly bound position in which we are all placed at birth. Huck did not ask to have such a father; he just found things that way. And he most certainly did not ask to be locked up; there was little he could do about it though. Hopefully, then, this selection illustrates the fact that birth is an accident. For we are all, at least initially, what others choose to make us. And nobody asked our permission.

Chapter 3

This chapter relates to the concept of identity—broadly, who and what am I?
—and to the anxiety that an individual almost inevitably encounters, particularly
in the modern world, in attempting to answer this most important question. Erik
Erikson writes "that ego identity, in its subjective aspect, is the awareness of the
fact that there is a self sameness and continuity to the ego's synthesizing methods,
the style of one's individuality, and that this style coincides with the sameness
and continuity of one's *meaning for significant others* in the immediate community."[1] Notice, therefore, that in *Demian,* Sinclair, quite early in his life, seems
to have asserted himself by denying the styles and significant others (except for
Demian and Beatrice) who surround him. Moreover, he has had an intensely
personal experience which seems to have opened wholly new vistas to him, "For
he had come home to himself again, even if only as the slave and servant of a
cherished image." And it might also be interesting to ask if it was inevitable
that Sinclair, in his confusion, would find an image. Witness Ortega y Gasset's
comment that "man adapts himself to everything, to the best and the worst. To
one thing only does he not adapt himself: to being not clear in his own mind
concerning what he believes about things."[2]

Antoine Thibault, on the other hand, cannot seem to decide what style he is
following or what his meaning is for others, not to mention himself. Is he really
the ruler of his own actions or is he really nothing but a creature of the bourgeois
herd? Is his style his own or his culture's? And was it inevitable that Antoine,
when faced with contradictions that threatened his identity, would allay the anxiety thus engendered, by self deception?

Kirilov, in *The Possessed,* is broaching problems of monumental significance.
For in his assertion of the "man-god" (not god-man) he is denying to God and
to his representatives the right to have anything at all to do with the style of anyone's individuality. Dostoyevsky characterized this as a "terrible freedom." There
are for example—at least to my knowledge—no really confused individuals in
all of Dostoyevsky's work who are able to solve their identity problems without
the aid of God and, more specifically, Jesus Christ. But the reader might want to
follow Nietzsche in his *Thus Spake Zarathustra* for a different view of the matter.
For taken together the two views (god or no god) are the poles within which
man operates. And they are crucial to a conception of identity. For if I am not
a creation of god, who am I? And where did I come from? And where am I
headed?

[1] Erik Erikson, *Youth, Identity and Anxiety* (New York, 1967), p. 51.
[2] Jose Ortega y Gasset, *Man and Crisis* (New York, 1957), p. 106.

5

Chapter 1

Motivation in Social Behavior

NIKOS KAZANTZAKIS

• *Saint Francis*

I shall not relate here how many days and weeks we worked. How can I remember! The time, raced by like a babbling brook and we babbled along with it, painting, chinking the tiles on the roof, wielding our hammers, trowels, and brushes. Each day the sun rose, mounted to the center of the heavens, set; the evening star appeared in the western sky, night fell, and we climbed up toward Assisi, happy, our hands spattered with cement. . . . The only thing I can say with certainty is that during each of those sacred days and weeks both of us experienced the sense of joy, urgency, and love possessed by the bird that is building its nest; we discovered, for the first time, the true meaning of "nest," "bird," and the exultation of realizing that your insides are filled with eggs! For the rest of our lives those days were to shine out, tender and lavish of grace, as though they had been a period of betrothal, the betrothal of our souls to God.

"What has happened, what has happened, Brother Leo?" Francis asked me one morning as we began work. "Did the world change or did we? I weep, I laugh, and weeping and laughing are the same thing. I believe I'm walking a man's height above the earth, suspended in the air! And what about you, Brother Leo?"

"Me? I believe I'm a caterpillar buried deep down under the ground. The entire earth is above me, crushing me, and I begin to bore through the soil, making a passage to the surface so that I can penetrate the crust and issue into the light. It's hard work boring through the entire earth, but I'm able to be patient

SOURCE. From *Saint Francis* by Nikos Kazantzakis. Copyright 1962, reprinted by permission of Simon and Schuster and Company.

9

because I have a strong premonition that as soon as I do issue into the light I shall become a butterfly."

"That's it! That's it!" shouted Francis joyfully. "Now I understand. God bless you, Brother Leo! We are two caterpillars and we want to become butterflies. So . . . to work! Mix cement, bring stones, hand me the trowel!"

Just as we were finally about to complete the rebuilding of San Damiano's, old Bernardone returned from his trip. He was taken aback when he did not find his son at the shop. Francis came no more to help with the business, but left at dawn, returned after dark, ate all by himself: Bernardone never saw him any more.

"Where does your darling go every morning instead of looking after the shop?" he asked his wife with irritation.

She lowered her gaze, not having the courage to face him directly.

"He had a dream," she answered. "San Damiano—great is his grace—came to him and ordered him to repair the church."

"And so . . . ?"

"He leaves every morning to go and build."

"By himself? With his own two hands?"

"With his own two hands."

"All alone?"

"No, with his friend the beggar."

Sior Bernardone frowned and clenched his fists.

"Your son is taking a bad road, Lady Pica," he said, "and you're the one to blame."

"Me?"

"You. Your blood! You have troubadours in your blood, and scatterbrains, and lunatics—and you know it."

The mother's eyes filled with tears. Bernardone took his walking stick.

"I'm going to go personally to retrieve him," he said. "He hasn't only your blood in him, he has mine also. There's hope for him yet."

He made his appearance at San Damiano's just before noon. His face was somber, his chest heaving from the exertion of the walk. Francis was perched on the church-roof, chinking the tiles. This was the day we were to finish our work, and he was singing troubadour songs in his mother's native tongue with even more gusto than usual.

Bernardone raised his stick. "Hey there, master craftsman," he shouted, "come down, I need you."

"Welcome to Sior Bernardone," answered Francis from high up on the roof. "What do you want?"

"My shop is falling to pieces too. Come down and repair it."

"I'm sorry, Sior Bernardone, but I don't repair shops, I demolish them."

Bernardone let out a howl and banged his stick furiously on the cobblestones of the yard. He wanted to speak but was unable to find the words, and his lips just twisted and turned.

"Come down here at once," he bellowed at last. "I command you to come down! Don't you know who I am? I'm your father."

"Sorry, Sior Bernardone, but my father is God, God and no one else."

"And what about me, then?" called Bernardone, froth coating his lips. Standing in the sun as he was, it was as if smoke were rising from his hair.

"And what about me?" he shouted again. "What am I? Who am I?"

"You are Sior Bernardone, the one who has the big shop on the square in Assisi and who stores up gold in his coffers and strips the people around him naked instead of clothing them."

The priest heard the shouting from his small house and came out. As soon as he saw old Bernardone he understood. Terrified, he stepped forward, reached under his frock, and brought forth the sack of money which Francis had given him to use to buy oil for the saint's lamp.

"This money is yours, Sior Bernardone," he said. "Forgive me. Your son gave it to me, but I haven't touched it."

Without even turning to look at the priest, Bernardone grabbed the sack and thrust it into his ample pocket. Then, brandishing his stick again toward the roof:

"Damn you, come down and get the thrashing you deserve!"

"I'm coming," Francis answered him, and he began to descend.

I put down my trowel and waited to see what would happen.

Shaking the dust and cement from his clothes, Francis started toward his father. Flames were darting from old Bernardone's eyes. He stood there glowering, ready to incinerate the rebellious boy. He did not move, did not speak, but, his stick raised in the air, simply waited for his son to come near him. Francis came, and as he bowed to greet his father, his hands crossed upon his breast, old Bernardone lifted his huge, weighty hand and gave him a strong slap on the right cheek; whereupon Francis turned the other.

"Strike the other cheek, Sior Bernardone," he said calmly. "Strike the other also; or else it might feel offended."

I started to run to my friend's defense, but he held out his hand. "Do not interfere with God's doings, Brother Leo," he said. "Sior Bernardone is helping his son find salvation. . . . Strike, Sior Bernardone!"

At this point old Bernardone became frantic. He raised his stick in order to baste his son squarely over the head, but his hand remained motionless in midair. Francis looked up in surprise. Fat grains of sweat had popped onto Bernardone's forehead, and his lips had turned blue. Fear deformed his face. You felt he was toiling to bring the stick down upon Francis' scalp. But his arm had turned to stone.

Francis saw how his father was staring into the air with protruding eyes, quaking from fright. Some infuriated angel must have swooped down upon the old man and restrained his arm. Francis did not see this angel and neither did I, but both of us heard wings beating angrily in the air.

"It's nothing, Father, nothing," said Francis. "Don't be afraid."

His heart pitied the man. He started to grasp him by the arm, but old Bernardone suddenly swayed and, with a single motion, crumpled onto the cobblestones.

When he came to, the sun was hanging at the zenith, the old priest still clasped the cup of water he had used to sprinkle the unconscious man's temples, and Francis, his head between his palms, was seated cross-legged next to his father and gazing at the sun-drenched flanks of Mount Subasio in the distance.

Old Bernardone sat up and retrieved his stick. I ran to help him rise to his feet, but he dismissed me with a wave of his hand. He got up, exhausted, and wiped away his sweat. Not breathing a word, not so much as glancing either at his son, who was still sitting on the ground, or at the tiny old priest with the cup of water, he shook out his clothes, leaned heavily upon his stick, and started slowly up the hill. Soon he had vanished behind a curve in the road.

That night Francis did not return home. I remained at his side. Searching in the vicinity of San Damiano's some days before, he had found a cave where every so often, abandoning his construction work, he would immure himself for hours on end. He must have spent the time praying, because when he emerged from the cave and returned to take up his work again there would be a nimbus of quivering light encircling his face, just like the halos we see on paintings of the saints: the flame of prayer had abided around his head.

We went to this cave and dragged ourselves inside. It was filled with the odor of damp soil. Placing two stones to serve as pillows, we lay down without eating, without exchanging a single word. I was exhausted and I slept immediately. It must have been already dawn when, waking up, I spied Francis seated at the mouth of the cave, his face wedged between his knees. I heard a persistent, muted murmuring; he seemed to be weeping softly, trying not to wake me up. I was destined many times in the succeeding years to hear Francis weep. But that morning his sobs were like those of an infant who desires to nurse and has no mother.

I crept to the entrance and knelt down next to him, riveting my eyes upon the sky. The stars had already begun to grow dim; several still hung in the milky heavens, and one, the biggest of all, was emitting flashes of green, rose, and blue light.

"Which star is that, Brother Francis?" I asked him to distract his thoughts. "Have you any idea?"

"It must be some archangel," he said, holding back his tears. "Who knows —perhaps the archangel Gabriel. It was such an archangel, gleaming with splendor, that came down one morning and pronounced the 'Hail, Mary.'"

He was quiet for a moment.

"And that star which is so bright—the one you see dancing there in the east and which is about to be smothered by the light of the sun—that is Lucifer!"

"Lucifer!" I exclaimed with surprise. "Why? Why? No, it's not right. He is more brilliant than the archangel Gabriel! Is that the way God punished him?"

"Exactly," answered Francis in a stifled voice. "There is no harsher means of punishment, Brother Leo, than to answer malice with kindness. . . .

"Why are you surprised?" he continued after a moment's silence. "Isn't that what God did with me—with me, vile, wretched, good-for-nothing Lucifer that I am? Instead of hurling down the thunderbolt to reduce me to ashes, one night when I was singing—gorged with food, drunk, debauched—what did He do? He sent San Damiano to me in my sleep and instructed me to place my back beneath the Church. 'It is in danger,' He said. 'Make it firm. I have faith in you.' I believed then that He was speaking about the ruined chapel, and I rebuilt it. But now—"

He sighed. Spreading out his arms, he took a deep breath.

"Now?" I asked, looking at him uneasily.

"Now my heart is still not calm. No, no, He wasn't speaking about the chapel—that is what has been on my mind all night. Brother Leo, I am beginning to understand the terrible hidden meaning."

He was silent.

"Can't I hear it too, Brother Francis? Tell me so that I can rejoice along with you."

"You won't rejoice, poor Brother Leo. No, you won't rejoice; you'll be terrified. Patience—come with me, have faith. Little by little you shall understand, and then you shall begin to weep, and you may even want to turn back. The uphill road is indeed severe. But—who knows?—perhaps by then it will be too late for you to turn back."

I grasped his hand. I wanted to kiss it, but he would not let me.

"Wherever you go I go too, Brother Francis. And I won't ask any more questions either. . . . Lead on!"

We remained silent, watching the ever-increasing light. Little by little the mountainside had turned from purple to rose, then from rose to brilliant white. Olive trees, stones, and soil were laughing. The sun appeared, seated itself on a rocky ledge, and we, at the entrance to the black cave, lifted our arms to greet it.

I rose to go to San Damiano's so that I could gather together our tools, sweep out the church, and put everything in order.

"Give the tools to the old curate," said Francis, "but first kiss them one by one: they did their duty well. We have no further need of them, because the Church that we are going to strengthen now cannot be strengthened with trowels and cement."

I began to open my mouth to ask why, but closed it immediately. One day I shall understand, I said to myself. Let's try and be patient.

"Go, and God be with you," said Francis. "I plan to spend the day here in the cave. I want to implore God—I have so very much to tell Him—I want to implore Him to give me strength. Before me is the abyss. How can I leap across it? And if I do not leap, how shall I ever be able to reach God?"

I departed. It was many years later, when Francis already had one foot in the grave and was preparing to take leave of this life, that I learned what had happened inside the cave that day. He was lying on the bare ground outside the Portiuncula, I remember, and was plagued by the wood mice that came and wanted to devour the little flesh that still remained to him. Unable to sleep, he called me to sit down next to him in order to chase them away, and also to keep him company. It was then, while I sat up with him that night, that he revealed to me what had happened inside the cave.

As soon as he had found himself alone he fell on his face and began to kiss the soil and call upon God. "I know Thou art everywhere," he called to Him. "Under whatever stone I lift, I shall find Thee; in whatever well I look, I shall see Thy face; on the back of every larva I gaze upon, at the spot where it is preparing to put forth its wings, I shall find Thy name engraved. Thou art therefore also in this cave and in the mouthful of earth which my lips are pressing against at this moment. Thou seest me and hearest me and takest pity on me.

"So, Father, listen to what I have to say. Last night in this cave I shouted joyfully: 'I did what Thou instructedst me to do. I rebuilt San Damiano's, made it firm!'

"And Thou answeredst me, 'Not enough!'

" 'Not enough? What more dost Thou wish me to do? Command me!'

"And then I heard Thy voice again: 'Francis, Francis—make Francis firm, rebuild the son of Bernardone!'

"How shall I make him firm, Lord? There are many roads. Which is my road? How shall I conquer the demons within me? They are many, and if Thou dost not come to my aid, I am lost! How can I push aside the flesh, Lord, so that it will not come between us and separate us? You saw for yourself, Lord, how troubled my heart was when I faced the young girl at San Damiano's, how troubled it was when I faced my father. How can I save myself from my mother and father, from women, friends, from comfortable living; and from pride, the yearning for glory, from happiness itself? The number of the mortal demons is seven, and all seven are sucking at my heart. How can I save myself, Lord, from Francis?"

He shouted and raved in this way the entire day, prostrate on the floor of the cave, throbbing convulsively. Toward evening, while I was still making the rounds of Assisi begging for alms, Francis heard a voice above him:

"Francis!"

"Here I am, Lord. Command me."

"Francis, can you go to Assisi—the place where you were born and where everyone knows you—can you go there, stand in front of your father's house and begin to sing, dance, and clap your hands, crying out My name?"

Francis listened, shuddering. He did not reply. Once more he heard the voice above him, but nearer now—in his ear: "Can you trample this Francis underfoot; can you humiliate him? This Francis is preventing our union. Destroy him! The children will run behind you and pelt you with stones; the young ladies will come to their windows and burst out laughing; and you, exultant, dripping with blood from the stoning, will stand your ground and cry, 'Whoever throws one stone at me, may he be once blessed by God; whoever throws two stones at me, may he be twice blessed by God; whoever throws three stones at me, may he be thrice blessed by God.' Can you do that? Can you? Why don't you speak?"

Francis listened, trembling. I can't, I can't, he was saying to himself, but he was ashamed to reveal his thought. Finally he opened his mouth:

"Lord, if I must dance in the middle of the square and cry out Thy name, couldst Thou not send me to some other city?"

But the voice, severe and full of scorn, answered, "No! Assisi!"

Francis' eyes filled with tears. He bit into the soil his lips had been resting upon. "Mercy, Lord," he cried. "Give me time to prepare my soul, to prepare my body. I ask three days of Thee, three days and three nights, nothing more."

And the voice thundered again, no longer in Francis' ear now, but within his bowels: "No, now!"

"Why art Thou in such a hurry, Lord? Why dost Thou wish to punish me so?"

"Because I love you . . ." said God's voice. It was soft now, tender, and it came from within Francis' heart.

Suddenly all the bitterness fled his breast and a force entered him, not his own force, but an omnipotent one. He rose. His face had begun to shine; his knees were firm. He stood for a moment at the entrance to the cave. The sun was about to set.

"I'm going," he said, and he crossed himself.

Just then I returned from my begging, my sack full of stale bread. I saw him standing in the opening of the cave. His face was like the rising sun; it was dazzling, and I had to place my hand over my eyes to shade them. I had planned to say to him: I've brought some bread, Francis; you must be hungry, you haven't had a thing all day, sit down and let's eat. But I was ashamed to say this, because the moment I beheld him I sensed that he had no need of bread.

As soon as he caught sight of me, he raised his hand.

"Let's go," he said.

"Where?"

"To leap!"

Once more I was too timid to ask him to explain. To leap? Over what— and why? I didn't understand. But he started out in front, striding hurriedly over stones and soil, and, together, we made our way to Assisi.

HONORE DE BALZAC

• *Gobseck*

"This adventure," Derville began after a pause, "brings the one romantic event in my life to my mind. You are laughing already," he went on; "it seems so ridiculous, doesn't it, that an attorney should speak of a romance in his life? But once I was five-and-twenty, like everybody else, and even then I had seen some queer things. I ought to begin at the beginning by telling you about some one whom it is impossible that you should have known. The man in question was a usurer.

"Can you grasp a clear notion of that sallow, wan face of his? I wish the *Académie* would give me leave to dub such faces the *lunar* type. It was like silver-gilt, with the gilt rubbed off. His hair was iron-gray, sleek, and carefully combed; his features might have been cast in bronze; Talleyrand himself was not more impassive than this money-lender. A pair of little eyes, yellow as a ferret's, and with scarce an eyelash to them, peered out from under the sheltering peak of a shabby old cap, as if they feared the light. He had the thin lips that you see in Rembrandt's or Metsu's portraits of alchemists and shrunken old men, and a nose so sharp at the tip that it put you in mind of a gimlet. His voice was low; he always spoke suavely; he never flew into a passion. His age was a problem; it was hard to say whether he had grown old before his time, or whether by economy of youth he had saved enough to last him his life.

"This room, and everything in it, from the green baize of his bureau to the strip of carpet by the bed, was as clean and threadbare as the chilly sanctuary of

SOURCE. From *Gobseck* by Honore de Balzac. Volume 10. Copyright 1901, Avil Publishing Company.

some elderly spinster who spends her days in rubbing her furniture. In winter time, the live brands of the fire smouldered all day in a bank of ashes; there was never any flame in his grate. He went through his day, from his uprising to his evening coughing-fit, with the regularity of a pendulum, and in some sort was a clockwork man, wound up by a night's slumber. Touch a wood-louse on an excursion across your sheet of paper, and the creature shams death; and in something the same way my acquaintance would stop short in the middle of a sentence, while a cart went by, to save the strain to his voice. Following the example of Fontenelle, he was thrifty of pulse-strokes, and concentrated all human sensibility in the innermost sanctuary of Self.

"His life flowed soundless as the sands of an hour-glass. His victims sometimes flew into a rage and made a great deal of noise, followed by a great silence; so is it in a kitchen after a fowl's neck has been wrung.

"Toward evening this bill of exchange incarnate would assume ordinary human shape, and his metals were metamorphosed into a human heart. When he was satisfied with his day's business, he would rub his hands; his inward glee would escape like smoke through every rift and wrinkle of his face;—in no other way is it possible to give an idea of the mute play of muscle which expressed sensations similar to the soundless laughter of *Leather Stocking.* Indeed, even in transports of joy, his conversation was confined to monosyllables; he wore the same non-committal countenance.

"This was the neighbor Chance found for me in the house in the Rue des Grès, where I used to live when as yet I was only a second clerk finishing my third year's studies. The house is damp and dark, and boasts no courtyard. All the windows look on the street; the whole dwelling, in claustral fashion, is divided into rooms or cells of equal size, all opening upon a long corridor dimly lit with borrowed lights. The place must have been part of an old convent once. So gloomy was it, that the gaiety of eldest sons forsook them on the stairs before they reached my neighbor's door. He and his house were much alike; even so does the oyster resemble his native rock.

"I was the one creature with whom he had any communication, socially speaking; he would come in to ask for a light, to borrow a book or a newspaper, and of an evening he would allow me to go into his cell, and when he was in the humor we would chat together. These marks of confidence were the results of four years of neighborhood and my own sober conduct. From sheer lack of pence, I was bound to live pretty much as he did. Had he any relations or friends? Was he rich or poor? Nobody could give an answer to these questions. I myself never saw money in his room. Doubtless his capital was safely stowed in the strong rooms of the Bank. He used to collect his bills himself as they fell due, running all over Paris on a pair of shanks as skinny as a stag's. On occasion he could be a martyr to prudence. One day, when he happened to have gold in his pockets, a double napoleon worked its way, somehow or other, out of his fob and fell, and another lodger following him up the stairs picked up the coin and returned it to its owner.

" 'That isn't mine!' said he, with a start of surprise. 'Mine indeed! If I were rich, should I live as I do!'

"He made his cup of coffee himself every morning on the cast-iron chafing dish which stood all day in the black angle of the grate; his dinner came in from a cookshop; and our old porter's wife went up at the prescribed hour to set his room in order. Finally, a whimsical chance, in which Sterne would have seen predestination, had named the man Gobseck. When I did business for him later, I came to know that he was about seventy-six years old at the time when we became acquainted. He was born about 1740, in some outlying suburb of Antwerp, of a Dutch father and a Jewish mother, and his name was Jean-Esther Van Gobseck. You remember how all Paris took an interest in that murder case, a woman named *La belle Hollandaise?* I happened to mention it to my old neighbor, and he answered without the slightest symptom of interest or surprise, 'She is my grandniece.'

"That was the only remark drawn from him by the death of his sole surviving next of kin, his sister's granddaughter. From reports of the case I found that *La belle Hollandaise* was in fact named Sara Van Gobseck. When I asked by what curious chance his grandniece came to bear his surname, he smiled:'

" 'The women never marry in our family.'

"Singular creature, he had never cared to find out a single relative among four generations counted on the female side. The thought of his heirs was abhorrent to him; and the idea that his wealth could pass into other hands after his death simply inconceivable.

"He was a child, ten years old, when his mother shipped him off as a cabin boy on a voyage to the Dutch Straits Settlements, and there he knocked about for twenty years. The inscrutable lines on that sallow forehead kept the secret of horrible adventures, sudden panic, unhoped-for luck, romantic cross events, joys that knew no limit, hunger endured and love trampled under foot, fortunes risked, lost, and recovered, life endangered time and time again, and saved, it may be, by one of the rapid, ruthless decisions absolved by necessity. He had known Admiral Simeuse, M. de Lally, M. de Kergarouët, M. d'Estaing, *le Bailli de Suffren,* M. de Portenduère, Lord Cornwallis, Lord Hastings, Tippoo Sahib's father, Tippoo Sahib himself. The bully who served Mahadaji Sindhia, King of Delhi, and did so much to found the power of the Mahrattas, had had dealings with Gobseck. Long residence at St. Thomas brought him in contact with Victor Hughes and other notorious pirates. In his quest of fortune he had left no stone unturned; witness an attempt to discover the treasure of that tribe of savages so famous in Buenos Ayres and its neighborhood. He had a personal knowledge of the events of the American War of Independence. But if he spoke of the Indies or of America, as he did very rarely with me, and never with any one else, he seemed to regard it as an indiscretion and to repent of it afterwards. If humanity and sociability are in some sort a religion, Gobseck might be ranked as an infidel; but though I set myself to study him, I must confess, to my shame, that his real nature was impenetrable up to the very last. I even felt doubts at times as to his sex. If all usurers are like this one, I maintain that they belong to the neuter gender.

"Did he adhere to his mother's religion? Did he look on Gentiles as his legitimate prey? Had he turned Roman Catholic, Lutheran, Mahometan, Brahmin, or what not? I never knew anything whatsoever about his religious opinions, and so far as I could see, he was indifferent rather than incredulous.

"One evening I went in to see this man who had turned himself to gold; the usurer, whom his victims (his clients, as he styled them) were wont to call Daddy Gobseck, perhaps ironically, perhaps by way of antiphrasis. He was sitting in his armchair, motionless as a statue, staring fixedly at the mantel-shelf, where he seemed to read the figures of his statements. A lamp, with a pedestal that had once been green, was burning in the room; but so far from taking color from its smoky light, his face seemed to stand out positively paler against the background. He pointed to a chair set for me, but not a word did he say.

" 'What thoughts can this being have in his mind?' said I to myself. 'Does he know that a God exists; does he know there are such things as feeling, woman, happiness?' I pitied him as I might have pitied a diseased creature. But, at the same time, I knew quite well that while he had millions of francs at his command, he possessed the world no less in idea—that world which he had explored, ransacked, weighed, appraised, and exploited.

" 'Good day, Daddy Gobseck,' I began.

"He turned his face towards me, with a slight contraction of his bushy, black eyebrows; this characteristic shade of expression in him meant as much as the most jubilant smile on a Southern face.

" 'You look just as gloomy as you did that day when the news came of the failure of that bookseller whose sharpness you admired so much, though you were one of his victims.'

" 'One of his victims?' he repeated, with a look of astonishment.

" 'Yes. Did you not refuse to accept composition at the meeting of creditors until he undertook privately to pay you your debt in full; and did he not give you bills accepted by the insolvent firm; and then, when he set up in business again, did he not pay you the dividend upon those bills of yours, signed as they were by the bankrupt firm?'

" 'He was a sharp one, but I had it out of him.'

" 'Then have you some bills to protest? To-day is the 30th, I believe.'

"It was the first time that I had spoken to him of money. He looked ironically up at me; then in those bland accents, not unlike the husky tones which the tyro draws from a flute, he answered, 'I am amusing myself.'

" 'So you amuse yourself now and again?'

" 'Do you imagine that the only poets in the world are those who print their verses?' he asked, with a pitying look and shrug of the shoulders.

" 'Poetry in that head!' thought I, for as yet I knew nothing of his life.

" 'What life could be as glorious as mine?' he continued, and his eyes lighted up. 'You are young, your mental visions are colored by youthful blood, you see women's faces in the fire, while I see nothing but coals in mine. You have all sorts of beliefs, while I have no beliefs at all. Keep your illusions—if you can. Now I will show you life with the discount taken off. Go wherever you like, or stay at home by the fireside with your wife, there always comes a time when you settle down in a certain groove, the groove of your preference; and then happiness consists in the exercise of your faculties by applying them to realities. Anything more in the way of precept is false. My principles have been various, among various men; I had to change them with every change of latitude. Things that we admire in Europe are punishable in Asia, and a vice in Paris becomes a necessity when you have passed the Azores. There are no such things as hard-and-fast rules; there are only conventions adapted to the climate. Fling a man headlong into one social melting pot after another, and convictions and forms and moral systems become so many meaningless words to him. The one thing that always remains, the one sure instinct that nature has implanted in us, is the instinct of self-preservation. In European society you call this instinct self-interest. If you had lived as long as I have, you would know that there is but one concrete reality invariable enough to be worth caring about, and that is—GOLD. Gold represents every form of human power. I have traveled. I found out that there were either hills or plains everywhere: the plains are monotonous, the hills a weariness; consequently, place may be left out of the question. As to manners; man is man all the world over. The same battle between the poor and the rich is going on everywhere; it is inevitable everywhere; consequently, it is better to exploit than to be exploited. Everywhere you find the man of thews and sinews who toils, and the lymphatic man who torments himself; and pleasures are everywhere the same, for when all sensations are exhausted, all that survives is Vanity—Vanity is the abiding substance of us, the *I* in us. Vanity is only to be satisfied by gold in floods. Our dreams need time and physical means and painstaking thought before they can be realized. Well, gold contains all things in embryo; gold realizes all things for us.

" 'None but fools and invalids can find pleasure in shuffling cards all evening long to find out whether they shall win a few pence at the end. None but driveling idiots could spend time in inquiring into all that is happening around them, whether Madame Such-an-One slept single on her couch or in company, whether she has more blood than lymph, more temperament than virtue. None but the dupes, who fondly imagine that they are useful to their like, can interest themselves in laying down rules for political guidance amid events which neither they nor any one else foresees, nor ever will foresee. None but simpletons can delight in talking about stage players and repeating their sayings; making the daily promenade of a caged animal over a rather larger area; dressing for others, eating for others, priding themselves on a horse or a carriage such as no neighbor can have until three days later. What is all this but Parisian life summed up in a few phrases? Let us find a higher outlook on life than theirs. Happiness consists either in strong emotions which drain our vitality, or in methodical occupation which makes existence like a bit of English machinery, working with the regularity of clockwork. A higher happiness than either consists in a curiosity, styled noble, a wish to learn Nature's secrets, or to attempt by artificial means to imitate Nature to some extent. What is this in two words but Science and Art, or passion or calm?—Ah! well, every human passion wrought up to its highest pitch in the struggle for existence comes to parade itself here before me—as I live in calm. As for your scientific curiosity, a kind of wrestling bout in which man is never uppermost, I replace it by an insight into all the springs of action in man and woman. To sum up, the world is mine without effort of mine, and the world has not the slightest hold on me. Listen to this,' he went on, 'I will tell you the history of my morning, and you will divine my pleasures.'

"He got up, pushed the bolt of the door, drew a tapestry curtain across it with a sharp grating sound of the rings on the rod, then he sat down again.

" 'This morning,' he said, 'I had only two amounts to collect; the rest of the bills that were due I gave away instead of cash to my customers yesterday. So much saved, you see, for when I discount a bill I always deduct two francs for a hired brougham—expenses of collection. A pretty thing it would be, would it not, if my clients were to set *me* trudging all over Paris for half-a-dozen francs of discount, when no man is my master, and I only pay seven francs in the shape of taxes?

" 'The first bill for a thousand francs was presented by a young fellow, a smart buck with a spangled waistcoat, and an eyeglass, and a tilbury and an English horse, and all the rest of it. The bill bore the signature of one of the prettiest women in Paris, married to a Count, a great landowner. Now, how came that Countess to put her name to a bill of exchange, legally not worth the paper it was written upon, but practically very good business; for these women, poor things, are afraid of the scandal that a protested bill makes in a family, and would give themselves away in payment sooner than fail? I wanted to find out what that bill of exchange really represented. Was it stupidity, imprudence, love, or charity?

" 'The second bill, bearing the signature "Fanny Malvaut," came to me from a linen-draper on the highway to bankruptcy. Now, no creature who has any credit with a bank comes to *me*. The first step to my door means that a man is desperately hard up; that the news of his failure will soon come out: and, most of all, it means that he has been everywhere else first. The stag is always at bay when I see him, and a pack of creditors are hard upon his track. The Countess lived in the Rue du Helder, and my Fanny in the Rue Montmartre. How many conjectures I made as I set out this morning! If these two women were not able to pay, they would show me more respect than they would show their own fathers. What tricks and grimaces would not the Countess try for a thousand francs! She would be so nice to me, she would talk to me in that ingratiating tone peculiar to endorsers of bills, she would pour out a torrent of coaxing words, perhaps she would beg and pray, and I . . .' (here the old man turned his pale eyes upon me—'and I not to be moved, inexorable!' he continued. 'I am there as the avenger, the apparition of Remorse. So much for hypotheses. I reached the house.

" ' "Madame la Comtesse is asleep," says the maid.

" ' "When can I see her?"

" ' "At twelve o'clock."

" ' "Is Madame la Comtesse ill?"

" ' "No, sir, but she only came home at three o'clock this morning from a ball."

" ' "My name is Gobseck, tell her that I shall call again at twelve o'clock," and out I went, leaving traces of my muddy boots on the carpet which covered the paved staircase. I like to leave mud on a rich man's carpet; it is not petty spite; I like to make them feel a touch of the claws of Necessity. In the Rue Montmartre I thrust open the old gateway of a poor-looking house, and looked into a dark courtyard where the sunlight never shines. The porter's lodge was grimy, the window looked like the sleeve of some shabby wadded gown—greasy, dirty, and full of holes.

" ' "Mlle. Fanny Malvaut?"

" ' "She has gone out; but if you have come about a bill, the money is waiting for you."

" ' "I will look in again," said I.

" ' "As soon as I knew that the porter had the money for me, I wanted to know what the girl was like; I pictured her as pretty. The rest of the morning I spent in looking at the prints in the shop windows along the boulevard; then, just as it struck twelve, I went through the Countess' antechamber.

" ' "Madame has just this minute rung for me," said the maid; "I don't think she can see you yet."

" ' "I will wait," said I, and sat down in an easy-chair.

" 'Venetian shutters were opened, and presently the maid came hurrying back.

" ' "Come in, sir."

" 'From the sweet tone of the girl's voice, I knew that the mistress could not be ready to pay. What a handsome woman it was that I saw in another moment! She had flung an Indian shawl hastily over her bare shoulders, covering herself with it completely, while it revealed the bare outlines of the form beneath. She wore a loose gown trimmed with snowy ruffles, which told plainly that her laundress' bills amounted to something like two thousand francs in the course of a year. Her dark curls escaped from beneath a bright Indian handkerchief, knotted carelessly about her head after the fashion of Creole women. The bed lay in disorder that told of broken slumber. A painter would have paid money to stay a while to see the scene that I saw. Under the luxurious hanging draperies, the pillow, crushed into the depths of an eider-down quilt, its lace border standing out in contrast against the background of blue silk, bore a vague impress that kindled the imagination. A pair of satin slippers gleamed from the great bear-skin rug spread by the carved mahogany lions at the bed-foot, where she had flung them off in her weariness after the ball. A crumpled gown hung over a chair, the sleeves touching the floor; stockings which a breath would have blown away were twisted about the leg of an easy-chair; while ribbon garters straggled over a settee. A fan of price, half unfolded, glittered on the chimney-piece. Drawers stood open; flowers, diamonds, gloves, a bouquet, a girdle, were littered about. The room was full of vague sweet perfume. And—beneath all the luxury and disorder, beauty and incongruity, I saw Misery crouching in wait for her or for her adorer, Misery rearing its head, for the Countess had begun to feel the edge of those fangs. Her tired face was an epitome of the room strewn with relics of past festival. The scattered gewgaws, pitiable this morning, when gathered together and coherent, had turned heads the night before.

" 'What efforts to drink of the Tantalus cup of bliss I could read in these traces of love stricken by the thunderbolt remorse—in this visible presentment of a life of luxury, extravagance, and riot. There were faint red marks on her young face, signs of the fineness of the skin; but her features were coarsened, as it were, and the circles about her eyes were unwontedly dark. Nature nevertheless was so vigorous in her, that these traces of past folly did not spoil her beauty. Her eyes glittered. She looked like some *Herodias* of da Vinci's (I have dealt in pictures), so magnificently full of life and energy was she; there was nothing starved nor stinted in feature or outline; she awakened desire; it seemed to me that there was some passion in her yet stronger than love. I was taken with her. It was a long while since my heart had throbbed; so I was paid then and there—for I would give a thousand francs for a sensation that should bring me back memories of youth.

" ' "Monsieur," she said, finding a chair for me, "will you be so good as to wait?"

" ' "Until this time to-morrow, madame," I said, folding up the bill again. "I cannot legally protest this bill any sooner." And within myself I said—"Pay the price of your luxury, pay for your name, pay for your ease, pay for the monopoly which you enjoy! The rich have invented judges and courts of law to secure their goods, and the guillotine—that candle in which so many an ignorant moth burns his wings. But for you who lie in silk, under silken coverlets, there is remorse, and grinding of teeth beneath a smile, and those fantastical lions' jaws are gaping to set their fangs in your heart."

" ' "Protest the bill! Can you mean it?" she cried, with her eyes upon me; "could you have so little consideration for me?"

" ' "If the King himself owed money to me, madame, and did not pay it, I should summons him even sooner than any other debtor."

" 'While we were speaking, somebody tapped gently at the door.

" ' "I cannot see any one," she cried imperiously.

" ' "But, Anastasie, I particularly wish to speak to you."

" ' "Not just now, dear," she answered in a milder tone, but with no sign of relenting.

" ' "What nonsense! You are talking to some one," said the voice, and in came a man who could only be the Count.

" 'The Countess gave me a glance. I saw how it was. She was thoroughly in my power. There was a time, when I was young, and might perhaps have been stupid enough not to protest the bill. At Pondicherry, in 1763, I let a woman off, and nicely she paid me out afterwards. I deserved it; what call was there for me to trust her?

" ' "What does this gentleman want?" asked the Count.

" 'I could see that the Countess was trembling from head to foot; the white satin skin of her throat was rough, "turned to goose flesh," to use the familiar expression. As for me, I laughed in myself without moving a muscle.

" ' "This gentleman is one of my tradesmen," she said.

" 'The Count turned his back on me; I drew the bill half out of my pocket. After that inexorable movement, she came over to me and put a diamond into my hands. "Take it," she said, "and be gone."

" 'We exchanged values, and I made my bow and went. The diamond was quite worth twelve hundred francs to me. Out in the courtyard I saw a swarm of flunkeys, brushing their liveries, waxing their boots, and cleaning sumptuous equipages.

" ' "This is what brings these people to me!" said I to myself. "It is to keep up this kind of thing that they steal millions with all due formalities, and betray their country. The great lord, and the little man who apes the great lord, bathes in mud once for all to save himself a splash or two when he goes afoot through the streets."

" 'Just then the great gates were opened to admit a cabriolet. It was the same young fellow who had brought the bill to me.

" ' "Sir," I said, as he alighted, "here are two hundred francs, which I beg you to return to Mme. la Comtesse, and have the goodness to tell her that I hold the pledge which she deposited with me this morning at her disposition for a week."

" 'He took the two hundred francs, and an ironical smile stole over his face; it was as if he had said, "Aha! so she has paid it, has she? . . . Faith, so much the better!" I read the Countess' future in his face. That good-looking, fair-haired young gentleman is a heartless gambler; he will ruin himself, ruin her, ruin her husband, ruin the children, eat up their portions, and work more havoc in Parisian salons than a whole battery of howitzers in a regiment.

" 'I went back to see Mlle. Fanny in the Rue Montmartre, climbed a very steep, narrow staircase, and reached a two-roomed dwelling on the fifth floor. Everything was as neat as a new ducat. I did not see a speck of dust on the furniture in the first room, where Mlle. Fanny was sitting. Mlle. Fanny herself was a young Parisian girl, quietly dressed, with a delicate fresh face, and a winning look. The arrangement of her neatly brushed chestnut hair in a double curve on her forehead lent a refined expression to blue eyes, clear as crystal. The broad daylight streaming in through the short curtains against the window pane fell with softened light on her girlish face. A pile of shaped pieces of linen told me that she was a sempstress. She looked like a spirit of solitude. When I held out the bill, I remarked that she had not been at home when I called in the morning.

" ' "But the money was left with the porter's wife," said she.

" 'I pretended not to understand.

" ' "You go out early, mademoiselle, it seems."

" ' "I very seldom leave my room; but when you work all night, you are obliged to take a bath sometimes."

" 'I looked at her. A glance told me all about her life. Here was a girl condemned by misfortune to toil, a girl who came of honest farmer folk, for she had still a freckle or two that told of country birth. There was an indefinable atmosphere of goodness about her; I felt as if I were breathing sincerity and frank innocence. It was refreshing to my lungs. Poor innocent child, she had faith in something; there was a crucifix and a sprig or two of green box above her poor little painted wooden bedstead; I felt touched, or somewhat inclined that way. I felt ready to offer to charge no more than twelve per cent, and so give something towards establishing her in a good way of business.

" ' "But maybe she has a little youngster of a cousin," I said to myself, "who would raise money on her signature and sponge on the poor girl."

" 'So I went away, keeping my generous impulses well under control; for I have frequently had occasion to observe that when benevolence does no harm to him who gives, it is the ruin of him who takes. When you came in I was thinking that Fanny Malvaut would make a nice little wife; I was thinking of the contrast between her pure, lonely life and the life of the Countess—she has sunk as low as a bill of exchange already, she will sink to the lowest depths of degradation before she has done!'—I scrutinized him during the deep silence that followed, but in a moment he spoke again. 'Well,' he said, 'do you think that it is nothing to have this power of insight into the deepest recesses of the human heart, to embrace so many lives, to see the naked truth underlying it all? There are no two dramas alike: there are hideous sores, deadly chagrins, love scenes, misery that soon will lie under the ripples of the Seine, young men's joys that lead to the scaffold, the laughter of despair, and sumptuous banquets. Yesterday it was a tragedy. A worthy soul of a father drowned himself because he could not support his family. To-morrow is a comedy; some youngster will try to re-hearse the scene of M. Dimanche, brought up to date. You have heard people extol the eloquence of our latter day preachers; now and again I have wasted my time by going to hear them; they produced a change in my opinions, but in my conduct (as somebody said, I can't recollect his name), in my conduct—never!— Well, well; these good priests and your Mirabeaus and Vergniauds and the rest of them, are mere stammering beginners compared with these orators of mine.

" 'Often it is some girl in love, some gray-headed merchant on the verge of bankruptcy, some mother with a son's wrongdoing to conceal, some starving artist, some great man whose influence is on the wane, and, for lack of money, is like to lose the fruit of all his labors—the power of their pleading has made me shudder. Sublime actors such as these play for me, for an audience of one, and they cannot deceive me. I can look into their inmost thoughts, and read them as God reads them. Nothing is hidden from me. Nothing is refused to the holder of the purse-strings to loose and to bind. I am rich enough to buy the consciences of those who control the action of ministers, from their office boys to their mistresses. Is not that power?—I can possess the fairest women, receive their softest caresses; is not that Pleasure? And is not your whole social economy summed up in terms of Power and Pleasure?

" 'There are ten of us in Paris, silent, unknown kings, the arbiters of your destinies. What is life but a machine set in motion by money? Know this for certain—methods are always confounded with results; you will never succeed in separating the soul from the senses, spirit from matter. Gold is the spiritual basis of existing society. The ten of us are bound by the ties of common interest; we meet on certain days of the week at the Café Thémis near the Pont Neuf, and there, in conclave, we reveal the mysteries of finance. No fortune can de-ceive us; we are in possession of family secrets in all directions. We keep a kind of Black Book, in which we note the most important bills issued, drafts on pub-lic credit, or on banks, or given and taken in the course of business. We are the Casuists of the Paris Bourse, a kind of Inquisition weighing and analyzing the most insignificant actions of every man of any fortune, and our forecasts are infallible. One of us looks out over the judicial world, one over the financial, another surveys the administrative, and yet another the business world. I myself keep an eye on eldest sons, artists, people in the great world, and gamblers—on the most sensational side of Paris. Every one who comes to us lets us into his neighbor's secrets. Thwarted passion and mortified vanity are great babblers. Vice and disappointment and vindictiveness are the best of all detectives. My colleagues, like myself, have enjoyed all things, are sated with all things, and have reached the point when power and money are loved for their own sake.

" 'Here,' he said, indicating his bare, chilly room, 'here the most high-mettled gallant, who chafes at a word and draws swords for a syllable elsewhere, will entreat with clasped hands. There is no city merchant so proud, no woman so vain of her beauty, no soldier of so bold a spirit, but that they entreat me here, one and all, with tears of rage or anguish in their eyes. Here they kneel —the famous artist, and the man of letters, whose name will go down to posterity. Here, in short' (he lifted his hand to his forehead), 'all the inheritances and all the concerns of all Paris are weighed in the balance. Are you still of the opinion that there are no delights behind the blank mask which so often has amazed you by its impassiveness?' he asked, stretching out that livid face which reeked of money.

"I went back to my room, feeling stupefied. The little, wizened old man had grown great. He had been metamorphosed under my eyes into a strange visionary symbol; he had come to be the power of gold personified. I shrank, shuddering, from life and my kind.

" 'Is it really so?' I thought; 'must everything be resolved into gold?'

"I remember that it was long before I slept that night. I saw heaps of gold all about me. My thoughts were full of the lovely Countess; I confess, to my shame, that the vision completely eclipsed another quiet, innocent figure, the figure of the woman who had entered upon a life of toil and obscurity; but on the morrow, through the clouds of slumber, Fanny's sweet face rose before me in all its beauty, and I thought of nothing else."

BENJAMIN CONSTANT

- *Adolphe*

Chapter Ten

I felt calmer for the next few days, having postponed indefinitely the
necessity to act. This necessity no longer haunted me like a spectre and I thought
I had plenty of time to prepare Ellenore. I meant to be kinder and more affectionate to her so as to preserve at any rate memories of friendship. My worry was
quite different from what I had felt hitherto. I had implored Heaven for some
insurmountable obstacle to come between Ellenore and me. This obstacle had
now arisen and I looked upon Ellenore as a being I was about to lose. The
tyranny I had so often found unbearable had ceased to have any terrors for me,
for I felt freed in advance, and hence found more freedom in giving way to her
still more, and felt none of that inner revolt which had formerly made me want
to tear everything to pieces. All my impatience had gone, and in its place there
was an unacknowledged desire to postpone the fateful moment.

Ellenore noticed that I was more affectionate and demonstrative, and she
became less bitter herself. I welcomed conversations I had previously avoided
and appreciated her loving words which so recently had irritated me, for now
that each time might be the last they had become precious.

One evening we had separated after a more than usually delightful talk. The
secret I kept locked in my heart made me sad but not excessively so. The very
uncertainty of the date of the separation I had been wishing for helped to keep

SOURCE. From *Adolphe* by Benjamin Constant. Translated by L. W. Tancock. Copyright
1964, reprinted with the permission of Penguin Books Limited.

the thought of it out of my mind. In the middle of the night I heard an unusual noise going on in the house, but it suddenly stopped, and I dismissed it
from my mind. In the morning, however, I thought about it again, and wondering what the reason was I made for Ellenore's room. To my utter astonishment I was told that for the past twelve hours she had been in a raging fever,
that a doctor sent for by her servants had declared her life in danger, and that
she had strictly forbidden my being informed or allowed to go to her.

I tried to insist. The doctor himself came out to impress upon me the
necessity of not exciting her in any way. He did not know the reason for the
order she had given, but put it down to her desire not to alarm me. I anxiously
tried to find out from the servants what could have plunged her so suddenly
into such a dangerous condition. After leaving me on the previous evening, I was
told, she received a letter brought from Warsaw by a man on horseback, and
as soon as she opened it and read it she fainted. On regaining consciousness she
flung herself upon her bed and refused to utter a word. One of her maids, worried by her agitated condition, stayed in the room without her knowing, and
towards midnight saw her overcome by a fit of trembling which shook the bed.
The maid wanted to send for me, but Ellenore forbade this with a kind of terror
so violent that nobody dared disobey. A doctor was sent for, but Ellenore refused,
and was still refusing, to answer him. All night long she uttered disconnected
words that nobody could understand, and often she clapped her handkerchief to
her mouth as though to prevent herself from speaking.

While I was being told all this another woman who had remained near
Ellenore ran out panic-stricken. Ellenore seemed to have lost the use of her
senses. She could not see anything round her. Sometimes she uttered piercing
screams and repeated my name; then, horrified, would make a gesture as if
asking for something hateful to be kept from her.

I went in. At the foot of the bed I saw two letters. One was mine to
Baron T—, the other was from him to Ellenore. The meaning of the terrible
mystery was all too clear. All my efforts to gain the time I wanted for our last
farewells had worked against the unhappy woman I had hoped to shield. She
had read in my own hand my promises to leave her, promises dictated only by
the desire to stay with her and which the very strength of that desire had made
me reiterate and enlarge upon in countless ways. M. de T—'s dispassionate eye
had easily read between the lines of these reiterated protestations the irresolution
I was disguising and the shifts of my own uncertainty, but he had had the
cruelty to calculate that Ellenore would take all that for an irrevocable decree.
I went up to her. She gazed at me with unseeing eyes. I spoke to her and she
shuddered. "What is that noise?" she asked. "It is the voice that has hurt me."
The doctor noticed that my presence was intensifying her delirium, and he urged
me to withdraw. How can I describe what I went through for three long hours?
At last the doctor came out. Ellenore had fallen into a heavy sleep. He did not
give up hope of saving her life provided the fever had abated when she woke.

She slept for a long time. When I heard that she had awakened I wrote her a note asking her to see me. She sent a message that I could go in. I wanted to speak, but she cut me short. "Don't let me hear a single hard word from you," she said. "I shall never ask for anything again, nor oppose anything; but that voice I have loved so much, that voice which used to echo in my heart, don't let it pierce my heart now. Adolphe, Adolphe, I have lacked self-control, I may have offended you, but you don't know what I have suffered, and please God you never will!"

She became extremely distressed. She put her forehead against my hand, and it felt burning hot. Her face was twisted in terrible suffering. "In Heaven's name, listen, dearest Ellenore," I cried. "Yes, I am guilty; that letter . . ." She shuddered and tried to move away, but I held her fast. "In my weakness and distress," I went on, "I may have given in momentarily to inexorable pressure, but have you not a thousand proofs that I am incapable of wanting anything that comes between us? I have been discontented, unhappy, unfair, but possibly, by the excessive violence with which you have fought to curb my wayward imagination, you have strengthened what were only passing inclinations which I now despise. But can you question my deep affection? Are not our souls linked by countless ties that nothing can break? Is not all the past shared between us? Can we look back over the last three years and not revive impressions we have shared, pleasures we have enjoyed, troubles we have been through together? Ellenore, let us begin a new chapter this very day, let us remember the hours of joy and love." She looked at me for some time with doubt in her eyes. "Your father," she said at length, "your duties, your family, what is expected of you. . . ." "Possibly," I answered, "some day, some time. . . ." But she noticed my hesitation. "Oh, God!" she cried, "why did he revive my hopes only to snatch them away again? Adolphe, I do thank you for your efforts, which have done me good, and all the more so because they will not cost you any sacrifice, I hope. But don't let us talk about the future, I beg of you. Don't reproach yourself, whatever happens. You have been good to me. I wanted the impossible. Love was my whole life, but it could not be yours. Now look after me for a few days longer." The tears flowed from her eyes, her breathing became less laboured and she rested her head on my shoulder. "This," she said, "is where I always wanted to die." I held her close to my heart and once again renounced all my plans and disavowed my insensate cruelties. "No," she said, "you must be free and happy." "How can I be if you are unhappy?" "I shall not be unhappy for long, you will not have to go on pitying me for long." I thrust aside fears I tried to think were illusory. "No, no, dear Adolphe, when you have been calling upon death for a long time Heaven sends, when the hour comes, a kind of infallible presentiment warning you that your prayer is heard." I swore I would never leave her. "That is what I always hoped for, and now I am sure."

It was one of those winter days when the sun seems to cast a dismal light over the greyish countryside, as though looking down in pity upon a world it has ceased to warm. Ellenore suggested we might go out. "It is very cold," I said. "Never mind, I should like to go for a walk with you." She took my arm and we went on for a long time without saying a word, she walking with difficulty and leaning heavily upon me. "Shall we stop for a moment?" "No," she said, "it is so pleasant to feel your support once again." We relapsed into silence. The sky was clear, but the trees were bare; there was not a breath of wind and no bird cleaved the still air. Everything was motionless, and the only sound to be heard was of the frozen grass being crunched beneath our feet. "How calm it all is!" said Ellenore. "Look how resigned nature is! Shouldn't our hearts learn resignation too?" She sat upon a boulder, then dropped on to her knees and buried her head in her hands. I heard a few whispered words and realized she was praying. At length she rose and said: "Let us go home. I have got cold and I am afraid of being ill. Don't say anything. I am not capable of taking it in."

From that day onwards Ellenore was visibly weakening and fading away. I called in all the doctors I could find. Some pronounced that she was incurably stricken, others lulled me with false hopes, but nature, dark and inscrutable, carried on her inexorable work with an invisible hand. Sometimes Ellenore seemed to be recovering, and then it was as if the iron hand weighing down upon her had been lifted. She raised her drooping head, her cheeks took on a little more colour and her eyes lit up; and then suddenly the deceptive improvement was wiped out by the cruel trick of some unknown power, the cause of which no doctor's art could discover. And so I watched her slowly moving towards her end; I saw the warning signs of death stamp themselves upon her noble and expressive features. I saw, and what a humiliating and dreadful sight it was, that proud, forceful character of hers suffer a thousand confused and incoherent transformations through bodily pain as though at this awful moment her soul, crushed by her physical being, was changing its shape in countless ways in order to adapt itself the less painfully to the dissolution of her body.

One sentiment alone never varied in her, and that was her feeling for me. She was too weak to be able to say much, but she looked at me in silence and at these times I had the impression that she was begging me to give her life, which I could no longer do. I was afraid of exciting her unduly, and invented pretexts for going out, when I wandered from one to another of the places where I had been with her, weeping at the sight of stones, beneath trees, in the presence of all the things which brought back memories of her.

It was not the mere heartache of love, but a deeper and more desolate emotion, for love so identifies itself with the beloved that even in its despair there is a certain charm. Love struggles against reality, the keenness of its desire makes it overrate its strength and uplifts it in the midst of woe. But my grief was dismal and solitary. I did not hope to die with Ellenore, but was going to live on without her in the wilderness of this world, in which I had so often wanted to be an independent traveller. I had crushed the one who loved me, broken this heart which like a twin soul had been unfailingly devoted to mine in tireless affection, and already I was overcome by loneliness. Ellenore was still alive but already past sharing my confidences; I was already alone in the world and no longer living in that atmosphere of love with which she had surrounded me, and the very air I breathed seemed harsher, the faces of the men I met seemed more unconcerned. All nature seemed to be telling me that soon I should cease to be loved, and for ever.

Ellenore's peril suddenly became more imminent, and unmistakable symptoms proclaimed that her end was near. She was warned of this by a priest of her own faith. She asked me to bring her a box containing a quantity of papers, had some of them burned in her presence, but appeared to be looking for one which she could not find and was in great distress. I begged her to give up the search which was upsetting her so much and during which she fainted twice. "Very well," she answered, "but, dear Adolphe, do not refuse me one request. You will find somewhere among my papers a letter addressed to you. Burn it unread, I do beseech you in the name of our love, in the name of these last moments which you have made easier for me." I promised, and she grew calmer. "And now leave me to devote myself to my religious duties," she said. "I have many sins to atone for—perhaps my love for you has been a sin, but I could not believe that if it made you happy."

I left her and only returned with all the household for the last solemn prayers. Kneeling in a corner of the room I was part of the time lost in my own thoughts, and part, impelled by an involuntary curiosity, watching all these people gathered together, studying the terror of some and the inattention of others, and that strange effect of habit which brings indifference into all prescribed formalities and makes us regard even the most august and awe-inspiring ceremonies as matters of routine and pure form. I heard these people mechanically repeating the words of the prayers for the dying as though they themselves were never to be actors some day in a similar scene, as if they themselves were not some day to die too. And yet I was far from scorning such practices, for is there a single one of them which man in his ignorance can dare to call useless? They were bringing Ellenore some peace of mind and helping her to cross that dread threshold towards which we are all moving without being able to foresee what our feelings will then be. What surprises me is not that man needs a religion, but rather that he should ever think himself strong enough or sufficiently secure from trouble to dare reject any one of them. I think he ought, in his weakness, to call upon them all. In the dense night that surrounds us is there any gleam of light we can afford to reject? In the torrent bearing us all away is there a single branch we dare refuse to cling to?

Ellenore seemed tired after going through such a lugubrious ceremony. She sank into a quite peaceful sleep and awoke in a less troubled state. I was alone in her room, and we exchanged a few words at long intervals. The doctor whose forecasts had been most reliable had warned me that she had not twenty-four hours to live, and I looked first at a clock marking the hours and then at Ellenore's face, on which I could see no fresh change. Each passing minute revived my hopes, and I was beginning to cast doubt upon the prophecies of a perfidious art. But suddenly Ellenore leaped up in bed; I caught her in my arms. Her whole body was shaking convulsively, her eyes were searching for me, but in them was a look of vague fear, as if she were begging mercy of something threatening her but invisible to me. She sat up, then fell back, clearly trying to escape; it was as if she were wrestling with some invisible physical power which, tired of waiting for her last moment, had seized and held her in order to dispatch her on her deathbed. She finally yielded to the determined attacks of hostile nature; her body became limp. She seemed to recover some consciousness and pressed my hand. She tried to weep, but the tears would not come; she tried to speak, but her voice had gone. In resignation she dropped her head upon the arm supporting it, and her breathing became slower. A few moments later she was gone.

For a long time I remained motionless beside the dead Ellenore. The certainty of her death had not yet penetrated my soul, and my eyes stared stupidly at this inanimate body. One of her women came in and then went to spread the awful news throughout the house. The noise going on round me roused me from the lethargy into which I had sunk. I rose to my feet, and then it was that I felt the rending grief and full horror of the final farewell. All this bustling activity of daily life, all these preoccupations and comings and goings which no longer concerned her, dispelled the illusion which I was prolonging, that illusion which allowed me to believe I was still living with Ellenore. I felt the last link snap and the awful reality come between her and me for ever. How irksome this liberty now was, that I had missed so grievously! How my heart now cried out for that independence which I had often hated! Only recently all my actions had one single object; each one of them, I was convinced, would dispel some sorrow or give some pleasure. But then I complained that it should be so and felt resentful that a benevolent eye should watch over all my movements and that another's happiness should depend upon them. There was nobody to watch over my movements now, they interested nobody; there was none to dispute my comings and goings, no voice to call me back as I was going out. I was free, truly, for I was no longer loved. I was a stranger to the whole world.

All Ellenore's papers were brought to me as she had ordered. In every line I found fresh proofs of her love, new sacrifices she had made for my sake and all unknown to me. At length I found the letter I had promised to burn. At first I did not know what it was; it was unaddressed and open so a few words caught my eye in spite of myself. Try as I would not to look I could not resist the temptation to read it all. I have not the strength to copy it all out. Ellenore had written it after one of those violent scenes which had preceded her illness. "Adolphe," she wrote, "why are you always against me? What crimes have I committed?

Loving you and being unable to exist without you. What misguided pity makes you afraid to break a tie you find irksome and yet go on torturing the unhappy soul you remain with because of that pity? Why do you deny me the paltry satisfaction of believing you to be at any rate generous? Why do you show yourself to be so hysterical and weak? You are haunted by the vision of my grief and yet the sight of this grief cannot stop you! What is your demand? That I should leave you? Don't you see that I have not the strength? Ah, it is you, who do not love me, you who must find the strength in a heart that is weary of me and that so much love cannot touch. You will never give me that strength, but will make me languish in tears and die at your feet."

"Tell mè," she wrote in another place, "is there any land where I would not follow you? Any retreat where I would not stay hidden so as to be near you without being a burden? No, no, you want no such thing. Any suggestion I make in fear and trembling (for you have struck terror into me), you impatiently reject. The best I can get from you is silence. So much hardness does not go with your character. You are good, and your actions are noble and kind, but what deeds could efface the memory of your words? Those biting words echo round me; I hear them in the night, they pursue me, torture me, and poison everything you do. Must I die then, Adolphe? Very well, you shall be satisfied. She will die, this poor creature you have protected but are now hurting again and again. She will die, this wearisome Ellenore whom you cannot bear to have anywhere near you, whom you regard as an obstacle, because of whom you cannot find a single spot on this earth that does not bore you. And you will walk on alone in the midst of this crowd you are so anxious to join. You will get to know what these people really are for whose indifference you are so grateful now, and perhaps some day, when you are wounded by their stony hearts, you will miss the heart that was yours, that lived on your affection and would have braved a thousand perils in your defence, and upon which you no longer deign to bestow a single rewarding glance."

Letter to the Publisher

Sir,

I return the manuscript you so kindly entrusted to me. I thank you for this kindness even though it has revived sad memories that time had dimmed. I knew most of the characters in this story, which is all too true. I often saw the strange and unhappy Adolphe, who is both the author and the hero; I tried to warn Ellenore—that charming woman worthy of a happier fate and a more faithful heart—against that mischievous person, no less unhappy than she, who dominated her by a kind of spell and broke her heart by his weakness. Alas, the last time I saw her I thought I had given her some strength and armed her reason against her heart. After far too long an absence I returned to the place where I had left her, to find nothing but a grave.

Sir, you should publish this anecdote. It can hurt nobody now, and in my view it might be very helpful. Ellenore's tragedy proves that even the most intense emotion cannot struggle against the accepted order of things. Society is too powerful, it has too many metamorphoses, mixes too much bitterness with any love it has not sanctioned; it favours the tendency to inconstancy, the bored impatience which are sicknesses of the soul that sometimes suddenly develop in the very midst of love. People unaffected themselves are remarkably eager to interfere in the name of morality and to hurt others by their zeal for virtue. It is as though the sight of affection were too much for them because they are incapable of it themselves, and when they can seize on an excuse they delight in attacking and destroying it. Woe betide the woman who puts her trust in a sentiment which everything conspires to poison, and against which society, once it is not obliged to respect it as legitimate, arms itself with all that is evil in the heart of man in order to discourage all that is good.

The example of Adolphe will be no less instructive if you add that after spurning the woman who loved him he was no less restless, upset, and unhappy; that he made no use of the liberty regained at the cost of so much grief and so many tears, and that by behaving in a thoroughly blameworthy manner he at the same time made himself worthy of pity.

If you want proofs of all this, Sir, read these letters which will acquaint you with Adolphe's later life. You will see him in many varied circumstances, but always the victim of the mingled selfishness and emotionalism which worked together in him for his own undoing and that of others; foreseeing the evil consequences of an act and yet doing it, and shrinking back in despair after having done it; punished for his qualities even more than for his defects because his qualities had their origin in his emotions and not in his principles; showing himself in turn the most affectionate and the most cruel of men, but as he always ended with cruelty after beginning with affection, he left no trace behind except of his misdeeds.

Reply

SIR,

Yes, I will certainly publish the manuscript you return, not that I share your view as to the service it might render; nobody in the world ever learns except at his own expense, and women who read it will all imagine they have met somebody better than Adolphe or that they themselves are better than Ellenore, but

I shall publish it as a true story of the misery of the human heart. If it has any instructive lesson, that lesson is for men, for it shows that intellect, which they are so proud of, can neither find happiness nor bestow it; that character, stead-fastness, fidelity, and kindness are the gifts we should pray for, and by kindness I do not mean that short-lived pity which cannot overcome impatience nor prevent it from reopening wounds which a moment of compunction had appeared to heal. The great question in life is the sorrow we cause, and the most ingenious metaphysics cannot justify a man who has broken the heart that loved him. [And besides, I hate the vanity of a mind which thinks it excuses what it explains, I hate the conceit which is concerned only with itself while narrating the evil it has done, which tries to arouse pity by self-destruction and which, soaring indestructible among the ruins, analyses itself when it should be repenting.] I hate that weakness which is always blaming others for its own impotence and which cannot see that the trouble is not in its surroundings but in itself. I might have guessed that Adolphe has since been punished for his character by his very character, that he has kept to no fixed path, adopted no useful career, that he has used up his gifts with no sense of direction beyond mere caprice, no other motive power than nervous reaction. All that, I repeat, I might have gussed even if you had not acquainted me with fresh details about his fate which I am not sure yet whether to make use of. Circumstances are quite unimportant, character is everything; in vain we break with outside things or people; we cannot break with ourselves. We change our circumstances, but we take with us into each new situation the torment we had hoped to leave behind, and as we cannot make ourselves any better by a change of scene, we simply find that we have added remorse to regrets and misdeeds to sufferings.

Chapter 2

Acquiring Motives and Attitudes

JAMES JOYCE

• *A Portrait of the Artist as a Young Man*

—*Remember only thy last things and thou shalt not sin for ever*—words taken, my dear little brothers in Christ, from the book of Ecclesiastes, seventh chapter, fortieth verse. In the name of the Father and of the Son and of the Holy Ghost. Amen.

Stephen sat in the front bench of the chapel. Father Arnall sat at a table to the left of the altar. He wore about his shoulders a heavy cloak; his pale face was drawn and his voice broken with rheum. The figure of his old master, so strangely rearisen, brought back to Stephen's mind his life at Clongowes: the wide playgrounds, swarming with boys, the square ditch, the little cemetery off the main avenue of limes where he had dreamed of being buried, the firelight on the wall of the infirmary where he lay sick, the sorrowful face of Brother Michael. His soul, as these memories came back to him, became again a child's soul.

—We are assembled here today, my dear little brothers in Christ, for one brief moment far away from the busy bustle of the outer world to celebrate and to honour one of the greatest of saints, the apostle of the Indies, the patron saint also of your college, saint Francis Xavier. Year after year for much longer than any of you, my dear little boys, can remember or than I can remember the boys of this college have met in this very chapel to make their annual retreat before the feast day of their patron saint. Time has gone on and brought with it its changes. Even in the last few years what changes can most of you not remember?

SOURCE. From *A Portrait of the Artist As a Young Man* by James Joyce. Copyright 1916 by B. W. Huebsch, renewed by Nora Joyce, reprinted with the permission of the Viking Press Incorporated.

Many of the boys who sat in those front benches a few years ago are perhaps now in distant lands, in the burning tropics or immersed in professional duties or in seminaries or voyaging over the vast expanse of the deep or, it may be, already called by the great God to another life and to the rendering up of their stewardship. And still as the years roll by, bringing with them changes for good and bad, the memory of the great saint is honoured by the boys of his college who make every year their annual retreat on the days preceding the feast day set apart by our holy mother the church to transmit to all the ages the name and fame of one of the greatest sons of catholic Spain.

—Now what is the meaning of this word *retreat* and why is it allowed on all hands to be a most salutary practice for all who desire to lead before God and in the eyes of men a truly christian life? A retreat, my dear boys, signifies a withdrawal for a while from the cares of our life, the cares of this workaday world, in order to examine the state of our conscience, to reflect on the mysteries of holy religion and to understand better why we are here in this world. During these few days I intend to put before you some thoughts concerning the four last things. They are, as you know from your catechism, death, judgment, hell and heaven. We shall try to understand them fully during these few days so that we may derive from the understanding of them a lasting benefit to our souls. And remember, my dear boys, that we have been sent into this world for one thing and for one thing alone: to do God's holy will and to save our immortal souls. All else is worthless. One thing alone is needful, the salvation of one's soul. What doth it profit a man to gain the whole world if he suffer the loss of his immortal soul? Ah, my dear boys, believe me there is nothing in this wretched world that can make up for such a loss.

—I will ask you therefore, my dear boys, to put away from your minds during these few days all worldly thoughts, whether of study or pleasure or ambition, and to give all your attention to the state of your souls. I need hardly remind you that during the days of the retreat all boys are expected to preserve a quiet and pious demeanour and to shun all loud unseemly pleasure. The elder boys, of course, will see that this custom is not infringed and I look especially to the prefects and officers of the sodality of Our Blessed Lady and of the sodality of the holy angels to set a good example to their fellowstudents.

—Let us try therefore to make this retreat in honour of saint Francis with our whole heart and our whole mind. God's blessing will then be upon all your year's studies. But, above and beyond all, let this retreat be one to which you can look back in after years when maybe you are far from this college and among very different surroundings, to which you can look back with joy and thankfulness and give thanks to God for having granted you this occasion of laying the first foundation of a pious honourable zealous christian life. And if, as may so happen, there be at this moment in these benches any poor soul who has had the unutterable misfortune to lose God's holy grace and to fall into grievous sin I fervently trust and pray that this retreat may be the turningpoint in the life of that soul. I pray to God through the merits of its zealous servant Francis Xavier that such a soul may be led to sincere repentance and that the holy communion on saint Francis' day of this year may be a lasting covenant between God and that soul. For just and unjust, for saint and sinner alike, may this retreat be a memorable one.

—Help me, my dear little brothers in Christ. Help me by your pious attention, by your own devotion, by your outward demeanour. Banish from your minds all worldly thoughts and think only of the last things, death, judgment, hell and heaven. He who remembers these things, says Ecclesiastes, shall not sin for ever. He who remembers the last things will act and think with them always before his eyes. He will live a good life and die a good death, believing and knowing that, if he has sacrificed much in this earthly life, it will be given to him a hundredfold and a thousandfold more in the life to come, in the kingdom without end—a blessing, my dear boys, which I wish you from my heart, one and all, in the name of the Father and of the Son and of the Holy Ghost. Amen.

As he walked home with silent companions a thick fog seemed to compass his mind. He waited in stupor of mind till it should lift and reveal what it had hidden. He ate his dinner with surly appetite and, when the meal was over and the greasestrewn plates lay abandoned on the table, he rose and went to the window, clearing the thick scum from his mouth with his tongue and licking it from his lips. So he had sunk to the state of a beast that licks his chaps after meat. This was the end; and a faint glimmer of fear began to pierce the fog of his mind. He pressed his face against the pane of the window and gazed out into the darkening street. Forms passed this way and that through the dull light. And that was life. The letters of the name of Dublin lay heavily upon his mind, pushing one another surlily hither and thither with slow boorish insistence. His soul was fattening and congealing into a gross grease, plunging ever deeper in its dull fear into a sombre threatening dusk, while the body that was his stood, listless and dishonoured, gazing out of darkened eyes, helpless, perturbed and human for a bovine god to stare upon.

The next day brought death and judgment, stirring his soul slowly from its listless despair. The faint glimmer of fear became a terror of spirit as the hoarse voice of the preacher blew death into his soul. He suffered its agony. He felt the deathchill touch the extremities and creep onward towards the heart, the film of death veiling the eyes, the bright centres of the brain extinguished one by one like lamps, the last sweat oozing upon the skin, the powerlessness of the dying limbs, the speech thickening and wandering and failing, the heart throbbing faintly and more faintly, all but vanquished, the breath, the poor breath, the poor helpless human spirit, sobbing and sighing, gurgling and rattling in the throat. No help! No help! He, he himself, his body to which he had yielded was dying. Into the grave with it! Nail it down into a wooden box, the corpse. Carry it out of the house on the shoulders of hirelings. Thrust it out of men's sight into a long hole in the ground, into the grave, to rot, to feed the mass of its creeping worms and to be devoured by scuttling plumpbellied rats.

And while the friends were still standing in tears by the bedside the soul of the sinner was judged. At the last moment of consciousness the whole earthly life passed before the vision of the soul and, ere it had time to reflect, the body had died and the soul stood terrified before the judgmentseat. God, who had long been merciful, would then be just. He had long been patient, pleading with the sinful soul, giving it time to repent, sparing it yet awhile. But that time had gone. Time was to sin and to enjoy, time was to scoff at God and at the warnings of His holy church, time was to defy His majesty, to disobey His commands, to hood-wink one's fellow men, to commit sin after sin and sin after sin and to hide one's corruption from the sight of men. But that time was over. Now it was God's turn: and He was not to be hoodwinked or deceived. Every sin would then come forth from its lurkingplace, the most rebellious against the divine will and the most degrading to our poor corrupt nature, the tiniest imperfection and the most hei-nous atrocity. What did it avail then to have been a great emperor, a great general, a marvellous inventor, the most learned of the learned? All were as one before the judgmentseat of God. He would reward the good and punish the wicked. One single instant was enough for the trial of a man's soul. One single instant after the body's death, the soul had been weighed in the balance. The particular judgment was over and the soul had passed to the abode of bliss or to the prison of purgatory or had been hurled howling into hell.

Nor was that all. God's justice had still to be vindicated before men: after the particular there still remained the general judgment. The last day had come. Doomsday was at hand. The stars of heaven were falling upon the earth like the figs cast by the figtree which the wind has shaken. The sun, the great luminary of the universe, had become as sackcloth of hair. The moon was bloodred. The firmament was as a scroll rolled away. The archangel Michael, the prince of the heavenly host, appeared glorious and terrible against the sky. With one foot on the sea and one foot on the land he blew from the archangelical trumpet the brazen death of time. The three blasts of the angel filled all the universe. Time is, time was but time shall be no more. At the last blast the souls of universal humanity throng towards the valley of Jehoshaphat, rich and poor, gentle and simple, wise and foolish, good and wicked. The soul of every human being that has ever existed, the souls of all those who shall yet be born, all the sons and daughters of Adam, all are assembled on that supreme day. And lo the supreme judge is coming! No longer the lowly Lamb of God, no longer the meek Jesus of Nazareth, no longer the Man of Sorrows, no longer the Good Shepherd, He is seen now coming upon the clouds, in great power and majesty, attended by nine choirs of angels, angels and archangels, principalities, powers and virtues, thrones and dominations, cherubim and seraphim, God Omnipotent, God Everlasting.

He speaks: and His voice is heard even at the farthest limits of space, even in the bottomless abyss. Supreme Judge, from His sentence there will be and can be no appeal. He calls the just to His side, bidding them enter into the kingdom, the eternity of bliss, prepared for them. The unjust He casts from Him, crying in His offended majesty: *Depart from me, ye cursed, into everlasting fire which was prepared for the devil and his angels.* O what agony then for the miserable sinners! Friend is torn apart from friend, children are torn from their parents, husbands from their wives. The poor sinner holds out his arms to those who were dear to him in this earthly world, to those whose simple piety perhaps he made a mock of, to those who counselled him and tried to lead him on the right path, to a kind brother, to a loving sister, to the mother and father who loved him so dearly. But it is too late: the just turn away from the wretched damned souls which now appear before the eyes of all in their hideous and evil character. O you hypocrites, O you whited sepulchres, O you who present a smooth smiling face to the world while your soul within is a foul swamp of sin, how will it fare with you in that terrible day?

And this day will come, shall come, must come; the day of death and the day of judgment. It is appointed unto man to die and after death the judgment. Death is certain. The time and manner are uncertain, whether from long disease or from some unexpected accident; the Son of God cometh at an hour when you little expect Him. Be therefore ready every moment, seeing that you may die at any moment. Death is the end of us all. Death and judgment, brought into the world by the sin of our first parents, are the dark portals that close our earthly existence, the portals that open into the unknown and the unseen, portals through which every soul must pass, alone, unaided save by its good works, without friend or brother or parent or master to help it, alone and trembling. Let that thought be ever before our minds, and then we cannot sin. Death, a cause of terror to the sinner, is a blessed moment for him who has walked in the right path, fulfilling the duties of his station in life, attending to his morning and evening prayers, approaching the holy sacrament frequently and performing good and merciful works. For the pious and believing catholic, for the just man, death is no cause of terror. Was it not Addison, the great English writer, who, when on his deathbed, sent for the wicked young earl of Warwick to let him see how a christian can meet his end. He it is and he alone, the pious and believing christian, who can say in his heart:

> *O grave, where is thy victory?*
> *O death, where is thy sting?*

Every word of it was for him. Against his sin, foul and secret, the whole wrath of God was aimed. The preacher's knife had probed deeply into his diseased conscience and he felt now that his soul was festering in sin. Yes, the preacher was right. God's turn had come. Like a beast in its lair his soul had lain down in its own filth but the blasts of the angel's trumpet had driven him forth from the darkness of sin into the light. The words of doom cried by the angel shattered in an instant his presumptuous peace. The wind of the last day blew through his mind; his sins, the jeweleyed harlots of his imagination, fled before the hurricane, squeaking like mice in their terror and huddled under a mane of hair.

As he crossed the square, walking homeward, the light laughter of a girl reached his burning ear. The frail gay sound smote his heart more strongly than a trumpetblast, and, not daring to lift his eyes, he turned aside and gazed, as he walked, into the shadow of the tangled shrubs. Shame rose from his smitten heart and flooded his whole being. The image of Emma appeared before him and, under her eyes, the flood of shame rushed forth anew from his heart. If she knew to what his mind had subjected her or how his brutelike lust had torn and trampled upon her innocence! Was that boyish love? Was that chivalry? Was that poetry? The sordid details of his orgies stank under his very nostrils: the soot-coated packet of pictures which he had hidden in the flue of the fireplace and in the presence of whose shameless or bashful wantonness he lay for hours sinning in thought and deed; his monstrous dreams, peopled by apelike creatures and by harlots with gleaming jewel eyes; the foul long letters he had written in the joy of guilty confession and carried secretly for days and days only to throw them under cover of night among the grass in the corner of a field or beneath some hingeless door or in some niche in the hedges where a girl might come upon them as she walked by and read them secretly. Mad! Mad! Was it possible he had done these things? A cold sweat broke out upon his forehead as the foul memories condensed within his brain.

When the agony of shame had passed from him he tried to raise his soul from its abject powerlessness. God and the Blessed Virgin were too far from him: God was too great and stern and the Blessed Virgin too pure and holy. But he imagined that he stood near Emma in a wide land and, humbly and in tears, bent and kissed the elbow of her sleeve.

In the wide land under a tender lucid evening sky, a cloud drifting west-ward amid a pale green sea of heaven, they stood together, children that had erred. Their error had offended deeply God's majesty though it was the error of two children, but it had not offended her whose beauty *is not like earthly beauty, dangerous to look upon, but like the morning star which is its emblem, bright and musical.* The eyes were not offended which she turned upon them nor reproachful. She placed their hands together, hand in hand, and said, speaking to their hearts:

—Take hands, Stephen and Emma. It is a beautiful evening now in heaven. You have erred but you are always my children. It is one heart that loves another heart. Take hands together, my dear children, and you will be happy together and your hearts will love each other.

The chapel was flooded by the dull scarlet light that filtered through the lowered blinds; and through the fissure between the last blind and the sash a shaft of wan light entered like a spear and touched the embossed brasses of the candlesticks upon the altar that gleamed like the battleworn mail armour of angels.

Rain was falling on the chapel, on the garden, on the college. It would rain for ever, noiselessly. The water would rise inch by inch, covering the grass and shrubs, covering the trees and houses, covering the monuments and the mountain tops. All life would be choked off, noiselessly: birds, men, elephants, pigs, children: noiselessly floating corpses amid the litter of the wreckage of the world. Forty days and forty nights the rain would fall till the waters covered the face of the earth.

It might be. Why not?

—*Hell has enlarged its soul and opened its mouth without any limits*— words taken, my dear little brothers in Christ Jesus, from the book of Isaias, fifth chapter, fourteenth verse. In the name of the Father and of the Son and of the Holy Ghost. Amen.

The preacher took a chainless watch from a pocket within his soutane and, having considered its dial for a moment in silence, placed it silently before him on the table.

He began to speak in a quiet tone.

—Adam and Eve, my dear boys, were, as you know, our first parents and you will remember that they were created by God in order that the seats in heaven left vacant by the fall of Lucifer and his rebellious angels might be filled again. Lucifer, we are told, was a son of the morning, a radiant and mighty angel; yet he fell: he fell and there fell with him a third part of the host of heaven: he fell and was hurled with his rebellious angels into hell. What his sin was we cannot say. Theologians consider that it was the sin of pride, the sinful thought conceived in an instant: *non serviam: I will not serve.* That instant was his ruin. He offended the majesty of God by the sinful thought of one instant and God cast him out of heaven into hell for ever.

—Adam and Eve were then created by God and placed in Eden, in the plain of Damascus, that lovely garden resplendent with sunlight and colour, teeming with luxuriant vegetation. The fruitful earth gave them her bounty: beasts and birds were their willing servants: they knew not the ills our flesh is heir to, disease and poverty and death: all that a great and generous God could do for them was done. But there was one condition imposed on them by God: obedience to His word. They were not to eat of the fruit of the forbidden tree.

—Alas, my dear little boys, they too fell. The devil, once a shining angel, a son of the morning, now a foul fiend, came in the shape of a serpent, the subtlest of all the beasts of the field. He envied them. He, the fallen great one, could not bear to think that man, a being of clay, should possess the inheritance which he by his sin had forfeited for ever. He came to the woman, the weaker vessel, and poured the poison of his eloquence into her ear, promising her—O, the blasphemy of that promise!—that if she and Adam ate of the forbidden fruit they would become as gods, nay as God Himself. Eve yielded to the wiles of the archtempter. She ate the apple and gave it also to Adam who had not the moral courage to resist her. The poison tongue of Satan had done its work. They fell.

—And then the voice of God was heard in that garden, calling His creature man to account: and Michael, prince of the heavenly host, with a sword of flame in his hand appeared before the guilty pair and drove them forth from Eden into the world, the world of sickness and striving, of cruelty and disappointment, of labour and hardship, to earn their bread in the sweat of their brow. But even then how merciful was God! He took pity on our poor degraded parents and promised that in the fulness of time He would send down from heaven One who would redeem them, make them once more children of God and heirs to the kingdom of heaven: and that One, that Redeemer of fallen man, was to be God's onlybegotten Son, the Second Person of the Most Blessed Trinity, the Eternal Word.

—He came. He was born of a virgin pure, Mary the virgin mother. He was born in a poor cowhouse in Judea and lived as a humble carpenter for thirty years until the hour of His mission had come. And then, filled with love for men, He went forth and called to men to hear the new gospel.

—Did they listen? Yes, they listened but would not hear. He was seized and bound like a common criminal, mocked at as a fool, set aside to give place to a public robber, scourged with five thousand lashes, crowned with a crown of thorns, hustled through the streets by the jewish rabble and the Roman soldiery, stripped of His garments and hanged upon a gibbet and His side was pierced with a lance and from the wounded body of Our Lord water and blood issued continually.

—Yet even then, in that hour of supreme agony, Our Merciful Redeemer had pity for mankind. Yet even there, on the hill of Calvary, He founded the holy catholic church against which, it is promised, the gates of hell shall not prevail. He founded it upon the rock of ages and endowed it with His grace, with sacraments and sacrifice, and promised that if men would obey the word of His church they would still enter into eternal life but if, after all that had been done for them, they still persisted in their wickedness there remained for them an eternity of torment: hell.

The preacher's voice sank. He paused, joined his palms for an instant, parted them. Then he resumed:

—Now let us try for a moment to realise, as far as we can, the nature of that abode of the damned which the justice of an offended God has called into existence for the eternal punishment of sinners. Hell is a strait and dark and foul-smelling prison, an abode of demons and lost souls, filled with fire and smoke. The straitness of this prisonhouse is expressly designed by God to punish those who refused to be bound by His laws. In earthly prisons the poor captive has at least some liberty of movement, were it only within the four walls of his cell or in the gloomy yard of his prison. Not so in hell. There, by reason of the great number of the damned, the prisoners are heaped together in their awful prison, the walls of which are said to be four thousand miles thick: and the damned are so utterly bound and helpless that, as a blessed saint, saint Anselm, writes in his book on similitudes, they are not even able to remove from the eye a worm that gnaws it.

—They lie in exterior darkness. For, remember, the fire of hell gives forth no light. As, at the command of God, the fire of the Babylonian furnace lost its heat but not its light so, at the command of God, the fire of hell, while retaining the intensity of its heat, burns eternally in darkness. It is a never-ending storm of darkness, dark flames and dark smoke of burning brimstone, amid which the bodies are heaped one upon another without even a glimpse of air. Of all the plagues with which the land of the Pharaohs was smitten one plague alone, that of darkness, was called horrible. What name, then, shall we give to the darkness of hell which is to last not for three days alone but for all eternity?

—The horror of this strait and dark prison is increased by its awful stench. All the filth of the world, all the offal and scum of the world, we are told, shall run there as to a vast reeking sewer when the terrible conflagration of the last day has purged the world. The brimstone too which burns there in such prodigious quantity fills all hell with its intolerable stench; and the bodies of the damned themselves exhale such a pestilential odour that as saint Bonaventure says, one of them alone would suffice to infect the whole world. The very air of this world, that pure element, becomes foul and unbreathable when it has been long enclosed. Consider then what must be the foulness of the air of hell. Imagine some foul and putrid corpse that has lain rotting and decomposing in the grave, a jellylike mass of liquid corruption. Imagine such a corpse a prey to flames, devoured by the fire of burning brimstone and giving off dense choking fumes of nauseous loathsome decomposition. And then imagine this sickening stench, multiplied a millionfold and a millionfold again from the millions upon millions of fetid carcasses massed together in the reeking darkness, a huge and rotting human fungus. Imagine all this and you will have some idea of the horror of the stench of hell.

—But this stench is not, horrible though it is, the greatest physical torment to which the damned are subjected. The torment of fire is the greatest torment to which the tyrant has ever subjected his fellowcreatures. Place your finger for a moment in the flame of a candle and you will feel the pain of fire. But our earthly fire was created by God for the benefit of man, to maintain in him the spark of life and to help him in the useful arts whereas the fire of hell is of another quality and was created by God to torture and punish the unrepentant sinner. Our earthly fire also consumes more or less rapidly according as the object which it attacks is more or less combustible so that human ingenuity has even succeeded in inventing chemical preparations to check or frustrate its action. But the sulphurous brimstone which burns in hell is a substance which is specially designed to burn for ever and for ever with unspeakable fury. Moreover our earthly fire destroys at the same time as it burns so that the more intense it is the shorter is its duration: but the fire of hell has this property that it preserves that which it burns and though it rages with incredible intensity it rages for ever.

—Our earthly fire again, no matter how fierce or widespread it may be, is always of a limited extent: but the lake of fire in hell is boundless, shoreless and bottomless. It is on record that the devil himself, when asked the question by a certain soldier, was obliged to confess that if a whole mountain were thrown into the burning ocean of hell it would be burned up in an instant like a piece of wax. And, this terrible fire will not afflict the bodies of the damned only from without but each lost soul will be a hell unto itself, the boundless fire raging in its very vitals. O, how terrible is the lot of those wretched beings! The blood seethes and boils in the veins, the brains are boiling in the skull, the heart in the breast glowing and bursting, the bowels a redhot mass of burning pulp, the tender eyes flaming like molten balls.

—And yet what I have said as to the strength and quality and boundlessness of this fire is as nothing when compared to its intensity, an intensity which it has as being the instrument chosen by divine design for the punishment of soul and body alike. It is a fire which proceeds directly from the ire of God, working not of its own activity but as an instrument of divine vengeance. As the waters of baptism cleanse the soul with the body so do the fires of punishment torture the spirit with the flesh. Every sense of the flesh is tortured and every faculty of the soul therewith: the eyes with impenetrable utter darkness, the nose with noisome odours, the ears with yells and howls and execrations, the taste with foul matter, leprous corruption, nameless suffocating filth, the touch with redhot goads and spikes, with cruel tongues of flame. And through the several torments of the senses the immortal soul is tortured eternally in its very essence amid the leagues upon leagues of glowing fires kindled in the abyss by the offended majesty of the Omnipotent God and fanned into everlasting and ever increasing fury by the breath of the anger of the Godhead.

—Consider finally that the torment of this infernal prison is increased by the company of the damned themselves. Evil company on earth is so noxious that even the plants, as if by instinct, withdraw from the company of whatsoever is deadly or hurtful to them. In hell all laws are overturned: there is no thought of family or country, of ties, of relationships. The damned howl and scream at one another, their torture and rage intensified by the presence of beings tortured and raging like themselves. All sense of humanity is forgotten. The yells of the suffering sinners fill the remotest corners of the vast abyss. The mouths of the damned are full of blasphemies against God and of hatred for their fellowsufferers and of curses against those souls which were their accomplices in sin. In olden times it was the custom to punish the parricide, the man who had raised his murderous hand against his father, by casting him into the depths of the sea in a sack in which were placed a cock, a monkey and a serpent. The intention of those lawgivers who framed such a law, which seems cruel in our times, was to punish the criminal by the company of hateful and hurtful beasts. But what is the fury of those dumb beasts compared with the fury of execration which bursts from the parched lips and aching throats of the damned in hell when they behold in their companions in misery those who aided and abetted them in sin, those whose words sowed the first seeds of evil thinking and evil living in their minds, those whose immodest suggestions led them on to sin, those whose eyes tempted and allured them from the path of virtue. They turn upon those accomplices and upbraid them and curse them. But they are helpless and hopeless: it is too late now for repentance.

—Last of all consider the frightful torment to those damned souls, tempters and tempted alike, of the company of the devils. These devils will afflict the damned in two ways, by their presence and by their reproaches. We can have no idea of how horrible these devils are. Saint Catherine of Siena once saw a devil and she has written that, rather than look again for one single instant on such a frightful monster, she would prefer to walk until the end of her life along a track of red coals. These devils, who were once beautiful angels, have become as hideous and ugly as they once were beautiful. They mock and jeer at the lost souls whom they dragged down to ruin. It is they, the foul demons, who are made in hell the voices of conscience. Why did you sin? Why did you lend an ear to the temptings of fiends? Why did you turn aside from your pious practices and good works? Why did you not shun the occasions of sin? Why did you not leave that evil companion? Why did you not give up that lewd habit, that impure habit? Why did you not listen to the counsels of your confessor? Why did you not, even after you had fallen the first or the second or the third or the fourth or the hundredth time, repent of your evil ways and turn to God who only waited for your repentance to absolve you of your sins? Now the time for repentance has gone by. Time is, time was, but time shall be no more! Time was to sin in secrecy, to indulge in that sloth and pride, to covet the unlawful, to yield to the promptings of your lower nature, to live like the beasts of the field, nay worse than the beasts of the field for they, at least, are but brutes and have not reason to guide them: time was but time shall be no more. God spoke to you by so many voices but you would not hear. You would not crush out that pride and anger in your heart, you would not restore those illgotten goods, you would not obey the precepts of your holy church nor attend to your religious duties, you would not abandon those wicked companions, you would not avoid those dangerous temptations. Such is the language of those fiendish tormentors, words of taunting and of reproach, of hatred and of disgust. Of disgust, yes! For even they, the very devils, when they sinned sinned by such a sin as alone was compatible with such angelical natures, a rebellion of the intellect: and they, even they, the foul devils must turn away, revolted and disgusted, from the contemplation of those unspeakable sins by which degraded man outrages and defiles the temple of the Holy Ghost, defiles and pollutes himself.

—O, my dear little brothers in Christ, may it never be our lot to hear that language! May it never be our lot, I say! In the last day of terrible reckoning I pray fervently to God that not a single soul of those who are in this chapel today may be found among those miserable beings whom the Great Judge shall command to depart for ever from His sight, that not one of us may ever hear ringing in his ears the awful sentence of rejection: *Depart from me, ye cursed, into everlasting fire which was prepared for the devil and his angels!*

He came down the aisle of the chapel, his legs shaking and the scalp of his head trembling as though it had been touched by ghostly fingers. He passed up the staircase and into the corridor along the walls of which the overcoats and waterproofs hung like gibbeted malefactors, headless and dripping and shapeless. And at every step he feared that he had already died, that his soul had been wrenched forth of the sheath of his body, that he was plunging headlong through space.

He could not grip the floor with his feet and sat heavily at his desk, opening one of his books at random and poring over it. Every word for him! It was true. God was almighty. God could call him now, call him as he sat at his desk, before he had time to be conscious of the summons. God had called him. Yes? What? Yes? His flesh shrank together as it felt the approach of the ravenous tongues of flames, dried up as it felt about it the swirl of stifling air. He had died. Yes. He was judged. A wave of fire swept through his body: the first. Again a wave. His brain began to glow. Another. His brain was simmering and bubbling within the cracking tenement of the skull. Flames burst forth from his skull like a corolla, shrieking like voices:

—Hell! Hell! Hell! Hell! Hell!

Voices spoke near him:

—On hell.

—I suppose he rubbed it into you well.

—You bet he did. He put us all into a blue funk.

—That's what you fellows want: and plenty of it to make you work.

He leaned back weakly in his desk. He had not died. God had spared him still. He was still in the familiar world of the school. Mr. Tate and Vincent

Heron stood at the window, talking, jesting, gazing out at the bleak rain, moving their heads.

—I wish it would clear up. I had arranged to go for a spin on the bike with some fellows out by Malahide. But the roads must be kneedeep.

—It might clear up, sir.

The voices that he knew so well, the common words, the quiet of the classroom when the voices paused and the silence was filled by the sound of softly browsing cattle as the other boys munched their lunches tranquilly, lulled his aching soul.

There was still time. O Mary, refuge of sinners, intercede for him! O Virgin Undefiled, save him from the gulf of death!

The English lesson began with the hearing of the history. Royal persons, favourites, intriguers, bishops, passed like mute phantoms behind their veil of names. All had died: all had been judged. What did it profit a man to gain the whole world if he lost his soul? At last he had understood: and human life lay around him, a plain of peace whereon antlike men laboured in brotherhood, their dead sleeping under quiet mounds. The elbow of his companion touched him and his heart was touched: and when he spoke to answer a question of his master he heard his own voice full of the quietude of humility and contrition.

His soul sank back deeper into depths of contrite peace, no longer able to suffer the pain of dread, and sending forth, as she sank, a faint prayer. Ah yes, he would still be spared; he would repent in his heart and be forgiven; and then those above, those in heaven, would see what he would do to make up for the past: a whole life, every hour of life. Only wait.

—All, God! All, all!

A messenger came to the door to say that confessions were being heard in the chapel. Four boys left the room; and he heard others passing down the corridor. A tremulous chill blew round his heart, no stronger than a little wind, and yet, listening and suffering silently, he seemed to have laid an ear against the muscle of his own heart, feeling it close and quail, listening to the flutter of its ventricles.

No escape. He had to confess, to speak out in words what he had done and thought, sin after sin. How? How?

—Father, I . . .

The thought slid like a cold shining rapier into his tender flesh: confession. But not there in the chapel of the college. He would confess all, every sin of deed and thought, sincerely: but not there among his school companions. Far away from there in some dark place he would murmur out his own shame: and he besought God humbly not to be offended with him if he did not dare to confess in the college chapel: and in utter abjection of spirit he craved forgiveness mutely of the boyish hearts about him.

Time passed.

He sat again in the front bench of the chapel. The daylight without was already failing and, as it fell slowly through the dull red blinds, it seemed that the sun of the last day was going down and that all souls were being gathered for the judgment.

—*I am cast away from the sight of Thine eyes:* words taken, my dear little brothers in Christ, from the Book of Psalms, thirtieth chapter, twentythird verse. In the name of the Father and of the Son and of the Holy Ghost. Amen.

The preacher began to speak in a quiet friendly tone. His face was kind and he joined gently the fingers of each hand, forming a frail cage by the union of their tips.

—This morning we endeavoured, in our reflection upon hell, to make what our holy founder calls in his book of spiritual exercises, the composition of place. We endeavoured, that is, to imagine with the senses of the mind, in our imagination, the material character of that awful place and of the physical torments which all who are in hell endure. This evening we shall consider for a few moments the nature of the spiritual torments of hell.

—Sin, remember, is a twofold enormity. It is a base consent to the promptings of our corrupt nature to the lower instincts, to that which is gross and beastlike; and it is also a turning away from the counsel of our higher nature, from all that is pure and holy, from the Holy God Himself. For this reason mortal sin is punished in hell by two different forms of punishment, physical and spiritual.

—Now of all these spiritual pains by far the greatest is the pain of loss, so great, in fact, that in itself it is a torment greater than all the others. Saint Thomas, the greatest doctor of the church, the angelic doctor, as he is called, says that the worst damnation consists in this that the understanding of man is totally deprived of divine light and his affection obstinately turned away from the goodness of God. God, remember, is a being infinitely good and therefore the loss of such a being must be a loss infinitely painful. In this life we have not a very clear idea of what such a loss must be but the damned in hell, for their greater torment, have a full understanding of that which they have lost and understand that they have lost it through their own sins and have lost it for ever. At the very instant of death the bonds of the flesh are broken asunder and the soul at once flies towards God. The soul tends towards God as towards the centre of her existence. Remember, my dear little boys, our souls long to be with God. We come from God, we live by God, we belong to God: we are His, inalienably His. God loves with a divine love every human soul and every human soul lives in that love. How could it be otherwise? Every breath that we draw, every thought of our brain, every instant of life proceed from God's inexhaustible goodness. And if it be pain for a mother to be parted from her child, for a man to be exiled from hearth and home, for friend to be sundered from friend, O think what pain, what anguish, it must be for the poor soul to be spurned from the presence of the supremely good and loving Creator Who has called that soul into existence from nothingness and sustained it in life and loved it with an immeasurable love. This, then, to be separated for ever from its greatest good, from God, and to feel the anguish of that separation, knowing full well that it is unchangeable, this is the greatest torment which the created soul is capable of bearing, *pœna damni,* the pain of loss.

—The second pain which will afflict the souls of the damned in hell is the pain of conscience. Just as in dead bodies worms are engendered by putrefaction so in the souls of the lost there arises a perpetual remorse from the putrefaction of sin, the sting of conscience, the worm, as Pope Innocent the Third calls it, of the triple sting. The first sting inflicted by this cruel worm will be the memory of past pleasures. O what a dreadful memory will that be! In the lake of alldevouring flame the proud king will remember the pomps of his court, the wise but wicked man his libraries and instruments of research, the lover of artistic pleasures his marbles and pictures and other art treasures, he who delighted in the pleasures of the table his gorgeous feasts, his dishes prepared with such delicacy, his choice wines; the miser will remember his hoard of gold, the robber his illgotten wealth, the angry and revengeful and merciless murderers their deeds of blood and violence in which they revelled, the impure and adulterous the unspeakable and filthy pleasures in which they delighted. They will remember all this and loathe themselves and their sins. For how miserable will all those pleasures seem to the soul condemned to suffer in hellfire for ages and ages. How they will rage and fume to think that they have lost the bliss of heaven for the dross of earth, for a few pieces of metal, for vain honours, for bodily comforts, for a tingling of the nerves. They will repent indeed: and this is the second sting of the worm of conscience, a late and fruitless sorrow for sins committed. Divine justice insists that the understanding of those miserable wretches be fixed continually on the sins of which they were guilty and moreover, as saint Augustine points out, God will impart to them His own knowledge of sin so that sin will appear to them in all its hideous malice as it appears to the eyes of God Himself. They will behold their sins in all their foulness and repent but it will be too late and then they will bewail the good occasions which they neglected. This is the last and deepest and most cruel sting of the worm of conscience. The conscience will say: You had time and opportunity to repent and would not. You were brought up religiously by your parents. You had the sacraments and graces and indulgences of the church to aid you. You had the minister of God to preach to you, to call you back when you had strayed, to forgive you your sins, no matter how many, how abominable, if only you had confessed and repented. No. You would not. You flouted the ministers of holy religion, you turned your back on the confessional, you wallowed deeper and deeper in the mire of sin. God appealed to you, threatened you, entreated you to return to Him. O what shame, what misery! The Ruler of the universe entreated you, a creature of clay, to love Him Who made you and to keep His law. No. You would not. And now, though you were to flood all hell with your tears if you could still weep, all that sea of repentance would not gain for you what a single tear of true repentance shed during your mortal life would have gained for you. You implore now a moment of earthly life wherein to repent: in vain. That time is gone: gone for ever.

—Such is the threefold sting of conscience, the viper which gnaws the very heart's core of the wretches in hell so that filled with hellish fury they curse themselves for their folly and curse the evil companions who have brought them to such ruin and curse the devils who tempted them in life and now mock them and torture them in eternity and even revile and curse the Supreme Being Whose goodness and patience they scorned and slighted but Whose justice and power they cannot evade.

—The next spiritual pain to which the damned are subjected is the pain of extension. Man, in this earthly life, though he be capable of many evils, is not capable of them all at once inasmuch as one evil corrects and counteracts another just as one poison frequently corrects another. In hell on the contrary one torment, instead of counteracting another, lends it still greater force: and moreover as the internal faculties are more perfect than the external senses, so are they more capable of suffering. Just as every sense is afflicted with a fitting torment so is every spiritual faculty; the fancy with horrible images, the sensitive faculty with alternate longing and rage, the mind and understanding with an interior darkness more terrible even than the exterior darkness which reigns in that dreadful prison. The malice, impotent though it be, which possesses these demon souls is an evil of boundless extension, of limitless duration, a frightful state of wickedness which we can scarcely realise unless we bear in mind the enormity of sin and the hatred God bears to it.

—Opposed to this pain of extension and yet coexistent with it we have the pain of intensity. Hell is the centre of evils and, as you know, things are more intense at their centres than at their remotest points. There are no contraries or admixtures of any kind to temper or soften in the least the pains of hell. Nay, things which are good in themselves become evil in hell. Company, elsewhere a source of comfort to the afflicted, will be there a continual torment: knowledge, so much longed for as the chief good of the intellect, will there be hated worse than ignorance: light, so much coveted by all creatures from the lord of creation down to the humblest plant in the forest, will be loathed intensely. In this life our sorrows are either not very long or not very great because nature either overcomes them by habits or puts an end to them by sinking under their weight. But in hell the torments cannot be overcome by habit. For while they are of terrible intensity they are at the same time of continual variety, each pain, so to speak, taking fire from another and reendowing that which has enkindled it with a still fiercer flame. Nor can nature escape from these intense and various tortures by succumbing to them for the soul is sustained and maintained in evil so that its suffering may be the greater. Boundless extension of torment, incredible intensity of suffering, unceasing variety of torture—this is what the divine majesty, so outraged by sinners, demands, this is what the holiness of heaven, slighted and set aside for the lustful and low pleasures of the corrupt flesh, requires, this is what the blood of the innocent Lamb of God, shed for the redemption of sinners, trampled upon by the vilest of the vile, insists upon.

—Last and crowning torture of all the tortures of that awful place is the eternity of hell. Eternity! O, dread and dire word. Eternity! What mind of man can understand it? And, remember, it is an eternity of pain. Even though the pains of hell were not so terrible as they are yet they would become infinite as they are destined to last for ever. But while they are everlasting they are at the same time, as you know, intolerably intense, unbearably extensive. To bear even the sting of an insect for all eternity would be a dreadful torment. What must it be, then, to bear the manifold tortures of hell for ever? For ever! For all eternity! Not for a year or for an age but for ever. Try to imagine the awful meaning of this. You have often seen the sand on the seashore. How fine are its tiny grains! And how many of those tiny little grains go to make up the small handful which a child grasps in its play. Now imagine a mountain of that sand, a million miles high, reaching from the earth to the farthest heavens, and a million miles broad, extending to remotest space, and a million miles in thickness: and imagine such an enormous mass of countless particles of sand multiplied as often as there are leaves in the forest, drops of water in the mighty ocean, feathers on birds, scales on fish, hairs on animals, atoms in the vast expanse of the air: and imagine that at the end of every million years a little bird came to that mountain and carried away in its beak a tiny grain of that sand. How many millions upon millions of centuries would pass before that bird had carried away even a square foot of that mountain, how many eons upon eons of ages before it had carried away all. Yet at the end of that immense stretch of time not even one instant of eternity could be said to have ended. At the end of all those billions and trillions of years eternity would have scarcely begun. And if that mountain rose again after it had been all carried away and if the bird came again and carried it all away again grain by grain: and if it so rose and sank as many times as there are stars in the sky, atoms in the air, drops of water in the sea, leaves on the trees, feathers upon birds, scales upon fish, hairs upon animals, at the end of all those innumerable risings and sinkings of that immeasurably vast mountain not one single instant of eternity could be said to have ended; even then, at the end of such a period, after that eon of time the mere thought of which makes our very brain reel dizzily, eternity would have scarcely begun.

—A holy saint (one of our own fathers I believe it was) was once vouchsafed a vision of hell. It seemed to him that he stood in the midst of a great hall, dark and silent save for the ticking of a great clock. The ticking went on unceasingly; and it seemed to this saint that the sound of the ticking was the ceaseless repetition of the words: ever, never; ever, never. Ever to be in hell, never to be in heaven; ever to be shut off from the presence of God, never to enjoy the beatific vision; ever to be eaten with flames, gnawed by vermin, goaded with burning spikes, never to be free from those pains; ever to have the conscience upbraid one, the memory enrage, the mind filled with darkness and despair, never to escape; ever to curse and revile the foul demons who gloat fiendishly over the misery of their dupes, never to behold the shining raiment of the blessed spirits; ever to cry out of the abyss of fire to God for an instant, a single instant, of respite from such awful agony, never to receive, even for an instant, God's pardon; ever to suffer, never to enjoy; ever to be damned, never to be saved; ever, never; ever, never. O what a dreadful punishment! An eternity of endless agony, of endless bodily and spiritual torment, without one ray of hope, without one moment of cessation, of agony limitless in extent, limitless in intensity, of torment infinitely lasting, infinitely varied, of torture that sustains eternally that which it eternally devours, of anguish that everlastingly preys upon the spirit while it racks the flesh, an eternity, every instant of which is itself an eternity, and that eternity an eternity of woe. Such is the terrible punishment decreed for those who die in mortal sin by an almighty and a just God.

—Yes, a just God! Men, reasoning always as men, are astonished that God should mete out an everlasting and infinite punishment in the fires of hell for a single grievous sin. They reason thus because, blinded by the gross illusion of the flesh and the darkness of human understanding, they are unable to comprehend the hideous malice of mortal sin. They reason thus because they are unable to comprehend that even venial sin is of such a foul and hideous nature that even if the omnipotent Creator could end all the evil and misery in the world, the wars, the diseases, the robberies, the crimes, the deaths, the murders, on condition that He allowed a single venial sin to pass unpunished, a single venial sin, a lie, an angry look, a moment of wilful sloth, He, the great omnipotent God, could not do so because sin, be it in thought or deed, is a transgression of His law and God would not be God if He did not punish the transgressor.

—A sin, an instant of rebellious pride of the intellect mad Lucifer and a third part of the cohorts of angels fall from their glory. A sin, an instant of folly and weakness, drove Adam and Eve out of Eden and brought death and suffering into the world. To retrieve the consequences of that sin the Only Begotten Son of God came down to earth, lived and suffered and died a most painful death, hanging for three hours on the cross.

—O, my dear little brethren in Christ Jesus, will we then offend that good Redeemer and provoke His anger? Will we trample again upon that torn and mangled corpse? Will we spit upon that face so full of sorrow and love? Will we too, like the cruel jews and the brutal soldiers, mock that gentle and compassionate Saviour Who trod alone for our sake the awful winepress of sorrow? Every word of sin is a wound in His tender side. Every sinful act is a thorn piercing His head. Every impure thought, deliberately yielded to, is a keen lance transfixing that sacred and loving heart. No, no. It is impossible for any human being to do that which offends so deeply the divine majesty, that which is punished by an eternity of agony, that which crucifies again the Son of God and makes a mockery of Him.

—I pray to God that my poor words may have availed today to confirm in holiness those who are in a state of grace, to strengthen the wavering, to lead back to the state of grace the poor soul that has strayed if any such be among you. I pray to God, and do you pray with me, that we may repent of our sins. I will ask you now, all of you, to repeat after me the act of contrition, kneeling here in this humble chapel in the presence of God. He is there in the tabernacle burning with love for mankind, ready to comfort the afflicted. Be not afraid. No matter how many or how foul the sins if only you repent of them they will be forgiven you. Let no worldly shame hold you back. God is still the merciful Lord Who wishes not the eternal death of the sinner but rather that he be converted and live.

—He calls you to Him. You are His. He made you out of nothing. He loved you as only a God can love. His arms are open to receive you even though you have sinned against Him. Come to Him, poor sinner, poor vain and erring sinner. Now is the acceptable time. Now is the hour.

The priest rose and, turning towards the altar, knelt upon the step before the tabernacle in the fallen gloom. He waited till all in the chapel had knelt and every least noise was still. Then, raising his head, he repeated the act of contrition, phrase by phrase, with fervour. The boys answered him phrase by phrase. Stephen, his tongue cleaving to his palate, bowed his head, praying with his heart.

> —*O my God!*—
> —*O my God!*—
> —*I am heartily sorry*—
> —*I am heartily sorry*—
> —*for having offended Thee*—
> —*for having offended Thee*—
> —*and I detest my sins*—
> —*and I detest my sins*—
> —*above every other evil*—
> —*above every other evil*—
> —*because they displease Thee, my God*—
> —*because they displease Thee, my God*—
> —*Who art so deserving*—

—Who art so deserving—
—of all my love—
—of all my love—
—and I firmly purpose—
—and I firmly purpose—
—by Thy holy grace—
—by Thy holy grace—
—never more to offend Thee—
—never more to offend Thee—
—and to amend my life—
—and to amend my life—

B. F. SKINNER

• *Walden Two*

29

Castle got his chance to take up "general issues" that afternoon. A walk to the summit of Stone Hill had been planned for a large party, which included Mr. and Mrs. Meyerson and three or four children. It seemed unlikely that any serious discussion would be possible. But a storm had been threatening all morning, and at lunch we heard it break. The afternoon was again open. I detected a certain activity in the dining room as plans were changed. As we were finishing dinner two young people approached our table and spoke to Rodge, Steve, and the girls.

"Do you play? Cornet, sax, trombone? We're getting up a concert. We even have a lonely tuba."

"You play, Steve," said Mary.

"Steve was the best little old trombone in the Philippines," said Rodge.

"Good! Anybody else? It's strictly amateur."

It appeared that Barbara could play popular tunes on the piano, mostly by ear, and it was thought that something might be arranged. They departed for the theater to look over the common stock of instruments, and Frazier, Castle, and I were left alone.

Castle immediately began to warm up his motors. He picked up an empty cigarette package which Barbara had left on the table, tore it in two, placed the

SOURCE. From *Walden Two* by B. F. Skinner. Copyright 1948 by B. F. Skinner, reprinted with the permission of the Macmillan Company.

halves together, and tore them again. Various husky noises issued from his throat. It was obvious that something was about to happen, and Frazier and I waited in silence.

"Mr. Frazier," Castle said at last, in a sudden roar, "I accuse you of one of the most diabolical machinations in the history of mankind!" He looked as steadily as possible at Frazier, but he was trembling, and his eyes were popping.

"Shall we go to my room?" Frazier said quietly.

It was a trick of Frazier's to adopt a contrasting tone of voice, and in this instance it was devastating. Castle came down to earth with a humiliating bump. He had prepared himself for a verbal battle of heroic dimensions, but he found himself humbly carrying his tray to the service window and trailing Frazier along the Walk.

I was not sure of the line Castle was going to take. Apparently he had done some thinking since morning, probably during the service, but I could not guess the result. Frazier's manner was also puzzling. His suggestion that we go to his room had sounded a little as if he were inviting a truculent companion to "step outside and say that again!" He had apparently expected the attack from Castle and had prepared the defenses to his satisfaction.

When we had settled ourselves in Frazier's room, with Frazier full-length on the bed, over which he had hastily pulled a cover, Castle began again in an unsuccessful attempt to duplicate the surprise and force of his first assault.

"A modern, mechanized, managerial Machiavelli—that is my final estimate of you, Mr. Frazier," he said, with the same challenging stare.

"It must be gratifying to know that one has reached a 'final estimate,' " said Frazier.

"An artist in power," Castle continued, "whose greatest art is to conceal art. The silent despot."

"Since we are dealing in 'M's,' why not sum it all up and say 'Mephistophelian'?" said Frazier, curiously reviving my fears of the preceding afternoon.

"I'm willing to do that!" said Castle. "And unless God is very sure of himself, I suspect He's by no means easy about this latest turn in the war of the angels. So far as I can see, you've blocked every path through which man was to struggle upward toward salvation. Intelligence, initiative—you have filled their places with a sort of degraded instinct, engineered compulsion. Walden Two is a marvel of efficient coordination—as efficient as an anthill!"

"Replacing intelligence with instinct—" muttered Frazier. "I had never thought of that. It's an interesting possibility. How's it done?" It was a crude maneuver. The question was a digression, intended to spoil Castle's timing and to direct our attention to practical affairs in which Frazier was more at home.

"The behavior of your members is carefully shaped in advance by a Plan," said Castle, not to be taken in, "and it's shaped to perpetuate that Plan. In-

tellectually Walden Two is quite as incapable of a spontaneous change of course
as the life within a beehive."

"I see what you mean," said Frazier distantly. But he returned to his strat-
egy. "And have you discovered the machinery of my power?"

"I have, indeed. We were looking in the wrong place. There's no *current*
contact between you and the members of Walden Two. You threw us off the
track very skillfully on that point last night. But you were behaving as a despot
when you first laid your plans—when you designed the social structure and drew
up the contract between community and member, when you worked out your educational practices and your guarantees against despotism—What a joke! Don't
tell me you weren't in control *then!* Burris saw the point. What about your career
as organizer? *There* was leadership! And the most damnable leadership in history, because you were setting the stage for the withdrawal of yourself as a personal force, knowing full well that everything that happened would still be your
doing. Hundreds—you predicted millions—of unsuspecting souls were to fall
within the scope of your ambitious scheme."

Castle was driving his argument home with great excitement, but Frazier
was lying in exaggerated relaxation, staring at the ceiling, his hands cupped behind his head.

"Very good, Mr. Castle," he said softly. "I gave you the clue, of course,
when we parted last night."

"You did, indeed. And I've wondered why. Were you led into that fatal
error by your conceit? Perhaps that's the ultimate answer to your form of despotism. No one could enjoy the power you have seized without wishing to display
it from time to time."

"I've admitted neither power nor despotism. But you're quite right in saying
that I've exerted an influence and in one sense will continue to exert it forever.
I believe you called me a *primum mobile*—not quite correctly, as I found upon
looking the term up last night. But I did plan Walden Two—not as an architect
plans a building, but as a scientist plans a long-term experiment, uncertain of
the conditions he will meet but knowing how he will deal with them when they
arise. In a sense, Walden Two is predetermined, but not as the behavior of a
beehive is determined. Intelligence, no matter how much is may be shaped and
extended by our educational system, will still function as intelligence. It will be
used to puzzle out solutions to problems to which a beehive would quickly suc-
cumb. What the plan does is to keep intelligence on the right track, for the good
of society rather than of the intelligent individual—or for the eventual rather
than the immediate good of the individual. It does this by making sure that the
individual will not forget his personal stake in the welfare of society."

"But you are forestalling many possibly useful acts of intelligence which
aren't encompassed by your plan. You have ruled out points of view which may

be more productive. You are implying that T. E. Frazier, looking at the world from the middle of the twentieth century, understands the best course for mankind forever."

"Yes, I suppose I do."

"But that's absurd!"

"Not at all. I don't say I foresee the course man will take a hundred years hence, let alone forever, but I know which he should take now."

"How can you be sure of it? It's certainly not a question you have answered experimentally."

"I think we're in the course of answering it," said Frazier. "But that's beside the point. There's no alternative. We must take that course."

"But that's fantastic. You who are taking it are in a small minority."

Frazier sat up.

"And the majority are in a big quandary," he said. "They're not on the road at all, or they're scrambling back toward their starting point, or sidling from one side of the road to the other like so many crabs. What do you think two world wars have been about? Something as simple as boundaries or trade? Nonsense. The world is trying to adjust to a new conception of man in relation to men."

"Perhaps it's merely trying to adjust to despots whose ideas are incompatible with the real nature of man."

"Mr. Castle," said Frazier very earnestly, "let me ask you a question. I warn you, it will be the most terrifying question of your life. *What would you do if you found yourself in possession of an effective science of behavior?* Suppose you suddenly found it possible to control the behavior of men as you wished. What would you do?"

"That's an assumption?"

"Take it as one if you like. *I* take it as a fact. And apparently you accept it as a fact too. I can hardly be as despotic as you claim unless I hold the key to an extensive practical control."

"What would I do?" said Castle thoughtfully. "I think I would dump your science of behavior in the ocean."

"And deny men all the help you could otherwise give them?"

"And give them the freedom they would otherwise lose forever!"

"How could you give them freedom?"

"By refusing to control them!"

"But you would only be leaving the control in other hands."

"Whose?"

"The charlatan, the demagogue, the salesman, the ward heeler, the bully, the cheat, the educator, the priest—all who are now in possession of the techniques of behavioral engineering."

"A pretty good share of the control would remain in the hands of the individual himself."

"That's an assumption, too, and it's your only hope. It's your only possible chance to avoid the implications of a science of behavior. If man is free, then a technology of behavior is impossible. But I'm asking you to consider the other case."

"Then my answer is that your assumption is contrary to fact and any further consideration idle."

"And your accusations——?"

"——were in terms of intention, not of possible achievement."

Frazier sighed dramatically.

"It's a little late to be proving that a behavioral technology is well advanced. How can you deny it? Many of its methods and techniques are really as old as the hills. Look at their frightful misuse in the hands of the Nazis! And what about the techniques of the psychological clinic? What about education? Or religion? Or practical politics? Or advertising and salesmanship? Bring them all together and you have a sort of rule-of-thumb technology of vast power. No, Mr. Castle, the science is there for the asking. But its techniques and methods are in the wrong hands——they are used for personal aggrandizement in a competitive world or, in the case of the psychologist and educator, for futilely corrective purposes. My question is, have you the courage to take up and wield the science of behavior for the good of mankind? You answer that you would dump it in the ocean!"

"I'd want to take it out of the hands of the politicians and advertisers and salesmen, too."

"And the psychologists and educators? You see, Mr. Castle, you can't have that kind of cake. The fact is, we not only *can* control human behavior, *we must.* But who's to do it, and what's to be done?"

"So long as a trace of personal freedom survives, I'll stick to my position," said Castle, very much out of countenance.

"Isn't it time we talked about freedom?" I said. "We parted a day or so ago on an agreement to let the question of freedom ring. It's time to answer, don't you think?"

"My answer is simple enough," said Frazier. "I deny that freedom exists at all. I must deny it——or my program would be absurd. You can't have a science about a subject matter which hops capriciously about. Perhaps we can never *prove* that man isn't free; it's an assumption. But the increasing success of a science of behavior makes it more and more plausible."

"On the contrary, a simple personal experience makes it untenable," said Castle. "The experience of freedom. I *know* that I'm free."

"It must be quite consoling," said Frazier.

"And what's more—you do, too," said Castle hotly. "When you deny your own freedom for the sake of playing with a science of behavior, you're acting in plain bad faith. That's the only way I can explain it." He tried to recover himself and shrugged his shoulders. "At least you'll grant that you *feel* free."

"The 'feeling of freedom' should deceive no one," said Frazier. "Give me a concrete case."

"Well, right now," Castle said. He picked up a book of matches. "I'm free to hold or drop these matches."

"You will, of course, do one or the other," said Frazier. "Linguistically or logically there seem to be two possibilities, but I submit that there's only one in fact. The determining forces may be subtle but they are inexorable. I suggest that as an orderly person you will probably hold—ah! you drop them! Well, you see, that's all part of your behavior with respect to me. You couldn't resist the temptation to prove me wrong. It was all lawful. You had no choice. The deciding factor entered rather late, and naturally you couldn't foresee the result when you first held them up. There was no strong likelihood that you would act in either direction, and so you said you were free."

"That's entirely too glib," said Castle. "It's easy to argue lawfulness after the fact. But let's see you predict what I will do in advance. Then I'll agree there's law."

"I didn't say that behavior is always predictable, any more than the weather is always predictable. There are often too many factors to be taken into account. We can't measure them all accurately, and we couldn't perform the mathematical operations needed to make a prediction if we had the measurements. The legality is usually an assumption—but none the less important in judging the issue at hand."

"Take a case where there's no choice, then," said Castle. "Certainly a man in jail isn't free in the sense in which I am free now."

"Good! That's an excellent start. Let us classify the kinds of determiners of human behavior. One class, as you suggest, is physical restraint—handcuffs, iron bars, forcible coercion. These are ways in which we shape human behavior according to our wishes. They're crude, and they sacrifice the affection of the controllee, but they often work. Now, what other ways are there of limiting freedom?"

Frazier had adopted a professorial tone and Castle refused to answer.

"The threat of force would be one," I said.

"Right. And here again we shan't encourage any loyalty on the part of the controllee. He has perhaps a shade more of the feeling of freedom, since he can always 'choose to act and accept the consequences,' but he doesn't feel exactly free. He knows his behavior is being coerced. Now what else?"

I had no answer.

"Force or the threat of force—I see no other possibility," said Castle after a moment.

"Precisely," said Frazier.

"But certainly a large part of my behavior has no connection with force at all. There's my freedom!" said Castle.

"I wasn't agreeing that there was no other possibility—merely that *you* could see no other. Not being a good behaviorist—or a good Christian, for that matter—you have no feeling for a tremendous power of a different sort."

"What's that?"

"I shall have to be technical," said Frazier. "But only for a moment. It's what the science of behavior calls 'reinforcement theory.' The things that can happen to us fall into three classes. To some things we are indifferent. Other things we like—we want them to happen, and we take steps to make them happen again. Still other things we don't like—we don't want them to happen and we take steps to get rid of them or keep them from happening again.

"*Now*," Frazier continued earnestly, "if it's in our power to create any of the situations which a person likes or to remove any situation he doesn't like, we can control his behavior. When he behaves as we want him to behave, we simply create a situation he likes, or remove one he doesn't like. As a result, the probability that he will behave that way again goes up, which is what we want. Technically it's called 'positive reinforcement.'

"The old school made the amazing mistake of supposing that the reverse was true, that by removing a situation a person likes or setting up one he doesn't like—in other words by punishing him—it was possible to *reduce* the probability that he would behave in a given way again. That simply doesn't hold. It has been established beyond question. What is emerging at this critical stage in the evolution of society is a behavioral and cultural technology based on positive reinforcement alone. We are gradually discovering—at an untold cost in human suffering—that in the long run punishment doesn't reduce the probability that an act will occur. We have been so preoccupied with the contrary that we always take 'force' to mean punishment. We don't say we're using force when we send shiploads of food into a starving country, though we're displaying quite as much *power* as if we were sending troops and guns."

"I'm certainly not an advocate of force," said Castle. "But I can't agree that it's not effective."

"It's *temporarily* effective, that's the worst of it. That explains several thousand years of bloodshed. Even nature has been fooled. We 'instinctively' punish a person who doesn't behave as we like—we spank him if he's a child or strike him if he's a man. A nice distinction! The immediate effect of the blow teaches us to strike again. Retribution and revenge are the most natural things on earth. But in the long run the man we strike is no less likely to repeat his act."

"But he won't repeat it if we hit him hard enough," said Castle.

"He'll still *tend* to repeat it. He'll *want* to repeat it. We haven't really altered his potential behavior at all. That's the pity of it. If he doesn't repeat it in our presence, he will in the presence of someone else. Or it will be repeated in the disguise of a neurotic symptom. If we hit hard enough, we clear a little place for ourselves in the wilderness of civilization, but we make the rest of the wilderness still more terrible.

"Now, early forms of government are naturally based on punishment. It's the obvious technique when the physically strong control the weak. But we're in the throes of a great change to positive reinforcement—from a competitive society in which one man's reward is another man's punishment, to a cooperative society in which no one gains at the expense of anyone else.

"The change is slow and painful because the immediate, temporary effect of punishment overshadows the eventual advantage of positive reinforcement. We've all seen countless instances of the temporary effect of force, but clear evidence of the effect of not using force is rare. That's why I insist that Jesus, who was apparently the first to discover the power of refusing to punish, must have hit upon the principle by accident. He certainly had none of the experimental evidence which is available to us today, and I can't conceive that it was possible, no matter what the man's genius, to have discovered the principle from casual observation."

"A touch of revelation, perhaps?" said Castle.

"No, accident. Jesus discovered one principle because it had immediate consequences, and he got another thrown in for good measure."

I began to see light.

"You mean the principle of 'love your enemies'?" I said.

"Exactly! To 'do good to those who despitefully use you' has two unrelated consequences. You gain the peace of mind we talked about the other day. Let the stronger man push you around—at least you avoid the torture of your own rage. *That's* the immediate consequence. What an astonishing discovery it must have been to find that in the long run you could *control the stronger man* in the same way!"

"It's generous of you to give so much credit to your early colleague," said Castle, "but why are we still in the throes of so much misery? Twenty centuries should have been enough for one piece of behavioral engineering."

"The conditions which made the principle difficult to discover made it difficult to teach. The history of the Christian Church doesn't reveal many cases of doing good to one's enemies. To inoffensive heathens, perhaps, but not enemies. One must look outside the field of organized religion to find the principle in practice at all. Church governments are devotees of *power,* both temporal and bogus."

"But what has all this got to do with freedom?" I said hastily.

Frazier took time to reorganize his behavior. He looked steadily toward the window, against which the rain was beating heavily.

"Now that we *know* how positive reinforcement works and why negative doesn't," he said at last, "we can be more deliberate, and hence more successful, in our cultural design. We can achieve a sort of control under which the controlled, though they are following a code much more scrupulously than was ever the case under the old system, nevertheless *feel free*. They are doing what they want to do, not what they are forced to do. That's the source of the tremendous power of positive reinforcement—there's no restraint and no revolt. By a careful cultural design, we control not the final behavior, but the *inclination* to behave —the motives, the desires, the wishes.

"The curious thing is that in that case *the question of freedom never arises*. Mr. Castle was free to drop the matchbook in the sense that nothing was preventing him. If it had been securely bound to his hand he wouldn't have been free. Nor would he have been quite free if I'd covered him with a gun and threatened to shoot him if he let it fall. The question of freedom arises when there is restraint—either physical or psychological.

"But restraint is only one sort of control, and absence of restraint isn't freedom. It's not control that's lacking when one feels 'free,' but the objectionable control of force. Mr. Castle felt free to hold or drop the matches in the sense that he felt no restraint—no threat of punishment in taking either course of action. He neglected to examine his positive reasons for holding or letting go, in spite of the fact that these were more compelling in this instance than any threat of force.

"We have no vocabulary of freedom in dealing with what we want to do," Frazier went on. "The question never arises. When men strike for freedom, they strike against jails and the police, or the threat of them—against oppression. They never strike against forces which make them want to act the way they do. Yet, it seems to be understood that governments will operate only through force or the threat of force, and that all other principles of control will be left to education, religion, and commerce. If this continues to be the case, we may as well give up. A government can never create a free people with the techniques now allotted to it.

"The question is: Can men live in freedom and peace? And the answer is: Yes, if we can build a social structure which will satisfy the needs of everyone and in which everyone will want to observe the supporting code. But so far this has been achieved only in Walden Two. Your ruthless accusations to the contrary, Mr. Castle, this is the freest place on earth. And it is free precisely because we make no use of force or the threat of force. Every bit of our research, from the nursery through the psychological management of our adult membership, is directed toward that end—to exploit every alternative to forcible control. By skillful planning, by a wise choice of techniques we *increase* the feeling of freedom.

"It's not planning which infringes upon freedom, but planning which uses force. A sense of freedom was practically unknown in the planned society of

Nazi Germany, because the planners made a fantastic use of force and the threat of force.

"No, Mr. Castle, when a science of behavior has once been achieved, there's no alternative to a planned society. We can't leave mankind to an accidental or biased control. But by using the principle of positive reinforcement—carefully avoiding force or the threat of force—we can preserve a personal sense of freedom."

Frazier threw himself back upon the bed and stared at the ceiling.

"But you haven't denied that you are in complete control," said Castle. "You are still the long-range dictator."

"As you will," said Frazier, waving his hands loosely in the air and then cupping them behind his head. "In fact, I'm inclined to agree. When you have once grasped the principle of positive reinforcement, you can enjoy a sense of unlimited power. It's enough to satisfy the thirstiest tyrant."

"There you are, then," said Castle. "That's my case."

"But it's a limited sort of despotism," Frazier went on. "And I don't think anyone should worry about it. The despot must wield his power for the good of others. If he takes any step which reduces the sum total of human happiness, his power is reduced by a like amount. What better check against a malevolent despotism could you ask for?"

"The check I ask for," said Castle, "is nothing less than democracy. Let the people rule and power will not be misused. I can't see that the nature of the power matters. As a matter of fact, couldn't this principle of 'positive reinforcement,' as you call it, be used by a democratic government just as well as by your dictatorship?"

"No principle is consistently used by a democratic government. What do you mean by democracy, anyway?"

"Government by the people or according to the will of the people, naturally," said Castle.

"As exemplified by current practices in the United States?"

"I suppose so. Yes, I'll take my stand on that. It's not a perfect democracy, but it's the best there is at the moment."

"Then I say that democracy is a pious fraud," said Frazier. "In what sense is it 'government by the people'?"

"In an obvious sense, I should say."

"It isn't obvious at all. How is the people's will ascertained? In an election. But what a travesty! In a small committee meeting, or even a town hall, I can see some point in voting, especially on a yes-or-no question. But fifty million voters choosing a president—that's quite another thing."

"I can't see that the number of voters changes the principle," said Castle.

"The chance that one man's vote will decide the issue in a national election," said Frazier, speaking very deliberately, "is less than the chance that he will be killed on his way to the polls. We pay no attention whatsoever to chances of that magnitude in our daily affairs. We should call a man a fool who bought a sweepstakes ticket with similar odds against him."

"It must mean something or people wouldn't vote," said Castle.

"How many of them would go on voting if they were free of a lot of extraneous pressures? Do you think a man goes to the polls because of any effect which casting a vote has ever had? By no means. He goes to avoid being talked about by his neighbors, or to 'knife' a candidate whom he dislikes, marking his X as he might defile a campaign poster—and with the same irrational spite. No, a man has no logical reason to vote whatsoever. The chances of affecting the issue are too small to alter his behavior in any appreciable way."

"I believe the mathematicians have a name for that fallacy," said Castle. "It's true that your chances of deciding the issue get smaller as the number of voters increases, but the stakes get larger at the same rate."

"But do they? Is a national election really an important issue? Does it really matter very much who wins? The platforms of the two parties are carefully made as much alike as possible, and when the election is over we're all advised to accept the result like good sports. Only a few voters go on caring very much after a week or two. The rest know there's no real threat. Things will go on pretty much the same. Elections are sometimes turned by a few million voters who can't make up their minds until election day. It can't be much of an issue if that's the case."

"Even so, it's important that the people *feel* they've chosen the government they want," said Castle.

"On the contrary, that's the worst of it. Voting is a device for blaming conditions on the people. The people aren't rulers, they're scapegoats. And they file to the polls every so often to renew their right to the title."

"I daresay there are defects in the machinery of democracy," said Castle. "No one wholly approves of the average presidential campaign. The will of the people is likely to be unduly influenced, and perhaps incorrectly determined. But that's a matter of technique. I think we will eventually work out a better system for ascertaining what the people want done. Democracy isn't a method of polling opinion, it's the assignment of power to that opinion. Let's assume that the will of the people can be ascertained. What then?"

"I should ask you that. What then, indeed? Are the people skilled governors? No. And they become less and less skilled, relatively speaking, as the science of government advances. It's the same point I raised in our discussion of the group nursery: when we've once acquired a behavioral technology, we can't leave the control of behavior to the unskilled. Your answer is to deny that the technology exists—a very feeble answer, it seems to me.

"The one thing the people know," Frazier continued, "and the one thing about which they should be heard is how they like the existing state of affairs, and perhaps how they would like some other state of affairs. What they conspicuously don't know is how to get what they want. That's a matter for specialists."

"But the people have solved some pretty important problems," I said.

"Have they, in fact? The actual practice in a democracy is to vote, not for a given state of affairs, but for a man who claims to be able to achieve that state. I'm not a historian"—Frazier laughed explosively—"quite the contrary—but I suspect that that's always what is meant by the rule of the people—rule by a man chosen by the people."

"Isn't that a possible way out, though?" said Castle. "Suppose we need experts. Why not elect them?"

"For a very simple reason. The people are in no position to evaluate experts. And elected experts are never able to act as they think best. They can't experiment. The amateur doesn't appreciate the need for experimentation. He wants his expert to *know*. And he's utterly incapable of sustaining the period of doubt during which an experiment works itself out. The experts must either disguise their experiments and pretend to know the outcome in advance or stop experimenting altogether and struggle to maintain the *status quo*."

" 'With all her faults, I love her still,' " said Castle. "I'll take democracy. We may have to muddle through. We may seem laughable to your streamlined Planners. But we have one thing on our side—freedom."

"I thought we had settled that," said Frazier.

"We had. But apparently not as you thought," said Castle. "I don't like despotism."

Frazier got up and went to the window. The rain had stopped, and the distant hills beyond the river had become visible. He stood with his back to us for perhaps a minute, which seemed very long against the energetic tempo of our conversation. Finally he turned.

"Can't I make you understand?" he said, holding out his hands in a gesture of appeal. "*I don't like despotism either!* I don't like the despotism of ignorance. I don't like the despotism of neglect, of irresponsibility, the despotism of accident, even. And I don't like the despotism of democracy!"

He turned back to the window.

"I don't think I follow you," said Castle, somewhat softened by Frazier's evident emotion.

"Democracy is the spawn of despotism," Frazier said, continuing to look out the window. "And like father, like son. Democracy is power and rule. It's not the will of the people, remember; it's the will of the majority." He turned and, in a husky voice which broke in flight like a tumbler pigeon on the word "out," he added, "My heart goes out to the everlasting minority." He seemed ready to cry, but I could not tell whether it was in sympathy for the oppressed or in rage at his failure to convince Castle.

"In a democracy," he went on, "there is *no* check against despotism, because the principle of democracy is supposed to be itself a check. But it guarantees only that the *majority* will not be despotically ruled."

"I don't agree that the minority has no say," said Castle. "But in any case it's better that at least half the people get what they want, instead of a small élite."

"There you are!" said Frazier, jumping up again just as he had started to sit down. "The majority are an élite. And they're despots. I want none of them! Let's have government for the benefit of all."

"But that isn't always possible," said Castle.

"It's possible much oftener than under a democracy. There are seldom any issues which have to be decided in an all-or-none fashion. A careful planner could work out a compromise which would be reasonably satisfying to everyone. But in a democracy, the majority solve the problem to their satisfaction, and the minority can be damned.

"The government of Walden Two," he continued, "has the virtues of democracy, but none of the defects. It's much closer to the theory or intent of democracy than the actual practice in America today. The will of the people is carefully ascertained. We have no election campaigns to falsify issues or obscure them with emotional appeals, but a careful study of the satisfaction of the membership is made. Every member has a direct channel through which he may protest to the Managers or even the Planners. And these protests are taken as seriously as the pilot of an airplane takes a sputtering engine. We don't need laws and a police force to compel a pilot to pay attention to a defective engine. Nor do we need laws to compel our Dairy Manager to pay attention to an epidemic among his cows. Similarly, our Behavioral and Cultural Managers need not be compelled to consider grievances. A grievance is a wheel to be oiled, or a broken pipe line to be repaired.

"Most of the people in Walden Two take no active part in running the government. And they don't want an active part. The urge to have a say in how the country should be run is a recent thing. It was not part of early democracy. The original victory over tyranny was a constitutional guarantee of personal rights, including the right to protest if conditions were not satisfactory. But the business of ruling was left to somebody else. Nowadays, everybody fancies himself an expert in government and wants to have a say. Let's hope it's a temporary cultural pattern. I can remember when everyone could talk about the mechanical principles according to which his automobile ran or failed to run. Everyone was an automotive specialist and knew how to file the points of a magneto and take the shimmy out of front wheels. To suggest that these matters might be left to experts would have been called Fascism, if the term had been invented. But today no one knows how his car operates and I can't see that he's any the less happy.

"In Walden Two no one worries about the government except the few to whom that worry has been assigned. To suggest that everyone should taken an interest would seem as fantastic as to suggest that everyone should become familiar with our Diesel engines. Even the constitutional rights of the members are seldom thought about, I'm sure. The only thing that matters is one's day-to-day happiness and a secure future. Any infringement there would undoubtedly 'arouse the electorate.' "

"I assume that your constitution at least can't be changed without a vote of the members," I said.

"Wrong again. It can be changed by a unanimous vote of the Planners and a two-thirds vote of the Managers. You're still thinking about government by the people. Get that out of your head. The people are in no better position to change the constitution than to decide upon current practices."

"Then what's to prevent your Planners from becoming despots?" I said. "Wouldn't it really be possible?"

"How?" said Frazier.

"Oh, in many ways, I imagine."

"Such as?"

"Well, if I were a Planner with a yen for despotism, I would begin by insinuating into the culture the notion that Planners were exceptional people. I would argue that they should be personally known to the members, and should therefore wear an identifying badge or uniform. This could be done under the guise of facilitating service to the members, but eventually the Planners would be set off as a separate caste. Then they'd be relieved from menial work on the ground that they were too busy with the affairs of the community. Then special quarters, perhaps quite luxurious, would be built for them. I'd bring the Managers around to this change in the constitution by giving them better quarters also. It would all be carefully propagandized, of course. Eventually more and more of the wealth of the community would be diverted to this élite, and I would come out with a true despotism. Isn't that possible?"

"If you mean, 'Isn't despotism possible?' the answer is yes," said Frazier. "Cultures which work for the advantage of a few last a long time. Look at India, where the oppressed aren't even aware that they are sick and miserable. But are the people strong, productive, progressive? If not, then the culture will eventually be replaced by competing cultures which work more efficiently. Our Planners know this. They know that any usurpation of power would weaken the community as a whole and eventually destroy the whole venture."

"A group of despotic planners might be willing to sacrifice the community," I said. "They wouldn't necessarily suffer if it failed. They could simply abscond with the funds."

"That would be a catastrophe. Like an earthquake, or a new and frightful epidemic, or a raid from another world. All we can do is take reasonable precautions. Your hypothetical case strikes me as implausible, that's all I can say."

"But isn't that just the weakness of your antidemocratic attitude?" Castle said. "Haven't you lost your guarantee against the usurpation of power?"

"There's no power to usurp," said Frazier. "There's no police, no military, no guns or bombs—tear-gas or atomic—to give strength to the few. In point of physical force the members are always clearly in power. Revolt is not only easy, it's inevitable if real dissatisfaction arises.

"And there's little real wealth to tempt anyone. It isn't true that the Planners could abscond with the funds. Our wealth is our happiness. The physical plant of the community would be practically worthless without the members.

"And then remember that the Planners are part of a noncompetitive culture in which a thirst for power is a curiosity. They have no reason to usurp. Their tradition is against it. Any gesture of personal domination would stand out as conspicuously as the theft of the bulletin board."

"But it's human to dominate," said Castle, "in any culture."

"That's an experimental question, Mr. Castle. You can't answer it from your armchair. But let's see what a usurpation of power would amount to. Insofar as the Planners rule at all, they do so through positive reinforcement. They don't use or threaten to use force. They have no machinery for that. In order to extend their power they would have to provide more and more satisfying conditions. A curious sort of despotism, Mr. Castle."

"But they might change to a different sort of power."

"That would require a unanimous vote. But the Planners are eventually demoted to simple citizenship. Their terms of office are staggered, and some of them are always so close to retirement that they wouldn't share in the selfish consequences. Why should they vote for the change?

"Usurpation of power is a threat only in a competitive culture," Frazier continued. "In Walden Two power is either destroyed or so diffused that usurpation is practically impossible. Personal ambition isn't essential in a good governor. As governmental technology advances, less and less is left to the decisions of governors, anyway. Eventually we shall have no use for Planners at all. The Managers will suffice."

Frazier turned to me in an open gesture of appeasement.

"Democracy is not a guarantee against despotism, Burris. Its virtues are of another sort. It has proved itself clearly superior to the despotic rule of a small élite. We have seen it survive in conflict with the despotic pattern in World War II. The democratic peoples proved themselves superior just because of their democracy. They could enlist the support of other peoples, who had less to fear from them than from an aggressive élite. They could marshal greater manpower in the long run because everyone had a stake in victory and few were suffering from the strain of forcible coercion. The despots couldn't convert the people they conquered while pretending to be a superior race. Every principle which seemed to strengthen the governmental structure of Fascism when the war began proved to be an eventual weakness.

"But the triumph of democracy doesn't mean it's the best government. It was merely the better in a contest with a conspicuously bad one. Let's not stop with democracy. It isn't, and can't be, the best form of government, because it's based on a scientifically invalid conception of man. It fails to take account of the fact that in the long run *man is determined by the state*. A *laissez-faire* philosophy which trusts to the inherent goodness and wisdom of the common man is incompatible with the observed fact that men are made good or bad and wise or foolish by the environment in which they grow."

"But which comes first," I asked, "the hen or the egg? Men build society and society builds men. Where do we start?"

"It isn't a question of starting. The start has been made. It's a question of what's to be done from now on."

"Then it's to be revolution, is that it?" said Castle. "If democracy can't change itself into something better—"

"Revolution? You're not a very rewarding pupil, Mr. Castle. The change won't come about through power politics at all. It will take place at another level altogether."

"What level?"

Frazier waved his hand toward the window, through which we could see the drenched landscape of Walden Two.

"Well," said Castle, "you'd better hurry up. It's not a job to be done on four hours a day."

"Four hours a day is exactly what it needs," said Frazier with a smile. He lay back upon the bed, looking rather tired.

"I can think of a conspicuous case in which the change you're advocating is coming about at the level of power politics," I said.

Frazier sat up quickly, with obvious effort. He looked at me suspiciously.

"Russia," I said.

"Ah, Russia," he said with relief. He showed no inclination to go on.

"What about Russia, though?"

"What about it, indeed?"

"Isn't there a considerable resemblance between Russian communism and your own philosophy?"

"Russia, Russia," Frazier murmured evasively. "Our visitors always ask that. Russia is our rival. It's very flattering—if you consider the resources and the numbers of people involved."

"But you're dodging my question. Hasn't Russia done what you're trying to do, but at the level of power politics? I can imagine what a Communist would say of your program at Walden Two. Wouldn't he simply tell you to drop the experiment and go to work for the Party?"

"He would and he does."

"And what's your answer?"

"I can see only four things wrong with Russia," Frazier said, clearly enjoying the condescension. "As originally conceived, it was a good try. It sprang from humanitarian impulses which are a commonplace in Walden Two. But it quickly developed certain weaknesses. There are four of them, and they were inevitable. They were inevitable just because the attempt was made at the level of power politics." He waited for me to ask him what the weaknesses were.

"The first," he said, as soon as I had done so, "is a decline in the experimental spirit. Many promising experiments have simply been dropped. The group care of children, the altered structure of the family, the abandonment of religion, new kinds of personal incentives—all these problems were 'solved' by dropping back to practices which have prevailed in capitalistic societies for centuries. It was the old difficulty. A government in power can't experiment. It must know the answers or at least pretend to know them. Today the Russians contend that an optimal cultural pattern has been achieved, if not yet fully implemented. They dare not admit to any serious need for improvement. Revolutionary experimentation is dead.

"In the second place, Russia has overpropagandized, both to its own people and to the outside world. Their propaganda is much more extensive than any which ever enslaved a working class. That's a serious defect, for it has made it impossible to evaluate their success. We don't know how much of the current vigor of Russian communism is due to a strong, satisfying way of life, and how much to indoctrination. You may call it a temporary expedient, to counteract the propaganda embedded in an older culture. But that need has long since passed, yet the propaganda continues. So long as it goes on, no valid data on the effectiveness of Russian communism can be obtained. For all we know, the whole culture would fall apart if the supporting attitudes were taken away. And what is worse, it's hard to see how they can ever be taken away. Propaganda makes it impossible to progress toward a form of society in which it is unnecessary.

"The third weakness of the Russian government is its use of heroes. The first function of the hero, in Russia as elsewhere, is to piece out a defective governmental structure. Important decisions aren't made by appeal to a set of principles; they are personal acts. The process of governing is an art, not a science, and the government is only as good or as long-lasting as the artist. As to the second function of the hero—how long would communism last if all the pictures of Lenin and Stalin were torn down? It's a question worth asking.

"But most important of all, the Russian experiment was based on power. You may argue that the seizure of power was also a temporary expedient, since the people who held it were intolerant and oppressive. But you can hardly defend the continued use of power in that way. The Russians are still a long way from a culture in which people behave as they *want* to behave, for their mutual good. In order to get its people to act as the communist pattern demands, the Russian government has had to use the techniques of capitalism. On the one hand it resorts to extravagant and uneven rewards. But an unequal distribution of wealth destroys more incentives than it creates. It obviously can't operate for the *common* good.

On the other hand, the government also uses punishment or the threat of it. What kind of behavioral engineering do you call that?"

Frazier spat into the flowerpot in a gesture of disgust. Then he held out his hands with an exaggerated shrug and drew himself slowly to his feet. He had evidently had enough of Castle's "general issues."

SAMUEL CLEMENS

• *Huckleberry Finn*

Chapter VI. Pap Struggles with the Death Angel

Well, pretty soon the old man was up and around again, and then he went for Judge Thatcher in the courts to make him give up that money, and he went for me, too, for not stopping school. He catched me a couple of times and thrashed me, but I went to school just the same, and dodged him or outrun him most of the time. I didn't want to go to school much before, but I reckoned I'd go now to spite pap. That law trial was a slow business—appeared like they warn't ever going to get started on it; so every now and then I'd borrow two or three dollars off of the judge for him, to keep from getting a cowhiding. Every time he got money he got drunk; and every time he got drunk he raised Cain around town; and every time he raised Cain he got jailed. He was just suited— this kind of thing was right in his line.

He got to hanging around the widow's too much, and so she told him at last that if he didn't quit using around there she would make trouble for him. Well, *wasn't* he mad? He said he would show who was Huck Finn's boss. So he watched out for me one day in the spring, and catched me, and took me up the river about three mile in a skiff, and crossed over to the Illinois shore where it was woody and there warn't no houses but an old log hut in a place where the timber was so thick you couldn't find it if you didn't know where it was.

He kept me with him all the time, and I never got a chance to run off. We lived in that old cabin, and he always locked the door and put the key under his

SOURCE. Samuel Clemens, *Huckleberry Finn,* Copyright 1931, Harper and Brothers.

head nights. He had a gun which he had stole, I reckon, and we fished and hunted, and that was what we lived on. Every little while he locked me in and went down to the store, three miles, to the ferry, and traded fish and game for whisky, and fetched it home and got drunk and had a good time, and licked me. The widow she found out where I was by and by, and she sent a man over to try to get hold of me; but pap drove him off with the gun, and it warn't long after that till I was used to being where I was, and liked it—all but the cowhide part.

It was kind of lazy and jolly, laying off comfortable all day, smoking and fishing, and no books nor study. Two months or more run along, and my clothes got to be all rags and dirt, and I didn't see how I'd ever got to like it so well at the widow's, where you had to wash, and eat on a plate, and comb up, and go to bed and get up regular, and be forever bothering over a book, and have old Miss Watson pecking at you all the time. I didn't want to go back no more. I had stopped cussing, because the widow didn't like it; but now I took to it again because pap hadn't no objections. It was pretty good times up in the woods there, take it all around.

But by and by pap got too handy with his hick'ry, and I couldn't stand it. I was all over welts. He got to going away so much, too, and locking me in. Once he locked me in and was gone three days. It was dreadful lonesome. I judged he had got drownded, and I wasn't every going to get out any more. I was scared. I made up my mind I would fix up some way to leave there. I had tried to get out of that cabin many a time, but I couldn't find no way. There warn't a window to it big enough for a dog to get through. I couldn't get up the chimbly; it was too narrow. The door was thick, solid oak slabs. Pap was pretty careful not to leave a knife or anything in the cabin when he was away; I reckon I had hunted the place over as much as a hundred times; well I was most all the time at it, because it was about the only way to put in the time. But this time I found something at last; I found an old rusty wood-saw without any handle; it was laid in between a rafter and the clapboards of the roof. I greased it up and went to work. There was an old horse-blanket nailed against the logs at the far end of the cabin behind the table, to keep the wind from blowing through the chinks and putting the candle out. I got under the table and raised the blanket, and went to work to saw a section of the big bottom log out—big enough to let me through. Well, it was a good long job, but I was getting toward the end of it when I heard pap's gun in the woods. I got rid of the signs of my work, and dropped the blanket and hid my saw, and pretty soon pap come in.

Pap warn't in a good humor—so he was his natural self. He said he was down-town, and everything was going wrong. His lawyer said he reckoned he would win his lawsuit and get the money if they ever got started on the trial; but then there was ways to put it off a long time, and Judge Thatcher knowed how to do it. And he said people allowed there'd be another trial to get me away from him and give me to the widow for my guardian, and they guessed it would win this time. This shook me up considerable, because I didn't want to go back to the widow's any more and be so cramped up and sivilized, as they called it. Then the old man got to cussing, and cussed everything and everybody he could think of, and then cussed them all over again to make sure he hadn't skipped any, and after that he polished off with a kind of general cuss all round, including a considerable parcel of people which he didn't know the names of, and so called them what's-his-name when he got to them, and went right along with his cussing.

He said he would like to see the widow get me. He said he would watch out, and if they tried to come any such game on him he knowed of a place six or seven mile off to stow me in, where they might hunt till they dropped and they couldn't find me. That made me pretty uneasy again, but only for a minute; I reckoned I wouldn't stay on hand till he got that chance.

The old man made me go to the skiff and fetch the things he had got. There was a fifty-pound sack of corn meal, and a side of bacon, ammunition, and a four-gallon jug of whisky, and an old book and two newspapers for wadding, besides some tow. I toted-up a load, and went back and set down on the bow of the skiff to rest. I thought it all over, and I reckoned I would walk off with the gun and some lines, and take to the woods when I run away. I guessed I wouldn't stay in one place, but just tramp right across the country, mostly night-times, and hunt and fish to keep alive, and so get so far away that the old man nor the widow couldn't ever find me any more. I judged I would saw out and leave that night if pap got drunk enough, and I reckoned he would. I got so full of it I didn't notice how long I was staying till the old man hollered and asked me whether I was asleep or drownded.

I got the things all up to the cabin, and then it was about dark. While I was cooking supper the old man took a swig or two and got sort of warmed up, and went to ripping again. He had been drunk over in town, and laid in the gutter all night, and he was a sight to look at. A body would 'a' thought he was Adam —he was just all mud. Whenever his liquor begun to work he most always went for the govment. This time he says:

"Call this a govment! why, just look at it and see what it's like. Here's the law a-standing ready to take a man's son away from him—a man's own son, which he has had all the trouble and all the anxiety and all the expense of raising. Yes, just as that man has got that son raised at last, and ready to go to work and begin to do suthin' for *him* and give him a rest, the law up and goes for him. And they call *that* govment! That ain't all, nuther. The law backs that old Judge Thatcher up and helps him to keep me out o' my property. Here's what the law does: The law takes a man worth six thousand dollars and up'ards, and jams him into an old trap of a cabin like this, and lets him go round in clothes that ain't fitten for a hog. They call that govment! A man can't get his rights in a govment like this. Sometimes I've a mighty notion to just leave the country for good and all. Yes, and I *told* 'em so; I told old Thatcher so to his face. Lots of 'em heard me, and can tell what I said. Says I, for two cents I'd leave the blamed country and never come a-near it ag'in. Them's the very words. I says, look at my hat—

if you call it a hat—but the lid raises up and the rest of it goes down till it's below my chin, and then it ain't rightly a hat at all, but more like my head was shoved up through a jint o' stove-pipe. Look at it, says I—such a hat for me to wear—one of the wealthiest men in this town if I could git my rights.

"Oh, yes, this is a wonderful govment, wonderful. Why, looky here. There was a free nigger there from Ohio—a mulatter, most as white as a white man. He had the whitest shirt on you ever see, too, and the shiniest hat; and there ain't a man in that town that's got as fine clothes as what he had; and he had a gold watch and chain, and a silver-headed cane—the awfulest old gray-headed nabob in the state. And what do you think? They said he was a p'fessor in a college, and could talk all kinds of languages, and knowed everything. And that ain't the wust. They said he could *vote* when he was at home. Well, that let me out. Thinks I, what is the country a-coming to? It was 'lection day, and I was just about to go and vote myself if I warn't too drunk to get there; but when they told me there was a state in this country where they'd let that nigger vote, I drawed out. I says I'll never vote ag'in. Them's the very words I said; they all heard me; and the country may rot for all me—I'll never vote ag'in as long as I live. And to see the cool way of that nigger—why, he wouldn't 'a' give me the road if I hadn't shoved him out o' the way. I says to the people, why ain't this nigger put up at auction and sold?—that's what I want to know. And what do you reckon they said? Why, they said he couldn't be sold till he'd been in the state six months, and he hadn't been there that long yet. There, now—that's a specimen. They call that a govment that can't sell a free nigger till he's been in the state six months. Here's a govment that calls itself a govment, and let's on to be a govment, and thinks it is a govment, and yet's got to set stock-still for six whole months before it can take a-hold of a prowling, thieving, infernal, white-shirted free nigger, and—"

Pap was a-going on so he never noticed where his old limber legs was taking him to, so he went head over heels over the tub of salt pork and barked both shins, and the rest of his speech was all the hottest kind of language—mostly hove at the nigger and the govment, though he give the tub some, too, all along, here and there. He hopped around the cabin considerable, first on one leg and then on the other, holding first one shin and then the other one, and at last he let out with his left foot all of a sudden and fetched the tub a rattling kick. But it warn't good judgment, because that was the boot that had a couple of his toes leaking out of the front end of it; so now he raised a howl that fairly made a body's hair raise, and down he went in the dirt, and rolled there, and held his toes; and the cussing he done then laid over anything he had ever done previous. He said so his own self afterwards. He had heard old Sowberry Hagan in his best days, and he said it laid over him, too; but I reckon that was sort of piling it on, maybe.

After supper pap took the jug, and said he had enough whisky there for two drunks and one delirium tremens. That was always his word. I judged he would be blind drunk in about an hour, and then I would steal the key, or saw myself out, one or t'other. He drank and drank, and tumbled down on his blankets by and by; but luck didn't run my way. He didn't go sound asleep, but was uneasy. He groaned and moaned and thrashed around this way and that for a long time. At last I got so sleepy I couldn't keep my eyes open all I could do, and so before I knowed what I was about I was sound asleep, and the candle burning.

I don't know how long I was asleep, but all of a sudden there was an awful scream and I was up. There was pap looking wild, and skipping around every which way and yelling about snakes. He said they was crawling up his legs; and then he would give a jump and scream, and say one had bit him on the cheek— but I couldn't see no snakes. He started and run round and round the cabin, hollering "Take him off! take him off! he's biting me on the neck!" I never see a man look so wild in the eyes. Pretty soon he was all fagged out, and fell down panting; then he rolled over and over wonderful fast, kicking things every which way, and striking and grabbing at the air with his hands, and screaming and saying there was devils a-hold of him. He wore out by and by, and laid still awhile, moaning. Then he laid stiller, and didn't make a sound. I could hear the owls and the wolves away off in the woods, and it seemed terrible still. He was laying over by the corner. By and by he raised up part way and listened, with his head to one side. He says, very low:

"Tramp—tramp—tramp; that's the dead; tramp—tramp—tramp; they're coming after me; but I won't go. Oh, they're here! don't touch me—don't! hands off—they're cold; let go. Oh, let a poor devil alone!"

Then he went down on all fours and crawled off, begging them to let him alone, and he rolled himself up in his blanket and wallowed in under the old pine table, still a-begging; and then he went to crying. I could hear him through the blanket.

By and by he rolled out and jumped up on his feet looking wild, and he see me and went for me. He chased me round and round the place with a clasp-knife, calling me the Angel of Death, and saying he would kill me, and then I couldn't come for him no more. I begged, and told him I was only Huck; but he laughed *such* a screechy laugh, and roared and cussed, and kept on chasing me up. Once when I turned short and dodged under his arm he made a grab and got me by the jacket between my shoulders, and I thought I was gone; but I slid out of the jacket quick as lightning, and saved myself. Pretty soon he was all tired out, and dropped down with his back against the door, and said he would rest a minute and then kill me. He put his knife under him, and said he would sleep and get strong, and then he would see who was who.

So he dozed off pretty soon. By and by I got the old split-bottom chair and clumb up as easy as I could, not to make any noise, and got down the gun. I slipped the ramrod down it to make sure it was loaded, and then I laid it across the turnip-barrel, pointing towards pap, and set down behind it to wait for him to stir. And how slow and still the time did drag along.

Chapter 3

Identity and Anxiety

HERMAN HESSE

• *Demian*

4) Beatrice

At the end of the holidays, and without having seen my friend again, I went to St. ———. My parents accompanied me and entrusted me to the care of a boy's boarding-house run by one of the teachers at the preparatory school. They would have been struck dumb with horror had they known into what world they were letting me wander.

The question remained: was I eventually to become a good son and useful citizen or did my nature point in an altogether different direction? My last attempt to achieve happiness in the shadow of the paternal home had lasted a long time, had on occasion almost succeeded, but had completely failed in the end.

The peculiar emptiness and isolation that I came to feel for the first time after Confirmation (oh, how familiar it was to become afterwards, this desolate, thin air!) passed only very slowly. My leave-taking from home was surprisingly easy, I was almost ashamed that I did not feel more nostalgic. My sisters wept for no reason; my eyes remained dry. I was astonished at myself. I had always been an emotional and essentially good child. Now I had completely changed. I behaved with utter indifference to the world outside and for days on end voices within preoccupied me, inner streams, the forbidden dark streams that roared below the surface. I had grown several inches in the last half year and I walked lanky and half-finished through the world. I had lost any charm I might ever have

SOURCE. From *Demian* by Herman Hesse. Copyright 1925 by S. Fischer Verlag. Copyright 1965 by Harper and Row Publishers, reprinted with the permission of Harper and Row.

had and felt that no one could possibly love me the way I was. I certainly had no love for myself. Often I felt a great longing for Max Demian, but no less often I hated him, accusing him of having caused the impoverishment of my life that held me in its sway like a foul disease.

I was neither liked nor respected in my boys' boarding-house. I was teased to begin with, then avoided and looked upon as a sneak and an unwelcome oddity. I fell in with this role, even exaggerated it, and grumbled myself into a self-isolation that must have appeared to outsiders like permanent and masculine contempt of the world, whereas, in truth, I often secretly succumbed to consuming fits of melancholy and despair. In school I managed to get by on the knowledge accumulated in my previous class—the present one lagged somewhat behind the one I had left—and I began to regard the students in my age group contemptuously as mere children.

It went on like this for a year or more. The first few visits back home left me cold. I was glad when I could leave again.

It was the beginning of November. I had become used to taking short meditative walks during all kinds of weather, walks on which I often enjoyed a kind of rapture tinged with melancholy, scorn of the world and self-hatred. Thus I roamed in the foggy dusk one evening through the town. The broad avenue of a public park stood deserted, beckoning me to enter; the path lay thickly carpeted with fallen leaves which I stirred angrily with my feet. There was a damp, bitter smell, and distant trees, shadowy as ghosts, loomed huge out of the mist.

I stopped irresolute at the far end of the avenue: staring into the dark foliage I greedily breathed the humid fragrance of decay and dying to which something within me responded with greeting.

Someone stepped out of one of the side paths, his coat billowing as he walked. I was about to continue when a voice called out:

"Hello, Sinclair."

He came up to me. It was Alfons Beck, the oldest boy in our boardinghouse. I was always glad to see him, had nothing against him except that he treated me, and all others who were younger, with an element of ironic and avuncular condescension. He was reputed to be strong as a bear and to have the teacher in our house completely under his thumb. He was the hero of many a student rumor.

"Well, what are you doing here?" he called out affably in that tone the bigger boys affected when they occasionally condescended to talk to one of us. "I'll bet anything you're making a poem."

"Wouldn't think of it," I replied brusquely.

He laughed out loud, walked beside me, and made small talk in a way I hadn't been used to for a long time.

"You don't need to be afraid that I wouldn't understand, Sinclair. There's something to walking with autumnal thoughts through the evening fog. One likes to compose poems at a time like that, I know. About moribund nature, of course, and one's lost youth, which resembles it. Heinrich Heine, for example."

"I'm not as sentimental as all that," I defended myself.

"All right, let's drop the subject. But it seems to me that in weather like this a man does the right thing when he looks for a quiet place where he can drink a good glass of wine or something. Will you join me? I happen to be all by myself at the moment. Or would you rather not? I don't want to be the one who leads you astray, mon vieux, that is, in case you happen to be the kind that keeps to the straight and narrow."

Soon afterwards we were sitting in a small dive at the edge of town, drinking a wine of doubtful quality and clinking the thick glasses. I didn't much like it to begin with, but at least it was something new. Soon, however, unused to the wine, I became very loquacious. It was as though an interior window had opened through which the world sparkled. For how long, for how terribly long hadn't I really talked to anyone? My imagination began to run away with me and eventually I even popped out with the story of Cain and Abel.

Beck listened with evident pleasure—finally here was someone to whom I was able to give something! He patted me on the shoulder, called me one hell of a fellow, and my heart swelled ecstatically at this opportunity to luxuriate in the release of a long pent-up need for talk and communication, for acknowledgment from an older boy. When he called me a damned clever little bastard, the words ran like sweet wine into my soul. The world glowed in new colors, thoughts gushed out of a hundred audacious springs. The fire of enthusiasm flared up within me. We discussed our teachers and fellow students and it seemed to me that we understood each other perfectly. We talked about the Greeks and the pagans in general and Beck very much wanted me to confess to having slept with girls. This was out of my league. I hadn't experienced anything, certainly nothing worth telling. And what I had felt, what I had constructed in imagination, ached within me but had not been loosened or made communicable by the wine. Beck knew much more about girls, so I listened to his exploits without being able to say a word. I heard incredible things. Things I had never thought possible became everyday reality, seemed normal. Alfons Beck, who was eighteen, seemed to be able to draw on a vast body of experience. For instance, he had learned that it was a funny thing about girls, they just wanted to flirt, which was all very well, but not the real thing. For the real thing one could hope for greater success with women. Women were much more reasonable. Mrs. Jaggelt, for example, who owned the stationery store, well, with her one could talk business, and all the things that had happened behind her counter wouldn't fit into a book.

I sat there enchanted and also dumbfounded. Certainly, I could never have loved Mrs. Jaggelt—yet the news was incredible. There seemed to be hidden sources of pleasure, at least for the older boys, of which I had not even dreamed. Something about it didn't sound right, and it tasted less appealing and more ordinary than love, I felt, was supposed to taste—but at least: this was reality, this was life and adventure, and next to me sat someone who had experienced it, to whom it seemed normal.

Once it had reached this height, our conversation began to taper off. I was no longer the damned clever little bastard; I'd shrunk to a mere boy listening to a man. Yet all the same—compared with what my life had been for months—this was delicious, this was paradise. Besides, it was, as I began to realize only gradually, very much prohibited—from our presence in the bar to the subject of our talk. At least for me it smacked of rebellion.

I can remember that night with remarkable clarity. We started on our way home through the damp, past gas lamps dimly lighting the late night: for the first time in my life I was drunk. It was not pleasant. In fact it was most painful, yet it had something, a thrill, a sweetness of rebellious orgy, that was life and spirit. Beck did a good job taking charge of me, even though he cursed me bitterly as a "bloody beginner," and half led, half carried me home. There he succeeded in smuggling me through an open window in the hallway.

The sober reality to which I awoke after a brief deathlike sleep coincided with a painful and senseless depression. I sat up in bed, still wearing my shirt. The rest of my clothes, strewn about on the floor, reeked of tobacco and vomit. Between fits of headache, nausea, and a raging thirst an image came to my mind which I had not viewed for a long time: I visualized my parents' house, my home, my father and mother, my sisters, the garden. I could see the familiar bedroom, the school, the market place, could see Demian and the Confirmation classes— everything was wonderful, godly pure, and everything, all of this—as I realized now—had still been mine yesterday, a few hours ago, had waited for me; yet now, at this very hour, everything looked ravaged and damned, was mine no longer, rejected me, regarded me with disgust. Everything dear and intimate, everything my parents had given me as far back as the distant gardens of my childhood, every kiss from my mother, every Christmas, each devout, light-filled Sunday morning at home, each and every flower in the garden—everything had been laid waste, everything had been trampled on *by me!* If the arm of the law had reached out for me now, had bound and gagged me and led me to the gallows as the scum of the earth and a desecrator of the temple, I would not have objected, would have gladly gone, would have considered it just and fair.

So that's what I looked like inside! I who was going about contemptuous of the world! I who was proud in spirit and shared Demian's thoughts! That's what I looked like, a piece of excrement, a filthy swine, drunk and filthy, loathsome and callow, a vile beast brought low by hideous appetites. That's what I looked like, I, who came out of such pure gardens where everything was cleanliness, radiance, and tenderness, I, who had loved the music of Bach and beautiful poetry. With nausea and outrage I could still hear my life, drunk and unruly, sputtering out of me in idiotic laughter, in jerks and fits. There I was.

In spite of everything, I almost reveled in my agonies. I had been blind and insensible and my heart had been silent for so long, had cowered impoverished in a corner, that even this self-accusation, this dread, all these horrible feelings were welcome. At least it was feeling of some kind, at least there were some flames, the heart at least flickered. Confusedly I felt something like liberation amid my misery.

Meanwhile, viewed from the outside, I was going rapidly downhill. My first drunken frenzy was soon followed by others. There was much going to bars and carousing in our school. I was one of the youngest to take part, yet soon enough I was not merely a fledgling whom one grudgingly took along, I had become the ringleader and star, a notorious and daring bar crawler. Once again I belonged entirely to the world of darkness and to the devil, and in this world I had the reputation of being one hell of a fellow.

Nonetheless, I felt wretched. I lived in an orgy of self-destruction and, while my friends regarded me as a leader and as a damned sharp and funny fellow, deep down inside me my soul grieved. I can still remember tears springing to my eyes when I saw children playing in the street on Sunday morning as I emerged from a bar, children with freshly combed hair and dressed in their Sunday best. Those friends who sat with me in the lowest dives among beer puddles and dirty tables I amused with remarks of unprecedented cynicism, often even shocked them; yet in my inmost heart I was in awe of everything I belittled and lay weeping before my soul, my past, my mother, before God.

There was good reason why I never became one with my companions, why I felt alone among them and was therefore able to suffer so much. I was a barroom hero and cynic to satisfy the taste of the most brutal. I displayed wit and courage in my ideas and remarks about teachers, school, parents, and church. I could also bear to hear the filthiest stories and even ventured an occasional one myself, but I never accompanied my friends when they visited women. I was alone and was filled with intense longing for love, a hopeless longing, while, to judge by my talk, I should have been a hard-boiled sensualist. No one was more easily hurt, no one more bashful than I. And when I happened to see the young well-brought-up girls of the town walking in front of me, pretty and clean, innocent and graceful, they seemed like wonderful pure dreams, a thousand times too good for me. For a time I could not even bring myself to enter Mrs. Jaggelt's stationery store because I blushed looking at her remembering what Alfons Beck had told me.

The more I realized that I was to remain perpetually lonely and different within my new group of friends the less I was able to break away. I really don't know any longer whether boozing and swaggering actually ever gave me any pleasure. Moreover, I never became so used to drinking that I did not always feel embarrassing after-effects. It was all as if I were somehow under a compulsion to do these things. I simply did what I had to do, because I had no idea what to do with myself otherwise. I was afraid of being alone for long, was afraid of the many tender and chaste moods that would overcome me, was afraid of the thoughts of love surging up in me.

What I missed above all else was a friend. There were two or three fellow students whom I could have cared for, but they were in good standing and my vices had long been an open secret. They avoided me. I was regarded by and large as a hopeless rebel whose ground was slipping from under his feet. The teachers were well-informed about me, I had been severely punished several times, my final expulsion seemed merely a matter of time. I realized myself that I had become a poor student, but I wriggled strenuously through one exam after the other, always feeling that it couldn't go on like this much longer.

There are numerous ways in which God can make us lonely and lead us back to ourselves. This was the way He dealt with me at that time. It was like a bad dream. I can see myself: crawling along in my odious and unclean way, across filth and slime, across broken beer glasses and through cynically wasted nights, a spellbound dreamer, restless and racked. There are dreams in which on your way to the princess you become stuck in quagmires, in back alleys full of foul odors and refuse. That was how it was with me. In this unpleasant fashion I was condemned to become lonely, and I raised between myself and my childhood a locked gateway to Eden with its pitilessly resplendent host of guardians. It was a beginning, an awakening of nostalgia for my former self.

Yet I had not become so callous as not to be startled into twinges of fear when my father, alarmed by my tutor's letters, appeared for the first time in St. ———— and confronted me unexpectedly. Later on that winter, when he came a second time, nothing could move me any more, I let him scold and entreat me, let him remind me of my mother. Finally toward the end of the meeting he became quite angry and said if I didn't change he would have me expelled from the school in disgrace and placed in a reformatory. Well, let him! When he went away that time I felt sorry for him; he had accomplished nothing, he had not found a way to me—and at moments I felt that it served him right.

I could not have cared less what became of me. In my odd and unattractive fashion, going to bars and bragging was my way of quarreling with the world— this was my way of protesting. I was ruining myself in the process but at times I understood the situation as follows: if the world had no use for people like me, if it did not have a better place and higher tasks for them, well, in that case, people like me would go to pot, and the loss would be the world's.

Christmas vacation was a joyless affair that year. My mother was deeply startled when she saw me. I had shot up even more and my lean face looked gray and wasted, with slack features and inflamed eyes. The first touch of a mustache and the eyeglasses I had just begun wearing made me look odder still. My sisters shied away and giggled. Everything was most unedifying. Disagreeable and bitter was the talk I had with my father in his study, disagreeable exchanging greetings with a handful of relatives, and particularly unpleasant was Christmas Eve itself. Ever since I had been a little child this had been the great day in our house. The evening was a festivity of love and gratitude, when the bond between child and parents was renewed. This time everything was merely oppressive and embarrassing. As usual my father read aloud the passage about the shepherds in the fields "watching their flocks," as usual my sisters stood radiantly before a table decked with gifts, but father's voice sounded disgruntled, his face looked old and strained, and mother was sad. Everything seemed out of place: the presents and Christmas greetings, Gospel reading and the lit-up tree. The gingerbread smelled sweet; it exuded a host of memories which were even sweeter. The fragrance of the Christmas tree told of a world that no longer existed. I longed for evening and for the holidays to be over.

It went on like this the entire winter. Only a short while back I had been given a stern warning by the teachers' council and been threatened with expulsion. It couldn't go on much longer. Well, I didn't care.

I held a very special grudge against Max Demian, whom I hadn't seen again even once. I had written him twice during my first months in St. ———— but had received no reply; so I had not called on him during the holidays.

In the same park in which I had met Alfons Beck in the fall, a girl came to my attention in early spring as the thorn hedges began to bud. I had taken a walk by myself, my head filled with vile thoughts and worries—for my health had deteriorated—and to make matters worse I was perpetually in financial difficulties, owed friends considerable sums and had thus continually to invent expenditures so as to receive money from home. In a number of stores I had allowed bills to mount for cigars and similar things. Not that this worried me much. If my existence was about to come to a sudden end anyway—if I drowned myself or was sent to the reformatory—a few small extras didn't make much difference. Yet I was forced to live face to face with these unpleasant details: they made me wretched.

On that spring day in the park I saw a young woman who attracted me. She was tall and slender, elegantly dressed, and had an intelligent and boyish face. I liked her at once. She was my type and began to fill my imagination. She probably was not much older than I but seemed far more mature, well-defined, a full-grown woman, but with a touch of exuberance and boyishness in her face, and this was what I liked above all.

I had never managed to approach a girl with whom I had fallen in love, nor did I manage in this case. But the impression she made on me was deeper than any previous one had been and the infatuation had a profound influence on my life.

Suddenly a new image had risen up before me, a lofty and cherished image. And no need, no urge was as deep or as fervent within me as the craving to worship and admire. I gave her the name Beatrice, for, even though I had not read Dante, I knew about Beatrice from an English painting of which I owned a reproduction. It showed a young pre-Raphaelite woman, long-limbed and slender, with long head and etherealized hands and features. My beautiful young woman did not quite resemble her, even though she, too, revealed that slender and boyish figure which I loved, and something of the ethereal, soulful quality of her face.

Although I never addressed a single word to Beatrice, she exerted a profound influence on me at that time. She raised her image before me, she gave me access to a holy shrine, she transformed me into a worshiper in a temple. From one day to the next I stayed clear of all bars and nocturnal exploits. I could be alone with myself again and enjoyed reading and going for long walks.

My sudden conversion drew a good deal of mockery in its wake. But now I had something I loved and venerated, I had an ideal again, life was rich with intimations of mystery and a feeling of dawn that made me immune to all taunts. I had come home again to myself, even if only as the slave and servant of a cherished image.

I find it difficult to think back to that time without a certain fondness. Once more I was trying most strenuously to construct an intimate "world of light" for myself out of the shambles of a period of devastation; once more I sacrificed everything within me to the aim of banishing darkness and evil from myself. And, furthermore, this present "world of light" was to some extent my own creation; it was no longer an escape, no crawling back to mother and the safety of irresponsibility; it was a new duty, one I had invented and desired on my own, with responsibility and self-control. My sexuality, a torment from which I was in constant flight, was to be transfigured into spirituality and devotion by this holy fire. Everything dark and hateful was to be banished, there were to be no more tortured nights, no excitement before lascivious pictures, no eavesdropping at forbidden doors, no lust. In place of all this I raised my altar to the image of Beatrice, and by consecrating myself to her I consecrated myself to the spirit and to the gods, sacrificing that part of life which I withdrew from the forces of darkness to those of light. My goal was not joy but purity, not happiness but beauty, and spirituality.

This cult of Beatrice completely changed my life. Yesterday a precocious cynic, today I was an acolyte whose aim was to become a saint. I not only avoided the bad life to which I had become accustomed, I sought to transform myself by introducing purity and nobility into every aspect of my life. In this connection I thought of my eating and drinking habits, my language and dress. I began my mornings with cold baths which cost me a great effort at first. My behavior became serious and dignified; I carried myself stiffly and assumed a slow and dignified gait. It may have looked comic to outsiders but to me it was a genuine act of worship.

Of all the new practices in which I sought to express my new conviction, one became truly important to me. I began to paint. The starting point for this was that the reproduction of the English picture I owned did not resemble my Beatrice closely enough. I wanted to try to paint her portrait for myself. With new joy and hopefulness I bought beautiful paper, paints, and brushes and carried them to my room—I had just been given one of my own—and prepared my palette, glass, porcelain dishes and pencils. The delicate tempera colors in the little tubes I had bought delighted me. Among them was a fiery chrome green that, I think, I can still see today as it flashed up for the first time in the small white dish.

I began with great care. Painting the likeness of a face was difficult. I wanted to try myself out first on something else. I painted ornaments, flowers, small imagined landscapes: a tree by a chapel, a Roman bridge with cypress trees. Sometimes I became so completely immersed in this game that I was as happy as a little child with his paintbox. Finally I set out on my portrait of Beatrice.

A few attempts failed completely and I discarded them. The more I sought to imagine the face of the girl I had encountered here and there on the street the less successful I was. Finally I gave up the attempt and contented myself with giving in to my imagination and intuition that arose spontaneously from the first strokes, as though out of the paint and brush themselves. It was a dream face that emerged and I was not dissatisfied with it. Yet I persisted and every new sketch was more distinct, approximated more nearly the type I desired, even if it in no way reproduced reality.

I grew more and more accustomed to idly drawing lines with a dreaming paintbrush and to coloring areas for which I had no model in mind, that were the result of playful fumblings of my subconscious. Finally, one day I produced, almost without knowing it, a face to which I responded more strongly than I had to any of the others. It was not the face of that girl—it wasn't supposed to be that any longer. It was something else, something unreal, yet it was no less valuable to me. It looked more like a boy's face than a girl's, the hair was not flaxen like that of my pretty girl, but dark brown with a reddish hue. The chin was strong and determined, the mouth like a red flower. As a whole it was somewhat stiff and masklike but it was impressive and full of a secret life of its own.

As I sat down in front of the completed painting, it had an odd effect on me. It resembled a kind of image of God or a holy mask, half male, half female, ageless, as purposeful as it was dreamy, as rigid as it was secretly alive. This face seemed to have a message for me, it belonged to me, it was asking something of me. It bore a resemblance to someone, yet I did not know whom.

For a time this portrait haunted my thoughts and shared my life. I kept it locked in a drawer so that no one would take it and taunt me with it. But as soon as I was alone in my small room I took it out and communed with it. In the evening I pinned it on the wall facing my bed and gazed on it until I fell asleep and in the morning it was the first thing my eyes opened on.

It was precisely at this time that I again began having many dreams, as I had always had as a child. It felt as though I had not dreamed for years. Now the dreams returned with entirely new images, and time after time the portrait appeared among them, alive and eloquent, friendly or hostile to me, sometimes distorted into a grimace, sometimes infinitely beautiful, harmonious, and noble.

Then one morning, as I awoke from one of these dreams, I suddenly recognized it. It looked at me as though it were fabulously familiar and seemed to call out my name. It seemed to know who I was, like a mother, as if its eyes had been fixed on me since the beginning of time. With a quivering heart I stared at the sheet, the close brown hair, the half-feminine mouth, the pronounced forehead with the strange brightness (it had dried this way of its own accord) and I felt myself coming nearer and nearer to the recognition, the rediscovery, the knowledge.

I leapt out of bed, stepped up to the face, and from inches away looked into its wide-open, greenish, rigid eyes, the right one slightly higher than the left. All at once the right eye twitched, ever so faintly and delicately but unmistakably, and I was able to recognize the picture. . . .

Why had it taken me so long? It was Demian's face.

Later I often compared the portrait with Demian's true features as I remembered them. They were by no means the same even though there was a resemblance. Nonetheless, it was Demian.

Once the early-summer sun slanted oblique and red into a window that faced westward. Dusk was growing in my room. It occurred to me to pin the portrait of Beatrice, or Demian, at the window crossbar and to observe the evening sun shine through it. The outlines of the face became blurred but the red-rimmed eyes, the brightness on the forehead, and the bright red mouth glowed deep and wild from the surface. I sat facing it for a long time, even after the sun had faded, and gradually I began to sense that this was neither Beatrice nor Demian but myself. Not that the picture resembled me—I did not feel that it should— but it was what determined my life, it was my inner self, my fate or my *daemon*. That's what my friend would look like if I were to find one ever again. That's what the woman I would love would look like if I were to love one. That's what my life and death would be like, this was the tone and rhythm of my fate.

During those weeks I had begun to read a book that made a more lasting impression on me than anything I had read before. Even later in life I have rarely experienced a book more intensely, except perhaps Nietzsche. It was a volume of Novalis, containing letters and aphorisms of which I understood only a few but which nevertheless held an inexpressible attraction for me. One of the aphorisms occurred to me now and I wrote it under the picture: "Fate and temperament are two words for one and the same concept." That was clear to me now.

I often caught sight of the girl I called Beatrice but I felt no emotion during these encounters, only a gentle harmony, a presentiment: you and I are linked, but not you, only your picture; you are a part of my fate.

My longing for Max Demian overwhelmed me again. I had had no news of him for years. Once I had met him during a vacation. I realized now that I suppressed this brief encounter in my notes and I realize that it was done out of vanity and shame. I have to make up for it.

Thus, during one of my holidays as I strolled through my home town, wearing the blasé, always slightly weary expression of my bar-crawling days, peering into the same old, despised faces of the philistines, I saw my former friend walking toward me. I had hardly seen him when I flinched. At the same moment I could not help thinking of Franz Kromer. If only Demian had really forgotten that episode! It was so unpleasant to be obligated to him. It was actually a silly children's story but an obligation nonetheless. . . .

He appeared to wait: would I greet him? When I did so as casually as possible he stretched out his hand. Yes, that was his grip! As firm, warm yet cool, and virile as ever!

He scrutinized my face and said. "You've grown, Sinclair." He himself seemed quite the same, as old or as young as ever.

He joined me and we took a walk, but talked of only inconsequential matters. It occurred to me that I had written him several times without getting a reply. I hoped that he'd forgotten that too, those stupid letters! He did not mention them.

At that time I had not yet met Beatrice and there was no portrait. I was still in the midst of my drunken period. At the outskirts of town I asked him to join me for a glass of wine and he did so. At once I made a big show of ordering a whole bottle, filled his glass, clinked mine with his, and displayed my great familiarity with student drinking customs by downing the first glass in one swallow.

"You spend a lot of time in bars, do you?" he asked.

"Well, yes," I replied. "What else is there to do? In the end it's more fun than anything else."

"You think? Maybe so. One part of it is of course very fine—the intoxication, the bacchanalian element. But I think most people that frequent bars have lost that entirely. It seems to me that going to bars is something genuinely philistine. Yes, for one night, with burning torches, a real wild drunk! But again and again, one little glass after the other, I wonder whether that's the real thing or not? Can you see Faust sitting night after night stooped over the bar?"

I took a swallow and looked at him with hostility.

"Well, not everybody's Faust," I said curtly.

He looked at me somewhat taken aback.

Then he laughed at me in his old lively and superior fashion. "Well, let's not fight over it! In any case, the life of a drunk is presumably livelier than that of the ordinary well-behaved citizen. And then—I read that once somewhere— the life of a hedonist is the best preparation for becoming a mystic. People like

St. Augustine are always the ones that become visionaries. He, too, was first a sensualist and man of the world."

I distrusted him and didn't want him to gain the upper hand under any circumstances. So I said superciliously: "Well, everybody to his own taste. As for me, I've no ambition to become a visionary or anything of the sort."

Demian gave me a brief shrewd look out of half-closed eyes.

"My dear Sinclair," he said slowly, "I didn't intend to tell you anything disagreeable. Besides—neither of us knows why you happen to be drinking wine at this moment. That which is within you and directs your life knows already. It's good to realize that within us there is someone who knows everything, wills everything, does everything better than we ourselves. But excuse me, I must go home."

We exchanged brief good-bys. I stayed on moodily and finished the bottle. When I wanted to leave I discovered that Demian had paid the bill—which put me in an even worse humor.

My thoughts returned to this small incident with Demian. I could not forget him. And the words he said to me in that bar at the edge of town would come to mind, strangely fresh and intact: "It's good to realize that within us there is someone who knows everything."

How I longed for Demian. I had no idea where he was nor how I could reach him. All I knew was that he was presumably studying at some university and that his mother had left town after he completed preparatory school.

I tried to remember whatever I could of Max Demian, reaching back as far as the Kromer episode. How much of what he had said to me over the years returned to mind, was still meaningful today, was appropriate and concerned me! And what he had said on our last and quite disagreeable meeting about a wasted life leading to sainthood suddenly also stood clearly before me. Wasn't that exactly what had happened to me? Hadn't I lived in drunkenness and squalor, dazed and lost, until just the opposite had come alive in me with a new zest for life, the longing for purity, the yearning for the sacred?

So I continued to pursue these memories. Night had long since come and now rain was falling. In my memories, too, I heard the rain: it was the hour under the chestnut trees when he had probed me about Franz Kromer and guessed my first secrets. One incident after another came back to me, conversations on the way to school, the Confirmation classes, and last of all my first meeting with him. What had we talked about? I couldn't find it at once, but I gave myself time, concentrating intensely. And now even that returned. We had stood before my parents' house after he had told me his version of the story of Cain. Then he had mentioned the old, half-hidden coat of arms situated in the keystone above our entrance. He had said that such things interested him and that one ought to attend to them.

That night I dreamed of Demian and the coat of arms. It kept changing continuously. Demian held it in his hand, often it was diminutive and gray, often powerful and varicolored, but he explained to me that it was always one and the same thing. In the end he obliged me to eat the coat of arms! When I had swallowed it, I felt to my horror that the heraldic bird was coming to life inside me, had begun to swell up and devour me from within. Deathly afraid I started up in bed, awoke.

I was wide awake; it was the middle of the night and I could hear rain pouring into the room. As I got up to close the window I stepped on something that shone bright on the floor. In the morning I discovered that it had been my painting. It lay in a puddle and the paper had warped. I placed it between two sheets of blotting paper inside a heavy book. When I looked at it again the next day it was dry, but had changed. The red mouth had faded and contracted a little. It now looked exactly like Demian's mouth.

I set about painting a fresh picture of the heraldic bird. I could not remember distinctly what it looked like and certain details, as I knew, could not be made out even from close up, because the thing was old an had often been painted over. The bird stood or perched on something, perhaps on a flower or on a basket or a nest, or on a treetop. I couldn't trouble myself over this detail and began with what I could visualize clearly. Out of an indistinct need I at once began to employ loud colors, painting the bird's head a golden yellow. Whenever the mood took me, I worked on the picture, bringing it to completion in several days.

Now it represented a bird of prey with a proud aquiline sparrow hawk's head, half its body stuck in some dark globe out of which it was struggling to free itself as though from a giant egg—all of this against a sky-blue background. As I continued to scrutinize the sheet it looked to me more and more like the many-colored coat of arms that had occurred to me in my dream.

I could not have written Demian even if I had known his address. I decided, however—in the same state of dreamlike presentiment in which I did everything—to send him the painting of the sparrow hawk, even if it would never reach him. I added no message, not even my name, carefully trimmed the edges and wrote my friend's former address on it. Then I mailed it.

I had an exam coming up and had to do more work than usual. The teachers had reinstated me in their favor since I had abruptly changed my previously despicable mode of life. Not that I had become an outstanding student, but now neither I nor anyone else gave it any further thought that half a year earlier my expulsion had seemed almost certain.

My father's letters regained some of their old tone, without reproaches or threats. Yet I felt no inclination to explain to him or anyone else how the change within me had come about. It was an accident that this transformation coincided with my parents' and teachers' wishes. This change did not bring me into the community of the others, did not make me closer to anyone, but actually made me even lonelier. My reformation seemed to point in the direction of Demian, but even this was a distant fate. *I* did not know myself, for I was too deeply involved. It had begun with Beatrice, but for some time I had been living in such an unreal world with my paintings and my thoughts of Demian that I'd forgotten all about her, too. I could not have uttered a single word about my dreams and expectations, my inner change, to anyone, not even if I had wanted to. But how could I have wanted to?

ROGER MARTIN DU GARD

• *The Thibaults*

XII

It was raining; Antoine took a taxi. As he neared the Faubourg Saint-Honoré his cheerfulness evaporated and a frown settled on his brows.

"If only it were all over!" he said to himself as, for the third time that day, he gloomily climbed the three flights of stairs. When he reached the door of the Héquets' flat he fancied for a moment that his wish had been fulfilled. The maid who opened the door looked at him in a peculiar manner and stepped forward hastily to whisper something in his ear. But it was only a private message from Mme. Héquet that she imparted; her mistress wanted Antoine to see her first, before going to the child.

There was no eluding it. The light was on in Nicole's room; the door stood open. As he entered he saw her head lying on the pillow. He walked up to the bedside. She did not stir. She had obviously dozed off, and it would have been brutal to disturb her. In repose she looked much younger, care-free, now that sleep had smoothed away the lines of grief and weariness. Antoine gazed at her, holding his breath, afraid to move; it startled him to read upon those features, whence sorrow had withdrawn itself only so short a while ago, this all so sudden ecstasy, so keen a longing for oblivion and happiness. The pearly lustre of her closed eyelids, fringed with fine-spun, tenuous strands of gold, her languid grace and air of unconcern—all the naked, self-revealing beauty of the face before him made his senses tingle. How fascinating, too, the drooping curve of

SOURCE. From *The Thibaults* by Roger Martin du Gard.

her mouth and the half-parted lips that now in their repose seemed to express only relief and hopefulness! "Why," Antoine asked himself, "why should the face of any young being seen asleep appeal to us so strongly? What instinct lies behind the thrill, the almost sensual thrill of pity it invokes in every one of us?"

Turning away, he tip-toed soundlessly from the room. Though the doors were shut the child's hoarse, incessant wailing came to his ears as he proceeded down the passage. With an effort he nerved himself to turn the handle, cross the threshold, and renew contact with the dark powers at work within.

The child's cradle had been placed in the middle of the room and Héquet was seated beside it, his hands resting on the edge, rocking it slowly, intently, to and fro. On the far side of the cradle the night-nurse, her hands pressed tight against her apron, her veiled grey forehead bent above the child, sat waiting like an effigy of disciplined, indomitable patience. Isaac Studler, ungainly as ever in his white linen coat, was leaning against the mantelpiece, with folded arms, stroking his jet-black beard.

The nurse rose as the doctor came in. But Héquet, his eyes fixed on the child, did not seem to notice anything. Not till Antoine went up to the cradle did Héquet raise his head towards him, with a sigh. Antoine had hastily grasped the burning little hand that fluttered on the coverlet, and, as he did so, the child's body seemed to shrink away, like some tiny insect trying to wriggle back into its hole. The child's face was red and mottled, almost the colour of the ice-bag placed behind her ear; her curls, as fair as Nicole's, clammy with sweat or wetted by the compresses, were smeared across her cheeks and forehead. Her eyes were half shut and between the eyelids the swimming pupils had a dull metallic lustre, like the eyes of butchered animals. The movement of the cradle rocked her head slowly to and fro, giving a rhythmic cadence to the moans that issued from the little parched throat.

The nurse made as if to fetch the stethoscope, but Antoine signed to her he did not need it.

"It's an idea of Nicole's," Héquet suddenly remarked in an unnatural, almost high-pitched tone. Then, seeing Antoine's puzzled look, he explained in a studiously level voice: "The cradle. Yes. It's Nicole's idea." He smiled uncertainly; across the twilight of his mind such details seemed to loom out in preternatural relief. "Yes," he added almost in the same breath, "we went and fetched it from the attic. Covered with dust. It's the only thing that calms her a bit, you see, being rocked like that."

Antoine gazed at him compassionately and, as he did so, realized how very far his pity, for all its deep sincerity, fell short of such a sorrow. He placed his hand on Héquet's arm.

"You're utterly fagged out, old man. You'd much better go and lie down for a while. What's the use of wearing yourself out?"

Studler put in a word.

"Yes, it's the third night you haven't slept."

"Do be reasonable now," Antoine insisted, bending towards his friend. "You'll be needing all the strength you have—very soon." He felt an almost physical impulsion to drag the unhappy man away from contact with the cradle, to plunge as soon as might be all that unavailing anguish in the anodynes of sleep.

Héquet did not answer, but went on rocking the cradle. His shoulders sagged more and more, as though Antoine's "very soon" had laid on them a burden not to be endured. Then, of his own accord, he rose, beckoned to the nurse to take his place beside the cradle, and, without waiting to dry his tear-stained cheeks, moved his head slowly round as if in search of something. At last he went up to Antoine and tried to look him in the face. Antoine was struck by the changed expression of his near-sighted eyes; their look of keen alertness had lost its edge, they seemed to move stiffly in their sockets, tending to settle down into a heavy, torpid stare.

Héquet gazed at Antoine and his lips moved before the words came out.

"Something—something *must* be done," he murmured. "She's in great pain, you know that. Why let her go on suffering? Don't . . . don't you agree? We must have the courage to . . . to do something." He paused, seeming to look to Studler for support; then once again his heavy gaze rested on Antoine. "Look here, Thibault, you *must* do something." Then, as though to elude Antoine's answer, he let his head fall, shambled across the room, and left the two men to themselves.

For some moments Antoine seemed incapable of movement; a sudden blush darkened his cheeks. His mind was a ferment of conflicting thoughts.

Studler tapped him on the shoulder.

"Well?" he asked in a low tone, watching Antoine's face. Studler's eyes resembled those of certain horses—over-large and elongated eyes, with languid pupils slackly floating in pools of watery whiteness. Just now, however, his look, like Héquet's, was searching, masterful.

"Well, what are you going to do about it?" he whispered.

In the brief silence that ensued each felt the impact of the other's thought.

"What will I do?" Antoine echoed evasively. But he knew that Studler would not let him off without an explanation. "Damn it!" he broke out. "Of course I realize. . . . But when he says 'do something' one daren't even appear to understand!"

"Hush!" Studler whispered, glancing towards the nurse; then he led Antoine into the passage and closed the door.

"You're convinced, aren't you, that nothing can be done?" he asked.

"Quite convinced."

"And that there's not the least, not the very faintest hope?"

"Not the faintest."

"Well, then?"

Antoine felt a mood of tense excitement gaining on him, and took refuge in an acrimonious silence.

"Well, then?" Studler insisted. "There's no use beating about the bush; the sooner it's ended, the better."

"And I assure you I want it to end quite as much as you do."

"Wanting's not enough."

Antoine raised his head and answered resolutely:

"That, unfortunately, is all that can be done."

"No!"

"Yes!"

The dialogue had grown so vehement that Studler kept silence for some seconds.

"Those injections," he presently observed. "I wonder now. . . . Supposing the doses were doubled? . . ."

Antoine cut him short.

"Hold your tongue, damn it!"

His mind was seething with exasperation. Studler watched him without speaking. Antoine's eyebrows stood out like an iron bar, in an almost straight line across his forehead, the muscles of his face twitched uncontrollably, dragging his mouth awry, and now and then a little stream of ripples fretted the tight-drawn skin, as though the nervous system just below the surface were in a state of violent commotion.

A minute passed.

"Hold your tongue!" Antoine repeated, but less harshly, stammering a little with excitement. "I know what you feel. We've all f-felt like that, wanted to cut things short; but that's just a beg-beginner's weakness. Only one consideration counts: the sanctity of human life. Yes. The sanctity of life. If you'd gone on with medicine, you'd see things in the same light as every other doctor. The necessity for certain fixed principles. A limit to our powers. Otherwise . . ."

"A limit? If a man's a man at all, the only limit is—his conscience."

"Exactly! His conscience; his professional conscience. But just think, man! Supposing doctors were to claim the right to . . . Anyhow, Isaac, there isn't one who would, not one. . . ."

"In that case—" Studler hissed the words out. Antoine cut him short.

"Héquet has dealt with cases every bit as hopeless, as pit-pitiful as this one, dozens of times. But he's never once deliberately . . . Never. Nor has Philip, nor Rigaud, nor Treuillard. No doctor worthy of the name would dream of it, do you hear me? Never!"

"In that case," Studler broke out, "you doctors may set up to be the high priests of the world today, but to my mind you're just a pack of scrimshankers!"

As he moved back a step the light from the hanging lamp fell on his face.

Its look conveyed more than his words had said; not only scorn and indignation but a sort of challenge, almost a threat—a secret will to *act*.

"That being so," Antoine said to himself, "I'll stay here till eleven and make the injection myself." He said no more but, with a shrug of his shoulders, went back to the bedroom and sat down.

The rain drummed on the shutters an endless monotone, and drippings from the eaves pattered incessantly upon the sill while, in the room, the swaying cradle timed the moaning of the dying child to its slow rhythm; and, across the hush of night, tense with death's immanence, all the sounds blended in a sad, persistent counterpoint.

"I stammered once or twice just now," Antoine, whose nerves were still on edge, muttered to himself. He was not often taken that way; it happened only when he had to keep up a distasteful pose—when, for example, he was forced to tell a complicated lie to some over-perspicacious patient, or when in conversation he was led to bolster up some conventional idea regarding which he had so far no personal convictions. "It's all the Caliph's fault!" With the corner of his eye he saw the "Caliph" back at his old place, leaning against the mantelpiece. He remembered Isaac Studler in his student days, when he had met him for the first time, ten years ago, in the neighbourhood of the School of Medicine. Bearded like a Persian king, with his silky voice and Rabelaisian laugh, the Caliph had been a familiar figure in the Latin Quarter of those days; then, too, there had been a truculent, subversive, and fanatical side to his character; half-measures were not the Caliph's way. An exceptionally brilliant future was predicted for him. Then one day the news went round that he had dropped his studies and set to earning his living; it was said that he had taken under his wing the wife and children of one of his brothers who had just killed himself after embezzling money from the bank where he was employed.

A shriller cry from the child cut short his musings. Antoine fixed his eyes for a moment on the writhing little body, trying to estimate the frequency of certain spasms, but there was nothing to be made of them; the movements were as incalculable as the palpitations of a chicken that is being bled. Then suddenly the feeling of unrest against which Antoine had been struggling ever since his passage of words with Studler grew to an acute distress. Ready though he always was to take the utmost risks when a patient's life was in danger, it was more than he could bear thus to come up against a hopeless situation, to feel so utterly at a loss for any form of action, condemned to watch the unseen enemy's triumphant progress with folded hands. And tonight the child's interminable struggle, her inarticulate cries, were working on Antoine's nerves with a peculiar urgency. Yet the sight of suffering, even the agony of little children, was nothing new to him. How was it that tonight he could not hold his feelings in? Confronted with the element of mystery and horror that attends a death-agony, he found himself tonight as impotent to curb his anguish as if he were the veriest novice. He was stirred to the depths of his being; his self-confidence was shaken —and, with it, his confidence in science, in activity, in life itself. Like a great wave, despair broke over him, dragging him down into the depths. In a ghastly pageant they streamed before his eyes, all the patients he had written down as "hopeless cases." Why, taking only those whom he had seen on this one day, the list was formidable in all conscience! Four or five hospital patients, Huguette, the Ernst boy, the blind baby, and now the child before him. And, doubtless, others too. Yes, his father; an old man with thick, milk-sodden lips, prisoned in an arm-chair. In a few weeks, after some days and nights of pain, the robust old veteran, too, would go their way. The way they all must go, one following the other. And in all this world-wide suffering there was no sense, no meaning. . . . "No, life's absurd, a beastly thing!" he adjured himself furiously, as though to argue down some quite incorrigible optimist; and who was that confirmed, pig-headed optimist if not—himself, his normal self?

The nurse rose soundlessly. Antoine glanced at his watch; was time for the injection. The pretext for moving, doing 'something, came as a vast relief; he felt almost cheerful, too, at the prospect of being able to get away from this room in a few minutes.

The nurse brought all he needed on a tray. Clipping off the tip of the ampoule, he plunged the needle in, filled the syringe to the prescribed level, then tipped out the contents of the ampoule (still three-quarters full) into the slop-pail. He could feel Studler's gaze intent on him.

After making the injection he sat down again; it seemed to have eased the pain a little. He bent over the child, took her pulse once more—it was terribly weak—and whispered some instructions to the nurse. Then he rose without haste, washed at the basin, shook Studler's hand without a word, and left the room.

He made his way out on tip-toe. The lights were on but no one was visible; Nicole's door was shut. As he moved away the sound of wailing seemed to grow fainter. He opened and shut the hall-door noiselessly. Outside, on the landing, he paused and listened. Not a sound. With a deep sigh of relief he sped briskly down the stairs.

Out in the street he could not refrain from gazing up towards the dark façade cut by a string of lighted windows as though a party were being given in the Héquets' flat.

The rain had just stopped and the pavements were streaming after the downpour. As far as eye could reach the empty streets shimmered with liquid light.

Antoine felt a sudden chill; turning up the collar of his coat, he quickened his steps.

XIII

A sound of water dripping; rain-drenched pavements. Suddenly the picture rose before him of a face streaming with tears, of Héquet standing there, Héquet's insistent gaze. "Look here, Thibault, you *must* do something!" For all his efforts to dispel it, the harrowing vision held his eyes a while. "A father's love," he mused; "yes, that's a feeling utterly unknown to me, however much I try to picture it." Suddenly the thought of Gise leapt to his mind. "A home. Children." An idle dream, all that, and, happily, unrealizable. That idea of marriage, why, now it struck him as more than premature; grotesque! "Am I an egoist?" he wondered. "Or is it simply cowardice?" His thoughts turned a new corner. "Anyhow, there's someone damns me for a coward just now, and that's the Caliph!" He remembered disgustedly the way Studler had cornered him in the passage, the man's hot, vulgar face and stubborn eyes. He struggled to brush away the swarm of ideas which ever since that moment had been buzzing in his brain. "A coward?" Rather an obnoxious word, that! "Over-cautious," perhaps. "Studler thought me over-cautious. The damned fool!"

He had reached the Elysée. A patrol of military police had just completed their circuit of the Palace. There was a clatter of rifle-butts on the sidewalk. Before he could avert their onset a horde of wild imaginings, like the protean pageant of a dream, streamed through his mind. He pictured Studler sending the nurse out of the room, taking a syringe from his pocket. Presently the nurse came back and passed her fingers over the little corpse. Then . . . ugly rumours; a report of the police; burial refused; an autopsy. The coroner; the police. "I'll take the blame." He was passing a sentry-box just then, and glared defiantly at the sentry within. "No," he heard himself affirming boldly to a phantom coroner, "no injections were made by anyone except myself. I administered an over-dose —deliberately. It was a hopeless case, and I take upon myself all the . . ." Shrugging his shoulders, he smiled and quickened his step. "What drivel I'm thinking!" But well he knew he had not laid the spectres of his mind. "If I'm so ready to take the blame for a fatal dose administered by another man, why did I so emphatically refuse to administer it myself?"

Whenever a brief but strenuous mental effort failed, if not to clarify a problem, at least to throw some light on it, he always felt intensely irritated. He recalled the passage of words with Studler, when he had lost his temper, stammered. He did not regret it in the least; yet he was unpleasantly aware that he had played a part and voiced opinions which were somehow out of keeping with his personality as a whole, disloyal to his truest self. He had, moreover, a vague but galling presentiment of a day to come when his outlook and conduct might well belie his attitude and words on this occasion. His sense of self-disapproval must have been keen indeed for Antoine now to feel so impotent to shake it off; as a rule he firmly refused to pass judgment on any of his acts; the feeling of remorse was wholly foreign to his nature. True, he enjoyed studying himself; of recent years, indeed, he had made a veritable hobby of self-analysis—but always from a strictly scientific point of view. Nothing could be more alien to his character than to sit in moral judgment on himself.

Another question shaped itself in his mind, adding to his perplexity. "Would it not have needed greater strength of mind to consent, than to refuse, to act?" Whenever he had to choose between two alternatives and when, all things considered, one seemed as cogent as the other, he usually chose the line of action involving the greater exercise of will-power; experience had taught him, so he averred, that this was almost always the better one to follow. But tonight he had to admit that he had chosen the line of least resistance, followed the beaten track.

Some of his own remarks still echoed in his ears. He had prated to Studler of "the sanctity of life." A ready-made phrase, and treacherous like all its kind. We "reverence" life, we say—or do we make a fetish of it?

He recalled an incident which had struck his imagination at the time—the case of the bicephalous child at Tréguineuc. Some fifteen years earlier, at the Breton seaport where the Thibaults were passing the summer holidays, a fisherman's wife had given birth to a freak of nature, with two separate, perfectly formed heads. Father and mother had begged the local doctor to put an end to the little monstrosity, and, when he refused to do so, the father, a notorious drunkard, had flung himself on the new-born child and attempted to strangle it. It had been necessary to secure him, lock him up. There was great excitement in the village and it was a burning topic at the dinner-tables of the summer visitors. Antoine, who was sixteen or seventeen at the time, had embarked on a heated discussion with his father (it was one of the first occasions on which father and son came into violent conflict), Antoine insisting, with the naïve intractability of youth, that the doctor should be permitted to cut short a life, doomed from the outset, without more ado.

It startled him to find how little his point of view regarding such a case had changed. "What view would Philip take?" he asked himself. The answer was not in doubt; Antoine could but admit that the idea of ending the child's life would never have crossed Philip's mind. What was more, did any dangerous malady develop, Philip would have strained every nerve to save its miserable life. Rigaud would have done the same thing. Terrignier, too. And Loiselle. So would every doctor. Wherever the least spark of life remains, the doctor's duty is imperative. Saviours of life, like trusty Saint Bernards! Philip's nasal voice droned in his ears: "You've no choice, my boy; you haven't the right . . . !"

Antoine rebelled. " 'The right'? Look here, you know as well as I do what they amount to, those ideas of 'right' and duty. The laws of nature are the only laws that count; they, I admit, are ineluctable. But all those so-called moral laws, what are they really? A complex of habits, foisted upon us by the past. Just that. Long ago they may have served their purpose, as furthering man's social progress. But what of today? Can you, as a thinking man, assign to all those antiquated rules of hygiene and public welfare a sort of divine right, the status of a categorical imperative?" And, as no answer was forthcoming from the chief, Antoine shrugged his shoulders and, thrusting his hands deeper into his overcoat pockets, crossed to the opposite sidewalk.

He walked blindly ahead, debating still—but only with himself. "One thing's sure: for me, morality simply doesn't exist! 'Ought' and 'ought not,' 'right' and 'wrong,' are meaningless to me—just words I use, like everyone else, as the small change of conversation; but in my heart I've always known they have no application to reality. Yes, I've *always* thought like that. No, that's going too far. I've thought like that since . . ." Rachel's face rose suddenly before his eyes. "Well, for quite a long time, anyhow." For a while he made a conscientious effort to sort out the principles governing his daily life. He could find none. "A kind of sincerity?" he ventured tentatively. He thought again and found a better definition. "Isn't it rather a kind of clear-sightedness?" His mind was still unsettled, but he was fairly satisfied with his discovery. "Yes. Obviously it doesn't amount to much. But, when I look into myself, my impulse to think clearly— well, it's about the only sure and solid thing I can find. Very likely I've made of it—unconsciously, no doubt—a kind of moral principle, my private creed. 'Complete freedom, provided I see clearly.' That sums it up, I imagine. Rather a risky principle, when you look into it. But it works out pretty well. The way one sees things, that's the only thing that matters. To profit by one's scientific training and examine oneself under the microscope coolly, impartially. To see oneself as one is; and, as a corollary, to accept oneself as one is. And then? Then I could almost say: Nothing is forbidden me! Nothing, provided I don't dupe myself; I know what I am doing and, as far as possible, why I am doing it."

But, almost at once, a wry smile pursed his lips. "The queerest thing is that, if I look into it carefully—my life, I mean, with its famous gospel of 'complete freedom' that does away with good and evil—the queer thing is, my life is almost entirely devoted to 'doing good,' as people call it! What has it brought me to, my precious emancipation? To acting not merely just like everybody else, but, oddly enough, in the very way which according to the present code of morals sets me among the best of men! The way I behaved just now is a case in point. Can it be that, for all practical purposes and despite myself, I've come to kotow to the cut-and-dried morality of those around me? Philip would smile. . . . No, I can't allow that our human obligation to behave as social animals should overrule our impulses as individuals. How then explain the line I took just now? It's fantastic how little the way we think fits in with, or even influences, the way we act. For, in my heart of hearts—why quibble over it?—I think Studler's right. The platitudes that I hurled at him carried no weight at all. It's he that has logic on his side; that poor child's sufferings are so much needless agony, the issue of her fight with death is a foregone conclusion, foregone and imminent, too. Well, then—the least reflection tells me that if her death can be accelerated, it's so much the better on every count. Not only for the child, but for her mother; it's obvious that in her present condition the sight of the baby's lingering agony may well prove dangerous to her—as Héquet, no doubt, is well aware. And there are no two ways about it; on a purely logical view the soundness of such arguments is as plain as daylight. But isn't it odd how mere logic seldom or never really satisfies us? I don't say that just to condone an act of cowardice; indeed, I know quite well that what drove me to act as I did this evening, or, rather, to refuse to act, was not mere cowardice. No, it was something as urgent, as imperative as a law of nature. But what it was, that urgency—that's what passes me." He ran over in his mind some possible explanations. Was it one of those inchoate ideas (he was convinced that such exist) that seem to sleep below the level of our lucid thoughts, but sometimes come awake and, rising to the surface, take control of us, impel us to an act—only to sink back once more, inexplicably, into the limbo of our unknown selves? Or—to take a simpler view —why not admit that a law of herd-morality exists and it is practically impossible for a man to act as if he were an isolated unit?

He seemed to be turning in a circle, his eyes blindfolded. He tried to recall the wording of Nietzsche's well-known dictum: that a man should not be a problem, but the solution of a problem. A self-evident axiom, he used to think, but one with which, year after year, he had found it ever harder to conform. He had already had occasion to observe that some of his decisions—the most spontaneous, as a rule; often the most important ones he made—clashed with his reasoned scheme of life; so much so, indeed, that he had sometimes wondered: "Can I be really the man I think I am?" The mere suspicion left him dazed and startled; it came like a lightning-flash that slits the shadows, leaving them the darker for its passing. But he was always quick to brush the thought aside, and now again he flouted it.

Chance befriended him. As he came into the Rue Royale a whiff of baking bread, warm as a living creature's breath, came to his nostrils from the vent-hole of a bakery, and started off his thoughts on a new tack. Yawning, he looked about him for an open tavern; then he was suddenly impelled to go and have something to eat at Zemm's, a little café near the Comédie Française which stayed open till dawn and where he sometimes dropped in at night before proceeding homewards across the river.

"Yes, it's a queer thing," he admitted to himself after a moment of no thoughts. "We can doubt, destroy, make a clean sweep of all our beliefs, but, whether we like it or not, there remains a solid kernel proof against every doubt, the human instinct to trust our reason. A truism of which I've been the living proof for the last hour or so!"

He felt tired, disconsolate, and hunted for a reassuring formula apt to restore his peace of mind. He fell back on an easy compromise. "Conflict is the common rule, and so it has always been. What is happening in my mind just now is going on throughout the universe: the clash of life with life."

For a while he walked on mechanically, thinking of nothing in particular. He was nearing the serried tumult of the boulevards and questing women here and there pressed on him their companionable charms; he shook them off good-humouredly.

But all the time his brain was unconsciously at work, his thoughts were crystallizing round an idea.

"I am a living being; in other words I am always choosing between alternatives and acting accordingly. So far so good. But there my quandary begins. What is the guiding principle on which I choose and act? I've no idea. Is it the clear-sightedness I was thinking of just now? No, hardly that. That's theory, not practice. My zeal for clarity has never really guided me to a decision or an act. It's only *after* I have acted that my lucidity comes into play—to justify to me what I have done. And yet, ever since I've been a sentient being, I've felt myself directed by a kind of instinct, a driving force that leads me almost all the time to choose this and not that, to act in this way, not in another. But—most puzzling thing of all!—I notice that all my acts follow precisely the same lines; everything takes place as if I were being controlled by an unalterable law. Exactly. But what law? I haven't a notion! Whenever at some critical moment of my life that driving force inside me leads me to take a certain course and act in consequence, I ask myself in vain: What was the principle that guided me? It's like running up against a wall of darkness! I feel sure of my ground, intensely alive, lawful in my occasions, so to speak—yet I'm outside the law. Lawful and lawless! Neither in the teaching of the past nor in any modern philosophy, not even in myself, can I find any satisfactory answer. I see clearly enough all the laws which I can't endorse, but I see none to which I could submit; not one of all the standard moral codes has ever seemed to me even approximately to fit my case, or to throw any light upon the way in which I act. Yet, all the same, I forge ahead, and at a good pace, too, without the least hesitation, and, what's more, keeping a pretty straight course. Yes, it's extraordinary! Driving full-steam ahead like a fast liner whose steersman's scapped the compass! It almost looks as if I were acting under orders. Yes, that's exactly what I feel; my way of life is ordered. Under orders, yes; but *whose* orders? . . . Meanwhile I don't complain; I'm happy. I've not the least wish to change; only I'd like to know why I am as I am. It's more than simple curiosity; there's a touch of apprehension in it. Has every man alive his mystery? I wonder. And shall I ever find the key to mine? Shall I know one day what it is: my guiding principle?"

He quickened his steps. Beyond the cross-roads a flashing shop-sign, Zemm's, had caught his eye, and hunger drove out thought.

So quickly did he dive into the entrance of the café that he stumbled over a pile of oyster-baskets that filled the passage with the sour smell of brine. The restaurant was in the basement, to which a narrow spiral staircase, picturesque and vaguely conspiratorial in appearance, gave access. At this late hour the room was full of night-birds taking their ease in a warm bath of vapour, thick with the fumes of alcohol, cigar-smoke, and odours from the kitchen, all churned up together by the whizzing fans. With its polished mahogany and green leather seats the long, low, windowless tavern had the aspect of a liner's smoking-room.

Antoine made for a corner of the room, deposited his overcoat beside him, and sat down. He felt a mood of calm well-being gaining on him. Then all at once there rose before his eyes a very different scene: the nursery, the little body bathed in sweat and vainly struggling against its unseen foe. He seemed to hear the rhythmic cadence of the swaying cradle, like a tragic football marking time. A spasm of horror gripped him and he shrank together.

"Supper, sir?"

"Yes. Roast beef and black bread. And some whisky in a big tumbler; iced water, please, not soda."

"Will you have some of our cheese-soup, sir?"

"Very well."

On each table stood a generous bowl of potato-chips, spangled with salt-flakes, brittle and thin as "honesty" pods, infallible thirst-producers. The zest with which he crunched the chips gave Antoine the measure of his hunger as he waited for the gruyère-soup to come; simmering and cheese-scummed, stringy and crisped with shreds of onion, it was one of Zemm's specialties.

At the cloak-room near his corner some people were calling for their coats. One of the noisy group, a girl, glanced covertly at Antoine and, as their eyes met, gave him a faint smile. Where was it he had seen that smooth, sleek face that brought to mind a Japanese print, with its etched-in eyebrows and tiny, slightly oblique eyes? He was amused by the clever way in which she had signalled to him without being noticed by the others. Why, of course, she was a model he had seen several times at Daniel de Fontanin's place—his old studio in the Rue Mazarine. It all came back to him now quite clearly: the sweltering summer afternoon, the model on her "throne"; why, he could remember even the hour it was, the lighting of the room, the model's pose—and then the emotion which had made him linger on, though he was pressed for time. His eyes followed her as she went out. What was it Daniel called her? Some name that sounded like a brand of tea. She looked back at him from the door. Yes, now he remembered how he had then been struck by the flatness of her body; an athlete's body, clean-limbed and sinewy.

While, during the last few months, he fancied himself in love with Gise, other women had hardly counted in his life. In fact, since he had broken off with Mme. Javenne—the liaison had lasted two months and all but ended in a catastrophe—he had dispensed with mistresses. Now, for a few seconds, he bitterly regretted it. He took a few sips of the whisky which had just been brought; then, lifting the lid of the soup-tureen, relished its appetizing fumes.

Just then the page-boy brought him a crumpled fragment of a music-hall programme, folded envelope-wise, in the corner of which some words were scrawled in pencil:

Zemm's tomorrow, 10 p.m.???

"Anybody waiting for an answer?" he asked with interest, but in some perplexity.

"No, sir. The lady's gone."

Antoine was determined to take no action on the assignation; all the same he slipped the note into his pocket before beginning his meal.

"What a damned fine thing life is!" he suddenly reflected as an unexpected rout of cheerful thoughts danced through his brain. "Yes, I'm in love with life!" He took a moment's thought. "And, in reality, I don't depend on anyone at all." Once more a memory of Gise flitted across his mind. Now he was sure that life itself, even if love were lacking, sufficed to make him happy. He honestly admitted to himself that when Gise had been away in England he had not felt her absence in the least. Truth to tell, had any woman ever held a large place in his life or in his happiness? Rachel? Yes. But what would have been the outcome, had not Rachel gone away? Anyhow, he had said good-bye to passions of that order once and for all. No, as he saw things now, he would no longer dare to describe his feeling towards Gise as "love." He tried to find another, apter word. "An attachment?" For a few moments yet Gise held the foreground of his thoughts and he resolved to clarify his feelings of the past few months. One thing was sure: he had imagined an ideal Gise, the mirror of his dreams, quite other than the flesh-and-blood Gise who, only this afternoon . . . But he declined to work out the comparison.

He took a pull of his whisky and water, tackled the roast beef, and told himself once more he was in love with life.

Life, as he saw it, was a vast, open arena into which the man of action has but to launch himself enthusiastically. By "love of life" he really meant self-love, self-confidence. Still, when he visualized his own life in particular, it presented itself as something far more definite than a wide field of action placed by some miracle at his disposal and offering an infinity of possible achievements; he saw it, rather, as a clean-cut track, a long, straight road leading infallibly towards a certain goal.

There was a familiar ring about the phrases he had just employed, but their sound was always welcome to his ears. "Thibault?" the inner voice went on. "He's thirty-two: the very age when great careers begin. What of his body? Remarkably fit; he's always in fine fettle, and strong as a cart-horse. And his mind? Quick in perception, adventurous, a pioneering intellect. His capacity for work? All but unlimited. . . . And comfortably off, into the bargain. All that a man can want, in fact! No vices, no bad habits, nothing to trammel his vocation. . . . On the crest of the wave!"

He stretched his limbs and lit a cigarette.

His vocation. . . . Since he was fifteen all things medical had always had a singular appeal for him. Even now it was his firm conviction that in the science of medicine we may see the fine flower of all man's intellectual efforts in the past, the most signal reward of twenty centuries' research in every branch of knowledge, and the richest field available for human genius. It knew no limits on the speculative side, yet it was founded on the very bedrock of reality and kept in close and constant contact with humanity itself. He had a special leaning towards its human aspect. Never would he have consented to shut himself up in a laboratory and glue his eyes upon a microscopic field; no, what most delighted him was the doctor's never-ending tussle with proteiform reality.

"What is needed," the inner voice resumed, "is that Thibault should work more on his own account and not, like Terrignier or Boistelot, let himself be hamstrung by his practice. He should find time to organize and follow up experiments, collate results, and thus evolve the outlines of a *system.*" For Antoine pictured for himself a career akin to those of the great masters of his profession; before he was fifty he would have a host of new discoveries to his credit and, above all, he would have laid the foundations of a system of his own, glimpses of which, vague though they were as yet, he seemed to have at certain moments. "Yes, soon, quite soon. . . ."

Leaping an interval of darkness, his father's death, his thoughts came out again into the cheerful sunlight of the near future. Between two puffs at his cigarette he contemplated his father's death from a new angle, without the least misgiving or distress. Rather, he saw it now as a prime condition of his long-awaited freedom, opening new horizons and favouring the swift ascension of his star. His brain teemed with new projects. "I'll have to thin out my practice at once so as to get some spare time for myself. Then I shall need an assistant for my research-work, or a secretary, why not? Not a collaborator; no, quite a youngster, someone open to ideas whom I could train, who'd do the spade-work for me. Then I could really get down to it, put everything I've got into it! And make discoveries. Yes, one day, that's certain, I'll bring off something *big!*" The ghost of a smile hovered on his lips, an upcrop of the optimistic mood that buoyed him.

He threw his cigarette away, struck by a sudden thought. "That's a queer thing, now that I think of it! The moral sense that I've cast out of my life, from which I felt only an hour ago that I'd escaped for good and all—why, here it is, all of a sudden, back again in its old place! Not skulking furtively in a dark byway of my awareness; no, on the contrary, solid and serene, and very much in evidence, standing up like a rock square in the centre of my active life—the nucleus of my professional career! No, it's no use beating about the bush; as a doctor and a scientist I've an absolutely rigid code of right and wrong and, what's more, I'm pretty certain I'll stand by it, come what may. But then—how the devil is one to fit that in with . . . ? Oh, after all," he consoled himself, "why want to make every blessed thing 'fit in'?" And very soon he gave up the attempt, letting his thoughts grow blurred, and indolently yielding to a mood of vague well-being mingled with fatigue, a comfortable lethargy.

Two motorists had just come in and settled down at a neighbouring table, depositing their bulky overcoats on the seat beside them. The man looked about twenty-five, the girl a year or two younger. A handsome couple, slim and athletic, dark-haired both, with forthright eyes, large mouths set with an array of valiant teeth, cheeks ruddied by the cold; a perfect match in age and health, in natural elegance and social standing, they shared, presumably, the same tastes. In any case their appetites ran neck and neck, for side by side and at exactly the same speed they munched their way through a pair of sandwiches as like as like could be; then, with the selfsame gesture, drained their beer-mugs, donned their furcoats, and, keeping step together, moved springily away. Antoine watched them with interest, so typical they seemed of the ideal couple, of cordial entente.

Just then he noticed that the room was almost empty. His eyes lit on the dial of a clock above his head, reflected in a distant mirror. "Ten past ten. No, the wrong way on. Eh? Nearly two."

Shaking off his lethargy, he rose. "A fine state I'll be in tomorrow morning!" he ruefully bethought himself.

As he went up the narrow staircase, passing the page-boy drowsing on a step, a cheerful thought flashed through his mind; so realistic was the picture it evoked that he smiled furtively. "Tomorrow, 10 p.m."

He hailed a taxi, and was home five minutes later.

On the hall-table where the evening mail awaited him a slip of paper was laid out, well in view. He recognized Léon's writing:

They rang up from Dr. Héquet's about 1 a.m. The little girl is dead.

He held up the sheet between his hands for some moments, then read it over again. "One a.m.? Very soon after I left. . . . Studler? With the nurse looking on? No. Most decidedly, no. What then? My injection? Possibly. A minimal dose, however. Still, the pulse was so weak. . . ."

Once the shock had spent itself, his feeling was one of relief. Hard though the blow must be for Héquet and his wife, at least it had cut short their horrible suspense. He remembered Nicole's face in sleep. Quite soon another little one would fill the absent place between them. So life is served, and every wound heals up at last. "Still, I'm sorry for them," he thought with a tightening of the heart. "I'll look them up on my way to the hospital."

In the kitchen the cat was mewing plaintively. "She'll keep me from sleeping, damn her!" Antoine grumbled. Then suddenly he remembered her kittens and opened the door. The cat flung herself across his legs and rubbed herself against him in a frenzy of caresses, with desperate importunity. Antoine stooped over her basket; it was empty.

"You'll drown them all, of course." Yes, those had been his words. Yet that too was life—why make a distinction? By what right—?

Shrugging his shoulders, he glanced at the clock, and yawned.

"Four hours' sleep. No time for dawdling!"

Léon's note was still in his hand; he rolled it into a ball and tossed it cheerfully onto the dresser.

"And now for a good cold shower. The Thibault system: Sluice away your tiredness before you go to bed!"

FYODOR DOSTOYEVSKY

• *The Possessed*

2

He first went home, and carefully, without haste, packed his trunk. At six o'clock in the morning there was a special train from the town. This early morning express only ran once a week, and was only a recent experiment. Though Pyotr Stepanovitch had told the members of the quintet that he was only going to be away for a short time in the neighbourhood, his intentions, as appeared later, were in reality very different. Having finished packing, he settled accounts with his landlady, to whom he had previously given notice of his departure, and drove in a cab to Erkel's lodgings, near the station. And then just upon one o'clock at night he walked to Kirillov's, approaching as before by Fedka's secret way.

Pyotr Stepanovitch was in a painful state of mind. Apart from other extremely grave reasons for dissatisfaction (he was still unable to learn anything of Stavrogin), he had, it seems—for I cannot assert it for a fact—received in the course of that day, probably from Petersburg, secret information of a danger awaiting him in the immediate future. There are, of course, many legends in the town relating to this period; but if any facts were known, it was only to those immediately concerned. I can only surmise as my own conjecture that Pyotr Stepanovitch may well have had affairs going on in other neighbourhoods as well as in our town, so that he really may have received such a warning. I am con-

SOURCE. From *The Possessed* by Fyodor Dostoyevsky. Translated by Constance Garnett. Copyright 1961, reprinted with the permission of the Macmillan Company.

vinced, indeed, in spite of Liputin's cynical and despairing doubts, that he really had two or three other quintets; for instance, in Petersburg and Moscow, and if not quintets at least colleagues and correspondents, and possibly was in very curious relations with them. Not more than three days after his departure an order for his immediate arrest arrived from Petersburg—whether in connection with what had happened among us, or elsewhere, I don't know. This order only served to increase the overwhelming, almost panic terror which suddenly came upon our local authorities and the society of the town, till then so persistently frivolous in its attitude, on the discovery of the mysterious and portentous murder of the student Shatov—the climax of the long series of senseless actions in our midst—as well as the extremely mysterious circumstances that accompanied that murder. But the order came too late: Pyotr Stepanovitch was already in Petersburg, living under another name, and, learning what was going on, he made haste to make his escape abroad. . . . But I am anticipating in a shocking way.

He went in to Kirillov, looking ill-humoured and quarrelsome. Apart from the real task before him, he felt, as it were, tempted to satisfy some personal grudge, to avenge himself on Kirillov for something. Kirillov seemed pleased to see him; he had evidently been expecting him a long time with painful impatience. His face was paler than usual; there was a fixed and heavy look in his black eyes.

"I thought you weren't coming," he brought out drearily from his corner of the sofa, from which he had not, however moved to greet him.

Pyotr Stepanovitch stood before him and, before uttering a word, looked intently at his face.

"Everything is in order, then, and we are not drawing back from our resolution. Bravo!" He smiled an offensively patronising smile. "But, after all," he added with unpleasant jocosity, "if I am behind my time, it's not for you to complain: I made you a present of three hours."

"I don't want extra hours as a present from you, and you can't make me a present . . . you fool!"

"What?" Pyotr Stepanovitch was startled, but instantly controlled himself. "What huffiness! So we are in a savage temper?" he rapped out, still with the same offensive superciliousness. "At such a moment composure is what you need. The best thing you can do is to consider yourself a Columbus and me a mouse, and not to take offence at anything I say. I gave you that advice yesterday."

"I don't want to look upon you as a mouse."

"What's that, a compliment? But the tea is cold—and that shows that everything is topsy-turvy. Bah! But I see something in the window, on a plate." He went to the window. "Oh, oh, boiled chicken and rice! But why haven't you begun upon it yet? So we are in such a state of mind that even chicken . . ."

"I've dined, and it's not your business. Hold your tongue!"

"Oh, of course; besides, it's no consequence—though for me at the moment it is of consequence. Only fancy, I scarcely had any dinner, and so if, as I suppose, that chicken is not wanted now . . . eh?"

"Eat it if you can."

"Thank you, and then I'll have tea."

He instantly settled himself at the other end of the sofa and fell upon the chicken with extraordinary greediness; at the same time he kept a constant watch on his victim. Kirillov looked at him fixedly with angry aversion, as though unable to tear himself away.

"I say, though," Pyotr Stepanovitch fired off suddenly, while he still went on eating, "what about our business? We are not crying off, are we? How about that document?"

"I've decided in the night that it's nothing to me. I'll write it. About the manifestoes?"

"Yes, about the manifestoes too. But I'll dictate it. Of course, that's nothing to you. Can you possibly mind what's in the letter at such a moment?"

"That's not your business."

"It's not mine, of course. It need only be a few lines, though: that you and Shatov distributed the manifestoes and with the help of Fedka, who hid in your lodgings. This last point about Fedka and your lodgings is very important—the most important of all, indeed. You see, I am talking to you quite openly."

"Shatov? Why Shatov? I won't mention Shatov for anything."

"What next! What is it to you? You can't hurt him now."

"His wife has come back to him. She has waked up and has sent to ask me where he is."

"She has sent to ask you where he is? H'm . . . that's unfortunate. She may send again; no one ought to know I am here."

Pyotr Stepanovitch was uneasy.

"She won't know, she's gone to sleep again. There's a midwife with her, Arina Virginsky."

"So that's how it was. . . . She won't overhear, I suppose? I say, you'd better shut the front door."

"She won't overhear anything. And if Shatov comes I'll hide you in another room."

"Shatov won't come; and you must write that you quarrelled with him because he turned traitor and informed the police . . . this evening . . . and caused his death."

"He is dead!" cried Kirillov, jumping up from the sofa.

"He died at seven o'clock this evening, or rather, at seven o'clock yesterday evening, and now it's one o'clock."

"You have killed him! . . . And I foresaw it yesterday!"

"No doubt you did! With this revolver here." (He drew out his revolver as though to show it, but did not put it back again and still held it in his right hand as though in readiness.) "You are a strange man, though, Kirillov; you knew yourself that the stupid fellow was bound to end like this. What was there to foresee in that? I made that as plain as possible over and over again. Shatov was meaning to betray us; I was watching him, and it could not be left like that. And you too had instructions to watch him; you told me so yourself three weeks ago. . . ."

"Hold your tongue! You've done this because he spat in your face in Geneva!"

"For that and for other things too—for many other things; not from spite, however. Why do you jump up? Why look like that? Oh, oh, so that's it, is it?"

He jumped up and held out his revolver before him. Kirillov had suddenly snatched up from the window his revolver, which had been loaded and put ready since the morning. Pyotr Stepanovitch took up his position and aimed his weapon at Kirillov. The latter laughed angrily.

"Confess, you scoundrel, that you brought your revolver because I might shoot you. . . . But I shan't shoot you . . . though . . . though . . ."

And again he turned his revolver upon Pyotr Stepanovitch, as it were rehearsing, as though unable to deny himself the pleasure of imagining how he would shoot him. Pyotr Stepanovitch, holding his ground, waited for him, waited for him till the last minute without pulling the trigger, at the risk of being the first to get a bullet in his head; it might well be expected of "the maniac." But at last "the maniac" dropped his hand, gasping and trembling and unable to speak.

"You've played your little game and that's enough." Pyotr Stepanovitch, too, dropped his weapon. "I knew it was only a game; only you ran a risk, let me tell you: I might have fired."

And he sat down on the sofa with a fair show of composure and poured himself out some tea, though his hand trembled a little. Kirillov laid his revolver on the table and began walking up and down.

"I won't write that I killed Shatov . . . and I won't write anything now. You won't have a document!"

"I shan't?"

"No, you won't."

"What meanness and what stupidity!" Pyotr Stepanovitch turned green with resentment. "I foresaw it, though. You've not taken me by surprise, let me tell you. As you please, however. If I could make you do it by force, I would. You are a scoundrel, though." Pyotr Stepanovitch was more and more carried away and unable to restrain himself. "You asked us for money out there and promised us no end of things. . . . I won't go away with nothing, however: I'll see you put the bullet through your brains first, anyway."

"I want you to go away at once." Kirillov stood firmly before him.

"No, that's impossible." Pyotr Stepanovitch took up his revolver again. "Now in your spite and cowardice you may think fit to put it off and to turn traitor to-morrow, so as to get money again; they'll pay you for that, of course. Damn it all, fellows like you are capable of anything! Only don't trouble yourself; I've provided for all contingencies: I am not going till I've dashed your brains out with this revolver, as I did to that scoundrel Shatov, if you are afraid to do it yourself and put off your intention, damn you!"

"You are set on seeing my blood, too?"

"I am not acting from spite; let me tell you, it's nothing to me. I am doing it to be at ease about the cause. One can't rely on men; you see that for yourself. I don't understand what fancy possesses you to put yourself to death. It wasn't my idea; you thought of it yourself before I appeared, and talked of your intention to the committee abroad before you said anything to me. And you know, no one has forced it out of you; no one of them knew you, but you came to confide in them yourself, from sentimentalism. And what's to be done if a plan of action here, which can't be altered now, was founded upon that with your consent and upon your suggestion? . . . your suggestion, mind that! You have put yourself in a position in which you know too much. If you are an ass and go off to-morrow to inform the police, that would be rather a disadvantage to us; what do you think about it? Yes, you've bound yourself; you've given your word, you've taken money. That you can't deny. . . ."

Pyotr Stepanovitch was much excited, but for some time past Kirillov had not been listening. He paced up and down the room, lost in thought again.

"I am sorry for Shatov," he said, stopping before Pyotr Stepanovitch again.

"Why so? I am sorry, if that's all, and do you suppose . . ."

"Hold your tongue, you scoundrel," roared Kirillov, making an alarming and unmistakable movement; "I'll kill you."

"There, there, there! I told a lie, I admit it; I am not sorry at all. Come, that's enough, that's enough." Pyotr Stepanovitch started up apprehensively, putting out his hand.

Kirillov subsided and began walking up and down again. "I won't put it off; I want to kill myself now: all are scoundrels."

"Well, that's an idea; of course all are scoundrels; and since life is a beastly thing for a decent man . . ."

"Fool, I am just such a scoundrel as you, as all, not a decent man. There's never been a decent man anywhere."

"He's guessed the truth at last! Can you, Kirillov, with your sense, have failed to see till now that all men are alike, that there are none better or worse, only some are stupider than others, and that if all are scoundrels (which is nonsense, though) there oughtn't to be any people that are not?"

"Ah! Why, you are really in earnest?" Kirillov looked at him with some wonder. "You speak with heat and simply. . . . Can it be that even fellows like you have convictions?"

"Kirillov, I've never been able to understand why you mean to kill yourself. I only know it's from conviction . . . strong conviction. But if you feel a yearning to express yourself, so to say, I am at your service. . . . Only you must think of the time."

"What time is it?"

"Oh, oh, just two." Pyotr Stepanovitch looked at his watch and lighted a cigarette.

"It seems we can come to terms after all," he reflected.

"I've nothing to say to you," muttered Kirillov.

"I remember that something about God comes into it . . . you explained it to me once—twice, in fact. If you shoot yourself, you become God; that's it, isn't it?"

"Yes, I become God."

Pyotr Stepanovitch did not even smile; he waited. Kirillov looked at him subtly.

"You are a political imposter and intriguer. You want to lead me on into philosophy and enthusiasm and to bring about a reconciliation so as to disperse my anger, and then, when I am reconciled with you, beg from me a note to say I killed Shatov."

Pyotr Stepanovitch answered with almost natural frankness.

"Well, supposing I am such a scoundrel. But at the last moments does that matter to you, Kirillov? What are we quarrelling about? Tell me, please. You are one sort of man and I am another—what of it? And what's more, we are both . . ."

"Scoundrels."

"Yes, scoundrels if you like. But you know that that's only words."

"All my life I wanted it not to be only words. I lived because I did not want it to be. Even now every day I want it to be not words."

"Well, every one seeks to be where he is best off. The fish . . . that is, every one seeks his own comfort, that's all. That's been a commonplace for ages and ages."

"Comfort, do you say?"

"Oh, it's not worth while quarrelling over words."

"No, you were right in what you said; let it be comfort. God is necessary and so must exist."

"Well, that's all right, then."

"But I know He doesn't and can't."

"That's more likely."

"Surely you must understand that a man with two such ideas can't go on living?"

"Must shoot himself, you mean?"

"Surely you must understand that one might shoot oneself for that alone? You don't understand that there may be a man, one man out of your thousands of millions, one man who won't bear it and does not want to."

"All I understand is that you seem to be hesitating. . . . That's very bad."

"Stavrogin, too, is consumed by an idea," Kirillov said gloomily, pacing up and down the room. He had not noticed the previous remark.

"What?" Pyotr Stepanovitch pricked up his ears. "What idea? Did he tell you something himself?"

"No, I guessed it myself: if Stavrogin has faith, he does not believe that he has faith. If he hasn't faith, he does not believe that he hasn't."

"Well, Stavrogin has got something else wiser than that in his head," Pyotr Stepanovitch muttered peevishly, uneasily watching the turn the conversation had taken and the pallor of Kirillov.

"Damn it all, he won't shoot himself!" he was thinking. "I always suspected it; it's a maggot in the brain and nothing more; what a rotten lot of people!"

"You are the last to be with me; I shouldn't like to part on bad terms with you," Kirillov vouchsafed suddenly.

Pyotr Stepanovitch did not answer at once. "Damn it all, what is it now?" he thought again.

"I assure you, Kirillov, I have nothing against you personally as a man, and always . . ."

"You are a scoundrel and a false intellect. But I am just the same as you are, and I will shoot myself while you will remain living."

"You mean to say, I am so abject that I want to go on living."

He could not make up his mind whether it was judicious to keep up such a conversation at such a moment or not, and resolved "to be guided by circumstances." But the tone of superiority and of contempt for him, which Kirillov had never disguised, had always irritated him, and now for some reason it irritated him more than ever—possibly because Kirillov, who was to die within an hour or so (Pyotr Stepanovitch still reckoned upon this), seemed to him, as it were, already only half a man, some creature whom he could not allow to be haughty.

"You seem to be boasting to me of your shooting yourself."

"I've always been surprised at every one's going on living," said Kirillov, not hearing his remark.

"H'm! Admitting that's an idea, but . . ."

"You ape, you assent to get the better of me. Hold your tongue; you won't understand anything. If there is no God, then I am God."

"There, I could never understand that point of yours: why are you God?"

"If God exists, all is His will and from His will I cannot escape. If not, it's all my will and I am bound to show self-will."

"Self-will? But why are you bound?"

"Because all will has become mine. Can it be that no one in the whole planet, after making an end of God and believing in his own will, will dare to express his self-will on the most vital point? It's like a beggar inheriting a fortune and being afraid of it and not daring to approach the bag of gold, thinking himself too weak to own it. I want to manifest my self-will. I may be the only one, but I'll do it."

"Do it by all means."

"I am bound to shoot myself because the highest point of my self-will is to kill myself with my own hands."

"But you won't be the only one to kill yourself; there are lots of suicides."

"With good cause. But to do it without any cause at all, simply for self-will, I am the only one."

"He won't shoot himself," flashed across Pyotr Stepanovitch's mind again.

"Do you know," he observed irritably, "if I were in your place I should kill some one else to show my self-will, not myself. You might be of use. I'll tell you whom, if you are not afraid. Then you needn't shoot yourself to-day, perhaps. We may come to terms."

"To kill some one would be the lowest point of self-will, and you show your whole soul in that. I am not you: I want the highest point and I'll kill myself."

"He's come to it of himself," Pyotr Stepanovitch muttered malignantly.

"I am bound to show my unbelief," said Kirillov, walking about the room. "I have no higher idea than disbelief in God. I have all the history of mankind on my side. Man has done nothing but invent God so as to go on living, and not kill himself; that's the whole of universal history up till now. I am the first one in the whole history of mankind who would not invent God. Let them know it once for all."

"He won't shoot himself," Pyotr Stepanovitch thought anxiously.

"Let whom know it?" he said, egging him on. "It's only you and me here; you mean Liputin?"

"Let every one know; all will know. There is nothing secret that will not be made known. *He* said so."

And he pointed with feverish enthusiasm to the image of the Saviour, before which a lamp was burning. Pyotr Stepanovitch lost his temper completely.

"So you still believe in Him, and you've lighted the lamp; 'to be on the safe side,' I suppose?"

The other did not speak.

"Do you know, to my thinking, you believe perhaps more thoroughly than any priest."

"Believe in whom? In *Him?* Listen." Kirillov stood still, gazing before him with fixed and ecstatic look. "Listen to a great idea: there was a day on earth, and in the midst of the earth there stood three crosses. One on the Cross had such faith that he said to another, 'To-day thou shalt be with me in Paradise.' The day ended; both died and passed away and found neither Paradise nor resurrection. His words did not come true. Listen: that Man was the loftiest of all on earth, He was that which gave meaning to life. The whole planet, with everything on it, is mere madness without that Man. There has never been any like Him before, or since, never, up to a miracle. For that is the miracle, that there never was or never will be another like Him. And if that is so, if the laws of nature did not spare even Him, have not spared even their miracle and made even Him live in a lie and die for a lie, then all the planet is a lie and rests on a lie and on mockery. So then, the very laws of the planet are a lie and the vaudeville of devils. What is there to live for? Answer, if you are a man."

"That's a different matter. It seems to me you've mixed up two different causes, and that's a very unsafe thing to do. But excuse me, if you are God? If the lie were ended and if you realised that all the falsity comes from the belief in that former God?"

"So at last you understand!" cried Kirillov rapturously. "So it can be understood if even a fellow like you understands. Do you understand now that the salvation for all consists in proving this idea to every one? Who will prove it? I! I can't understand how an atheist could know that there is no God and not kill himself on the spot. To recognise that there is no God and not to recognise at the same instant that one is God oneself is an absurdity, else one would certainly kill oneself. If you recognise it you are sovereign, and then you won't kill yourself but will live in the greatest glory. But one, the first, must kill himself, for else who will begin and prove it? So I must certainly kill myself, to begin and prove it. Now I am only a god against my will and I am unhappy, because I am *bound* to assert my will. All are unhappy because all are afraid to express their will. Man has hitherto been so unhappy and so poor because he has been afraid to assert his will in the highest point and has shown his self-will only in little things, like a school-boy. I am awfully unhappy, for I'm awfully afraid. Terror is the curse of man. . . . But I will assert my will, I am bound to believe that I don't believe. I will begin and will make an end of it and open the door, and will save. That's the only thing that will save mankind and will re-create the next generation physically; for with his present physical nature man can't get on without his former God, I believe. For three years I've been seeking for the attribute of my godhead and I've found it; the attribute of my godhead is self-will! That's all I can do to prove in the highest point my independence and my new terrible freedom. For it is very terrible. I am killing myself to prove my independence and my new terrible freedom."

His face was unnaturally pale, and there was a terrible heavy look in his eyes. He was like a man in delirium. Pyotr Stepanovitch thought he would drop on to the floor.

"Give me the pen!" Kirillov cried suddenly, quite unexpectedly, in a positive frenzy. "Dictate; I'll sign anything. I'll sign that I killed Shatov even. Dictate while it amuses me. I am not afraid of what the haughty slaves will think! You will see for yourself that all that is secret shall be made manifest! And you will be crushed. . . . I believe, I believe!"

Pyotr Stepanovitch jumped up from his seat and instantly handed him an inkstand and paper, and began dictating, seizing the moment, quivering with anxiety.

"I, Alexey Kirillov, declare . . ."

"Stay; I won't! To whom am I declaring it?"

Kirillov was shaking as though he were in a fever. This declaration and the sudden strange idea of it seemed to absorb him entirely, as though it were a means of escape by which his tortured spirit strove for a moment's relief.

"To whom am I declaring it? I want to know to whom?"

"To no one, every one, the first person who reads it. Why define it? The whole world!"

"The whole world! Bravo! And I won't have any repentance. I don't want penitence and I don't want it for the police!"

"No, of course, there's no need of it, damn the police! Write, if you are in earnest!" Pyotr Stepanovitch cried hysterically.

"Stay! I want to put at the top a face with the tongue out."

"Ech, what nonsense," cried Pyotr Stepanovitch crossly, "you can express all that without the drawing, by—the tone."

"By the tone? That's true. Yes, by the tone, by the tone of it. Dictate, the tone."

"I, Alexey Kirillov," Pyotr Stepanovitch dictated firmly and peremptorily, bending over Kirillov's shoulder and following every letter which the latter formed with a hand trembling with excitement, "I, Kirillov, declare that to-day, the —th October, at about eight o'clock in the evening, I killed the student Shatov in the park for turning traitor and giving information of the manifestoes and of Fedka, who has been lodging with us for ten days in Filipov's house. I am shooting myself to-day with my revolver, not because I repent and am afraid of you, but because when I was abroad I made up my mind to put an end to my life."

"Is that all?" cried Kirillov with surprise and indignation.

"Not another word," cried Pyotr Stepanovitch, waving his hand, attempting to snatch the document from him.

"Stay." Kirillov put his hand firmly on the paper. "Stay, it's nonsense! I want to say with whom I killed him. Why Fedka? And what about the fire? I want it all and I want to be abusive in tone, too, in tone!"

"Enough, Kirillov, I assure you it's enough," cried Pyotr Stepanovitch almost imploringly, trembling lest he should tear up the paper; "that they may believe you, you must say it as obscurely as possible, just like that, simply in hints. You must only give them a peep of the truth, just enough to tantalise them. They'll tell a story better than ours, and of course they'll believe themselves more than they would us; and you know, it's better than anything—better than anything! Let me have it, it's splendid as it is; give it to me, give it to me!"

And he kept trying to snatch the paper. Kirillov listened open-eyed and appeared to be trying to reflect, but he seemed beyond understanding now.

"Damn it all," Pyotr Stepanovitch cried all at once, ill-humouredly, "he hasn't signed it! Why are you staring like that? Sign!"

"I want to abuse them," muttered Kirillov. He took the pen, however, and signed. "I want to abuse them."

"Write *'Vive la république,'* and that will be enough."

"Bravo!" Kirillov almost bellowed with delight. *'Vive la république démocratique sociale et universelle ou la mort!'* No, no, that's not it. *Liberté, égalité, fraternité ou la mort.'* There, that's better, that's better." He wrote it gleefully under his signature.

"Enough, enough," repeated Pyotr Stepanovitch.

"Stay, a little more. I'll sign it again in French, you know. *'De Kirilloff, gentilhomme russe et citoyen du monde.'* Ha ha!" He went off in a peal of laughter. "No, no, no; stay. I've found something better than all. Eureka! *'Gentilhomme, séminariste russe et citoyen du monde civilisé!'* That's better than any. . . ." He jumped up from the sofa and suddenly, with a rapid gesture, snatched up the revolver from the window, ran with it into the next room, and closed the door behind him. Pyotr Stepanovitch stood for a moment, pondering and gazing at the door.

"If he does it at once, perhaps he'll do it, but if he begins thinking, nothing will come of it."

Meanwhile he took up the paper, sat down, and looked at it again. The wording of the document pleased him again.

"What's needed for the moment? What's wanted is to throw them all off the scent and keep them busy for a time. The park? There's no park in the town and they'll guess its Skvoreshniki of themselves. But while they are arriving at that, time will be passing; then the search will take time too; then when they find the body it will prove that the story is true, and it will follow that it's all true, that it's true about Fedka too. And Fedka explains the fire, the Lebyadkins; so that it was all being hatched here, at Filipov's, while they overlooked it and saw nothing —that will quite turn their heads! They will never think of the quintet; Shatov and Kirillov and Fedka and Lebyadkin, and why they killed each other—that will be another question for them. Oh, damn it all, I don't hear the shot!"

Though he had been reading and admiring the wording of it, he had been listening anxiously all the time, and he suddenly flew into a rage. He looked anxiously at his watch; it was getting late and it was fully ten minutes since Kirillov had gone out. . . . Snatching up the candle, he went to the door of the room where Kirillov had shut himself up. He was just at the door when the thought struck him that the candle had burnt out, that it would not last another twenty minutes, and that there was no other in the room. He took hold of the handle and listened warily; he did not hear the slightest sound. He suddenly opened the door and lifted up the candle: something uttered a roar and rushed at him. He slammed the door with all his might and pressed his weight against it; but all sounds died away and again there was deathlike stillness.

He stood for a long while irresolute, with the candle in his hand. He had been able to see very little in the second he held the door open, but he had caught a glimpse of the face of Kirillov standing at the other end of the room by the window, and the savage fury with which the latter had rushed upon him. Pyotr Stepanovitch started, rapidly set the candle on the table, made ready his revolver, and retreated on tiptoes to the farthest corner of the room, so that if Kirillov opened the door and rushed up to the table with the revolver he would still have time to be the first to aim and fire.

Pyotr Stepanovitch had by now lost all faith in the suicide. "He was standing in the middle of the room, thinking," flashed like a whirlwind through Pyotr Stepanovitch's mind, "and the room was dark and horrible too. . . . He roared and rushed at me. There are two possibilities: either I interrupted him at the very second when he was pulling the trigger or . . . or he was standing planning how to kill me. Yes, that's it, he was planning it. . . . He knows I won't go away without killing him if he funks it himself—so that he would have to kill me first to prevent my killing him. . . . And again, again there is silence. I am really frightened: he may open the door all of a sudden. . . . The nuisance of it is that he believes in God like any priest. . . . He won't shoot himself for anything! There are lots of these people nowadays 'who've come to it of themselves.' A rotten lot! Oh, damn it, the candle, the candle! It'll go out within a quarter of an hour for certain. . . . I must put a stop to it; come what may, I must put a stop to it. . . . Now I can kill him. . . . With that document here no one would think of my killing him. I can put him in such an attitude on the floor with an unloaded revolver in his hand that they'd be certain he'd done it himself. . . . Ach, damn it! how is one to kill him? If I open the door he'll rush out again and shoot me first. Damn it all, he'll be sure to miss!"

He was in agonies, trembling at the necessity of action and his own indecision. At last he took up the candle and again approached the door with the revolver held up in readiness; he put his left hand, in which he held the candle, on the doorhandle. But he managed awkwardly: the handle clanked, there was a rattle and a creak. "He will fire straightway," flashed through Pyotr Stepanovitch's mind. With his foot he flung the door open violently, raised the candle, and held out the revolver; but no shot nor cry came from within. . . . There was no one in the room.

He started. The room led nowhere. There was no exit, no means of escape from it. He lifted the candle higher and looked about him more attentively: there was certainly no one. He called Kirillov's name in a low voice, then again louder; no one answered.

"Can he have got out by the window?" The casement in one window was, in fact, open. "Absurd! He couldn't have got away through the casement." Pyotr Stepanovitch crossed the room and went up to the window. "He couldn't possibly." All at once he turned round quickly and was aghast at something extraordinary.

Against the wall facing the windows on the right of the door stood a cupboard. On the right side of this cupboard, in the corner formed by the cupboard and the wall, stood Kirillov, and he was standing in a very strange way; motionless, perfectly erect, with his arms held stiffly at his sides, his head raised and pressed tightly back against the wall in the very corner, he seemed to be trying to conceal and efface himself. Everything seemed to show that he was hiding, yet somehow it was not easy to believe it. Pyotr Stepanovitch was standing a little sideways to the corner, and could only see the projecting parts of the figure. He could not bring himself to move to the left to get a full view of Kirillov and solve the mystery. His heart began beating violently, and he felt a sudden rush of blind fury: he started from where he stood, and, shouting and stamping with his feet, he rushed to the horrible place.

But when he reached Kirillov he stopped short again, still more overcome, horror-stricken. What struck him most was that, in spite of his shout and his furious rush, the figure did not stir, did not move in a single limb—as though it were of stone or of wax. The pallor of the face was unnatural, the black eyes were quite unmoving and were staring away at a point in the distance. Pyotr Stepanovitch lowered the candle and raised it again, lighting up the figure from all points of view and scrutinising it. He suddenly noticed that, although Kirillov was looking straight before him, he could see him and was perhaps watching him out of the corner of his eye. Then the idea occurred to him to hold the candle right up to the wretch's face, to scorch him and see what he would do. He suddenly fancied that Kirillov's chin twitched and that something like a mocking smile passed over his lips—as though he had guessed Pyotr Stepanovitch's thought. He shuddered and, beside himself, clutched violently at Kirillov's shoulder.

Then something happened so hideous and so soon over that Pyotr Stepanovitch could never afterwards recover a coherent impression of it. He had hardly touched Kirillov when the latter bent down quickly and with his head knocked the candle out of Pyotr Stepanovitch's hand; and candlestick fell with a clang on the ground and the candle went out. At the same moment he was conscious of a fearful pain in the little finger of his left hand. He cried out, and all that he could remember was that, beside himself, he hit out with all his might and struck three blows with the revolver on the head of Kirillov, who had bent down to him and had bitten his finger. At last he tore away his finger and rushed headlong to get out of the house, feeling his way in the dark. He was pursued by terrible shouts from the room.

"Directly, directly, directly, directly." Ten times. But he still ran on, and was running into the porch when he suddenly heard a loud shot. Then he stopped short in the dark porch and stood deliberating for five minutes; at last he made his way back into the house. But he had to get the candle. He had only to feel on the floor on the right of the cupboard for the candlestick; but how was he to light the candle? There suddenly came into his mind a vague recollection: he recalled that when he had run into the kitchen the day before to attack Fedka he had noticed in passing a large red box of matches in a corner on a shelf. Feeling with his hands, he made his way to the door on the left leading to the kitchen, found it, crossed the passage, and went down the steps. On the shelf, on the very spot where he had just recalled seeing it, he felt in the dark a full unopened box of matches. He hurriedly went up the steps again without striking a light, and it was only when he was near the cupboard, at the spot where he had struck Kirillov with the revolver and been bitten by him, that he remembered his bitten finger, and at the same instant was conscious that it was unbearably painful. Clenching his teeth, he managed somehow to light the candle-end, set it in the candlestick again, and looked about him: near the open casement, with his feet towards the right-hand corner, lay the dead body of Kirillov. The shot had been fired at the right temple and the bullet had come out at the top on the left, shattering the skull. There were splashes of blood and brains. The revolver was still in the suicide's hand on the floor. Death must have been instantaneous. After a careful look around, Pyotr Stepanovitch got up and went out on tiptoe, closed the door, left the candle on the table in the outer room, thought a moment, and resolved not to put it out, reflecting that it could not possibly set fire to anything. Looking once more at the document left on the table, he smiled mechanically and then went out of the house, still for some reason walking on tiptoe. He crept through Fedka's hole again and carefully replaced the posts after him.

PART 2

Personality in Culture

Culture, says Edward Tylor, consists of the complex whole of everything that we think, do, and have as members of society. In Part 2 we are concerned with the ways in which what we think (democracy versus monarchy), do (eating with a knife and fork as opposed to chop sticks), and have (a technologically dominated rather than an agriculturally dominated society) affect our personalities. Personalities are unique entities. There will never be another me just as there will never be another you. Still, any adequate understanding of the nature of the human condition requires the recognition of the fact that we are all, at one and the same time, both unique and typical, both what we have made of ourselves and what others have made of us. Often, it is quite difficult to decide which is which—that is exactly the point of the following selections.

Chapter 4

Chapter 4 pertains to social roles and social norms. Essential topics in a course in social psychology, their importance is perhaps best emphasized by Robert Nisbet's comment that "from the very beginnings of life one's interaction with others is normatively bounded, normatively inspired, and normatively maintained. For what has been called for thousands of years human nature is actually human normative nature."[1] Culture, then, provides the firm structures for human life that are lacking biologically, and the norms and the roles that spring from them are culture's vital core.[2]

The Turgenev selection not only gives a good description of the rights and obligations of a nineteenth century landowner but it also calls our attention to the often brutal norms of conduct that prevailed between lord and serf. The reader might want to follow another version of the norms of this relationship in Tolstoy's *Master and Man.*

The selection from Hawthorne not only demonstrates the harsh manner in which the community (and the norms which stand behind it) has treated our heroine but it also highlights the fact that the Parson, aware that he had committed an act which his fellows considered grievously wrong, was unable to remain quiet. For the internalization of the community's norms (here mores) demanded that *he also* wear a scarlet letter.

The chapters drawn from *Babbitt* are concerned with the "domestic manners" which prevailed in the Babbitt home and in Zenith at large. At the time these chapters were written, they were, and they remain, acute observations about the nature of American society. Remember, for example, that the twenties produced

1 Robert Nisbet, *The Social Bond* (New York, 1970), p. 222.
2 Peter Berger, *The Sacred Canopy* (New York, 1968), p. 7.

Bruce Barton's *The Man Nobody Knows,* which argued the thesis that Jesus Christ was "the founder of modern business." It led the best seller lists in America for two straight years (1925 and 1926).

Chapter 5

Chapter 5 calls our attention to yet other culturally related personality differences. John Steinbeck's description of Cannery Row is a fine picture of the nature of a "lower class" environment and of the people who live in and spring from it. Consider also Steinbeck's question: "What can it profit a man to gain the whole world and to come to his property with a gastric ulcer, a blown prostrate, and bifocals?" Is money that important? Or is that just the Protestant Ethic internalized and now transformed into its twentieth century form? For who was it that had the temerity to refer to the people of Cannery Row as "lower class?"

The selection from *War and Peace* relates to a social gathering in which class and caste (here synonomous with social honor) conflict. It is noteworthy that the uniqueness of personality is relatively unimportant in this instance. The characters are being judged rather by the social standards they do or do not live up to. For it is a qualitative judgment which makes Anna Pavlovna better than Pierre. Notice particularly her reaction to Pierre's remarks about Napoleon.

The *Ice Palace* is a particularly nice story which describes a complaint of many Southerners come North: Northerners are just too cold-hearted. Incidentally, this was a phenomenon that Fitzgerald knew at first hand. His wife was from the South (a Southern belle if you will), and the habits that she acquired there meshed well with the manner in which the Fitzgerald's spent their early married life.

Chapter 6

Chapter 6 concerns the concept of reference group. I note here, following Professor Kelley, that there are two types of reference groups: first, the "normative type," which sets and maintains standards for the individual, and, second, the "comparison type," which provides a frame of comparison relative to which the individual evaluates himself and others.[3] The first is a source of values, and the second is a context for evaluating the relative position of oneself and others. Of course, the distinction is only an analytical one since a particular group can serve both functions.[4]

[3] Robert Merton, *Social Theory and Social Structure* (New York, 1957), pp. 283–284.
[4] *Ibid.,* p. 284.

In the first two selections, both Madame Bovary and Jacques Thibault are referring to groups of the "comparison type," although it should be noted that in his discussion of the capitalist classes Jacques' and his friends' references are *negative,* while Madame Bovary's references to Romantics and to the people associated with the "ball" are definitely *positive.* It is essential, then, to understand that the reference group can function in either manner.

The selection from *The Persian Letters* should clarify further the importance of the concept of reference group. Here, Rica and Uzbek are "strangers" to the world of France, and thus, in the words of Alfred Schutz, their "contour lines of relevance" are manifestly different. The letters demonstrate that while both Rica and Uzbek use the French for the purposes of comparison, they still refer those comparisons to the normative standards of their own group. For, in their eyes, bishops are dervishes and Christians a group of people who live within the shadow of idolatry—and who is to say that they are wrong?

Chapter 4

Social Roles and Social Norms

IVAN TURGENEV

• *Sketches from a Hunter's Album*

Two Landowners

I have already had the honour, kind readers, of acquainting you with some of my neighbouring landowners; please permit me now, appropriately (for the likes of us writers everything is appropriate), to acquaint you with two further landowners, on whose lands I have frequently hunted, men who are highly esteemed and well-intentioned, and who enjoy universal respect in several counties.

To begin with, I will describe to you the retired Major-General Vyacheslav Illarionovich Khvalynsky. Imagine a tall man, at one time possessing a graceful build, though now a little flabby, but by no means decrepit, not even really old— a man of mature age, in his prime, as they say. True, the formerly straight—even so, still pleasing—features of his face have changed a little, his cheeks have sagged, frequent wrinkles form ray-like surrounds to his eyes, here and there a tooth is gone, as Saadi[1] was reputed to have said, according to Pushkin; the auburn hair—at least, what has remained of it—has turned a lilac grey, thanks to a preparation bought at the Romen horse fair from a Jew who passed himself off as an Armenian; but Vyacheslav Illarionovich has a lively manner of speaking, laughs boisterously, jingles his spurs, twirls his moustache and—to cap it all— speaks of himself as an old cavalry officer, whereas it is common knowledge that real oldsters never speak of themselves as old. He usually wears a coat buttoned up to the neck, a tall cravat with starched collar and wide grey speckled trousers

SOURCE. From *Sketches from A Hunter's Album* by Ivan Turgenev. Translated by Richard Freeborn. Copyright 1967, reprinted with the permission of Penguin Books Limited.

of military cut; his cap he wears pulled straight down over his forehead, leaving the back of his head completely bare.

He is a man of great kindness, but with some fairly strange notions and habits. For example: he can never treat impoverished noblemen or those with no rank as people who are his equals. Conversing with them, he usually looks at them sideways, leaning his cheek strongly against his firm, white collar, or he suddenly ups and glowers at them with a lucid and unwavering stare, stops talking and starts twitching the skin all over his scalp; he even takes to pronouncing words differently and does not say, for instance: "Thank you, Pavel Vasilych," or "Please approach, Mikhaylo Ivanych," but: "Sonk you, Pall Asilich," or "Pl-laase apprarch, Mikhal Vanych." He deals even more oddly with those who occupy the lowest rungs of society: he does not look at them at all and, prior to explaining to them what he wants or giving an order, he has a way of repeating, several times in a row and with a perplexed and dreamy look on his face: "What's your name? . . . What's your name?," placing unusually sharp emphasis on the first word "what" and uttering the rest very rapidly, which gives his manner of speaking a fairly close resemblance to the cry of a male quail. He is a terrible one for fussing and frightfully grasping, but he is poor at managing his own affairs, having taken on as administrator of his estate a retired sergeant-major who is a Little Russian and an extraordinarily stupid man.

In the matter of estate-management, by the way, not one of us has yet outdone a certain important St Petersburg official who, having observed from the reports of his steward that the store-barns on his estate were frequently catching fire (as a result of which a great deal of his grain was being lost), issued the strictest edict to the effect that corn sheaves should not be placed in the barns until all fires were completely extinguished. This very same personage took it into his head to sow all his fields with poppies on the evidently very simple principle, so he claimed, that poppy-seed was dearer than rye, consequently poppies were more profitable. It was he who also ordered all his peasant women to wear tall head-dresses designed according to a pattern sent from St Petersburg and in fact, right up to the present day, the womenfolk on his estates still wear such head-dresses—except that the tall tops have been folded down . . . But we must return to Vyacheslav Illarionovich.

Vyacheslav Illarionovich is terribly keen on the fair sex and he no sooner catches sight of some pretty girl or other on the street of his local town than he at once sets off in hot pursuit, only to develop a sudden limp—which is a remarkable state of affairs. He likes to play cards, but only with people of lower rank, so that they will address him as "Your Excellency" while he can huff and puff at them and abuse them as much as he wishes. Whenever he happens to be playing with the Governor or some high-ranking official, a surprising change comes over him: he even smiles and nods his head and looks them intently in the eyes—he positively exudes honey and sweetness. . . . He even loses without grumbling.

Vyacheslav Illarionovich reads little and, when he does, he continuously moves his moustache and eyebrows—first his moustache, then his eyebrows, just as if a wave was passing upwards across his face. This wave-like movement on the face of Vyacheslav Illarionovich is particularly noteworthy when he happens—in the presence of guests, naturally—to be reading through the columns of the *Journal des Debats*. At the elections of marshals of nobility he plays a fairly important role, but out of meanness he always refuses the honourable title of marshal. "Gentlemen," he says to the members of the nobility who usually approach him on the subject, and he says it in a voice redolent with condescension and self-confidence, "I am much obliged for the honour; but I have resolved to devote my leisure hours to solitude." And, having once uttered these words, he will jerk his head several times to right and left, and then, with dignity, let the flesh of his chin and cheeks lap over his cravat.

In the days of his youth he was adjutant to some important personage, whom he never addressed otherwise than by his name and patronymic. They say that he assumed rather more than the duties of an adjutant, that decked out, for example, in full parade uniform, with everything buttoned-up and in place, he used to attend to his master's needs in the bath-house—but one can't believe everything one hears. Besides, General Khvalynsky is himself by no means fond of mentioning his service career, which is in general a somewhat odd circumstance; he also, it seems, has no experience of war. He lives, does General Khvalynsky, in a small house, by himself; he has had no experience of married happiness in his life, and consequently is regarded as an eligible bachelor even now—indeed, an advantageous match. Yet he has a housekeeper, a woman of about thirty-five, black-eyed and black-browed, buxom, fresh-faced and bewhiskered, who walks about on weekdays in starched dresses, adding muslin sleeves on Sundays.

Splendid is Vyacheslav Illarionovich's behaviour at large banquets given by landowners in honour of Governors and other persons in authority: on such occasions, it might be said, he is truly in his element. It is usual for him on such occasions to sit, if not directly to the Governor's right, then not far from him; at the beginning of the banquet he is concerned more than anything with preserving a sense of his own dignity and, leaning back, though without turning his head, directs his eyes sideways at the stand-up collars of the guests and the round napes of their necks; then, towards the end of the sitting, he grows expansively gay, smiles in all directions (he had smiled in the Governor's direction from the beginning of the meal) and even occasionally proposes a toast in honour of the fair sex—an ornament to our planet, as he puts it. Likewise, General Khvalynsky makes a good showing on all solemn and public occasions, at inquiries, assemblies and exhibitions; masterly, also, is his fashion of receiving a blessing from a priest. At the end of theatrical performances, at river-crossings and other such places, Vyacheslav Illarionovich's servants never make a noise or shout; on the contrary, making a path for him through a crowd or summoning a carriage, they always say in pleasant, throaty baritones: "If you please, if you please, make way for General Khvalynsky" or "General Khvalynsky's carriage. . . ." His carriage, if the truth be told, is of fairly ancient design; his footmen wear fairly tattered livery (it is hardly worth mentioning that it is grey with red piping); his horses are also fairly antiquated and have given service in their time; but Vyacheslav Illarionovich makes no pretensions to dandyishness and does not even consider it proper for a man of his rank to throw dust in people's eyes.

Khvalynsky has no particular gifts for words, or it may be that he has no chance of displaying his eloquence since he cannot tolerate either disputes or rebuttals and studiously avoids all lengthy conversations, particularly with young people. Indeed, this is the proper way to handle things; any other way would be disastrous with the people as they are today: in no time at all they'd stop being servile and start losing respect for you. In the presence of those of higher rank Khvalynsky is mostly taciturn, but to those of lower rank, whom he evidently despises but who are the only ones he knows, he delivers sharp, abrupt speeches, endlessly using such expressions as: "You are, however, talking rubbish," or "At last I find it necessary, my good fellah, to put you in your place," or "Now, damn it all, you surely ought to know who you're talking to," and so on. Postmasters, committee chairmen and station-masters are especially awed by him. He never receives guests at home and lives, so rumour has it, like a regular Scrooge. Despite all this, he is an excellent landowner. Neighbours refer to him as "an old fellow who's done his service, a man who's quite selfless, with principles, *vieux grognard,* old grouser that he is." The public prosecutor of the province is the only man to permit himself a smile when mention is made in his presence of General Khvalynsky's splendid and solid qualities—but, then, such is the power of envy!

Let me pass now to another landowner.

Mardary Apollonych Stegunov bore no resemblance at all to Khvalynsky; he was hardly likely to have served anywhere and was never accounted handsome. Mardary Apollonych is a squat little old man, roly-poly and bald, with a double chin, soft little hands and a thoroughgoing paunch. He is a great one for entertaining and has a fondness for pranks; he lives, as they say, in clover; and winter and summer he walks about in a striped quilted dressing-gown. In only one respect is he similar to General Khvalynsky: he is also a bachelor. He has five hundred serfs. Mardary Apollonych takes a fairly superficial interest in his estate; ten years ago, so as not to be too far behind the times, he bought from the Butenops in Moscow a threshing machine, locked it in his barn and then rested content. On a fine summer day he may indeed order his racing buggy to be harnessed and then ride out into the field to see how the grain is ripening and to pick cornflowers.

He lives, does Mardary Apollonych, completely in the old style. Even his house is of antiquated construction: the entrance hall, as one might expect, smells of *kvas,* tallow candles and leather; on the right stands a sideboard with pipes and hand-towels; the dining-room contains family portraits, flies, a large pot of geraniums and a down-in-the-mouth piano; the drawing-room has three divans, three tables, two mirrors and a wheezy clock of blackened enamel with fretted, bronze hands; the study has a table piled with papers, a bluish draught-screen pasted with pictures cut from various works of the last century, cupboards full of stinking books, spiders and thick black dust, a stuffed arm-chair and an Italian window and a door into the garden that has been nailed up. . . . In a word, everything is quite appropriate. Mardary Apollonych has a mass of servants, and they are all dressed in old-fashioned style: long blue coats with high collars, trousers of some muddy colouring and short yellowish waistcoats. They use the old-fashioned address "good master" in speaking to guests. His estate is managed by a bailiff drawn from among his peasants, a man with a beard as long as his sheepskin coat; his house is run by an old woman, wrinkled and tight-fisted, with a brown kerchief wound round her head. His stables contain thirty horses of various sizes; he rides out in a home-made carriage weighing well over two and a half tons. He receives guests with the utmost warmth and entertains them lavishly—that is to say, thanks to the stupefying characteristics of Russian cookery, he deprives them, until right up to the evening, of any opportunity of doing anything apart from playing preference. He himself never occupies himself with anything and has even given up reading his dream-book. But we still have a good many such landowners in Russia. It may be asked: what's led me to mention him and why? In place of a straight answer, let me tell you about one of my visits to Mardary Apollonych.

I went over to his place one summer, about seven o'clock in the evening. Evening prayers had just concluded, and the priest, a young man, evidently very shy and only recently graduated from his seminary, was sitting in the drawing-room beside the door, perched on the very edge of a chair. Mardary Apollonych, as was his custom, received me exceptionally fondly: he was genuinely delighted to receive guests and, by and large, he was the kindest of men. The priest rose and picked up his hat.

"One moment, one moment, my good fellow," said Mardary Apollonych without leaving hold of my arm. "You mustn't be going. I've ordered them to bring you some vodka."

"I don't drink, sir," the priest mumbled in confusion and reddened up to his ears.

"What rubbish! You say you're a priest and you don't drink!" Mardary Apollonych retorted. "Mishka! Yushka! Vodka for the gentleman!"

Yushka, a tall and emaciated old man of about eighty, came in with a glass of vodka on a dark-painted tray covered with a variety of flesh-coloured splodges.

The priest proceeded to refuse.

"Drink, my good fellow, and no fussing, it's not proper," the landowner remarked in a reproachful tone.

The poor young man acquiesced.

"Well now, my good fellow, you can go."

The priest started bowing.

"All right, all right, be off with you. . . . An excellent fellow," Mardary Apollonych continued, watching him depart, "and I'm very satisfied with him. The only thing is—he's still young. Preaches sermons all the time, and he doesn't drink. But how are you, my good fellow? What're you doing, how're things? Let's go out on to the balcony—you see what a fine evening it is."

We went out on to the balcony, sat down and began to talk. Mardary Apollonych glanced downwards and suddenly became frightfully excited.

"Whose are these chickens? Whose are these chickens?" he started shouting. "Whose are these chickens walking about the garden? Yushka! Yushka! Off with you and find out at once whose are these chickens walking about the garden. Whose are these chickens? How many times I've forbidden this, how many times I've said so!"

Yushka ran off.

"What disorders there are!" repeated Mardary Apollonych. "It's terrible!"

The unfortunate chickens—as I recall it now, there were two speckled and one white one with a crest—continued walking under the apple trees with the utmost lack of concern, occasionally expressing their feelings by making prolonged cluckings, when suddenly Yushka, hatless and armed with a stick, and three other house-serfs who were well on in years made a combined attack on them. A riot followed. The chickens squawked, flapped their wings, leapt about and cackled deafeningly; the house-serfs ran to and fro, stumbling and falling; and their master shouted from the balcony like one possessed: "Catch them, catch them! Catch them, catch them! Catch them, catch them, catch them! Whose are these chickens, whose are these chickens?" Finally, one of the house-serfs succeeded in catching the crested chicken by forcing its breast to the ground, and at that very moment a girl of about eleven years of age, thoroughly dishevelled and with a switch in her hand, jumped over the garden fence from the street.

"So that's who the chickens belong to!" the landowner exclaimed triumphantly. "They're Yermila the coachman's! See, he's sent his little Natalya to drive them back! It's not likely he'd send Parasha," the landowner interjected under his breath and grinned meaningfully. "Hey, Yushka! Forget the chickens and bring little Natalya here."

But before the puffing Yushka could reach the terrified little girl, she was grabbed by the housekeeper, who had appeared from nowhere, and given several slaps on her behind.

"That's right, that's right," the landowner said, accompanying the slaps. "Yes, yes, yes! Yes, yes, yes! And mind you take the chickens off, Avdotya," he added in a loud voice and turned to me with a shining face: "Quite a chase, my good fellow, what? I've even worked myself into a sweat—just look at me!"

And Mardary Apollonych rattled off into thunderous laughter.

We remained on the balcony. The evening was really unusually beautiful. Tea was served to us.

"Tell me," I began, "Mardary Apollonych, are they yours, those settlements out there on the road, beyond the ravine?"

"They're mine. What of it?"

"How could you allow such a thing, Mardary Apollonych? It's quite wrong. The tiny huts allotted to the peasants are horrible, cramped things; there's not a tree to be seen anywhere; there's nothing in the way of a pond; there's only one well, and that's no use. Surely you could have found somewhere else? And rumour has it that you've even taken away their old hemp-fields."

"But what's one to do about these redistributions of the land?" Mardary Apollonych asked me in turn. "This redistribution's got me right here." He pointed to the back of his neck. "And I don't foresee any good coming from it. And as to whether I took away their hemp-fields and didn't dig out a pond for them there—about such matters, my good fellow, I haven't the foggiest. I'm just a simple man and I have old-fashioned ways. In my way of thinking, if you're the master, you're the master, and if you're a peasant, you're a peasant. And that's that."

It goes without saying that such a lucid and convincing argument was unanswerable.

"What's more," he continued, "those peasants are a bad sort, not in my good books. Particularly two families over there. Even my late father, God rest his soul in the Kingdom of Heaven, even he wasn't fond of them, not at all fond of them. And I'll tell you something I've noticed: if the father's a thief, then the son'll be a thief, it doesn't matter how much you want things to be otherwise. . . . Oh, blood-ties, blood-ties—they're the big thing! I tell you quite frankly that I've sent men from those two families to be recruits out of their turn and shoved them around here, there and everywhere. But what's one to do? They won't give up breeding. They're so fertile, damn them!"

In the meantime, the air grew completely quiet. Only occasionally a light breeze eddied around us and, on the last occasion, as it died down around the house it brought to our ears the sound of frequent and regular blows which resounded from the direction of the stables. Mardary Apollonych had only just raised a full saucer to his lips and was already on the point of distending his nostrils, without which, as everyone knows, no true Russian can imbibe his tea, when he stopped, pricked up his ears, nodded his head, drank and, setting the saucer down on the table, uttered with the kindest of smiles and as if unconsciously in time with the blows: "Chooky-chooky-chook! Chooky-chook! Chooky-chook!"

"What on earth is that?" I asked in astonishment.

"It's a little rascal being punished on my orders. Do you by any chance know Vasya the butler?"

"Which Vasya?"

"The one who's just been waiting on us at dinner. He's the one who sports those large side-whiskers."

The fiercest sense of outrage could not have withstood Mardary Apollonych's meek and untrammeled gaze.

"What's bothering you, young man, eh?" he said, shaking his head. "You think I'm wicked, is that why you're staring at me like that? Spare the rod and spoil the child, you know that as well as I do."

A quarter of an hour later I said good-bye to Mardary Apollonych. On my way through the village I saw Vasya the butler. He was walking along the street and chewing nuts. I ordered my driver to stop the horses and called to him.

"Did they give you a beating today, my friend?" I asked him.

"How did you know about it?" Vasya answered.

"Your master told me."

"The master did?"

"Why did he order you to be beaten?"

"It served me right, good master, it served me right. You don't get beaten for nothing here. That's not how things are arranged here—oh, no. Our master's not like that, our master's . . . you won't find another master like ours anywhere else in the province."

"Let's go!" I told my driver. *Well, that's old-style Russia for you!* I thought as I travelled home.

NATHANIEL HAWTHORNE

• *The Scarlet Letter*

XXIII. The Revelation of the Scarlet Letter

The eloquent voice, on which the souls of the listening audience had been borne aloft as on the swelling waves of the sea, at length came to a pause. There was a momentary silence, profound as what should follow the utterance of oracles. Then ensued a murmur and half-hushed tumult; as if the auditors, released from the high spell that had transported them into the region of another's mind, were returning into themselves, with all their awe and wonder still heavy on them. In a moment more, the crowd began to gush forth from the doors of the church. Now that there was an end, they needed other breath, more fit to support the gross and earthly life into which they relapsed, than that atmosphere which the preacher had converted into words of flame, and had burdened with the rich fragrance of his thought.

In the open air their rapture broke into speech. The street and the market-place absolutely babbled, from side to side, with applauses of the minister. His hearers could not rest until they had told one another of what each knew better than he could tell or hear. According to their united testimony, never had man spoken in so wise, so high, and so holy a spirit, as he that spake this day; nor had inspiration ever breathed through mortal lips more evidently than it did through his. Its influence could be seen, as it were, descending upon him, and possessing him, and continually lifting him out of the written discourse that lay before him, and filling him with ideas that must have been as marvellous to himself as to his

SOURCE. From *The Scarlet Letter* by Nathaniel Hawthorne. Cuneo Press, N.D.

audience. His subject, it appeared, had been the relation between the Deity and the communities of mankind, with a special reference to the New England which they were here planting in the wilderness. And as he drew toward the close, a spirit as of prophecy had come upon him, constraining him to its purpose as mightily as the old prophets of Israel were constrained; only with this difference, that, whereas the Jewish seers had denounced judgments and ruin on their country, it was his mission to foretell a high and glorious destiny for the newly gathered people of the Lord. But, throughout it all, and through the whole discourse, there had been a certain deep, sad undertone of pathos, which could not be interpreted otherwise than as the natural regret of one soon to pass away. Yes; their minister whom they so loved—and who so loved them all, that he could not depart heavenward without a sigh—had the foreboding of untimely death upon him, and would soon leave them in their tears! This idea of his transitory stay on earth gave the last emphasis to the effect which the preacher had produced; it was as if an angel, in his passage to the skies, had shaken his bright wings over the people for an instant—at once a shadow and a splendor—and had shed down a shower of golden truths upon them.

Thus there had come to the Reverend Mr. Dimmesdale—as to most men in their various spheres, though seldom recognized until they see it far behind them —an epoch of life more brilliant and full of triumph than any previous one, or than any which could hereafter be. He stood at this moment, on the very proudest eminence of superiority, to which the gifts of intellect, rich lore, prevailing eloquence, and a reputation of whitest sanctity could exalt a clergyman in New England's earliest days, when the professional character was of itself a lofty pedestal. Such was the position which the minister occupied, as he bowed his head forward on the cushions of the pulpit, at the close of his Election Sermon. Meanwhile Hester Prynne was standing beside the scaffold of the pillory, with the scarlet letter still burning on her breast.

Now was heard again the clangor of music and the measured tramp of the military escort issuing from the church door. The procession was to be marshalled thence to the town hall, where a solemn banquet would complete the ceremonies of the day.

Once more, therefore, the train of venerable and majestic fathers was seen moving through a broad pathway of the people, who drew back reverently on either side as the Governor and magistrates, the old and wise men, the holy ministers, and all that were eminent and renowned, advanced into the midst of them. When they were fairly in the market-place, their presence was greeted by a shout. This—though doubtless it might acquire additional force and volume from the childlike loyalty which the age awarded to its rulers—was felt to be an irrepressible outburst of enthusiasm kindled in the auditors by that high strain of eloquence which was yet reverberating in their ears. Each felt the impulse in himself, and, in the same breath, caught it from his neighbor. Within the church, it had hardly been kept down; beneath the sky, it pealed upward to the zenith. There were human beings enough, and enough of highly wrought and symphonious feeling to produce that more impressive sound than the organ tones of the blast, or the thunder, or the roar of the sea; even that mighty swell of many voices, blended into one great voice by the universal impulse which makes likewise one vast heart out of the many. Never, from the soil of New England, had gone up such a shout! Never, on New England soil, had stood the man so honored by his mortal brethren as the preacher!

How fared it with him then? Were there not the brilliant particles of a halo in the air about his head? So etherealized by spirit as he was, and so apotheosized by worshiping admirers, did his footsteps, in the procession really tread upon the dust of earth?

As the ranks of military men and civil fathers moved onward, all eyes were turned toward the point where the minister was seen to approach among them. The shout died into a murmur, as one portion of the crowd after another obtained a glimpse of him. How feeble and pale he looked amid all his triumph! The energy—or say, rather, the inspiration which had held him up, until he should have delivered the sacred message that brought its own strength along with it from heaven—was withdrawn, now that it had so faithfully performed its office. The glow which they had just before beheld burning on his cheek, was extinguished, like a flame that sinks down hopelessly, among the late-decaying embers. It seemed hardly the face of a man alive, with such a deathlike hue; it was hardly a man with life in him, that tottered on his path so nervelessly, yet tottered, and did not fall!

One of his clerical brethren—it was the venerable John Wilson—observing the state in which Mr. Dimmesdale was left by the retiring wave of intellect and sensibility, stepped forward hastily to offer his support. The minister tremulously, but decidedly, repelled the old man's arm. He still walked onward, if that movement could be so described, which rather resembled the wavering effort of an infant, with its mother's arms in view, outstretched to tempt him forward. And now, almost imperceptible as were the latter steps of his progress, he had come opposite the well-remembered and weather-darkened scaffold, where, long since, with all that dreary lapse of time between, Hester Prynne had encountered the world's ignominious stare. There stood Hester, holding little Pearl by the hand! And there was the scarlet letter on her breast! The minister here made a pause; although the music still played the stately and rejoicing march to which the procession moved. It summoned him onward—onward to the festival!—but here he made a pause.

Bellingham, for the last few moments, had kept an anxious eye upon him. He now left his own place in the procession, and advanced to give assistance; judging, from Mr. Dimmesdale's aspect, that he must otherwise inevitably fall. But there was something in the latter's expression that warned back the magistrate, although a man not readily obeying the vague intimations that pass from one spirit to another. The crowd, meanwhile, looked on with awe and wonder. This earthly faintness was, in their view, only another phase of the minister's celestial strength; nor would it have seemed a miracle too high to be wrought for one so holy, had he ascended before their eyes, waxing dimmer and brighter, and fading at last into the light of Heaven!

He turned toward the scaffold, and stretched forth his arms.

"Hester," said he, "come hither! Come, my little Pearl!"

It was a ghastly look with which he regarded them; but there was something at once tender and strangely triumphant in it. The child, with the bird-like motion which was one of her characteristics, flew to him, and clasped her arms about his knees. Hester Prynne—slowly, as if impelled by inevitable fate, and against her strongest will—likewise drew near, but paused before she reached him. At this instant, old Roger Chillingworth thrust himself through the crowd —or perhaps, so dark, disturbed, and evil was his look, he rose up out of some nether region—to snatch back his victim from what he sought to do! Be that as it might, the old man rushed forward, and caught the minister by the arm.

"Madman, hold! what is your purpose?" whispered he. "Wave back that woman! Cast off this child! All shall be well! Do not blacken your fame, and perish in dishonor! I can yet save you! Would you bring infamy on your sacred profession?"

"Ha, tempter! Methinks thou art too late!" answered the minister, encountering his eye, fearfully, but firmly. "Thy power is not what it was! With God's help, I shall escape thee now!"

He again extended his hand to the woman of the scarlet letter.

"Hester Prynne," cried he, with a piercing earnestness, "in the name of Him, so terrible and so merciful, who gives me grace, at this last moment, to do what—for my own heavy sin and miserable agony—I withheld myself from doing seven years ago, come hither now, and twine thy strength about me! Thy strength, Hester; but let it be guided by the will which God hath granted me! This wretched and wronged old man is opposing it with all his might!—with all his own might, and the fiend's! Come Hester, come! Support me up yonder scaffold!"

The crowd was in a tumult. The men of rank and dignity, who stood more immediately around the clergyman, were so taken by surprise, and so perplexed as to the purport of what they saw—unable to receive the explanation which most readily presented itself, or to imagine any other—that they remained silent and inactive spectators of the judgment which Providence seemed about to work. They beheld the minister, leaning on Hester's shoulder, and supported by her arm around him, approach the scaffold, and ascend its steps; while still the little hand of the sin-born child was clasped in his. Old Roger Chillingworth followed, as one intimately connected with the drama of guilt and sorrow in which they had all been actors, and well entitled, therefore, to be present, at its closing scene.

"Hadst thou sought the whole earth over," said he, looking darkly at the clergyman, "there was no one place so secret—no high place nor lowly place, where thou couldst have escaped me—save on this very scaffold!"

"Thanks be to Him who hath led me hither!" answered the minister.

Yet he trembled, and turned to Hester, with an expression of doubt and anxiety in his eyes, not the less evidently betrayed, that there was a feeble smile upon his lips.

"Is not this better," murmured he, "than what we dreamed of in the forest?"

"I know not! I know not!" she hurriedly replied. "Better? Yea; so we may both die, and little Pearl die with us!"

"For thee and Pearl, be it as God shall order," said the minister; "and God is merciful! Let me now do the will which he hath made plain before my sight. For, Hester, I am a dying man. So let me make haste to take my shame upon me!"

Partly supported by Hester Prynne, and holding one hand of little Pearl's, the Reverend Mr. Dimmesdale turned to the dignified and venerable rulers; to the holy ministers, who were his brethren; to the people, whose great heart was thoroughly appalled, yet overflowing with tearful sympathy, as knowing that some deep life-matter—which, if full of sin, was full of anguish and repentance likewise—was now to be laid open to them. The sun, but little past its meridian, shone down upon the clergyman, and gave a distinctness to his figure, as he stood out from all the earth, to put in his plea of guilty at the bar of Eternal Justice.

"People of New England!" cried he, with a voice that rose over them, high, solemn, and majestic—yet had always a tremor through it, and sometimes a shriek, struggling up out of a fathomless depth of remorse and woe—ye, that have loved me!—ye, that have deemed me holy!—behold me here, the one sinner of the world! At last!—at last!—I stand upon the spot where, seven years since, I should have stood; here with this woman, whose arm, more than the little strength wherewith I have crept hitherward, sustains me, at this dreadful moment, from grovelling down upon my face! Lo, the scarlet letter which Hester wears! Ye have all shuddered at it? Wherever her walk hath been—wherever, so miserably burdened, she may have hoped to find repose—it hath cast a lurid gleam of awe and horrible repugnance round about her. But there stood one in the midst of you, at whose brand of sin and infamy ye have not shuddered!"

It seemed, at this point, as if the minister must leave the remainder of his secret undisclosed. But he fought back the bodily weakness—and, still more, the faintness of heart—that was striving for the mastery with him. He threw off all assistance, and stepped passionately forward a pace before the woman and the child.

"It was on him!" he continued, with a kind of fierceness; so determined was he to speak out the whole. "God's eye beheld it! The angels were forever pointing at it! The Devil knew it well, and fretted it continually with the touch of his burning finger! But he hid it cunningly from men, and walked among you with the mien of a spirit, mournful, because so pure in a sinful world!—and sad, because he missed his heavenly kindred! Now, at the death-hour, he stands up before you! He bids you look again at Hester's scarlet letter! He tells you, that with all its mysterious horror, it is but the shadow of what he bears on his own breast, and that even this, his own red stigma, is no more than the type of what has seared his inmost heart! Stand any here that question God's judgment on a sinner? Behold! Behold a dreadful witness of it!"

With a convulsive motion, he tore away the ministerial band from before his breast. It was revealed! but it were irreverent to describe that revelation. For an instant the gaze of the horror-stricken multitude was concentrated on the ghastly miracle; while the minister stood, with a flush of triumph in his face, as one who, in the crisis of acutest pain, had won a victory. Then, down he sank upon the scaffold. Hester partly raised him, and supported his head against her bosom. Old Roger Chillingworth knelt down beside him, with a blank, dull countenance, out of which the life seemed to have departed.

"Thou hast escaped me!" he repeated more than once. "Thou hast escaped me!"

"May God forgive thee!" said the minister. "Thou, too, hast deeply sinned."

He withdrew his dying eyes from the old man, and fixed them on the woman and the child.

"My little Pearl," said he, feebly—and there was a sweet and gentle smile over his face, as of a spirit sinking into deep repose; nay, now that the burden was removed, it seemed almost as if he would be sportive with the child—"dear little Pearl, wilt thou kiss me now? Thou wouldst not, yonder in the forest. But now thou wilt?"

Pearl kissed his lips. A spell was broken. The great scene of grief, in which the wild infant bore a part, had developed all her sympathies, and as her tears fell upon her father's cheek, they were the pledge that she would grow up amid human joy and sorrow, nor forever do battle with the world, but be a woman in it. Toward her mother, too, Pearl's errand as a messenger of anguish was all fulfilled.

"Hester," said the clergyman, "farewell."

"Shall we not meet again?" whispered she, bending her face down close to his. "Shall we not spend our immortal life together? Surely, surely, we have ransomed one another, with all this woe! Thou lookest far into eternity, with those bright dying eyes. Then, tell me what thou seest?"

"Hush, Hester, hush!" said he, with tremulous solemnity. "The law we broke!—the sin here so awfully revealed!—let these alone be in thy thoughts. I fear! I fear! It may be that, when we forget our God—when we violated our reverence each for the other's soul—it was thenceforth vain to hope that we could meet hereafter in an everlasting and pure reunion. God knows, and he is merciful! He hath proved his mercy, most of all, in my afflictions. By giving me this burning torture to bear upon my breast! By sending yonder dark and ter-rible old man, to keep the torture always at red-heat! By bringing me hither, to die this death of triumphant ignominy before the people! Had either of these agonies been wanting, I had been lost forever! Praised be his name! His will be done! Farewell!"

That final word came forth with the minister's expiring breath. The multi-tude, silent till then, broke out in a strange, deep voice of awe and wonder, which could not as yet find utterance, save in this murmur that rolled so heavily after the departed spirit.

SINCLAIR LEWIS

• *Babbitt*

Chapter 8

The great events of Babbitt's spring were the secret buying of real-estate options in Linton for certain street-traction officials, before the public announcement that the Linton Avenue Car Line would be extended, and a dinner which was, as he rejoiced to his wife, not only "a regular society spread but a real sure-enough highbrow affair, with some of the keenest intellects and the brightest bunch of little women in town." It was so absorbing an occasion that he almost forgot his desire to run off to Maine with Paul Riesling.

Though he had been born in the village of Catawba, Babbitt had risen to that metropolitan social plane on which hosts have as many as four people at dinner without planning it for more than an evening or two. But a dinner of twelve, with flowers from the florist's and all the cut-glass out, staggered even the Babbitts.

For two weeks they studied, debated, and arbitrated the list of guests.

Babbitt marveled, "Of course we're up-to-date ourselves, but still, think of us entertaining a famous poet like Chum Frink, a fellow that on nothing but a poem or so every day and just writing a few advertisements pulls down fifteen thousand berries a year!"

"Yes, and Howard Littlefield. Do you know, the other evening Eunice told me her papa speaks three languages!" said Mrs. Babbitt.

SOURCE. From *Babbitt* by Sinclair Lewis. Copyright 1922 by Harcourt, Brace and World, Incorporated; renewed 1950 by Sinclair Lewis, reprinted with the permission of Harcourt, Brace and World.

"Huh! That's nothing! So do I—American, baseball, and poker!"

"I don't think it's nice to be funny about a matter like that. Think how wonderful it must be to speak three languages, and so useful and—And with people like that, I don't see why we invite the Orville Joneses."

"Well now, Orville is a mighty up-and-coming fellow!"

"Yes, I know, but—A laundry!"

"I'll admit a laundry hasn't got the class of poetry or real estate, but just the same, Orvy is mighty deep. Ever start him spieling about gardening? Say, that fellow can tell you the name of every kind of tree, and some of their Greek and Latin names too! Besides, we owe the Joneses a dinner. Besides, gosh, we got to have some boob for audience, when a bunch of hot-air artists like Frink and Littlefield get going."

"Well, dear—I meant to speak of this—I do think that as host you ought to sit back and listen, and let your guests have a chance to talk once in a while!"

"Oh, you do, do you! Sure! I talk all the time! And I'm just a business man—oh sure!—I'm no Ph.D. like Littlefield, and no poet, and I haven't anything to spring! Well, let me tell you, just the other day your darn Chum Frink comes up to me at the club begging to know what I thought about the Springfield school-bond issue. And who told him? I did! You bet your life I told him! Little me! I certainly did! He came up and asked me, and I told him' all about it! You bet! And he was darn glad to listen to me and—Duty as a host! I guess I know my duty as a host and let me tell you—"

In fact, the Orville Joneses were invited.

II

On the morning of the dinner, Mrs. Babbitt was restive.

"Now, George, I want you to be sure and be home early tonight. Remember, you have to dress."

"Uh-huh, I see by the *Advocate* that the Presbyterian General Assembly has voted to quit the Interchurch World Movement. That—"

"George! Did you hear what I said? You must be home in time to dress to-night."

"Dress? Hell! I'm dressed now! Think I'm going down to the office in my B.V.D.'s?"

"I will not have you talking indecently before the children! And you do have to put on your dinner-jacket!"

"I guess you mean my Tux. I tell you, of all the doggone nonsensical nuisances that was ever invented—"

Three minutes later, after Babbitt had wailed, "Well, I don't know whether

I'm going to dress or *not*" in a manner which showed that he was going to dress, the discussion moved on.

"Now, George, you musn't forget to call in at Vecchia's on the way home and get the ice cream. Their delivery-wagon is broken down, and I don't want to trust them to send it by—"

"All right! You told me that before breakfast!"

"Well, I don't want you to forget. I'll be working my head off all day long, training the girl that's to help with the dinner—"

"All nonsense, anyway, hiring an extra girl for the feed. Matilda could perfectly well—"

"—and I have to go out and buy the flowers, and fix them, and set the table, and order the salted almonds, and look at the chickens, and arrange for the children to have their supper upstairs and—And I simply must depend on you to go to Vecchia's for the ice cream."

"All riiiiiight! Gosh, I'm going to get it!"

"All you have to do is to go in and say you want the ice cream that Mrs. Babbitt ordered yesterday by 'phone, and it will be all ready for you."

At ten-thirty she telephoned to him not to forget the ice cream from Vecchia's.

He was surprised and blasted then by a thought. He wondered whether Floral Heights dinners were worth the hideous toil involved. But he repented the sacrilege in the excitement of buying the materials for cocktails.

Now this was the manner of obtaining alcohol under the reign of righteousness and prohibition:

He drove from the severe rectangular streets of the modern business center into the tangled byways of Old Town—jagged blocks filled with sooty warehouses and lofts; on into The Arbor, once a pleasant orchard but now a morass of lodging-houses, tenements, and brothels. Exquisite shivers chilled his spine and stomach, and he looked at every policeman with intense innocence, as one who loved the law, and admired the Force, and longed to stop and play with them. He parked his car a block from Healey Hanson's saloon, worrying, "Well, rats, if anybody did see me, they'd think I was here on business."

He entered a place curiously like the saloons of ante-prohibition days, with a long greasy bar with sawdust in front and streaky mirror behind, a pine table at which a dirty old man dreamed over a glass of something which resembled whisky, and with two men at the bar, drinking something which resembled beer, and giving that impression of forming a large crowd which two men always give in a saloon. The bartender, a tall pale Swede with a diamond in his lilac scarf, stared at Babbitt as he stalked plumply up to the bar and whispered, "I'd, uh— Friend of Hanson's sent me here. Like to get some gin."

The bartender gazed down on him in the manner of an outraged bishop. "I guess you got the wrong place, my friend. We sell nothing but soft drinks here." He cleaned the bar with a rag which would itself have done with a little cleaning, and glared across his mechanically moving elbow.

The old dreamer at the table petitioned the bartender, "Say, Oscar, listen." Oscar did not listen.

"Aw, say, Oscar, listen, will yuh? Say, lis-sen!"

The decayed and drowsy voice of the loafer, the agreeable stink of beer-dregs, threw a spell of inanition over Babbitt. The bartender moved grimly toward the crowd of two men. Babbitt followed him as delicately as a cat, and wheedled, "Say, Oscar, I want to speak to Mr. Hanson."

"Whajuh wanta see him for?"

"I just want to talk to him. Here's my card."

It was a beautiful card, an engraved card, a card in the blackest black and the sharpest red, announcing that Mr. George F. Babbitt was Estates, Insurance, Rents. The bartender held it as though it weighed ten pounds, and read it as though it were a hundred words long. He did not bend from his episcopal dignity, but he growled, "I'll see if he's around."

From the back room he brought an immensely old young man, a quiet sharp-eyed man, in tan silk shirt, checked vest hanging open, and burning brown trousers—Mr. Healey Hanson. Mr. Hanson said only "Yuh?" but his implacable and contemptuous eyes queried Babbitt's soul, and he seemed not at all impressed by the new dark-gray suit for which (as he had admitted to every acquaintance at the Athletic Club) Babbitt had paid a hundred and twenty-five dollars.

"Glad meet you, Mr. Hanson. Say, uh—I'm George Babbitt of the Babbitt-Thompson Realty Company. I'm a great friend of Jake Offutt's."

"Well, what of it?"

"Say, uh, I'm going to have a party, and Jake told me you'd be able to fix me up with a little gin." In alarm, in obsequiousness, as Hanson's eyes grew more bored, "You telephone to Jake about me, if you want to."

Hanson answered by jerking his head to indicate the entrance to the back room, and strolled away. Babbitt melodramatically crept into an apartment containing four round tables, eleven chairs, a brewery calendar, and a smell. He waited. Thrice he saw Healey Hanson saunter through, humming, hands in pockets, ignoring him.

By this time Babbitt had modified his valiant morning vow, "I won't pay one cent over seven dollars a quart" to "I might pay ten." On Hansons next weary entrance he besought, "Could you fix that up?" Hanson scowled, and grated, "Just a minute—Pete's sake—just a min-ute!" In growing meekness Babbitt went on waiting till Hanson casually reappeared with a quart of gin—what is euphemistically known as a quart—in his disdainful long white hands.

"Twelve bucks," he snapped.

"Say, uh, but say, cap'n, Jake thought you'd be able to fix me up for eight or nine a bottle."

"Nup. Twelve. This is the real stuff, smuggled from Canada. This is none o' your neutral spirits with a drop of juniper extract," the honest merchant said virtuously. "Twelve bones—if you want it. Course y' understand I'm just doing this anyway as a friend of Jake's."

"Sure! Sure! I understand!" Babbitt gratefully held out twelve dollars. He felt honored by contact with greatness as Hanson yawned, stuffed the bills, uncounted, into his radiant vest, and swaggered away.

He had a number of titillations out of concealing the gin-bottle under his coat and out of hiding it in his desk. All afternoon he snorted and chuckled and gurgled over his ability to "give the Boys a real shot in the arm to-night." He was, in fact, so exhilarated that he was within a block of his house before he remembered that there was a certain matter, mentioned by his wife, of fetching ice cream from Vecchia's. He explained, "Well, darn it—" and drove back.

Vecchia was not a caterer, he was The Caterer of Zenith. Most coming-out parties were held in the white and gold ballroom of the Maison Vecchia; at all nice teas the guests recognized the five kinds of Vecchia sandwiches and the seven kinds of Vecchia cakes; and all really smart dinners ended, as on a resolving chord, in Vecchia Neapolitan ice cream in one of the three reliable molds—the melon mold, the round mold like a layer cake, and the long brick.

Vecchia's shop had pale blue woodwork, tracery of plaster roses, attendants in frilled aprons, and glass shelves of "kisses" with all the refinement that inheres in whites of eggs. Babbitt felt heavy and thick amid this professional daintiness, and as he waited for the ice cream he decided, with hot prickles at the back of his neck, that a girl customer was giggling at him. He went home in a touchy temper. The first thing he heard was his wife's agitated:

"George! *Did* you remember to go to Vecchia's and get the ice cream?"

"Say! Look here! Do I ever forget to do things?"

"Yes! Often!"

"Well now, it's darn seldom I do, and it certainly makes me tired, after going into a pink-tea joint like Vecchia's and having to stand around looking at a lot of half-naked young girls, all rouged up like they were sixty and eating a lot of stuff that simply ruins their stomachs—"

"Oh, it's too bad about you! I've noticed how you hate to look at pretty girls!"

With a jar Babbitt realized that his wife was too busy to be impressed by that moral indignation with which males rule the world, and he went humbly up-stairs to dress. He had an impression of a glorified dining-room, of cut-glass, candles, polished wood, lace, silver, roses. With the awed swelling of the heart suitable to so grave a business as giving a dinner, he slew the temptation to wear his plaited dress-shirt for a fourth time, took out an entirely fresh one, tightened his black bow, and rubbed his patent-leather pumps with a handkerchief. He glanced with pleasure at his garnet and silver studs. He smoothed and patted his ankles, transformed by silk socks from the sturdy shanks of George Babbitt to the elegant limbs of what is called a Clubman. He stood before the pier-glass, viewing his trim dinner-coat, his beautiful triple-braided trousers; and murmured in lyric beatitude, "By golly, I don't look so bad. I certainly don't look like Catawba. If the hicks back home could see me in this rig, they'd have a fit!"

He moved majestically down to mix the cocktails. As he chipped ice, as he squeezed oranges, as he collected vast stores of bottles, glasses, and spoons at the sink in the pantry, he felt as authoritative as the bartender at Healey Hanson's saloon. True, Mrs. Babbitt said he was under foot, and Matilda and the maid hired for the evening brushed by him, elbowed him, shrieked "Pleasopn door," as they tottered through with trays, but in this high moment he ignored them.

Besides the new bottle of gin, his cellar consisted of one half-bottle of Bourbon whisky, a quarter of a bottle of Italian vermouth, and approximately one hundred drops of orange bitters. He did not possess a cocktail-shaker. A shaker was proof of dissipation, the symbol of a Drinker, and Babbitt disliked being known as a Drinker even more than he liked a Drink. He mixed by pouring from an ancient gravy-boat into a handleless pitcher; he poured with a noble dignity, holding his alembics high beneath the powerful Mazda globe, his face hot, his shirt-front a glaring white, the copper sink a scoured red-gold.

He tasted the sacred essence. "Now, by golly, if that isn't pretty near one fine old cocktail! Kind of a Bronx, and yet like a Manhattan. Ummmmmm! Hey, Myra, want a little nip before the folks come?"

Bustling into the dining-room, moving each glass a quarter of an inch, rushing back with resolution implacable on her face, her gray and silver-lace party frock protected by a denim towel, Mrs. Babbitt glared at him, and rebuked him, "Certainly not!"

"Well," in a loose, jocose manner, "I think the old man will!"

The cocktail filled him with a whirling exhilaration behind which he was aware of devastating desires—to rush places in fast motors, to kiss girls, to sing, to be witty. He sought to regain his lost dignity by announcing to Matilda:

"I'm going to stick this pitcher of cocktails in the refrigerator. Be sure you don't upset any of 'em."

"Yeh."

"Well, be sure now. Don't go putting anything on this top shelf."

"Yeh."

"Well, be—" He was dizzy. His voice was thin and distant. "Whee!" With enormous impressiveness he commanded, "Well, be sure now," and minced into the safety of the living-room. He wondered whether he could persuade "as slow a bunch as Myra and the Littlefields to go some place aft' dinner and raise Cain and maybe dig up smore booze." He perceived that he had gifts of profligacy which had been neglected.

By the time the guests had come, including the inevitable late couple for whom the others waited with painful amiability, a great gray emptiness had replaced the purple swirling in Babbitt's head, and he had to force the tumultuous greetings suitable to a host on Floral Heights.

The guests were Howard Littlefield, the doctor of philosophy who furnished publicity and comforting economics to the Street Traction Company; Vergil Gunch, the coal-dealer, equally powerful in the Elks and in the Boosters' Club; Eddie Swanson, the agent for the Javelin Motor Car, who lived across the street; and Orville Jones, owner of the Lily White Laundry, which justly announced itself "the biggest, busiest, bulliest cleanerie shoppe in Zenith." But, naturally, the most distinguished of all was T. Cholmondeley Frink, who was not only the author of "Poemulations," which, syndicated daily in sixty-seven leading newspapers, gave him one of the largest audiences of any poet in the world, but also an optimistic lecturer and the creator of "Ads that Add." Despite the searching philosophy and high morality of his verses, they were humorous and easily understood by any child of twelve; and it added a neat air of pleasantry to them that they were set not as verse but as prose. Mr. Frink was known from Coast to Coast as "Chum."

With them were six wives, more or less—it was hard to tell, so early in the evening, as at first glance they all looked alike, and as they all said, "Oh, *isn't* this nice!" in the same tone of determined liveliness. To the eye, the men were less similar: Littlefield, a hedge-scholar, tall and horse-faced; Chum Frink, a trifle of a man with soft and mouse-like hair, advertising his profession as poet by a silk cord on his eyeglasses; Vergil Gunch, broad, with coarse black hair *en brosse*; Eddie Swanson, a bald and bouncing young man who showed his taste for elegance by an evening waistcoat of figured black silk with glass buttons; Orville Jones, a steady-looking, stubby, not very memorable person, with a hemp-colored toothbrush mustache. Yet they were all so well fed and clean, they all shouted " 'Evenin', Georgie!" with such robustness, that they seemed to be cousins, and the strange thing is that the longer one knew the women, the less alike they seemed; while the longer one knew the men, the more alike their bold patterns appeared.

The drinking of the cocktails was as canonical a rite as the mixing. The company waited, uneasily, hopefully, agreeing in a strained manner that the weather had been rather warm and slightly cold, but still Babbitt said nothing about drinks. They became despondent. But when the late couple (the Swansons) had arrived, Babbitt hinted, "Well, folks, do you think you could stand breaking the law a little?"

They looked at Chum Frink, the recognized lord of language. Frink pulled at his eye-glass cord as at a bell-rope, he cleared his throat and said that which was the custom:

"I'll tell you, George: I'm a law-abiding man, but they do say Verg Gunch is a regular yegg, and of course he's bigger 'n I am, and I just can't figure out what I'd do if he tried to force me into anything criminal!"

Gunch was roaring, "Well, I'll take a chance—" when Frink held up his hand and went on, "So if Verg and you insist, Georgie, I'll park my car on the wrong side of the street, because I take it for granted that's the crime you're hinting at!"

There was a great deal of laughter. Mrs. Jones asserted, "Mr. Frink is simply too killing! You'd think he was so innocent!"

Babbitt clamored, "How did you guess it, Chum? Well, you-all just wait a moment while I go out and get the—keys to your cars!" Through a froth of merriment he brought the shining promise, the mighty tray of glasses with the cloudy yellow cocktails in the glass pitcher in the center. The men babbled, "Oh, gosh, have a look!" and "This gets me right where I live!" and "Let me at it!" But Chum Frink, a traveled man and not unused to woes, was stricken by the thought that the potion might be merely fruit-juice with a little neutral spirits. He looked timorous as Babbitt, a moist and ecstatic almoner, held out a glass, but as he tasted it he piped, "Oh, man, let me dream on! It ain't true, but don't waken me! Jus' lemme slumber!"

Two hours before, Frink had completed a newspaper lyric beginning:

> *I sat alone and groused and thunk, and scratched my head and sighed and wunk, and groaned, "There still are boobs, alack, who'd like the old-time gin-mill back; that den that makes a sage a loon, the vile and smelly old saloon!" I'll never miss their poison booze, whilst I the bubbling spring can use, that leaves my head at merry morn as clear as any babe new-born!*

Babbitt drank with the others; his moment's depression was gone; he perceived that these were the best fellows in the world; he wanted to give them a thousand cocktails. "Think you could stand another?" he cried. The wives refused, with giggles, but the men, speaking in a wide, elaborate, enjoyable manner, gloated, "Well, sooner than have you get sore at me, Georgie—"

"You got a little dividend coming," said Babbitt to each of them, and each intoned, "Squeeze it, Georgie, squeeze it!"

When, beyond hope, the pitcher was empty, they stood and talked about prohibition. The men leaned back on their heels, put their hands in their trousers-pockets, and proclaimed their views with the booming profundity of a prosperous male repeating a thoroughly hackneyed statement about a matter of which he knows nothing whatever.

"Now, I'll tell you," said Vergil Gunch; "way I figure it is this, and I can speak by the book, because I've talked to a lot of doctors and fellows that ought to know, and the way I see it is that it's a good thing to get rid of the saloon, but they ought to let a fellow have beer and light wines."

Howard Littlefield observed, "What isn't generally realized is that it's a dangerous prop'sition to invade the rights of personal liberty. Now, take this for instance: The King of—Bavaria? I think it was Bavaria—yes, Bavaria, it was—in 1862, March, 1862, he issued a proclamation against public grazing of live-stock. The peasantry had stood for overtaxation without the slightest complaint, but when this proclamation came out, they rebelled. Or it may have been Saxony. But it just goes to show the dangers of invading the rights of personal liberty."

"That's it—no one got a right to invade personal liberty," said Orville Jones.

"Just the same, you don't want to forget prohibition is a mighty good thing for the working-classes. Keeps 'em from wasting their money and lowering their productiveness," said Vergil Gunch.

"Yes, that's so. But the trouble is the manner of enforcement," insisted Howard Littlefield. "Congress didn't understand the right system. Now, if I'd been running the thing, I'd have arranged it so that the drinker himself was licensed, and then we could have taken care of the shiftless workman—kept him from drinking—and yet not 've interfered with the rights—with the personal liberty—of fellows like ourselves."

They bobbed their heads, looked admiringly at one another, and stated, "That's so, that would be the stunt."

"The thing that worries me is that a lot of these guys will take to cocaine," sighed Eddie Swanson.

They bobbed more violently, and groaned, "That's so, there is a danger of that."

Chum Frink chanted, "Oh, say, I got hold of a swell new receipt for home-made beer the other day. You take—"

Gunch interrupted, "Wait! Let me tell you mine!" Littlefield snorted, "Beer! Rats! Thing to do is to ferment cider!" Jones insisted, "I've got the receipt that does the business!" Swanson begged, "Oh, say, lemme tell you the story—" But Frink went on resolutely, "You take and save the shells from peas, and pour six gallons of water on a bushel of shells and boil the mixture till—"

Mrs. Babbitt turned toward them with yearning sweetness; Frink hastened to finish even his best beer-recipe; and she said gaily, "Dinner is served."

There was a good deal of friendly argument among the men as to which should go in last, and while they were crossing the hall from the living-room to the dining-room Vergil Gunch made them laugh by thundering, "If I can't sit next to Myra Babbitt and hold her hand under the table, I won't play—I'm goin' home." In the dining-room they stood embarrassed while Mrs. Babbitt fluttered, "Now, let me see—Oh, I was going to have some nice hand-painted placecards for you but—Oh, let me see; Mr. Frink, you sit there."

The dinner was in the best style of women's-magazine art, whereby the salad was served in hollowed apples, and everything but the invincible fried chicken resembled something else.

Ordinarily the men found it hard to talk to the women; flirtation was an art unknown on Floral Heights, and the realms of offices and of kitchens had no alliances. But under the inspiration of the cocktails, conversation was violent. Each of the men still had a number of important things to say about prohibition, and now that each had a loyal listener in his dinner-partner he burst out:

"I found a place where I can get all the hootch I want at eight a quart—"

"Did you read about this fellow that went and paid a thousand dollars for ten cases of red-eye that proved to be nothing but water? Seems this fellow was standing on the corner and fellow comes up to him—"

"They say there's a whole raft of stuff being smuggled across at Detroit—"

"What I always say is—what a lot of folks don't realize about prohibition—"

"And then you get all this awful poison stuff—wood alcohol and everything—"

"Course I believe in it on principle, but I don't propose to have anybody telling me what I got to think and do. No American 'll ever stand for that!"

But they all felt that it was rather in bad taste for Orville Jones—and he not recognized as one of the wits of the occasion anyway—to say, "In fact, the whole thing about prohibition is this: it isn't the initial cost, it's the humidity."

Not till the one required topic had been dealt with did the conversation become general.

It was often and admiringly said of Vergil Gunch, "Gee, that fellow can get away with murder! Why, he can pull a Raw One in mixed company and all the ladies 'll laugh their heads off, but me, gosh, if I crack anything that's just the least bit off color I get the razz for fair!" Now Gunch delighted them by crying to Mrs. Eddie Swanson, youngest of the women, "Louetta! I managed to pinch Eddie's doorkey out of his pocket, and what say you and me sneak across the street when the folks aren't looking? Got something," with a gorgeous leer, "awful important to tell you!"

The women wriggled, and Babbitt was stirred to like naughtiness. "Say, folks, I wished I dared show you a book I borrowed from Doc Patten!"

"Now, George! The idea!" Mrs. Babbitt warned him.

"This book—racy isn't the word! It's some kind of an anthropological report about—about Customs, in the South Seas, and what it doesn't *say*! It's a book you can't buy. Verg, I'll lend it to you."

"Me first!" insisted Eddie Swanson. "Sounds spicy!"

Orville Jones announced, "Say, I heard a Good One the other day about a coupla Swedes and their wives," and, in the best Jewish accent, he resolutely carried the Good One to a slightly disinfected ending. Gunch capped it. But the cocktails waned, the seekers dropped back into cautious reality.

Chum Frink had recently been on a lecture-tour among the small towns, and he chuckled, "Awful good to get back to civilization! I certainly been seeing some hick towns! I mean—Course the folks there are the best on earth, but, gee whiz, those Main Street burgs are slow, and you fellows can't hardly appreciate what it means to be here with a bunch of live ones!"

"You bet!" exulted Orville Jones. "They're the best folks on earth, those small-town folks, but, oh, mama! what conversation! Why, say, they can't talk about anything but the weather and the ne-oo Ford, by heckalorum!"

"That's right. They all talk about just the same things," said Eddie Swanson.

"Don't they, though! They just say the same things over and over," said Vergil Gunch.

"Yes, it's really remarkable. They seem to lack all power of looking at things impersonally. They simply go over and over the same talk about Fords and the weather and so on," said Howard Littlefield.

"Still, at that, you can't blame 'em. They haven't got any intellectual stimulus such as you get up here in the city," said Chum Frink.

"Gosh, that's right," said Babbitt. "I don't want you high-brows to get stuck on yourselves but I must say it keeps a fellow right up on his toes to sit in with a poet and with Howard, the guy that put the con in economics! But these small-town boobs, with nobody but each other to talk to, no wonder they get so sloppy and uncultured in their speech, and so balled-up in their thinking!"

Orville Jones commented, "And, then take our other advantages—the movies, frinstance. These Yapville sports think they're all-get-out if they have one change of bill a week, where here in the city you got your choice of a dozen diff'rent movies any evening you want to name!"

"Sure, and the inspiration we get from rubbing up against high-class hustlers every day and getting jam full of ginger," said Eddie Swanson.

"Same time," said Babbitt, "no sense excusing these rube burgs too easy. Fellow's own fault if he doesn't show the initiative to up and beat it to the city, like we done—did. And, just speaking in confidence among friends, they're jealous as the devil of a city man. Every time I go up to Catawba I have to go around apologizing to the fellows I was brought up with because I've more or less succeeded and they haven't. And if you talk natural to 'em, way we do here, and show finesse and what you might call a broad point of view, why, they think you're putting on side. There's my own half-brother Martin—runs the little ole general store my Dad used to keep. Say, I'll bet he don't know there is such a thing as a Tux—as a dinner-jacket. If he was to come in here now, he'd think we were a bunch of—of—Why, gosh, I swear, he wouldn't know what to think! Yes, sir, they're jealous!"

Chum Frink agreed, "That's so. But what I mind is their lack of culture and appreciation of the Beautiful—if you'll excuse me for being highbrow. Now, I like to give a high-class lecture, and read some of my best poetry—not the news-paper stuff but the magazine things. But say, when I get out in the tall grass, there's nothing will take but a lot of cheesy old stories and slang and junk that if any of us were to indulge in it here, he'd get the gate so fast it would make his head swim."

Vergil Gunch summed it up: "Fact is, we're mightly lucky to be living among a bunch of city-folks, that recognize artistic things and business-punch equally. We'd feel pretty glum if we got stuck in some Main Street burg and tried to wise up the old codgers to the kind of life we're used to here. But, by golly, there's this you got to say for 'em: Every small American town is trying to get population and modern ideals. And darn if a lot of 'em don't put it across! Somebody starts panning a rube crossroads, telling how he was there in 1900 and it consisted of one muddy street, count 'em, one, and nine hundred hu-man clams. Well, you go back there in 1920, and you find pavements and a swell little hotel and a first-class ladies' ready-to-wear shop—real perfection, in fact! You don't want to just look at what these small towns are, you want to look at what they're aiming to become, and they all got an ambition that in the long run is going to make 'em the finest spots on earth—they all want to be just like Zenith!"

III

However intimate they might be with T. Cholmondeley Frink as a neigh-bor, as a borrower of lawn-mowers and monkey-wrenches, they knew that he was also a Famous Poet and a distinguished advertising-agent; that behind his easi-ness were sultry literary mysteries which they could not penetrate. But to-night, in the gin-evolved confidence, he admitted them to the arcanum:

"I've got a literary problem that's worrying me to death. I'm doing a series of ads for the Zeeco Car and I want to make each of 'em a real little gem— reg'lar stylistic stuff. I'm all for this theory that perfection is the stunt, or noth-ing at all, and these are as tough things as I ever tackled. You might think it'd be harder to do my poems—all these Heart Topics: home and fireside and happi-ness—but they're cinches. You can't go wrong on 'em; you know what senti-ments any decent go-ahead fellow must have if he plays the game, and you stick right to 'em. But the poetry of industrialism, now there's a literary line where you got to open up new territory. Do you know the fellow who's really *the* American genius? The fellow who you don't know his name and I don't either, but his work ought to be preserved so's future generations can judge our Amer-ican thought and originality to-day? Why, the fellow that writes the Prince Albert Tobacco ads! Just listen to this:

It's P.A. that jams such joy in jimmy pipes. Say—bet you've often bent-an-ear to that spill-of-speech about hopping from five to f-i-f-t-y p-e-r by "stepping on her a bit!" Guess that's going some, all right—BUT—just among ourselves, you better start a rapidwhiz system to keep tabs as to how fast you'll buzz from low smoke spirits to tip-top-high—once you line up behind a jimmy pipe that's all aglow with that peach-of-a-pal, Prince Albert.

Prince Albert is john-on-the-job—always joy'usly more-ish in flavor; always delightfully cool and fragrant! For a fact, you never hooked such double-decked, copper-riveted, two-fisted smoke enjoyment!

Go to a pipe—speed-o-quick like you light on a good thing! Why—packed with Prince Albert you can play a joy'us jimmy straight across the boards! And you know what that means!"

"Now that," caroled the motor agent, Eddie Swanson, "that's what I call he-literature! That Prince Albert fellow—though, gosh, there can't be just one fellow that writes 'em; must be a big board of classy ink-slingers in conference, but anyway: now, him, he doesn't write for long-haired pikers, he writes for Regular Guys, he writes for *me*, and I tip my benny to him! The only thing is: I wonder if it sells the goods? Course, like all these poets, this Prince Albert fellow lets his idea run away with him. It makes elegant reading, but it don't say nothing. I'd never go out and buy Prince Albert Tobacco after reading it, because it doesn't tell me anything about the stuff. It's just a bunch of fluff."

Frink faced him: "Oh, you're crazy! Have I got to sell you the idea of Style? Anyway, that's the kind of stuff I'd like to do for the Zeeco. But I simply can't. So I decided to stick to the straight poetic, and I took a shot at a high-brow ad for the Zeeco. How do you like this:

The long white trail is calling—calling—and it's over the hills and far away for every man or woman that has red blood in his veins and on his lips the ancient song of the buccaneers. It's away with dull drudging, and a fig for care. Speed—glorious Speed—it's more than just a moment's exhilaration—it's Life for you and me! This great new truth the makers of the Zeeco Car have considered as much as price and style. It's fleet as the antelope, smooth as the glide of a swallow, yet powerful as the charge of a bull-elephant. Class breathes in every line. Listen, brother! You'll never know what the high art of hiking is till you TRY LIFE'S ZIPPINGEST ZEST—THE ZEECO!

"Yes," Frink mused, "that's got an elegant color to it, if I do say so, but it ain't got the originality of 'spill-of-speech!' "

The whole company sighed with sympathy and admiration.

Chapter 9

Babbitt was fond of his friends, he loved the importance of being host and shouting, "Certainly, you're going to have smore chicken—the idea!" and he appreciated the genius of T. Cholmondeley Frink, but the vigor of the cocktails was gone, and the more he ate the less joyful he felt. Then the amity of the dinner was destroyed by the nagging of the Swansons.

In Floral Heights and the other prosperous sections of Zenith, especially in the "young married set," there were many women who had nothing to do. Though they had few servants, yet with gas stoves, electric ranges and dishwashers and vacuum cleaners, and tiled kitchen walls, their houses were so convenient that they had little housework, and much of their food come from bakeries and delicatessens. They had but two, one, or no children; and despite the myth that the Great War had made work respectable, their husbands objected to their "wasting time and getting a lot of crank ideas" in unpaid social work, and still more to their causing a rumor, by earning money, that they were not adequately supported. They worked perhaps two hours a day, and the rest of the time they ate chocolates, went to the motion-pictures, went window-shopping, went in gossiping twos and threes to card-parties, read magazines, thought timorously of the lovers who never appeared, and accumulated a splendid restlessness which they got rid of by nagging their husbands. The husbands nagged back.

Of these naggers the Swansons were perfect specimens.

Throughout the dinner Eddie Swanson had been complaining, publicly, about his wife's new frock. It was, he submitted, too short, too low, too immodestly thin, and much too expensive. He appealed to Babbitt:

"Honest, George, what do you think of that rag Louetta went and bought? Don't you think it's the limit?"

"What's eating you, Eddie? I call it a swell little dress."

"Oh, it is, Mr. Swanson. It's a sweet frock," Mrs. Babbitt protested.

"There now, do you see, smarty! You're such an authority on clothes!" Louetta raged, while the guests ruminated and peeped at her shoulders.

"That's all right now," said Swanson. "I'm authority enough so I know it was a waste of money, and it makes me tired to see you not wearing out a whole closetful of clothes you got already. I've expressed my idea about this before, and you know good and well you didn't pay the least bit of attention. I have to camp on your trail to get you to do anything—"

There was much more of it, and they all assisted, all but Babbitt. Everything about him was dim except his stomach, and that was a bright scarlet disturbance. "Had too much grub; oughtn't to eat this stuff," he groaned—while he went on eating, while he gulped down a chill and glutinous slice of the ice-cream brick, and cocoanut cake as oozy as shaving-cream. He felt as though he had been stuffed with clay; his body was bursting, his throat was bursting, his brain was hot mud; and only with agony did he continue to smile and shout as became a host on Floral Heights.

He would, except for his guests, have fled outdoors and walked off the intoxication of food, but in the haze which filled the room they sat forever, talking, talking, while he agonized, "Darn fool to be eating all this—not 'nother mouthful," and discovered that he was again tasting the sickly welter of melted ice cream on his plate. There was no magic in his friends; he was not uplifted when Howard Littlefield produced from his treasure-house of scholarship the information that the chemical symbol for raw rubber is $C_{10}H_{16}$, which turns into isoprene, or $2C_5H_8$. Suddenly, without precedent, Babbitt was not merely bored but admitting that he was bored. It was ecstacy to escape from the table, from the torture of a straight chair, and loll on the davenport in the living-room.

The others, from their fitful unconvincing talk, their expressions of being slowly and painfully smothered, seemed to be suffering from the toil of social life and the horror of good food as much as himself. All of them accepted with relief the suggestion of bridge.

Babbitt recovered from the feeling of being boiled. He won at bridge. He was again able to endure Vergil Gunch's inexorable heartiness. But he pictured loafing with Paul Riesling beside a lake in Maine. It was as overpowering and imaginative as homesickness. He had never seen Maine, yet he beheld the shrouded mountains, the tranquil lake of evening. "That boy Paul's worth all these ballyhooing highbrows put together," he muttered; and, "I'd like to get away from—everything."

Even Louetta Swanson did not rouse him.

Mrs. Swanson was pretty and pliant. Babbitt was not an analyst of women, except as to their tastes in Furnished Houses to Rent. He divided them into Real Ladies, Working Women, Old Cranks, and Fly Chickens. He mooned over their charms but he was of opinion that all of them (save the women of his own family) were "different" and "mysterious." Yet he had known by instinct that Louetta Swanson could be approached. Her eyes and lips were moist. Her face tapered from a broad forehead to a pointed chin, her mouth was thin but strong and avid, and between her brows were two outcurving and passionate wrinkles. She was thirty, perhaps, or younger. Gossip had never touched her, but every man naturally and instantly rose to flirtatiousness when he spoke to her, and every woman watched her with stilled blankness.

Between games, sitting on the davenport, Babbitt spoke to her with the requisite gallantry, that sonorous Floral Heights gallantry which is not flirtation but a terrified flight from it:

"You're looking like a new soda-fountain to-night, Louetta."

"Am I?"

"Ole Eddie kind of on the rampage."

"Yes. I get so sick of it."

"Well, when you get tired of hubby, you can run off with Uncle George."

"If I ran away—Oh, well—"

"Anybody ever tell you your hands are awful pretty?"

She looked down at them, she pulled the lace of her sleeves over them, but otherwise she did not heed him. She was lost in unexpressed imaginings.

Babbitt was too languid this evening to pursue his duty of being a captivating (though strictly moral) male. He ambled back to the bridge-tables. He was not much thrilled when Mrs. Frink, a small twittering woman, proposed that they "try and do some spiritualism and table-tipping—you know Chum can make the spirits come—honest, he just scares me!"

The ladies of the party had not emerged all evening, but now, as the sex given to things of the spirit while the men warred against base things material, they took command and cried, "Oh, let's!" In the dimness the men were rather solemn and foolish, but the goodwives quivered and adored as they sat about the table. They laughed, "Now, you be good or I'll tell!" when the men took their hands in the circle.

Babbitt tingled with a slight return of interest in life as Louetta Swanson's hand closed on his with quiet firmness.

All of them hunched over, intent. They startled as some one drew a strained breath. In the dusty light from the hall they looked unreal, they felt disembodied. Mrs. Gunch squeaked, and they jumped with unnatural jocularity, but at Frink's hiss they sank into subdued awe. Suddenly, incredibly, they heard a knocking. They stared at Frink's half-revealed hands and found them lying still. They wriggled, and pretended not to be impressed.

Frink spoke with gravity: "Is some one there?" A thud. "Is one knock to be the sign for 'yes'?" A thud. "And two for 'no'?" A thud.

"Now, ladies and gentlemen, shall we ask the guide to put us into communication with the spirit of some great one passed over?" Frink mumbled.

Mrs. Orville Jones begged, "Oh, let's talk to Dante! We studied him at the Reading Circle. You know who he was, Orvy."

"Certainly I know who he was! The Wop poet. Where do you think I was raised?" from her insulted husband.

"Sure—the fellow that took the Cook's Tour to Hell. I've never waded through his po'try, but we learned about him in the U.," said Babbitt.

"Page Mr. Dannnnnty!" intoned Eddie Swanson.

"You ought to get him easy, Mr. Frink, you and he being fellow-poets," said Louetta Swanson.

"Fellow-poets, rats! Where d' you get that stuff?" protested Vergil Gunch. "I suppose Dante showed a lot of speed for an old-timer—not that I've actually read him, of course—but to come right down to hard facts, he wouldn't stand one-two-three if he had to buckle down to practical literature and turn out a poem for the newspaper-syndicate every day, like Chum does!"

"That's so," from Eddie Swanson. "Those old birds could take their time. Judas Priest, I could write poetry myself if I had a whole year for it, and just wrote about that old-fashioned junk like Dante wrote about."

Frink demanded, "Hush, now! I'll call him. . . . O, Laughing Eyes, emerge forth into the, uh, the ultimates and bring hither the spirit of Dante, that we mortals may list to his words of wisdom."

"You forgot to give um the address: 1658 Brimstone Avenue. Fiery Heights, Hell," Gunch chuckled, but the others felt that this was irreligious. And besides—"probably it was just Chum making the knocks, but still, if there did happen to be something to all this, be exciting to talk to an old fellow belonging to—way back in early times—"

A thud. The spirit of Dante had come to the parlor of George F. Babbitt.

He was, it seemed, quite ready to answer their questions. He was "glad to be with them, this evening."

Frink spelled out the messages by running through the alphabet till the spirit interpreter knocked at the right letter.

Littlefield asked, in a learned tone, "Do you like it in the Paradiso, Messire?"

"We are very happy on the higher plane, Signor. We are glad that you are studying this great truth of spiritualism," Dante replied.

The circle moved with an awed creaking of stays and shirt-fronts. "Suppose—suppose there were something to this?"

Babbitt had a different worry. "Suppose Chum Frink was really one of these spiritualists! Chum had, for a literary fellow, always seemed to be a Regular Guy; he belonged to the Chatham Road Presbyterian Church and went to the Boosters' lunches and liked cigars and motors and racy stories. But suppose that secretly—After all, you never could tell about these darn highbrows; and to be an out-and-out spiritualist would be almost like being a socialist!"

No one could long be serious in the presence of Vergil Gunch. "Ask Dant' how Jack Shakespeare and old Verg'—the guy they named after me—are gettin' along, and don't they wish they could get into the movie game!" he blared, and instantly all was mirth. Mrs. Jones shrieked, and Eddie Swanson desired to know whether Dante didn't catch cold with nothing on but his wreath.

The pleased Dante made humble answer.

But Babbitt—the curst discontent was torturing him again, and heavily, in the impersonal darkness, he pondered, "I don't—. We're all so flip and think we're so smart. There'd be—A fellow like Dante—I wish I'd read some of his pieces. I don't suppose I ever will, now."

He had, without explanation, the impression of a slaggy cliff and on it, in silhouette against menacing clouds, a lone and austere figure. He was dismayed by a sudden contempt for his surest friends. He grasped Louetta Swanson's hand, and found the comfort of human warmth. Habit came, a veteran warrior; and he shook himself. "What the deuce is the matter with me, this evening?"

He patted Louetta's hand, to indicate that he hadn't meant anything improper by squezing it, and demanded of Frink, "Say, see if you can get old Dant' to spiel us some of his poetry. Talk up to him. Tell him, '*Buena giorna, señor, com sa va, wie geht's? Keskersaykersa* a little pome, *señor?*' "

II

The lights were switched on; the women sat on the fronts of their chairs in that determined suspense whereby a wife indicates that as soon as the present speaker has finished, she is going to remark brightly to her husband, "Well, dear, I think per-*haps* it's about time for us to be saying goodnight." For once Babbitt did not break out in blustering efforts to keep the party going. He had—there was something he wished to think out—But the psychical research had started them off again. ("Why didn't they go home! Why didn't they go home!") Though he was impressed by the profundity of the statement, he was only half-enthusiastic when Howard Littlefield lectured, "The United States is the only nation in which the government is a Moral Ideal and not just a social arrangement." ("True—true—weren't they *ever* going home?") He was usually delighted to have an "inside view" of the momentous world of motors but tonight he scarcely listened to Eddie Swanson's revelation: "If you want to go above the Javelin class, the Zeeco is a mighty good buy. Couple weeks ago, and mind you, this was a fair, square test, they took a Zeeco stock touring-car and they slid up the Tonawanda hill on high, and fellow told me—" ("Zeeco—good boat but—Were they planning to stay all night?")

They really were going, with a flutter of "We did have the best time!"

Most aggressively friendly of all was Babbitt, yet as he burbled he was reflecting, "I got through it, but for a while there I didn't hardly think I'd last out." He prepared to taste that most delicate pleasure of the host: making fun

of his guests in the relaxation of midnight. As the door closed he yawned voluptuously, chest out, shoulders wriggling, and turned cynically to his wife.

She was beaming. "Oh, it was nice, wasn't it! I know they enjoyed every
minute of it. Don't you think so?"

He couldn't do it. He couldn't mock. It would have been like sneering at
a happy child. He lied ponderously: "You bet! Best party this year, by a long
shot."

"Wasn't the dinner good! And honestly I thought the fried chicken was
delicious!"

"You bet! Fried to the Queen's taste. Best fried chicken I've tasted for a
coon's age."

"Didn't Matilda fry it beautifully! And don't you think the soup was simply
delicious?"

"It certainly was! It was corking! Best soup I've tasted since Heck was a
pup!" But his voice was seeping away. They stood in the hall, under the electric
light in its square box-like shade of red glass bound with nickel. She stared at
him.

"Why, George, you don't sound—you sound as if you hadn't really enjoyed
it."

"Sure I did! Course I did!"

"George! What is it?"

"Oh, I'm kind of tired, I guess. Been pounding pretty hard at the office.
Need to get away and rest up a little."

"Well, we're going to Maine in just a few weeks now, dear."

"Yuh—" Then he was pouring it out nakedly, robbed of reticence. "Myra:
I think it'd be a good thing for me to get up there early."

"But you have this man you have to meet in New York about business."

"What man? Oh, sure. Him. Oh, that's all off. But I want to hit Maine
early—get in a little fishing, catch me a big trout, by golly!" A nervous, artificial laugh.

"Well, why don't we do it? Verona and Matilda can run the house between them, and you and I can go any time, if you think we can afford it."

"But that's—I've been feeling so jumpy lately, I thought maybe it might
be a good thing if I kind of got off by myself and sweat it out of me."

"George! Don't you *want* me to go along?" She was too wretchedly in
earnest to be tragic, or gloriously insulted, or anything save dumpy and defense-
less and flushed to the red steaminess of a boiled beet.

"Of course I do! I just meant—" Remembering that Paul Riesling had
predicted this, he was as desperate as she. "I mean, sometimes it's a good thing
for an old grouch like me to go off and get it out of his system." He tried to
sound paternal. "Then when you and the kids arrive—I figured maybe I might
skip up to Maine just a few days ahead of you—I'd be ready for a real bat, see

how I mean?" He coaxed her with large booming sounds, with affable smiles, like a popular preacher blessing an Easter congregation, like a humorous lecturer completing his stint of eloquence, like all perpetrators of masculine wiles.

She stared at him, the joy of festival drained from her face. "Do I bother you when we go on vacations? Don't I add anything to your fun?"

He broke. Suddenly, dreadfully, he was hysterical, he was a yelping baby. "Yes, yes, yes! Hell, yes! But can't you understand I'm shot to pieces? I'm all in! I got to take care of myself! I tell you, I got to—I'm sick of everything and everybody! I got to—"

It was she who was mature and protective now. "Why, of course! You shall run off by yourself! Why don't you get Paul to go along, and you boys just fish and have a good time?" She patted his shoulder—reaching up to it—while he shook with palsied helplessness, and in that moment was not merely by habit fond of her but clung to her strength.

She cried cheerily, "Now up-stairs you go, and pop into bed. We'll fix it all up. I'll see to the doors. Now skip!"

For many minutes, for many hours, for a bleak eternity, he lay awake, shivering, reduced to primitive terror, comprehending that he had won freedom, and wondering what he could do with anything so unknown and so embarrassing as freedom.

Chapter 5

Differences in Class, Caste, and Region

JOHN STEINBECK

• *Cannery Row*

Cannery Row in Monterey in California is a poem, a stink, a grating noise, a quality of light, a tone, a habit, a nostalgia, a dream. Cannery Row is the gathered and scattered, tin and iron and rust and splintered wood, chipped pavement and weedy lots and junk heaps, sardine canneries of corrugated iron, honky tonks, restaurants and whore houses, and little crowded groceries, and laboratories and flophouses. Its inhabitants are, as the man once said, "whores, pimps, gamblers, and sons of bitches, by which he meant Everybody. Had the man looked through another peephole he might have said, "Saints and angels and martyrs and holy men," and he would have meant the same thing.

In the morning when the sardine fleet has made a catch, the purse-seiners waddle heavily into the bay blowing their whistles. The deep-laden boats pull in against the coast where the canneries dip their tails into the bay. The figure is advisedly chosen, for if the canneries dipped their mouths into the bay the canned sardines which emerge from the other end would be metaphorically, at least, even more horrifying. Then cannery whistles scream and all over the town men and women scramble into their clothes and come running down to the Row to go to work. Then shining cars bring the upper classes down: superintendents, accountants, owners who disappear into offices. Then from the town pour Wops and Chinamen and Polaks, men and women in trousers and rubber coats and oilcloth aprons. They come running to clean and cut and pack and cook and can

SOURCE. From *Cannery Row* by John Steinbeck. Copyright 1945 by John Steinbeck, reprinted with the permission of the Viking Press.

the fish. The whole street rumbles and groans and screams and rattles while the silver rivers of fish pour in out of the boats and the boats rise higher and higher in the water until they are empty. The canneries rumble and rattle and squeak until the last fish is cleaned and cut and cooked and canned and then the whistles scream again and the dripping, smelly, tired Wops and Chinamen and Polaks, men and women, straggle out and droop their ways up the hill into the town and Cannery Row becomes itself again—quiet and magical. Its normal life returns. The bums who retired in disgust under the black cypress tree come out to sit on the rusty pipes in the vacant lot. The girls from Dora's emerge for a bit of sun if there is any. Doc strolls from the Western Biological Laboratory and crosses the street to Lee Chong's grocery for two quarts of beer. Henri the painter noses like an Airedale through the junk in the grass-grown lot for some part or piece of wood or metal he needs for the boat he is building. Then the darkness edges in and the street light comes on in front of Dora's—the lamp which makes perpetual moonlight in Cannery Row. Callers arrive at Western Biological to see Doc, and he crosses the street to Lee Chong's for five quarts of beer.

How can the poem and the stink and the grating noise—the quality of light, the tone, the habit and the dream—be set down alive? When you collect marine animals there are certain flat worms so delicate that they are almost impossible to capture whole, for they break and tatter under the touch. You must let them ooze and crawl of their own will onto a knife blade and then lift them gently into your bottle of sea water. And perhaps that might be the way to write this book—to open the page and let the stories crawl in by themselves.

Chapter I

Lee Chong's grocery, while not a model of neatness, was a miracle of supply. It was small and crowded but within its single room a man could find everything he needed or wanted to live and to be happy—clothes, food, both fresh and canned, liquor, tobacco, fishing equipment, machinery, boats, cordage, caps, pork chops. You could buy at Lee Chong's a pair of slippers, a silk kimono, a quarter pint of whiskey and a cigar. You could work out combinations to fit almost any mood. The one commodity Lee Chong did not keep could be had across the lot at Dora's.

The grocery opened at dawn and did not close until the last wandering vagrant dime had been spent or retired for the night. Not that Lee Chong was avaricious. He wasn't, but if one wanted to spend money, he was available. Lee's position in the community surprised him as much as he could be surprised. Over the course of the years everyone in Cannery Row owed him money. He never pressed his clients, but when the bill became too large, Lee cut off credit. Rather than walk into the town up the hill, the client usually paid or tried to.

Lee was round-faced and courteous. He spoke a stately English without ever using the letter R. When the tong wars were going on in California, it happened now and then that Lee found a price on his head. Then he would go secretly to San Francisco and enter a hospital until the trouble blew over. What he did with his money, no one ever knew. Perhaps he didn't get it. Maybe his wealth was entirely in unpaid bills. But he lived well and he had the respect of all his neighbors. He trusted his clients until further trust became ridiculous. Sometimes he made business errors, but even these he turned to advantage in good will if in no other way. It was that way with the Palace Flophouse and Grill. Anyone but Lee Chong would have considered the transaction a total loss.

Lee Chong's station in the grocery was behind the cigar counter. The cash register was then on his left and the abacus on his right. Inside the glass case were the brown cigars, the cigarettes, the Bull Durham, the Duke's mixture, the Five Brothers, while behind him in racks on the wall were the pints, half pints and quarters of Old Green River, Old Town House, Old Colonel, and the favorite—Old Tennessee, a blended whiskey guaranteed four months old, very cheap and known in the neighborhood as Old Tennis Shoes. Lee Chong did not stand between the whiskey and the customer without reason. Some very practical minds had on occasion tried to divert his attention to another part of the store. Cousins, nephews, sons and daughters-in-law waited on the rest of the store, but Lee never left the cigar counter. The top of the glass was his desk. His fat delicate hands rested on the glass, the fingers moving like small restless sausages. A broad golden wedding ring on the middle finger of his left hand was his only jewelry and with it he silently tapped on the rubber change mat from which the little rubber tits had long been worn. Lee's mouth was full and benevolent and the flash of gold when he smiled was rich and warm. He wore half-glasses and since he looked at everything through them, he had to tilt his head back to see in the distance. Interest and discounts, addition, subtraction he worked out on the abacus with his little restless sausage fingers, and his brown friendly eyes roved over the grocery and his teeth flashed at the customers.

On an evening when he stood in his place on a pad of newspapers to keep his feet warm, he contemplated with humor and sadness a business deal that had been consummated that afternoon and reconsummated later that same afternoon. When you leave the grocery, if you walk catty-cornered across the grass-grown lot, threading your way among the great rusty pipes thrown out of the canneries, you will see a path worn in the weeds. Follow it past the cypress tree, across the railroad track, up a chicken walk with cleats, and you will come to a long low building which for a long time was used as a storage place for fish meal. It was just a great big roofed room and it belonged to a worried gentleman named Horace Abbeville. Horace had two wives and six children and over a period of years he had managed through pleading and persuasion to build a grocery debt second to none in Monterey. That afternoon he had come into the grocery and his sensitive tired face had flinched at the shadow of sternness that crossed Lee's face. Lee's fat finger tapped the rubber mat. Horace laid his hands palm up on the cigar counter. "I guess I owe you plenty of dough," he said simply.

Lee's teeth flashed up in appreciation of an approach so different from any he had ever heard. He nodded gravely, but he waited for the trick to develop.

Horace wet his lips with his tongue, a good job from corner to corner. "I hate to have my kids with that hanging over them," he said. "Why, I bet you wouldn't let them have a pack of spearmint now."

Lee Chong's face agreed with this conclusion. "Plenty dough," he said.

Horace continued. "You know that place of mine across the track up there where the fish meal is."

Lee Chong nodded. It was his fish meal.

Horace said earnestly, "If I was to give you that place—would it clear me up with you?"

Lee Chong tilted his head back and stared at Horace through his half-glasses while his mind flicked among accounts and his right hand moved restlessly to the abacus. He considered the construction which was flimsy and the lot which might be valuable if a cannery ever wanted to expand. "Shu," said Lee Chong.

"Well, get out the accounts and I'll make you a bill of sale on that place," Horace seemed in a hurry.

"No need papers," said Lee. "I make paid-in-full paper."

They finished the deal with dignity and Lee Chong threw in a quarter pint of Old Tennis Shoes. And then Horace Abbeville walking very straight went across the lot and past the cypress tree and across the track and up the chicken walk and into the building that had been his, and he shot himself on a heap of fish meal. And although it has nothing to do with this story, no Abbeville child, no matter who its mother was, knew the lack of a stick of spearmint ever afterward.

But to get back to the evening. Horace was on the trestles with the embalming needles in him, and his two wives were sitting on the steps of his house with their arms about each other (they were good friends until after the funeral, and then they divided up the children and never spoke to each other again). Lee Chong stood in the back of the cigar counter and his nice brown eyes were turned inward on a calm eternal Chinese sorrow. He knew he could not have helped it, but he wished he might have known and perhaps tried to help. It was deeply a part of Lee's kindness and understanding that man's right to kill himself is inviolable, but sometimes a friend can make it unnecessary. Lee had already underwritten the funeral and sent a wash basket of groceries to the stricken families.

Now Lee Chong owned the Abbeville building—a good roof, a good floor, two windows and a door. True it was piled high with fish meal and the smell of it was delicate and penetrating. Lee Chong considered it as a storehouse for groceries, as a kind of warehouse, but he gave that up on second thought. It was too far away and anyone can go in through a window. He was tapping the rubber mat with his gold ring and considering the problem when the door opened and Mack came in. Mack was the elder, leader, mentor, and to a small extent the exploiter of a little group of men who had in common no families, no money, and no ambitions beyond food, drink, and contentment. But whereas most men in their search for contentment destroy themselves and fall wearily short of their targets, Mack and his friends approached contentment casually, quietly, and absorbed it gently. Mack and Hazel, a young man of great strength, Eddie who filled in as a bartender at La Ida, Hughie and Jones who occasionally collected frogs and cats for Western Biological, were currently living in those large rusty pipes in the lot next to Lee Chong's. That is, they lived in the pipes when it was damp but in fine weather they lived in the shadow of the black cypress tree at the top of the lot. The limbs folded down and made a canopy under which a man could lie and look at the flow and vitality of Cannery Row.

Lee Chong stiffened ever so slightly when Mack came in and his eyes glanced quickly about the store to make sure that Eddie or Hazel or Hughie or Jones had not come in too and drifted away among the groceries.

Mack laid out his cards with a winning honesty. "Lee," he said, "I and Eddie and the rest heard you own the Abbeville place."

Lee Chong nodded and waited.

"I and my friends thought we'd ast you if we could move in there. We'll keep up the property," he added quickly. "Wouldn't let anybody break in or hurt anything. Kids might knock out the windows, you know—" Mack suggested. "Place might burn down if somebody don't keep an eye on it."

Lee tilted his head back and looked into Mack's eyes through the half-glasses and Lee's tapping finger slowed its tempo as he thought deeply. In Mack's eyes there was good will and good fellowship and a desire to make everyone happy. Why then did Lee Chong feel slightly surrounded? Why did his mind pick its way as delicately as a cat through cactus? It had been sweetly done, almost in a spirit of philanthropy. Lee's mind leaped ahead at the possibilities—no, they were probabilities, and his finger tapping slowed still further. He saw himself refusing Mack's request and he saw the broken glass from the windows. Then Mack would offer a second time to watch over and preserve Lee's property—and at the second refusal, Lee could smell the smoke, could see the little flames creeping up the walls. Mack and his friends would try to help to put it out. Lee's finger came to a gentle rest on the change mat. He was beaten. He knew that. There was left to him only the possibility of saving face and Mack was likely to be very generous about that. Lee said, "You like pay lent my place? You like live there same hotel?"

Mack smiled broadly and he was generous. "Say—" he cried. "That's an idear. Sure. How much?"

Lee considered. He knew it didn't matter what he charged. He wasn't going to get it anyway. He might just as well make it a really sturdy face-saving sum. "Fi dolla' week," said Lee.

Mack played it through to the end. "I'll have to talk to the boys about it," he said dubiously. "Couldn't you make that four dollars a week?"

"Fi dolla'," said Lee firmly.

"Well, I'll see what the boys say," said Mack.

And that was the way its was. Everyone was happy about it. And if it be thought that Lee Chong suffered a total loss, at least his mind did not work that way. The windows were not broken. Fire did not break out, and while no rent was ever paid, if the tenants ever had any money, and quite often they did have, it never occurred to them to spend it any place except at Lee Chong's grocery. What he had was a little group of active potential customers under wraps. But it went further than that. If a drunk caused trouble in the grocery, if the kids swarmed down from New Monterey intent on plunder, Lee Chong had only to call and his tenants rushed to his aid. One further bond it established—you cannot steal from your benefactor. The saving to Lee Chong in cans of beans and tomatoes and milk and watermelons more than paid the rent. And if there was a sudden and increased leakage among the groceries in New Monterey that was none of Lee Chong's affair.

The boys moved in and the fish meal moved out. No one knows who named the house that has been known ever after as the Palace Flophouse and Grill. In the pipes and under the cypress tree there had been no room for furniture and the little niceties which are not only the diagnosis but the boundaries of our civilization. Once in the Palace Flophouse, the boys set about furnishing it. A chair appeared and a cot and another chair. A hardware store supplied a can of red paint not reluctantly because it never knew about it, and as a new table or or footstool appeared it was painted, which not only made it very pretty but also disguised it to a certain extent in case a former owner looked in. And the Palace Flophouse and Grill began to function. The boys could sit in front of their door and look down across the track and across the lot and across the street right into the front windows of Western Biological. They could hear the music from the laboratory at night. And their eyes followed Doc across the street when he went to Lee Chong's for beer. And Mack said, "That Doc is a fine fellow. We ought to do something for him."

Chapter II

The word is a symbol and a delight which sucks up men and scenes, trees, plants, factories, and Pekinese. Then the Thing becomes the Word and back to Thing again, but warped and woven into a fantastic pattern. The Word sucks up

Cannery Row, digests it and spews it out, and the Row has taken the shimmer of the green world and the sky-reflecting seas. Lee Chong is more than a Chinese grocer. He must be. Perhaps he is evil balanced and held suspended by good—an Asiatic planet held to its orbit by the pull of Lao Tze and held away from Lao Tze by the centrifugality of abacus and cash register—Lee Chong suspended, spinning, whirling among groceries and ghosts. A hard man with a can of beans —a soft man with the bones of his grandfather. For Lee Chong dug into the grave on China Point and found the yellow bones, the skull with gray ropy hair still sticking to it. And Lee carefully packed the bones, femurs, and tibias really straight, skull in the middle, with pelvis and clavicle surrounding it and ribs curving on either side. Then Lee Chong sent his boxed and brittle grandfather over the western sea to lie at last in ground made holy by his ancestors.

Mack and the boys, too, spinning in their orbits. They are the Virtues, the Graces, the Beauties of the hurried mangled craziness of Monterey and the cosmic Monterey where men in fear and hunger destroy their stomachs in the fight to secure certain food, where men hungering for love destroy everything lovable about them. Mack and the boys are the Beauties, the Virtues, the Graces. In the world ruled by tigers with ulcers, rutted by strictured bulls, scavenged by blind jackals, Mack and the boys dine delicately with the tigers, fondle the frantic heifers, and wrap up the crumbs to feed the sea gulls of Cannery Row. What can it profit a man to gain the whole world and to come to his property with a gastric ulcer, a blown prostate, and bifocals? Mack and the boys avoid the trap, walk around the poison, step over the noose while a generation of trapped, poisoned, and trussed-up men scream at them and call them no-goods, come-to-bad-ends, blots-on-the-town, thieves, rascals, bums. Our Father who art in nature, who has given the gift of survival to the coyote, the common brown rat, the English sparrow, the house fly and the moth, must have a great and overwhelming love for no-goods and blots-on-the-town and bums, and Mack and the boys. Virtues and graces and laziness and zest. Our Father who art in nature.

Chapter III

Lee Chong's is to the right of the vacant lot (although why it is called vacant when it is piled high with old boilers, with rusting pipes, with great square timbers, and stacks of five-gallon cans, no one can say). Up in back of the vacant lot is the railroad track and the Palace Flophouse. But on the left-hand boundary of the lot is the stern and stately whore house of Dora Flood; a decent, clean, honest, old-fashioned sporting house where a man can take a glass of beer among friends. This is no fly-by-night cheap clip-joint but a sturdy, virtuous club, built, maintained, and disciplined by Dora who, madam and girl for fifty years, has through the exercise of special gifts of tact and honesty, charity and a certain realism, made herself respected by the intelligent, the learned, and the kind. And by the same token she is hated by the twisted and lascivious sisterhood of married spinsters whose husbands respect the home but don't like it very much.

Dora is a great woman, a great big woman with flaming orange hair and a taste for Nile green evening dresses. She keeps an honest, one price house, sells no hard liquor, and permits no loud or vulgar talk in her house. Of her girls some are fairly inactive due to age and infirmities, but Dora never puts them aside although, as she says, some of them don't turn three tricks a month but they go right on eating three meals a day. In a moment of local love Dora named her place the Bear Flag Restaurant and the stories are many of people who have gone in for a sandwich. There are normally twelve girls in the house, counting the old ones, a Greek cook, and a man who is known as a watchman but who undertakes all manner of delicate and dangerous tasks. He stops fights, ejects drunks, soothes hysteria, cures headaches, and tends bar. He bandages cuts and bruises, passes the time of day with cops, and since a good half of the girls are Christian Scientists, reads aloud his share of *Science and Health* on a Sunday morning. His predecessor, being a less well-balanced man, came to an evil end as shall be reported, but Alfred has triumphed over his environment and has brought his environment up with him. He knows what men should be there and what men shouldn't be there. He knows more about the home life of Monterey citizens than anyone in town.

As for Dora—she leads a ticklish existence. Being against the law, at least against its letter, she must be twice as law abiding as anyone else. There must be no drunks, no fighting, no vulgarity, or they close Dora up. Also being illegal Dora must be especially philanthropic. Everyone puts the bite on her. If the police give a dance for their pension fund and everyone else gives a dollar, Dora has to give fifty dollars. When the Chamber of Commerce improved its gardens, the merchants each gave five dollars but Dora was asked for and gave a hundred. With everything else it is the same, Red Cross, Community Chest, Boy Scouts, Dora's unsung, unpublicized, shameless dirty wages of sin lead the list of donations. But during the depression she was hardest hit. In addition to the usual charities, Dora saw the hungry children of Cannery Row and the jobless fathers and the worried women and Dora paid grocery bills right and left for two years and very nearly went broke in the process. Dora's girls are well trained and pleasant. They never speak to a man on the street although he may have been in the night before.

Before Alfy the present watchman took over, there was a tragedy in the Bear Flag Restaurant which saddened everyone. The previous watchman was named William and he was a dark and lonesome-looking man. In the daytime when his duties were few he would grow tired of female company. Through the windows he could see Mack and the boys sitting on the pipes in the vacant lot, dangling their feet in the mallow weeds and taking the sun while they discoursed slowly and philosophically of matters of interest but of no importance. Now and then as he watched them he saw them take out a pint of Old Tennis Shoes and wiping the neck of the bottle on a sleeve, raise the pint one after another. And William began to wish he could join that good group. He walked out one day and sat on the pipe. Conversation stopped and an uneasy and hostile silence fell on the group. After a while William went disconsolately back to the Bear Flag and through the window he saw the conversation spring up again and it saddened him. He had a dark and ugly face and a mouth twisted with brooding.

The next day he went again and this time he took a pint of whiskey. Mack and the boys drank the whiskey, after all they weren't crazy, but all the talking they did was "Good luck," and "Lookin' at you."

After a while William went back to the Bear Flag and he watched them through the window and he heard Mack raise his voice saying, "But God damn it, I hate a pimp!" Now this was obviously untrue although William didn't know that. Mack and the boys just didn't like William.

Now William's heart broke. The bums would not receive him socially. They felt that he was too far beneath them. William had always been introspective and self-accusing. He put on his hat and walked out along the sea, clear out to the Lighthouse. And he stood in the pretty little cemetery where you can hear the waves drumming always. William thought dark and broody thoughts. No one loved him. No one cared about him. They might call him a watchman but he was a pimp—a dirty pimp, the lowest thing in the world. And then he thought how he had a right to live and be happy just like anyone else, by God he had. He walked back angrily but his anger went away when he came to the Bear Flag and climbed the steps. It was evening and the juke box was playing *Harvest Moon* and William remembered that the first hooker who ever gaffed for him used to like that song before she ran away and got married and disappeared. The song made him awfully sad. Dora was in the back parlor having a cup of tea when William came in. She said, "What's the matter, you sick?"

"No," said William. "But what's the percentage? I feel lousy. I think I'll bump myself off."

Dora had handled plenty of neurotics in her time. Kid 'em out of it was her motto. "Well, do it on your own time and don't mess up the rugs," she said.

A gray damp cloud folded over William's heart and he walked slowly out and down the hall and knocked on Eva Flanegan's door. She had red hair and went to confession every week. Eva was quite a spiritual girl with a big family of brothers and sisters but she was an unpredictable drunk. She was painting her nails and messing them pretty badly when William went in and he knew she was bagged and Dora wouldn't let a bagged girl work. Her fingers were nail polish to the first joint and she was angry. "What's eating you?" she said. William grew angry too. "I'm going to bump myself off," he said fiercely.

Eva screeched at him. "That's a dirty, lousy, stinking sin," she cried, and then, "Wouldn't it be like you to get the joint pinched just when I got almost enough kick to take a trip to East St. Louis. You're a no-good bastard." She was still screaming at him when William shut her door after him and went to the kitchen. He was very tired of women. The Greek would be restful after women.

The Greek, big apron, sleeves rolled up, was frying pork chops in two big skillets, turning them over with an ice pick. "Hello, Kits. How is going things?" The pork chops hissed and swished in the pan.

"I don't know, Lou," said William. "Sometimes I think the best thing to do would be—kluck!" He drew his finger across his throat.

The Greek laid the ice pick on the stove and rolled his sleeves higher. "I tell you what I hear, Kits," he said. "I hear like the fella talks about it don't never do it." William's hand went out for the ice pick and he held it easily in his hand. His eyes looked deeply into the Greek's dark eyes and he saw disbelief and amusement and then as he stared the Greek's eyes grew troubled and then worried. And William saw the change, saw first how the Greek knew he could do it and then the Greek knew he would do it. As soon as he saw that in the Greek's eyes William knew he had to do it. He was sad because now it seemed silly. His hand rose and the ice pick snapped into his heart. It was amazing how easily it went in. William was the watchman before Alfred came. Everyone liked Alfred. He could sit on the pipes with Mack and the boys any time. He could even visit up at the Palace Flophouse.

LEO TOLSTOY

• War and Peace

I

"Well, Prince, Genoa and Lucca are now no more than private estates of the Bonaparte family. No, I warn you, that if you do not tell me we are at war, if you again allow yourself to palliate all the infamies and atrocities of this Antichrist (upon my word, I believe he is), I don't know you in future, you are no longer my friend, no longer my faithful slave, as you say. There, how do you do, how do you do? I see I'm scaring you, sit down and talk to me."

These words were uttered in July 1805 by Anna Pavlovna Scherer, a distinguished lady of the court, and confidential maid-of-honour to the Empress Marya Fyodorovna. It was her greeting to Prince Vassily, a man high in rank and office, who was the first to arrive at her *soirée*. Anna Pavlovna had been coughing for the last few days; she had an attack of *la grippe*, as she said—*grippe* was then a new word only used by a few people. In the notes she had sent round in the morning by a footman in red livery, she had written to all indiscriminately:

"If you have nothing better to do, count (or prince), and if the prospect of spending an evening with a poor invalid is not too alarming to you, I shall be charmed to see you at my house between 7 and 10. Annette Scherer."

"Heavens! what a violent outburst!" the prince responded, not in the least disconcerted at such a reception. He was wearing an embroidered court uniform,

SOURCE. From *War and Peace* by Leo Tolstoy. The Modern Library, N.D.

stockings and slippers, and had stars on his breast, and a bright smile on his flat face.

He spoke in that elaborately choice French, in which our forefathers not only spoke but thought, and with those slow, patronising intonations peculiar to a man of importance who has grown old in court society. He went up to Anna Pavlovna, kissed her hand, presenting her with a view of his perfumed, shining bald head, and complacently settled himself on the sofa.

"First of all, tell me how you are, dear friend. Relieve a friend's anxiety," he said, with no change of his voice and tone, in which indifference, and even irony, was perceptible through the veil of courtesy and sympathy.

"How can one be well when one is in moral suffering? How can one help being worried in these times, if one has any feeling?" said Anna Pavlovna. "You'll spend the whole evening with me, I hope?"

"And the fête at the English ambassador's? To-day is Wednesday. I must put in an appearance there," said the prince. "My daughter is coming to fetch me and take me there."

"I thought to-day's fête had been put off. I confess that all these festivities and fireworks are beginning to pall."

"If they had known that it was your wish, the fête would have been put off," said the prince, from habit, like a wound-up clock, saying things he did not even wish to be believed.

"Don't tease me. Well, what has been decided in regard to the Novosiltsov dispatch? You know everything."

"What is there to tell?" said the prince in a tired, listless tone. "What has been decided? It has been decided that Bonaparte has burnt his ships, and I think that we are about to burn ours."

Prince Vassily always spoke languidly, like an actor repeating his part in an old play. Anna Pavlovna Scherer, in spite of her forty years, was on the contrary brimming over with excitement and impulsiveness. To be enthusiastic had become her pose in society, and at times even when she had, indeed, no inclination to be so, she was enthusiastic so as not to disappoint the expectations of those who knew her. The affected smile which played continually about Anna Pavlovna's face, out of keeping as it was with her faded looks, expressed a spoilt child's continual consciousness of a charming failing of which she had neither the wish nor the power to correct herself, which, indeed, she saw no need to correct.

In the midst of a conversation about politics, Anna Pavlovna became greatly excited.

"Ah, don't talk to me about Austria! I know nothing about it, perhaps, but Austria has never wanted, and doesn't want war. She is betraying us. Russia alone is to be the saviour of Europe. Our benefactor knows his lofty destiny, and will be true to it. That's the one thing I have faith in. Our good and sublime emperor has the greatest part in the world to play, and he is so virtuous and noble that

God will not desert him, and he will fulfil his mission—to strangle the hydra of revolution, which is more horrible than ever now in the person of this murderer and miscreant. . . . Whom can we reckon on, I ask you? . . . England with her commercial spirit will not comprehend and cannot comprehend all the loftiness of soul of the Emperor Alexander. She has refused to evacuate Malta. She tries to detect, she seeks a hidden motive in our actions. What have they said to Novo-siltsov? Nothing. They didn't understand, they're incapable of understanding the self-sacrifice of our emperor, who desires nothing for himself, and everything for the good of humanity. And what have they promised? Nothing. What they have promised even won't come to anything! Prussia has declared that Bonaparte is invincible, and that all Europe can do nothing against him. . . . And I don't be-lieve a single word of what was said by Hardenberg or Haugwitz. That famous Prussian neutrality is a mere snare. I have no faith but in God and the lofty des-tiny of our adored emperor. He will save Europe!" She stopped short abruptly, with a smile of amusement at her own warmth.

"I imagine," said the prince, smiling, "that if you had been sent instead of our dear Wintsengerode, you would have carried the Prussian king's consent by storm,—you are so eloquent. Will you give me some tea?"

"In a moment. By the way," she added, subsiding into calm again, "there are two very interesting men to be here to-night, the vicomte de Mortemart; he is connected with the Montmorencies through the Rohans, one of the best families in France. He is one of the good emigrants, the real ones. Then Abbé Morio; you know that profound intellect? He has been received by the emperor. Do you know him?"

"Ah! I shall be delighted," said the prince. "Tell me," he added, as though he had just recollected something, speaking with special nonchalance, though the question was the chief motive of his visit: "it is true that the dowager empress desires the appointment of Baron Funke as first secretary to the Vienna legation? He is a poor creature, it appears, that baron." Prince Vassily would have liked to see his son appointed to the post, which people were trying, through the Empress Marya Fyodorovna, to obtain for the baron.

Anna Pavlovna almost closed her eyes to signify that neither she nor any one else could pass judgment on what the empress might be pleased or see fit to do.

"Baron Funke has been recommended to the empress-mother by her sister," was all she said in a dry, mournful tone. When Anna Pavlovna spoke of the em-press her countenance suddenly assumed a profound and genuine expression of devotion and respect, mingled with melancholy, and this happened whenever she mentioned in conversation her illustrious patroness. She said that her Imperial Majesty had been graciously pleased to show great esteem to Baron Funke, and again a shade of melancholy passed over her face. The prince preserved an in-different silence. Anna Pavlovna, with the adroitness and quick tact of a courtier and a woman, felt an inclination to chastise the prince for his temerity in referring in such terms to a person recommended to the empress, and at the same time to console him.

"But about your own family," she said, "do you know that your daughter, since she has come out, charms everybody? People say she is as beautiful as the day."

The prince bowed in token of respect and acknowledgment.

"I often think," pursued Anna Pavlovna, moving up to the prince and smiling cordially to him, as though to mark that political and worldly conversation was over and now intimate talk was to begin: "I often think how unfairly the blessings of life are sometimes apportioned. Why has fate given you two such splendid children—I don't include Anatole, your youngest—him I don't like" (she put in with a decision admitting of no appeal, raising her eyebrows)—"such charming children? And you really seem to appreciate them less than any one, and so you don't deserve them."

And she smiled her ecstatic smile.

"What would you have? Lavater would have said that I have not the bump of paternity," said the prince.

"Don't keep on joking. I wanted to talk to you seriously. Do you know I'm not pleased with your youngest son. Between ourselves" (her face took its mournful expression), "people have been talking about him to her majesty and commiserating you . . ."

The prince did not answer, but looking at him significantly, she waited in silence for his answer. Prince Vassily frowned.

"What would you have me do?" he said at last. "You know I have done everything for their education a father could do, and they have both turned out *des imbéciles*. Ippolit is at least a quiet fool, while Anatole's a fool that won't keep quiet, that's the only difference," he said, with a smile, more unnatural and more animated than usual, bringing out with peculiar prominence something surprisingly brutal and unpleasant in the lines about his mouth.

"Why are children born to men like you? If you weren't a father, I could find no fault with you," said Anna Pavlovna, raising her eyes pensively.

"I am your faithful slave and to you alone I can confess. My children are the bane of my existence. It's the cross I have to bear, that's how I explain it to myself. What would you have?" . . . He broke off with a gesture expressing his resignation to a cruel fate. Anna Pavlovna pondered a moment.

"Have you never thought of marrying your prodigal son Anatole? People say," she said, "that old maids have a mania for matchmaking. I have never been conscious of this failing before, but I have a little person in my mind, who is very unhappy with her father, a relation of ours, the young Princess Bolkonsky."

Prince Vassily made no reply, but with the rapidity of reflection and memory characteristic of worldly people, he signified by a motion of the head that he had taken in and was considering what she said.

"No, do you know that the boy is costing me forty thousand roubles a year?" he said, evidently unable to restrain the gloomy current of his thoughts. He paused. "What will it be in five years if this goes on? These are the advantages of being a father. . . . Is she rich, your young princess?"

"Her father is very rich and miserly. He lives in the country. You know that notorious Prince Bolkonsky, retired under the late emperor, and nicknamed the 'Prussian King.' He's a very clever man, but eccentric and tedious. The poor little thing is as unhappy as possible. Her brother it is who has lately been married to Liza Meinen, an adjutant of Kutuzov's. He'll be here this evening."

"Listen, dear Annette," said the prince, suddenly taking his companion's hand, and for some reason bending it downwards. "Arrange this matter for me and I am your faithful slave for ever and ever. She's of good family and well off. That's all I want."

And with the freedom, familiarity, and grace that distinguished him, he took the maid-of-honour's hand, kissed it, and as he kissed it waved her hand, while he stretched forward in his low chair and gazed away into the distance.

"Wait," said Anna Pavlovna, considering. "I'll talk to Lise (the wife of young Bolkonsky) this very evening, and perhaps it can be arranged I'll try my prentice hand as an old maid in your family."

II

Anna Pavlovna's drawing-room gradually began to fill. The people of the highest distinction in Petersburg were there, people very different in ages and characters, but alike in the set in which they moved. The daughter of Prince Vassily, the beauty, Ellen, came to fetch her father and go with him to the ambassador's fête. She was wearing a ball-dress with an imperial badge on it. The young Princess Bolkonsky was there, celebrated as the most seductive woman in Petersburg. She had been married the previous winter, and was not now going out into the great world on account of her interesting condition, but was still to be seen at small parties. Prince Ippolit, the son of Prince Vassily, came too with Mortemart, whom he introduced. The Abbé Morio was there too, and many others.

"Have you not yet seen, or not been introduced to *ma tante?*" Anna Pavlovna said to her guests as they arrived, and very seriously she led them up to a little old lady wearing tall bows, who had sailed in out of the next room as soon as the guests began to arrive. Anna Pavlovna mentioned their names, deliberately turning her eyes from the guest to *ma tante,* and then withdrew. All the guests performed the ceremony of greeting the aunt, who was unknown, uninteresting and unnecessary to every one. Anna Pavlovna with mournful, solemn sympathy, followed these greetings, silently approving them. *Ma tante* said to each person the same words about his health, her own health, and the health of her majesty, who was, thank God, better to-day. Every one, though from politeness showing no undue haste, moved away from the old lady with a sense of relief at a tiresome duty accomplished, and did not approach her again all the evening. The young Princess Bolkonsky had come with her work in a gold-embroidered velvet bag. Her pretty little upper lip, faintly darkened with down, was very short over her teeth, but was all the more charming when it was lifted, and still more charming when it was at times drawn down to meet the lower lip. As is always the case with perfectly charming women, her defect—the shortness of the lip and the half-opened mouth—seemed her peculiar, her characteristic beauty. Every one took delight in watching the pretty creature full of life and gaiety, so soon to be a mother, and so lightly bearing her burden. Old men and bored, depressed young men gazing at her felt as though they were becoming like her, by being with her and talking a little while to her. Any man who spoke to her, and at every word saw her bright little smile and shining white teeth, gleaming continually, imagined that he was being particularly successful this evening. And this each thought in turn.

The little princess, moving with a slight swing, walked with rapid little steps round the table with her work-bag in her hand, and gaily arranging the folds of her gown, sat down on a sofa near the silver samovar; it seemed as though everything she did was a festival for herself and all around her.

"I have brought my work," she said, displaying her reticule, and addressing the company generally. "Mind, Annette, don't play me a nasty trick," she turned to the lady of the house; "you wrote to me that it was quite a little gathering. See how I am got up."

And she flung her arms open to show her elegant grey dress, trimmed with lace and girt a little below the bosom with a broad sash.

"Never mind, Lise, you will always be prettier than any one else," answered Anna Pavlovna.

"You know my husband is deserting me," she went on in just the same voice, addressing a general; "he is going to get himself killed. Tell me what this nasty war is for," she said to Prince Vassily, and without waiting for an answer she turned to Prince Vassily's daughter, the beautiful Ellen.

"How delightful this little princess is!" said Prince Vassily in an undertone to Anna Pavlovna.

Soon after the little princess, there walked in a massively built, stout young man in spectacles, with a cropped head, light breeches in the mode of the day, with a high lace ruffle and a ginger-coloured coat. This stout young man was the illegitimate son of a celebrated dandy of the days of Catherine, Count Bezuhov, who was now dying at Moscow. He had not yet entered any branch of the service; he had only just returned from abroad, where he had been educated, and this was his first appearance in society. Anna Pavlovna greeted him with a nod reserved for persons of the very lowest hierarchy in her drawing-room. But, in spite of this greeting, Anna Pavlovna's countenance showed signs on seeing Pierre of uneasiness and alarm, such as is shown at the sight of something too big and out of place. Though Pierre certainly was somewhat bigger than any of the other men in the room, this expression could only have reference to the clever, though shy, observant and natural look that distinguished him from every one else in the drawing-room.

"It is very kind of you, M. Pierre, to have come to see a poor invalid," Anna Pavlovna said to him, exchanging anxious glances with her aunt, to whom she was conducting him.

Pierre murmured something unintelligible, and continued searching for something with his eyes. He smiled gleefully and delightedly, bowing to the little princess as though she were an intimate friend, and went up to the aunt. Anna Pavlovna's alarm was not without grounds, for Pierre walked away from the aunt without waiting to the end of her remarks about her majesty's health. Anna Pavlovna stopped him in dismay with the words: "You don't know Abbé Morio? He's a very interesting man," she said.

"Yes, I have heard of his scheme for perpetual peace, and it's very interesting, but hardly possible . . ."

"You think so?" said Anna Pavlovna in order to say something and to get away again to her duties as hostess, but Pierre committed the opposite incivility. Just now he had walked off without listening to the lady who was addressing him; now he detained by his talk a lady who wanted to get away from him. With head bent and legs planted wide apart, he began explaining to Anna Pavlovna why he considered the abbé's scheme chimerical.

"We will talk of it later," said Anna Pavlovna, smiling.

And getting rid of this unmannerly young man she returned to her duties, keeping her eyes and ears open, ready to fly to the assistance at any point where the conversation was flagging. Just as the foreman of a spinning-mill settles the work-people in their places, walks up and down the works, and noting any stoppage or unusual creaking or too loud a whir in the spindles, goes up hurriedly, slackens the machinery and sets it going properly, so Anna Pavlovna, walking about her drawing-room, went up to any circle that was pausing or too loud in conversation and by a single word or change of position set the conversational machine going again in its regular, decorous way. But in the midst of these cares a special anxiety on Pierre's account could still be discerned in her. She kept an anxious watch on him as he went up to listen to what was being said near Mortemart, and walked away to another group where the abbé was talking. Pierre had been educated abroad, and this party at Anna Pavlovna's was the first at which he had been present in Russia. He knew all the intellectual lights of Petersburg gathered together here, and his eyes strayed about like a child's in a toy-shop. He was afraid at every moment of missing some intellectual conversation which he might have heard. Gazing at the self-confident and refined expressions of the personages assembled here, he was continually expecting something exceptionally clever. At last he moved up to Abbé Morio. The conversation seemed interesting, and he stood still waiting for an opportunity of expressing his own ideas, as young people are fond of doing.

III

Anna Pavlovna's *soirée* was in full swing. The spindles kept up their regular hum on all sides without pause. Except the aunt, beside whom was sitting no one but an elderly lady with a thin, careworn face, who seemed rather out of her element in this brilliant society, the company was broken up into three groups. In one of these, the more masculine, the centre was the abbé; in the other, the group of young people, the chief attractions were the beautiful Princess Ellen, Prince Vassily's daughter, and the little Princess Bolkonsky, with her rosy prettiness, too plump for her years. In the third group were Mortemart and Anna Pavlovna.

The vicomte was a pretty young gentleman with soft features and manners, who obviously regarded himself as a celebrity, but with good breeding modestly allowed the company the benefit of his society. Anna Pavlovna unmistakably regarded him as the chief entertainment she was giving her guests. As a clever *maître d'hôtel* serves as something superlatively good the piece of beef which no one would have cared to eat seeing it in the dirty kitchen, Anna Pavlovna that evening served up to her guests—first, the vicomte and then the abbé, as something superlatively subtle. In Mortemart's group the talk turned at once on the execution of the duc d'Enghien. The vicomte said that the duc d'Enghien had been lost by his own magnanimity and that there were special reasons for Bonaparte's bitterness against him.

"Ah, come! Tell us about that, vicomte," said Anna Pavlovna gleefully, feeling that the phrase had a peculiarly Louis Quinze note about it: *"Contez-nous cela, vicomte."*

The vicomte bowed and smiled courteously in token of his readiness to obey. Anna Pavlovna made a circle round the vicomte and invited every one to hear his story.

"The vicomte was personally acquainted with his highness," Anna Pavlovna whispered to one. "The vicomte tells a story perfectly," she said to another. "How one sees the man of quality," she said to a third, and the vicomte was presented to the company in the most elegant and advantageous light, like the roast-beef on the hot dish garnished with green parsley.

The vicomte was about to begin his narrative, and he smiled subtly.

"Come over here, *chère Hélène*," said Anna Pavlovna to the young beauty who was sitting a little way off, the centre of another group.

Princess Ellen smiled. She got up with the same unchanging smile of the acknowledged beauty with which she had entered the drawing-room. Her white ball-dress adorned with ivy and moss rustled lightly; her white shoulders, glossy hair, and diamonds glittered, as she passed between the men who moved apart to make way for her. Not looking directly at any one, but smiling at every one, as it were courteously allowing to all the right to admire the beauty of her figure, her full shoulders, her bosom and back, which were extremely exposed in the mode of the day, she moved up to Anna Pavlovna, seeming to bring with her the brilliance of the ballroom. Ellen was so lovely that she was not merely free from the slightest shade of coquetry, she seemed on the contrary ashamed of the too evident, too violent and all-conquering influence of her beauty. She seemed to wish but to be unable to soften the effect of her beauty.

"What a beautiful woman!" every one said on seeing her. As though struck by something extraordinary, the vicomte shrugged his shoulders and dropped his eyes, when she seated herself near him and dazzled him too with the same unchanging smile.

"Madame, I doubt my abilities before such an audience," he said, bowing with a smile.

The princess leaned her plump, bare arm on the table and did not find it necessary to say anything. She waited, smiling. During the vicomte's story she sat upright, looking from time to time at her beautiful, plump arm, which lay with its line changed by pressure on the table, then at her still lovelier bosom, on which she set straight her diamond necklace. Several times she settled the folds of her gown, and when the narrative made a sensation upon the audience, she glanced at Anna Pavlovna and at once assumed the expression she saw on the maid-of-honour's face, then she relapsed again into her unvarying smile. After Ellen the little princess too moved away from the tea-table.

"Wait for me, I will take my work," she said. "Come, what are you thinking of?" she said to Prince Ippolit. "Bring me my reticule."

The little princess, smiling and talking to every one, at once effected a change of position, and settling down again, gaily smoothed out her skirts.

"Now I'm comfortable," she said, and begging the vicomte to begin, she took up her work. Prince Ippolit brought her reticule, moved to her side, and bending close over her chair, sat beside her.

Le charmant Hippolyte struck every one as extraordinarily like this sister, and, still more, as being, in spite of the likeness, strikingly ugly. His features were like his sister's, but in her, everything was radiant with joyous life, with the complacent, never-failing smile of youth and life and an extraordinary antique beauty of figure. The brother's face on the contrary was clouded over by imbecility and invariably wore a look of aggressive fretfulness, while he was thin and feebly built. His eyes, his nose, his mouth—everything was, as it were, puckered up in one vacant, bored grimace, while his arms and legs always fell into the most grotesque attitudes.

"It is not a ghost story," he said, sitting down by the princess and hurriedly fixing his eyeglass in his eye, as though without that instrument he could not begin to speak.

"Why, no, my dear fellow," said the astonished vicomte, with a shrug.

"Because I detest ghost stories," said Prince Ippolit in a tone which showed that he uttered the words before he was aware of their meaning.

From the self-confidence with which he spoke, no one could tell whether what he said was very clever or very stupid. He was dressed in a dark-green frock coat, breeches of the colour of the *cuisse de nymphe effrayée,* as he called it, stockings and slippers. The vicomte very charmingly related the anecdote then current, that the duc d'Enghien had secretly visited Paris for the sake of an interview with the actress, Mlle. Georges, and that there he met Bonaparte, who also enjoyed the favours of the celebrated actress, and that, meeting the duc, Napoleon had fallen into one of the fits to which he was subject and had been completely in the duc's power, how the duc had not taken advantage of it, and Bonaparte had in the sequel avenged his magnanimity by the duc's death.

The story was very charming and interesting, especially at the point when the rivals suddenly recognise each other and the ladies seemed to be greatly excited by it. *"Charmant!"* said Anna Pavlovna, looking inquiringly at the little princess. "Charming!" whispered the little princess, sticking her needle into her work as an indication that the interest and charm of the story prevented her working. The vicomte appreciated this silent homage, and smiling gratefully, resumed his narrative. But meanwhile Anna Pavlovna, still keeping a watch on the dreadful young man, noticed that he was talking too loudly and too warmly with the abbé and hurried to the spot of danger. Pierre had in fact succeeded in getting into a poltical conversation with the abbé on the balance of power, and the abbé, evidently interested by the simple-hearted fervour of the young man, was unfolding to him his cherished idea. Both were listening and talking too eagerly and naturally, and Anna Pavlovna did not like it.

"The means?—the balance of power in Europe and the rights of the people," said the abbé. "One powerful state like Russia—with the prestige of barbarism—need only take a disinterested stand at the head of the alliance that aims at securing the balance of power in Europe, and it would save the world!" "How are you going to get such a balance of power?" Pierre was beginning; but at that moment Anna Pavlovna came up, and glancing severely at Pierre, asked the Italian how he was supporting the climate. The Italian's face changed instantly and assumed the look of offensive, affected sweetness, which was evidently its habitual expression in conversation with women. "I am so enchanted by the wit and culture of the society—especially of the ladies—in which I have had the happiness to be received, that I have not yet had time to think of the climate," he said. Not letting the abbé and Pierre slip out of her grasp, Anna Pavlovna, for greater convenience in watching them, made them join the bigger group.

At that moment another guest walked into the drawing-room. This was the young Prince Andrey Bolkonsky, the husband of the little princess. Prince Bolkonsky was a very handsome young man, of medium height, with clear, clean-cut features. Everything in his appearance, from his weary, bored expression to his slow, measured step, formed the most striking contrast to his lively little wife. Obviously all the people in the drawing-room were familiar figures to him, and more than that, he was unmistakably so sick of them that even to look at them and to listen to them was a weariness to him. Of all the wearisome faces the face of his pretty wife seemed to bore him most. With a grimace that distorted his handsome face he turned away from her. He kissed Anna Pavlovna's hand, and with half-closed eyelids scanned the whole company.

"You are enlisting for the war, prince?" said Anna Pavlovna.

"General Kutuzov has been kind enough to have me as an aide-de-camp," said Bolkonsky.

"And Lise, your life?——"

"She is going into the country."

"Isn't it too bad of you to rob us of your charming wife?"

"*André,*" said his wife, addressing her husband in exactly the same coquettish tone in which she spoke to outsiders, "the vicomte has just told us such a story about Mlle. Georges and Bonaparte!"

Prince Andrey scowled and turned away. Pierre, who had kept his eyes joyfully and affectionately fixed on him ever since he came in, went up to him and took hold of his arm. Prince Andrey, without looking round, twisted his face into a grimace of annoyance at any one's touching him, but seeing Pierre's smiling face, he gave him a smile that was unexpectedly sweet and pleasant.

"Why, you! . . . And in such society too," he said to Pierre.

"I knew you would be here," answered Pierre. "I'm coming to supper with you," he added in an undertone, not to interrupt the vicomte who was still talking. "Can I?"

"Oh no, impossible," said Prince Andrey, laughing, with a squeeze of his hand giving Pierre to understand that there was no need to ask. He would have said something more, but at that instant Prince Vassily and his daughter got up and the two young men rose to make way for them.

"Pardon me, my dear vicomte," said Prince Vassily in French, gently pulling him down by his sleeve to prevent him from getting up from his seat. "This luckless fête at the ambassador's deprives me of a pleasure and interrupts you. I am very sorry to leave your enchanting party," he said to Anna Pavlovna.

His daughter, Princess Ellen, lightly holding the folds of her gown passed between the chairs, and the smile glowed more brightly than ever on her handsome face. Pierre looked with rapturous, almost frightened eyes at this beautiful creature as she passed them.

"Very lovely!" said Prince Andrey.

"Very," said Pierre.

As he came up to them, Prince Vassily took Pierre by the arm, and addressing Anna Pavlovna:

"Get this bear into shape for me," he said. "Here he has been staying with me for a month, and this is the first time I have seen him in society. Nothing's so necessary for a young man as the society of clever women."

IV

Anna Pavlovna smiled and promised to look after Pierre, who was, she knew, related to Prince Vassily on his father's side. The elderly lady, who had been till then sitting by the aunt, got up hurriedly, and overtook Prince Vassily in the hall. All the affectation of interest she had assumed till now vanished. Her kindly, careworn face expressed nothing but anxiety and alarm.

"What have you to tell me, prince, of my Boris?" she said, catching him in the hall. "I can't stay any longer in Petersburg. Tell me what news am I to take to my poor boy?"

Although Prince Vassily listened reluctantly and almost uncivilly to the elderly lady and even showed signs of impatience, she gave him an ingratiating and appealing smile, and to prevent his going away she took him by the arm. "It is nothing for you to say a word to the Emperor, and he will be transferred at once to the Guards," she implored.

"Believe me, I will do all I can, princess," answered Prince Vassily; "but it's not easy for me to petition the Emperor. I should advise you to apply to Rumyantsov, through Prince Galitsin; that would be the wisest course."

The elderly lady was a Princess Drubetskoy, one of the best families in Russia; but she was poor, had been a long while out of society, and had lost touch with her former connections. She had come now to try and obtain the appointment of her only son to the Guards. It was simply in order to see Prince Vassily that she had invited herself and come to Anna Pavlovna's party, simply for that she had listened to the vicomte's story. She was dismayed at Prince Vassily's words; her once handsome face showed exasperation, but that lasted only one moment. She smiled again and grasped Prince Vassily's arm more tightly.

"Hear what I have to say, prince," she said. "I have never asked you a favour, and never will I ask one; I have never reminded you of my father's affection for you. But now, for God's sake, I beseech you, do this for my son, and I shall consider you my greatest benefactor," she added hurriedly. "No, don't be angry, but promise me. I have asked Galitsin; he has refused. Be as kind as you used to be," she said, trying to smile, though there were tears in her eyes.

"Papa, we are late," said Princess Ellen, turning her lovely head on her statuesque shoulders as she waited at the door.

But influence in the world is a capital, which must be carefully guarded if it is not to disappear. Prince Vassily knew this, and having once for all reflected that if he were to beg for all who begged him to do so, he would soon be unable to beg for himself, he rarely made use of his influence. In Princess Drubetskoy's case, however, he felt after her new appeal something akin to a conscience-prick. She had reminded him of the truth; for his first step upwards in the service he had been indebted to her father. Besides this, he saw from her manner that she was one of those women—especially mothers—who having once taken an idea into their heads will not give it up till their wishes are fulfilled, and till then are prepared for daily, hourly persistence, and even for scenes. This last consideration made him waver.

"*Chère* Anna Mihalovna," he said, with his invariable familiarity and boredom in his voice, "it's almost impossible for me to do what you wish; but to show you my devotion to you, and my reverence for your dear father's memory, I will do the impossible—your son shall be transferred to the Guards; here is my hand on it. Are you satisfied?"

"My dear prince, you are our benefactor. I expected nothing less indeed; I know how good you are——" He tried to get away. "Wait a moment, one word. Once in the Guards . . ." She hesitated. "You are on friendly terms with Mihail Ilarianovitch Kutuzov, recommend Boris as his adjutant. Then my heart will be set at rest, then indeed . . ."

Prince Vassily smiled. "That I can't promise. You don't know how Kutuzov has been besieged ever since he has been appointed commander-in-chief. He told me himself that all the Moscow ladies were in league together to give him all their offspring as adjutants."

"No, promise me; I can't let you off, kind, good friend, benefactor . . ."

"Papa," repeated the beauty in the same tone, "we are late."

"Come, *au revoir,* good-bye. You see how it is."

"To-morrow then you will speak to the Emperor?"

"Certainly; but about Kutuzov I can't promise."

"Yes; do promise, promise, *Basile,*" Anna Mihalovna said, pursuing him with the smile of a coquettish girl, once perhaps characteristic, but now utterly incongruous with her careworn face. Evidently she had forgotten her age and from habit was bringing out every feminine resource. But as soon as he had gone out her face assumed once more the frigid, artificial expression it had worn all the evening. She went back to the group in which the vicomte was still talking, and again affected to be listening, waiting for the suitable moment to get away, now that her object had been attained.

"And what do you think of this latest farce of the coronation at Milan?" said Anna Pavlovna. "And the new comedy of the people of Lucca and Genoa coming to present their petitions to Monsieur Buonaparte. Monsieur Buonaparte sitting on a throne and granting the petitions of nations! Adorable! Why, it is enough to drive one out of one's senses! It seems as though the whole world had lost its head."

Prince Andrey smiled sarcastically, looking straight into Anna Pavlovna's face.

"God gives it me; let man beware of touching it," he said (Bonaparte's words uttered at the coronation). "They say that he was very fine as he spoke those words," he added, and he repeated the same words in Italian: *"Dio me l'ha data, e quai a chi la tocca."*

"I hope that at last," pursued Anna Pavlovna, "this has been the drop of water that will make the glass run over. The sovereigns cannot continue to endure this man who is a threat to everything."

"The sovereigns! I am not speaking of Russia," said the vicomte, deferentially and hopelessly. "The sovereigns! . . . Madame! What did they do for Louis the Sixteenth, for the queen, for Madame Elisabeth? Nothing," he went on with more animation; "and believe me, they are undergoing the punishment of their treason to the Bourbon cause. The sovereigns! . . . They are sending ambassadors to congratulate the usurper."

And with a scornful sigh he shifted his attitude again. Prince Ippolit, who had for a long time been staring through his eyeglass at the vicomte, at these words suddenly turned completely round, and bending over the little princess asked her for a needle, and began showing her the coat-of-arms of the Condé family, scratching it with the needle on the table. He explained the coat-of-arms with an air of gravity, as though the princess had asked him about it. "Staff, gules; engrailed with gules of azure—house of Condé," he said. The princess listened smiling.

"If Bonaparte remains another year on the throne of France," resumed the vicomte, with the air of a man who, being better acquainted with the subject than any one else, pursues his own train of thought without listening to other people, "things will have gone too far. By intrigue and violence, by exiles and executions, French society—I mean good society—will have been destroyed for ever, and then . . ."

He shrugged his shoulders, and made a despairing gesture with his hand. Pierre wanted to say something—the conversation interested him—but Anna Pavlovna, who was keeping her eye on him, interposed.

"And the Emperor Alexander," she said with the pathetic note that always accompanied all her references to the imperial family, "has declared his intention of leaving it to the French themselves to choose their own form of government. And I imagine there is no doubt that the whole nation, delivered from the usurper, would fling itself into the arms of its lawful king," said Anna Pavlovna, trying to be agreeable to an *émigré* and loyalist.

"That's not certain," said Prince Andrey. "*M. le vicomte* is quite right in supposing that things have gone too far by now. I imagine it would not be easy to return to the old régime."

"As far as I could hear," Pierre, blushing, again interposed in the conversation, "almost all the nobility have gone over to Bonaparte."

"That's what the Bonapartists assert," said the vicomte without looking at Pierre. "It's a difficult matter now to find out what public opinion is in France."

"Bonaparte said so," observed Prince Andrey with a sarcastic smile. It was evident that he did not like the vicomte, and that though he was not looking at him, he was directing his remarks against him.

"'I showed them the path of glory; they would not take it,'" he said after a brief pause, again quoting Napoleon's words. "'I opened my anterooms to them; they crowded in.' . . . I do not know in what degree he had a right to say so."

"None!" retorted the vicomte. "Since the duc's murder even his warmest partisans have ceased to regard him as a hero. If indeed some people made a hero of him," said the vicomte addressing Anna Pavlovna, "since the duke's assassination there has been a martyr more in heaven, and a hero less on earth."

Anna Pavlovna and the rest of the company hardly had time to smile their appreciation of the vicomte's words, when Pierre again broke into the conversation, and though Anna Pavlovna had a foreboding he would say something inappropriate, this time she was unable to stop him.

"The execution of the duc d'Enghien," said Monsieur Pierre, "was a political necessity, and I consider it a proof of greatness of soul that Napoleon did not hesitate to take the whole responsibility of it upon himself."

"*Dieu! mon Dieu!*" moaned Anna Pavlovna, in a terrified whisper.

"What, Monsieur Pierre! you think assassination is greatness of soul?" said the little princess, smiling and moving her work nearer to her.

"Ah! oh!" cried different voices.

"Capital!" Prince Ippolit said in English, and he began slapping his knee. The vicomte merely shrugged his shoulders.

Pierre looked solemnly over his spectacles at his audience.

"I say so," he pursued desperately, "because the Bourbons ran away from the Revolution, leaving the people to anarchy; and Napoleon alone was capable of understanding the Revolution, of overcoming it, and so for the public good he could not stop short at the life of one man."

"Won't you come over to this table?" said Anna Pavlovna. But Pierre went on without answering her.

"Yes," he said, getting more and more eager, "Napoleon is great because he has towered above the Revolution, and subdued its evil tendencies, preserving all that was good—the equality of all citizens, and freedom of speech and of the press, and only to that end has he possessed himself of supreme power."

"Yes, if on obtaining power he had surrendered it to the lawful king, instead of making use of it to commit murder," said the vicomte, "then I might have called him a great man."

"He could not have done that. The people gave him power simply for him to rid them of the Bourbons, and that was just why the people believed him to be a great man. The Revolution was a grand fact," pursued Monsieur Pierre, betraying by this desperate and irrelevantly provocative statement his extreme youth and desire to give full expression to everything.

"Revolution and regicide a grand fact? . . . What next? . . . but won't you come to this table?" repeated Anna Pavlovna.

"*Contrat social,*" said the vicomte with a bland smile.

"I'm not speaking of regicide. I'm speaking of the idea."

"The idea of plunder, murder, and regicide!" an ironical voice put in.

"Those were extremes, of course; but the whole meaning of the Revolution did not lie in them, but in the rights of man, in emancipation from conventional ideas, in equality; and all these Napoleon has maintained in their full force."

"Liberty and equality," said the vicomte contemptuously, as though he had at last made up his mind to show this youth seriously all the folly of his assertions: "all high-sounding words, which have long since been debased. Who does not love liberty and equality? Our Saviour indeed preached liberty and equality. Have men been any happier since the Revolution? On the contrary. We wanted liberty, but Bonaparte has crushed it."

Prince Andrey looked with a smile first at Pierre, then at the vicomte, then at their hostess.

For the first minute Anna Pavlovna had, in spite of her social adroitness, been dismayed by Pierre's outbreak; but when she saw that the vicomte was not greatly discomposed by Pierre's sacrilegious utterances, and had convinced herself that it was impossible to suppress them, she rallied her forces and joined the vicomte in attacking the orator.

"*Mais, mon cher Monsieur Pierre,*" said Anna Pavlovna, "what have you to say for a great man who was capable of executing the duc—or simply any human being—guiltless and untried?"

"I should like to ask," said the vicomte, "how *monsieur* would explain the 18th of Brumaire? Was not that treachery?"

"It was a juggling trick, not at all like a great man's way of acting."

"And the wounded he killed in Africa?" said the little princess; "that was awful!" And she shrugged her shoulders.

"He's a plebeian, whatever you may say," said Prince Ippolit.

Monsieur Pierre did not know which to answer. He looked at them all and smiled. His smile was utterly unlike the half-smile of all the others. When he smiled, suddenly, instantaneously, his serious, even rather sullen, face vanished completely, and a quite different face appeared, childish, good-humoured, even rather stupid, that seemed to beg indulgence. The vicomte, who was seeing him for the first time, saw clearly that this Jacobin was by no means so formidable as his words. Every one was silent.

"How is he to answer every one at once?" said Prince Andrey. "Besides, in the actions of a statesman, one must distinguish between his acts as a private person and as a general or an emperor. So it seems to me."

"Yes, yes, of course," put in Pierre, delighted at the assistance that had come to support him.

"One must admit," pursued Prince Andrey, "that Napoleon as a man was great at the bridge of Arcola, or in the hospital at Jaffa, when he gave his hand to the plague-stricken, but . . . but there are other actions it would be hard to justify."

Prince Andrey, who obviously wished to relieve the awkwardness of Pierre's position, got up to go, and made a sign to his wife.

Suddenly Prince Ippolit got up, and with a wave of his hands stopped every one, and motioning to them to be seated, began:

"Ah, I heard a Moscow story to-day; I must entertain you with it. You will excuse me, vicomte, I must tell it in Russian. If not, the point of the story will be lost." And Prince Ippolit began speaking in Russian, using the sort of jargon Frenchmen speak after spending a year in Russia. Every one waited expectant; Prince Ippolit had so eagerly, so insistently called for the attention of all for his story.

"In Moscow there is a lady, *une dame.* And she is very stingy. She wanted to have two footmen behind her carriage. And very tall footmen. That was her taste. And she had a lady's maid, also very tall. She said . . ."

Here Prince Ippolit paused and pondered, apparently collecting his ideas with difficulty.

"She said . . . yes, she said: 'Girl,' to the lady's maid, 'put on *livrée,* and get up behind the carriage, to pay calls.' "

Here Prince Ippolit gave a loud guffaw, laughing long before any of his audience, which created an impression by no means flattering to him. Several persons, among them the elderly lady and Anna Pavlovna, did smile, however.

"She drove off. Suddenly there was a violent gust of wind. The girl lost her hat, and her long hair fell down . . ."

At this point he could not restrain himself, and began laughing violently, articulating in the middle of a loud guffaw, "And all the world knew . . ."

There the anecdote ended. Though no one could understand why he had told it, and why he had insisted on telling it in Russian, still Anna Pavlovna and several other people appreciated the social breeding of Prince Ippolit in so agreeably putting a close to the disagreeable and ill-bred outbreak of Monsieur Pierre. The conversation after this episode broke up into small talk of no interest concerning the last and the approaching ball, the theatre, and where and when one would meet so-and-so again.

F. SCOTT FITZGERALD

• The Ice Palace

The sunlight dripped over the house like golden paint over an art jar, and the freckling shadows here and there only intensified the rigor of the bath of light. The Butterworth and Larkin houses flanking were intrenched behind great stodgy trees; only the Happer house took the full sun, and all day long faced the dusty road-street with a tolerant kindly patience. This was the city of Tarleton in southernmost Georgia, September afternoon.

Up in her bedroom window Sally Carrol Happer rested her nineteen-year-old chin on a fifty-two-year-old sill and watched Clark Darrow's ancient Ford turn the corner. The car was hot—being partly metallic it retained all the heat it absorbed or evolved—and Clark Darrow sitting bolt upright at the wheel wore a pained, strained expression as though he considered himself a spare part, and rather likely to break. He laboriously crossed two dust ruts, the wheels squeeking indignantly at the encounter, and then with a terrifying expression he gave the steering-gear a final wrench and deposited self and car approximately in front of the Happer steps. There was a plaintive heaving sound, a death-rattle, followed by a short silence; and then the air was rent by a startling whistle.

Sally Carrol gazed down sleepily. She started to yawn, but finding this quite impossible unless she raised her chin from the window-sill, changed her

SOURCE. From *The Ice Palace* by F. Scott Fitzgerald. Copyright 1920, Curtis Publishing Company; renewal copyright 1948; copyright 1956, Francis S. Fitzgerald Lanahan. Reprinted with the permission of Charles Scribner's Sons, Publishers.

mind and continued silently to regard the car, whose owner sat brilliantly if perfunctorily at attention as he waited for an answer to his signal. After a moment the whistle once more split the dusty air.

"Good mawnin'."

With difficulty Clark twisted his tall body round and bent a distorted glance on the window.

" 'Tain't mawnin', Sally Carrol."

"Isn't it, sure enough?"

"What you doin'?"

"Eatin' 'n apple."

"Come on go swimmin'—want to?"

"Reckon so."

"How 'bout hurryin' up?"

"Sure enough."

Sally Carrol sighed voluminously and raised herself with profound inertia from the floor, where she had been occupied in alternately destroying parts of a green apple and painting paper dolls for her younger sister. She approached a mirror, regarded her expression with a pleased and pleasant languor, dabbed two spots of rouge on her lips and a grain of powder on her nose, and covered her bobbed corn-colored hair with a rose-littered sunbonnet. Then she kicked over the painting water, said, "Oh, damn!"—but let it lay—and left the room.

"How you, Clark?" she inquired a minute later as she slipped nimbly over the side of the car.

"Mighty fine, Sally Carrol."

"Where we go swimmin'?"

"Out to Walley's Pool. Told Marylyn we'd call by an' get her an' Joe Ewing."

Clark was dark and lean, and when on foot was rather inclined to stoop. His eyes were ominous and his expression somewhat petulant except when startlingly illuminated by one of his frequent smiles. Clark had "a income"—just enough to keep himself in ease and his car in gasoline—and he had spent the two years since he graduated from Georgia Tech in dozing round the lazy streets of his home town, discussing how he could best invest his capital for an immediate fortune.

Hanging round he found not at all difficult; a crowd of little girls had grown up beautifully, the amazing Sally Carrol foremost among them; and they enjoyed being swum with and danced with and made love to in the flower-filled summery evenings—and they all liked Clark immensely. When feminine company palled there were half a dozen other youths who were always just about to do something, and meanwhile were quite willing to join him in a few holes of golf, or a game of billiards, or the consumption of a quart of "hard yella licker." Every once in a while one of these contemporaries made a farewell round of calls before going up to New York or Philadelphia or Pittsburgh to go into business, but mostly they just stayed round in this languid paradise of dreamy skies and firefly evenings and noisy niggery street fairs—and especially of gracious, soft-voiced girls, who were brought up on memories instead of money.

The Ford having been excited into a sort of restless resentful life Clark and Sally Carrol rolled and rattled down Valley Avenue into Jefferson Street, where the dust road became a pavement; along opiate Millicent Place, where there were half a dozen prosperous, substantial mansions; and on into the downtown section. Driving was perilous here, for it was shopping time; the population idled casually across the streets and a drove of low-moaning oxen were being urged along in front of a placid street-car; even the shops seemed only yawning their doors and blinking their windows in the sunshine before retiring into a state of utter and finite coma.

"Sally Carrol," said Clark suddenly, "it a fact that you're engaged?"

She looked at him quickly.

"Where'd you hear that?"

"Sure enough, you engaged?"

" 'At's a nice question!"

"Girl told me you were engaged to a Yankee you met up in Asheville last summer."

Sally Carrol sighed.

"Never saw such an old town for rumors."

"Don't marry a Yankee, Sally Carrol. We need you round here." Sally Carrol was silent a moment.

"Clark," she demanded suddenly, "who on earth shall I marry?"

"I offer my services."

"Honey, you couldn't support a wife," she answered cheerfully. "Anyway, I know you too well to fall in love with you."

" 'At doesn't mean you ought to marry a Yankee," he persisted.

"S'pose I love him?"

He shook his head.

"You couldn't. He'd be a lot different from us, every way."

He broke off as he halted the car in front of a rambling, dilapidated house. Marylyn Wade and Joe Ewing appeared in the doorway.

" 'Lo, Sally Carrol."

"Hi!"

"How you-all?"

"Sally Carrol," demanded Marylyn as they started off again, "you engaged?"

"Lawdy, where'd all this start? Can't I look at a man 'thout everybody in town engagin' me to him?"

Clark stared straight in front of him at a bolt on the clattering windshield.

"Sally Carrol," he said with a curious intensity, "don't you like us?"

"What?"

"Us down here?"

"Why, Clark, you know I do. I adore all you boys."

"Then why you gettin' engaged to a Yankee?"

"Clark, I don't know. I'm not sure what I'll do, but—well, I want to go places and see people. I want my mind to grow. I want to live where things happen on a big scale."

"What you mean?"

"Oh, Clark, I love you, and I love Joe here, and Ben Arrot, and you-all, but you'll—you'll——"

"We'll all be failures?"

"Yes. I don't mean only money failures, but just sort of—of ineffectual and sad, and—oh, how can I tell you?"

"You mean because we stay here in Tarleton?"

"Yes, Clark; and because you like it and never want to change things or think or go ahead."

He nodded and she reached over and pressed his hand.

"Clark," she said softly, "I wouldn't change you for the world. You're sweet the way you are. The things that'll make you fail I'll love always—the living in the past, the lazy days and nights you have, and all your carelessness and generosity."

"But you're goin' away?"

"Yes—because I couldn't every marry you. You've a place in my heart no one else ever could have, but tied down here I'd get restless. I'd feel I was—wastin' myself. There's two sides to me, you see. There's the sleepy old side you love; an' there's a sort of energy—the feelin' that makes me do wild things. That's the part of me that may be useful somewhere, that'll last when I'm not beautiful any more."

She broke off with characteristic suddenness and sighed, "Oh, sweet cooky!" as her mood changed.

Half closing her eyes and tipping back her head till it rested on the seat-back she let the savory breeze fan her eyes and ripple the fluffy curls of her bobbed hair. They were in the country now, hurrying between tangled growths of bright-green coppice and grass and tall trees that sent sprays of foliage to hang a cool welcome over the road. Here and there they passed a battered Negro cabin, its oldest white-haired inhabitant smoking a corncob pipe beside the door, and half a dozen scantily clothed pickaninnies parading tattered dolls on the wild-grown grass in front. Farther out were lazy cotton-fields, where even the workers seemed intangible shadows lent by the sun to the earth, not for toil, but to while away some age-old tradition in the golden September fields. And round the drowsy picturesqueness, over the trees and shacks and muddy rivers, flowed the heat, never hostile, only comforting, like a great warm nourishing bosom for the infant earth.

"Sally Carrol, we're here!"

"Poor chile's soun' asleep."

"Honey, you dead at last outa sheer laziness?"

"Water, Sally Carrol! Cool water waitin' for you!"

Her eyes opened sleepily.

"Hi!" she murmured, smiling.

II

In November Harry Bellamy, tall, broad, and brisk, came down from his Northern city to spend four days. His intention was to settle a matter that had been hanging fire since he and Sally Carrol had met in Asheville, North Carolina, in midsummer. The settlement took only a quiet afternoon and an evening in front of a glowing open fire, for Harry Bellamy had everything she wanted; and, besides, she loved him—loved him with that side of her she kept especially for loving. Sally Carrol had several rather clearly defined sides.

On his last afternoon they walked, and she found their steps tending half-unconsciously toward one of her favorite haunts, the cemetery. When it came in sight, gray-white and golden-green under the cheerful late sun, she paused, irresolute, by the iron gate.

"Are you mournful by nature, Harry?" she asked with a faint smile.

"Mournful? Not I."

"Then let's go in here. It depresses some folks, but I like it."

They passed through the gateway and followed a path that led through a wavy valley of graves—dusty-gray and mouldy for the fifties; quaintly carved with flowers and jars for the seventies; ornate and hideous for the nineties, with fat marble cherubs lying in sodden sleep on stone pillows, and great impossible growths of nameless granite flowers. Occasionally they saw a kneeling figure with tributary flowers, but over most of the graves lay silence and withered leaves with only the fragrance that their own shadowy memories could waken in living minds.

They reached the top of a hill where they were fronted by a tall, round head-stone, freckled with dark spots of damp and half grown over with vines.

"Margery Lee," she read; "1844–1873. Wasn't she nice? She died when she was twenty-nine. Dear Margery Lee," she added softly. "Can't you see her, Harry?"

"Yes, Sally Carrol."

He felt a little hand insert itself into his.

"She was dark, I think; and she always wore her hair with a ribbon in it, and gorgeous hoop-skirts of alice blue and old rose."

"Yes."

"Oh, she was sweet, Harry! And she was the sort of girl born to stand on a wide, pillared porch and welcome folks in. I think perhaps a lot of men went away to war meanin' to come back to her; but maybe none of 'em ever did."

He stooped down close to the stone, hunting for any record of marriage.

"There's nothing here to show."

"Of course not. How could there be anything there better than just 'Margery Lee,' and that eloquent date?"

She drew close to him and an unexpected lump came into his throat as her yellow hair brushed his cheek.

"You see how she was, don't you, Harry?"

"I see," he agreed gently. "I see through your precious eyes. You're beautiful now, so I know she must have been."

Silent and close they stood, and he could feel her shoulders trembling a little. An ambling breeze swept up the hill and stirred the brim of her floppidy hat.

"Let's go down there!"

She was pointing to a flat stretch on the other side of the hill where along the green turf were a thousand grayish-white crosses stretching in endless, ordered rows like the stacked arms of a battalion.

"Those are the Confederate dead," said Sally Carrol simply.

They walked along and read the inscriptions, always only a name and a date, sometimes quite indecipherable.

"The last row is the saddest—see, 'way over there. Every cross has just a date on it, and the word 'Unknown.' "

She looked at him and her eyes brimmed with tears.

"I can't tell you how real it is to me, darling—if you don't know."

"How you feel about it is beautiful to me."

"No, no, it's not me, it's them—that old time that I've tried to have live in me. These were just men, unimportant evidently or they wouldn't have been 'unknown'; but they died for the most beautiful thing in the world—the dead South. You see," she continued, her voice still husky, her eyes glistening with tears, "people have these dreams they fasten onto things, and I've always grown up with that dream. It was so easy because it was all dead and there weren't any disillusions comin' to me. I've tried in a way to live up to those past standards of noblesse oblige—there's just the last remnants of it, you know, like the roses of an old garden dying all round us—streaks of strange courtliness and chivalry in some of these boys an' stories I used to hear from a Confederate soldier who lived next door, and a few old darkies. Oh, Harry, there was something, there was something! I couldn't ever make you understand, but it was there."

"I understand," he assured her again quietly.

Sally Carrol smiled and dried her eyes on the tip of a handkerchief protruding from his breast pocket.

"You don't feel depressed, do you, lover? Even when I cry I'm happy here, and I get a sort of strength from it."

Hand in hand they turned and walked slowly away. Finding soft grass she drew him down to a seat beside her with their backs against the remnants of a low broken wall.

"Wish those three old women would clear out," he complained. "I want to kiss you, Sally Carrol."

"Me, too."

They waited impatiently for the three bent figures to move off, and then she kissed him until the sky seemed to fade out and all her smiles and tears to vanish in an ecstasy of eternal seconds.

Afterward they walked slowly back together, while on the corners twilight played at somnolent black-and-white checkers with the end of day.

"You'll be up about mid-January," he said, "and you've got to stay a month at least. It'll be slick. There's a winter carnival on, and if you've never really seen snow it'll be like fairy-land to you. There'll be skating and skiing and tobogganing and sleigh-riding, and all sorts of torchlight parades on snow-shoes. They haven't had one for years, so they're going to make it a knock-out."

"Will I be cold, Harry?" she asked suddenly.

"You certainly won't. You may freeze your nose, but you won't be shivery cold. It's hard and dry, you know."

"I guess I'm a summer child. I don't like any cold I've ever seen."

She broke off and they were both silent for a minute.

"Sally Carrol," he said very slowly, "what do you say to—March?"

"I say I love you."

"March?"

"March, Harry."

III

All night in the Pullman it was very cold. She rang for the porter to ask for another blanket, and when he couldn't give her one she tried vainly, by squeezing down into the bottom of her berth and doubling back the bedclothes, to snatch a few hours' sleep. She wanted to look her best in the morning.

She rose at six and sliding uncomfortably into her clothes stumbled up to the diner for a cup of coffee. The snow had filtered into the vestibules and covered the floor with a slippery coating. It was intriguing, this cold, it crept in everywhere. Her breath was quite visible and she blew into the air with a naïve enjoyment. Seated in the diner she stared out the window at white hills and valleys and scattered pines whose every branch was a green platter for a cold feast of snow. Sometimes a solitary farmhouse would fly by, ugly and bleak and lone on the white waste; and with each one she had an instant of chill compassion for the souls shut in there waiting for spring.

As she left the diner and swayed back into the Pullman she experienced a surging rush of energy and wondered if she was feeling the bracing air of which Harry had spoken. This was the North, the North—her land now!

> "Then blow, ye winds, heigho!
> A-roving I will go,"

she chanted exultantly to herself.

"What's 'at?" inquired the porter politely.

"I said: 'Brush me off.' "

The long wires of the telegraph-poles doubled; two tracks ran up beside the train—three—four; came a succession of white-roofed houses, a glimpse of a trolley-car with frosted windows, streets—more streets—the city.

She stood for a dazed moment in the frosty station before she saw three fur-bundled figures descending upon her.

"There she is!"

"Oh, Sally Carrol!"

Sally Carrol dropped her bag.

"Hi!"

A faintly familiar icy-cold face kissed her, and then she was in a group of faces all apparently emitting great clouds of heavy smoke; she was shaking hands. There were Gordon, a short, eager man of thirty who looked like an amateur knocked-about model for Harry, and his wife, Myra, a listless lady with flaxen hair under a fur automobile cap. Almost immediately Sally Carrol thought of her as vaguely Scandinavian. A cheerful chauffeur adopted her bag, and amid ricochets of half-phrases, exclamations, and perfunctory listless "my dears" from Myra, they swept each other from the station.

Then they were in a sedan bound through a crooked succession of snowy streets where dozens of little boys were hitching sleds behind grocery wagons and automobiles.

"Oh," cried Sally Carrol, "I want to do that! Can we, Harry?"

"That's for kids. But we might——"

"It looks like such a circus!" she said regretfully.

Home was a rambling frame house set on a white lap of snow, and there she met a big, gray-haired man of whom she approved, and a lady who was like an egg, and who kissed her—these were Harry's parents. There was a breath-less indescribable hour crammed full of half-sentences, hot water, bacon and eggs and confusion; and after that she was alone with Harry in the library, asking him if she dared smoke.

It was a large room with a Madonna over the fireplace and rows upon rows of books in covers of light gold and dark gold and shiny red. All the chairs had little lace squares where one's head should rest, the couch was just comfortable, the books looked as if they had been read—some—and Sally Carrol had an in-stantaneous vision of the battered old library at home, with her father's huge medical books, and the oil-paintings of her three great-uncles, and the old couch that had been mended up for forty-five years and was still luxurious to dream in. This room struck her as being neither attractive nor particularly otherwise. It was simply a room with a lot of fairly expensive things in it that all looked about fifteen years old.

"What do you think of it up here?" demanded Harry eagerly. "Does it surprise you? Is it what you expected, I mean?"

"You are, Harry," she said quietly, and reached out her arms to him.

But after a brief kiss he seemed anxious to extort enthusiasm from her.

"The town, I mean. Do you like it? Can you feel the pep in the air?"

"Oh, Harry," she laughed, "you'll have to give me time. You can't just fling questions at me."

She puffed at her cigarette with a sigh of contentment.

"One thing I want to ask you," he began rather apologetically; "you South-erners put quite an emphasis on family, and all that—not that it isn't quite all right, but you'll find it a little different here. I mean—you'll notice a lot of things that'll seem to you sort of vulgar display at first, Sally Carrol; but just remember that this is a three-generation town. Everybody has a father, and about half of us have grandfathers. Back of that we don't go."

"Of course," she murmured.

"Our grandfathers, you see, founded the place, and a lot of them had to take some pretty queer jobs while they were doing the founding. For instance, there's one woman who at present is about the social model for the town; well, her father was the first public ash man—things like that."

"Why," said Sally Carrol, puzzled, "did you s'pose I was goin' to make remarks about people?"

"Not at all," interrupted Harry; "and I'm not apologizing for any one either. It's just that—well, a Southern girl came up here last summer and said some unfortunate things, and—oh, I just thought I'd tell you."

Sally Carrol felt suddenly indignant—as though she had been unjustly spanked—but Harry evidently considered the subject closed, for he went on with a great surge of enthusiasm.

"It's carnival time, you know. First in ten years. And there's an ice palace they're building now that's the first they've had since eighty-five. Built out of blocks of the clearest ice they could find—on a tremendous scale."

She rose and walking to the window pushed aside the heavy Turkish portières and looked out.

"Oh!" she cried suddenly. "There's two little boys makin' a snow man! Harry, do you reckon I can go out an' help 'em?"

"You dream! Come here and kiss me."

She left the window rather reluctantly.

"I don't guess this is a very kissable climate, is it? I mean, it makes you so you don't want to sit round, doesn't it?"

"We're not going to. I've got a vacation for the first week you're here, and there's a dinner-dance to-night."

"Oh, Harry," she confessed, subsiding in a heap, half in his lap, half in the pillows, "I sure do feel confused. I haven't got an idea whether I'll like it or not, an' I don't know what people expect, or anythin'. You'll have to tell me, honey."

"I'll tell you," he said softly, "if you'll just tell me you're glad to be here."

"Glad—just awful glad!" she whispered, insinuating herself into his arms in her own peculiar way. "Where you are is home for me, Harry."

And as she said this she had the feeling for almost the first time in her life that she was acting a part.

That night, amid the gleaming candles of a dinner-party, where the men seemed to do most of the talking while the girls sat in a haughty and expensive aloofness, even Harry's presence on her left failed to make her feel at home.

"They're a good-looking crowd, don't you think?" he demanded. "Just look round. There's Spud Hubbard, tackle at Princeton last year, and Junie Morton—he and the red-haired fellow next to him were both Yale hockey captains; Junie was in my class. Why, the best athletes in the world come from these States round here. This is a man's country, I tell you. Look at John J. Fishburn!"

"Who's he?" asked Sally Carrol innocently.

"Don't you know?"

"I've heard the name."

"Greatest wheat man in the Northwest, and one of the greatest financiers in the country."

She turned suddenly to a voice on her right.

"I guess they forgot to introduce us. My name's Roger Patton."

"My name is Sally Carrol Happer," she said graciously.

"Yes, I know. Harry told me you were coming."

"You a relative?"

"No, I'm a professor."

"Oh," she laughed.

"At the university. You're from the South, aren't you?"

"Yes; Tarleton, Georgia."

She liked him immediately—a reddish-brown mustache under watery blue eyes that had something in them that these other eyes lacked, some quality of appreciation. They exchanged stray sentences through dinner, and she made up her mind to see him again.

After coffee she was introduced to numerous good-looking young men who danced with conscious precision and seemed to take it for granted that she wanted to talk about nothing except Harry.

"Heavens," she thought, "they talk as if my being engaged made me older than they are—as if I'd tell their mothers on them!"

In the South an engaged girl, even a young married woman, expected the same amount of half-affectionate badinage and flattery that would be accorded a débutante, but here all that seemed banned. One young man, after getting well started on the subject of Sally Carrol's eyes, and how they had allured him ever since she entered the room, went into a violent confusion when he found she was visiting the Bellamys—was Harry's fiancée. He seemed to feel as though he had made some risqué and inexcusable blunder, became immediately formal, and left her at the first opportunity.

She was rather glad when Roger Patton cut in on her and suggested that they sit out a while.

"Well," he inquired, blinking cheerily, "how's Carmen from the South?"

"Mighty fine. How's—how's Dangerous Dan McGrew? Sorry, but he's the only Northerner I know much about."

He seemed to enjoy that.

"Of course," he confessed, "as a professor of literature I'm not supposed to have read Dangerous Dan McGrew."

"Are you a native?"

"No, I'm a Philadelphian. Imported from Harvard to teach French. But I've been here ten years."

"Nine years, three hundred an' sixty-four days longer than me."

"Like it here?"

"Uh-huh. Sure do!"

"Really?"

"Well, why not? Don't I look as if I were havin' a good time?"

"I saw you look out the window a minute ago—and shiver."

"Just my imagination," laughed Sally Carrol. "I'm used to havin' everythin' quiet outside, an' sometimes I look out an' see a flurry of snow, an' it's just as if somethin' dead was movin'."

He nodded appreciatively.

"Ever been North before?"

"Spent two Julys in Asheville, North Carolina."

"Nice-looking crowd, aren't they?" suggested Patton, indicating the swirling floor.

Sally Carrol started. This had been Harry's remark.

"Sure are! They're—canine."

"What?"

She flushed.

"I'm sorry; that sounded worse than I meant it. You see I always think of people as feline or canine, irrespective of sex."

"Which are you?"

"I'm feline. So are you. So are most Southern men an' most of these girls here."

"What's Harry?"

"Harry's canine distinctly. All the men I've met to-night seem to be canine."

"What does 'canine' imply? A certain conscious masculinity as opposed to subtlety?"

"Reckon so. I never analyzed it—only I just look at people an' say 'canine' or 'feline' right off. It's right absurd, I guess."

"Not at all. I'm interested. I used to have a theory about these people. I think they're freezing up."

"What?"

"I think they're growing like Swedes—Ibsenesque, you know. Very gradually getting gloomy and melancholy. It's these long winters. Ever read any Ibsen?"

She shook her head.

"Well, you find in his characters a certain brooding rigidity. They're righteous, narrow, and cheerless, without infinite possibilities for great sorrow or joy."

"Without smiles or tears?"

"Exactly. That's my theory. You see there are thousands of Swedes up here. They come, I imagine, because the climate is very much like their own, and there's been a gradual mingling. There're probably not half a dozen here to-night, but—we've had four Swedish governors. Am I boring you?"

"I'm mighty interested."

"Your future sister-in-law is half Swedish. Personally I like her, but my theory is that Swedes react rather badly on us as a whole. Scandinavians, you know, have the largest suicide rate in the world."

"Why do you live here if it's so depressing?"

"Oh, it doesn't get me. I'm pretty well cloistered, and I suppose books mean more than people to me anyway."

"But writers all speak about the South being tragic. You know—Spanish señoritas, black hair and daggers an' haunting music."

He shook his head.

"No, the Northern races are the tragic races—they don't indulge in the cheering luxury of tears."

Sally Carrol thought of her graveyard. She supposed that that was vaguely what she had meant when she said it didn't depress her.

"The Italians are about the gayest people in the world—but it's a dull subject," he broke off. "Anyway, I want to tell you you're marrying a pretty fine man."

Sally Carrol was moved by an impulse of confidence.

"I know. I'm the sort of person who wants to be taken care of after a certain point, and I feel sure I will be."

"Shall we dance? You know," he continued as they rose, "it's encouraging to find a girl who knows what she's marrying for. Nine-tenths of them think of it as a sort of walking into a moving-picture sun-set."

She laughed, and liked him immensely.

Two hours later on the way home she nestled near Harry in the back seat.

"Oh, Harry," she whispered, "it's so co-old!"

"But it's warm in here, darling girl."

"But outside it's cold; and oh, that howling wind!"

She buried her face deep in his fur coat and trembled involuntarily as his cold lips kissed the tip of her ear.

IV

The first week of her visit passed in a whirl. She had her promised toboggan-ride at the back of an automobile through a chill January twilight. Swathed in furs she put in a morning tobogganing on the country-club hill; even tried skiing, to sail through the air for a glorious moment and then land in a tangled laughing bundle on a soft snowdrift. She liked all the winter sports, except an afternoon spent snowshoeing over a glaring plain under pale yellow sunshine, but she soon realized that these things were for children—that she was being humored and that the enjoyment round her was only a reflection of her own.

At first the Bellamy family puzzled her. The men were reliable and she liked them; to Mr. Bellamy especially, with his iron-gray hair and energetic dignity, she took an immediate fancy, once she found that he was born in Kentucky, this made of him a link between the old life and the new. But toward the women she felt a definite hostility. Myra, her future sister in law, seemed the essence of spiritless conventionality. Her conversation was so utterly devoid of personality that Sally Carrol, who came from a country where a certain amount of charm and assurance could be taken for granted in the women, was inclined to despise her.

"If those women aren't beautiful," she thought, "they're nothing. They just fade out when you look at them. They're glorified domestics. Men are the centre of every mixed group."

Lastly there was Mrs. Bellamy, whom Sally Carrol detested. The first day's impression of an egg had been confirmed—an egg with a cracked, veiny voice and such an ungracious dumpiness of carriage that Sally Carrol felt that if she once fell she would surely scramble. In addition, Mrs. Bellamy seemed to typify the town in being innately hostile to strangers. She called Sally Carrol "Sally," and could not be persuaded that the double name was anything more than a tedious ridiculous nickname. To Sally Carrol this shortening of her name was like presenting her to the public half clothed. She loved "Sally Carrol"; she loathed "Sally." She knew also that Harry's mother disapproved of her bobbed hair; and she had never dared smoke down-stairs after that first day when Mrs. Bellamy had come into the library sniffing violently.

Of all the men she met she preferred Roger Patton, who was a frequent visitor at the house. He never again alluded to the Ibsenesque tendency of the populace, but when he came in one day and found her curled upon the sofa bent over "Peer Gynt" he laughed and told her to forget what he'd said—that it was all rot.

And then one afternoon in her second week she and Harry hovered on the edge of a dangerously steep quarrel. She considered that he precipitated it entirely, though the Serbia in the case was an unknown man who had not had his trousers pressed.

They had been walking homeward between mounds of high-piled snow and under a sun which Sally Carrol scarcely recognized. They passed a little girl done up in gray wool until she resembled a small Teddy bear, and Sally Carrol could not resist a gasp of maternal appreciation.

"Look! Harry!"

"What?"

"That little girl—did you see her face?"

"Yes, why?"

"It was red as a little strawberry. Oh, she was cute!"

"Why, your own face is almost as red as that already! Everybody's healthy here. We're out in the cold as soon as we're old enough to walk. Wonderful climate!"

She looked at him and had to agree. He was mighty healthy-looking; so was his brother. And she had noticed the new red in her own cheeks that very morning.

Suddenly their glances were caught and held, and they stared for a moment at the street-corner ahead of them. A man was standing there, his knees bent, his eyes gazing upward with a tense expression as though he were about to make a leap toward the chilly sky. And then they both exploded into a shout of laughter, for coming closer they discovered it had been a ludicrous momentary illusion produced by the extreme bagginess of the man's trousers.

"Reckon that's one on us," she laughed.

"He must be a Southerner, judging by those trousers," suggested Harry mischievously.

"Why, Harry!"

Her surprised look must have irritated him.

"Those damn Southerners!"

Sally Carrol's eyes flashed.

"Don't call 'em that!"

"I'm sorry, dear," said Harry, malignantly apologetic, "but you know what I think of them. They're sort of—sort of degenerates—not at all like the old Southerners. They've lived so long down there with all the colored people that they've gotten lazy and shiftless."

"Hush your mouth, Harry!" she cried angrily. "They're not! They may be lazy—anybody would be in that climate—but they're my best friends, an' I don't want to hear 'em criticised in any such sweepin' way. Some of 'em are the finest men in the world."

"Oh, I know. They're all right when they come North to college, but of all the hangdog, ill-dressed, slovenly lot I ever saw, a bunch of small-town Southerners are the worst!"

Sally Carrol was clinching her gloved hands and biting her lip furiously.

"Why," continued Harry, "there was one in my class at New Haven, and we all thought that at last we'd found the true type of Southern aristocrat, but it turned out that he wasn't an aristocrat at all—just the son of a Northern carpetbagger, who owned about all the cotton round Mobile."

"A Southerner wouldn't talk the way you're talking now," she said evenly.

"They haven't the energy!"

"Or the somethin' else."

"I'm sorry, Sally Carrol, but I've heard you say yourself that you'd never marry——"

"That's quite different. I told you I wouldn't want to tie my life to any of the boys that are round Tarleton now, but I never made any sweepin' gen-eralities."

They walked along in silence.

"I probably spread it on a bit thick, Sally Carrol. I'm sorry."

She nodded but made no answer. Five minutes later as they stood in the hallway she suddenly threw her arms round him.

"Oh, Harry," she cried, her eyes brimming with tears, "let's get married next week. I'm afraid of having fusses like that. I'm afraid, Harry. It wouldn't be that way if we were married."

But Harry, being in the wrong, was still irritated.

"That'd be idiotic. We decided on March."

The tears in Sally Carrol's eyes faded; her expression hardened slightly.

"Very well—I suppose I shouldn't have said that."

Harry melted.

"Dear little nut!" he cried. "Come and kiss me and let's forget."

That very night at the end of a vaudeville performance the orchestra played "Dixie" and Sally Carrol felt something stronger and more enduring than her tears and smiles of the day brim up inside her. She leaned forward gripping the arms of her chair until her face grew crimson.

"Sort of get you, dear?" whispered Harry.

But she did not hear him. To the spirited throb of the violins and the inspiring beat of the kettledrums her own old ghosts were marching by and on into the darkness, and as fifes whistled and sighed in the low encore they seemed so nearly out of sight that she could have waved good-by.

> "Away, away,
> Away down South in Dixie!
> Away, away,
> Away down South in Dixie!"

V

It was a particularly cold night. A sudden thaw had nearly cleared the streets the day before, but now they were traversed again with a powdery wraith of loose snow that travelled in wavy lines before the feet of the wind, and filled the lower air with a fine-particled mist. There was no sky—only a dark, ominous tent that draped in the tops of the streets and was in reality a vast approaching army of snowflakes—while over it all, chilling away the comfort from the brown-and-green glow of lighted windows and muffling the steady trot of the horse pulling their sleigh, interminably washed the north wind. It was a dismal town after all, she thought—dismal.

Sometimes at night it had seemed to her as though no one lived here—they had all gone long ago—leaving lighted houses to be covered in time by tombing heaps of sleet. Oh, if there should be snow on her grave! To be beneath great piles of it all winter long, where even her headstone would be a light shadow against light shadows. Her grave—a grave that should be flower-strewn and washed with sun and rain.

She thought again of those isolated country houses that her train had passed, and of the life there the long winter through—the ceaseless glare through the windows, the crust forming on the soft drifts of snow, finally the slow, cheerless melting, and the harsh spring of which Roger Patton had told her. Her spring—to lose it forever—with its lilacs and the lazy sweetness it stirred in her heart. She was laying away that spring—afterward she would lay away that sweetness.

With a gradual insistence the storm broke. Sally Carrol felt a film of flakes melt quickly on her eyelashes, and Harry reached over a furry arm and drew down her complicated flannel cap. Then the small flakes came in skirmish-line, and the horse bent his neck patiently as a transparency of white appeared momentarily on his coat.

"Oh, he's cold, Harry," she said quickly.

"Who? The horse? Oh, no, he isn't. He likes it!"

After another ten minutes they turned a corner and came in sight of their destination. On a tall hill outlined in vivid glaring green against the wintry sky stood the ice palace. It was three stories in the air, with battlements and embrasures and narrow icicled windows, and the innumerable electric lights inside make a gorgeous transparency of the great central hall. Sally Carrol clutched Harry's hand under the fur robe.

"It's beautiful!" he cried excitedly. "My golly, it's beautiful, isn't it! They haven't had one here since eighty-five!"

Somehow the notion of there not having been one since eighty-five oppressed her. Ice was a ghost, and this mansion of it was surely peopled by those shades of the eighties, with pale faces and blurred snow-filled hair.

"Come on, dear," said Harry.

She followed him out of the sleigh and waited while he hitched the horse. A party of four—Gordon, Myra, Roger Patton, and another girl—drew up beside them with a mighty jingle of bells. There were quite a crowd already, bundled in fur or sheepskin, shouting and calling to each other as they moved through the snow, which was now so thick that people could scarcely be distinguished a few yards away.

"It's a hundred and seventy feet tall," Harry was saying to a muffled figure beside him as they trudged toward the entrance; "covers six thousand square yards."

She caught snatches of conversation: "One main hall"—"walls twenty to forty inches thick"—"and the ice cave has almost a mile of—"—"this Canuck who built it——"

They found their way inside, and dazed by the magic of the great crystal walls Sally Carrol found herself repeating over and over two lines from "Kubla Khan":

> "It was a miracle of rare device,
> A sunny pleasure-dome with caves of ice!"

In the great glittering cavern with the dark shut out she took a seat on a wooden bench, and the evening's oppression lifted. Harry was right—it was beautiful; and her gaze travelled the smooth surface of the walls, the blocks for which had been selected for their purity and clearness to obtain this opalescent, translucent effect.

"Look! Here we go—oh, boy!" cried Harry.

A band in a far corner struck up "Hail, Hail, the Gang's All Here!" which echoed over to them in mild muddled acoustics, and then the lights suddenly went out; silence seemed to flow down the icy sides and sweep over them. Sally Carrol could still see her white breath in the darkness, and a dim row of pale faces over on the other side.

The music eased to a sighing complaint, and from outside drifted in the full throated resonant chant of the marching clubs. It grew louder like some pæan of a viking tribe traversing an ancient wild; it swelled—they were coming nearer; then a row of torches appeared, and another and another, and keeping time with their moccasined feet a long column of gray-mackinawed figures swept in, snowshoes slung at their shoulders, torches soaring and flickering as their voices rose along the great walls.

The gray column ended and another followed, the light streaming luridly this time over red toboggan caps and flaming crimson mackinaws, and as they entered they took up the refrain; then came a long platoon of blue and white, of green, of white, of brown and yellow.

"Those white ones are the Wacouta Club," whispered Harry eagerly. "Those are the men you've met round at dances."

The volume of the voices grew; the great cavern was a phantasmagoria of torches waving in great banks of fire, of colors and the rhythm of soft-leather steps. The leading column turned and halted, platoon deployed in front of platoon until the whole procession made a solid flag of flame, and then from thousands of voices burst a mighty shout that filled the air like a crash of thunder, and sent the torches wavering. It was magnificent, it was tremendous! To Sally Carrol it was the North offering sacrifice on some mighty altar to the gray pagan God of Snow. As the shout died the band struck up again and there came more singing, and then long reverberating cheers by each club. She sat very quiet listening while the staccato cries rent the stillness; and then she started, for there was a volley of explosion, and great clouds of smoke went up here and there through the cavern—the flash-light photographers at work—and the council was over. With the band at their head the clubs formed in column once more, took up their chant, and began to march out.

"Come on!" shouted Harry. "We want to see the labyrinths downstairs before they turn the lights off!"

They all rose and started toward the chute—Harry and Sally Carrol in the lead, her little mitten buried in his big fur gantlet. At the bottom of the chute was a long empty room of ice, with the ceiling so low that they had to stoop— and their hands were parted. Before she realized what he intended Harry had darted down one of the half-dozen glittering passages that opened into the room and was only a vague receding blot against the green shimmer.

"Harry!" she called.

"Come on!" he cried back.

She looked round the empty chamber; the rest of the party had evidently decided to go home, were already outside somewhere in the blundering snow. She hesitated and then darted in after Harry.

"Harry!" she shouted.

She had reached a turning-point thirty feet down; she heard a faint muffled answer far to the left, and with a touch of panic fled toward it. She passed another turning, two more yawning alleys.

"Harry!"

No answer. She started to run straight forward, and then turned like lightning and sped back the way she had come, enveloped in a sudden icy terror.

She reached a turn—was it here?—took the left and came to what should have been the outlet into the long, low room, but it was only another glittering passage with darkness at the end. She called again but the walls gave back a flat, lifeless echo with no reverberations. Retracing her steps she turned another corner, this time following a wide passage. It was like the green lane between the parted waters of the Red Sea, like a damp vault connecting empty tombs.

She slipped a little now as she walked, for ice had formed on the bottom of her overshoes; she had to run her gloves along the half-slippery, half-sticky walls to keep her balance.

"Harry!"

Still no answer. The sound she made bounced mockingly down to the end of the passage.

Then on an instant the lights went out, and she was in complete darkness. She gave a small, frightened cry, and sank down into a cold little heap on the ice. She felt her left knee do something as she fell, but she scarcely noticed it as some deep terror far greater than any fear of being lost settled upon her. She was alone with this presence that came out of the North, the dreary loneliness that rose from ice-bound whalers in the Arctic seas, from smokeless, trackless wastes where were strewn the whitened bones of adventure. It was an icy breath of death; it was rolling down low across the land to clutch at her.

With a furious, despairing energy she rose again and started blindly down the darkness. She must get out. She might be lost in here for days, freeze to death and lie embedded in the ice like corpses she had read of, kept perfectly preserved until the melting of a glacier. Harry probably thought she had left with the others—he had gone by now; no one would know until late next day. She reached pitifully for the wall. Forty inches thick, they had said—forty inches thick!

"Oh!"

On both sides of her along the walls she felt things creeping, damp souls that haunted this palace, this town, this North.

"Oh, send somebody—send somebody!" she cried aloud.

Clark Darrow—he would understand; or Joe Ewing; she couldn't be left here to wander forever—to be frozen, heart, body, and soul. This her—this Sally Carrol! Why, she was a happy thing. She was a happy little girl. She liked warmth and summer and Dixie. These things were foreign—foreign.

"You're not crying," something said aloud. "You'll never cry any more. Your tears would just freeze; all tears freeze up here!"

She sprawled full length on the ice.

"Oh, God!" she faltered.

A long single file of minutes went by, and with a great weariness she felt her eyes closing. Then some one seemed to sit down near her and take her face in warm, soft hands. She looked up gratefully.

"Why, it's Margery Lee," she crooned softly to herself. "I knew you'd come." It really was Margery Lee, and she was just as Sally Carrol had known she would be, with a young, white brow, and wide, welcoming eyes, and a hoop-skirt of some soft material that was quite comforting to rest on.

"Margery Lee."

It was getting darker now and darker—all those tombstones ought to be repainted, sure enough, only that would spoil 'em, of course. Still, you ought to be able to see 'em.

Then after a succession of moments that went fast and then slow, but seemed to be ultimately resolving themselves into a multitude of blurred rays converging toward a pale-yellow sun, she heard a great cracking noise break her new-found stillness.

It was the sun, it was a light; a torch, and a torch beyond that, and another one, and voices; a face took flesh below the torch, heavy arms raised her, and she felt something on her cheek—it felt wet. Some one had seized her and was rubbing her face with snow. How ridiculous—with snow!

"Sally Carrol! Sally Carrol!"

It was Dangerous Dan McGrew; and two other faces she didn't know.

"Child, child! We've been looking for you for two hours! Harry's half-crazy!"

Things came rushing back into place—the singing, the torches, the great shout of the marching clubs. She squirmed in Patton's arms and gave a long low cry.

"Oh, I want to get out of here! I'm going back home. Take me home"—her voice rose to a scream that sent a chill to Harry's heart as he came racing down the next passage—"to-morrow!" she cried with delirious, unrestrained passion—"To-morrow! To-morrow! To-morrow!"

VI

The wealth of golden sunlight poured a quite enervating yet oddly comforting heat over the house where day long it faced the dusty stretch of road. Two birds were making a great to-do in a cool spot found among the branches of a tree next door, and down the street a colored woman was announcing herself melodiously as a purveyor of strawberries. It was April afternoon.

Sally Carrol Happer, resting her chin on her arm, and her arm on an old window-seat gazed sleepily down over the spangled dust whence the heat waves were rising for the first time this spring. She was watching a very ancient Ford turn a perilous corner and rattle and groan to a jolting stop at the end of the walk. She made no sound, and in a minute a strident familiar whistle rent the air. Sally Carrol smiled and blinked.

"Good mawnin'."

A head appeared tortuously from under the car-top below.

" 'Tain't mawnin', Sally Carrol."

"Sure enough!" she said in affected surprise. "I guess maybe not."

"What you doin'?"

"Eatin' green peach. 'Spect to die any minute."

Clark twisted himself a last impossible notch to get a view of her face.

"Water's warm as a kettla steam, Sally Carrol. Wanta go swimmin'?"

"Hate to move," sighed Sally Carrol lazily, "but I reckon so."

Chapter 6

Reference Group

GUSTAVE FLAUBERT

• Madame Bovary

VI

She had read *Paul and Virginia* and dreamed about the bamboo cottage, the Negro Domingo, and the dog Fidèle, but most of all about the sweet friendship of some dear little brother who gathers ripe fruit for you in huge trees taller than steeples or who runs barefoot over the sand, bringing you a bird's nest.

When she was thirteen, her father took her to the city to enter her in the convent. They stopped at an inn in the Saint-Gervais section, where they were served their supper on painted dishes depicting Mademoiselle de La Vallière's story. The explanatory legends, interrupted in several places by knife scratches, accorded equal glory to religion, the delicacy of the heart, and courtly pomp.

Far from being bored in the convent, she was happy at first in the company of the kind sisters who, to amuse her, would take her into the chapel, which was connected to the refectory by a long corridor. She played very little during recess periods and understood the catechism well; and it was she who always answered the vicar's difficult questions. Living thus, without ever leaving the drowsy atmosphere of the classroom and among these white-faced women wearing rosaries with copper crosses, she succumbed peacefully to the mystic languor emanating from the fragrances of the altar, from the freshness of the font and the glow of

SOURCE. From *Madame Bovary* by Gustave Flaubert. Translated by Mildred Marmur. Copyright 1964, New American Library.

the candles. Instead of following the Mass, she looked at the pious vignettes edged in azure in her book, and she loved the sick lamb, the Sacred Heart pierced with sharp arrows, and poor Jesus stumbling as He walked under His cross. She tried to fast one entire day to mortify her soul. She attempted to think of some vow to fulfill.

When she went to confession, she would invent trivial sins in order to prolong her stay there, on her knees in the shadow, hands clasped, her face at the grill as the priest whispered above her. The references to fiancé, husband, heavenly lover, and eternal marriage that recur in sermons awakened unexpected joys within her.

In the evening, before prayers, some religious selection would be read at study. During the week it was a summary of Abbé Frayssinous's religious-history lectures and on Sunday, for relaxation, passages from *le Génie du Christianisme*. How she listened, those first times, to the sonorous lamentation of romantic melancholy being echoed throughout the world and unto eternity! Had her childhood been spent in an apartment behind a store in some business district, she might have been receptive to nature's lyric effusions that ordinarily reach us only via the interpretations of writers. But she knew the countryside too well; she knew the lowing of the flocks, the milking, and the plowing. Accustomed to the calm life, she turned away from it toward excitement. She loved the sea only for its storms, and greenery only when it was scattered among ruins. She needed to derive immediate gratification from things and rejected as useless everything that did not supply this satisfaction. Her temperament was more sentimental than artistic. She sought emotions and not landscapes.

There was an old maid who came to the convent for one week every month to work in the laundry. Protected by the archbishop because she belonged to an old aristocratic family ruined during the Revolution, she ate in the refectory at the good sisters' table and would chat with them for a while after dinner before returning to her work. The girls would often steal out of class to visit her. She knew the romantic songs of the past century by heart and would sing them softly as she plied her needle. She told stories, brought in news of the outside world, ran errands in the city, and would secretly lend the older girls some novel that she always kept in the pocket of her apron, of which the good creature herself devoured long chapters between tasks. It was always love, lovers, mistresses, persecuted women fainting in solitary little houses, postilions expiring at every relay, horses killed on every page, gloomy forests, romantic woes, oaths, sobs, tears and kisses, small boats in the moonlight, nightingales in the groves, gentlemen brave as lions, gentle as lambs, impossibly virtuous, always well dressed, who wept copiously. For six months, at the age of fifteen, Emma soiled her hands with these dusty remains of old reading rooms. Later, with Walter Scott, she grew enamored of historic events, dreamed of traveling chests, guardrooms, and minstrels. She wished that she had lived in some old manor, like those long-waisted ladies of the manor who spent their days under the trefoil of pointed arches, elbows on the rampart and chin in hand, watching a cavalier with a white feather emerge from the horizon on a galloping black charger. During that period she had a passion for Mary Stuart and adored unfortunate or celebrated women. Joan of Arc, Héloise, Agnès Sorel, La Belle Ferronnière, and Clémence Isaure blazed for her like comets over the murky immensity of history, on which, still standing out in relief, but more lost in the shadow and with no relationship to each other, were Saint Louis with his oak, the dying Bayard, a few vicious crimes of Louis XI, a bit of the Saint Bartholomew Massacre, Henri IV's plume, and the continuing memory of the painted plates praising Louis XIV.

In the ballads she sang in music class there were only tiny angels with golden wings, madonnas, lagoons, gondoliers—gentle compositions that enabled her to perceive, through the foolishness of the style and the weaknesses of the music, the attractive fantasy of sentimental realities. Several of her friends brought to the convent keepsake books they had received as gifts. They made a great to-do about hiding them. They would read them in the dormitory. Handling their lovely satin bindings delicately, Emma would focus her dazzled eyes on the names of the unknown authors, who usually signed their pieces "count" or "viscount." She would tremble as she breathed gently on the tissue paper covering the illustrations. It would lift in a double fold and then fall back gently against the page. Behind a balcony balustrade there would be a young man in a short coat holding tight in his arms a girl in a white dress with an alms purse on her sash, or anonymous portraits of English ladies with blond curls who looked at you with bright eyes from under their round straw hats. Some were relaxing in their carriages, gliding through parks while a greyhound jumped in front of the team being led at a trot by two small postilions in white breeches. Others, dreaming on sofas near an opened letter, were gazing at the moon through an open window half draped by a black curtain. The naïve ones were revealed with a tear on their cheek, feeding a turtledove through the bars of a Gothic cage or smiling, head to one side, and pulling daisy leaves with their tapered fingers, which curved like pointed slippers. And you were also there, you sultans with long pipes, swooning with delight in bowers in the arms of dancing girls! You giaours, Turkish sabers, fezzes! And you especially, pale landscapes of fabulous lands, which often show us at one and the same time palm trees and evergreens, tigers to the right, a lion to the left, Tartar minarets against the horizon, Roman ruins in the foreground, and camels crouching; the whole framed by a well-kept virgin forest with a large ray of perpendicular sunshine shimmering on the water upon which, like white gashes on a steel-gray background, swans are swimming into the distance.

And the lampshade, attached to the wall above Emma's head, shed light on all these tableaux of the world that passed before her one after the other in the silence of the dormitory to the sound of rumbles in the distance of some late fiacre still rolling down the boulevards.

She cried a great deal the first days after her mother's death. She had a memorial picture made with the dead woman's hair, and in a letter that she sent to Les Bertaux, all filled with sad reflections about life, she asked to be buried in the same tomb when she died. Her father thought she must be ill and came to see her. Emma was inwardly pleased to feel that she had achieved at her first attempt this rare ideal of pallid existences that mediocre hearts never achieve. She let herself glide into Lamartinian meanderings, listened to all the harps on the lake, to the songs of the dying swans, to all the falling leaves, the pure virgins rising to heaven, and the voice of the Eternal reverberating in the valleys. She tired of this, didn't want to admit it, continued first out of habit, then out of vanity, and was finally surprised to find herself soothed and with as little sadness in her heart as wrinkles on her forehead.

The good sisters, who had been so sure about her vocation, realized with great astonishment that Mademoiselle Rouault seemed to be eluding their influence. They had, in fact, lavished on her so many prayers, retreats, novenas, and sermons, had so well preached the veneration that is owed to saints and martyrs, and given so much good advice about bodily modesty and the salvation of her soul that she responded as do tightly reined horses; she stopped short and the bit slipped from her teeth. This temperament, positive in the midst of its enthusiasms, which had loved the church for its flowers, the music for the romantic lyrics, and literature for its passion-inspiring stimulation, rebelled before the mysteries of faith in proportion to her growing irritation against the discipline, which was antipathetic to her nature. When her father came to take her from the convent, they were not sorry to see her go. The Mother Superior even found that toward the end Emma had become quite irreverent toward the community.

Back home Emma amused herself at first by taking charge of the servants, then she began disliking the country and missed the convent. When Charles came to Les Bertaux for the first time, she felt quite disillusioned, having nothing more to learn, nothing more to feel.

But the uneasiness at a new role or perhaps the disturbance caused by the presence of this man, had been sufficient to make her believe that she finally felt that marvelous passion that until now had been like a huge pink-winged bird soaring through the splendor of poetic skies. She could not believe that the calm in which she was now living was the happiness of which she had dreamed.

VII

Yet sometimes she thought that these were the most beautiful days of her life—the honeymoon, as it was called. To savor its sweetness, it would have doubtless been necessary to go off to one of those sonorous-sounding countries where the first days of married life are languorously spent. Behind the blue silk shades of the mail coaches they would slowly climb up steep roads, listening to the song of the postilion being echoed through the mountain together with the sound of goat bells and the muffled roar of a waterfall. At sunset they would inhale the scent of the lemon trees by the shores of the gulfs; then, in the evening, on the terraces of the villas, alone, fingers intertwined, they would gaze at the stars and dream. She felt that certain places on the earth must produce happiness, just as a plant that languishes everywhere else thrives only in special soil. Why couldn't she be leaning her elbow on the balcony of a Swiss chalet or indulging her moods in a Scottish cottage with a husband dressed in a black velvet suit with long coattails, soft boots, a pointed hat, and elegant cuffs!

She might have wanted to confide all these things to someone. But how do you describe an intangible uneasiness that changes shape like a cloud and blows about like the wind? Words failed her—as well as the opportunity and the courage.

If Charles only suspected, if his gaze had even once penetrated her thought, it seemed to her that a sudden abundance would have broken away from her heart, as the fruit falls from a tree when you shake it. But as their life together brought increased physical intimacy, she built up an inner emotional detachment that separated her from him.

Charles's conversation was as flat as a sidewalk, with everyone's ideas walking through it in ordinary dress, arousing neither emotion, nor laughter, nor dreams. He had never been curious, he said, the whole time he was living in Rouen to go see a touring company of Paris actors at the theater. He couldn't swim, or fence, or shoot, and once he couldn't even explain to Emma a term about horseback riding she had come across in a novel.

But a man should know everything, shouldn't he? Excel in many activities, initiate you into the excitements of passion, into life's refinements, into all its mysteries? Yet this man taught nothing, knew nothing, hoped for nothing. He thought she was happy, and she was angry at him for this placid stolidity, for this leaden serenity, for the very happiness she gave to him.

Sometimes she would draw. Charles was always happy watching her lean over her drawing board, squinting in order to see her work better, or rolling little bread pellets between her fingers. As for the piano, the faster her fingers flew over it, the more he marveled. She struck the keys with aplomb and ran from one end of the keyboard to the other without a stop. The old instrument, with its frayed strings, could then be heard at the other end of the village if the window were open; and often the bailiff's clerk passing over the highway, bareheaded and in moccasins, would stop to listen to her, his sheet of paper in his hand.

On the other hand, Emma did know how to run the house. She sent patients statements of their visits in well-written letters that didn't look like bills. When some neighbor came to dine on Sundays, she managed to offer some tasty dish, would arrange handsome pyramids of greengages on vine leaves, serve fruit preserves on a dish, and even spoke of buying finger bowls for dessert. All this reflected favorably on Bovary.

Charles ended up by thinking all the more highly of himself for possessing such a wife. In the living room he pointed with pride to her two small pencil sketches that he had mounted in very large frames and hung against the wallpaper on long green cords. People returning from Mass would see him at his door wearing handsome needlepoint slippers.

He would come home late, at ten o'clock, sometimes at midnight. Then he would want something to eat, and Emma would serve him because the maid was asleep. He would remove his coat in order to eat more comfortably. He would report on all the people he had met one after the other, the villages he had been to, the prescriptions he had written, and, content with himself, would eat the remainder of the stew, peel his cheese, bite into an apple, empty the decanter, then go to sleep, lying on his back and snoring.

Since he had been accustomed for a long time to wearing a nightcap, his scarf would not stay put around his ears, and in the morning his hair was all disheveled about his face and whitened by the down from his pillow, the ties of which would become undone during the night. He always wore heavy boots, which had at the instep two thick folds slanting obliquely toward the ankles whereas the rest of the upper continued in a straight line, as taut as if stretched on a wooden leg. He said that it was "good enough for the country."

His mother approved his economy. She came to visit him as before, after some violent battle at her home. Yet, she seemed rather prejudiced against her daughter-in-law. She found her "a bit too haughty for their station in life"; wood, sugar, and candles were consumed "as if it were a great mansion" and the amount of charcoal that was burned in the kitchen would have sufficed for twenty-five meals! She arranged Emma's linens in the cupboards and taught her to keep an eye on the butcher when he delivered the meat. Emma accepted the lessons; Madame Bovary lavished them. And the words "daughter" and "mother" were exchanged all day long, accompanied by a tiny quivering of the lips, each of them offering gentle phrases in a voice trembling with anger.

During Madame Dubuc's day, the old woman still felt herself the favorite. But now Charles's love for Emma seemed to her desertion, an encroachment on that which belonged to her; and she observed her son's happiness with a sad silence like a ruined person who watches, through the windowpanes, people sitting around the table of his former home. She would recall her exertions and her sacrifices to him in the form of reminiscences, and comparing them to Emma's neglectful habits, would conclude that it was not reasonable for him to adore her in such an exclusive way.

Charles didn't know what to say. He respected his mother, and he loved his wife boundlessly. He considered the former's judgment infallible but found the other irreproachable. When his mother had left he would try timidly, and in the same terms, one or two of the milder observations he had heard her make. Emma would show him in but few words that he was mistaken and send him off to his patients.

And yet, in line with the theories she admired, she wanted to give herself up to love. In the moonlight of the garden she would recite all the passionate poetry she knew by heart and would sing melancholy adagios to him with sighs, but she found herself as calm afterward as before and Charles didn't appear more amorous or moved because of it.

After she had several times struck the flint on her heart without eliciting a single spark, incapable as she was of understanding that which she did not feel or of believing things that didn't manifest themselves in conventional forms, she convinced herself without difficulty that Charles's passion no longer offered anything extravagant. His effusions had become routine; he embraced her at certain hours. It was one habit among others, like the established custom of eating dessert after the monotony of dinner.

A gamekeeper, having been cured by Charles of a chest inflammation, had given Emma a small Italian greyhound; she would take it out to walk since she went out occasionally in order to escape for a moment and not have the eternal garden with the dusty road constantly before her eyes.

She would go as far as the Banneville beech grove, near the abandoned pavilion that forms an angle of the wall at the side of the fields. Sharp-edged leaves from the reeds would be scattered through the vegetation in the ditch.

First she would look all around to see if anything had changed since her last visit. She would find again, in the same places, foxglove and wallflowers, beds of nettles surrounding the huge stones, and patches of lichen along the three windows whose perpetually closed shutters were rattling away on their rusty iron bars. Her thoughts, at first unfocused, wandered at random like her greyhound, who ran around in circles through the countryside, yapping at yellow butterflies, chasing shrewmice, and nibbling the poppies on the edge of a wheat field. Then her thoughts would start to crystallize. She would sit on the grass into which she would dig the tip of her parasol with brief thrusts and would ask herself: "My God, why did I get married?"

She would ask herself if there might not be a way, by other combinations of fate, to meet some other man, and she tried to imagine what these unrealized events, this different life, this husband she did not know, would be like. None of them resembled her present husband. He might have been handsome, witty, distinguished, attractive, as, doubtless, were all the men her old friends from the convent had married. What were they doing now? In the city, with the s'reet noises, the hum of the theaters, and the lights of the ballroom, they were living lives in which the heart expands, in which the senses blossom. But her life was as cold as an attic with northern exposure, and boredom, that silent spider, was spinning its web in all the dark corners of her heart. She remembered the days on which prizes were distributed, when she climbed to the platform to receive her small wreaths. With her braided hair, white dress, and openwork shoes, she had a gentle manner, and when she was back in her seat the gentlemen leaned over to compliment her. The courtyard was filled with carriages; the people said good-bye to her through the windows; the music master greeted her as he passed by with his violin case. How far it all was! How far!

She signaled to her greyhound, Djali, took her between her knees, passed her fingers along the long delicate head, and said: "Come kiss your mistress; you have no worries."

Then as she looked at the melancholy expression of the graceful animal, who was slowly yawning, she softened and spoke aloud to her, as to someone in need of consolation.

Sometimes there were gusts of wind, breezes from the sea, that, rolling over the entire plateau of the Caux country all the way into the fields, carried with them a salty freshness. Close to the ground the rushes whistled and the beech leaves rustled, while their tops, continually swaying, kept up their deep murmuring. Emma tightened her shawl around her shoulders and arose.

In the avenue between the trees a green light filtered by the foliage lit up the moss that was gently crackling under her feet. The sun was setting; the sky was red between the branches, and the uniform trunks of trees planted in a straight line seemed a dark colonnade standing out against a golden background. Fear came over her, she called to Djali, went rapidly back to Tostes by the highway, collapsed into an armchair, and did not say one word the entire evening.

But toward the end of September something extraordinary happened in her life; she was invited to Vaubyessard, to the home of the Marquis d'Andervilliers.

The marquis, secretary of state during the Restoration, seeking to reenter political life, was preparing his candidacy for the office of deputy well in advance. He distributed a great deal of wood during the winter and was always eloquently demanding new roads for his district in the General Council. During the hot weather he had an abscess in his mouth that Charles had miraculously cured with a touch of the lancet. The clerk he sent to Tostes to pay for the operation reported that evening that he had seen some superb cherries in the doctor's little garden. Now, cherry trees did not grow well in Vaubyessard; the marquis asked Bovary for a few slips, made it a point to thank him in person, noticed Emma, thought she had a pretty figure and a manner not at all like a peasant's, so much so that he did not feel he was going beyond the bounds of condescension nor on the other hand that he was making a mistake by inviting the young couple to the château.

One Wednesday at three o'clock, Monsieur and Madame Bovary set off in their buggy for Vaubyessard with a large trunk attached in the rear and a hatbox set in front on the dashboard. Charles also had a handbox between his knees.

They arrived at nightfall, just as the lamps in the park were being lit to illuminate the way for the carriages.

VIII

The château, of modern construction, in the Italian sytle, had two projecting wings and three front entrances. It was spread out at the back of an immense lawn on which several cows were grazing between clumps of large, evenly spaced trees while groups of shrubs, rhododendron, syringa, and snowballs projected their unequal tufts of foliage along the winding sandy road. A stream passed under a bridge. Through the haze could be seen the thatch-roofed buildings scattered across the meadow. This latter was set in between the gentle slopes of two tree-covered hills. In the groves behind the house, set on two parallel lines, were the coach houses and stables, sole remains of the old, demolished château.

Charles's carriage arrived at the middle flight of steps; servants appeared; the marquis came forward, and offering his arm to the doctor's wife, he led her into the foyer.

It was high ceilinged and paved with marble tiles, and the combined noise of steps and voices echoed in it as in a church. A staircase faced it, and to the left a gallery overlooking the garden led to a billiard room, from which you could hear the ivory balls clicking as soon as you approached the door.

As she was crossing it to get to the drawing room, Emma noticed the serious-faced men, chins set over cravats folded high and all wearing decorations, standing around the table. They would smile silently as they hit with their cues. On the dark wood panels were large gilded frames with names written in black letters on their lower borders. She read: "Jean-Antoine d'Andervilliers d'Yverbonville, Count de la Vaubyessard, and Baron de la Fresnaye, killed in the battle of Coutras, October 20, 1587." And on another: "Jean-Antoine-Henri-Guy d'Andervilliers de la Vaubyessard, Admiral of France and Knight of the Order of St. Michael, wounded in the battle of La Hougue-Saint-Vaast, May 29, 1692, died at La Vaubyessard, January 23, 1693." Those that followed could barely be made out because the light from the lamps, directed on the green cloth of the billiard table, left the rest of the room in shadow. It turned the hanging canvases brown and highlighted only the cracks in the varnish; and from all the large gilt-edged black squares only some lighter part of the painting would emerge here and there—a pale forehead, two eyes staring at you, wigs unfurling over the powdered shoulders, red suits, or perhaps the buckle of a garter at the top of a fleshy calf.

The marquis opened the drawing-room door; one of the women arose (the marquise herself), came forward to meet Emma, and sat her down beside her on a small settee, where she began to chat amiably, as if she had known her a long time. She was a woman of about forty, with handsome shoulders, an aquiline nose, and a drawling voice; she wore a simple lace shawl that fell back in a point over her chestnut hair. A fair-haired young woman was sitting beside her in a high-backed chair, and gentlemen with tiny flowers in their lapels were talking to the ladies gathered around the fireplace.

Dinner was served at seven. The men, who outnumbered the ladies, sat down at the first table, in the hall, and the women were placed at the second, in the dining room with the marquis and the marquise.

As she entered, Emma felt herself enveloped in a warm atmosphere, a mixture of flower scent and the aroma of fine linens, of well-seasoned meat and truffles. The candles in the candelabra played their elongated flames over the silver platter covers; crystal pieces misted over reflected each other with pale glimmers. There were bunches of flowers set in a line along the entire table, and in the wide-bordered dishes napkins folded in the shape of bishop's miters held small oval-shaped rolls.

The red claws of the lobsters hung over the dishes; huge pieces of fruit were piled on each other in openwork baskets; the quails still bore their plumage; clouds of steam kept rising; and the butler, in silk stockings, knee breeches, white cravat, and frilled shirt, solemn as a judge, passing the already carved platters between the guests' shoulders, would make the piece you selected jump with one flick of the knife. On the large porcelain stove with its copper fittings, a statue of a woman draped to the chin stared steadily at the roomful of people.

Madame Bovary noticed that several of the women had not put their gloves in their wineglasses.

At the upper end of the table, alone among all the women, there was one old man eating, bending over his well-filled platter with his napkin knotted in back like a child, drops of sauce dribbling from his mouth. His eyes were bloodshot and he wore a small pigtail tied with a black ribbon. It was the marquis' father-in-law, the old Duke of Laverdière, once favorite of the Count d'Artois in the days of the Marquis de Conflans's hunting parties in Vaudreuil; it was said he had been Marie-Antoinette's lover between Messieurs de Coigny and de Lauzun. He had led a thoroughly debauched life, filled with duels, wagers, and abductions, had run through his fortune and been the terror of his entire family. A servant behind his chair was shouting into his ear the names of dishes that the old man would point to with his finger, mumbling. Emma could not keep herself from staring at the slack-mouthed old man as on someone extraordinary and august. He had lived at Court and slept in the bed of queens!

Iced champagne was served. Emma shivered all over at the prickly sensation in her mouth. She had never seen pomegranates before nor eaten pineapple. Even the granulated sugar seemed to her whiter and finer than elsewhere.

After dinner the ladies went up to their rooms to get ready for the ball. Emma dressed with the meticulous care of an actress making her debut. She arranged her hair as the hairdresser had suggested and pulled on the *barège* dress that had been spread out on the bed. Charles's pants were too tight around the stomach.

"The shoe straps are going to be in my way when I dance," he said.

"Dance?" she asked.

"Yes."

"You're out of your mind! They'll laugh at you. Stay in your place. Besides, it's more suitable for a doctor," she added.

Charles said no more. He paced up and down the room waiting for Emma to finish dressing.

Her back was turned to him, and he looked at her reflection in the mirror between the two candles. Her black eyes seemed even blacker. Her hair, gently puffed toward the ears, gleamed with a bluish luster; a rose in her chignon was trembling on its fragile stem. It had artificial dewdrops at the tips of its leaves. She wore a pale saffron-colored dress, set off by three bunches of pompon roses mingled with greenery.

Charles went over to kiss her on the shoulder.

"Let go of me!" she said. "You'll wrinkle my dress!"

A violin flourish and the sounds of a horn could be heard. She descended the staircase, restraining herself from running.

The quadrilles had begun. More people were arriving, jostling each other. She stationed herself on a settee near the door.

When the quadrille was over, the floor remained free. Groups of men stood and chatted while the liveried servants brought in large trays. Along the row of seated women, painted fans were fluttering, bouquets half concealed smiling faces, and gold-stoppered perfume bottles were being turned in half-opened hands whose tight white gloves revealed the shape of the fingernails and hugged the wrists. Lace trimmings, diamond brooches, and bracelets with lockets trembled on bodices, sparkled on breasts, jingled on bare arms. The hairdos, securely arranged and twisted at the napes, were crowned with clusters or bunches of forget-me-nots, jasmine, pomegranate blossoms, wheat ears, or cornflowers. The mothers, sitting quietly in their places, wore red turbans and frowning expressions.

Emma's heart was beating a bit faster when, her partner holding her by the tips of his fingers, she took her place in line and awaited the fiddler's stroke to begin. But the emotion soon disappeared, and swaying to the rhythm of the orchestra, she glided forward, moving her neck lightly. A smile came to her lips at certain delicate strains of the violin during its solo moments; you could hear the clinking of gold coins dropping onto the card tables in the next room; then everything began at once, the cornet emitted a loud blast, feet fell in measure, skirts swirled out and rustled against each other, hands joined, then separated; the same eyes that lowered before you looked up again at yours.

Several men (about fifteen) between twenty-five and forty years of age, scattered among the dancers or chatting at the entrances, distinguished themselves from the crowd by their family resemblance despite the differences in their ages, dress, and facial features.

Their clothes, better made, seemed of a finer cloth, and their hair, made to gleam by more refined pomades, was brought forward in curls toward the temples. They had the complexion of wealth, that whiteness that is accentuated by the pallor of porcelain, the sheen of watered satin, the varnish of fine furniture, and that is nurtured by a diet of exquisitely prepared food. Their necks turned in relaxed manner over low-folded cravats, their long sideburns fell over turned-down collars; they wiped their lips with elegantly scented handkerchiefs embroidered with large monograms. Those who were beginning to age looked young, and a certain maturity lay over the faces of the young ones. The calm of daily satisfied passions showed in their indifferent glances, but their gentle manners did not completely mask that special brutality that stems from their relatively easy conquests, the handling of thoroughbred horses and the company of fallen women, in which the muscles are flexed and vanity sated.

A few feet from Emma a gentleman in a blue coat was talking about Italy with a pale young woman wearing a pearl necklace. They were praising the size of the pillars at St. Peter's, Tivoli, Vesuvius, Castellamare, and the Cascine; the roses of Genoa; the Colosseum in the moonlight. Emma listened with her other ear to a conversation full of words she did not understand. In the center of a group was a very young man who had beaten Miss Arabelle and Romulus the week before and won two thousand louis by jumping a ditch in England. One man was complaining that his racers were getting fat; another, about the way a printing error had garbled his horse's name.

The air in the ballroom grew heavy; the lights were fading. People began moving toward the billiard room. A servant climbing on a chair broke two windowpanes; at the noise of the shattered glass, Madame Bovary looked round and saw some peasants, their faces pressed to the window, staring at her from the garden. Then the memory of Les Bertaux came back to her. She saw the farm again, the muddy pond, her father in a smock under the apple trees, and she saw once more herself in the dairy skimming the cream from the milk cans with her finger. But in the splendor of the present hour, her past life, so clear until now, was disappearing completely, and she almost doubted that she had lived it. She was here, and outside the ballroom there was merely shadow cast over all the rest. She ate a maraschino-flavored ice, which she held in her left hand in a silver-gilt shell, and half closed her eyes, the spoon between her teeth.

A woman near her dropped her fan as a man danced by. "Would you be so kind, Monsieur," the woman said, "and pick my fan up from under the sofa?" The gentleman kneeled down, and as he reached out, Emma saw the young woman's hand throw something white, folded into a triangle, into his hat. The gentleman picked up the fan and held it out to the woman respectfully; she thanked him with a nod and began to sniff her bouquet.

After supper, at which many Spanish and Rhine wines were served, along with bisque and cream-of-almond soups, Trafalgar puddings, and all sorts of cold meats, surrounded by jellied molds, quivering on the plates, the carriages began going off, one after the other. By pulling the muslin curtain away from the corner one could see the light of their lanterns gliding through the night. The settees began to empty; there were still some card players; the musicians moistened the tips of their fingers on their tongues; Charles was leaning against a door, half asleep.

The cotilion began at three in the morning. Emma did not know how to waltz. Everyone was waltzing, even Mademoiselle d'Andervilliers and the marquise; there remained now only the château guests, about a dozen people.

One of the dancers, familiarly addressed as viscount, whose extremely low-cut waistcoat seemed molded on his chest, came a second time to invite Madame Bovary, assuring her that he would lead her and that she would manage well.

They began slowly, then moved more rapidly. Everything was turning around them, the lights, furniture, paneling, and the floor, like a disk on a pivot. Passing near the doors, the hem of Emma's dress flared out against her partner's trousers; their legs intertwined; he looked down at her, she raised her eyes to him; a numbness overcame her, she stopped. They started again and the viscount, with a more rapid movement, swept her away, disappeared with her to the end of the gallery, where, out of breath, she almost fell and for one moment leaned her head on his chest. And then, still turning, but more gently now, he led her back to her place; she leaned back against the wall and put her hand before her eyes.

When she opened them again, there was a woman seated on a stool in the middle of the floor with three dancers on their knees before her. She chose the viscount and the violin struck up again.

They were stared at. Up and down they went, she with her body held rigid, chin down, and he always in the same pose, holding himself erect, elbow rounded, face jutting forward. How she could waltz! They continued for a long time and tired out the others.

People chatted a while and after the "good nights," or rather "good mornings," the house guests went to sleep.

Charles dragged himself upstairs, clinging to the banister; his legs "couldn't stand up another minute." He had spent five solid hours standing near the tables watching the whist games without understanding a thing about them. And so he heaved a great sigh of relief when his boots were finally removed.

Emma wrapped a shawl around her shoulders, opened the window, and leaned out.

The night was black. A few drops of rain were falling. She breathed in the humid breeze that was refreshing her eyelids. With the ball music still humming in her ears, she was trying to stay awake in order to prolong the illusion of this luxurious life that she would have to abandon in a short while.

Day broke. She looked at the château windows for a long time, trying to guess which were the bedrooms of the various people she had noticed the night before. She would have liked to know about their lives, to enter into them, to become involved with them.

But she was shivering with cold. She undressed and snuggled between the sheets against Charles, who was asleep.

There were a lot of people at breakfast; the doctor was amazed that no liquor was served. Later Mademoiselle d'Andervilliers picked up what was left of the rolls in a basket to carry them to the swans on the lake, and they went for a walk in the hothouses, where exotic plants bristling with hairy leaves rose in pyramids beneath hanging vases, which, like over-crowded serpents' nests, dropped long, twisted green tendrils over their edges. The orangery at the far end via a covered passage to the outhouses. The marquis took Emma to the stable to amuse her. Above the basket-shaped racks, porcelain plaques bore the horses' names in black. When they passed by, each animal stirred in its stall and clicked its tongue. The floor of the saddle room glistened like a drawing-room floor. Coach harnesses were set in the middle on two revolving columns and the bits, whips, stirrups, and curbs were all lined up along the wall.

Meanwhile, Charles went to ask a servant to ready his buggy. They brought it around to the front, and when all their luggage had been packed in, the Bovarys took leave of the marquis and marquise and headed back to Tostes.

Emma said nothing and watched the wheels turn. Charles, seated on the edge of the seat, was driving with his arms outstretched, and the small horse ambled along between its oversized shafts. The slack reins hitting its crupper grew moist with its lather, and the box roped on behind kept making loud, steady thuds against the body.

They were on the heights of Thibourville when suddenly some horsemen passed before them, laughing, with cigars in their mouths. Emma thought she recognized the viscount; she turned around and saw nothing on the horizon but heads moving up and down in rhythm with the uneven cadence of the trot and gallop.

Half a mile later they had to stop to tie a cord around the breech band, which had broken. As Charles took one last look at the harness, he saw something on the ground between the horse's legs; and he picked up a cigar case edged with green silk and emblazoned with a coat of arms in the center as on a coach door.

"There are still two cigars inside," he said. "They'll be for tonight after dinner."

"You smoke?" she asked.

"Sometimes, when I have the chance."

He put his find in his pocket and whipped the horse.

Dinner was not ready when they arrived home. Madame became furious. Nastasie answered with insolence.

"Get out!" Emma said. "You brazen creature! I'm sending you away!"

For dinner there was onion soup with a bit of veal cooked in sorrel. Facing Emma, Charles said, rubbing his hands together with a contented look: "It feels good to be home again!"

They could hear Nastasie crying. He was rather fond of the poor girl. In the old days when he had been a widower, she had kept him company on many an empty evening. She was his first patient, his oldest acquaintance in the district.

"Have you sent her away for good?" he said finally.

"Yes. Who's stopping me?" she answered.

They warmed themselves in the kitchen while their bedroom was being readied. Charles began to smoke. He smoked with his lips puckered, spitting every minute, recoiling at each puff.

"You'll make yourself sick," she said disdainfully.

He put his cigar down and ran off to gulp down a glass of cold water from the pump. Emma, seizing the cigar case, threw it hastily into the bottom of the cupboard.

The next day was long. She walked about in her garden, passing back and forth over the same paths, stopping in front of the flower beds, the fruit-tree trellises, the plaster curé, staring with bewilderment at all these once familiar things. How far away the ball already seemed! Why should there be such a distance between yesterday morning and tonight? Her trip to Vaubyessard had made a gap in her life like one of those great crevices that a storm sometimes carves out in the mountains in a single night. She resigned herself, however; reverently she packed away in the chest of drawers her lovely dress and even her satin slippers, whose soles had yellowed from the floor wax. Her heart was like them; the wealth had rubbed off on her, something that would never be erased.

And so the memory of the ball became a preoccupation for Emma. Every Wednesday she would say to herself on awakening: "Ah! A week ago today— two weeks ago—three weeks ago, I was there." Little by little the faces blurred in her memory; she forgot the quadrille tunes; she no longer saw the livery and the rooms so clearly; some of the details faded away, but the regret remained.

ROGER MARTIN DU GARD

- ## *Summer 1914*

V

The Headquarters, or "Talking Shop" as Meynestrel's intimates usually called it, was discreetly situated in the heart of the upper city, in the old Rue des Barrières flanking the Cathedral.

Seen from outside, the building gave the impression of being disused. It was one of several ramshackle old houses that had somehow survived in that decorous quarter of the town. The front, three stories high, was plastered a dingy pink; the wall was crannied, pocked with damprot, and the dusty, shutterless sash-windows suggested an abandoned tenement-house. Between it and the street was a narrow, walled-in front yard, littered with refuse, scrap-iron, and rubble, among which a large elder tree rose in solitary grace. The entrance-gate had vanished, and a band of metal linked the two stone pillars, bearing in still legible characters the inscription: "Brass Foundry." The foundry had long since been transferred elsewhere, but the premises were still being used as a warehouse by the proprietors.

Behind the empty house there was a second yard, invisible from the street, in which stood the two-story building that was known as Headquarters. The only access to it was through a long, vaulted corridor crossing the former foundry from end to end. The ground floor had been used as stabling in earlier days, and in it Monier, the handyman, now lived. The upper floor consisted of four adjoining rooms opening on a long, dark passage. The smallest of the rooms, at the end

SOURCE. From *Summer 1914* by Roger Martin du Gard.

of the passage, had been, at the suggestion of Alfreda, set apart as a sort of private office for the Pilot. The others, which were fairly spacious, served as common rooms. In each were ten or a dozen chairs, some benches, and tables strewn with newspapers and magazines. For at Headquarters was available not only the whole Socialist press of Europe but also the majority of those sporadic revolutionary periodicals which, after several successive issues to bring themselves to notice, lapsed into an eclipse that lasted from a few months to years, because funds had run out or their staff was languishing in jail.

No sooner had Jacques emerged from the cloisterlike corridor and entered the back yard than a buzz of heated conversation on the upper floor apprised him that the Talking Shop had a full house that evening.

At the foot of the staircase three men were carrying on an animated discussion in what sounded vaguely like Italian or Spanish. They were three enthusiastic Esperantists, one of whom, Charpentier, a teacher at Lausanne—he had come to Geneva to hear Janotte's speech—was the editor of a review that had some success in revolutionary circles, *L'Espérantiste du Léman*. He never missed an opportunity of declaring that one of the most crying needs of the internationalists was a universal tongue, and that the adoption of Esperanto as a second language by men of every nationality would simplify intercourse between the people on the intellectual plane no less than on the material. He was fond of invoking the high authority of Descartes, who in a letter to a friend explicitly preconized a "universal language, very easy to learn, to speak, and to write, and apt—this being the most important thing—to aid the understanding."

After shaking hands with the Esperantists, Jacques went up the stairs. On the landing he found Monier on his knees, busy sorting out on the floor a pile of numbers of *Vorwärts*. Monier was a professional waiter, but though he always wore, in season and out, the low-cut waistcoat and celluloid dicky appropriate to his calling, he rarely followed it. The utmost he did was, for one week every month, to work as an extra hand at a beer-house, thus ensuring three weeks' leisure, all of which he devoted to the "revolutionary cause." He displayed an equal zeal for all and sundry tasks—running errands, cleaning up, sorting out periodicals, and operating the mimeograph.

The door of the room at the top of the stairs stood open. Alfreda and Paterson were by themselves, talking near the window. Jacques had already observed that, when she was with the Englishman, Alfreda seemed to drop her usual role of silent onlooker and blossom out into a young woman with a mind of her own —an aspect of her that, presumably out of shyness, she never revealed in other circumstances. She had Meynestrel's brief-case under her arm and in her hand a pamphlet, a passage from which she was reading out in a low tone to Paterson. Puffing at his pipe, the young man seemed to be listening absent-mindedly. His eyes were studying the bent face with the jet-black fringe and the pale cheeks on which the long lashes cast wavering shadows; he was wondering, perhaps, how the curious dull sheen of that white skin could be realized on canvas. Neither of them noticed Jacques walking past the door.

In the second room he saw a number of familiar faces. Old Boissonis was sitting near the door, his fat paunch sagging over his thighs. Near him stood Mithoerg, Guérin, and Charcovsky, the bookseller.

Boissonis shook Jacques's hand, without interrupting a rejoinder he was making.

"But, in that case . . . well, what does it prove? The same old story: not enough driving force behind the revolutionary movement. And why? They don't *think* enough." He threw himself back in his chair, his hands splayed on his knees, and grinned aggressively.

Daily he was one of the first-comers. Discussion was the breath of life to him. Sometime professor of natural science at the Bordeaux University, he had been led on from anthropology to sociological research, and, the boldness of his views having got him into bad odour at the university, he had moved to Geneva. What caught the eye in his appearance was the disproportion between his tiny features and his enormous head. The vast, bald, dome-shaped forehead, the heavy jowl, and several layers of chin formed a zone of superfluous fat which seemed to dwarf preposterously all the rest: the eyes sparkling with mischievous good nature; a snub, inquisitive nose with large, gaping nostrils; and fleshly lips always in readiness to smile. All the fat man's vitality seemed concentrated in the small oasis of eyes, nose, and mouth, lost in a Sahara of gross flesh.

"I've said it before, and I say it again," he oracled, licking his plump lips, "we've got to launch our attack, to start with, on the philosophic front."

Mithoerg rolled disapproving eyes behind his glasses, and shook his shaggy mane.

"Thought and action must march hand in hand."

"Look at what happened in Germany in the nineteenth century," Charcovsky began.

Old Boissonis slapped his thighs. "That's just it!" he cried, chuckling already with the satisfaction of having made his point. "Yes, let us take the case of the Germans. . . ."

Jacques knew in advance everything they were going to say; the only variations would be in the way they bandied arguments and counter-arguments, like pawns on a chess-board.

Standing in the middle of the room, Zelavsky, Périnet, Saffrio, and Skada formed an animated quartet. Jacques went up to them.

"Everything hangs together, everything fits in so perfectly, in the capitalist system," declared Zelavsky, a Russian with a long flaxen moustache.

"And zat is vy ve only need to vait, Sergei Pavlovitch," put in Skada, sharply enunciating each word in a tone pitched deliberately low. "Ze bourgeois vorld vill of its own accord crumple into pieces."

Skada, the Levantine Jew, was a man in the early fifties. He was extremely near-sighted, and glasses thick as telescope lenses straddled the putty-coloured hooked nose. The face was an ugly one, with short, fuzzy hair closely plastered over the egg-shaped skull and enormous ears; but the thoughtful eyes glowed with an infinite kindliness. Skada led an ascetic life. Meynestrel had nicknamed him "the Pundit."

"How's yourself?" a gruff voice inquired, and a sledge-hammer hand crashed on Jacques's shoulder. "Hot as hell, ain't it?"

Quilleuf, who had just come in, walked round the room, slapping backs and shaking hands with his hearty "How's yourself?" He never waited for an answer and, in winter as in summer, invariably followed up with "Hot as hell, ain't it?" Nothing short of a raging blizzard could make him change the formula.

"It may take time to crumple," Skada went on, "but crumple it must one day —in-ev-i-ta-bly. Zat's vy one can die vithout regrets." His flabby eyelids dropped and a quiet smile that vouched for his serene confidence in the future set the long, plump lips slowly writhing across each other, like two tangled snakes.

Jean Périnet greeted the Pundit's speech with a series of little, emphatic nods. "Yes, time's on our side. Everywhere. Even in France."

Périnet had a rapid, high-pitched voice with ringing tones, and a way of saying everything that crossed his mind with artless unconcern. His broad Parisian accent struck an amusing note in these international confabulations. He looked twenty-eight or thirty, a typical young workman from the Parisian suburbs, with alert eyes, the ghost of a moustache, a quizzical nose, and a general air of health and cleanliness. The son of a Paris furniture-maker, he had got into trouble over a woman and run away from home when little more than a boy. He had known hard luck, frequented anarchist circles, and done time in jail. When, as the sequel to a street affray, the Lyon police were on his tracks, he had crossed the frontier. Jacques greatly liked him. The non-French members of the group, however, tended to keep him at arm's length; they were put off by his overready laugh, his caustic wit, and, most of all, by his regrettable habit of naming his friends in terms of their national fare: the "Macaronis," the "German Sausages," the "Rosbifs," and so forth. He meant no harm by it, and himself had taken no offence on hearing an Englishman refer to him as "the Frog."

He turned to Jacques, as if calling him to witness. "In France, even in big business circles, the new generation's caught on to it. They know damn well, deep down inside them, that the game is up; that they won't be able to live on the backs of the workers much longer; that one of these fine days the land and mines and factories and railways, the whole bag of tricks, has got to come back to the workers. The younger ones, anyhow, know it. Ain't that so, Thibault?"

Zelavsky and Skada spun quickly round and fixed keenly questioning eyes on Jacques, as if the point were one of extreme urgency and they were only waiting for Jacques's reply before making some momentous decision. Jacques smiled.

True, he attached no less importance than they did to every symptom of impending social upheaval, but he was less convinced than they of the utility of such conversations.

"That's so," he agreed. "Many young Frenchmen of the middle class, I imagine, have developed secret doubts of the future of capitalism. The capitalist system still keeps their pockets lined, and they hope it will last out their lifetime. Still, they're beginning to feel uneasy. But that's all. It's a mistake to jump to the conclusion that they're on the point of deserting their class. On the contrary, I expect they'll put up a very stiff fight for their privileges, and they're still devilishly well entrenched. For one thing, oddly enough, they have the tacit consent of the poor devils whom they exploit; that's a big help."

"And don't forget," Périnet put in, "that they keep all the top jobs for their own selves, they run the show."

"Not only," Jacques observed, "do they run it but, for the time being, one might say they have a sort of right to run it. For, after all, where could we find —?"

A sudden bellow from Quilleuf interrupted him. *"Memories of a Proletarian!* Ha! Ha!" At the far end of the room Quilleuf was standing beside the table on which Charcovsky, the bookseller—who held the post of librarian—laid out each evening the new books, magazines, and newspapers that had just come in. All that could be seen of Quilleuf was his bent back and big shoulders quaking in a vast guffaw.

Jacques completed his remark. "Where could we find, at a moment's notice, men with enough expert knowledge to take their place? Why are you laughing, Sergei?"

For some moments Zelavsky had been contemplating Jacques with a look of mingled amusement and affection.

"In every Frenchman," he said, wagging his head, "dwells a sceptic who never sleeps but with one eye open."

Quilleuf had swung round abruptly. After a hasty glance at the other groups, he marched straight on Jacques, brandishing a book he had picked up from the table.

"Emile Pouchard. *Memories of a Proletarian Childhood.* What d'you make of this, eh, boys?" Guffawing, rolling his eyes, and thrusting forward his plump, jovial face to peer at each in turn, he comically overdid his fury for their entertainment.

"Here's another of these half-baked 'comrades,' some miserable whippersnapper with his precious problems! Some dud pen-pusher who dumps his garbage on the workers' doorsteps!"

Quilleuf, hailed by his friends as "the Tribune"—alternatively, "the Cobbler"—came from the South of France. After many years at sea in the merchant marine and spells of multifarious work in Mediterranean ports, this rolling stone had fetched up at Geneva. His little bootshop was always thronged with work-less militants who found there, after closing time at Headquarters, a fire in win-ter, soft drinks in summer, and at all times tobacco and good company.

There was a pleasant magic—which instinctively he turned to excellent ac-count—in his melodious southern voice. Sometimes at public meetings, after fidgeting in his seat for a couple of hours, he would rush onto the platform and, though he had nothing new to put forward and merely clad the arguments of previous speakers in the glamour of his tempestuous eloquence, in a few phrases he would carry his hearers with him and persuade them to vote for measures for which the cleverest orators had until then failed to get a majority. The difficult thing was to dam this spate of eloquence, once the flood-gates were opened; for the release of his pent-up enthusiasm and the sense of power that, radiating from his personality, swept his audience off their feet—not to say the sound of his own voice—gave him a physical pleasure so intense that he could never have enough of it.

Now he was fluttering the pages of the *Memories,* scanning the chapter headings, and sliding his fat forefinger under certain passages, like a child spell-ing out the words.

" 'The joys of family life'! 'The charm of home'! Oh, the son of a bitch!"

He shut the book, and with the neat precision of an expert on the bowling green, flexing his knees and swinging his arms, pitched it across the room onto the table.

"Look here!" He turned to Jacques again. "I don't see why I shouldn't write my memoirs, too. Don't I know all about 'the joys of family life'! And I've plenty of memories of childhood, and to spare, for those who haven't any!"

Drawn by the stentorian voice, others were strolling up to join the group around the Tribune, whose yarns always brought a gust of breezy realism into the rather academic atmosphere of these gatherings.

Half closing his eyes, he cast a swift glance round his audience, then began adroitly in a low, confidential tone. "Everyone here knows the Old Town at Mar-seilles, don't they? Well, that's where we lived, the six of us, at the end of a blind alley. In two rooms which, put together, made about half the size of this one. One of 'em hadn't no window. My dad had to get up by candlelight every morning, before the sun rose, and bitter cold it was. He'd haul me out of the heap of old rags where I slept with my brothers; seems he couldn't bear to see anyone else taking it easy while he was up and about. Every night he'd roll in very late, half drunk, after a god-awful day loading barrels on the docks, poor devil. Ma was always ailing and wondering how to make both ends meet. Ma was as scared of him as we were. She, too, was out all day—doing chores, most likely, down in the town. As I'd the honour to be the first-born of the bunch, I had to keep the other three kids in order. And didn't I wallop it into them, seeing as how they got on my nerves, puling and mewling and snuffling and scrapping all the time.

Nary a hot stew for us kids; a hunk of bread, an onion, and a dozen olives was all that came our way, with a rasher thrown in once in a blue moon. Never a square meal, never a kind word, never a lark, never a bloody thing! From morn till night we mooched about the streets, fighting like wildcats when we'd spotted a rotten orange in the gutter. Or we'd go sniffing the shells the lucky ones who were digging into sea-urchins chucked down on the sidewalk. At thirteen we'd started in with little girls, in the empty lots behind the billboards. My 'joys of family life'—to hell with them! Cold, hunger, injustice, jealousy, revolt! I'd been put to work as an apprentice at a blacksmith's; the only pay I got was kicks in the beam. My fingers were raw with burns, and my arms ached from tugging at the bellows, and my cheeks were scorched all day by the big, roaring forge." He had raised his tone; his voice was vibrant with indignation, and with pleasure at its own sound. Again with a swift glance he reviewed his audience. "Aye, I could tell some 'memories of childhood' if I set to it."

Jacques caught an amused twinkle in Zelavsky's eye. The Russian gently raised his arm toward Quilleuf, and asked: "How did you come to join the Party?"

"It's ancient history," Quilleuf said. "When I was at sea, I'd the luck to have two shipmates who bunked with me, who *knew,* and did a bit of propagandizing. I started reading, finding out about it. So did some of the others. We lent each other books, we talked things over. Cutting our wisdom teeth, eh? In six months' time there was a whole bunch of us that *knew.* When I left the ship, I'd grown up; I was—a man!"

He fell silent, staring before him into the middle distance.

"Yes, we were a group—a real gang of tough 'uns. What's become of all the others? Anyhow, they ain't written their 'Memoirs'—not they! . . . Hello, girls! And how's yourselves?" He turned gallantly toward two young women who were coming up. "Hot today, ain't it?"

The ring of listeners parted to include the two Swiss comrades, Anaïs Julian and Emilie Cartier. One was a schoolmistress, the other a Red Cross nurse. They shared a flat, and usually came together to these gatherings. Anaïs, the teacher, spoke several languages and made translations of foreign revolutionary articles for the radical Swiss papers.

They were very different in appearance. Emilie, the younger, was a small, plump brunette. Set off by the blue veil that suited her so well and which she almost always wore, her complexion had the creamy pink-and-whiteness of an English child's. She was a merry, mildly flirtatious girl, quick in her gestures and retorts, though the latter never had a sting. Her patients adored her. So did Quilleuf, who gave her no peace from his semi-paternal banter. In the broadest accents but with the utmost gravity, he would declare: "It ain't that she's exactly pretty, but our Emilie's a treat to look at."

Anaïs, the other girl, was also dark; she had prominent cheekbones, a high colour, and there was a hint of surliness in the long, horselike face. But both alike gave an impression of perfect mental balance and vast reserves of strength —the fine serenity of those for whom what they think is in perfect harmony with what they are and do.

The conversation had taken a new turn.

Skada, the dreamer, was discoursing on justice.

"*Ach,* but ve should alvays spread more and more justice round us," he pleaded, in his slow, ingratiating voice. "Zat, zat is ze great thing to make men keep peace between zemselves."

"Stuff!" Quilleuf burst in. "When you ask for justice, I'm with you till hell freezes—that's sure. But, as for it making men keep peace, I wouldn't reckon too much on that; there's no fussier, more quarrelsome fellow on earth than one who has justice on the brain."

"Nothing lasts that isn't based on love," murmured little Vanheede, who had just moved to Jacques's side. "Peace is the work of faith, of faith and charity." He stayed motionless for a few moments, then walked away, an enigmatic smile upon his lips.

Jacques noticed Paterson and Alfreda slowly crossing the room together, still engrossed in a low-voiced conversation; they were going toward the other room, where presumably Meynestrel was to be found. Alfreda looked tinier than ever beside the Englishman; tall and lithe, his pipe as usual to the fore, he was bending toward her as they walked. His clean-shaven face, delicately moulded features, and the cut of his clothes, threadbare though they were, always made him seem better turned out than the others. As she passed, Alfreda cast at the group of men including Jacques that soft, brooding glance of hers in which sometimes, as now, there shone an unexpected gleam, a slumberous fire that seemed to mark her out for some high destiny.

Paterson smiled to Jacques. He was obviously in good spirits, which made him look more boyish than ever.

"Look what Richardley's given me!" he cried gleefully, holding out a small pack of tobacco. "Roll yourself a cigarette, Thibault. No? You're wrong." He took a puff and voluptuously rolled the smoke out through his nostrils. "I assure you, old boy, tobacco is the greatest boon on earth."

Smiling, Jacques watched his receding form. Then unthinkingly he too began to move toward the door which had just closed behind them. But on the threshold he halted and leaned against the doorjamb.

Meynestrel's voice was coming to him, harsh, cutting, with an ironic lift at the close of certain phrases.

"That goes without saying. I'm not against what are called 'reforms' as a matter of course. The struggle for reforms may serve in some countries as a fighting platform. And the improved conditions of life thus obtained by the proletariat may tend to speed up its revolutionary education to some extent. But your reformers always imagine that reforms are the only means to attain their ends. They're only one of many means. Your reformers think that social legislation and victories on the economic front are bound to increase not only the well-being of the masses but their striking-power. I wonder! They assume that reforms will be enough to bring about a state of affairs in which the proletariat need only make a quiet gesture and political power will drop into its hands like a ripe plum. That's as it may be! But no child is born without some very painful birth-pangs for the mother."

"And no revolution," a voice put in, "without a *Wirbelsturm,* a phase of storm and stress." Jacques recognized the voice as Mithoerg's.

"Your reformers," Meynestrel went on, "are grievously mistaken. Mistaken in two ways. Firstly, because they overestimate the proletariat; secondly, because they underestimate capitalism. The proletariat is still far short of the stage of development they fancy it has reached. It hasn't enough cohesion, not enough class-consciousness, not enough—heaps of other things, to be able to take the offensive and seize the reins of power. As for capitalism, your reformers imagine that because it's giving ground it will let itself be nibbled away piecemeal, by re-form after reform, till nothing's left. That's nonsense. Its anti-revolutionary zeal, its powers of resistance are intact. And all the time it's preparing the ground, with diabolical cunning, for a counter-attack. Do you think the capitalists don't know what they're about when they accept reforms which win over to them the Party officials and divide the working class by making distinctions between the workers —and all the rest of it? Of course I know that capitalism's divided against itself; I know that, appearances notwithstanding, the mutual hostility between capitalist groups is steadily increasing. That's another reason why we may be sure capital-ism, before throwing in its hand, will play all the cards it has up its sleeve. *All!* And one of the trump cards on which, rightly or wrongly, it most relies is—war! War, it reckons, will restore to it, at one swoop, all the ground it has been losing to the socialist advance. War will enable it to divide and crush the proletariat. Firstly, to divide it—because the masses are not at one in being immune from patriotic sentiments, and a war would set those who thought nationally (no small number, I should say) at loggerheads with those who were faithful to the inter-national ideal. Secondly, to crush it—because considerable numbers of the workers on both sides would fall at the front and such as survived would be either dispirited, in the country that was beaten; or, in the victor country, easy to lull into a state of lethargy. . . ."

MONTESQUIEU

• *The Persian Letters*

Letter XXVIII

Rica to ——

I saw yesterday a rather strange thing, even though it happens daily in Paris.

Toward the end of an afternoon, all the people come together and proceed to play a sort of scene that I heard called *comedy*. The movement takes place on a platform, which they call the *stage*. To the two sides of this can be seen, in little alcoves called *loges,* men and women who are playing mute scenes almost like those that are the custom in our own Persia.

Here, there is a woman in the throes of love, expressing her languor; there, another, more lively, consumes with her eyes a lover who looks at her in the same way. Every passion is imprinted on these faces and expressed with an eloquence no whit less animated for being mute. Over there, actresses appear in heavy décolleté, carrying usually a muff, out of modesty, to hide their arms. Below stands a crowd of people who poke fun at those upon the stage, while these laugh in their turn at the people below.

However, those who take the greatest pains are certain people chosen for the

SOURCE. From *The Persian Letters* by Montesquieu. Translated by Robert Joy. Copyright 1961, reprinted with the permission of Meridian Books.

role at a tender age, so as to bear up under the strain. They are obliged to be everywhere at once. They pass from place to place by paths they alone know; they climb with astounding skill from floor to floor. They are up, they are down —in all the loges. They dive, so to speak, and seem lost; then they reappear. Often they leave one stage to go play on another. There are even some of them, by a miracle you wouldn't dare hope for from their crutches, who can be seen walking and getting about like the others. Finally everyone goes to rooms where an intimate comedy is played. It starts with bows and reverences and continues with embraces. It is said that the flimsiest acquaintance gives a man the right practically to stifle another. The environment seems to encourage affection. And, in sooth, it is said that the princesses reigning there are not at all cruel, and if you discount two or three hours out of the day when they are rather unsociable, it can be said that the rest of the time they are amenable and that the difficult moments are an intoxication that leaves them easily.

Everything I have told you so far takes place in almost the same way in another place, called the *opera*. The only difference is that in one place they talk and in the other they sing. The other day, one of my friends took me into a loge where one of the leading actresses was undressing. We struck up such a close acquaintance that, the next day, I received from her the following letter:

Monsieur,

I am the most unhappy girl in the world. I have always been the most virtuous actress at the opera. Seven or eight months ago I was in the loge where you saw me yesterday. As I was in the midst of dressing for the role of a priestess of Diana, a young abbé came into me, and with no respect for my white costume, veil, and headband, ravished me of my innocence. I stress the sacrifice I made for him as much as I can; he only starts to laugh and points out that he found me most profane. Meanwhile, I have grown so pregnant that I scarcely dare appear any more on the stage, for, as to the whole question of honor, I am of unbelievable delicacy and have always held that a young lady of good birth can be brought to lose her virtue more easily than her decorum. With such delicacy of feeling, you can be sure that the young abbé would never have succeeded if he had not promised to marry me. Such a legitimate motive made me pass over the usual minor formalities and start where I should have finished. Now, however, since his faithlessness has dishonored me, I wish no longer to live at the opera, where, between you and me, I am barely given enough to live on; for now, when I am no longer young and am losing out in the matter of charms, my annuity, which remains the same, seems to grow smaller every day. I have learned, through a gentleman in your entourage, that much is made in your country of a good dancer and that if I were in Ispahan, my fortune would be quickly made. If you were to be willing to accord your protection to me and take me with you into your country, you would have the distinct advantage of performing a kindness to a girl who by reason of her virtue and decorous conduct, would not make herself unworthy of your favors. I am, sir . . .

From Paris, the 2nd of the
Moon of Shalval, 1712.

Letter XXIX

Rica to Ibben in Smyrna

The Pope is the head of the Christians. He is an old idol worshipped out of habit. Formerly he was to be feared even by kings, for he deposed them as easily as our magnificent sultans depose the kings of Imirette and Georgia. But now he is no longer feared. He claims that he is the successor of one of the first Christians, who is called Saint Peter, and his is most certainly a rich succession, for he has immense treasures and a great country under his domination.

Bishops are lawyers subordinate to him, and they have, under his authority, two quite different functions. When they are assembled together they create, as does he, articles of faith. When they are acting individually they have scarcely any other function except to give dispensation from fulfilling the law. For you must know that the Christian religion is weighed down with an infinity of very difficult practices. And since it has been decided that it is less easy to fulfill these duties than to have bishops around who can dispense with them, this last alternative was chosen out of a sense of common good. In this way, if you don't wish to keep Ramadan, if you don't choose to be subjected to the formalities of marriage, if you wish to break your vows, if you would like to marry in contravention of the prohibitions of the law, even sometimes if you want to break a sworn oath —you go to the bishop or the Pope and you are given immediate dispensation.

Bishops do not create articles of faith by their own decision. There are countless doctors, most of them dervishes, who introduce among themselves thousands of new questions touching upon religion. They are allowed to dispute at great length, and the war goes on until a decision comes along to finish it.

And thus I can assure you that there never has been a kingdom where there are so many civil wars as in the Kingdom of Christ.

Those who propose some new proposition are called at first *heretics*. Each heresy has its own name, and this name becomes for those who are involved, something like a rallying cry. But no one has to be a heretic. One needs only split the difference in half and give some distinction to those who make accusations of heresy, and whatever the distinction—logical or not—it makes a man white as snow, and he may have himself called *orthodox*.

What I am telling you is valid for France and Germany, for I have heard it said that in Spain and Portugal there are certain dervishes who stand for no nonsense and will have a man burned as if he were straw. When people fall into the hands of those fellows, happy is he who has always prayed to God with little wooden beads in his hand, who has worn on his person two strips of cloth attached to two ribbons, or who has at some time been in a province called Galicia. Without that, the poor devil is in bad straits. Even should he swear like a pagan that he is orthodox, they might quite possibly disagree with him on his qualifications and burn him for a heretic. He could talk all he likes of distinctions to be made—there is no distinction, for he would be in ashes before they even considered listening to him.

Other judges assume that an accused man is innocent until proved guilty; these judges always assume him guilty. When in doubt, they have as their rule always to decide on the side of severity, apparently because they believe men to be bad. But then, from another point of view, they have such a good opinion of men that they never judge them capable of lying, for they receive the testimony of professed enemies, of women of evil repute, of those who ply an infamous profession. In their sentences they include a little compliment for those clad in the brimstone shirt by telling them that they are very vexed to see them so badly dressed, that they as judges are gentle people and abhor blood and are truly grieved to have condemned them. However, to console their grief, they confiscate all the property of these wretches to their own advantage.

Happy the land inhabited by the sons of the prophets! These sad spectacles are unknown there. The holy religion brought to that land by the angels is protected by its very truth; it needs none of these violent means to preserve itself.

From Paris, the 4th of the
Moon of Shalval, 1712.

Letter XXX

Rica to the same in Smyrna

The inhabitants of Paris are curious to the point of extravagance. When I arrived, they looked upon me as if I had been sent from heaven: old men, young men, women, children—they all wanted to see me. Whenever I went out, everybody appeared at the windows. If I were in the Tuileries, I would see a group circle about me immediately: the women formed a rainbow, shaded through a thousand colors, as they surrounded me. If I were to go to the theater, I would immediately find a hundred lorgnettes turned on me. In short, no man was ever more looked at than myself. I would sometimes smile to hear people who had practically never strayed from their rooms say among themselves: "You must admit that he looks very Persian." What an admirable business! I found portraits of myself everywhere; I saw myself multiplied in every shop, on every mantel. So frightened were they not to have their fill of seeing enough of me.

So much honor cannot go long without becoming a burden. I did not think of myself as being such a curious and rare man, and however good the opinion I may have of myself, I should never have imagined that I was to upset the tranquility of a big city where I was totally unknown. All this made me decide to put off the Persian costume and change over to one in European style, just to see if there would remain anything admirable in my face. That test made me understand what I was really worth. Free of all foreign embellishment, I found that I was more soberly judged. I had every reason to complain of my tailor, who in one moment, made me lose the attentions of public esteem, for I immediately fell into a frightful void. I could stay sometimes for a whole hour in a social gathering without being looked at, without being given any occasion to open my mouth. But if, by chance, someone in the group learned that I was Persian, I would immediately hear a humming all about me: "Ah, ah! So Monsieur is a Persian? What an extraordinary thing! How can anyone be a Persian?"

From Paris, the 6th of the
Moon of Shalval, 1712.

Letter XXXI

Rhedi to Usbek

For the present, my dear Usbeck, I am in Venice. A man could have seen all the cities in the world and still be surprised upon arriving in Venice. It will always be a surprise to see a city and its towers and mosques rising from beneath the water and to look upon masses of people in a place where there should be only fish.

But this worldly city lacks the most precious treasure in the world—I mean fresh water. It is impossible to accomplish a single legal ablution here. This city is an abomination to our Holy Prophet and he looks down upon it from heaven with nothing but rage.

If it were not for that, my dear Usbek, I should be delighted to live in a city where my mind is developing every day. I am ferreting out for myself secrets of commerce; I learn about the motives of princes and the form of their government. I do not even neglect popular European superstitions. I apply myself to medicine, physics, and astronomy, and I am studying the arts. In short,

I am beginning to come out from behind the clouds that covered my eyes in the land of my birth.

From Venice, the 16th of the
Moon of Shalval, 1712.

Letter XXXII

Rica to ——

The other day I went to see a home where some three hundred persons are being rather poorly cared for. The visit did not take long, for the church and the buildings are not worth looking at. The inmates of the place are rather gay; several of them were playing cards or other games I didn't recognize at all. As I was leaving, one of these men left too, and having heard me ask the road to the Marais, the most outlying section of Paris, he said: "I am going there, and I shall take you along; follow me." He led me beautifully, extricated me from all the bottlenecks, and cleverly saved me from carriages and carts. We were about to arrive at our goal when curiosity got the better of me.

"My good friend," I asked, "couldn't I find out who you are?"

"I am a blind man, sir," he replied.

"What! you are blind!" I exclaimed. "Why then didn't you ask that good man playing cards with you to bring us here?"

"He is blind, too," he replied. "For four hundred years now, three hundred of us blind men have been living in that home where you saw me. But I must leave you. There is the street you were looking for. I am going into the crowd, into that church there. And I assure you I shall embarrass people more than they embarrass me."

From Pairs, the 17th of the
Moon of Shalval, 1712.

Letter XXXIII

Usbek to Rhedi in Venice

Wine is so expensive in Paris, by reason of all the taxes put on it, that it would seem likely the authorities have undertaken to carry out the precept of the divine Koran, which forbids drinking.

When I think of all the deadly effects of that liquor, I cannot but consider it the most dreadful gift Nature ever made to man. If anything has dishonored the life and reputation of our monarchs, it has been their intemperance. It is the most envenomed source of their injustice and cruelty.

I shall dare to say it to the shame of mankind: the law forbids the use of wine to our princes, and yet they drink it to an excess that debases them lower than humanity itself. The use of wine is, on the contrary, permissible to Christian princes, and it cannot be noticed that it does them any harm. The human mind is contradiction personified: in licentious debauch, people rebel with fury against precept, and the law, established to make us more virtuous, often serves only to make us more blameworthy.

However, if I disapprove of the use of the sort of liquor that causes loss of reason, I do not condemn in the same way drinks that brighten it up. It is Oriental wisdom to search out remedies against melancholy with as much care as those against the most dangerous diseases. When some misfortune strikes a European, he has no other resource save to read a philosopher called Seneca. But the Asiatics are more reasonable and better physicians in that quarter, and they take brews capable of making a man gay and of charming away the memory of his afflictions.

Nothing can be more distressing than consolation drawn from the necessity of evil, the futility of all remedy, the fatality of destiny, the order of providence, and the sad plight of the human lot. It is ridiculous to try to attenuate evil by considering that we are born miserable. Better to lift the spirit above its own reflections and treat a man as a sentient rather than as a rational being.

The soul, united as it is to the body, is forever the victim of its tyranny. If the blood flows too lethargically, if the humors are not sufficiently purified, if they do not exist in sufficient quantity, we fall into depression and melancholy. But if we swallow brews capable of changing the disposition of our body, our soul becomes once more capable of receiving cheering impressions, and it experiences a secret pleasure at seeing its machinery recover, so to speak, its movement and its life.

From Paris, the 25th of the
Moon of Zilcade, 1713.

Letter XXXIV

Usbek to Ibben in Smyrna

Persian women are more beautiful than those of France, but French women are prettier. Impossible not to love the former, and equally impossible not to be happy with the latter. The first are more gentle and more modest; the others are gayer and more sprightly.

What keeps the bloodline so handsome in Persia is the orderly life led by women there. They neither gamble nor stay up late; they drink no wine and are practically never exposed to the air. One must admit that the seraglio is made more for hygiene than for pleasure. It is a uniform existence, without excitement. Everything smells of obedience and duty. Even the pleasures taken there are sober, and the joys severe, and they are practically never relished except as manifestations of authority and subservience.

Even the men in Persia lack the gaiety of Frenchmen. You simply cannot find there the freedom of mind and the complacent attitude that I see here in every rank and profession.

It is even worse in Turkey, where families could be found in which, from father to son, no one has laughed since the foundation of the monarchy.

This Asiatic sobriety derives from the dearth of intercourse between people. They see each other only when forced to do so by ceremony. Friendship, that sweet bond of hearts which creates a gentleness of existence here, is practically unknown to them. They withdraw to their houses where they always find a social company awaiting them, so that each family group lives, so to speak, in isolation.

One day when I was discussing these things with a man of this country, he said to me: "What shocks me most in your way of life is that you are forced to live with slaves whose hearts and minds always reflect the baseness of their social position. These cowardly people weaken in you feelings of virtue which stem from nature, and they have been destroying such feelings in you since the very childhood they tyrannize.

"For you must eventually cast off your prejudices. What can a man hope for from an education received at the hands of a miserable fellow whose whole honor consists in guarding the women of another man, and who prides himself on having the basest position one can hold among humankind? A man who is to be scorned for his very loyalty (his sole virtue) because he is brought to that loyalty by envy, jealousy, and despair? A man who, burning to avenge himself on the two sexes from which he is an outcast, consents to the tyranny of the stronger so long as he can harass the weaker; who, drawing the whole renown of his calling from his own imperfection, ugliness, and deformity, is held in esteem only because he does not deserve to be? A man, finally, who, forever chained to the door to which his duty attaches him, is harder than the hinges and bolts that hold it up, and who dares boast of his fifty years of life in such an unworthy post, during which, while responsible to his master's jealousy, he has exercised his utter baseness?"

From Paris, the 14th of the
Moon of Zilhage, 1713.

Letter XXXV

Usbek to Jasheed, his cousin, dervish at the shining monastery of Tabriz

What thinkest thou of Christians, sublime dervish? Dost thou believe that, at the Judgment Day, they will be like the infidel Turks, who will be used as asses for riding off the Jews to hell at a trot? I am quite aware that they will certainly not go to the sojourn of the prophets, and that the great Ali never came for them. But just because they were not fortunate enough to find proper mosques in their own countries, dost think they will be condemned to eternal punishment and that God will chastise them for not practicing a religion he did not make known unto them? I can tell thee I have many times examined these Christians, I have questioned to see if they had some idea of the great Ali, the most beautiful among men. I discovered that they had never even heard him mentioned.

They do not at all resemble the infidels whom our saints caused to pass under the sword's edge because they refused to believe in the miracles of heaven. They are more like those unfortunate people who lived within the shadow of idolatry before the divine light came to illumine the face of our great Prophet.

Moreover, if thou but examine their religion closely, thou canst find there in seed, as it were, our dogmas. I have often admired the secrets of providence, which seems thereby to have wished to prepare them all for a general conversion. I have heard talk about a book of their own doctors, called *Polygamy Triumphant*, in which it is shown that polygamy is enjoined upon Christians. Their baptism is the very image of our legal ablutions, and the Christians err only in the efficacity they grant to this first ablution, which, they believe, suffices for all the others. Their priests and their monks, like ourselves, pray seven times a day. They hope to enjoy a paradise where they will partake of a thousand delights by means of the resurrection of the body. Like ourselves, they have set aside days for fasting and mortification of the flesh, by which they hope to sway divine mercy. They offer up worship to the good angels and shun the evil ones. They possess a blessed credulity for miracles performed by God through the ministry of his servants. Like ourselves, they admit to the insufficiency of their good works and to the need they feel for an intercessor in the presence of God. I can see Mohammedanism everywhere, although I cannot find Mohammed here at all. Do what you will, Truth will out and will ever pierce the shadows that surround her. The day will come when the Eternal will see upon the face of the Earth only true believers. Time, which consumes all, will destroy the very errors themselves. All men will be surprised to find themselves under the same standard. Everything, including the law, will be fulfilled. The divine exemplars will be lifted up from the earth and carried off to the celestial archives.

From Paris, the 20th of the
Moon of Zilhage, 1713.

Letter XXXVI

Usbek to Rhedi in Venice

Coffee is very popular in Paris. There are a great number of public houses where it is served. In some of these houses news is reported; in others, chess is played. There is one of them where the coffee is prepared in such a way as to give wit to those who drink it. At least, of all the people who come out of that place there is no man who does not think that he has four times more than when he went in.

What shocks me, however, in these wits is that they do not make themselves useful to their country and that they exercise their talents in puerile things. For example, when I arrived in Paris I found them warmed up over a dispute that couldn't imaginably have been slighter. The whole matter revolved about the reputation of an old Greek poet: for the past two thousand years no one has even been sure of his country or of the date of his death. Both sides admitted that he was an excellent poet; the real question was precisely what degree of excellence should be assigned to him. Everybody wanted to give the final assessment, but among those distributors of reputation, some had more weight on their side than others. And the quarrel started! It was most animated, for, on both sides, such vulgar insults were made and such bitter jests exchanged so cordially that I admired the manner of disputing no less than the subject. "If anyone," I said to myself, "were to be so rash as to approach one of this Greek poet's defenders and to attack the reputation of some honest citizen, he would be soundly rebuked, for I believe that such delicate zeal for the reputation of the dead would flare up nicely to defend that of a living man. However that may be," I added, "God forbid that I should ever draw on my head the enmity of the censors of this poet whom two thousand years in the tomb has not spared from such implacable hate! As things now stand, they are striking out emptily into the air. But what would be their fury if it were fanned by the living presence of their enemy?"

The people I have just spoken to you about discuss in the vulgar tongue, and they must be distinguished from another sort of disputants, who use a foreign tongue that appears to add something to the fury and obstinacy of the combatants. There are some quarters where they draw sustenance from drawing distinctions; they live from obscure reasoning and false conclusions. This profession, in which you might really suppose people would die of hunger, is far from nonlucrative. Members of an entire nation, expelled from their country, have been observed to cross the seas to settle in France, bringing with them for provision against the necessities of life, nothing except a fearful talent for dispute.

Farewell.

From Paris, the last of the
Moon of Zilhage, 1713.

PART 3

Group Membership

In his very suggestive *Civilization and Its Discontents,* Freud writes "that the word civilization describes the whole sum of the achievements and the regulations which distinguish our lives from those of our animal ancestors and which serve two purposes—namely to protect men against nature and to adjust their mutual relations." In this context groups (for in its larger sense that is what civilization is composed of) serve a very vital function. They provide a degree of aid unavailable to the solitary individual and, in addition, they engender a sense of community which enables a man to transcend himself. It is equally obvious, though, that the compromises that group life necessitates will always generate, in many, a sense of discontent. Inevitably, some will affirm the group's principles in conversation and deny them in practice; and others will find the group's codes not only constraining but untenable. Still, if men are to live together with some degree of harmony it is necessary that there be differentiations of power rooted in the groups that give that power substance.

Let there be no doubt about it, therefore: no man is or can be an island entire to himself. For we are all, whether we like it or not, implicated in the humanity of a number of others. We may be discontented but if (for example) power and competition are to be kept in at least some sort of check, and if conflicts are to be solved without resort to force, there is no recourse but group life. In sum, I may even go so far as to call the group a necessary evil, but at least I have seen that it is necessary, indeed, essential.

Chapter 7

Chapter 7 illustrates the enormous power of the group. James Baldwin depicts a religious ceremony in which the emotional intensity of the respondents is at a fever pitch. It is remarkably easy to feel at one with the group when reading these pages. It is also remarkably easy to give into the group in such an emotionally charged atmosphere—even if one does *not* really believe. Indeed, one could almost say that given the conditions described it was almost inevitable that the group would dominate.

Eugene Zamiatin's novel is an anti-Utopian piece written in the early twenties in Russia. Frightened of too much organization, and particularly of the influence of none other than an American (Frederick Taylor, famous for his *The Principles of Scientific Management*), Zamiatin shows the extent to which the concept of the group can be taken. These pages tell us that under such a system "the status *is* the person." The group is not concerned with how I feel or with what I believe; it is only concerned that my functionally rational and functionally specific performance will contribute to the larger group efficiency.

Certainly, any student in possession of his IBM card can understand, to at least some degree, what is so very frightening to Zamiatin.

The selection from Melville shows the group as an agency of social control. Notice particularly the "anguish" of the judge. For everyone is aware that Billy had ample justification for his action, and yet the laws state that he must be punished. There is, then, no alternative for the judge if the group standards are to be upheld. Billy Budd "must" be hanged. Clearly, Billy was, in Melville's apt phrasing, "a martyr to martial discipline."

Chapter 8

The Dreiser and Stendhal selections concern some of the means of competition; but both pieces are also useful descriptions of how power is organized and utilized. In addition, it is noteworthy that, while Stendhal deals with early nineteenth century French society, and Dreiser with early twentieth century American society, the situation does not seem to have changed very much. We are still trying (as in Stendhal) to rig elections and (as in Dreiser) to get in "on the ground plan," however unscrupulously, of new civic and industrial developments. It might be well to ask here if such abuses are merely characteristic of a capitalistic society or if they are endemic in man's human *social* nature or both.

In the selection from Arthur Koestler we see a tragic manifestation of the misuse of power, and of the crimes which are so very often committed under the guise of righteousness. The selection concerns, of course, not only past but also contemporary Russian society. The recent crackdown in Eastern Europe and the treatment of Alexander Solzhenitsyn (author of, among other things, *The First Circle,* which is a brilliant portrayal of life under the Stalin "penal" system) unfortunately bears this contention out. Moreover, it must be noted that such misuse is not confined to Russia. The Inquisition and the McCarthy era are also instances, among a multitude of others, in which the misuse of power has been sanctioned in the name of righteousness.

Chapter 9

Chapter 9 offers examples of types of leaders. In the selection from Ken Kesey, there is no doubt as to who the boss is. McMurphy comes into that room and, not at all maliciously, he just plain takes over. His charisma is overpowering. Consider also, though, that charisma, at least in the work of Max Weber, referred to a leader who did not operate within a system of rules. On the contrary, the hallmark of the charismatic leader was his proclamation: "it is written, but I say unto you." McMurphy then (or Kennedy or Castro) may have charisma, but it is seriously constrained if used within the confines of a particular system. In that case it will be the laws, and not the charisma, that will dominate.

The Nietzsche selection, on the other hand, calls our attention to a figure who, although he has attempted to preach a new ethic, also refuses to solve the problems of his disciples. This is consistent with the individualistic ethic of Zarathustra, but it *is* contrary to the manner in which leaders usually conduct themselves. To wit, it must not be forgotten that Zarathustra was among the very first, if not the first, to proclaim: "do your own thing."

Finally, the selection from Emile Zola refers to a leader who fears that he has led all too well. Indeed, Etienne finds that in the end the group was on its own. He had completely lost control of it. It had become a mob. Unfortunately, this is a point which is sometimes forgotten. For there will always be a difference between what the leader says, and what the people think and feel the leader says. Perception, remember, is an interpolated act.[1]

Chapter 10

Here we are concerned with group conflict. The selection from Homer deals with a battle between two of literature's most famous heroes. Its literary merit should not blind us, though, to the very important issues it raises. For the topic in question—WAR—is the most serious one presently confronting world civilization. George Thayer, for example, notes that there have been fifty-five wars since 1945.[2] Is it really possible, therefore, to speak of being civilized? For were not Achilles and Hector, and the culture of which they are symbols, a great deal more civilized than we? And can one really speak of sanity when men not only think about the unthinkable but, indeed, actually broach the unthinkable as an instrument of national policy? Is Lorenz correct, then, when he asserts "that militant enthusiasm is an instinctive response with a phylogenetically determined releasing mechanism and that the only point at which intelligent and responsible supervision can get control is in the conditioning of the response to an object which proves to be a genuine value under the scrutiny of the categorical question?"[3]

The last two selections refer to what can broadly be characterized as manifestations of class conflicts. The Kazantzakis novel, a splendid one by the way, refers to the recent Greek civil war (in the late forties), and the one by Dickens refers to the French Revolution. Both are telling examples of what unsolved and lingering inequities can lead to.

[1] Harry Stack Sullivan, *Interpersonal Theory of Psychiatry* (New York, 1953), p. 27.
[2] George Thayer, *The War Business* (New York, 1968).
[3] Konrad Lorenz, *On Aggression* (New York, 1966), p. 262.

Chapter 7

Group as a System

JAMES BALDWIN

• *Go Tell It on the Mountain*

Then I buckled up my shoes,
And I started.

He knew, without knowing how it had happened, that he lay on the floor, in the dusty space before the altar which he and Elisha had cleaned; and knew that above him burned the yellow light which he had himself switched on. Dust was in his nostrils, sharp and terrible, and the feet of the saints, shaking the floor beneath him, raised small clouds of dust that filmed his mouth. He heard their cries, so far, so high above him—he could never rise that far. He was like a rock, a dead man's body, a dying bird, fallen from an awful height; something that had no power of itself, any more, to turn.

And something moved in John's body which was not John. He was invaded, set at naught, possessed. This power had struck John, in the head or in the heart; and, in a moment, wholly, filling him with an anguish that he could never in his life have imagined, that he surely could not endure, that even now he could not believe, had opened him up; had cracked him open, as wood beneath the axe cracks down the middle, as rocks break up; had ripped him and felled him in a moment, so that John had not felt the wound, but only the agony, had not felt the fall, but only the fear; and lay here, now, helpless, screaming, at the very bottom of darkness.

He wanted to rise—a malicious, ironic voice insisted that he rise—and, at once, to leave this temple and go out into the world.

He wanted to obey the voice, which was the only voice that spoke to him; he tried to assure the voice that he would do his best to rise; he would only lie here a moment, after his dreadful fall, and catch his breath. It was at this moment, precisely, that he found he could not rise; something had happened to his arms, his legs, his feet—ah, something had happened to John! And he began to scream again in his great, bewildered terror, and felt himself, indeed, begin to move— not upward, toward the light, but down again, a sickness in his bowels, a tightening in his loin-strings; he felt himself turning, again and again, across the dusty floor, as though God's toe had touched him lightly. And the dust made him cough and retch; in his turning the center of the whole earth shifted, making of space a sheer void and a mockery of order, and balance, and time. Nothing remained: all was swallowed up in chaos. And: *Is this it?* John's terrified soul inquired—*What is it?*—to no purpose, receiving no answer. Only the ironic voice insisted yet once more that he rise from that filthy floor if he did not want to become like all the other niggers.

Then the anguish subsided for a moment, as water withdraws briefly to dash itself once more against the rocks: he knew that it subsided only to return. And he coughed and sobbed in the dusty space before the altar, lying on his face. And still he was going down, farther and farther from the joy, the singing, and the light above him.

He tried, but in such despair!—the utter darkness does not present any point of departure, contains no beginning, and no end—to rediscover, and, as it were, to trap and hold tightly in the palm of his hand, the moment preceding his fall, his change. But that moment was also locked in darkness, was wordless, and would not come forth. He remembered only the cross: he had turned again to kneel at the altar, and had faced the golden cross. And the Holy Ghost was speaking—seeming to say, as John spelled out the so abruptly present and gigantic legend adorning the cross: *Jesus Saves*. He had stared at this, an awful bitterness in his heart, wanting to curse—and the Spirit spoke, and spoke in him. Yes: there was Elisha, speaking from the floor, and his father, silent, at his back. In his heart there was a sudden yearning tenderness for holy Elisha; desire, sharp and awful as a reflecting knife, to usurp the body of Elisha, and lie where Elisha lay; to speak in tongues, as Elisha spoke, and, with that authority, to confound his father. Yet this had not been the moment; it was as far back as he could go, but the secret, the turning, the abysmal drop was farther back, in darkness. As he cursed his father, as he loved Elisha, he had, even then, been weeping; he had already passed his moment, was already under the power, had been struck, and was going down.

Ah, down!—and to what purpose, where? To the bottom of the sea, the bowels of the earth, to the heart of the fiery furnace? Into a dungeon deeper than

Hell, into a madness louder than the grave? What trumpet sound would awaken him, what hand would lift him up? For he knew, as he was struck again, and screamed again, his throat like burning ashes, and as he turned again, his body hanging from him like a useless weight, a heavy, rotting carcass, that if he were not lifted he would never rise.

His father, his mother, his aunt, Elisha—all were far above him, waiting, watching his torment in the pit. They hung over the golden barrier, singing behind them, light around their heads, weeping, perhaps, for John, struck down so early. And, no, they could not help him any more—nothing could help him any more. He struggled, struggled to rise up, and meet them—he wanted wings to fly upward and meet them in that morning, that morning where they were. But his struggles only thrust him downward, his cries did not go upward, but rang in his own skull.

Yet, though he scarcely saw their faces, he knew that they were there. He felt them move, every movement causing a trembling, an astonishment, a horror in the heart of darkness where he lay. He could not know if they wished him to come to them as passionately as he wished to rise. Perhaps they did not help him because they did not care—because they did not love him.

Then his father returned to him, in John's changed and low condition; and John thought, but for a moment only, that his father had come to help him. In the silence, then, that filled the void, John looked on his father. His father's face was black—like a sad, eternal night; yet in his father's face there burned a fire— a fire eternal in an eternal night. John trembled where he lay, feeling no warmth for him from this fire, trembled, and could not take his eyes away. A wind blew over him, saying: "Whosoever loveth and maketh a lie." And he knew that he had been thrust out of the holy, the joyful, the blood-washed community, that his father had thrust him out. His father's will was stronger than John's own. His power was greater because he belonged to God. Now, John felt no hatred, nothing, only a bitter, unbelieving despair: all prophecies were true, salvation was finished, damnation was real!

Then Death is real, John's soul said, and Death will have his moment.

"Set thine house in order," said his father, "for thou shalt die and not live."

And then the ironic voice spoke again, saying: "Get up, John. Get up, boy. Don't let him keep you here. You got everything your daddy got."

John tried to laugh—John thought that he was laughing—but found, instead, that his mouth was filled with salt, his ears were full of burning water. Whatever was happening in his distant body now, he could not change or stop; his chest heaved, his laughter rose and bubbled at his mouth, like blood.

And his father looked on him. His father's eyes looked down on him, and John began to scream. His father's eyes stripped him naked, and hated what they saw. And as he turned, screaming, in the dust again, trying to escape his father's eyes, those eyes, that face, and all their faces, and the far-off yellow light, all departed from his vision as though he had gone blind. He was going down again. There is, his soul cried out again, no bottom to the darkness!

He did not know where he was. There was silence everywhere—only a perpetual, distant, faint trembling far beneath him—the roaring, perhaps, of the fires of Hell, over which he was suspended, or the echo, persistent, invincible still, of the moving feet of the saints. He thought of the mountaintop, where he longed to be, where the sun would cover him like a cloth of gold, would cover his head like a crown of fire, and in his hands he would hold a living rod. But this was no mountain where John lay, here, no robe, no crown. And the living rod was uplifted in other hands.

"I'm going to beat sin out of him. I'm going to beat it out."

Yes, he had sinned, and his father was looking for him. Now, John did not make a sound, and did not move at all, hoping that his father would pass him by.

"Leave him be. Leave him alone. Let him pray to the Lord."

"Yes, Mama. I'm going to try to love the Lord."

"He done run off somewhere. I'm going to find him. I'm going to beat it out."

Yes, he had sinned: one morning, alone, in the dirty bathroom, in the square, dirt-gray cupboard room that was filled with the stink of his father. Sometimes, leaning over the cracked, "tattle-tale gray" bathtub, he scrubbed his father's back; and looked, as the accursed son of Noah had looked, on his father's hideous nakedness. It was secret, like sin, and slimy, like the serpent, and heavy, like the rod. Then he hated his father, and longed for the power to cut his father down.

Was this why he lay here, thrust out from all human or heavenly help tonight? This, and not that other, his deadly sin, having looked on his father's nakedness and mocked and cursed him in his heart? Ah, that son of Noah's had been cursed, down to the present groaning generation: *A servant of servants shall he be unto his brethren.*

Then the ironic voice, terrified, it seemed, of no depth, no darkness, demanded of John, scornfully, if he believed that he was cursed. All niggers had been cursed, the ironic voice reminded him, all niggers had come from this most undutiful of Noah's sons. How could John be cursed for having seen in a bathtub what another man—*if* that other man had ever lived—had seen ten thousand years ago, lying in an open tent? Could a curse come down so many ages? Did it live in time, or in the moment? But John found no answer for this voice, for he was in the moment, and out of time.

And his father approached. "I'm going to beat sin out of him. I'm going to beat it out." All the darkness rocked and wailed as his father's feet came closer; feet whose tread resounded like God's tread in the garden of Eden, searching the covered Adam and Eve. Then his father stood just above him, looking down. Then John knew that a curse was renewed from moment to moment, from father to son. Time was indifferent, like snow and ice; but the heart, crazed wanderer in the driving waste, carried the curse forever.

"John," said his father, "come with me."

Then they were in a straight street, a narrow, narrow way. They had been walking for many days. The street stretched before them, long, and silent, going down, and whiter than the snow. There was no one on the street, and John was frightened. The buildings on this street, so near that John could touch them on either side, were narrow, also, rising like spears into the sky, and they were made of beaten gold and silver. John knew that these buildings were not for him—not today—*no, nor tomorrow, either!* Then, coming up this straight and silent street, he saw a woman, very old and black, coming toward them, staggering on the crooked stones. She was drunk, and dirty, and very old, and her mouth was bigger than his mother's mouth, or his own; her mouth was loose and wet, and he had *never* seen anyone so black. His father was astonished to see her, and beside himself with anger; but John was glad. He clapped his hands and cried:

"See! She's uglier than Mama! She's uglier than me!"

"You mighty proud, ain't you," his father said, "to be the Devil's son?"

But John did not listen to his father. He turned to watch the woman pass. His father grabbed his arm.

"You see that? That's sin. That's what the Devil's son runs after."

"Whose son are you?" John asked.

His father slapped him. John laughed, and moved a little away.

"I seen it. I seen it. I ain't the Devil's son for nothing."

His father reached for him, but John was faster. He moved backward down the shining street, looking at his father—his father who moved toward him, one hand outstretched in fury.

"And I *heard* you—all the nighttime long. I know what you do in the dark, black man, when you think the Devil's son's asleep. I heard you, spitting, and groaning, and choking—and I *seen* you, riding up and down, and going in and out. I ain't the Devil's son for nothing."

The listening buildings, rising upward yet, leaned, closing out the sky. John's feet began to slip; tears and sweat were in his eyes; still moving backward before his father, he looked about him for deliverance; but there was no deliverance in this street for him.

"And I hate you. I hate you. I don't care about your golden crown. I don't care about your long white robe. I seen you under the robe, I seen you!"

Then his father was upon him; at his touch there was singing, and fire. John lay on his back in the narrow street, looking up at his father, that burning face beneath the burning towers.

"I'm going to beat it out of you. I'm going to beat it out."

His father raised his hand. The knife came down. John rolled away, down the white, descending street, screaming:

"Father! Father!"

These were the first words he uttered. In a moment there was silence, and his father was gone. Again, he felt the saints above him—and dust was in his mouth. There was singing somewhere; far away, above him; singing slow and mournful. He lay silent, racked beyond endurance, salt drying on his face, with nothing in him any more, no lust, no fear, no shame, no hope. And yet he knew that it would come again—the darkness was full of demons crouching, waiting to worry him with their teeth again.

Then I looked in the grave and I wondered.

Ah, down!—what was he searching here, all alone in darkness? But now he knew, for irony had left him, that he was searching something, hidden in the darkness, that must be found. He would die if it was not found; or, he was dead already, and would never again be joined to the living, if it was not found.

And the grave looked so sad and lonesome.

In the grave where he now wandered—he knew it was the grave, it was so cold and silent, and he moved in icy mist—he found his mother and his father, his mother dressed in scarlet, his father dressed in white. They did not see him: they looked backward, over their shoulders, at a cloud of witnesses. And there was his Aunt Florence, gold and silver flashing on her fingers, brazen earrings dangling from her ears; and there was another woman, whom he took to be that wife of his father's called Deborah—who had, as he had once believed, so much to tell him. But she, alone, of all that company, looked at him and signified that there was no speech in the grave. He was a stranger there—they did not see him pass, they did not know what he was looking for, they could not help him search. He wanted to find Elisha, who knew, perhaps, who would help him—but Elisha was not there. There was Roy: Roy also might have helped him, but he had been stabbed with a knife, and lay now, brown and silent, at his father's feet.

Then there began to flood John's soul the waters of despair. *Love is as strong as death, as deep as the grave.* But love, which had, perhaps, like a benevolent monarch, swelled the population of his neighboring kingdom, Death, had not himself descended: they owed him no allegiance here. Here there was no speech or language, and there was no love; no one to say: You are beautiful, John; no one to forgive him, no matter what his sin; no one to heal him, and lift him up. No one: father and mother looked backward, Roy was bloody, Elisha was not here.

Then the darkness began to murmur—a terrible sound—and John's ears trembled. In this murmur that filled the grave, like a thousand wings beating on the air, he recognized a sound that he had always heard. He began, for terror, to weep and moan—and this sound was swallowed up, and yet was magnified by the echoes that filled the darkness.

This sound had filled John's life, so it now seemed, from the moment he had first drawn breath. He had heard it everywhere, in prayer and in daily speech, and wherever the saints were gathered, and in the unbelieving streets. It was in his father's anger, and in his mother's calm insistence, and in the vehement mockery of his aunt; it had rung, so oddly, in Roy's voice this afternoon, and when Elisha played the piano it was there; it was in the beat and jangle of Sister McCandless's tambourine, it was in the very cadence of her testimony, and invested that testimony with a matchless, unimpeachable authority. Yes, he had heard it all his life, but it was only now that his ears were opened to this sound that came from darkness, that could only come from darkness, that yet bore such sure witness to the glory of the light. And now in his moaning, and so far from any help, he heard it in himself—it rose from his bleeding, his cracked-open heart. It was a sound of rage and weeping which filled the grave, rage and weeping from time set free, but bound now in eternity; rage that had no language, weeping with no voice—which yet spoke now, to John's startled soul, of boundless melancholy, of the bitterest patience, and the longest night; of the deepest water, the strongest chains, the most cruel lash; of humility most wretched, the dungeon most absolute, of love's bed defiled, and birth dishonored, and most bloody, unspeakable, sudden death. Yes, the darkness hummed with murder: the body in the water, the body in the fire, the body on the tree. John looked down the line of these armies of darkness, army upon army, and his soul whispered: *Who are these? Who are they?* And wondered: *Where shall I go?*

There was no answer. There was no help or healing in the grave, no answer in the darkness, no speech from all that company, They looked backward. And John looked back, seeing no deliverance.

I, John, saw the future, way up in the middle of the air.

Were the lash, the dungeon, and the night for him? And the sea for him? And the grave for him?

I, John, saw a number, way in the middle of the air.

And he struggled to flee—out of this darkness, out of this company—into the land of the living, so high, so far away. Fear was upon him, a more deadly fear than he had ever known, as he turned and turned in the darkness, as he moaned, and stumbled, and crawled through darkness, finding no hand, no voice, finding no door. *Who are these? Who are they?* They were the despised and rejected, the wretched and the spat upon, the earth's offscouring; and he was in their company, and they would swallow up his soul. The stripes they had endured would scar his back, their punishment would be his, their portion his, his their humiliation, anguish, chains, their dungeon his, their death his. *Thrice was I beaten with rods, once I was stoned, thrice I suffered shipwreck, a night and a day I have been in the deep.*

And their dread testimony would be his!

"In journeyings often, in perils of waters, in perils of robbers, in perils by mine own countrymen, in perils by the heathen, in perils in the city, in perils in the wilderness, in perils in the sea, in perils among false brethren.

And their desolation, his:

In weariness and painfulness in watchings often, in hunger and thirst, in fastings often, in cold and nakedness.

And he began to shout for help, seeing before him the lash, the fire, and the depthless water, seeing his head bowed down forever, he, John, the lowest among these lowly. And he looked for his mother, but her eyes were fixed on this dark army—she was claimed by this army. And his father would not help him, his father did not see him, and Roy lay dead.

Then he whispered, not knowing that he whispered: "Oh, Lord, have mercy on me. Have mercy on me."

And a voice, for the first time in all his terrible journey, spoke to John, through the rage and weeping, and fire, and darkness, and flood:

"Yes," said the voice, "go through. Go through."

"Lift me up," whispered John, "lift me up. I can't go through."

"Go through," said the voice, "go through."

Then there was silence. The murmuring ceased. There was only this trembling beneath him. And he knew there was a light somewhere.

"Go through."

"Ask Him to take you through."

But he could never go through this darkness, through this fire and this wrath. He could never go through. His strength was finished, and he could not move. He belonged to the darkness—the darkness from which he had thought to flee had claimed him. And he moaned again, weeping, and lifted up his hands.

"Call on Him. Call on Him."

"Ask Him to take you through."

Dust rose again in his nostrils, sharp as the fumes of Hell. And he turned again in the darkness, trying to remember something he had heard, something he had read.

Jesus saves.

And he saw before him the fire, red and gold, and waiting for him—yellow, and red, and gold, and burning in a night eternal, and waiting for him. He must go through this fire, and into this night.

Jesus saves.
Call on Him.
Ask Him to take you through.

He could not call, for his tongue would not unlock, and his heart was silent, and great with fear. In the darkness, how to move?—with death's ten thousand jaws agape, and waiting in the darkness. On any turning whatsoever the beast may spring—to move in the darkness is to move into the waiting jaws of death. And yet, it came to him that he must move; for there was a light somewhere, and life, and joy, and singing—somewhere, somewhere above him.

And he moaned again: "Oh, Lord, have mercy. Have mercy, Lord."

There came to him again the communion service at which Elisha had knelt at his father's feet. Now this service was in a great, high room, a room made golden by the light of the sun; and the room was filled with a multitude of people, all in long, white robes, the women with covered heads. They sat at a long, bare, wooden table. They broke at this table flat, unsalted bread, which was the body of the Lord, and drank from a heavy silver cup the scarlet wine of His blood. Then he saw that they were barefoot, and that their feet were stained with this same blood. And a sound of weeping filled the room as they broke the bread and drank the wine.

Then they rose, to come together over a great basin filled with water. And they divided into four groups, two of women and two of men; and they began, woman before woman, and man before man, to wash each other's feet. But the blood would not wash off; many washings only turned the crystal water red; and someone cried: *"Have you been to the river?"*

Then John saw the river, and the multitude was there. And now they had undergone a change; their robes were ragged, and stained with the road they had traveled, and stained with unholy blood; the robes of some barely covered their nakedness; and some indeed were naked. And some stumbled on the smooth stones at the river's edge, for they were blind; and some crawled with a terrible wailing, for they were lame; some did not cease to pluck at their flesh, which was rotten with running sores. All struggled to get to the river, in a dreadful hardness of heart: the strong struck down the weak, the ragged spat on the naked, the naked cursed the blind, the blind crawled over the lame. And someone cried: *"Sinner, do you love my Lord?"*

Then John saw the Lord—for a moment only; and the darkness, for a moment only, was filled with a light he could not bear. Then, in a moment, he was set free; his tears sprang as from a fountain; his heart, like a fountain of waters, burst. Then he cried: "Oh, blessed Jesus! Oh, Lord Jesus! Take me through!"

Of tears there was, yes, a very fountain—springing from a depth never sounded before, from depths John had not known were in him. And he wanted to rise up, singing, singing in that great morning, the morning of his new life. Ah, how his tears ran down, how they blessed his soul!—as he felt himself, out of the darkness, and the fire, and the terrors of death, rising upward to meet the saints.

"Oh, yes!" cried the voice of Elisha. "Bless our God forever!"

And a sweetness filled John as he heard this voice, and heard the sound of singing: the singing was for him. For his drifting soul was anchored in the love of God; in the rock that endured forever. The light and the darkness has kissed each other, and were married now, forever, in the life and the vision of John's soul.

I, John, saw a city, way in the middle of the air,
Waiting, waiting, waiting up there.

He opened his eyes on the morning, and found them, in the light of the morning, rejoicing for him. The trembling he had known in darkness had been the echo of their joyful feet—these feet, bloodstained forever, and washed in many rivers—they moved on the bloody road forever, with no continuing city, but seeking one to come: a city out of time, not made with hands, but eternal in the heavens. No power could hold this army back, no water disperse them, no fire consume them. One day they would compel the earth to heave upward, and surrender the waiting dead. They sang, where the darkness gathered, where the lion waited, where the fire cried, and where blood ran down:

My soul, don't you be uneasy!

They wandered in the valley forever; and they smote the rock, forever; and the waters sprang, perpetually, in the perpetual desert. They cried unto the Lord forever, and lifted up their eyes forever, they were cast down forever, and He lifted them up forever. No, the fire could not hurt them, and yes, the lion's jaws were stopped; the serpent was not their master, the grave was not their resting-place, the earth was not their home. Job bore them witness, and Abraham was their father, Moses had elected to suffer with them rather than glory in sin for a season. Shadrach, Meshach, and Abednego had gone before them into the fire, their grief had been sung by David, and Jeremiah had wept for them. Ezekiel had prophesied upon them, these scattered bones, these slain, and, in the fulness of time, the prophet, John, had come out of the wilderness, crying that the promise was for them. They were encompassed with a very cloud of witnesses: Judas, who had betrayed the Lord; Thomas, who had doubted Him; Peter, who had trembled at the crowing of a cock; Stephen, who had been stoned; Paul, who had been bound; the blind man crying in the dusty road, the dead man rising from the grave. And they looked unto Jesus, the author and the finisher of their faith, running with patience the race He had set before them; they endured the cross, and they despised the shame, and waited to join Him, one day, in glory, at the right hand of the Father.

My soul! don't you be uneasy!
Jesus going to make up my dying bed!

"Rise up, rise up, Brother Johnny, and talk about the Lord's deliverance."

It was Elisha who had spoken; he stood just above John, smiling; and behind him were the saints—Praying Mother Washington, and Sister McCandless, and Sister Price. Behind these, he saw his mother, and his aunt; his father, for the moment, was hidden from his view.

"Amen!" cried Sister McCandless, "rise up, and praise the Lord!"

He tried to speak, and could not, for the joy that rang in him this morning.

He smiled up at Elisha, and his tears ran down; and Sister McCandless began to sing:

> *"Lord, I ain't*
> *No stranger now!"*

"Rise up, Johnny," said Elisha, again. "Are you saved, boy?"

"Yes," said John, "oh, yes!" And the words came upward, it seemed, of themselves, in the new voice God had given him. Elisha stretched out his hand, and John took the hand, and stood—so suddenly, and so strangely, and with such wonder!—once more on his feet.

> *"Lord, I ain't*
> *No stranger now!"*

Yes, the night had passed, the powers of darkness had been beaten back. He moved among the saints, he, John, who had come home, who was one of their company now; weeping, he yet could find no words to speak of his great gladness; and he scarcely knew how he moved, for his hands were new, and his feet were new, and he moved in a new and Heaven-bright air. Praying Mother Washington took him in her arms, and kissed him, and their tears, his tears and the tears of the old, black woman, mingled.

"God bless you, son. Run on, honey, and don't get weary!"

> *"Lord, I been introduced*
> *To the Father and the Son,*
> *And I ain't*
> *No stranger now!"*

Yet, as he moved among them, their hands touching, and tears falling, and the music rising—as though he moved down a great hall, full of a splendid company—something began to knock in that listening, astonished, newborn, and fragile heart of his; something recalling the terrors of the night, which were not finished, his heart seemed to say; which, in this company, were now to begin. And, while his heart was speaking, he found himself before his mother. Her face was full of tears, and for a long while they looked at each other, saying nothing. And once again, he tried to read the mystery of that face—which, as it has never before been so bright and pained with love, had never seemed before so far from him, so wholly in communion with a life beyond his life. He wanted to comfort her, but the night had given him no language, no second sight, no power to see into the heart of any other. He knew only—and now, looking at his mother, he knew that he could never tell it—that the heart was a fearful place. She kissed him, and she said: "I'm mighty proud, Johnny. You keep the faith, I'm going to be praying for you till the Lord puts me in my grave."

Then he stood before his father. In the moment that he forced himself to raise his eyes and look into his father's face, he felt in himself a stiffening, and a panic, and a blind rebellion, and a hope for peace. The tears still on his face, and smiling still, he said: "Praise the Lord."

"Praise the Lord," said his father. He did not move to touch him, did not kiss him, did not smile. They stood before each other in silence, while the saints rejoiced; and John struggled to speak the authoritative, the living word that would conquer the great division between his father and himself. But it did not come, the living word; in the silence something died in John, and something came alive. It came to him that he must testify: his tongue only could bear witness to the wonders he had seen. And he remembered, suddenly, the text of a sermon he had once heard his father preach. And he opened his mouth, feeling, as he watched his father, the darkness roar behind him, and the very earth beneath him seem to shake; yet he gave to his father their common testimony. "I'm saved," he said, "and I know I'm saved." And then, as his father did not speak, he repeated his father's text: "My witness is in Heaven and my record is on high."

"It come from your mouth," said his father then. "I want to see you live it. It's more than a notion."

"I'm going to pray God," said John—and his voice shook, whether with joy or grief he could not say—"to keep me, and make me strong . . . to stand . . . to stand against the enemy . . . and against everything and everybody . . . that wants to cut down my soul."

Then his tears came down again, like a wall between him and his father. His Aunt Florence came and took him in her arms. Her eyes were dry, and her face was old in the savage, morning light. But her voice, when she spoke, was gentler than he had ever known it to be before.

"You fight the good fight," she said, "you hear? Don't you get weary, and don't you get scared. Because I *know* the Lord's done laid His hands on you."

"Yes," he said, weeping, "yes. I'm going to serve the Lord."

"Amen!" cried Elisha. "Bless our God!"

EUGENE ZAMIATIN

• *We*

Record Thirty-eight

I Don't Know What Title—Perhaps the Whole
Synopsis May Be Called a Castoff Cigarette Butt

I awoke. A bright glare painful to look at. I half-closed my eyes. My head
seemed filled with some caustic blue smoke. Everything was enveloped in fog,
and through the fog:
"But I did not turn on the light . . . then how is it . . ."
I jumped up. At the table, leaning her chin on her hand and smiling, sat
I-330, looking at me.

She was at the very table at which I am now writing. Those ten or fifteen
minutes are already well behind me, cruelly twisted into a very firm spring. Yet
it seems to me that the door closed after her only a second ago, and that I could
still overtake her and grasp her hand, and that she might laugh out and say . . .

I-330 was at the table. I rushed toward her.
"You? You! I have been . . . I saw your room. . . . I thought you . . ." But
midway I hurt myself upon the sharp, motionless spears of her eyelashes, and I
stopped. I remembered: she had looked at me in the same way before, in the
Integral. I felt I had to tell her everything in one split second, and in such a way
that she would surely believe, or she would never . . .

"Listen, I-330, I must . . . I must . . . everything! No, no, one moment—let me have a glass of water first."

My mouth was as dry as if it were lined with blotting paper. I poured a glass of water but I couldn't . . . I put the glass back upon the table, and with both hands firmly grasped the carafe.

Now I noticed that the blue smoke came from a cigarette. She brought the cigarette to her lips, and eagerly drew in and swallowed the smoke as I did water; then she said:

"Don't. Be silent. Don't you see it matters very little? I came, anyway. They are waiting for me below. . . . Do you want these minutes, which are our last . . . ?"

Abruptly she threw the cigarette on the floor and bent backward, over the side of the chair, to reach the button in the wall (it was quite difficult to do), and I remember how the chair swayed slightly, how two of its legs were lifted. Then the curtains fell.

She came close to me and embraced me. Her knees, through her dress, were like a slow, gentle, warm, enveloping, and permeating poison . . .

Suddenly (it happens at times) you plunge into sweet, warm sleep—when all at once, as if something pricks you, you tremble and your eyes are again widely open. So it was now; there on the floor in her room were the pink checks stamped with traces of footsteps, some of them bore the letter F- and some figures . . . Plus and minus fused within my mind into one lump . . . I could not say even now what sort of feeling it was, but I crushed her so that she cried out with pain . . .

One more minute out of those ten or fifteen; her head thrown back, lying on the bright yellow pillow, her eyes half-closed, a sharp, sweet line of teeth . . . And all this reminded me in an irresistible, absurd, torturing way about something forbidden, something not permissible at that moment. More tenderly, more cruelly, I pressed her to myself, brighter grew the blue traces of my fingers . . .

She said, without opening her eyes (I noticed this), "They say you went to see the Well-Doer yesterday; is it true?"

"Yes."

Then her eyes opened widely and with delight I looked at her and saw that her face grew quickly paler and paler, that it effaced itself, disappearing—only the eyes remained.

I told her everything. Only for some reason, why I don't know (no, that's not true, I know the reason), I was silent about one thing: His assertion at the end that they needed me only in order . . .

Like the image on a photographic plate in a developing fluid, her face gradually reappeared: the cheeks, the white line of teeth, the lips. She stood up and went to the mirror door of the closet. My mouth was dry again. I poured water but it was revolting to drink it; I put the glass back on the table and asked:

"Did you come to see me because you wanted to inquire . . . ?"

A sharp, mocking triangle of brows drawn to the temples looked at me from the mirror. She turned around to say something, but said nothing.

It was not necessary; I knew.

To bid her good-by, I moved my foreign limbs, struck the chair with them. It fell upside down, dead, like the table in her room. Her lips were cold . . . just as cold was once the floor, here, near my bed . . .

When she left I sat down on the floor, bent over the cigarette butt . . .

I cannot write any more—I no longer want to!

Record Thirty-nine

The End

All this was like the last crystal of salt thrown into a saturated solution; quickly, needle-like crystals began to appear, to grow more substantial and solid. It was all clear to me; the decision was made, and tomorrow morning I *shall do it!* It amounts to suicide, but perhaps then I shall be reborn. For only what is killed can be reborn.

Every second the sky twitched convulsively there in the west. My head was burning and pulsating inside; I was up all night, and I fell asleep only at about seven o'clock in the morning, when the darkness of the night was already dispelled and becoming gray, and the roofs crowded with birds became visible . . .

I woke up; ten o'clock. Evidently the bell did not ring today. On the table —left from yesterday—stood the glass of water. I gulped the water eagerly and I ran; I had to do it quickly, as quickly as possible.

The sky was deserted, blue, all eaten up by the storm. Sharp corners of shadows . . . Everything seemed to be cut out of blue autumnal air—thin, dangerous to touch; it seemed so brittle, ready to disperse into glass dust. Within me something similar; I must not think; it was dangerous to think, for . . .

And I did not think, perhaps I did not even see properly; I only registered impressions. There on the pavement, thrown from somewhere, branches were strewn; their leaves were green, amber, and cherry-red. Above, crossing each other, birds and aeros were tossing about. Here below heads, open mouths, hands waving branches . . . All this must have been shouting, buzzing, chirping . . .

Then—streets empty as if swept by a plague. I remember I stumbled over something disgustingly soft, yielding yet motionless. I bent down—a corpse. It was lying flat, the legs apart. The face . . . I recognized the thick Negro lips, which even now seemed to sprinkle with laughter. His eyes, firmly screwed in, laughed into my face. One second . . . I stepped over him and ran: I could no longer . . . I had to have everything done as soon as possible, or else I felt I would snap, I would break in two like an overloaded sail. . .

Luckily it was not more than twenty steps away; I already saw the sign with the golden letters: "The Bureau of Guardians." At the door I stopped for a moment to gulp down as much air as I could, and I stepped in.

Inside, in the corridor, stood an endless chain of Numbers, holding small sheets of paper and heavy notebooks. They moved slowly, advancing a step or two and stopping again. I began to be tossed about along the chain; my head was breaking to pieces. I pulled them by the sleeves, I implored them as a sick man implores to be given something that would, even at the price of sharpest pain, end everything forever.

A woman with a belt tightly clasped around her waist and with two distinctly protruding, squatty hemispheres tossing about as if she had eyes on them, chuckled at me:

"He has a bellyache! Show him to the room second door to the right!"

Everybody laughed, and because of that laughter something rose in my throat; I felt I would either scream or . . . or . . .

Suddenly from behind me someone touched my elbow. I turned around. Transparent wing ears! But they were not pink as usual; they were purplish red; his Adam's apple was tossing about as though ready to tear the covering . . .

Quickly boring into me: "What are you here for?"

I seized him.

"Quickly! Please! Quickly! . . . into your office . . . I must tell everything . . . right away . . . I am glad that you . . . It may be terrible that it should be you to whom . . . But it is good, it is good. . . ."

He, too, knew *her*; this made it even more tormenting for me. But perhaps he, too, would tremble when he heard . . . And we would both be killing . . . And I would not be alone at that, my supreme second . . .

The door closed with a slam. I remember a piece of paper was caught beneath the door, and it rustled on the floor when the door closed. And then a strange, airless silence covered us as if a glass bell had been put over us. If only he had uttered a single, most insignificant word, no matter what, I would have told him everything at once. But he was silent. So keyed up that I heard a noise in my ears, I said without looking at him:

"I think I always hated her from the very beginning . . . I struggled . . . Or, no, no, don't believe me; I could have, but I did not want to save myself. I wanted to perish; this was dearer to me than anything else . . . and even now, even this minute, when I already know everything . . . Do you know that I was summoned to the Well-Doer?"

"Yes, I do."

"But what he told me! Please realize that it was equivalent to . . . it was as if someone should remove the floor from under you this minute, and you and everything here on the desk, the papers, the ink . . . the ink would splash out and cover everything with blots . . ."

"What else? What further? Hurry up, others are waiting!"

Then, stumbling, muttering, I told him everything that is recorded in these pages . . . About my real self, and about my hairy self, and about my hands . . . yes . . . exactly, that was the beginning . . . And how I lied to myself, and how she obtained false certificates for me, and how I grew worse and worse, every day, and about the long corridors underground, and there beyond the Wall . . .

All this I threw out in formless pieces and lumps. I would stutter and fail to find words. The lips double-curved in a smile would prompt me with the word I needed, and I would nod gratefully: "Yes, yes!" . . . Suddenly, what was it? He was talking for me, and I only listened and nodded: "Yes, yes," and then, "Yes, exactly so, . . . yes, yes . . ."

I felt cold around my mouth as though it were wet with ether, and I asked with difficulty:

"But how is it . . . You could not learn anywhere . . ."

He smiled a smile growing more and more curved; then:

"But I see that you do want to conceal something from me. For example, you enumerated everything you saw beyond the Wall, but you failed to mention one thing. You deny it? But don't you remember that once, just in passing, just for a second, you saw me there? Yes, yes, *me*!"

Silence.

Suddenly, like a flash of lightning, it became shamelessly clear to me: he— he, too— And everything about myself, my torment, all that I had brought here, crushed by the burden, plucking up my last strength as if performing a great feat, all appeared to me only funny—like the ancient anecdote about Abraham and Isaac: Abraham all in a cold sweat, with the knife already raised over his son, over himself, and suddenly a voice from above: "Never mind . . . I was only joking."

Without taking my eyes from the smile that grew more and more curved, I put my hands on the edge of the desk and slowly, very slowly pushed myself with my chair away from him. Then instantly gathering myself into my own hands, I dashed madly out, past loud voices, past steps and mouths . . .

I do not remember how I got into one of the public rest rooms, in a station of the Underground Railway. Above, everything was perishing; the greatest civilization, the most rational in human history was crumbling, but here, by some irony, everything remained as before, beautiful. The walls shone; water murmured cozily; and like the water, the unseen, transparent music . . . Only think of it! All this is doomed; all this will be covered with grass someday; only myths will remain . . .

I moaned aloud. At the same instant I felt someone gently patting my knee. It was from the left; it was my neighbor who occupied a seat on my left —an enormous forehead, a bald parabola, yellow, unintelligible lines of wrinkles on his forehead, those lines about me.

"I understand you. I understand completely," he said. "Yet you must calm yourself. You must. It will return. It will inevitably return. It is only important that everybody should learn of my discovery. You are the first to whom I talk about it. I have calculated that there is *no infinity*! No!"

I looked at him wildly.

"Yes, yes, I tell you so. There is no infinity. If the universe is infinite, then the average density of matter must equal zero; but since we know it is not zero, therefore the universe is finite; it is spherical in form, and the square of its radius—R^2—is equal to the average density multiplied by . . . The only thing left is to calculate the numerical coefficient and then . . . Do you realize what it means? It means that everything is final, everything is simple . . . But you, my honored sir, you disturb me, you prevent my finishing my calculations by your yelling!"

I do not know which shattered me more, his discovery, or his positiveness at that apocalyptic hour. Only then did I notice that he had a notebook in his hands, and a logarithmic dial. I understood then that even if everything was perishing it was my duty (before you, my unknown and beloved) to leave these records in a finished form.

I asked him to give me some paper, and here in the rest room, to the accompaniment of the quiet music, transparent like water, I wrote down these last lines.

I was about to put down a period as the ancients would put a cross over the caves into which they used to throw their dead, when all of a sudden my pencil trembled and fell from between my fingers . . .

"Listen!" I pulled my neighbor. "Yes, listen, I say. There, where your finite universe ends, what is there? What?"

He had no time to answer. From above, down the steps stamping . . .

Record Forty

Facts
The Bell
I Am Certain

Daylight. It is clear. The barometer—760 mm. Is it possible that I, D-503, really wrote these—pages? Is it possible that I ever felt, or imagined I felt, all this?

The handwriting is mine. And what follows is all in my handwriting. Fortunately, only the handwriting. No more delirium, no absurd metaphors, no feelings—only facts. For I am healthy—perfectly, absolutely healthy . . . I am smiling; I cannot help smiling; a splinter has been taken out of my head, and I feel so light, so empty! To be more exact, not empty, but there is nothing foreign, nothing that prevents me from smiling. (Smiling is the normal state for a normal human being.)

The facts are as follows: That evening my neighbor who discovered the finiteness of the universe, and I, and all others who did not have a certificate showing that we had been operated on, all of us were taken to the nearest auditorium. (For some reason the number of the auditorium, 112, seemed familiar to me.) There they tied us to the tables and performed the great operation. Next day, I, D-503, appeared before the Well-Doer and told him everything known to me about the enemies of happiness. Why, before, it had seemed hard for me to go, I cannot understand. The only explanation seems to be my illness—my soul.

That same evening, sitting at the same table with Him, with the Well-Doer, I saw for the first time in my life the famous Gas Chamber. They brought in that woman. She was to testify in my presence. She remained stubbornly silent and smiling. I noticed that she had sharp and very white teeth which were very pretty.

Then she was brought under the Bell. Her face became very white, and as her eyes were large and dark, all was very pretty. When they began pumping the air from under the Bell she threw her head back and half-closed her eyes; her lips were pressed together. This reminded me of something. She looked at me, holding the arms of the chair firmly. She continued to look until her eyes closed. Then she was taken out and brought back to consciousness by means of electrodes, and again she was put under the Bell. The procedure was repeated three times, yet she did not utter a word.

The others who were brought in with that woman proved to be more honest; many of them began to speak after the first trial. Tomorrow they will all ascend the steps to the Machine of the Well-Doer. No postponement is possible, for there still is chaos, groaning, cadavers, beasts in the western section; and to our regret there are still quantities of Numbers who have betrayed Reason.

But on the transverse avenue Forty we have succeeded in establishing a temporary Wall of high-voltage waves. And I hope we win. More than that; I am certain we shall win. For Reason must prevail.

HERMAN MELVILLE

• *Billy Budd*

XXIII

It was Captain Vere himself who of his own motion communicated the finding of the court to the prisoner; for that purpose going to the compartment where he was in custody and bidding the marine there to withdraw for the time.

Beyond the communication of the sentence what took place at this interview was never known. But in view of the character of the twain briefly closeted in that stateroom, each radically sharing in the rarer qualities of our nature—so rare indeed as to be all but incredible to average minds however much cultivated— some conjectures may be ventured.

It would have been in consonance with the spirit of Captain Vere should he on this occasion have concealed nothing from the condemned one—should he indeed have frankly disclosed to him the part he himself had played in bringing about the decision, at the same time revealing his actuating motives. On Billy's side it is not improbable that such a confession would have been received in much the same spirit that prompted it. Not without a sort of joy indeed he might have appreciated the brave opinion of him implied in his captain making such a confidant of him. Nor, as to the sentence itself could he have been insensible that it was imparted to him as to one not afraid to die. Even more may have been.

SOURCE. From *Billy Budd* by Herman Melville. Copyright 1962, Washington Square Press.

Captain Vere in the end may have developed the passion sometimes latent under an exterior stoical or indifferent. He was old enough to have been Billy's father. The austere devotee of military duty letting himself melt back into what remains primeval in our formalized humanity may in the end have caught Billy to his heart even as Abraham may have caught young Isaac on the brink of resolutely offering him up in obedience to the exacting behest. But there is no telling the sacrament, seldom if in any case revealed to the gadding world wherever under circumstances at all akin to those here attempted to be set forth two of great Nature's nobler order embrace. There is privacy at the time, inviolable to the survivor, and holy oblivion the sequel to each diviner magnanimity, providentially covers all at last.

The first to encounter Captain Vere in act of leaving the compartment was the senior lieutenant. The face he beheld, for the moment one expressive of the agony of the strong, was to that officer, though a man of fifty, a startling revelation. That the condemned one suffered less than he who mainly had effected the condemnation was apparently indicated by the former's exclamation in the scene soon perforce to be touched upon.

XXIV

Of a series of incidents within a brief term rapidly following each other, the adequate narration may take up a term less brief, especially if explanation or comment here and there seem requisite to the better understanding of such incidents. Between the entrance into the cabin of him who never left it alive, and him who when he did leave it left it as one condemned to die; between this and the closeted interview just given less than an hour and a half had elapsed. It was an interval long enough however to awaken speculation among no few of the ship's company as to what it was that could be detaining in the cabin the master-at-arms and the sailor; for a rumor that both of them had been seen to enter it and neither of them had been seen to emerge, this rumor had got abroad upon the gundecks and in the tops; the people of a great warship being in one respect like villagers taking microscopic note of every outward movement or nonmovement going on. When therefore in weather not at all tempestuous all hands were called in the second dogwatch, a summons under such circumstances not usual in those hours, the crew were not wholly unprepared for some announcement extraordinary, one having connection too with the continued absence of the two men from their wonted haunts.

There was a moderate sea at the time; and the moon, newly risen and near to being at its full, silvered the white spardeck wherever not blotted by the clear-cut shadows horizontally thrown of fixtures and moving men. On either side the quarter-deck the marine guard under arms was drawn up; and Captain Vere standing in his place surrounded by all the wardroom officers, addressed his men. In so doing his manner showed neither more nor less than that property pertaining to his supreme position aboard his own ship. In clear terms and concise he told them what had taken place in the cabin; that the master-at-arms was dead; that he who had killed him had been already tried by a summary court and condemned to death; and that the execution would take place in the early morning watch. The word *mutiny* was not named in what he said. He refrained too from making the occasion an opportunity for any preachment as to the maintenance of discipline, thinking perhaps that under existing circumstances in the navy the consequence of violating discipline should be made to speak for itself.

Their captain's announcement was listened to by the throng of standing sailors in a dumbness like that of a seated congregation of believers in hell listening to the clergyman's announcement of his Calvinistic text.

At the close, however, a confused murmur went up. It began to wax. All but instantly, then, at a sign, it was pierced and suppressed by shrill whistles of the boatswain and his mates piping down one watch.

To be prepared for burial Claggart's body was delivered to certain petty-officers of his mess. And here, not to clog the sequel with lateral matters, it may be added that at a suitable hour, the master-at-arms was committed to the sea with every funeral honor properly belonging to his naval grade.

In this proceeding as in every public one growing out of the tragedy strict adherence to usage was observed. Nor in any point could it have been at all deviated from, either with respect to Claggart or Billy Budd, without begetting undesirable speculations in the ship's company, sailors, and more particularly men-of-war's men, being of all men the greatest sticklers for usage.

For similar cause, all communication between Captain Vere and the condemned one ended with the closeted interview already given, the latter being now surrendered to the ordinary routine preliminary to the end. This transfer under guard from the captain's quarters was effected without unusual precautions—at least no visible ones.

If possible not to let the men so much as surmise that their officers anticipate aught amiss from them is the tacit rule in a military ship. And the more that some sort of trouble should really be apprehended the more do the officers keep that apprehension to themselves; though not the less unostentatious vigilance may be augmented.

In the present instance the sentry placed over the prisoner had strict orders to let no one have communication with him but the chaplain. And certain unobtrusive measures were taken absolutely to insure this point.

XXV

In a seventy-four of the old order the deck known as the upper gundeck was the one covered over by the spardeck which last though not without its armament was for the most part exposed to the weather. In general it was at all hours free from hammocks; those of the crew swinging on the lower gundeck, and berthdeck, the latter being not only a dormitory but also the place for the stowing of the sailors' bags, and on both sides lined with the large chests or movable pantries of the many messes of the men.

On the starboard side of the *Indomitable's* upper gundeck, behold Billy Budd under sentry lying prone in irons in one of the bays formed by the regular spacing of the guns comprising the batteries on either side. All these pieces were of the heavier caliber of that period. Mounted on lumbering wooden carriages they were hampered with cumbersome harness of breeching and strong side-tackles for running them out. Guns and carriages, together with the long rammers and shorter lintstocks lodged in loops overhead—all these, as customary, were painted black; and the heavy hempen breechings tarred to the same tint, wore the like livery of the undertakers. In contrast with the funereal hue of these surroundings the prone sailor's exterior apparel, white jumper and white duck trousers, each more or less soiled, dimly glimmered in the obscure light of the bay like a patch of discolored snow in early April lingering at some upland cave's black mouth. In effect he is already in his shroud or the garments that shall serve him in lieu of one. Over him but scarce illuminating him, two battle lanterns swing from two massive beams of the deck above. Fed with the oil supplied by the war-contractors (whose gains, honest or otherwise, are in every land an anticipated portion of the harvest of death) with flickering splashes of dirty yellow light they pollute the pale moonshine, all but ineffectually struggling in obstructed flecks through the open ports from which the tompioned[1] cannon protrude. Other lanterns at intervals serve but to bring out somewhat the obscurer bays which like small confessionals or side-chapels in a cathedral branch from the long dim-vistaed broad aisle between the two batteries of that covered tier.

Such was the deck where now lay the Handsome Sailor. Through the rose-tan of his complexion, no pallor could have shown. It would have taken days of sequestration from the winds and the sun to have brought about the effacement of that. But the skeleton in the cheekbone at the point of its angle was just beginning delicately to be defined under the warm-tinted skin. In fervid hearts

---

[1] Usually, "tampioned"; plugged with a tampion, as the muzzle of a gun not in use.

self-contained some brief experiences devour our human tissue as secret fire in a ship's hold consumes cotton in the bale.

But now lying between the two guns, as nipped in the vice of fate, Billy's agony, mainly proceeding from a generous young heart's virgin experience of the diabolical incarnate and effective in some men—the tension of that agony was over now. It survived not the something healing in the closeted interview with Captain Vere. Without movement, he lay as in a trance. That adolescent expression previously noted as his, taking on something akin to the look of a slumbering child in the cradle when the warm hearth-glow of the still chamber at night plays on the dimples that at whiles mysteriously form in the cheek, silently coming and going there. For now and then in the gyved one's trance a serene happy light born of some wandering reminiscence or dream would diffuse itself over his face, and then wane away only anew to return.

The chaplain coming to see him and finding him thus, and perceiving no sign that he was conscious of his presence, attentively regarded him for a space, then slipping aside, withdrew for the time, peradventure feeling that even he the minister of Christ though receiving his stipend from Mars had no consolation to proffer which could result in a peace transcending that which he beheld. But in the small hours he came again. And the prisoner now awake to his surroundings noticed his approach and civilly, all but cheerfully, welcomed him. But it was to little purpose that in the interview following the good man sought to bring Billy Budd to some godly understanding that he must die, and at dawn. True, Billy himself freely referred to his death as a thing close at hand; but it was something in the way that children will refer to death in general, who yet among their other sports will play a funeral with hearse and mourners.

Not that like children Billy was incapable of conceiving what death really is. No, but he was wholly without irrational fear of it, a fear more prevalent in highly civilized communities than those so-called barbarous ones which in all respects stand nearer to unadulterate Nature. And, as elsewhere said, a barbarian Billy radically was; as much so, for all the costume, as his countrymen the British captives, living trophies, made to march in the Roman triumph of Germanicus.[2] Quite as much so as those later barbarians, young men probably, and picked specimens among the earlier British converts to Christianity, at least nominally such and taken to Rome (as today converts from lesser isles of the sea may be taken to London) of whom the Pope of that time, admiring the strangeness of their personal beauty so unlike the Italian stamp, their clear ruddy complexion and curled flaxen locks, exclaimed, "Angles" (meaning *English* the modern derivative) "Angles do you call them? And is it because they look so like angels?" Had it been later in time one would think that the

---

[2] Germanicus Caesar (15 B.C.–19 A.D.), Roman general and conqueror, whose triumphs were spectacularly celebrated in Rome in 17 A.D.

Pope had in mind Fra Angelico's[3] seraphs some of whom, plucking apples in gardens of the Hesperides have the faint rose-bud complexion of the more beautiful English girls.

If in vain the good chaplain sought to impress the young barbarian with ideas of death akin to those conveyed in the skull, dial, and crossbones on old tombstones; equally futile to all appearance were his efforts to bring home to him the thought of salvation and a Saviour. Billy listened, but less out of awe or reverence perhaps than from a certain natural politeness; doubtless at bottom regarding all that in much the same way that most mariners of his class take any discourse abstract or out of the common tone of the work-a-day world. And this sailor way of taking clerical discourse is not wholly unlike the way in which the pioneer of Christianity full of transcendent miracles was received long ago on tropic isles by any superior *savage* so called—a Tahitian, say of Captain Cook's time or shortly after that time.[4] Out of natural courtesy he received, but did not appropriate. It was like a gift placed in the palm of an outreached hand upon which the fingers do not close.

But the *Indomitable's* chaplain was a discreet man possessing the good sense of a good heart. So he insisted not in his vocation here. At the instance of Captain Vere, a lieutenant had apprised him of pretty much everything as to Billy; and since he felt that innocence was even a better thing than religion wherewith to go to judgment, he reluctantly withdrew; but in his emotion not without first performing an act strange enough in an Englishman, and under the circumstances yet more so in any regular priest. Stooping over, he kissed on the fair cheek his fellowman, a felon in martial law, one who though on the confines of death he felt he could never convert to a dogma; nor for all that did he fear for his future.

Marvel not that having been made acquainted with the young sailor's essential innocence (an irruption of heretic thought hard to suppress) the worthy man lifted not a finger to avert the doom of such a martyr to martial discipline. So to do would not only have been as idle as invoking the desert, but would also have been an audacious transgression of the bounds of his function, one as exactly prescribed to him by military law as that of the boatswain or any other naval officer. Bluntly put, a chaplain is the minister of the Prince of Peace serving in the host of the god of war—Mars. As such, he is as incongruous as that musket of Blücher etc.[5] at Christmas. Why then is he there? Because he indirectly

---

[3] Italian friar-painter of the fifteenth century, famous for his religious frescoes. The Hesperides, in classical myth, were fabulous gardens where grew golden apples, guarded by a dragon.

[4] Captain James Cook (1728–1779), British explorer, made remarkable discoveries in the Pacific, visiting the Marquesas Islands and Tahiti, where Melville adventured in 1842.

[5] The manuscript is illegible; "Blücher etc." is a conjectural reading. Prussian Field Mar-

subserves the purpose attested by the cannon; because, too, he lends the sanction of the religion of the meek to that which practically is the abrogation of everything but brute force.

XXVI

The night so luminous on the spardeck but otherwise on the cavernous ones below, levels so like the tiered galleries in a coalmine—the luminous night passed away. But, like the prophet in the chariot disappearing in heaven and dropping his mantle to Elisha, the withdrawing night transferred its pale robe to the breaking day. A meek shy light appeared in the East, where stretched a diaphanous fleece of white furrowed vapor. That light slowly waxed. Suddenly eight bells was struck aft, responded to by one louder metallic stroke from forward. It was four o'clock in the morning. Instantly the silver whistles were heard summoning all hands to witness punishment. Up through the great hatchways rimmed with racks of heavy shot, the watch below came pouring over-spreading with the watch already on deck the space between the mainmast and foremast including that occupied by the capacious launch and the black booms tiered on either side of it, boat and booms making a summit of observation for the powder boys and younger tars. A different group comprising one watch of topmen leaned over the rail of that sea balcony, no small one in a seventy-four, looking down on the crowd below. Man or boy none spake but in whisper, and few spake at all. Captain Vere—as before, the central figure among the assembled commissioned officers—stood nigh the break of the poopdeck facing forward. Just below him on the quarterdeck the marines in full equipment were drawn up much as at the scene of the promulgated sentence.

At sea in the old time, the execution by halter of a military sailor was generally from the foreyard. In the present instance, for special reasons the mainyard was assigned. Under an arm of that lee yard[6] the prisoner was presently brought up, the chaplain attending him. It was noted at the time and remarked upon afterwards that in this final scene the good man evinced little or nothing of the perfunctory. Brief speech indeed he had with the condemned one, but the genuine Gospel was less on his tongue than in his aspect and manner toward him. The final preparations personal to the latter being speedily brought to an end by two boatswain's-mates, the consummation impended. Billy stood facing

shal Gebhard von Blücher (1742–1819), who had aided Wellington at Waterloo, was still famous.

[6] Melville wrote both "weather" and "lee" above the word "yard," and failed to cancel either of these opposites. The lee yard would be more likely, as being more sheltered.

aft. At the penultimate moment, his words, his only ones, words wholly unob-structed in the utterance were these—"God bless Captain Vere!" Syllables so unanticipated coming from one with the ignominious hemp about his neck—a con-ventional felon's benediction directed aft towards the quarters of honor; syllables too delivered in the clear melody of a singing bird on the point of launching from the twig, had a phenomenal effect, not unenhanced by the rare personal beauty of the young sailor spiritualized now through late experiences so poig-nantly profound.

Without volition as it were, as if indeed the ship's populace were but the vehicles of some vocal current electric, with one voice from alow and aloft came a resonant sympathetic echo—"God bless Captain Vere!" And yet at that instant Billy alone must have been in their hearts, even as he was in their eyes.

At the pronounced words and the spontaneous echo that voluminously re-bounded them, Captain Vere, either through stoic self-control or a sort of mo-mentary paralysis induced by emotional shock, stood erectly rigid as a musket in the ship armorer's rack.

The hull deliberately recovering from the periodic roll to leeward was just regaining an even keel, when the last signal, a preconcerted dumb one, was given. At the same moment it chanced that the vapory fleece hanging low in the East, was shot through with a soft glory as of the fleece of the Lamb of God seen in mystical vision, and simultaneously therewith, watched by the wedged mass of upturned faces, Billy ascended; and, ascending, took the full rose of the dawn.

In the pinioned figure, arrived at the yard end, to the wonder of all no motion was apparent, none save that created by the ship's motion, in moderate weather so majestic in a great ship ponderously cannoned.

Chapter 8

Competition and Power

THEODORE DREISER

• *The Titan*

Chapter XXI

A Matter of Tunnels

The question of Sohlberg adjusted thus simply, if brutally, Cowperwood turned his attention to Mrs. Sohlberg. But there was nothing much to be done. He explained that he had now completely subdued Aileen and Sohlberg, that the latter would make no more trouble, that he was going to pension him, that Aileen would remain permanently quiescent. He expressed the greatest solicitude for her, but Rita was now sickened of this tangle. She had loved him, as she thought, but through the rage of Aileen she saw him in a different light, and she wanted to get away. His money, plentiful as it was, did not mean as much to her as it might have meant to some women; it simply spelled luxuries, without which she could exist if she must. His charm for her had, perhaps, consisted mostly in the atmosphere of flawless security which seemed to surround him—a glittering bubble of romance. That, by one fell attack, was now burst. He was seen to be quite as other men, subject to the same storms, the same danger of shipwreck. Only he was a better sailor than most. She recuperated gradually; left for home; left for Europe; details too long to be narrated. Sohlberg, after much meditating and fuming, finally accepted the offer of Cowperwood and re-

SOURCE. From *The Titan* by Theodore Dreiser. Copyright 1914 by John Lane; 1925 by Horace Liverright, reprinted by permission of World Publishing Company by arrangement with the Dreiser Estate.

turned to Denmark. Aileen, after a few days of quarreling in which he agreed to dispense with Antoinette Nowak, returned home.

Cowperwood was in no wise pleased by this rough denouement. Aileen had not raised her own attractions in his estimation, and yet, strange to relate, he was not unsympathetic with her. He had no desire to desert her as yet, though for some time he had been growing in the feeling that Rita would have been a much better type of wife for him. But what he could not have, he could not have. He turned his attention with renewed force to his business; but it was with many a backward glance at those radiant hours when, with Rita in his presence or enfolded by his arms, he had seen life from a new and poetic angle. She was so charming, so naive—but what could he do?

For several years thereafter Cowperwood was busy following the Chicago street-railway situation with increasing interest. He knew it was useless to brood over Rita Sohlberg—she would not return—and yet he could not help it; but he could work hard, and that was something. His natural aptitude and affection for street-railway work had long since been demonstrated, and it was now making him restless. One might have said of him quite truly that the tinkle of car bells and the plop of plodding horses' feet was in his blood. He surveyed these extending lines, with their jingling cars, as he went about the city, with an almost hungry eye. Chicago was growing fast, and these little horsecars on certain streets were crowded night and morning—fairly bulging with people at the rush hours. If he could only secure an octopus-grip on one or all of them; if he could combine and control them all! What a fortune! That, if nothing else, might salve him for some of his woes—a tremendous fortune—nothing less. He forever busied himself with various aspects of the scene quite as a poet might have concerned himself with rocks and rills. To own these street-railways! To own these street-railways! So rang the song of his mind.

Like the gas situation, the Chicago street-railway situation was divided into three parts—three companies representing and corresponding with the three different sides or divisions of the city. The Chicago City Railway Company, occupying the South Side and extending as far south as Thirty-ninth Street, had been organized in 1859, and represented in itself a mine of wealth. Already it controlled some seventy miles of track, and was annually being added to on Indiana Avenue, on Wabash Avenue, on State Street, and on Archer Avenue. It owned over 150 cars of the old-fashioned, straw-strewn, no-stove type, and over 1,000 horses; it employed 170 conductors, 160 drivers, a hundred stablemen, and blacksmiths, harness-makers, and repairers in interesting numbers. Its snowplows were busy on the street in winter, its sprinkling cars in summer. Cowperwood calculated its shares, bonds, rolling stock, and other physical properties as totaling in the vicinity of over 2 million dollars. The trouble with this company was that its outstanding stock was principally controlled by Norman Schryhart, who was now decidedly inimical to Cowperwood or anything he might wish to do, and by Anson Merrill, who had never manifested any signs of friendship. He did not see how he was to get control of this property. Its shares were selling around $250.

The North Chicago City Railway was a corporation which had been organized at the same time as the South Side company, but by a different group of men. Its management was old, indifferent, and incompetent, its equipment about the same. The Chicago West Division Railway had originally been owned by the Chicago City or South Side Railway, but was now a separate corporation. It was not yet so profitable as the other divisions of the city, but all sections of the city were growing. The horse bell was heard everywhere tinkling gaily.

Standing on the outside of this scene, contemplating its promise, Cowperwood, much more than anyone else connected financially with the future of these railways at this time, was impressed with their enormous possibilities—their enormous future if Chicago continued to grow, and was concerned with the various factors which might further or impede their progress.

Not long before he had discovered that one of the chief handicaps to street-railway development, on the North and West Sides, lay in the congestion of traffic at the bridges spanning the Chicago River. Between the street ends that abutted on it and connected the two sides of the city ran this amazing stream—dirty, odorous, picturesque, compact—of a heavy, delightful, constantly crowding and moving boat traffic, which kept the various bridges momentarily turning and tied up the street traffic on either side of the river until it seemed at times as though the tangle of teams and boats would never anymore be straightened out. It was lovely, human, natural, Dickensesque—a fit subject for a Daumier, a Turner, or a Whistler. The idlest of bridge-tenders judged for himself when the boats and when the teams should be made to wait, and how long, while in addition to the regular pedestrians a group of idlers stood at gaze fascinated by the crowd of masts, the crush of wagons, and the picturesque tugs in the foreground below. Cowperwood, as he sat in his light runabout, annoyed by a delay, or dashed swiftly forward to get over before a bridge turned, had long since noted that the streetcar service in the North and West Sides was badly hampered. The unbroken South Side, unthreaded by a river, had no such problem, and was growing rapidly.

Because of this he was naturally interested to observe one day, in the course of his peregrinations, that there existed in two places under the Chicago River—in the first place at La Salle Street, running north and south, and in the second at Washington Street, running east and west—two now soggy and rat-infested tunnels which were never used by anybody—dark, dank, dripping affairs only vaguely lighted with oil lamps, and oozing with water. Upon investigation he learned that they had been built years before to accommodate this same tide of wagon traffic which now congested at the bridges, and which even then had been rapidly rising. Being forced to pay a toll in time to which a slight toll in cash, exacted for the privilege of using a tunnel, had seemed to the investors and public infinitely to be preferred, this traffic had been offered this opportunity of avoiding the delay. However, like many another handsome commercial scheme on paper or bubbling in the human brain, the plan did not work exactly. These tunnels might have proved profitable if they had been properly built with long, low percent grades, wide roadways, and a sufficiency of light and air; but, as a matter of fact, they had not been judiciously adapted to public convenience. Norman Schryhart's father had been an investor in these tunnels, and Anson Merrill. When they had proved unprofitable, after a long period of pointless manipulation—cost, one million dollars—they had been sold to the city for exactly that sum each, it being poetically deemed that a growing city could better afford to lose so disturbing an amount than any of its humble, ambitious, and respectable citizens. That was a little affair by which members of council had profited years before; but that also is another story.

After discovering these tunnels Cowperwood walked through them several times—for though they were now boarded up, there was still an uninterrupted footpath—and wondered why they could not be utilized. It seemed to him that if the streetcar traffic were heavy enough, profitable enough, and these tunnels, for a reasonable sum, could be made into a lower grade, one of the problems which now hampered the growth of the North and West Sides would be obviated. But how? He did not own the tunnels. He did not own the street-railways. The cost of leasing and rebuilding the tunnels would be enormous. Helpers and horses and extra drivers on any grade, however slight, would have to be used, and that meant an extra expense. With streetcar horses as the only means of traction, and with the long, expensive grades, he was not so sure that this venture would be a profitable one.

However, in the fall of 1880, or a little earlier (when he was still very much entangled with the preliminary sex affairs that led eventually to Rita Sohlberg), he became aware of a new system of traction relating to streetcars, which together with the arrival of the arc light, the telephone, and other inventions, seemed destined to change the character of city life entirely.

Recently in San Francisco, where the presence of hills made the movement of crowded street-railway cars exceedingly difficult, a new type of traction had been introduced—that of the cable, which was nothing more than a traveling rope of wire running over guttered wheels in a conduit, and driven by immense engines conveniently located in adjacent stations, or powerhouses. The cars carried a readily manipulated grip lever, or steel hand, which reached down through a slot into a conduit and gripped the moving cable. This invention solved the problem of hauling heavily laden streetcars up and down steep grades. About the same time he also heard, in a roundabout way, that the Chicago City Railway, of which Schryhart and Merrill were the principal owners, was about to introduce this mode of traction on its lines—to cable State Street, and attach the cars of other lines running farther out into unprofitable districts as trailers. At once the solution of the North and West Side problems flashed upon him—cables.

Outside of the bridge crush and the tunnels above mentioned, there was one other special condition which had been for some time past attracting Cowperwood's attention. This was the waning energy of the North Chicago City Railway Company—the lack of foresight on the part of its directors which prevented them from perceiving the proper solution of their difficulties. The road was in a rather unsatisfactory state financially—really open to a coup of some sort. In the beginning it had been considered unprofitable, so thinly populated was the territory it served, and so short the distance from the business heart. Later, however, as the territory filled up, it did better; only then the long waits at the bridges occurred. The management, feeling that the lines were likely to be poorly patronized, had put down poor little lightweight rails, and run slimpsy cars which were as cold as ice in winter and as hot as stove ovens in summer. No attempt had been made to extend the downtown terminus of the several lines into the business center—they stopped just over the river which bordered it at the north. (On the South Side Mr. Schryhart had done much better for his patrons. He had already installed a loop for his cable about Merrill's store.) As on the West Side, straw was strewn in the bottom of all the cars in winter to keep the feet of the passengers warm, and but few open cars were used in summer. The directors were averse to introducing them because of the expense. So they had gone on and on, adding lines only where they were sure they would make a good profit from the start, putting down the same style of cheap rail that had been used in the beginning, and employing the same antique type of car, which rattled and trembled as it ran until the patrons were enraged to the point of anarchy. Only recently, because of various suits and complaints inaugurated, the company had been greatly annoyed, but they scarcely knew what to do, how to meet the onslaught. Though there was here and there a man of sense—such as Terrence Mulgannon, the general superintendent; Edwin Kaffrath, a director; William Johnson, the constructing engineer of the company—yet such other men as Onias C. Skinner, the president, and Walter Parker, the vice-president, were reactionaries of an elderly character, conservative, meditative, stingy, and worst of all, fearful or without courage for great adventure. It is a sad commentary that age almost invariably takes away the incentive to new achievement and makes "Let well enough alone" the most appealing motto.

Mindful of this, Cowperwood, with a now splendid scheme in his mind, one day invited John J. McKenty over to his house to dinner on a social pretext. When the latter, accompanied by his wife, had arrived, and Aileen had smiled on them both sweetly, and was doing her best to be nice to Mrs. McKenty, Cowperwood remarked:

"McKenty, do you know anything about these two tunnels that the city owns under the river at Washington and La Salle streets?"

"I know that the city took them over when it didn't need them, and that they're no good for anything. That was before my time, though," explained McKenty cautiously. "I think the city paid a million for them. Why?"

"Oh, nothing much," replied Cowperwood, evading the matter for the present. "I was wondering whether they were in such condition that they couldn't be used for anything. I see occasional references in the papers to their uselessness."

"They're in pretty bad shape, I'm afraid," replied McKenty. "I haven't been through either of them in years and years. The idea was originally to let the wagons go through them and break up the crowding at the bridges. But it didn't work. They made the grade too steep and the tolls too high, and so the drivers preferred to wait for the bridges. They were pretty hard on horses. I can testify to that myself. I've driven a wagonload through them more than once. The city should never have taken them over at all by rights. It was a deal. I don't know who all was in it. Carmody was mayor then, and Aldrich was in charge of public works."

He relapsed into silence, and Cowperwood allowed the matter of the tunnels to rest until after dinner when they had adjourned to the library. There he placed a friendly hand on McKenty's arm, an act of familiarity which the politician rather liked.

"You felt pretty well satisfied with the way that gas business came out last year, didn't you?" he inquired.

"I did," replied McKenty warmly. "Never more so. I told you that at the time." The Irishman liked Cowperwood, and was grateful for the swift manner in which he had been made richer by the sum of several hundred thousand dollars.

"Well, now, McKenty," continued Cowperwood abruptly and with a seeming lack of connection, "has it ever occurred to you that things are shaping up for a big change in the street-railway situation here? I can see it coming. There's going to be a new motor power introduced on the South Side within a year or two. You've heard of it?"

"I read something of it," replied McKenty, surprised and a little questioning. He took a cigar and prepared to listen. Cowperwood, never smoking, drew up a chair.

"Well, I'll tell you what that means," he explained. "It means that eventually every mile of street-railway track in this city—to say nothing of all the additional miles that will be built before this change takes place—will have to be done over on an entirely new basis. I mean this cable-conduit system. These old companies that are hobbling along now with any old equipment will have to make the change. They'll have to spend millions and millions before they can bring their equipment up-to-date. If you've paid any attention to the matter you must have seen what a condition these North and West Side lines are in."

"It's pretty bad; I know that," commented McKenty.

"Just so," replied Cowperwood emphatically. "Well, now, if I know any-thing about these old managements from studying them, they're going to have a hard time bringing themselves to do this. Two to three million are two to three million, and it isn't going to be an easy matter for them to raise the money—not as easy, perhaps, as it would be for some of the rest of us, supposing we wanted to go into the street-railway business."

"Yes, supposing," replied McKenty jovially. "But how are you to get in it? There's no stock for sale that I know of."

"Just the same," said Cowperwood, "we can if we want to, and I'll show you how. But at present there's just one thing in particular I'd like you to do for me. I want to know if there is any way that we can get control of either of those two old tunnels that I was talking to you about a little while ago. I'd like both if I might. Do you suppose that is possible?"

"Why, yes," replied McKenty, wondering; "but what have they got to do with it? They're not worth anything. Some of the boys were talking about filling them in some time ago—blowing them up. The police think crooks hide in them."

"Just the same, don't let anyone touch them—don't lease them or any-thing," replied Cowperwood forcefully. "I'll tell you frankly what I want to do. I want to get control, just as soon as possible, of all the street-railway lines I can on the North and West Sides—new or old franchises. Then you'll see where the tunnels come in."

He paused to see whether McKenty caught the point of all he meant, but the latter failed.

"You don't want much, do you?" he said cheerfully. "But I don't see how you can use the tunnels. However, that's no reason why I shouldn't take care of them for you, if you think that's important."

"It's this way," said Cowperwood thoughtfully. "I'll make you a preferred partner in all the ventures that I control if you do as I suggest. The street-rail-ways, as they stand now, will have to be taken up lock, stock, and barrel and thrown into the scrap heap within eight or nine years at the latest. You see what the South Side company is beginning to do now. When it comes to the West and North Side companies they won't find it so easy. They aren't earning as much as the South Side, and besides they have those bridges to cross. That means a severe inconvenience to a cable line. In the first place, the bridges will have to be rebuilt to stand the extra weight and strain. Now the question arises at once—at whose expense? The city's?"

"That depends on who's asking for it," replied Mr. McKenty amiably.

"Quite so," assented Cowperwood. "In the next place, this river traffic is becoming impossible from the point of view of a decent streetcar service. There are waits now of from eight to fifteen minutes while these tows and vessels get through. Chicago has five hundred thousand population today. How much will it have in 1890? In 1900? How will it be when it has eight hundred thousand or a million?"

"You're quite right," interpolated McKenty. "It will be pretty bad."

"Exactly. But what is worse, the cable lines will carry trailers, or single cars, from feeder lines. There won't be single cars waiting at these draws—there will be trains, crowded trains. It won't be advisable to delay a cable train from eight to fifteen minutes while boats are making their way through a draw. The public won't stand for that very long, will it, do you think?"

"Not without making a row, probably," replied McKenty.

"Well, that means what, then?" asked Cowperwood. "Is the traffic going to get any lighter? Is the river going to dry up?"

Mr. McKenty stared. Suddenly his face lighted. "Oh, I see," he said shrewdly. "It's those tunnels you're thinking about. Are they in any shape to be used?"

"They can be made over cheaper than new ones can be built."

"True for you," replied McKenty, "and if they're in any sort of repair they'd be just what you'd want." He was emphatic, almost triumphant. "They belong to the city. They cost pretty near a million apiece, those things."

"I know it," said Cowperwood. "Now, do you see what I'm driving at?"

"Do I see!" smiled McKenty. "That's a real idea you have, Cowperwood. I take off my hat to you. Say what you want."

"Well, then, in the first place," replied Cowperwood genially, "it is agreed that the city won't part with those two tunnels under any circumstances until we can see what can be done about this other matter?"

"It will not."

"In the next place, it is understood, is it, that you won't make it any easier than you can possibly help for the North and West Side companies to get ordinances extending their lines, or anything else, from now on? I shall want to introduce some franchises for feeders and outlying lines myself."

"Bring in your ordinances," replied McKenty, "and I'll do whatever you say. I've worked with you before. I know that you keep your word."

"Thanks," said Cowperwood warmly. "I know the value of keeping it. In the meanwhile I'll go ahead and see what can be done about the other matter. I don't know just how many men I will need to let in on this, or just what form the organization will take. But you may depend upon it that your interests will be properly taken care of, and that whatever is done will be done with your full knowledge and consent."

"All very good," answered McKenty, thinking of the new field of activity before them. A combination between himself and Cowperwood in a matter like this must prove very beneficial to both. And he was satisfied, because of their previous relations, that his own interests would not be neglected.

"Shall we go and see if we can find the ladies?" asked Cowperwood jauntily, laying hold of the politician's arm.

"To be sure," assented McKenty gaily. "It's a fine house you have here—beautiful. And your wife is as pretty a woman as I ever saw, if you'll pardon the familiarity."

"I have always thought she was rather attractive myself," replied Cowperwood innocently.

Chapter XXII

Street-Railways at Last

Among the directors of the North Chicago City company there was one man, Edwin L. Kaffrath, who was young and of a forward-looking temperament. His father, a former heavy stockholder of this company, had recently died and left all his holdings and practically his directorship to his only son. Young Kaffrath was by no means a practical street-railway man, though he fancied he could do very well at it if given a chance. He was the holder of nearly eight hundred of the five thousand shares of stock; but the rest of it was so divided that he could only exercise a minor influence. Nevertheless, from the day of his entrance into the company—which was months before Cowperwood began seriously to think over the situation—he had been strong for improvements—extensions, more franchises, better cars, better horses, stoves in the cars in winter, and the like, all of which suggestions sounded to his fellow directors like mere manifestations of the reckless impetuosity of youth, and were almost uniformly opposed.

"What's the matter with them cars?" asked Albert Thorsen, one of the elder directors, at one of the meetings at which Kaffrath was present and offering his usual protest. "I don't see anything the matter with 'em. I ride in 'em."

Thorsen was a heavy, dusty, tobacco-bestrewn individual of sixty-six, who was a little dull but genial. He was in the paint business, and always wore a very light steel-gray suit much crinkled in the seat and arms.

"Perhaps that's what's the matter with them, Albert," chirped up Solon Kaempfaert, one of his cronies on the board.

The sally drew a laugh.

"Oh, I don't know. I see the rest of you on board often enough."

"Why, I tell you what's the matter with them," replied Kaffrath. "They're dirty, and they're flimsy, and the windows rattle so you can't hear yourself think. The track is no good, and the filthy straw we keep in them in winter is enough to make a person sick. We don't keep the track in good repair. I don't wonder people complain. I'd complain myself."

"Oh, I don't think things are as bad as all that," put in Onias C. Skinner, the president, who had a face which with its very short side-whiskers was as bland as a Chinese god. He was sixty-eight years of age. "They're not the best cars in the world, but they're good cars. They need painting and varnishing pretty badly, some of them, but outside of that there's many a good year's wear in them yet. I'd be very glad if we could put in new rolling stock, but the item of expense will be considerable. It's these extensions that we have to keep building and the long hauls for five cents which eat up the profits." The so-called long hauls were only two or three miles at the outside, but they seemed long to Mr. Skinner.

"Well, look at the South Side," persisted Kaffrath. "I don't know what you people are thinking of. Here's a cable system introduced in Philadelphia. There's another in San Francisco. Someone has invented a car, as I understand it, that's going to run by electricity, and here we are running cars—barns, I call them— with straw in them. Good Lord, I should think it was about time that some of us took a tumble to ourselves!"

"Oh, I don't know," commented Mr. Skinner. "It seems to me we have done pretty well by the North Side. We have done a good deal."

Directors Solon Kaempfaert, Albert Thorsen, Isaac White, Anthony Ewer, Arnold C. Benjamin, and Otto Matjes, being solemn gentlemen all, merely sat and stared.

The vigorous Kaffrath was not to be so easily repressed, however. He repeated his complaints on other occasions. The fact that there was also considerable complaint in the newspapers from time to time in regard to this same North Side service pleased him in a way. Perhaps this would be the proverbial fire under the terrapin which would cause it to move along.

By this time, owing to Cowperwood's understanding with McKenty, all possibility of the North Side company's securing additional franchises for unoccupied streets, or even the use of the La Salle Street tunnel, had ended. Kaffrath did not know this. Neither did the directors or officers of the company, but it was true. In addition, McKenty, through the aldermen, who were at his beck and call on the North Side, was beginning to stir up additional murmurs and complaints in order to discredit the present management. There was a great to-do in council over a motion on the part of somebody to compel the North Side company to throw out its old cars and lay better and heavier tracks. Curiously, this did not apply so much to the West and South Sides, which were in the same condition. The rank and file of the city, ignorant of the tricks which were constantly being employed in politics to effect one end or another, were greatly cheered by this so-called public uprising. They little knew the pawns they were in the game, or how little sincerity constituted the primal impulse.

Quite by accident, apparently, one day, Addison, thinking of the different men in the North Side company who might be of service to Cowperwood, and having finally picked young Kaffrath as the ideal agent, introduced himself to the latter at the Union League.

"That's a pretty heavy load of expense that's staring you North and West Side street-railway people in the face," he took occasion to observe.

"How's that?" asked Kaffrath curiously, anxious to hear anything which concerned the development of the business.

"Well, unless I'm greatly mistaken, you, all of you, are going to be put to the expense of doing over your lines completely in a very little while—so I hear —introducing this new motor or cable system that they are getting on the South Side." Addison wanted to convey the impression that the city council or public sentiment or something was going to force the North Chicago company to indulge in this great and expensive series of improvements.

Kaffrath pricked up his ears. What was the city council going to do? He wanted to know all about it. They discussed the whole situation—the nature of the cable conduits, the cost of the powerhouses, the need of new rails, and the necessity of heavier bridges, or some other means of getting over or under the river. Addison took very good care to point out that the Chicago City or South Side Railway was in a much more fortunate position than either of the other two by reason of its freedom from the river-crossing problem. Then he again commiserated the North Side company on its rather difficult position. "Your company will have a very great deal to do, I fancy," he reiterated.

Kaffrath was duly impressed and appropriately depressed, for his eight hundred shares would be depressed in value by the necessity of heavy expenditures for tunnels and other improvements. Nevertheless, there was some consolation in the thought that such betterment, as Addison now described, would in the long run make the lines more profitable. But in the meantime there might be rough sailing. The old directors ought to act soon now, he thought. With the South Side company being done over, they would have to follow suit. But would they? How could he get them to see that even though it were necessary to mortgage the lines for years to come, it would pay in the long run? He was sick of old, conservative, cautious methods.

After the lapse of a few weeks Addison, still acting for Cowperwood, had a second and private conference with Kaffrath. He said, after exacting a promise of secrecy for the present, that since their previous conversation he had become aware of new developments. In the interval he had been visited by several men of long connection with street-railways in other localities. They had been visiting various cities, looking for a convenient outlet for their capital, and had finally picked on Chicago. They had looked over the various lines here, and had decided that the North Chicago City railway was as good a field as any. He then elaborated with exceeding care the idea which Cowperwood had outlined to him. Kaffrath, dubious at first, was finally won over. He had too long chafed under the dusty, poky attitude of the old regime. He did not know who these new men were, but this scheme was in line with his own ideas. It would require, as Addison pointed out, the expenditure of several millions of dollars, and he did not see how the money could be raised without outside assistance, unless the lines were heavily mortgaged. If these new men were willing to pay a high rate for 51 percent of this stock for ninety-nine years and would guarantee a satisfactory rate of interest on all the stock as it stood, besides inaugurating a forward policy, why not let them? It would be just as good as mortgaging the soul out of the old property, and the management was of no value, anyhow. Kaffrath could not see how fortunes were to be made for these new investors out of subsidiary construction and equipment companies, in which Cowperwood would be interested, how by issuing watered stock on the old and new lines the latter need scarcely lay down a dollar once he had the necessary opening capital (the "talking capital," as he was fond of calling it) guaranteed. Cowperwood and Addison had by now agreed, if this went through, to organize the Chicago Trust Company with millions back of it to manipulate all their deals. Kaffrath only saw a better return on his stock, possibly a chance to get in on the ground plan, as a new phrase expressed it, of the new company.

"That's what I've been telling these fellows for the past three years," he finally exclaimed to Addison, flattered by the latter's personal attention and awed by his great influence; "but they never have been willing to listen to me. The way this North Side system has been managed is a crime. Why, a child could do better than we have done. They've saved on track and rolling stock, and lost on population. People are what we want up there, and there is only one way that I know of to get them, and that is to give them decent car service. I'll tell you frankly we've never done it."

Not long after this Cowperwood had a short talk with Kaffrath, in which he promised the latter not only six hundred dollars a share for all the stock he possessed or would part with on lease, but a bonus of new company stock for his influence. Kaffrath returned to the North Side jubilant for himself and for his company. He decided after due thought that a roundabout way would best serve Cowperwood's ends, a line of subtle suggestion from some seemingly disinterested party. Consequently he caused William Johnson, the directing engineer, to approach Albert Thorsen, one of the most vulnerable of the directors, declaring he had heard privately that Isaac White, Arnold C. Benjamin, and Otto Matjes, three other directors and the heaviest owners, had been offered a very remarkable price for their stock, and that they were going to sell, leaving the others out in the cold.

Thorsen was beside himself with grief. "When did you hear that?" he asked.

Johnson told him, but for the time being kept the source of his information secret. Thorsen at once hurried to his friend, Solon Kaempfaert, who in turn went to Kaffrath for information.

"I have heard something to that effect," was Kaffrath's only comment, "but really I do not know."

Thereupon Thorsen and Kaempfaert imagined that Kaffrath was in the conspiracy to sell out and leave them with no particularly valuable pickings. It was very sad.

Meanwhile, Cowperwood, on the advice of Kaffrath, was approaching Isaac White, Arnold C. Benjamin, and Otto Matjes direct—talking with them as if they were the only three he desired to deal with. A little later Thorsen and Kaempfaert were visited in the same spirit, and agreed in secret fear to sell out, or rather lease at the very advantageous terms Cowperwood offered, providing he could get the others to do likewise. This gave the latter a strong backing of sentiment on the board. Finally Isaac White stated at one of the meetings that he had been approached with an interesting proposition, which he then and there outlined. He was not sure what to think, he said, but the board might like to consider it. At once Thorsen and Kaempfaert were convinced that all Johnson had suggested was true. It was decided to have Cowperwood come and explain to the full board just what his plan was, and this he did in a long, bland, smiling talk. It was made plain that the road would have to be put in shape in the near future, and that this proposed plan relieved all of them of work, worry, and care. Moreover, they were guaranteed more interest at once than they had expected to earn in the next twenty or thirty years. Thereupon it was agreed that Cowperwood and his plan should be given a trial. Seeing that if he did not succeed in paying the proposed interest promptly the property once more became theirs, so they thought, and that he assumed all obligations—taxes, water rents, old claims, a few pensions—it appeared in the light of a rather idyllic scheme.

"Well, boys, I think this is a pretty good day's work myself," observed Anthony Ewer, laying a friendly hand on the shoulder of Mr. Albert Thorsen. "I'm sure we can all unite in wishing Mr. Cowperwood luck with his adventure." Mr. Ewer's seven hundred and fifteen shares, worth seventy-one thousand, five hundred dollars, having risen to a valuation of four hundred and twenty-nine thousand dollars, he was naturally jubilant.

"You're right," replied Thorsen, who was parting with four hundred and eighty shares out of a total of seven hundred and ninety, and seeing them all bounce in value from two hundred dollars to six hundred dollars. "He's an interesting man. I hope he succeeds."

ARTHUR KOESTLER

• *Darkness at Noon*

The day before the term set by Ivanov expired, at the serving out of supper, Rubashov had the feeling that there was something unusual in the air. He could not explain why; the food was doled out according to routine, the melancholy tune of the bugle sounded punctually at the prescribed time; yet it seemed to- Rubashov that there was something tense about the atmosphere. Perhaps one of the orderlies had looked at him a shade more expressively than usual; perhaps the voice of the old warder had had a curious undertone. Rubashov did not know, but he was unable to work; he felt the tension in his nerves, as rheumatic people feel a storm.

After the "Last Post" had died away, he spied out into the corridor; the electric bulbs, lacking current, burnt at half strength and shed their dim light on to the tiles; the silence of the corridor seemed more final and hopeless than ever. Rubashov lay down on his bunk, stood up again, forced himself to write a few lines, stubbed out his cigarette and lit a new one. He looked down into the yard: it was thawing, the snow had become dirty and soft, the sky was clouded over; on the parapet opposite, the sentinel with his rifle was marching up and down. Once more Rubashov looked through the judas into the corridor: silence, desolation and electric light.

Against his custom, and in spite of the late hour, he started a conversation with No. 402. ARE YOU ASLEEP? he tapped.

SOURCE. From *Darkness At Noon* by Arthur Koestler. Translated by Daphne Hardy. Copyright 1941, reprinted with the permission of the Macmillan Company.

For a while there was no answer and Rubashov waited with a feeling of disappointment. Then it came—quieter and slower than usual:

NO. DO YOU FEEL IT TOO?

FEEL—WHAT? asked Rubashov. He breathed heavily; he was lying on the bunk, tapping with his pince-nez.

Again No. 402 hesitated a while. Then he tapped so subduedly that it sounded as if he were speaking in a very low voice:

IT'S BETTER FOR YOU TO SLEEP. . . .

Rubashov lay still on his bunk and was ashamed that No. 402 should speak to him in such a paternal tone. He lay on his back in the dark and looked at his pince-nez, which he held against the wall in his half-raised hand. The silence outside was so thick that he heard it humming in his ears. Suddenly the wall ticked again:

FUNNY—THAT YOU FELT IT AT ONCE. . . .

FELT WHAT? EXPLAIN! tapped Rubashov, sitting up on the bunk.

No. 402 seemed to think it over. After a short hesitation he tapped:

TO-NIGHT POLITICAL DIFFERENCES ARE BEING SETTLED. . . .

Rubashov understood. He sat leaning against the wall, in the dark, waiting to hear more. But No. 402 said no more. After a while, Rubashov tapped:

EXECUTIONS?

YES, answered 402 laconically.

HOW DO YOU KNOW? asked Rubashov.

FROM HARE-LIP.

AT WHAT TIME?

DON'T KNOW. And, after a pause: SOON.

KNOW THE NAMES? asked Rubashov.

NO, answered No. 402. After another pause he added: OF YOUR SORT. POLITICAL DIVERGENCIES.

Rubashov lay down again and waited. After a while he put on his pince-nez, then he lay still, one arm under his neck. From outside nothing was to be heard. Every movement in the building was stifled, frozen into the dark.

Rubashov had never witnessed an execution—except, nearly, his own; but that had been during the Civil War. He could not well picture to himself how the same thing looked in normal circumstances, as part of an orderly routine. He knew vaguely that the executions were carried out at night in the cellars, and that the delinquent was killed by a bullet in the neck; but the details of it he did not know. In the Party death was no mystery, it had no romantic aspect. It was a logical consequence, a factor with which one reckoned and which bore rather an abstract character. Also death was rarely spoken of, and the word "execution" was hardly ever used; the customary expression was "physical liquidation". The words "physical liquidation" again evoked only one concrete idea: The cessation of political activity. The act of dying in itself was a technical detail, with no claim to interest; death as a factor in a logical equation had lost any intimate bodily feature.

Rubashov stared into the darkness through his pince-nez. Had the proceedings already started? Or was it still to come? He had taken off shoes and socks; his bare feet at the other end of the blanket stuck up palely in the darkness. The silence became even more unnatural. It was not the usual comforting absence of noise; it was a silence which had swallowed all sound and smothered it, a silence vibrating like a taut drum-skin. Rubashov stared at his bare feet and slowly moved the toes. It looked grotesque and uncanny, as though the white feet led a life of their own. He was conscious of his own body with unusual intensity, felt the lukewarm touch of the blanket on his legs and the pressure of his hand under his neck. Where did the "physical liquidation" take place? He had the vague idea that it must take place below under the stairs which led down, beyond the barber's room. He smelled the leather of Gletkin's revolver belt and heard the crackling of his uniform. What did he say to his victim? "Stand with your face to the wall"? Did he add "please"? Or did he say: "Don't be afraid. It won't hurt . . ."? Perhaps he shot without any warning, from behind, while they were walking along—but the victim would be constantly turning his head round. Perhaps he hid the revolver in his sleeve, as the dentist hides his forceps. Perhaps others were also present. How did they look? Did the man fall forwards or backwards? Did he call out? Perhaps it was necessary to put a second bullet in him to finish him off.

Rubashov smoked and looked at his toes. It was so quiet that one heard the crackling of the burning cigarette paper. He took a deep pull on his cigarette. Nonsense, he said to himself. Penny novelette. In actual fact, he had never believed in the technical reality of "physical liquidation". Death was an abstraction, especially one's own. Probably it was now all over, and what is past has no reality. It was dark and quiet, and No. 402 had stopped tapping.

He wished that outside somebody might scream to tear this unnatural silence. He sniffed and noticed that for some time already he had the scent of Arlova in his nostrils. Even the cigarettes smelled of her; she had carried a leather case in her bag and every cigarette out of it had smelled of her powder. . . . The silence persisted. Only the bunk creaked slightly when he moved.

Rubashov was just thinking of getting up and lighting another cigarette when the ticking in the wall started again. THEY ARE COMING, said the ticking.

Rubashov listened. He heard his pulses hammering in his temples and nothing else. He waited. The silence thickened. He took off his pince-nez and tapped:

I HEAR NOTHING. . . .

For a whole while No. 402 did not answer. Suddenly he tapped, loudly and sharply:

NO. 380. PASS IT ON.

Rubashov sat up quickly. He understood: the news had been tapped on through eleven cells, by the neighbours of No. 380. The occupants of the cells between 380 and 402 formed an acoustic relay through darkness and silence. They were defenceless, locked within their four walls; this was their form of solidarity. Rubashov jumped from his trunk, pattered over bare-footed to the other wall, posted himself next to the bucket, and tapped to No. 406:

ATTENTION. NO. 380 IS TO BE SHOT NOW. PASS IT ON.

He listened. The bucket stank; its vapours had replaced the scent of Arlova. There was no answer. Rubashov pattered hastily back to the bunk. This time he tapped not with the pince-nez, but with his knuckles:

WHO IS NO. 380?

There was again no answer. Rubashov guessed that, like himself, No. 402 was moving pendulum-like between the two walls of his cell. In the eleven cells beyond him, the inhabitants were hurrying noiselessly, with bare feet, backwards and forwards between the walls. Now No. 402 was back again at his wall; he announced:

THEY ARE READING THE SENTENCE TO HIM. PASS IT ON.

Rubashov repeated his previous question:

WHO IS HE?

But No. 402 had gone again. It was no use passing the message on to Rip Van Winkle, yet Rubashov pattered over to the bucket side of the cell and tapped it through; he was driven by an obscure sense of duty, the feeling that the chain must not be broken. The proximity of the bucket made him feel sick. He pattered back to the bed and waited. Still not the slightest sound was heard from outside. Only the wall went on ticking:

HE IS SHOUTING FOR HELP.

HE IS SHOUTING FOR HELP, Rubashov tapped to 406. He listened. One heard nothing. Rubashov was afraid that the next time he went near the bucket he would be sick.

THEY ARE BRINGING HIM. SCREAMING AND HITTING OUT. PASS IT ON, tapped No. 402.

WHAT IS HIS NAME? Rubashov tapped quickly, before 402 had quite finished his sentence. This time he got an answer:

BOGROV. OPPOSITIONAL. PASS IT ON.

Rubashov's legs suddenly became heavy. He leant against the wall and tapped through to No. 406:

MICHAEL BOGROV, FORMER SAILOR ON BATTLESHIP POTEM-KIN, COMMANDER OF THE EASTERN FLEET, BEARER OF THE FIRST REVOLUTIONARY ORDER, LED TO EXECUTION.

He wiped the sweat from his forehead, was sick into the bucket and ended his sentence:

PASS IT ON.

He could not call back to his memory the visual image of Bogrov, but he saw the outlines of his gigantic figure, his awkward, trailing arms, the freckles on his broad, flat face with the slightly turned-up nose. They had been room-mates in exile after 1905; Rubashov had taught him reading, writing and the fundamentals of historical thought; since then, wherever Rubashov might hap-pen to be, he received twice a year a hand-written letter, ending invariably with the words: "Your comrade, faithful unto the grave, Bogrov."

THEY ARE COMING, tapped No. 402 hastily, and so loudly that Ruba-shov, who was still standing next to the bucket with his head leaning against the wall, heard it across the cell! STAND AT THE SPY-HOLE. DRUM. PASS IT ON.

Rubashov stiffened. He tapped the message through to No. 406: STAND AT THE SPY-HOLE. DRUM. PASS IT ON. He pattered through the dark to the cell door and waited. All was silent as before.

In a few seconds there came again the ticking in the wall: NOW.

Along the corridor came the low, hollow sound of subdued drumming. It was not tapping nor hammering: the men in the cells 380 to 402, who formed the acoustic chain and stood behind their doors like a guard of honour in the dark, brought out with deceptive resemblance the muffled, solemn sound of a roll of drums, carried by the wind from the distance. Rubashov stood with his eyes pressed to the spy-hole, and joined the chorus by beating with both hands rhythmically against the concrete door. To his astonishment, the stifled wave was carried on to the right, through No. 406 and beyond; Rip Van Winkle must have understood after all; he too was drumming. At the same time Rubashov heard to his left, at some distance still from the limits of his range of vision, the grinding of iron doors being rolled back on their slidings. The drumming to his left became slightly louder; Rubashov knew that the iron door which separated the isolation cells from the ordinary ones, had been opened. A bunch of keys jangled, now the iron door was shut again; now he heard the approach of steps, accompanied by sliding and slipping noises on the tiles. The drumming to the left rose in a wave, a steady, muffled crescendo. Rubashov's field of vision, limited by cells No. 401 and 407, was still empty. The sliding and squealing sounds approached quickly, now he distinguished also a moaning and whimper-ing, like the whimpering of a child. The steps quickened, the drumming to the left faded slightly, to the right it swelled.

Rubashov drummed. He gradually lost the sense of time and of space, he heard only the hollow beating as of jungle tom-toms; it might have been apes that stood behind the bars of their cages, beating their chests and drumming; he pressed his eye to the judas, rising and falling rhythmically on his toes as he drummed. As before, he saw only the stale, yellowish light of the electric bulb in the corridor; there was nothing to be seen save the iron doors of Nos. 401 to 407, but the roll of drums rose, and the creaking and whimpering approached.

Suddenly shadowy figures entered his field of vision: they were there. Rubashov ceased to drum and stared. A second later they had passed.

What he had seen in these few seconds, remained branded on Rubashov's memory. Two dimly lit figures had walked past, both in uniform, big and indistinct, dragging between them a third, whom they held under the arms. The middle figure hung slack and yet with doll-like stiffness from their grasp, stretched out at length, face turned to the ground, belly arched downwards. The legs trailed after, the shoes skated along on the toes, producing the squealing sound which Rubashov had heard from the distance. Whitish strands of hair hung over the face turned towards the tiles, with the mouth wide open. Drops of sweat clung to it; out of the mouth spittle ran thinly down the chin. When they had dragged him out of Rubashov's field of vision, further to the right and down the corridor, the moaning and whimpering gradually faded away; it came to him only as a distant echo, consisting of three plaintive vowels: "u-a-o". But before they had turned the corner at the end of the corridor, by the barber's shop, Bogrov bellowed out loudly twice, and this time Rubashov heard not only the vowels, but the whole word; it was his own name, he heard it clearly: Ru-ba-shov.

Then, as if at a signal, silence fell. The electric lamps were burning as usual, the corridor was empty as usual. Only in the wall No. 406 was ticking:

ARIE, YE WRETCHED OF THE EARTH.

Rubashov was lying on his bunk again, without knowing how he had got there. He still had the drumming in his ears, but the silence was now a true silence, empty and relaxed. No. 402 was presumably asleep. Bogrov, or what had remained of him, was presumably dead by now.

"Rubashov, Rubashov. . . ." That last cry was branded ineffaceably in his acoustic memory. The optic image was less sharp. It was still difficult for him to identify with Bogrov that doll-like figure with wet face and stiff, trailing legs, which had been dragged through his field of vision in those few seconds. Only now did the white hair occur to him. What had they done to Bogrov? What had they done to this sturdy sailor, to draw this childish whimpering from his throat? Had Arlova whimpered in the same way when she was dragged along the corridor?

Rubashov sat up and leant his forehead against the wall behind which No. 402 slept; he was afraid he was going to be sick again. Up till now, he had never imagined Arlova's death in such detail. It had always been for him an abstract occurrence; it had left him with a feeling of strong uneasiness, but he had never doubted the logical rightness of his behaviour. Now, in the nausea which turned his stomach and drove the wet perspiration from his forehead, his past mode of thought seemed lunacy. The whimpering of Bogrov unbalanced the logical equation. Up till now Arlova had been a factor in this equation, a small factor compared to what was at stake. But the equation no longer stood. The vision of Arlova's legs in their high-heeled shoes trailing along the corridor upset the mathematical equilibrium. The unimportant factor had grown to the immeasurable, the absolute; Bogrov's whining, the inhuman sound of the voice which had called out his name, the hollow beat of the drumming, filled his ears; they smothered the thin voice of reason, covered it as the surf covers the gurgling of the drowning.

Exhausted, Rubashov fell asleep, sitting—his head leaning against the wall, the pince-nez before his shut eyes.

STENDHAL

• *The Telegraph*

Chapter Thirteen

There was nothing but business for Lucien that day from the beginning to the end; for he hastened to Madame Grandet's in the evening as he would have gone to his office to keep a belated appointment. Lightly he crossed the court-yard, mounted the stairs, went through the antechamber, smiling all the time at the simplicity of the venture he was about to engage in. He knew the same pleasure he might have felt at recovering some document that had disappeared at the moment he wanted to attach it to a report for the King.

He found Madame Grandet surrounded by her faithful admirers, and suddenly distaste extinguished his youthful smile. The gentlemen were arguing: a M. Greslin, who was Referendary at the Court of Accounts (thanks to twelve thousand francs presented to the cousin of the mistress of the Comte de Vaize), questioned whether the corner grocer, M. Béranville, who was purveyor to the General Staff of the National Guard, would dare displease such *good customers* by voting in accordance with his newspaper. One of the other gentlemen, a Jesuit before 1830 and now a Lieutenant of Grenadiers, and decorated, had just offered the information that one of Béranville's clerks subscribed to the *National,* a thing

SOURCE. From *Lucien Leuwen* (The Telegraph) by Stendhal. Translated by Louise Varese. Copyright 1950 by Louise Varese, reprinted by permission of the New Directions Publishing Corporation.

he certainly would never have dared to do if his employer had had a proper horror of that rhapsodical and disruptive republican sheet.

With each word, Madame Grandet's beauty perceptibly faded in Lucien's estimation. And the worst of it was that she was taking a very active part in a discussion which would not have been out of place in a porter's lodge. She voted that the grocer be indirectly threatened with loss of patronage by the Drum-Major of the company of Grenadiers, whom she knew very well.

"Instead of enjoying their enviable position," Lucien thought, "these people waste their time *being afraid,* like my friends, the nobles of Nancy, and, furthermore, they make me sick at my stomach."

Lucien was leagues away from that youthful smile with which he had entered the magnificent drawing room, now transformed into a porter's lodge.

"I am sure that the conversation of the young ladies of the Opera is less vulgar. What a curious age! These Frenchmen who are normally so brave, as soon as they become rich spend their lives being afraid. But perhaps these noble souls of the *Juste-milieu* are incapable of serenity as long as any possibility of danger exists in the world."

And he stopped listening to them. It was only then that he noticed that Madame Grandet was receiving him very coolly; this amused him.

"I thought," he said to himself, "that I would remain in favor for at least a couple of weeks. But it doesn't take that long for this featherbrain to tire of an idea."

This brisk and breezy reasoning of Lucien's would have seemed pretty ridiculous to any politician. It was he who was the featherbrain: he had failed to divine Madame Grandet's character. This woman, so fresh, so young, and apparently so taken up with the frescoes of her summer gallery, copies of those of Pompeii, was almost constantly engrossed in the most profound political calculations. She was as rich as a Rothschild and longed to be a Montmorency!

"This young Leuwen, Master of Petitions, is not bad. If half of his real merit could be exchanged for an inherited position in the world, a position no one could dispute, he would be good for something in society. Just as he is, with that simplicity amounting almost to naïveté, yet not lacking in nobility by any means, he would suit to perfection one of those little women who look for gallantry, and not for a distinguished position in society."

And she was quite horrified by this vulgar way of thinking.

"He has no name. He is an insignificant young man, the son of a rich banker who has acquired the reputation of being clever because he has a malicious tongue. But his father is nothing but a beginner in the career in which M. Grandet has advanced so far. He is without a name or a family solidly established in society. It is not in his power to add anything to my position. Every time he is invited to the Tuileries I shall also be invited, and before he is. He has never yet had the honor of being invited to dance with the Princesses."

Such were Madame Grandet's thoughts as she studied Lucien, who all the time believed her to be entirely engrossed by the question of the crimes of the corner grocer and the means of punishing him by withdrawing the patronage of the General Staff of the National Guard.

Suddenly Madame Grandet laughed to herself, something very unusual for her.

"If, as Madame de Thémines so generously believes, he has such a passion for me, the thing to do is to drive him completely mad. And I believe, to begin with, harsh treatment would best suit this handsome young man, and it will certainly suit me very well."

At the end of half an hour, seeing that he was really being treated with marked coolness, Lucien found himself, in regard to the beautiful Madame Grandet, in the same position as a connoisseur who is bargaining for a mediocre painting; as long as he thinks he can have it for a few louis he exaggerates its beauties; but if the salesman sets an exorbitant value on it, the painting begins to seem absurd to him, he finds nothing but flaws in it and thinks only of ridiculing it.

"I am here," Lucien admonished himself, "to make plain to fools that I am hopelessly in love. Let's see, what does one do when one is consumed by such a passion and has been badly received by so pretty a woman? Naturally one sinks into a melancholy silence."

And he didn't utter another word.

"How well the world understands passion!" he thought, smiling to himself and becoming really melancholy. "When I was actually in the state I am now assuming, no one was noisier than I at the Café Charpentier!"

Lucien remained seated on his chair in the most praiseworthy immobility. Unhappily he could not shut his ears.

About ten o'clock M. de Torpet, an ex-Deputy, a very handsome young man, and the eloquent editor of a government newspaper, arrived.

"Have you read the *Messager*, Madam?" he said, coming up to the mistress of the house with a vulgar and almost familiar air, as though showing off his intimacy with this young society woman who was so much talked about. "Have you read the *Messager*? They won't be able to find a reply to those few lines I launched this morning on the latest crazy idea of the reformists. In a few brief words I dealt with the question of the increase in the number of voters. England has eight hundred thousand, and we have a hundred eighty thousand. But if I take a quick glance at England, what is it that strikes me first of all, what preeminently and startlingly meets my eye? A powerful and respected aristocracy, an aristocracy which has its roots deep in the customs of that supremely serious people; serious because they are a Biblical people. And on this side of the Channel what do I see? People who have wealth and nothing more! Perhaps in two years the heirs to their wealth and to their names will be in Sainte-Pélagie. . . ."

Addressed to a rich bourgeois woman whose grandfather had certainly not kept a carriage, this discourse amused Lucien for a while. Unfortunately, M. de Torpet did not have the wit to be witty in a few words, he required endless periods.

"This impudent Gascon thinks it incumbent on him to talk like M. de Chateaubriand's books," thought Lucien impatiently. He put in two or three little remarks himself, which, had they been carefully explained to this audience, might have been considered amusing. But he quickly cut himself short. "I am forgetting that I am hopelessly in love. Silence and sadness are the only fitting attitudes to assume, after the reception Madame Grandet has given me tonight."

Reduced to silence, Lucien heard so many stupidities and, above all, witnessed the proud display of so many base sentiments that he had the feeling that he was in his father's servants' hall.

"When my mother finds her lackeys talking like M. de Torpet, she dismisses them."

He began to feel a distinct dislike for all the elegant appointments of Madame Grandet's little oval drawing room. He was wrong: nothing could have been more charming and less theatrical; if it had not been for the oval form and some of the gay ornaments skillfully placed there by the architect, this delicious little drawing room would have been a perfect temple; artists would have agreed, "It borders on the solemn." But the impudence of M. de Torpet spoiled everything for Lucien. The youth, the freshness of the mistress of the house, although somewhat enhanced for him by her cool reception, seemed that of a chambermaid.

Lucien continued to think of himself as a philosopher, and failed to see that it was simply a question of not being able to stand effrontery. This attribute, so indispensable to success and carried to the extreme by M. de Torpet, filled him with a loathing that came very near to anger. This loathing for so necessary an attribute was the symptom which alarmed M. Leuwen about his son.

"He is not made for this age," Lucien's father used to say to himself, "and will never be anything but an insignificant man of merit."

When the inevitable pool at billiards was suggested, Lucien saw that M. de Torpet was disposed to take a ball. Lucien's ears were really offended by the loud voice of this handsome man. His disgust was so great that he felt incapable of dancing attendance at the billiard table and silently took his leave, but remembering to walk with dragging steps as befitted his sorrow.

"It is only eleven o'clock," he said with delight, and for the first time that season hastened toward the Opera with pleasure at the thought of arriving.

He found Mademoiselle Raimonde in her father's latticed box. She had been alone for the last quarter of an hour and was dying to talk to someone. Lucien listened to her with umistakable pleasure which surprised her. He was altogether charming to her.

"She has real wit," he said to himself in his state of infatuation. "What a contrast to the slow, monotonous pomposity of the Grandet drawing room!"

"You are charming, my lovely Raimonde, or at least I am charmed. Now tell me all about the dispute between Madame —— and her husband, and about the duel."

While Raimonde's soft little voice, that was as clear as a bell, went flitting from one detail of her story to another, Lucien's thoughts were still occupied with the scene he had just left.

"How heavy and sad those people are, exchanging their specious arguments which both listener and speaker know to be false! But it would shock all the proprieties of that confraternity not to exchange this counterfeit money of theirs. One has to swallow I don't know how many imbecilities, but never laugh at the fundamental verities of their religion, or all is lost." He then surprised his companion by interrupting her chatter to say:

"In your company, my lovely Raimonde, a Torpet would be impossible."

"Where have you come from?" she asked.

"With your impetuous, fearless disposition, it wouldn't take you long to make a fool of him, you would tear his grandiloquence to tatters. . . . What a pity I can't have you both to lunch together! My father would deserve to be present at such a luncheon. Never could your lively spirit endure that man's long pompous periods, which are in perfect keeping with the manners of the provinces."

Our hero fell silent.

"Perhaps," he thought, "I should transfer my consuming passion from Madame Grandet to Mademoiselle Elssler or Mademoiselle Gosselin? They, too, are very famous; neither Mademoiselle Elssler nor Mademoiselle Gosselin has the wit nor the unexpectedness of Mademoiselle Raimonde, but at least at Mademoiselle Gosselin's, a Torpet would be impossible. And that is why society in France has fallen into decadence. We have reached the age of Seneca; we no longer dare act or speak as in the time of Madame de Sévigné and the great Condé. Spontaneity has taken refuge in the corps-de-ballet. I wonder which would be less troublesome as the object of my hopeless passion, Madame Grandet or Mademoiselle Gosselin? Am I really to be condemned to write inanities all morning and to listen to them all evening?"

In the midst of this self-examination, while Lucien half-listened to Mademoiselle Raimonde's foolish chatter, the door of the box burst open, giving entrance to no less a personage than His Excellency, M. le Comte de Vaize.

"I have been looking for you," he said to Lucien in a solemn tone, not without a touch of self-importance. "I must talk to you! But . . . this young lady . . . can she be trusted?"

Although he had lowered his voice, Mademoiselle Raimonde caught his words.

"That is a question no one has ever asked without regretting it," she cried. "And since I can't ask Your Excellency to get out, I'll postpone my revenge till the next session of the Chamber." And she disappeared.

"Not bad," said Lucien, laughing. "Really not bad at all."

"But how can anyone be so frivolous, engaged, as you are, in affairs of such importance?" the Minister exclaimed with the ill humor of a man beset by grave difficulties who sees himself put off with a jest.

"I have sold myself body and soul to Your Excellency during the day, but it is now eleven o'clock at night and, by gad, my evenings are my own. But," he continued jokingly, "what am I offered for them?"

"I will make you a Lieutenant instead of a Second-Lieutenant."

"Alas! A very pretty offer, but I wouldn't know what to do with it."

"There will come a time when you will appreciate its full value. Can you lock this box?"

"Nothing could be easier," replied Lucien, bolting the door.

Meanwhile the Minister looked to see if people in the adjoining box could hear them. It was empty. His Excellency was careful to hide behind a column.

"Entirely through your own merit you have become my aide-de-camp," he began with an air of gravity. "The office you hold was nothing, and my only reason for placing you there was to please your father. You have created the office yourself, it is at present not without importance, and I have just spoken of you to the King."

He paused, expecting this last declaration to have a great effect. He looked at Lucien intently and found nothing but a somewhat listless attention.

"Unhappy monarchy!" he thought. "The name *King* has been shorn of all its magical effect. It is really impossible to govern with all these little newspapers demolishing everything. We have to pay everything in cash or preferments. . . . And it is ruining us: the Treasury is not infinite, nor preferments either."

There followed a little silence of ten seconds during which the Minister's face took on a somber expression. In his early youth at Coblentz, the four letters K I N G had still produced an effect.

"Is he about to make some proposition like the Caron affair?" Lucien wondered. "In that case, the army will never have a Lieutenant by the name of Leuwen."

"My friend," said the Minister finally, "the King approves my sending you on this double electoral mission."

("Elections again!" thought Lucien. "Tonight I am like M. de Pourceaugnac.")

"Your Excellency," he rejoined firmly, "is not ignorant of the fact that such missions are not looked upon by a disabused public as altogether honorable."

"That is what I am far from admitting," the Minister replied. "And, allow me to add, I have had more experience than you."

This last was said with an air of self-complacency in the worst possible taste, nor was the retort slow in coming:

"And I, M. le Comte, have less interest in power, and beg Your Excellency to confide such missions to someone more worthy than myself."

"But, my friend," the Minister replied, trying to restrain his ministerial vanity, "it is one of the duties of your office, that office which you have succeeded in making something of . . . "

"In that case I have a second request to add to my first, that of asking you to accept my resignation, together with my thanks for all your kindness to me."

"Unhappy monarchical principle!" the Minister said almost to himself.

As it did not suit him to part either with Lucien or his father he added in the most courteous tone:

"Permit me to say, my dear sir, that the question of your resignation can only be discussed with M. Leuwen, your father."

"I should be happy not always to have recourse to my father's talents. If Your Excellency would be good enough to explain these missions to me, and if there is no danger of a Rue Transnonain at the end of the affair, I might accept them."

"I deplore no less than you the terrible accidents that can happen in the precipitate use of even perfectly legitimate force. But you must surely feel that an accident, deplored and rectified as far as was possible, proves nothing against a system. Is a man who shoots his friend while hunting, a murderer?"

"M. de Torpet talked to us for an endless half hour this evening about such misadventures, exaggerated by a wicked press."

"Torpet is a fool, and it is because we haven't a Leuwen, and the others are wanting in flexibility, that we are forced to use a Torpet. For, after all, the machine must function. The arguments and torrents of eloquence, for which these gentlemen are paid, are not intended for intelligences such as yours. But in a large army you cannot expect all the soldiers to be marvels of delicacy."

"But who will guarantee that another Minister will not employ in my honor the same terms Your Excellency has used in your panegyric of M. de Torpet?"

"Really, my friend, you *are* intractable!"

This was said so naturally and so good-naturedly, and Lucien was still so young, that this tone brought a response:

"No, M. le Comte. Indeed, in order not to disappoint my father, I am ready to accept your missions provided there is no bloodshed at the end of them."

"But do you really suppose we have the power to shed blood?" the Minister exclaimed in a very different tone of voice and with something like reproach, and even regret.

This remark coming from the heart struck Lucien.

"What a perfect inquisitor," he thought.

"The object of your mission is twofold," the Minister continued, assuming an altogether official tone, and at the same time thinking to himself: "I shall have to watch my words so as not to offend our young Leuwen. And this is what we are reduced to with *our inferiors* today. If we find one who is deferential he is untrustworthy, ready to sell us to the *National* or to Henri V."

"As I say, your mission is twofold, my dear aide-de-camp," he continued out loud. "First of all you must put in an appearance at Champagnier in the Cher, where your father has large estates, talk to your father's agents and, with their assistance, try to find out what makes M. Blondeau's nomination so uncertain. The Prefect, M. de Riquebourg, is a worthy man, pious and completely devoted, but he seems to me to be an imbecile. You will have letters to him. You will have money to distribute on the banks of the Loire and, in addition, three tobacco concessions. I think there will also be two post-office directorships. The Minister of Finance has not yet replied on the subject, but I shall inform you later by telegraph. In addition you may remove from office just about anyone you choose. You are intelligent and will make use of all your powers with discretion. Conciliate the ancient nobility and the clergy: the life of a child is all that stands between them and us. No mercy for the republicans, especially for those young men who have received a good education and who do not have one penny to their names. Not all of them are in Mont-Saint-Michel. You know how my departments are honeycombed with spies, so you will address all important communications to your father.

"But Champagnier does not worry me inordinately. M. Malot, the liberal rival of Blondeau, is a braggart, a swaggerer, but no longer young, and he has had himself painted in the uniform of a Captain of the National Guard complete with bearskin on his head. He is not a man on the stern and energetic side. To play a good joke on him, I suppressed his Guard a week after he was made Captain. Such a man cannot be indifferent to a red ribbon that will make a fine effect in the portrait. In any case, he is an imprudent, fatuous boaster who, in the Chamber, would do his party more harm than good. You must study the means of winning Malot over, in the event of the failure of the faithful Blondeau.

"The crucial point, however, is Caen in the Calvados. You will give a day or two to the business of Champagnier, and then get on to Caen with all possible dispatch. At any cost, M. Mairobert must not be elected. He has both intelligence and wit. With a dozen or more heads like that, the Chamber would become unmanageable. I give you practically carte blanche in the matter of money, as well as offices to be given and taken away. Only, in the latter case, there might be some objections from two Peers belonging to us who are great landowners in that region. In any case, the Chamber of Peers is not troublesome, but I don't want M. Mairobert under any consideration. He is rich, he has no poor relations, and he already has the Cross. So there is no way of getting at him.

"The Prefect of Caen, M. Boucaut de Séranville, is rabid with all the zeal you lack. He himself has written a pamphlet against M. Mairobert, and has been rash enough to have it printed down there, right in the county-seat of his Prefecture. I have just issued an order to be sent to him by tomorrow's telegraph, not to distribute a single copy. Since M. Mairobert has public opinion in his favor, it is through that means we must attack him. M. de Torpet has also written a pamphlet. You will take three hundred copies with you in your carriage. Two more pamphlets by our regular writers, MM. D—— and F——, will be ready at midnight. All this is of very little value but costs a great deal. M. D——'s pamphlet, which is insulting and sarcastic, cost me six hundred francs; the other, which, according to the author, is subtle, ingenious and in good taste, cost me fifty louis. You will distribute either one or both of these pamphlets according to circumstances. The Normans are very canny. In short, you are at liberty to distribute or not to distribute them. If you care to write one yourself, either an entirely new one or adapted from the others, you would be doing me a great service. In a word, do anything on earth to prevent the election of M. Mairobert. Write me twice a day, and I give you my word that I will read your letters to the King."

Lucien smiled.

"An anachronism, M. le Comte. We are no longer living in the days of Samuel Bernard. What can the King do for me in a concrete way? As for distinctions, M. de Torpet dines once or twice a week with Their Majesties. No, really, your monarchy is lacking in rewards, bribes and means of seduction."

"Not so lacking as you think. If, in spite of your good and loyal services, M. Mairobert is elected, you will be made a Lieutenant. If he is not elected you will be made a Lieutenant of the General Staff, with the ribbon."

"M. de Torpet did not neglect to inform us this evening that he had been made an Officer of the Legion of Honor a week ago, apparently because of his long article on the houses demolished by cannon-fire at Lyons. Moreover, I remember the advice given by Marshal Bournonville to the King of Spain, Ferdinand VII. It is now midnight; I shall leave at two o'clock in the morning."

"Bravo, bravo, my friend! Write out your instructions in the way I have suggested and your letters to the Prefects and Generals. I will sign everything at one-thirty before going to bed. I shall probably have to be up the whole night again because of these infernal elections. So don't be afraid of disturbing me. Then, too, you will always have the telegraph."

"Does that mean that I can send you messages without showing them to the Prefects?"

"To be sure! In any case, they will always be kept informed by the telegraph operator. But it would be wise not to offend the Prefects. If they are good sorts tell them only as much as you see fit. If they seem inclined to view your mission with a jealous eye, try not to provoke them: we must not divide our army on the eve of battle."

"I shall try to act with all prudence," Lucien said, "but, in plain words, am I to telegraph Your Excellency without communicating my dispatch to the Prefect?"

"Yes, I agree, but don't quarrel with the Prefects. I wish you were fifty years old instead of twenty-four."

"Your Excellency is certainly free to choose a man of fifty who would be less susceptible, perhaps, to the insults of the press."

"You shall have all the money you need. If your pride will allow me the satisfaction, you shall have that and more. In a word, we must succeed. My private opinion is that it is better to spend five hundred thousand francs than to be faced with Mairobert in the Chamber. He is tenacious, wise, respected—a terrible man. He despises money, of which he has a great deal. In short, we couldn't have anyone worse."

"I shall do my best to save you from him," Lucien coldly replied.

The Minister rose and, followed by Lucien, left the box. He had to return at least fifty bows and shake eight or nine hands before reaching his carriage. He invited Lucien to get in with him.

"Handle this as well as you did the Kortis affair," he said to Lucien, whom he insisted on taking to the Place de la Madeleine, "and I shall tell the King that his government has no subject superior to you. And you are not yet twenty-five. There is nothing you cannot aspire to. I see only two obstacles: will you have the courage to speak before four hundred Deputies of whom three hundred are imbeciles? And can you control that first impulse which in you is so terrible? Above all, let it be understood, and make the Prefects understand, that you must never appeal to those so-called magnanimous sentiments so closely allied to mass insurrection."

"Ah!" Lucien painfully ejaculated.

"What is the trouble?"

"It doesn't sound very alluring."

"Remember that your Napoleon, even in 1814 when the enemy had crossed the Rhine, would have none of them."

"May I take M. Coffe with me? He has enough sang-froid for two."

"But then I should be left with no one!"

"With only four hundred clerks! What about M. Desbacs, for example?"

"He's a little schemer, far too ingratiating, who will betray more than one Minister before he gets to be a Councilor of State. And I shall do my best not to be one of those Ministers. That is why, despite all your asperity, I call upon your aid. Desbacs is your exact opposite. . . . However, take with you whomever you please, even M. Coffe. No Mairobert at any price! I shall expect you within an hour and a half. Ah! youth, with all its activity! What a happy time!"

Chapter 9

Leadership

KEN KESEY

• *One Flew over the Cuckoo's Nest*

The new man stands looking a minute, to get the set-up of the day room.

One side of the room younger patients, known as Acutes because the doctors figure them still sick enough to be fixed, practice arm wrestling and card tricks where you add and subtract and count down so many and it's a certain card. Billy Bibbit tries to learn to roll a tailormade cigarette, and Martini walks around, discovering things under the tables and chairs. The Acutes move around a lot. They tell jokes to each other and snicker in their fists (nobody ever dares let loose and laugh, the whole staff'd be in with notebooks and a lot of questions) and they write letters with yellow, runty, chewed pencils.

They spy on each other. Sometimes one man says something about himself that he didn't aim to let slip, and one of his buddies at the table where he said it yawns and gets up and sidles over to the big log book by the Nurses' Station and writes down the piece of information he heard—of therapeutic interest to the whole ward, is what the Big Nurse says the book is for, but I know she's just waiting to get enough evidence to have some guy reconditioned at the Main Building, overhauled in the head to straighten out the trouble.

The guy that wrote the piece of information in the log book, he gets a star by his name on the roll and gets to sleep late the next day.

Across the room from the Acutes are the culls of the Combine's product, the Chronics. Not in the hospital, these, to get fixed, but just to keep them from walk-

SOURCE. From *One Flew over the Cuckoo's Nest* by Ken Kesey. Copyright 1962 by Ken Kesey, reprinted with the permission of the Viking Press.

ing around the streets giving the product a bad name. Chronics are in for good, the staff concedes. Chronics are divided into Walkers like me, can still get around if you keep them fed, and Wheelers and Vegetables. What the Chronics are—or most of us—are machines with flaws inside that can't be repaired, flaws born in, or flaws beat in over so many years of the guy running head-on into solid things that by the time the hospital found him he was bleeding rust in some vacant lot.

But there are some of us Chronics that the staff made a couple of mistakes on years back, some of us who were Acutes when we came in, and got changed over. Ellis is a Chronic came in an Acute and got fouled up bad when they overloaded him in that filthy brain-murdering room that the black boys call the "Shock Shop." Now he's nailed against the wall in the same condition they lifted him off the table for the last time, in the same shape, arms out, palms cupped, with the same horror on his face. He's nailed like that on the wall, like a stuffed trophy. They pull the nails when it's time to eat or time to drive him in to bed when they want him to move so's I can mop the puddle where he stands. At the old place he stood so long in one spot the piss ate the floor and beams away under him and he kept falling through to the ward below, giving them all kinds of census headaches down there when roll check came around.

Ruckly is another Chronic came in a few years back as an Acute, but him they overloaded in a different way: they made a mistake in one of their head installations. He was being a holy nuisance all over the place, kicking the black boys and biting the student nurses on the legs, so they took him away to be fixed. They strapped him to that table, and the last anybody saw of him for a while was just before they shut the door on him; he winked, just before the door closed, and told the black boys as they backed away from him, "You'll pay for this, you damn tarbabies."

And they brought him back to the ward two weeks later, bald and the front of his face an oily purple bruise and two little button-sized plugs stitched one above each eye. You can see by his eyes how they burned him out over there; his eyes are all smoked up and gray and deserted inside like blown fuses. All day now he won't do a thing but hold an old photograph up in front of that burned-out face, turning it over and over in his cold fingers, and the picture wore gray as his eyes on both sides with all his handling till you can't tell any more what it used to be.

The staff, now, they consider Ruckly one of their failures, but I'm not sure but what he's better off than if the installation had been perfect. The installations they do nowadays are generally successful. The technicians got more skill and experience. No more of the button holes in the forehead, no cutting at all—they go in through the eye sockets. Sometimes a guy goes over for an installation, leaves the ward mean and mad and snapping at the whole world and comes back a few weeks later with black-and-blue eyes like he'd been in a fist-fight, and he's the sweetest, nicest, best-behaved thing you ever saw. He'll maybe even go home in a month or two, a hat pulled low over the face of a sleepwalker wandering round in a simple, happy dream. A success, they say, but I say he's just another robot for the Combine and might be better off as a failure, like Ruckly sitting there fumbling and drooling over his picture. He never does much else. The dwarf black boy gets a rise out of him from time to time by leaning close and asking, "Say, Ruckly, what you figure your little wife is doing in town tonight?" Ruckly's head comes up. Memory whispers someplace in that jumbled machinery. He turns red and his veins clog up at one end. This puffs him up so he can just barely make a little whistling sound in his throat. Bubbles squeeze out the corner of his mouth, he's working his jaw so hard to say something. When he finally does get to where he can say his few words it's a low, choking noise to make your skin crawl—"Ffffff*fuck* da wife! Ffffff*fuck* da wife!" and passes out on the spot from the effort.

Ellis and Ruckly are the youngest Chronics. Colonel Matterson is the oldest, an old, petrified cavalry soldier from the First War who is given to lifting the skirts of passing nurses with his cane, or teaching some kind of history out of the text of his left hand to anybody that'll listen. He's the oldest on that ward, but not the one's been here longest—his wife brought him in only a few years back, when she got to where she wasn't up to tending him any longer.

I'm the one been here on the ward the longest, since the Second World War. I been here on the ward longer'n anybody. Longer'n any of the other patients. The Big Nurse has been here longer'n me.

The Chronics and the Acutes don't generally mingle. Each stays on his own side of the day room the way the black boys want it. The black boys say it's more orderly that way and let everybody know that's the way they'd like it to stay. They move us in after breakfast and look at the grouping and nod. "That's right, gennulmen, that's the way. Now you keep it that way."

Actually there isn't much need for them to say anything, because, other than me, the Chronics don't move around much, and the Acutes say they'd just as leave stay over on their own side, give reasons like the Chronic side smells worse than a dirty diaper. But I know it isn't the stink that keeps them away from the Chronic side so much as they don't like to be reminded that here's what could happen to *them* someday. The Big Nurse recognizes this fear and knows how to put it to use; she'll point out to an Acute, whenever he goes into a sulk, that you boys be good boys and cooperate with the staff policy which is engineered for your *cure,* or you'll end up over on *that* side.

(Everybody on the ward is proud of the way the patients cooperate. We got a little brass tablet tacked to a piece of maple wood that has printed on it: CONGRATULATIONS FOR GETTING ALONG WITH THE SMALLEST NUMBER OF PERSONNEL OF ANY WARD IN THE HOSPITAL. It's a prize for cooperation. It's hung on the wall right above the log book, right square in the middle between the Chronics and Acutes.)

338 · GROUP MEMBERSHIP

This new redheaded Admission, McMurphy, knows right away he's not a Chronic. After he checks the day room over a minute, he sees he's meant for the Acute side and goes right for it, grinning and shaking hands with everybody he comes to. At first I see that he's making everybody over there feel uneasy, with all his kidding and joking and with the brassy way he hollers at that black boy who's still after him with a thermometer, and especially with that big wide-open laugh of his. Dials twitch in the control panel at the sound of it. The Acutes look spooked and uneasy when he laughs, the way kids look in a schoolroom when one ornery kid is raising too much hell with the teacher out of the room and they're all scared the teacher might pop back in and take it into her head to make them all stay after. They're fidgeting and twitching, responding to the dials in the control panel; I see McMurphy notices he's making them uneasy, but he don't let it slow him down.

"Damn, what a sorry-looking outfit. You boys don't look so crazy to me." He's trying to get them to loosen up, the way you see an auctioneer spinning jokes to loosen up the crowd before the bidding starts. "Which one of you claims to be the craziest? Which one is the biggest loony? Who runs these card games? It's my first day, and what I like to do is make a good impression straight off on the right man if he can prove to me he *is* the right man. Who's the bull goose loony here?"

He's saying this directly to Billy Bibbit. He leans down and glares so hard at Billy that Billy feels compelled to stutter out that he isn't the buh-buh-buh-bull goose loony yet, though he's next in luh-luh-line for the job.

McMurphy sticks a big hand down in front of Billy, and Billy can't do a thing but shake it. "Well, buddy," he says to Billy, "I'm truly glad you're next in luh-line for the job, but since I'm thinking about taking over this whole show myself, lock, stock, and barrel, maybe I better talk with the top man." He looks round to where some of the Acutes have stopped their card-playing, covers one of his hands with the other, and cracks all his knuckles at the sight. "I figure, you see, buddy, to be sort of the gambling baron on this ward, deal a wicked game of blackjack. So you better take me to your leader and we'll get it straightened out who's gonna be boss around here."

Nobody's sure if this barrel-chested man with the scar and the wild grin is play-acting or if he's crazy enough to be just like he talks, or both, but they are all beginning to get a big kick out of going along with him. They watch as he puts that big red hand on Billy's thin arm, waiting to see what Billy will say. Billy sees how it's up to him to break the silence, so he looks around and picks out one of the pinochle-players: "Harding," Billy says, "I guess it would b-b-be you. You're p-president of Pay-Pay-Patient's Council. This m-man wants to talk to you."

The Acutes are grinning now, not so uneasy any more, and glad that something out of the ordinary's going on. They all razz Harding, ask him if he's bull goose loony. He lays down his cards.

Harding is a flat, nervous man with a face that sometimes makes you think you seen him in the movies, like it's a face too pretty to just be a guy on the street. He's got wide, thin shoulders and he curves them in around his chest when he's trying to hide inside himself. He's got hands so long and white and dainty I think they carved each other out of soap, and sometimes they get loose and glide around in front of him free as two white birds until he notices them and traps them between his knees; it bothers him that he's got pretty hands.

He's president of the Patient's Council on account of he has a paper that says he graduated from college. The paper's framed and sits on his nightstand next to a picture of a woman in a bathing suit who also looks like you've seen her in the moving pictures—she's got very big breasts and she's holding the top of the bathing suit up over them with her fingers and looking sideways at the camera. You can see Harding sitting on a towel behind her, looking skinny in his bathing suit, like he's waiting for some big guy to kick sand on him. Harding brags a lot about having such a woman for a wife, says she's the sexiest woman in the world and she can't get enough of him nights.

When Billy points him out Harding leans back in his chair and assumes an important look, speaks up at the ceiling without looking at Billy or McMurphy. "Does this . . . gentleman have an appointment, Mr. Bibbit?"

"Do you have an appointment, Mr. McM-m-murphy? Mr. Harding is a busy man, nobody sees him without an ap-appointment."

"This busy man Mr. Harding, is he the bull goose loony?" He looks at Billy with one eye, and Billy nods his head up and down real fast; Billy's tickled with all the attention he's getting.

"Then you tell Bull Goose Loony Harding that R. P. McMurphy is waiting to see him and that this hospital ain't big enough for the two of us. I'm accustomed to being top man. I been a bull goose catskinner for every gyppo logging operation in the Northwest and bull goose gambler all the way from Korea, was even bull goose pea weeder on that pea farm at Pendleton—so I figure if I'm bound to be a loony, then I'm bound to be a stompdown dadgum good one. Tell this Harding that he either meets me man to man or he's a yaller skunk and better be outta town by sunset."

Harding leans farther back, hooks his thumbs in his lapels. "Bibbit, you tell this young upstart McMurphy that I'll meet him in the main hall at high noon and we'll settle this affair once and for all, libidos a-blazin'." Harding tries to drawl like McMurphy; it sounds funny with his high, breathy voice. "You might also warn him, just to be fair, that I have been bull goose loony on this ward for nigh onto two years, and that I'm crazier than any man alive."

"Mr. Bibbit, you might warn this Mr. Harding that I'm so crazy I admit to voting for Eisenhower."

"Bibbit! You tell Mr. McMurphy I'm so crazy I voted for Eisenhower *twice!*"

"And you tell Mr. Harding right back"—he puts both hands on the table and leans down, his voice getting low—"that I'm so crazy I plan to vote for Eisenhower again this *November*."

"I take off my hat," Harding says, bows his head, and shakes hands with McMurphy. There's no doubt in my mind that McMurphy's won, but I'm not sure just what.

All the other Acutes leave what they've been doing and ease up close to see what new sort this fellow is. Nobody like him's ever been on the ward before. They're asking him where he's from and what his business is in a way I've never seen them do before. He says he's a dedicated man. He says he was just a wanderer and logging bum before the Army took him and taught him what his natural bent was; just like they taught some men to goldbrick and some men to goof off, he says, they taught him to play poker. Since then he's settled down and devoted himself to gambling on all levels. Just play poker and stay single and live where and how he wants to, if people would let him, he says, "but you know how society persecutes a dedicated man. Ever since I found my callin' I done time in so many small-town jails I could write a brochure. They say I'm a habitual hassler. Like I fight some. Sheeut. They didn't mind so much when I was a dumb logger and got into a hassle; that's *excusable,* they say, that's a hard-workin' feller blowing off steam, they say. But if you're a gambler, if they know you to get up a back-room game now and then, all you have to do is spit slantwise and you're a goddamned criminal. Hooee, it was breaking up the budget drivin' me to and from the pokey for a while there."

He shakes his head and puffs out his cheeks.

"But that was just for a period of time. I learned the ropes. To tell the truth, this 'sault and battery I was doing in Pendleton was the first hitch in close to a year. That's why I got busted. I was outa practice; this guy was able to get up off the floor and get to the cops before I left town. A very tough individual . . ."

He laughs again and shakes hands and sits down to arm wrestle every time that black boy gets too near him with the thermometer, till he's met everybody on the Acute side. And when he finishes shaking hands with the last Acute he comes right on over to the Chronics, like we aren't no different. You can't tell if he's really this friendly or if he's got some gambler's reason for trying to get acquainted with guys so far gone a lot of them don't even know their names.

He's there pulling Ellis's hand off the wall and shaking it just like he was a politician running for something and Ellis's vote was good as anybody's. "Buddy," he says to Ellis in a solemn voice, "my name is R. P. McMurphy and I don't like to see a full-grown man sloshin' around in his own water. Whyn't you go get dried up?"

Ellis looks down at the puddle around his feet in pure surprise. "Why, I thank you," he says and even moves off a few steps toward the latrine before the nails pull his hands back to the wall.

McMurphy comes down the line of Chronics, shakes hands with Colonel Matterson and with Ruckly and with Old Pete. He shakes the hands of Wheelers and Walkers and Vegetables, shakes hands that he has to pick up out of laps like picking up dead birds, mechanical birds, wonders of tiny bones and wires that have run down and fallen. Shakes hands with everybody he comes to except Big George the water freak, who grins and shies back from that unsanitary hand, so McMurphy just salutes him and says to his own right hand as he walks away, "Hand, how do you suppose that old fellow knew all the evil you been into?"

Nobody can make out what he's driving at, or why he's making such a fuss with meeting everybody, but it's better'n mixing jigsaw puzzles. He keeps saying it's a necessary thing to get around and meet the men he'll be dealing with, part of a gambler's job. But he must know he ain't going to be dealing with no eighty-year-old organic who couldn't do any more with a playing card than put it in his mouth and gum it awhile. Yet he looks like he's enjoying himself, like he's the sort of guy that gets a laugh out of people.

I'm the last one. Still strapped in the chair in the corner. McMurphy stops when he gets to me and hooks his thumbs in his pockets again and leans back to laugh, like he sees something funnier about me than about anybody else. All of a sudden I was scared he was laughing because he knew the way I was sitting there with my knees pulled up and my arms wrapped around them, staring straight ahead as though I couldn't hear a thing, was all an act.

"Hooeee," he said, "look what we got here."

I remember all this part real clear. I remember the way he closed one eye and tipped his head back and looked down across that healing wine-colored scar on his nose, laughing at me. I thought at first that he was laughing because of how funny it looked, an Indian's face and black, oily Indian's hair on somebody like me. I thought maybe he was laughing at how weak I looked. But then's when I remember thinking that he was laughing because he wasn't fooled for one minute by my deaf-and-dumb act; it didn't make any difference *how* cagey the act was, he was onto me and was laughing and winking to let me know it.

"What's your story, Big Chief? You look like Sittin' Bull on a sitdown strike." He looked over to the Acutes to see if they might laugh about his joke; when they just sniggered he looked back to me and winked again. "What's your name, Chief?"

Billy Bibbit called across the room. "His n-n-name is Bromden. Chief Bromden. Everybody calls his Chief Buh-Broom, though, because the aides have him sweeping a l-large part of the time. There's not m-much else he can do, I guess. He's deaf." Billy put his chin in hands. "If I was d-d-deaf"—he sighed—"I would kill myself."

McMurphy kept looking at me. "He gets his growth, he'll be pretty good-sized, won't he? I wonder how tall he is."

"I think somebody m-m-measured him once at s-six feet seven; but even if he is big, he's scared of his own sh-sh-shadow. Just a bi-big deaf Indian."

"When I saw him sittin' here I *thought* he looked some Indian. But Bromden ain't an Indian name. What tribe is he?"

"I don't know," Billy said. "He was here wh-when I c-came."

"I have information from the doctor," Harding said, "that he is only half Indian, a Columbia Indian, I believe. That's a defunct Columbia Gorge tribe. The doctor said his father was the tribal leader, hence this fellow's title, 'Chief.' As to the 'Bromden' part of the name, I'm afraid my knowledge in Indian lore doesn't cover that."

McMurphy leaned his head down near mine where I had to look at him. "Is that right? You deef, Chief?"

"He's de-de-deef and dumb."

McMurphy puckered his lips and looked at my face a long time. Then he straightened back up and stuck his hand out.

"Well, what the hell, he can shake hands can't he? Deef or whatever. By God, Chief, you may be big, but you shake my hand or I'll consider it an insult. And it's not a good idea to insult the new bull goose loony of the hospital."

When he said that he looked back over to Harding and Billy and made a face, but he left that hand in front of me, big as a dinner plate.

I remember real clear the way that hand looked: there was carbon under the fingernails where he'd worked once in a garage; there was an anchor tattooed back from the knuckles; there was a dirty Band-Aid on the middle knuckle, peeling up at the edge. All the rest of the knuckles were covered with scars and cuts, old and new. I remember the palm was smooth and hard as bone from hefting the wooden handles of axes and hoes, not the hand you'd think could deal cards. The palm was callused, and the calluses were cracked, and dirt was worked in the cracks. A road map of his travels up and down the West. That palm made a scuffling sound against my hand. I remember the fingers were thick and strong closing over mine, and my hand commenced to feel peculiar and went to swelling up out there on my stick of an arm, like he was transmitting his own blood into it. It rang with blood and power. It blowed up near as big as his, I remember. . . .

"Mr. McMurry."

It's the Big Nurse.

"Mr. McMurry, could you come here please?"

It's the Big Nurse. That black boy with the thermometer has gone and got her. She stands there tapping that thermometer against her wrist watch, eyes whirring while she tries to gauge this new man. Her lips are in that triangle shape, like a doll's lips ready for a fake nipple.

"Aide Williams tells me, Mr. McMurry, that you've been somewhat difficult about your admission shower. Is this true? Please understand, I appreciate the way you've taken it upon yourself to orient with the other patients on the ward, but everything in its own good time, Mr. McMurry. I'm sorry to interrupt you and Mr. Bromden, but you do understand: *everyone* . . . must follow the rules."

He tips his head back and gives that wink that she isn't fooling him any more than I did, that he's onto her. He looks up at her with one eye for a minute.

"Ya know, ma'am," he says, "ya know—that is the ex-*act* thing somebody *always* tells me about the rules . . ."

He grins. They both smile back and forth at each other, sizing each other up.

". . . just when they figure I'm about to do the dead opposite."

Then he lets go my hand.

FRIEDRICH NIETZSCHE

• *Thus Spake Zarathustra*

On the Gift-Giving Virtue

1

When Zarathustra had said farewell to the town to which his heart was attached, and which was named The Motley Cow, many who called themselves his disciples followed him and escorted him. Thus they came to a crossroads; then Zarathustra told them that he now wanted to walk alone, for he liked to walk alone. His disciples gave him as a farewell present a staff with a golden handle on which a serpent coiled around the sun. Zarathustra was delighted with the staff and leaned on it; then he spoke thus to his disciples:

Tell me: how did gold attain the highest value? Because it is uncommon and useless and gleaming and gentle in its splendor; it always gives itself. Only as the image of the highest virtue did gold attain the highest value. Goldlike gleam the eyes of the giver. Golden splendor makes peace between moon and sun. Uncommon is the highest virtue and useless; it is gleaming and gentle in its splendor: a gift-giving virtue is the highest virtue.

SOURCE. From *The Portable Nietzsche* translated by Walter Kaufmann. Copyright 1954, reprinted with the permission of the Viking Press.

Verily, I have found you out, my disciples: you strive, as I do, for the gift-giving virtue. What would you have in common with cats and wolves? This is your thirst: to become sacrifices and gifts yourselves; and that is why you thirst to pile up all the riches in your soul. Insatiably your soul strives for treasures and gems, because your virtue is insatiable in wanting to give. You force all things to and into yourself that they may flow back out of your well as the gifts of your love. Verily, such a gift-giving love must approach all values as a robber; but whole and holy I call this selfishness.

There is also another selfishness, an all-too-poor and hungry one that always wants to steal—the selfishness of the sick: sick selfishness. With the eyes of a thief it looks at everything splendid; with the greed of hunger it sizes up those who have much to eat; and always it speaks around the table of those who give. Sickness speaks out of such craving and invisible degeneration; the thievish greed of this selfishness speaks of a diseased body.

Tell me, my brothers: what do we consider bad and worst of all? Is it not *degeneration?* And it is degeneration that we always infer where the gift-giving soul is lacking. Upward goes our way, from genus to overgenus. But we shudder at the degenerate sense which says, "Everything for me." Upward flies our sense: thus it is a parable of our body, a parable of elevation. Parables of such elevations are the names of the virtues.

Thus the body goes through history, becoming and fighting. And the spirit —what is that to the body? The herald of its fights and victories, companion and echo.

All names of good and evil are parables: they do not define, they merely hint. A fool is he who wants knowledge of them!

Watch for every hour, my brothers, in which your spirit wants to speak in parables: there lies the origin of your virtue. There your body is elevated and resurrected; with its rapture it delights the spirit so that it turns creator and esteemer and lover and benefactor of all things.

When your heart flows broad and full like a river, a blessing and a danger to those living near: there is the origin of your virtue.

When you are above praise and blame, and your will wants to command all things, like a lover's will: there is the origin of your virtue.

When you despise the agreeable and the soft bed and cannot bed yourself far enough from the soft: there is the origin of your virtue.

When you will with a single will and you call this cessation of all need "necessity": there is the origin of your virtue.

Verily, a new good and evil is she. Verily, a new deep murmur and the voice of a new well!

Power is she, this new virtue; a dominant thought is she, and around her a wise soul: a golden sun, and around it the serpent of knowledge.

2

Here Zarathustra fell silent for a while and looked lovingly at his disciples. Then he continued to speak thus, and the tone of his voice had changed:

Remain faithful to the earth, my brothers, with the power of your virtue. Let your gift-giving love and your knowledge serve the meaning of the earth. Thus I beg and beseech you. Do not let them fly away from earthly things and beat with their wings against eternal walls. Alas, there has always been so much virtue that has flown away. Lead back to the earth the virtue that flew away, as I do—back to the body, back to life, that it may give the earth a meaning, a human meaning.

In a hundred ways, thus far, have spirit as well as virtue flown away and made mistakes. Alas, all this delusion, and all these mistakes still dwell in our body: they have there become body and will.

In a hundred ways, thus far, spirit as well as virtue has tried and erred. Indeed, an experiment was man. Alas, much ignorance and error have become body within us.

Not only the reason of millennia, but their madness too, breaks out in us. It is dangerous to be an heir. Still we fight step by step with the giant, accident; and over the whole of humanity there has ruled so far only nonsense—no sense.

Let your spirit and your virtue serve the sense of the earth, my brothers; and let the value of all things be posited newly by you. For that shall you be fighters! For that shall you be creators!

With knowledge, the body purifies itself; making experiments with knowledge, it elevates itself; in the lover of knowledge all instincts become holy; in the elevated, the soul becomes gay.

Physician, help yourself: thus you help your patient too. Let this be his best help that he may behold with his eyes the man who heals himself.

There are a thousand paths that have never yet been trodden—a thousand healths and hidden isles of life. Even now, man and man's earth are unexhausted and undiscovered.

Wake and listen, you that are lonely! From the future come winds with secret wing-beats; and good tidings are proclaimed to delicate ears. You that are lonely today, you that are withdrawing, you shall one day be the people: out of you, who have chosen yourselves, there shall grow a chosen people—and out of them, the overman. Verily, the earth shall yet become a site of recovery. And even now a new fragrance surrounds it, bringing salvation—and a new hope.

3

When Zarathustra had said these words he became silent, like one who has not yet said his last word; long he weighed his staff in his hand, doubtfully. At last he spoke thus, and the tone of his voice had changed.

Now I go alone, my disciples. You too go now, alone. Thus I want it. Verily, I counsel you: go away from me and resist Zarathustra! And even better: be ashamed of him! Perhaps he deceived you.

The man of knowledge must not only love his enemies, he must also be able to hate his friends.

One repays a teacher badly if one always remains nothing but a pupil. And why do you not want to pluck at my wreath?

You revere me; but what if your reverence tumbles one day? Beware lest a statue slay you.

You say you believe in Zarathustra? But what matters Zarathustra? You are my believers—but what matter all believers? You had not yet sought yourselves: and you found me. Thus do all believers; therefore all faith amounts to so little.

Now I bid you lose me and find yourselves; and only when you have all denied me will I return to you.

Verily, my brothers, with different eyes shall I then seek my lost ones; with a different love shall I then love you.

And once again you shall become my friends and the children of a single hope—and then shall I be with you the third time, that I may celebrate the great noon with you.

And that is the great noon when man stands in the middle of his way between beast and overman and celebrates his way to the evening as his highest hope: for it is the way to a new morning.

Then will he who goes under bless himself for being one who goes over and beyond; and the sun of his knowledge will stand at high noon for him.

"Dead are all gods: now we want the overman to live"—on that great noon, let this be our last will.

Thus spoke Zarathustra.

EMILE ZOLA

• *Germinal*

[6]

Catherine's blows had sobered Étienne, but he was still at the head of his
comrades. Yet even while he was hoarsely urging them on against Montsou, he
could hear another voice within him, the voice of reason, asking in amazement
what was the meaning of all this? He had not meant any of this to happen. How
had it come about that having set out for Jean-Bart with the object of keeping a
cool head and preventing disaster, he now found himself ending a day of violence
upon violence by besieging the manager's house?

And yet he it was who had cried halt. But at first his sole idea had been to
protect the Company's yards where they were talking of going to smash everything up. And now that stones were beginning to graze the walls of the house,
he cast about in vain for some legitimate prey against which to unleash the mob
and so prevent still more serious disasters. As he was standing in the middle of
the road, feeling alone and powerless, he heard a voice calling him. It was a man
in the doorway of Tison's bar, the proprietress of which had hastily put up her
shutters, leaving only the door open.

"Yes, it's me . . . now listen a moment."

It was Rasseneur. Some thirty men and women, almost all from Village 240,
had stayed at home in the morning and had now come out for news. At the

SOURCE. From *Germinal* by Emile Zola. Translated by L. W. Tancock. Copyright 1954, reprinted with the permission of Penguin Books Limited.

approach of the strikers they had rushed into the bar. Zacharie was at a table with his wife Philomène, and further in, with their backs turned to the road and their faces hidden, were Pierron and Pierronne. Nobody was drinking, they had simply sought refuge.

Recognizing Rasseneur, Étienne was turning away, but the latter added:

"You don't want to see me, do you? . . . Well, I warned you and now the trouble is beginning. You can ask for bread now, but you'll get bullets."

Étienne turned back and answered:

"What annoys me is to see cowards looking on with folded arms while we risk our lives."

"So your idea is pillage over there?" asked Rasseneur.

"My idea is to stick by my friends to the end, and die with them if need be."

Sick at heart, Étienne went back into the crowd, prepared to die. Three children in the road were throwing stones, and he gave them a good kick, saying very loud, for the benefit of his mates, that smashing windows would do no good to anyone.

Bébert and Lydie had rejoined Jeanlin, who was teaching them how to work the sling. Each one aimed a stone, and the game was to see who would do the most damage. Lydie bungled her throw and cut open a woman's head in the crowd, which made the two boys helpless with merriment. Bonnemort and Mouque were sitting behind them on a bench, watching. Bonnemort's swollen legs were now so bad that he had only dragged himself as far as this with the greatest difficulty, and God knows what curiosity had brought him there, for his face had the ashen hue it wore on the days when nobody could get a word out of him.

Anyhow they had all long since given up obeying Étienne. Despite his order, stones went on flying, and he was dismayed at the sight of these brutes whom he had unleashed, for if they were slow to anger they were terrible when roused, and their ferocity was implacable. All the old Flemish blood was there, thick and placid, taking months to warm up, but then working itself up to unspeakable cruelties and refusing to listen to any arguments until the beast in them was sated with atrocities. In the south, where he came from, mobs flared up more quickly but they did far less damage. He had to fight Levaque to get the axe away from him, and he had lost control of the Maheus, who were throwing stones with both hands. It was above all the women who frightened him: la Levaque, Mouquette, and the rest, who were possessed with murderous fury and fighting tooth and nail, yelping like a pack of bitches and egged on by Ma Brûlé, whose skinny form towered above them.

But there was a sudden lull. A moment of surprise had produced some of the calm that all Étienne's supplications failed to impose. It was simply that the Grégoires had decided to take leave of the notary and cross the road to the manager's house; and they looked so peaceful, as though they thought all this was just a joke on the part of their worthy miners, whose resignation had fed them for a century, that the crowd in its amazement had stopped throwing stones for fear of hitting this old gentleman and old lady who had dropped from the sky. They were allowed to enter the garden, walk up the steps and ring at the barricaded door which nobody was anxious to open. But just then Rose was returning from her afternoon off, joking with the enraged miners, every one of whom she knew, for she was a Montsou girl. And she it was who banged on the door with her fist and forced Hippolyte to open it a few inches. Only just in time, too, for the hail of stones began again as the Grégoires were disappearing inside. The crowd had recovered from its astonishment and was now chanting louder than ever:

"Death to the bourgeois! Up with Socialism!"

In the hall Rose was still laughing, very tickled by the adventure, and she repeated to the terrified manservant:

"They won't hurt you! I know them."

Monsieur Grégoire methodically hung up his coat and helped Madame Grégoire out of her thick winter wrap. Then he said:

"Oh, I'm sure there is no real malice in them. When they have had a good shout they'll go home with a better appetite for supper!"

Monsieur Hennebeau was coming down from the second floor. Having witnessed the scene he was now hastening to welcome his guests with his customary formal politeness, with only a slight pallor betraying his recent storm of tears. The man in him had been overcome and only the administrator was left, perfectly behaved and determined to do his duty.

"You know," he said, "the ladies are not back yet."

For the first time the Grégoires felt some anxiety. Cécile not back! How could she get in if the miners went on with this nonsense?

"I though of having a space cleared in front of the house, but unfortunately I am on my own here, and in any case I don't know where to send my man for four men and a corporal to come and clear this rabble away."

Rose, who was still there, ventured to say yet again:

"Oh, sir, they're all right really!"

The manager shook his head as the tumult outside increased in volume and stones could be heard thudding against the walls.

"I don't bear them any ill-will, in fact I can excuse them, for anybody who can believe that we are out to do them harm must be as foolish as they are. But all the same I am responsible for keeping the peace. To think that there are gendarmes parading the roads, or so I'm told, and yet ever since this morning I have been trying in vain to find one!"

He broke off and stepped back to allow Madame Grégoire to pass, saying:

"But please don't stay here, Madame. Come into the drawing-room."

They were kept in the hall, however, by cook who came up from the basement in a towering rage, declaring that she could no longer answer for the dinner, as she was still waiting for the vol-au-vent cases she had ordered for four o'clock from the pastrycook's at Marchiennes. Obviously he had got lost on the way—scared of the bandits, she supposed. His baskets might even have been pillaged. She had visions of the vol-au-vents held up behind some bushes, besieged by these three thousand ne'er-do-wells who were clamouring for bread, and destined to blow out their bellies. Howsoever be it, the master had been warned: she would rather chuck the whole dinner into the fire than have it spoilt because of the revolution.

"Do be patient," said Monsieur Hennebeau. "All is not lost. The pastry-cook may still come."

He was turning back to Madame Grégoire and opening the drawing-room door for her when to his great surprise he saw a man sitting on the hall seat. In the deepening twilight he had not noticed him before.

"What, you, Maigrat? What brings you here?"

Maigrat had risen, and his heavy features were livid and quite changed by fear. Gone was his four-square, calm solidity as he diffidently explained that he had slipped over to the manager's house to ask for help and protection if the brigands attacked his shop.

"You can see that I am in danger too and have nobody here," answered Monsieur Hennebeau. "You would have done better to stay at home and guard your stock."

"Oh, I have put up iron bars and left my wife there!"

The manager was annoyed and made no effort to hide his contempt. A nice guard indeed, that puny creature, worn to a skeleton by beatings!

"Anyhow, there's nothing I can do about it. Try and fend for yourself. And I advise you to get back at once, for they are still shouting for bread. Listen to them."

The tumult was starting up again with renewed violence, and Maigrat thought he heard his own name. It was too late to go back now—he would be lynched. But on the other hand he was appalled by the prospect of ruin. He glued his face to the glass panel in the front door, sweating and trembling, expecting disaster at any moment. Meanwhile the Grégoires decided to go into the drawing-room.

Monsieur Hennebeau calmly played the attentive host. But in vain did he beg his guests to be seated. This room, closed and boarded up, with two lamps burning while it was still broad daylight outside, was filled with fresh terror at every shout from the street. Muffled by the curtains, the roaring anger of the mob was all the more frightening for being vague. But they made conversation which, however, always came back to this extraordinary revolt. He was amazed at his own lack of foresight, but his information was so at fault that he singled out

Rasseneur for abuse, claiming that he recognized the man's hateful influence. Of course the gendarmes were bound to come, for it was impossible that he could be so completely let down. The Grégoires had no thought except for their daughter: poor little dear, and she took fright so easily! Perhaps, in view of the danger, the carriage had gone back to Marchiennes. The wait lasted another quarter of an hour, with the tension increasing because of the noise in the street and the impact of stones on the shutters resounding like drums. The situation was becoming intolerable, and Monsieur Hennebeau was talking of going out single-handed to drive away these bawling creatures and meet the carriage, when Hippolyte appeared, shouting:

"Sir! Sir! Here is Madame! They are killing Madame!"

The carriage had not been able to get out of the Réquillart lane because of threatening groups, and Négrel had carried out his plan of walking the hundred metres from there to the house and knocking at the little garden gate near the outbuildings, for he was confident that the gardener would hear them, or at any rate that there would be somebody to open it for them. At first the plan had worked perfectly, and Madame Hennebeau and the young ladies were actually knocking when some of the women who had got wind of the manoeuvre rushed round into the lane. From then onwards everything went wrong. Nobody opened the gate and Négrel tried in vain to burst it open with his shoulder. The crowd of women was rapidly swelling, and fearing he might be overwhelmed, he took the desperate measure of pushing his aunt and the girls in front of him and trying to force a way through the assailants to the front steps. But this move led to a scrimmage, for the howling mob would not let go of them, and veered to and fro, not yet understanding why these fashionably dressed ladies were in the middle of the fray. At that moment the confusion was so great that one of those inexplicable misunderstandings occurred. Lucie and Jeanne had reached the steps and slipped through the door which the maid was holding ajar, Madame Hennebeau had managed to follow them in, and Négrel had brought up the rear and bolted the door behind him, under the impression that he had seen Cécile go in first. She was not there. She had disappeared on the way, so panic-stricken that she had turned her back on the house and rushed of her own accord right into the danger.

At once a shout arose:

"Up with the people! Death to the bourgeois! Death!"

Her face was hidden by a veil, and some of them took her at a distance for Madame Hennebeau. Others thought she was a friend of the manager's wife, the young wife of a neighbouring industrialist whom his workmen loathed. In any case it did not matter, for what infuriated them was her silk dress, fur coat and the white feather in her hat. She smelled of scent, she had a watch, she had the tender skin of an idle creature who never touched coal.

"Just you wait!" screamed Ma Brûlé. "We'll stick that lace up your arse!"

"Those bitches pinch all that stuff from us," added la Levaque. "They stick fur on their skins while we die of cold. Strip her bloody well naked, just to show her what life is!"

Mouquette rushed forward.

"Yes, yes, let's whip her!"

The women vied with each other in abominations, choking with rage, displaying their own rags and each trying to get a piece of this rich man's daughter. Her bum was no better than anyone else's you bet! More than one of them was rotten underneath her fine feathers. This injustice had lasted long enough, and now they would be made to dress the same as the working people, these harlots who had the sauce to spend fifty sous to have a skirt cleaned!

Surrounded by these furies Cécile was shaking with terror and on the point of collapse. Over and over again she stammered out the same words:

"Ladies—please, ladies! Please don't hurt me!"

But her voice turned into a strangled scream: cold hands had closed round her throat. The crowd had pushed her up close to old Bonnemort who had seized her. Hunger had made him light-headed, he was stupefied by long years of misery, and now he had suddenly emerged from half a century of resignation, spurred on by some mysterious impulse to get his own back. The man who had saved a dozen of his mates from death and risked his life in fire-damp and falls of rock, was now giving way to things he could never have explained, an urge to act like this, the fascination of this girl's white throat. As it was one of his silent days he kept his teeth clenched, looking like some sick and aged animal chewing over his memories.

"No, no!" yelled the women. "Turn her up, arse in the air!"

As soon as they had seen what was happening, Négrel and Monsieur Hennebeau had courageously opened the door again to rush to Cécile's rescue. But the crowd was now storming the garden fence, and it was not easy to get out. A pitched battle began, watched by the terrified Grégoires, who had come out on to the steps.

"Leave her alone, old boy, it's the young lady from La Piolaine," said Maheude to Grandpa Bonnemort, recognizing Cécile whose veil had been torn off by one of the women.

Étienne, horrified by these reprisals on a mere child, cast round for some way of heading off the mob. He had an inspiration and, brandishing the axe he had taken from Levaque, cried out:

"To Maigrat's, by God! There's bread there! Down with Maigrat's bloody shack!"

He aimed the first blow at random against the shop door. Some of the men followed suit, Levaque, Maheu, and a few more. But the women were not to be put off, and Cécile had fallen from the hands of Bonnemort into those of Ma Brûlé. Lydie and Bébert, led by Jeanlin, were crawling on all fours under her skirt to see the lady's bottom. Already she was being mauled and her clothes torn, when a man on horseback rode up, forcing his animal on and using the whip on anybody who did not stand back at once.

"You lot of swine! So you're hitting our daughters now!"

It was Deneulin, arriving in time for dinner. He jumped down, put one arm round Cécile's waist, and with the other steered his horse with such strength and skill that he used it as a living wedge and split the crowd which fell back before the shying beast. The battle was still raging at the railings, but he won through, breaking limbs right and left. This unforeseen help relieved Négrel and Monsieur Hennebeau, who were in great danger amid the curses and blows. And while the young man at last took the swooning Cécile indoors, Deneulin, covering the manager with his burly frame, reached the top of the steps, but was hit by a stone which nearly dislocated his shoulder.

"That's right!" he shouted. "Break my bones now you have broken my machines!"

He slammed the door. A volley of stones cut into the wood.

"What a lot of madmen!" he cried. "Another two seconds and they would have split my head open like a pumpkin. There's nothing you can say to them, is there? They are past understanding and all you can do is mow them down!"

In the drawing-room the Grégoires tearfully watched Cécile come round. She was quite unhurt, without even a scratch, but had merely lost her veil. Their dismay was greater than ever, though, when they realized that their own cook, Mélanie, was standing in front of them, describing how the mob had wrecked La Piolaine. Mad with terror, she had rushed to warn her master and mistress and had slipped in unnoticed through the open door during the confusion. As her interminable story unfolded itself, the single stone thrown by Jeanlin which had broken one window-pane became a full-scale bombardment which had rent the walls asunder. All Monsieur Grégoire's ideas were by now topsy-turvy: they slew his daughter and razed his home to the ground, so it must be true, then, that these miners were capable of resenting his living peacefully on their work!

The maid, who had brought a towel and some Eau de Cologne, remarked yet again:

"It's funny, though, because they're all right really."

Madame Hennebeau, looking deathly pale as she sat in her chair, could not shake off the shock, but she did manage to smile when Négrel was congratulated. Cécile's parents were particularly grateful to the young man, and the marriage was as good as settled. Monsieur Hennebeau silently glanced from his wife to this lover of hers whom that very morning he had sworn to kill, and then to this girl who would probably soon take him out of the way. He has not in any hurry, but the only thing he feared now was that his wife would sink still lower —some servant, perhaps.

"And what about you, my dears," Deneulin asked his daughters, "no bones broken?"

Lucie and Jeanne had had a great fright, but they were glad to have seen it all, and were now merrily laughing.

"Gosh!" their father went on. "What a day we've had! If you want a dowry you would do well to earn it yourselves, and, what's more, you can count on having to keep me as well."

He spoke flippantly, but his voice was unsteady, and when his daughters threw themselves into his arms, his eyes filled with tears.

Monsieur Hennebeau had overheard this confession of ruin, and a sudden thought lit up his face. Of course Vandame would now belong to Montsou. Here was the long hoped-for compensation, the stroke of luck that would put him back into favour with the Directors. At every crisis in his life he took refuge in the strict execution of orders, and found his small share of happiness in the military discipline in which he lived.

By now the tension was relaxing and a weary peace was descending upon the room, with the soft light of the two lamps and the warm and deadening effect of hangings. What could be happening outside? The shoutings had almost died away and no more stones were hitting the walls. Only heavy thuds could be heard, like the distant sound of an axe in the forest. They felt a curiosity to know and went back into the hall to peep through the glass panel in the front door. Even the ladies went upstairs to look through the shutters on the first floor.

"Do you see that scoundrel Rasseneur standing at the door of the pub over there?" Monsieur Hennebeau said to Deneulin. "I guessed as much, he must be behind it."

But it was not Rasseneur. It was Étienne, smashing in Maigrat's shop with an axe. He kept on calling to his mates: didn't the provisions in the shop belong to the miners? Hadn't they the right to claim back their own from this robber who had been exploiting them for so long and who starved them whenever the Company told him to? Gradually they all left the manager's house and ran to sack the neighbouring shop. The cry "We want bread!" began again. They would find plenty of it behind this door. A frenzy of hunger seized them all, as though they had suddenly found out that they could last out no longer without dying there and then in the road. They pressed in such crowds against the door that Étienne was afraid of hurting somebody with each swing of the axe.

Meanwhile Maigrat had left the hall and had first sought refuge in the kitchen. But from there he could not hear anything, and visualized abominable attacks on his shop. So he had come up again and hidden behind the pump in the yard, whence he could clearly hear his door cracking and voices urging each other on to the pillage and pronouncing his own name. It was not a nightmare, then, for although he could not see he could now hear, and he followed each stage of the attack with outraged ears. Each blow of the axe struck at his heart. One hinge must have gone: five more minutes now and the whole shop must be in their hands. He had mental pictures of appalling realism—the brigands rushing in, drawers forced, sacks ripped open, everything eaten and drunk and his home plundered into the bargain—nothing left, not even a stick to go begging with in the villages. No! he would not let them finish him off, he would sooner leave his dead body there. Since he had been standing there he had seen through a side window of the house the puny figure of his wife, pale and distorted through the glass; she was no doubt passively watching the attack like the poor, beaten, dumb animal she was. Below the window there was a shed in such a position that from the garden of the manager's house it could be reached by climbing up the palings on the party wall, and from there it was simple to crawl along the tiles as far as the window. He became obsessed by the idea of getting back home by this route, for he was cursing himself for ever having left. He might still be in time to barricade the shop with furniture—he even thought of other heroic means of defence such as boiling oil or burning paraffin poured down from above. A desperate struggle ensued between love of his stock and fear for his life, and his breath came thick in the battle against cowardice. Suddenly a still louder blow of the axe made up his mind for him. Avarice won: he and his wife would cover the sacks with their dead bodies rather than give up a single loaf.

Almost at once there was a burst of catcalls:

"Look, look! There's the tomcat up there! After him!"

They had caught sight of Maigrat on the shed roof. In spite of his corpulence he had leaped up the palings with feverish agility, heedless of what wood he smashed, and now he was flat on the tiles, working his way towards the window. But the pitch of the roof was steep, his stomach was in the way and his nails were breaking off. Nevertheless he would have dragged himself to the top had not his fear of stones started a fit of trembling, for the crowd, which he could no longer see, was still shouting:

"After him! After the cat! Let's do him in!"

All of a sudden both hands lost their grip, he rolled down like a ball, bounced over the gutter and fell across the party wall so awkwardly that he rebounded from there to the road, where his skull was split open on the point of a stone post, and his brains gushed out. He was killed instantly. The pale, dim form of his wife was still looking down through the window-pane.

For a moment everyone was horror-struck. Étienne stopped short and the axe fell from his hands. Maheu, Levaque, and the others forgot all about the shop, and all eyes were fixed on the wall, down which a thin red streak was slowly trickling. The shouting had died and a hush spread through the deepening shadows.

Then the yelling began again. It was the women who rushed forward, seized with a thirst for blood.

"Then there is a God after all! You swine, you're done for now!"

They surrounded the warm body and insulted it with jeers, called his smashed head an ugly mug, screaming into his face all the long pent-up hatred of their starved lives.

"I owed you sixty francs. Well, you're paid now, you thief!" said Maheude, now as frenzied as anybody else. "You won't refuse me any more credit. Just wait a minute, I must fatten you up a bit more!"

With her ten fingers she scratched up the earth, took two handfuls and rammed them into his mouth.

"Here you are, eat it! Go on, eat away like you used to eat us!"

Insults rained thick and fast while the dead man lay on his back, gazing with staring eyes at the wide sky from which night was falling. This earth in his mouth was the bread he had denied them, and it was the only bread he would eat henceforth. A lot of good it had done him to starve poor folk!

But the women had other scores to settle. They sniffed round him like she-wolves, trying to think of some outrage some obscenity to relieve their feelings.

The shrill voice of Ma Brûlé was heard:

"Doctor him like a tomcat!"

"Yes, yes, like a cat! The dirty old sod has done it once too often!"

Mouquette was already undoing his trousers and pulling them down, helped by la Levaque who lifted the legs. And Ma Brûlé, with her withered old hands, parted his naked thighs and grasped his dead virility. She took hold of the lot and pulled so hard that she strained her skinny back and her long arms cracked with the effort. The soft skin resisted and she had to try again, but she managed in the end to pull away the lump of hairy, bleeding flesh which she waved aloft with a snarl of triumph.

"I've got it! I've got it!"

The horrible trophy was greeted with shrill imprecations.

"You bugger, you won't fill up our girls any more!"

"Yes, no more paying you with our bodies! Never again shall we have to go through that, offering our backsides for a loaf of bread!"

"Oh, by the way, I owe you ten francs. Would you like something on account? I'm willing if you still can!"

These witticisms made them shake with terrible mirth. They pointed out to each other the bloody piece of flesh as though it were some nasty animal that had hurt them all and which they had at last squashed to death and now had lying there inert in their power. They spat on it, thrusting forward their jaws, repeating in a furious outburst of contempt:

"He can't do it now! He can't do it now! It isn't even a man they've got left to shove in the ground. Go and rot, you're no good for anything now!"

Then Ma Brûlé stuck the whole thing on the end of her stick, raised it on high and carried it like a standard down the street, followed by a rout of shrieking women. Drops of blood spattered down, and this miserable bit of flesh hung down like an odd piece of meat on a butcher's stall. Up at the window Madame Maigrat was still motionless, but the last rays of the setting sun caught her pale face, and through the distorting glass it seemed to be grinning. Beaten, continually deceived, with her back bent over a ledger from morn till night, perhaps she really was laughing as the band of women hurtled by, with the evil beast crushed at last and stuck on a pole.

This frightful mutilation had been performed in an atmosphere of icy horror. Neither Étienne, Maheu, nor anybody else had had time to intervene, but stood motionless before this stampede of furies. Faces appeared at the door of Tison's: Rasseneur livid with disgust, Zacharie and Philomène horrified at having seen it. The two old men, Bonnemort and Mouque, sagely shook their heads. The only one to giggle was Jeanlin, who nudged Bébert and forced Lydie to look up. But already the women had turned back and were passing the manager's windows. Behind the shutters the ladies were craning their necks. They had not been able to see the scene which had been hidden from them by the wall, and now they could not see anything clearly because it was getting dark.

"Whatever have they got on the end of that stick!" asked Cécile, who had now plucked up courage to look out.

Lucie and Jeanne declared that it must be a rabbit-skin.

"No, no," murmured Madame Hennebeau, "they must have looted the butcher's. It looks like a bit of pork."

Then she shuddered and stopped. Madame Grégoire had nudged her with her knee. They both stood stock still, open mouthed. The girls, deathly pale, asked no more questions, but their eyes watched the red vision disappear into the darkness.

Étienne brandished his axe again. But the feeling of horror could not be dispelled, and now the corpse was in the way, protecting the shop. Many of them had turned away, as though now that their appetites were sated they had lost interest. Maheu was standing in glum silence when a voice whispering in his ear told him to make off at once. He turned and saw Catherine, still in her man's coat, with coal on her face and gasping with anxiety. He pushed her aside refused to listen and threatened to hit her. She hesitated, made a despairing gesture and then run up to Étienne.

"Run, run! The police!"

He also made as if to drive her off with curses, feeling the blood rush back to his cheeks at the places where she had hit them. But she would not be put off, forced him to drop the axe, and exerting all her strength dragged him along irresistibly by both arms.

"I tell you it's the police! Listen. Chaval went for them and is bringing them, if you want to know. I was disgusted at him, and so I've come. . . . Clear off, I don't want you to be caught."

Catherine led him away just as a heavy galloping could be heard some way off along the road. At once a shout went up: "The police the police!" It was a rout, such a wild stampede that in two minutes the road was cleared, absolutely empty, as though it had been swept by a hurricane. Only Maigrat's corpse remained, a dark patch on the white roadway. There was nobody left in front of Tison's except Rasseneur, whose face had lit up with relief and approval of the easy victory of the sabres, whilst in the darkened and deserted town of Montsou, behind their silent, shuttered walls, the bourgeois, with sweating bodies and chattering teeth, still dared not look out. The plain had disappeared in the dense night, and far away in the tragic sky only the glare of the furnaces and coke-ovens remained. The heavy gallop of the gendarmes came nearer and they entered the street in an indistinguishable dark mass. Behind them and entrusted to their protection, came the pastry-cook's van from Marchiennes at long last: a light two-wheeled cart out of which jumped an errand-boy who calmly proceeded to unload the vol-au-vent cases.

Chapter 10

Group Conflict

HOMER

• *The Iliad*

Book XXII

How Achilles fought with Hector, and slew him, and brought his body to the ships.

Thus they throughout the city, scared like fawns, were cooling their sweat and drinking and slaking their thirst, leaning on the fair battlements, while the Achaians drew near the wall, setting shields to shoulders. But Hector deadly fate bound to abide in his place, in front of Ilios and the Skaian gates. Then to the son of Peleus spake Phoebus Apollo: "Wherefore, son of Peleus, pursuest thou me with swift feet, thyself being mortal and I a deathless god? Thou hast not even yet known me, that I am a god, but strivest vehemently. Truly thou regardest not thy task among the affliction of the Trojans whom thou affrightedst, who now are gathered into the city, while thou hast wandered hither. Me thou wilt never slay, for I am not subject unto death."

Then mightily moved spake unto him Achilles fleet of foot: "Thou hast baulked me, Far-darter, most mischievous of all the gods, in that thou hast turned me hither from the wall: else should full many yet have bitten the dust or ever within Ilios had they come. Now hast thou robbed me of great renown, and lightly hast saved them, because thou hadst no vengeance to fear thereafter. Verily I would avenge me on thee, had I but the power."

Thus saying toward the city he was gone in pride of heart, rushing like

SOURCE. From *The Iliad* by Homer. The Modern Library, N.D.

some victorious horse in a chariot, that runneth lightly at full speed over the plain; so swiftly plied Achilles in his feet and knees. Him the old man Priam first beheld as he sped across the plain, blazing as the star that cometh forth at harvest-time, and plain seen his rays shine forth amid the host of stars in the darkness of night, the star whose name men call Orion's Dog. Brightest of all is he, yet for an evil sign is he set, and bringeth much fever upon hapless men. Even so on Achilles' breast the bronze gleamed as he ran. And the old man cried aloud and beat upon his head with his hands, raising them on high, and with a cry called aloud beseeching his dear son; for he before the gates was standing, all hot for battle with Achilles. And the old man spake piteously unto him, stretching forth his hands: "Hector, beloved son, I pray thee await not this man alone with none beside thee, lest thou quickly meet thy doom, slain by the son of Peleus, since he is mightier far, a merciless man. Would the gods loved him even as do I! then quickly would dogs and vultures devour him on the field—thereby would cruel pain go from my heart—the man who hath bereft me of many valiant sons, slaying them and selling them captive into far-off isles. Ay even now twain of my children, Lykaon and Polydoros, I cannot see among the Trojans that throng into the fastness, sons whom Laothoë bare me, a princess among women. If they be yet alive amid the enemy's host, then will we ransom them with bronze and gold, for there is store within, for much goods gave the old man famous Altes to his child. If they be dead, then even in the house of Hades shall they be a sorrow to my soul and to their mother, even to us who gave them birth, but to the rest of the folk a briefer sorrow, if but thou die not by Achilles' hand. Nay, come within the wall, my child, that thou preserve the men and women of Troy, neither give great triumph to the son of Peleus, and be thyself bereft of sweet life. Have compassion also on me, the helpless one, who still can feel, ill-fated; whom the father, Kronos' son, will bring to nought by a grievous doom in the path of old age, having seen full many ills, his sons perishing and his daughters carried away captive, and his chambers laid waste and infant children hurled to the ground in terrible war, and his sons' wives dragged away by the ruinous hands of the Achaians. Myself then last of all at the street door will ravening dogs tear, when some one by stroke or throw of the sharp bronze hath bereft my limbs of life—even the dogs I reared in my halls about my table and to guard my door, which then having drunk my blood, maddened at heart shall lie in the gateway. A young man all beseemeth, even to be slain in war, to be torn by the sharp bronze and lie on the field; though he be dead yet is all honourable to him, whate'er be seen: but when dogs defile the hoary head and hoary beard and the secret parts of an old man slain, this is the most piteous thing that cometh upon hapless men."

Thus spake the old man, and grasped his hoary hairs, plucking them from his head, but he persuaded not Hector's soul. Then his mother in her turn wailed tearfully, loosening the folds of her robe, while with the other hand she showed her breast; and through her tears spake to him winged words: "Hector, my child, have regard unto this bosom and pity me, if ever I gave thee consolation of my breast. Think of it, dear child, and from this side of the wall drive back the foe, nor stand in front to meet him. He is merciless; if he slay thee it will not be on a bed that I or thy wife wooed with many gifts shall bewail thee, my own dear child, but far away from us by the ships of the Argives will swift dogs devour thee."

Thus they with wailing spake to their dear son, beseeching him sore, yet they persuaded not Hector's soul, but he stood awaiting Achilles as he drew nigh in giant might. As a serpent of the mountains upon his den awaiteth a man, having fed on evil poisons, and fell wrath hath entered into him, and terribly he glareth as he coileth himself about his den, so Hector with courage unquenchable gave not back, leaning his shining shield against a jutting tower. Then sore troubled he spake to his great heart: "Ay me, if I go within the gates and walls, Polydamas will be first to bring reproach against me, since he bade me lead the Trojans to the city during this ruinous night, when noble Achilles arose. But I regarded him not, yet surely it had been better far. And now that I have undone the host by my wantonness, I am ashamed before the men of Troy and women of trailing robes, lest at any time some worse man than I shall say: 'Hector by trusting his own might undid the host.' So will they speak; then to me would it be better far to face Achilles and either slay him and go home, or myself die gloriously before the city. Or what if I lay down my bossy shield and my stout helm, and lean my spear against the wall, and go of myself to meet noble Achilles and promise him that Helen, and with her all possessions that Alexandros brought in hollow ships to Troy, the beginning of strife, we will give to the sons of Atreus to take away, and therewithal to divide in half with the Achaians all else that this city holdeth: and if thereafter I obtain from the Trojans an oath of the Elders that they will hide nothing but divide all in twain [whatever wealth the pleasant city hold within]? But wherefore doth my heart debate thus? I might come unto him and he would not pity or regard me at all, but presently slay me unarmed as, it were but a woman, if I put off my armour. No time is it now to dally with him from oak-tree or from rock, like youth with maiden, as youth and maiden hold dalliance one with another. Better is it to join battle with all speed: let us know upon which of us twain the Olympian shall bestow renown."

Thus pondered he as he stood, but nigh on him came Achilles, peer of Enyalios warrior of the waving helm, brandishing from his right shoulder the Pelian ash, his terrible spear; and all around the bronze on him flashed like the gleam of blazing fire or of the Sun as he ariseth. And trembling seized Hector as he was aware of him, nor endured he to abide in his place, but left the gates behind him and fled in fear. And the son of Peleus darted after him, trusting in his swift feet. As a falcon upon the mountains, swiftest of winged things, swoopeth fleetly after a trembling dove; and she before him fleëth, while he with shrill screams hard at hand still darteth at her, for his heart urgeth him to seize her; so Achilles in hot haste flew straight for him, and Hector fled beneath the Trojans' wall, and plied swift knees. They past the watch-place and wind-waved wild fig-tree sped ever, away from under the wall, along the waggon-track, and came to the two fair-flowing springs, where two fountains rise that feed deep-eddying Skamandros. The one floweth with warm water, and smoke goeth up therefrom around as it were from a blazing fire, while the other even in summer floweth forth like cold hail or snow or ice that water formeth. And there beside the springs are broad washing-troughs hard by, fair troughs of stone, where wives and fair daughters of the men of Troy were wont to wash bright raiment, in the old time of peace, before the sons of the Achaians came. Thereby they ran, he flying, he pursuing. Valiant was the flier but far mightier he who fleetly pursued him. For not for beast of sacrifice or for an ox-hide were they striving, such as are prizes for men's speed of foot, but for the life of horse-taming Hector was their race. And as when victorious whole-hooved horses run rapidly round the turning-points, and some great prize lieth in sight, be it a tripod or a woman, in honour of a man that is dead, so thrice around Priam's city circled those twain with flying feet, and all the gods were gazing on them. Then among them spake first the father of gods and men: "Ay me, a man beloved I see pursued around the wall. My heart is woe for Hector, who hath burnt for me many thighs of oxen amid the crests of many-folded Ida, and other times on the city-height; but now is goodly Achilles pursuing him with swift feet round Priam's town. Come, give your counsel, gods, and devise whether we shall save him from death or now at last slay him, valiant though he be, by the hand of Achilles Peleus' son."

Then to him answered the bright-eyed goddess Athene: "O Father, Lord of the bright lightning and the dark cloud, what is this thou hast said? A man that is a mortal, doomed long ago by fate, wouldst thou redeem back from ill-boding death? Do it, but not all we other gods approve."

And unto her in answer spake cloud-gathering Zeus: "Be of good cheer, Trito-born, dear child: not in full earnest speak I, and I would fain be kind to thee. Do as seemeth good to thy mind, and draw not back."

Thus saying he roused Athene, that already was set thereon, and from the crests of Olympus she darted down.

But after Hector sped fleet Achilles chasing him vehemently. And as when on the mountains a hound hunteth the fawn of a deer, having started it from its covert, through glens and glades, and if it crouch to baffle him under a bush, yet scenting it out the hound runneth constantly until he find it; so Hector baffled not Peleus' fleet-footed son. Oft as he set himself to dart under the well-built walls over against the Dardanian gates, if haply from above they might succour him with darts, so oft would Achilles gain on him and turn him toward the plain, while himself he sped ever on the city-side. And as in a dream one faileth in chase of a flying man—the one faileth in his flight and the other in his chase—so failed Achilles to overtake him in the race, and Hector to escape. And thus would Hector have avoided the visitation of death, had not this time been utterly the last wherein Apollo came nigh to him, who nerved his strength and his swift knees. For to the host did noble Achilles sign with his head, and forbade them to hurl bitter darts against Hector, lest any smiting him should gain renown, and he himself come second. But when the fourth time they had reached the springs, then the Father hung his golden balances, and set therein two lots of dreary death, one of Achilles, one of horse-taming Hector, and held them by the midst and poised. Then Hector's fated day sank down, and fell to the house of Hades, and Phoebus Apollo left him. But to Peleus' son came the bright-eyed goddess Athene, and standing near spake to him winged words: "Now verily, glorious Achilles dear to Zeus, I have hope that we twain shall carry off great glory to the ships for the Achaians, having slain Hector, for all his thirst for fight. No longer is it possible for him to escape us, not even though far-darting Apollo should travail sore, grovelling before the Father, aegis-bearing Zeus. But do thou now stand and take breath, and I will go and persuade this man to confront thee in fight."

Thus spake Athene, and he obeyed, and was glad at heart, and stood leaning on his bronze-pointed ashen-spear. And she left him and come to noble Hector, like unto Deiphobos in shape and in strong voice, and standing near spake to him winged words: "Dear brother, verily fleet Achilles doth thee violence, chasing thee round Priam's town with swift feet: but come let us make a stand and await him on our defence."

Then answered her great Hector of the glancing helm: "Deiphobos, verily aforetime wert thou far dearest of my brothers, whom Hekabe and Priam gendered, but now methinks I shall honour thee even more, in that thou hast dared for my sake, when thou sawest me, to come forth of the wall, while the others tarry within."

Then to him again spake the bright-eyed goddess Athene: "Dear brother, of a truth my father and lady mother and my comrades around besought me much, entreating me in turn, to tarry there, so greatly do they all tremble before him; but my heart within was sore with dismal grief. And now fight we with straight-set resolve and let there be no sparing of spears, that we may know whether Achilles is to slay us and carry our bloody spoils to the hollow ships, or whether he might be vanquished by thy spear."

Thus saying Athene in her subtlety led him on. And when they were come nigh in onset on one another, to Achilles first spake great Hector of the glancing helm: "No longer, son of Peleus, will I fly thee, as before I thrice ran round the great town of Priam, and endured not to await thy onset. Now my heart biddeth me stand up against thee; I will either slay or be slain. But come hither and let us pledge us by our gods, for they shall be best witnesses and beholders of covenants: I will entreat thee in no outrageous sort, if Zeus grant me to outstay thee, and if I take thy life, but when I have despoiled thee of thy glorious armour, O Achilles, I will give back thy dead body to the Achaians, and do thou the same."

But unto him with grim gaze spake Achilles fleet of foot: "Hector, talk not to me, thou madman, of covenants. As between men and lions there is no pledge of faith, nor wolves and sheep can be of one mind, but imagine evil continually against each other, so is it impossible for thee and me to be friends, neither shall be any pledge between us until one or other shall have fallen and glutted with blood Ares, the stubborn god of war. Bethink thee of all thy soldiership: now behoveth it thee to quit thee as a good spearman and valiant man of war. No longer is there way of escape for thee, but Pallas Athene will straightway subdue thee to my spear; and now in one hour shalt thou pay back for all my sorrows for my friends whom thou hast slain in the fury of thy spear."

He said, and poised his far-shadowing spear and hurled. And noble Hector watched the coming thereof and avoided it; for with his eye on it he crouched, and the bronze spear flew over him, and fixed itself in the earth; but Pallas Athene caught it up and gave it back to Achilles, unknown of Hector shepherd of hosts. Then Hector spake unto the noble son of Peleus: "Thou hast missed, so nowise yet, godlike Achilles, hast thou known from Zeus the hour of my doom, though thou thoughtest it. Cunning of tongue art thou and a deceiver in speech, that fearing thee I might forget my valour and strength. Not as I flee shalt thou plant thy spear in my reins, but drive it straight through my breast as I set on thee, if God hath given thee to do it. Now in thy turn avoid my spear of bronze. O that thou mightst take it all into thy flesh! Then would the war be lighter to the Trojans, if but thou wert dead, for thou art their greatest bane."

He said, and poised his long-shadowed spear and hurled it, and smote the midst of the shield of Peleus' son, and missed him not: but far from the shield the spear leapt back. And Hector was wroth that his swift weapon had left his hand in vain, and he stood downcast, for he had no second ashen spear. And he called with a loud shout to Deiphobos of the white shield, and asked of him a long spear, but he was nowise nigh. Then Hector knew the truth in his heart, and spake and said: "Ay me, now verily the gods have summoned me to death. I deemed the warrior Deiphobos was by my side, but he is within the wall, and it was Athene who played me false. Now therefore is evil death come very nigh me, not far off, nor is there way of escape. This then was from of old the pleasure of Zeus and of the far-darting son of Zeus, who yet before were fain to succour me: but now my fate hath found me. At least let me not die without a struggle or ingloriously, but in some great deed of arms whereof men yet to be born shall hear."

Thus saying he drew his sharp wood sword that by his flank hung great and strong, and gathered himself and swooped like a soaring eagle that darteth to the plain through the dark clouds to seize a tender lamb or crouching hare. So Hector swooped, brandishing his sharp sword. And Achilles made at him, for his heart was filled with wild fierceness, and before his breast he made a covering with his fair graven shield, and tossed his bright four-plated helm; and round it waved fair golden plumes [that Hephaistos had set thick about the crest]. As a star goeth among stars in the darkness of night, Hesperos, fairest of all stars set in heaven, so flashed there forth a light from the keen spear Achilles poised in his right hand, devising mischief against noble Hector, eyeing his fair flesh to find the fittest place. Now for the rest of him his flesh was covered by the fair bronze armour he stripped from strong Patroklos when he slew him, but there was an opening where the collar bones coming from the shoulders clasp the neck, even at the gullet, where destruction of life cometh quickliest; there, as he came on, noble Achilles drave at him with his spear, and right through the tender neck went the point. Yet the bronze-weighted ashen spear clave not the windpipe, so that he might yet speak words of answer to his foe. And he fell down in the dust, and noble Achilles spake exultingly: "Hector, thou thoughtest, whilst thou wert spoiling Patroklos, that thou wouldst be safe, and didst reck nothing of me who was afar, thou fool. But away among the hollow ships his comrade, a mightier far, even I, was left behind, who now have unstrung thy knees. Thee shall dogs and birds tear foully, but his funeral shall the Achaians make."

Then with faint breath spake unto him Hector of the glancing helm: "I pray thee by thy life and knees and parents leave me not for dogs of the Achaians to devour by the ships, but take good store of bronze and gold, gifts that my father and lady mother shall give to thee, and give them home my body back again, that the Trojans and Trojans' wives give me my due of fire after my death."

But unto him with grim gaze spake Achilles fleet of foot: "Entreat me not, dog, by knees or parents. Would that my heart's desire could so bid me myself to carve and eat raw thy flesh, for the evil thou hast wrought me, as surely as there none that shall keep the dogs from thee, not even should they bring ten or twenty fold ransom and here weigh it out, and promise even more, not even were Priam Dardanos' son to bid pay thy weight in gold, not even so shall thy lady mother lay thee on a bed to mourn her son, but dogs and birds shall devour thee utterly."

Then dying spake unto him Hector of the glancing helm: "Verily I know thee and behold thee as thou art, nor was I destined to persuade thee; truly thy heart is iron in thy breast. Take heed now lest I draw upon thee wrath of gods, in the day when Paris and Phoebus Apollo slay thee, for all thy valour, at the Skaian gate."

He ended, and the shadow of death came down upon him, and his soul flew forth of his limbs and was gone to the house of Hades, wailing her fate, leaving her vigour and youth. Then to the dead man spake noble Achilles: "Die: for my death, I will accept it whensoever Zeus and the other immortal gods are minded to accomplish it."

He said, and from the corpse drew forth his bronze spear, and set it aside, and stripped the bloody armour from the shoulders. And other sons of Achaians ran up around, who gazed upon the stature and marvellous goodliness of Hector. Nor did any stand by but wounded him, and thus would many a man say looking toward his neighbour: "Go to, of a truth far easier to handle is Hector now than when he burnt the ships with blazing fire." Thus would many a man say, and wound him as he stood hard by. And when fleet noble Achilles had despoiled him, he stood up among the Achaians and spake winged words: "Friends, chiefs and counsellors of the Argives, since the gods have vouchsafed us to vanquish this man who hath done us more evil than all the rest together, come let us make trial in arms round about the city, that we may know somewhat of the Trojans' purpose, whether since he hath fallen they will forsake the citadel, or whether they are minded to abide, albeit Hector is no more. But wherefore doth my heart debate thus? There lieth by the ships a dead man unbewailed, unburied, Patroklos; him will I not forget, while I abide among the living and my knees can stir. Nay if even in the house of Hades the dead forget their dead, yet will I even there be mindful of my dear comrade. But come, ye sons of the Achaians, let us now, singing our song of victory, go back to the hollow ships and take with us our foe. Great glory have we won; we have slain the noble Hector, unto whom the Trojans prayed throughout their city, as he had been a god."

He said, and devised foul entreatment of noble Hector. The tendons of both feet behind he slit from heel to ankle-joint, and thrust therethrough thongs of ox-hide, and bound him to his chariot, leaving his head to trail. And when he had mounted the chariot and lifted therein the famous armour, he lashed his horses to speed, and they nothing loth flew on. And dust rose around him that was dragged, and his dark hair flowed loose on either side, and in the dust lay all his once fair head, for now had Zeus given him over to his foes to entreat foully in his own native land.

Thus was his head all grimed with dust. But his mother when she beheld her son, tore her hair and cast far from her her shining veil, and cried aloud with an exceeding bitter cry. And piteously moaned his father, and around them the folk fell to crying and moaning throughout the town. Most like it seemed as though all beetling Ilios were burning utterly in fire. Scarcely could the folk keep back the old man in his hot desire to get him forth of the Dardanian gates. For he besought them all, casting himself down in the mire, calling on each man by his name: "Hold, friends, and though you love me leave me to get me forth of the city alone and go unto the ships of the Achaians. Let me pray this accursed horror-working man, if haply he may feel shame before his age-fellows and pity an old man. He also hath a father such as I am, Peleus, who begat and reared him to be a bane of Trojans—and most of all to me hath he brought woe. So many sons of mine hath he slain in their flower—yet for all my sorrow for the rest I mourn them all less than this one alone, for whom my sharp grief will bring me down to the house of Hades—even Hector. Would that he had died in my arms; then would we have wept and wailed our fill, his mother who bore him to her ill hap, and I myself."

Thus spake he wailing, and all the men of the city made moan with him. And among the women of Troy, Hekabe led the wild lament: "My child, ah, woe is me! wherefore should I live in my pain, now thou art dead, who night and day wert my boast through the city, and blessing to all, both men and women of Troy throughout the town, who hailed thee as a god, for verily an exceeding glory to them wert thou in thy life:—now death and fate have over-taken thee."

Thus spake she wailing. But Hector's wife knew not as yet, for no true messenger had come to tell her how her husband abode without the gates, but in an inner chamber of the lofty house she was weaving a double purple web, and broidering therein manifold flowers. Then she called to her goodly-haired handmaids through the house to set a great tripod on the fire, that Hector might have warm washing when he came home out of the battle—fond heart, and was unaware how, far from all washings, bright-eyed Athene had slain him by the hand of Achilles. But she heard shrieks and groans from the battlements, and her limbs reeled, and the shuttle fell from her hands to earth. Then again among her goodly-haired maids she spake: "Come two of ye this way with me that I may see what deeds are done. It was the voice of my husband's noble mother that I heard, and in my own breast my heart leapeth to my mouth and my knees are numbed beneath me: surely some evil thing is at hand against the children of Priam. Would that such word might never reach my ear! yet terribly I dread lest noble Achilles have cut off bold Hector from the city by himself and chased him to the plain and ere this ended his perilous pride that possessed him, for never would he tarry among the throng of men but ran out before them far, yielding place to no man in his hardihood."

Thus saying she sped through the chamber like one mad, with beating heart, and with her went her handmaidens. But when she came to the battlements and the throng of men, she stood still upon the wall and gazed, and beheld him dragged before the city:—swift horses dragged him recklessly toward the hollow ships of the Achaians. Then dark night came on her eyes and shrouded her, and she fell backward and gasped forth her spirit. From off her head she shook the bright attiring thereof, frontlet and net and woven band, and veil, the veil that golden Aphrodite gave her on the day when Hector of the glancing helm led her forth of the house of Eëtion, having given bride-gifts untold. And around her thronged her husband's sisters and his brothers' wives, who held her up among them, distraught even to death. But when at last she came to herself and her soul returned into her breast, then wailing with deep sobs she spake among the women of Troy: "O Hector, woe is me! to one fate then were we both born, thou in Troy in the house of Priam, and I in Thebe under woody Plakos, in the house of Eëtion, who reared me from a little one—ill-fated sire of cruel-fated child. Ah, would he had begotten me not. Now thou to the house of Hades beneath the secret places of the earth departest, and me in bitter mourning thou leavest a widow in thy halls: and thy son is but an infant child—son of unhappy parents, thee and me—nor shalt thou profit him, Hector, since thou art dead, neither he thee. For even if he escape the Achaians' woful war, yet shall labour and sorrow cleave unto him hereafter, for other men shall seize his lands. The day of orphanage sundereth a child from his fellows, and his head is bowed down ever, and his cheeks are wet with tears. And in his need the child seeketh his father's friends, plucking this one by cloak and that by coat, and one of them that pity him holdeth his cup a little to his mouth, and moisteneth his lips, but his palate he moisteneth not. And some child unorphaned thrusteth him from the feast with blows and taunting words, 'Out with thee! no farther of thine is at our board.' Then weeping to his widowed mother shall he return, even Astyanax, who erst upon his father's knee ate only marrow and fat flesh of sheep; and when sleep fell on him and he ceased from childish play, then in bed in his nurse's arms he would slumber softly nested, having satisfied his heart with good things: but now that he hath lost his father he will suffer many ills, Astyanax— that name the Trojans gave him, because thou only wert the defence of their gates and their long walls. But now by the beaked ships, far from thy parents, shall coiling worms devour thee when the dogs have had their fill, as thou liest naked; yet in these halls lieth raiment of thine, delicate and fair, wrought by the hands of women. But verily all these will I consume with burning fire—to thee no profit, since thou wilt never lie therein, yet that this be honour to thee from the men and the women of Troy."

Thus spake she wailing, and the women joined their moan.

NIKOS KAZANTZAKIS

• *The Fratricides*

20

The sky began to pale, the morning star struggled and slowly faded in the growing light. A sad and gentle smile spread softly over the lonely rocks. A solitary hawk balanced itself in the peak of heaven; it, too, was waiting for the sun to appear and thaw its wings.

In the cool rose-light of dawn came the sound of a bell pealing joyfully— Christ had risen from the dead! The proud fighters entered the village and began to sing. The hymn leaped from their manly chests and rolled over the hillsides; it trod the village like a chieftain with his heavy boots, his bandoliers, his curling mustache. The crowd pushed forward, the doors of the church opened; Father Yánaros came down from the portals of the iconostas, walked toward the great arched gate in the courtyard, holding the heavy silver-bound Bible tightly in his arms. At that very moment the guerrillas, their rifles slung over their shoulders, stepped out of the shadowy side streets into the early light of dawn. They had stopped singing, and walked cautiously; they looked around in apprehension—they trusted no one yet.

The villagers, uneasy now, poured out of the church; they, too, were mistrustful. They saw the rifles gleaming and the eyes glowing in the half-light, and they were frightened. They kept looking back and forth, from the priest to the

SOURCE. From *The Fratricides* by Nikos Kazantzakis. Copyright 1962, reprinted with the permission of Simon and Schuster and Company.

armed beasts he had brought into the village. The savage guests from the hills came in increasing numbers and filled Castello by the minute. They entered and overflowed the church.

The guerrillas, both men and women, stepped back to make a path for the tall, heavy, fearsome captain who appeared. He raised his fist in greeting: "Welcome, to us!" he shouted.

"Blessed be he who cometh in the name of the Lord!" Father Yánaros replied, and held out the Bible for the captain to kiss.

But Drakos turned to the crowd, stroking his beard, and his voice echoed under the dome of the church.

"We are happy that you have finally seen the light. We bring you justice and order, and soon after, freedom!"

"Not before?" Father Yánaros asked, controlling his turmoil. "After? Not before, Captain?"

"Justice and order first," he said again, and crimson flooded his hairy face. "We must bring order first. Freedom is a strong wine, Father Yánaros, and it can go to one's head. Everyone can't take it, I'll have to choose!"

"May God place His hand," murmured the priest, and threw a secretive, inquiring glance at Christ there on the right of the iconostas. He bit his lips to control himself.

"God is the great Judge—He will decide—we place our trust in Him."

Captain Drakos laughed sarcastically. "We've knocked God off His throne, Father Yánaros, don't you know that yet? Man is sitting on God's throne now. We used to hold Him responsible for all things—right and wrong—but now we are to blame for whatever happens—good or bad. We formed our own government and we take the responsibility."

Father Yánaros groaned; he wanted to cry out, to shout an anathema at this bear who blasphemed, but he held back his heart. He was afraid for the people and he smothered his anger.

These are only words that others put in their mouths, he thought, they only say them to frighten us. But God works within them, even though they do not know it. We must be patient.

"Let us finish the sacrament of giving and receiving the kiss of love; your heart may soften then, Captain."

Father Yánaros began the Holy Liturgy of the Resurrection; never did his voice echo so joyfully, never did his chest shake with such strength, as though Christ were really inside, as though his chest were the tombstone and it was rising to let Christ out. Christ took on a new meaning: it was man who had been crucified, and died, and now cried out to be resurrected.

Father Yánaros opened the Bible; he held it tightly in his arms as he walked out into the courtyard. Behind him came the rebels; further back the crowd of people holding the unlit candles. The priest climbed upon the stone ledge, raised his voice to shout the holy words of the Resurrection. As he stood there, dressed in silk, with the gold vestment stole, his chest swelled and his throat strained; he looked like a golden rooster who stands in the courtyard to crow for the sun to rise.

The people extended their candles, ready to pounce on Father Yánaros to receive a light. The priest spread his palm on the open Bible; he did not look at it—he knew the words by heart—and his voice resounded triumphantly in the morning wind of spring: "And when the Sabbath passed, Mary Magdalene . . ."

The rebel leader coughed; Father Yánaros turned and threw him a quick glance. He stood erect, unbending in the center of the courtyard, surrounded by his men, and a triumphant smile spread over his face.

"God help us," murmured Father Yánaros, raising the lighted candles and summoning all his strength as the mournful pleading, the paean of the Resurrection, came from his puffed-out chest: "Christ has risen from the dead!"

The crowd leaped to light their candles from Father Yánaros' flame; Drakos turned to the men beside him, lowered his voice, and gave a command. Ten of them grabbed their rifles and strode toward the outer door. The crowd moved, shaken. A sense of evil passed through the air. He turned to leave, but Father Yánaros stretched out his hand. "Do not go," he said, "I want to talk to you."

The people stopped short, impatiently, as though choking from the rebels' breathing around them. Drakos turned to the priest. "Make it short, priest," he said, "we have work to do."

As he stood on the ledge, Father Yánaros opened his arms wide, turned to the right and to the left, as though he wanted to embrace the villagers who were gathered in the courtyard, the rebels, and all of Castello, all of Greece.

His voice leaped from his chest like joyful bubbling water.

"My children," he cried, "I have been resurrecting Christ for forty years but I have never felt a more joyous, more complete, more heart-filled Resurrection. Because for the first time I realize that Christ and Greece and man's soul are one. And when we say, 'Christ is risen,' it means that Greece is risen, that the soul of man has risen. Only yesterday, on this very hill, brothers were killing brothers. The rocks echoed from the moans and curses. And now—look! Reds and blacks have united in brotherhood and share together their understanding of 'Christ has risen.' This is the true meaning of the Resurrection—this is the true meaning of love. For years now this is what I have waited for; and now it has come. Glory to the Almighty! Captain, the people's eyes are upon you; they await your words; speak to them, this great moment!"

The captain raised his hand. "Go to your homes—go!"

"Is that all you have to say, Captain?" the priest growled angrily. "Is that the way Christ is resurrected? Is that what unity and brotherhood mean?"

"Yes, that's it. We said order and justice must come first. There are enemies of the cause here; I asked to have them brought before me. All of you leave; I will remain here in the courtyard with my men and pass judgment."

The crowd swarmed, pushing and shoving toward the gate; the courtyard soon emptied.

"I will remain here with you, Captain," Father Yánaros said as he folded his vestments—his hands trembled from anger.

Captain Drakos shrugged his shoulders. "Stay and give them last rites," he said, and laughed.

Fury swept over Father Yánaros; his voice came stern and hoarse: "Captain Drakos, the two of us made a bargain. I kept my word and turned over the village to you. Now it's your turn. I gave—now you give! You're the debtor now—I'm staying here to collect."

Enraged at the words, Loukas grabbed the priest by the shoulder. "What are you trying to prove, old man? And what gives you the right to talk to a guerrilla on equal terms? Who's behind you that makes you talk with such assurance?"

"I have God behind me, my son," the older man replied. "I have God behind me, and that's why I talk with such assurance. I have God in front of me, God to the right of me, God to the left of me; I'm encircled by God; all your rifles and all your swords and all your threats will never be able to touch me."

He enthroned himself, alone, on the edge of the stone ledge. As they spoke, the sound of footsteps came from the narrow street, followed by moans, cries, and curses. In a few moments the open gate filled. Old Mandras was at the head, thin and erect, his long neck stretching like a pelican's. Behind him were his three sons and four family men, followed by three of the town elders: Barba Tassos, old Stamatis, and Hadjis. Their faces were drained, their lips drooping, their sashes loose; they were crying. Behind the notables, limping, dragged Mitros the sergeant. He had resisted and the rebels had beaten him. He could barely drag his legs and he was held up by Nionios. Behind them came the other soldiers, torn, ragged, unarmed. At the end, covered with mud and blood was the captain. He had been shot while resisting capture. Blood ran from his wounds. Two fighters held him up. But as they entered the courtyard, he fell to the ground in a heap.

Captain Drakos jumped at sight of the captain. He approached him, craned his neck and looked. The light had now caught the dome of the church and slowly fell over the courtyard; the faces of the men shone and there, among the guerrillas, the light showed the pale, dark-eyed army captain's wife, who stood tight-lipped and bare-necked.

Drakos bent over, watching the captain hungrily, silent for a long while. At last he opened his mouth: "Is it you, Captain? You, sir? What's happened to you?" He turned to his men. "Untie him," he ordered, "cut the ropes! Lift him up." Then he turned to the captain. "You! You've aged, you've rotted away —why is your hair so white?"

The captain bit his mustache with fury; he would not speak. Blood ran from his eyebrow, and a bullet was lodged in his right heel; it must have pierced the bone for he was in great pain. But he gritted his teeth to prevent from crying out.

Drakos watched him with admiration, with compassion, with horror. Was this the raven-mustached, silent, brave warrior whose name resounded throughout the Albanian hills? What a shame, Drakos thought, what a pity that men of such spirit are not on our side! All the virtues should be among our own fighters, all the cowardices and dishonors within the others. But we have many cowards and dishonest ones among us, and the others have many brave men with them. I think that God shuffled the cards wrong and we're all mixed up . . .

"Do you remember me, sir?" he asked. "Look at me closely; don't you remember me?"

The captain wiped the blood from his eyes, turned his face away, and remained silent.

"I served in your company during the Albanian war," Drakos went on. "I had another name then; you were very fond of me and you called me Pirate. When there was a dangerous mission you always called on me. 'Go on, Pirate,' you'd say, 'perform your miracle!' And when you were wounded in both legs during one of the battles, remember, you fell, and the others left you; but I put you on my shoulders, carried you for five hours, and brought you to the hospital. You had put your arms around my neck and said, 'I owe my life to you—I owe my life to you!' And now the wheel's turned—damn it—and we're killing each other."

The captain's knees buckled; he fell to the ground, silent.

"Why did you go with them, Captain?" Drakos continued, and his voice was filled with grief and complaint. "You, a hero, an honorable Greek! Didn't you shed your blood for freedom, in Albania? Why do you betray it now? Why do you fight against it? Come with us—I'll turn my men over to you— I'll serve under your command again. Send me on the difficult missions; we'll fight together again to free our people. Don't you pity the Greeks who are being destroyed? Come, join us!"

Blood rose to the captain's pale cheeks. "Kill me," he murmured at last. "Kill me so I can be free."

He paused a moment and then he added: "If you were my prisoner, traitor, I'd have killed you—so kill me, too. That's all I have to say!"

"I respect you," Drakos replied, and now his voice was filled with mercy and anger. "I respect you and I feel sorry for you, but I'm going to kill you anyway."

"That's the way it should be," the captain replied.

Drakos clenched his fist and turned to his men: "Line them up against the wall," he ordered, "all of them! Captain, can you stand up?"

"Yes, I can," he replied and mustered all his strength to rise, but his knees gave in, and he fell back. Two men ran to help him, but he waved his hand in anger.

"Don't touch me," he growled, "I'll get up alone." He grabbed hold of a stone in the wall, summoned all his strength and stood up. Sweat poured over him, and he turned paler still. He looked around him; below, on the slates of the courtyard sat the guerrillas with crossed legs. On the stone ledge across, sat Drakos with Loukas. At one end Father Yánaros, and at the other . . . The captain's blood whirled, his eyes dulled; black lightning tore through his brain, as he saw that the woman sitting on the other end of the ledge was his wife. Once upon a time he had a wife . . . How quickly fifteen years of happiness had passed—like a flash! It seemed like only yesterday when the two of them had climbed the rocky hills of Roumeli. His elderly mother had stood there at the threshold, dressed in white—her wedding dress, and the same one she would wear when she died. She had waited for them, she waited and waited, since daybreak, and now she cried with joy. The newlyweds began to cry, too, because they were young and it was spring and the ground smelled sweet; and a partridge that was in a cage in the courtyard paced back and forth behind its bars. It watched the new arrivals and cackled sadly, as though she, too, wanted to be married, but her groom was in the hills, and the cage stood between them, preventing their union. So she beat against her prison with her beak and her red feet, trying to escape. "Mother," the bride said, "I want to ask a favor of you. I can't stand to see the partridge imprisoned; give me your permission to open her cage and set her free."

"She's yours, daughter," the old woman replied, "she's yours to do with as you please." And the bride opened the cage, and took the plumed partridge in her palm. She admired her coral legs, the wild, yet gentle, eyes, the puffed-up breast, and quickly she tossed her hand high and released her in the air. "Go on," she told it, "you're free!"

Drakos' voice rang in the air. "Line them up against the wall!" The three elders were crying, spattering saliva and tears on their beards. The soldiers, gathered in a group, were whispering and looking toward the gate; old Mandras spat at Father Yánaros as he passed in front of him. "Traitor," he said, and spat again.

Father Yánaros rose, walked toward the wall where the men stood in a line at the right and left of Drakos. His heart trembled, but he controlled himself.

"Don't be afraid, my children," the priest cried, "the rebel leader did not come to our village for revenge—he came in friendship. He is a man, a brave lad; he gave his word that he would harm no one—his word of honor—have faith! He only wants to frighten you, and rightly so, because of your resistance to a reconciliation. He wants to scold you and then he'll let you go free—he came for freedom's sake didn't he? Do not fear!"

Old Mandras turned a wild, poisonous look at the priest. "To hell with you, you traitor, you Judas! Do you think they believe in such a thing as honor, you fool?"

Drakos threw his cigarette down and stamped on it with his heavy boot. Then he turned to the captain and to his own men.

"Captain," he said, "you've acted like a man. You have last Castello, but you have not lost your honor. And those of you who remained—you fought us and killed my men, but it was war, so it's understandable. I take the sponge and wipe all this away; now I offer you my hand, listen to me! Those who decide to put on the rebel cap and fight for freedom are welcome to join us. Those who refuse, die!" He turned to Mandras. "You, old man Mandras, you heartless elder who's taken over the whole village and drained the blood of the poor, I'm not asking you to come along—you, I'm going to kill!"

The old man half closed his small, runny eyes and looked over his shoulder at Captain Drakos. "I made sons and grandsons, I've lived my life, my work is done; I'm not afraid of you, rebel! Only one thing bothers me"—he turned to Father Yánaros—"that I didn't get a chance to skin you alive, you scoundrel!"

Then he turned to his sons. "Do whatever you want. Both honor and dishonor stand before you—choose!"

He turned, lastly, to the young family men. "You family men go with them, you poor souls, save your skins." Then he grabbed his shirt and tore it open, showing the bony, hairy chest. "I'm ready," he said.

Father Yánaros stretched his neck, yanked at his beard, and listened; he could not believe his ears. Is this, then, the freedom they bring us? "Surrender and you are free; resist and you die!" If they go back on their word, I will rise and shout; let them put me up against the wall, too. "Onward, Father Yánaros —both redhoods and blackhoods fight you. But don't complain, you want to be free, don't you? Then pay!"

Mitros the sergeant closed his eyes; he could see the little house in the ravine, the oak in the middle of the yard, and in the shade of the tree his wife Margo, with her thick stockings, her embroidered skirt, and the red shoes. He could see her sitting, unbuttoning her blouse, and taking out her breast to feed his son.

He opened his eyes and saw the captain standing before him. "Will you let me go, sir?" he said softly, shamefully, to the captain. "Won't you let me go back to my village, to Roumeli? I want no part of war, damn it! I want no part of it! I wasn't meant to kill . . ."

The captain threw back his head to hear him. "Mitros!" he growled reprimandingly, and his eyebrows arched.

"Captain," Mitros replied, stammering, "command me, sir."

"Aren't you ashamed? Come with me!"

"I'm coming, Captain," the sergeant answered, and at once the hill and the oak tree and his wife and their son disappeared.

The three family men stepped forward. "We're coming with you, Captain Drakos," they said. "Life is too sweet."

Mandras turned his head the other way and spat, but he remained silent.

The three elders—Barba Tassos, old Stamatis, and Hadjis—took a step and staggered; the oldest—Hadjis—spoke up. "Don't you want to take our possessions, Captain Drakos?" he asked, whimpering.

"I don't like haggling," growled the rebel leader, and shoved the three old men back against the wall. "What would I do with you old wrecks? Stand up against the wall!"

Vassos, a soldier with lines in his cheeks, with crooked shoulders, with wide calloused hands, with small sad eyes, stood despairingly, first on one leg, then on the other; he could not come to a decision. Only today he had received a letter from his four sisters, and his heart had filled with poison.

"Captain Drakos," he said, "I have four sisters; I've got to marry them off. Don't kill me."

"Will you join us?"

Vassos swallowed hard. "I'll come."

Three other soldiers from the seven stepped from the wall and came forward. Stratis, the first and most agile, spoke up. "Captain Drakos, we were always on your side. Our rifles were in Castello, but our hearts were in the hills. We'll come with you."

One of the remaining soldiers, Nionios of Zante, spoke. "Captain Drakos," he said, "I'm not coming with you. Not because I don't love life, but because I am ashamed. I'm ashamed to be subjected by force. So kill me."

"If you were ashamed, you'd join us. I pity your wasted youth."

"My dignity as a man does not allow me to be forced into obedience," Nionios replied, and stood up against the wall.

Old Mandras' youngest son, Milton, sighed and looked first at his father, then at the rebel leader, and then at the gate. Oh if he were only a bird, to fly away! He was twenty-five years old and unmarried. All the village girls were his; he loved wine and he played the tambour drum. Every Sunday he would place a flower behind his ear and make the rounds of the neighborhoods. He was chubby, rosy-cheeked, with a lock of hair that bounced over his forehead.

Milton sighed; his mind went to the wine and young women, then to honor and country and to the heroes who sacrificed their lives and became immortal. The poor soldier was dazed; he could not decide which was stronger and more real, which to choose.

Drakos stood before him and watched. "Well?" he asked. "Make up your mind—decide!" The young man bowed his head; his face turned crimson. A cluster of basil that a girl from the village had given him last night still hung over his ear. "I'll join you," he said, and walked away from the wall.

Mandras bowed his head and did not speak.

"The devil take you," his two brothers shouted, and spat at him.

Drakos approached the captain. How can I help him? How can I help him? he thought, and watched him silently. There's nothing I can do, since he's not afraid of death.

He turned to his men who waited with raised rifles. "Ready?" he asked, and raised his hand to give the word. Father Yánaros' eyes bulged as he leaned against the wall; his insides were tearing. Within his fist he felt the hand of the Almighty trembling.

"What is this that trembles? Are You frightened, too?" he said to God, softly. "Are You afraid for me? Courage, my Lord!"

As Captain Drakos raised his hand to give the signal, Father Yánaros jumped up, growling, and walked slowly, heavily, toward the rebel leader. He felt that he had suddenly become one hundred years old; his body had become lead; he felt an unbearable weight on his shoulders. He took two steps, three, and stopped in front of the leader. He did not know what to say; his throat had clogged; he was choking. Finally, with great effort, his lips unsealed. "Are you going to kill them?" he said, and his whole body trembled. Drakos turned and looked at him. The priest's face had become ashen, his mouth slanted, he was breathing with difficulty. "Are you going to kill them?" The old man's voice, short and hoarse, was heard again.

"Yes, death to all who stand in the way of freedom!"

"Those who do not allow others to have their own opinion stand in the way of freedom, too," Father Yánaros reprimanded. "What about the promise you made me? Is this the freedom you bring?"

"Don't meddle in the affairs of this world, old man!" the rebel leader said, exasperated.

"This world and the next world are one; you can win and lose this world, you can win and lose the other, too. I meddle in your affairs because they're my affairs, too, Captain Drakos. I spread my arms over these Christians that you've pushed against the wall and I say to you, "You're not going to kill them! I, Father Yánaros, won't let you kill them!"

"Calm down, old man, for your sake I tell you to calm down! If we let everyone go free now, we're lost; we won't be a nation, we'll be a pack of dogs. Freedom will come in due time, don't rush things; it never comes at the beginning, it always comes last."

"Tyranny, then?" The old man threw his hands in the air and shouted,

"Tyranny, force and the whip? Is that how we get freedom? No, no, I won't accept that. I'll rise and shout through all the villages, 'Tyrants, degraders, cursed enemies of the people!' "

"Be quiet! Or I'll stand you up against the wall, too!"

"I was always up against the wall, my boy. I've been expecting the bullet from the moment I saw the truth, so let it come!"

Loukas, who seemed to be sitting on hot coals throughout the scene, could control himself no longer. He jumped up and grabbed the priest by the neck. "Don't shout, priest, you think we respect your black robes? I'll twist your neck, scoundrel!"

"Don't try to frighten me, redhood," the old man replied. "Death only frightens the unbelievers. I believe in God. I'm not afraid of death. I've already dug my grave, there, in front of you, and I've carved on my tombstone the words, 'Death, I fear you not!' "

"I'm going to kill you, you old goat, shut up!" Loukas growled.

Five or six rebels jumped up and encircled the priest, slipping the rifles from their shoulders.

"Kill me, you're welcome to it, my boys. You think that because you carry rifles you carry justice, too? Kill me! You can kill the last free man, but you'll never kill freedom." He walked back to the wall and stood beside the captain.

"Get away from the wall, old man," Drakos said. "And stop talking. Close your mouth, or we'll close it for you."

"My place is here. You cheated me and I cheated the village. I betrayed it. How can I show my face before those people again? I'm anxious to appear before God, to tell Him of my pain, to inform on you and your men, you charlatan! You think you're going to shape the new world, eh? With lies, with slavery, with dishonesty?"

"Father Yánaros, I don't want to ordain you a hero and have you become a ghost," Drakos growled as he grabbed the priest's arm and yanked him away from the wall.

"If you let me live, I'll cry out! If you kill me, I'll cry out! You'll never escape me," the priest said, and as he spoke, the first rays of the sun fell on him and his beard turned a rose hue.

Again Father Yánaros felt the Almighty trembling inside his fist. Anger seized him. "Now, at this crucial moment," he cried within himself, "Now, you are overcome with fear? This is when we need strength; get up, help me save them! You forget that You're not only the crucified Christ, but the resurrected Christ as well! The world has no need of crucified Christs any longer, it needs fighting Christs! Take a lesson from me. Enough of tears and passions, and crucifixions; get up I say, call out for the army of angels to descend; bring justice! Enough they've spit on us, beaten us, made us wear a crown of thorns, crucified us; now it's the turn of the resurrected Christ.

"We want the Second Coming here, here on earth, before we die. Get up, rise!" And a deep sad voice came from the depths of his inner being: "I cannot . . ."

Father Yánaros' hands fell paralyzed. "You cannot? You want to, but You cannot? You are good and just; You love the people, You want to bring justice and freedom and love to the world and You say You cannot?"

The priest's eyes filled. "How sad," he murmured, "so freedom is not almighty, it is not immortal, it, too, is the child of man and it needs him!"

His inner being flooded with bitterness, with compassion, with tenderness; never, never had he loved Christ as he loved Him at this moment. "My child . . ." he murmured, and closed his eyes.

Captain Drakos turned and looked at him; he watched his father's tears running down his cheeks and on his beard. He knew that Father Yánaros was not crying out of fear—he placed little value on his life—he was crying for all men, friends and enemies, blacks and reds. He looked and looked at the old man's tears falling, and suddenly without knowing from where the warm wind of compassion blew, his heart ached for the twelve men who stood waiting against the wall. Their lives hung on one word from him, on one movement of his hand. What should he do? Which was the shortest road to victory? Was it to kill, to kill and bring no end to hate? Or to open his arms, too, like his father, the priest, and conquer hatred through love? He made a move toward the condemned men. "I am keeping my word," he wanted to say, "I bring freedom, you're free!" But his eyes met Loukas' stare, wild and mocking. A demon leaped within him; it was dark, hairy, covered with blood. Drakos raised his hand. "Fire!" he growled in a voice that was not his own.

The rifles cracked, and the twelve bodies fell on the churchyard slates. The captain's body quivered like a fish, then it rolled to a stop at his wife's feet; she shoved it away with her foot.

Father Yánaros let out a cry; for a moment his brain jolted; he turned toward the church, but his mind was reeling, and with it reeled the village and the hill around it, and Greece. Slowly, dragging himself, he moved toward the twelve corpses; he bent over, scooped up a fistful of blood and daubed it on his beard, making it fiery red. He bent over again, took another fistful of blood, and poured it over his head.

"Your blood, my children," he groaned, "your blood is on my hands; I killed you!"

The rebels turned and looked at him, and they laughed.

He went into the church, bowed before the Holy Altar; the blood-spattered rock still lay beside the crucifixion; he worshiped it. Whose blood was on it, a redhood's? a blackhood's? He did not question; he had taken the rock from the hill after one of the first battles. He had placed it on the Holy Altar beside Christ on the cross and before every liturgy, he prayed to it.

He removed his vestment stole, folded it, wrapped it around the Bible, and put it under his arm. He made the sign of the cross as he took his staff from the corner. He felt his heart opening and an inexhaustible river of love spilling out, flowing from Castello to the valleys and the seashores of Greece. Love flowed— it flowed, and Father Yánaros felt relief in his heart.

Who knows, he thought, perhaps Christ entrusted me, the unworthy one, with this great duty. In the name of God, His will be done. He turned to his right.

"Come," he said to the Invisible One. "Let us go!"

He walked out of the church and stood in the middle of the courtyard. "I am leaving," he shouted. "I will do as I said, I will go from village to village and I will shout: 'Brothers, do not believe the reds, do not believe the blacks, unite in brotherhood!' A village without a village idiot is nothing; I will become the village idiot, the lunatic of Greece, and I will go about shouting."

The old man glowed in the morning light; there in the center of the courtyard he looked like a giant with his bloodied beard, with his black, bushy eyebrows, with his heavy staff and large boots.

He turned to Captain Drakos. "I've taken my vestment stole and the Bible with me, Captain Charlatan. I'm taking with me all the slaughtered battalions and regiments; and all the mothers, murderer, who are dressed in mourning, and all the orphans and all the war's cripples, the lame, the blind, the paralytics, the insane. I'm taking them and going on."

"What are you saving him for, Captain?" shouted Loukas angrily. "Kill him!"

Father Yánaros shrugged his shoulders scornfully. "Do you think that I'm afraid of death? What can that bogeyman do to me? He can take me from this vain life to the eternal one—the poor thing can do nothing more. Death is only a mule; you mount it, and it takes you to eternal life."

He raised his hands to the sky. "If I live," he cried, "if they let me live, I will never crucify You again, I swear; I will never leave You again, unprotected, to the mercy of Anna and Kayafas, my Lord Jesus! You said You hold a dagger —where is it? How long will You go on being crucified? Enough of this! Come down to earth armed, this time. After such pain and bloodshed, I understand man's duty. Virtue!—arm yourself! Christ!— arm yourself! I am going to preach through towns and villages—I am going to preach about the new Christ, the armed Christ!"

He stretched out his hand to the right, to the Invisible One. "Let us be on our way," he said.

The rebels watched him with surprise. "The priest has gone mad." Several of them laughed. "Who's he talking to? Who's he saying 'Let us go' to?"

Father Yánaros raised his hand to Drakos. "Captain Murderer, till we meet again!" And with a steady stride, he was over the threshold.

No one moved; Loukas looked sarcastically at his leader. "He's going to set fires now," he said. "Are you going to let him? Or do you feel sorry for him?"

But Drakos was silent as he watched the old man walk away, tapping his cane on the cobbles. He walked in large strides, his robes fluttering in the wind; his white hair swung over his shoulders as he walked; he was heading for the path to Prastova and he descended hurriedly. The stones dragged under his heavy shoes; beneath his arm, the gold-embroidered stole and the silver Bible gleamed in the rays of the morning sun. The blood of the dead which he had poured over himself had run down his head and dripped on his sunburned nape.

Captain Drakos watched him, and his mind moved far away, to one of the shores of the Black Sea; to a village filled with peace, with Christianity and greenery. This old man had crow-black hair then, and was dark and slender—a handsome priest; how he had stood up to the Turk and defended Christ and Christianity! And when the day came, the holiday of the patron saint who held the village in his palm, how this old man entered those flames and clapped his hands and danced and never condescended to go out into the dangerless wind again!

How Drakos hated him, how he loved him, how he admired him!

And then he had lost sight of him; father and son had separated, and they met in the Albanian war years later. How he had rolled back his robes and climbed the hills, calling to the Virgin! And as he called Her, the soldiers saw Her climbing the rocks, carrying the wounded boys in Her arms. This old man could shape anything he wanted in the air, because he believed, because he pained. And his soul came out of his body and at times became the Virgin, at times St. George the Rider, at times a loud voice that cried, "Christ conquers!" And the inner beings of the soldiers would fill with assault.

Father Yánaros had descended now and was ready to take the path to Prastova; within the still-slanted rays of the sun his shadow fell like a giant on the rose-colored stones and continued on. A little more and he woud pass the rocks and disappear behind them.

Loukas jumped over to the middle of the road and raised his rifle.

"Eh, Captain," he called, "now let's see the stuff you're made of! So he's your father: so what? Steel your heart! You have a duty to perform and a report to give. Didn't you hear him? He says he wants to be free!"

Father Yánaros heard the rifle trigger cock behind him; he understood. Reaching to his right, he took Christ by the hand and placed Him in front to shield Him from the bullet.

"Come here, my Son," he said softly, tenderly to Him. "Come, so that they will not hurt You."

Two or three guerrillas came up and stood beside Loukas; they, too, raised their rifles and took aim as they looked at the captain. Drakos stood by the gate, not speaking, admiring the way his father strode over the rocks, handsome and forceful as an old Archangel.

"Eh, Captain," Loukas called again. "I tell you he's going to set fires—stop him!" He paused for a moment and giggled. "Can it be that you feel sorry for him?"

The captain's blood simmered; the eyes of all his men were fixed upon him, waiting. Loukas laughed again; he winked at his comrades, then turned to his leader.

"Now let's see what you're going to do, Captain," he said, but he did not get a chance to finish.

Drakos raised his hand. "Shoot him!" he commanded in a choked voice, and his eyes filled.

"Eh, priest," Loukas shouted, "eh, Father Yánaros, wait!"

The old man heard the call and turned. His bloodied beard gleamed a deep red in the sun. Loukas pushed aside his comrades and steadied his rifle butt on his shoulder. The bullet caught Father Yánaros in the forehead. The old man opened his arms, and without uttering a sound, fell, face down, on the stones.

CHARLES DICKENS

• *A Tale of Two Cities*

Echoing Footsteps

A wonderful corner for echoes, it has been remarked, that corner where the Doctor lived. Ever busily winding the golden thread which bound her husband, and her father, and herself, and her old directress and companion, in a life of quiet bliss, Lucie sat in the still house on the tranquilly resounding corner, listening to the echoing footsteps of years.

At first, there were times, though she was a perfectly happy young wife, when her work would slowly fall from her hands, and her eyes would be dimmed. For, there was something coming in the echoes, something light, afar off, and scarcely audible yet, that stirred her heart too much. Fluttering hopes and doubts —hopes, of a love as yet unknown to her; doubts, of her remaining upon earth, to enjoy that new delight—divided her breast. Among the echoes then, there would arise the sound of footsteps at her own early grave; and thoughts of the husband who would be left so desolate, and who would mourn for her so much, swelled to her eyes, and broke like waves.

That time passed, and her little Lucie lay on her bosom. Then, among the advancing echoes, there was the tread of her tiny feet and the sound of her prattling words. Let greater echoes resound as they would, the young mother at the cradle side could always hear those coming. They came, and the shady house

SOURCE. From *A Tale of Two Cities* by Charles Dickens. Copyright 1962, Crowell Collier Books, Incorporated.

387

was sunny with a child's laugh, and the Divine friend of children, to whom in her trouble she had confided hers, seemed to take her child in His arms, as He took the child of old, and made it a sacred joy to her.

Ever busily winding the golden thread that bound them all together, weaving the service of her happy influence through the tissue of all their lives, and making it predominate nowhere, Lucie heard in the echoes of years none but friendly and soothing sounds. Her husband's step was strong and prosperous among them; her father's firm and equal. Lo, Miss Pross, in harness of string, awakening the echoes, as an unruly charger, whip-corrected, snorting and pawing the earth under the plane-tree in the garden!

Even when there were sounds of sorrow among the rest, they were not harsh nor cruel. Even when golden hair, like her own, lay in a halo on a pillow round the worn face of a little boy, and he said, with a radiant smile, "Dear papa and mamma, I am very sorry to leave you both, and to leave my pretty sister; but I am called, and I must go!" those were not tears all of agony that wetted his young mother's cheek as the spirit departed from her embrace that had been entrusted to it. Suffer them and forbid them not. They see my Father's face. O Father, blessed words!

Thus, the rustling of an Angel's wings got blended with the other echoes, and they were not wholly of earth, but had in them that breath of Heaven. Sighs of the winds that blew over a little garden-tomb were mingled with them also, and both were audible to Lucie, in a hushed murmur—like the breathing of a summer sea asleep upon a sandy shore—as the little Lucie, comically studious at the task of the morning, or dressing a doll at her mother's footstool, chattered in the tongues of the Two Cities that were blended in her life.

The echoes rarely answered to the actual tread of Sydney Carton. Some half-dozen times a year, at most, he claimed his privilege of coming in uninvited, and would sit among them through the evening, as he had once done often. He never came there heated with wine. And one other thing regarding him was whispered in the echoes, which has been whispered by all true echoes for ages and ages.

No man ever really loved a woman, lost her, and knew her with a blameless though an unchanged mind, when she was a wife and a mother, but her children had a strange sympathy with him—an instinctive delicacy of pity for him. What fine hidden sensibilities are touched in such a case, no echoes tell; but it is so, and it was so here. Carton was the first stranger to whom little Lucie held out her chubby arms, and he kept his place with her as she grew. The little boy had spoken of him, almost at the last. "Poor Carton! Kiss him for me!"

Mr. Stryver shouldered his way through the law, like some great engine forcing itself through turbid water, and dragged his useful friend in his wake, like a boat towed astern. As the boat so favoured is usually in a rough plight, and mostly under water, so, Sydney had a swamped life of it. But, easy and strong custom, unhappily so much easier and stronger in him than any stimulating sense of desert or disgrace, made it the life he was to lead; and he no more thought of emerging from his state of lion's jackal, than any real jackal may be supposed to think of rising to be a lion. Stryver was rich; had married a florid widow with property and three boys, who had nothing particularly shining about them but the straight hair of their dumpling heads.

These three young gentlemen, Mr. Stryver, exuding patronage of the most offensive quality from every pore, had walked before him like three sheep to the quiet corner in Soho, and had offered as pupils to Lucie's husband: delicately saying, "Halloa! here are three lumps of bread-and-cheese towards your matrimonial picnic, Darnay!" The polite rejection of the three lumps of bread-and-cheese had quite bloated Mr. Stryver with indignation, which he afterwards turned to account in the training of the young gentlemen, by directing them to beware of the pride of Beggars, like that tutor-fellow. He was also in the habit of declaiming to Mrs. Stryver, over his full-bodied wine, on the arts Mrs. Darnay had once put in practice to "catch" him, and on the diamond-cut-diamond arts in himself, madam, which had rendered him "not to be caught." Some of his King's Bench familiars, who were occasionally parties to the full-bodied wine, and the lie, excused him for the latter by saying that he had told it so often, that he believed it himself—which is surely such an incorrigible aggravation of an originally bad offence, as to justify any such offender's being carried off to some suitably retired spot, and there hanged out of the way.

These were among the echoes to which Lucie, sometimes pensive, sometimes amused and laughing, listened in the echoing corner, until her little daughter was six years old. How near to her heart the echoes of her child's tread came, and those of her own dear father's, always active and self-possessed, and those of her dear husband's, need not be told. Nor, how the lightest echo of their united home, directed by herself with such a wise and elegant thrift that it was more abundant than any waste, was music to her. Nor, how there were echoes all about her, sweet in her ears, of the many times her father had told her that he found her more devoted to him married (if that could be) than single, and of the many times her husband had said to her that no cares and duties seemed to divide her love for him or her help to him, and asked her "What is the magic secret, my darling, of your being everything to all of us, as if there were only one of us, yet never seeming to be hurried, or to have too much to do?"

But, there were other echoes, from a distance, that rumbled menacingly in the corner all through this space of time. And it was now, about little Lucie's sixth birthday, that they began to have an awful sound, as of a great storm in France with a dreadful rea rising.

On a night in mid-July, one thousand seven hundred and eighty-nine, Mr. Lorry came in late, from Tellson's, and sat himself down by Lucie and her husband in the dark window. It was a hot, wild night, and they were all three re-minded of the old Sunday night when they had looked at the lightning from the same place.

"I began to think," said Mr. Lorry, pushing his brown wig back, "that I should have to pass the night at Tellson's. We have been so full of business all day, that we have not known what to do first, or which way to turn. There is such an uneasiness in Paris, that we have actually a run of confidence upon us! Our customers over there, seem not to be able to confide their property to us fast enough. There is positively a mania among some of them for sending it to England."

"That has a bad look," said Darnay.

"A bad look, you say, my dear Darnay? Yes, but we don't know what reason there is in it. People are so unreasonable! Some of us at Tellson's are getting old, and we really can't be troubled out of the ordinary course without due occasion."

"Still," said Darnay, "you know how gloomy and threatening the sky is."

"I know that, to be sure," assented Mr. Lorry, trying to persuade himself that his sweet temper was soured, and that he grumbled, "but I am determined to be peevish after my long day's botheration. Where is Manette?"

"Here he is," said the Doctor, entering the dark room at the moment.

"I am quite glad you are at home; for these hurries and forebodings by which I have been surrounded all day long, have made me nervous without reason. You are not going out, I hope?"

"No; I am going to play backgammon with you, if you like," said the Doctor.

"I don't think I do like, if I may speak my mind. I am not fit to be pitted against you to-night. Is the teaboard still there, Lucie? I can't see."

"Of course, it has been kept for you."

"Thank ye, my dear. The precious child is safe in bed?"

"And sleeping soundly."

"That's right; all safe and well! I don't know why anything should be otherwise than safe and well here, thank God; but I have been so put out all day, and I am not as young as I was! My tea, my dear! Thank ye. Now, come and take your place in the circle, and let us sit quiet, and hear the echoes about which you have your theory."

"Not a theory; it was a fancy."

"A fancy, then, my wise pet," said Mr. Lorry, patting her hand. "They are very numerous and very loud, though, are they not? Only hear them!"

Headlong, mad, and dangerous footsteps to force their way into anybody's life, footsteps not easily made clean again if once stained red, the footsteps raging in Saint Antoine afar off, as the little circle sat in the dark London window.

Saint Antoine had been, that morning, a vast dusky mass of scarecrows heaving to and fro, with frequent gleams of light above the billowy heads, where steel blades and bayonets shone in the sun. A tremendous roar arose from the throat of Saint Antoine, and a forest of naked arms struggled in the air like shrivelled branches of trees in a winter wind; all the fingers convulsively clutching at every weapon or semblance of a weapon that was thrown up from the depths below, no matter how far off.

Who gave them out, whence they last came, where they began, through what agency they crookedly quivered and jerked, scores at a time, over the heads of the crowd, like a kind of lightning, no eye in the throng could have told; but, muskets were being distributed—so were cartridges, powder and ball, bars of iron and wood, knives, axes, pikes, every weapon that distracted ingenuity could discover or devise. People who could lay hold of nothing else, set themselves with bleeding hands to force stones and bricks out of their places in walls. Every pulse and heart in Saint Antoine was on high-fever strain and at high-fever heat. Every living creature there held life as of no account, and was demented with a passionate readiness to sacrifice it.

As a whirlpool of boiling waters has a centre point, so, all this raging circled round Defarge's wine-shop, and every human drop in the caldron had a tendency to be sucked towards the vortex where Defarge himself, already begrimed with gunpowder and sweat, issued orders, issued arms, thrust this man back, dragged this man forward, disarmed one to arm another, laboured and strove in the thickest of the uproar.

"Keep near to me, Jacques Three," cried Defarge; "and do you, Jacques One and Two, separate and put yourselves at the head of as many patriots as you can. Where is my wife?"

"Eh, well! Here you see me!" said madame, composed as ever, but not knitting to-day. Madame's resolute right hand was occupied with an axe, in place of the usual softer implements, and in her girdle were a pistol and a cruel knife.

"Where do you go, my wife?"

"I go," said madame, "with you at present. You shall see me at the head of women, by-and-by."

"Come then!" cried Defarge, in a resounding voice. "Patriots and friends, we are ready! The Bastille!"

With a roar that sounded as if all the breath in France had been shaped into the detested word, the living sea rose, wave on wave, depth on depth, and overflowed the city to that point. Alarm-bells ringing, drums beating, the sea raging and thundering on its new beach, the attack begun.

Deep ditches, double drawbridge, massive stone walls, eight great towers, cannon, muskets, fire and smoke. Through the fire and through the smoke—in the fire and in the smoke, for the sea cast him up and against a cannon, and on the instant he became a cannonier—Defarge of the wine-shop worked like a manful soldier, two fierce hours.

Deep ditch, single drawbridge, massive stone walls, eight great towers, cannon, muskets, fire and smoke. One drawbridge down! "Work, comrades all, work! Work, Jacques One, Jacques Two, Jacques One Thousand, Jacques Two Thousand, Jacques Five-and-Twenty Thousand; in the name of all the Angels or the Devils—which you prefer—work!" Thus Defarge of the wine-shop, still at his gun, which had long grown hot.

"To me, women!" cried madame his wife, "What! We can kill as well as the men when the place is taken!" And to her, with a shrill thirsty cry, trooping women variously armed, but all armed alike in hunger and revenge.

Cannon, muskets, fire and smoke; but still the deep ditch, the single drawbridge, the massive stone walls, and the eight great towers. Slight displacements of the raging sea, made by the falling wounded. Flashing weapons, blazing torches, smoking waggonloads of wet straw, hard work at neighbouring barricades in all directions, shrieks, volleys, execrations, bravery without stint, boom smash and rattle, and the furious sounding of the living sea; but, still the deep ditch, and the single drawbridge, and the massive stone walls, and the eight great towers, and still Defarge of the wine-shop at his gun, grown doubly hot by the service of four fierce hours.

A white flag from within the fortress, and a parley—this dimly perceptible through the raging storm, nothing audible in it—suddenly the sea rose immeasurably, wider and higher, and swept Defarge of the wine-shop over the lowered drawbridge, past the massive stone outer walls, in among the eight great towers surrendered!

So resistless was the force of the ocean bearing him on, that even to draw his breath or turn his head was as impracticable as if he had been struggling in the surf at the South Sea, until he was landed in the outer courtyard of the Bastille. There, against an angle of a wall, he made a struggle to look about him. Jacques Three was nearly at his side; Madame Defarge, still heading some of her women, was visible in the inner distance, and her knife was in her hand. Everywhere was tumult, exultation, deafening and maniacal bewilderment, astounding noise, yet furious dumb-show.

"The Prisoners!"

"The Records!"

"The secret cells!"

"The instruments of torture!"

"The Prisoners!"

Of all these cries, and ten thousand incoherencies, "The Prisoners!" was the cry most taken up by the sea that rushed in, as if there were an eternity of people, as well as of time and space. When the foremost billows rolled past, bearing the prison officers with them, and threatening them all with instant death if any secret nook remained undisclosed. Defarge laid his strong hand on the breast of one of these men—a man with a grey head, who had a lighted torch in his hands —separated him from the rest, and got him between himself and the wall.

"Show me the North Tower!" said Defarge. "Quick!"

"I will faithfully," replied the man, "if you will come with me. But there is no one there."

"What is the meaning of One Hundred and Five, North Tower?" asked Defarge. "Quick!"

"The meaning, monsieur?"

"Does it mean a captive, or a place of captivity? Or do you mean that I shall strike you dead?"

"Kill him!" croaked Jacques Three, who had come close up.

"Monsieur, it is a cell."

"Show it me!"

"Pass this way, then."

Jacques Three, with his usual craving on him, and evidently disappointed by the dialogue taking a turn that did not seem to promise bloodshed, held by Defarge's arm as he held by the turnkey's. Their three heads had been close together during their brief discourse, and it had been as much as they could do to hear one another, even then: so tremendous was the noise of the living ocean, in its irruption into the Fortress, and its inundation of the courts and passages and staircases. All around outside too, it beat the walls with a deep hoarse roar, from which, occasionally, some partial shouts of tumult broke and leaped into the air like spray.

Through gloomy vaults where the light of day had never shone, past hideous doors of dark dens and cages, down cavernous flights of steps, and again up steep rugged ascents of stone and brick, more like dry waterfalls than staircases. Defarge, the turnkey, and Jacques Three, linked hand and arm, went with all the speed they could make. Here and there, especially at first, the inundation started on them and swept by; but when they had done descending, and were winding and climbing up a tower, they were alone. Hemmed in here by the massive thickness of walls and arches, the storm within the fortress and without was only audible to them in a dull, subdued way, as if the noise out of which they had come had almost destroyed their sense of hearing.

The turnkey stopped at a low door, put a key in a clashing lock, swung the door slowly open, and said, as they all bent their heads and passed in——

"One Hundred and Five, North Tower!"

There was a small, heavily-grated, unglazed window high in the wall, with a stone screen before it, so that the sky could be only seen by stooping low and looking up. There was a small chimney, heavily barred across, a few feet within. There was a heap of old feathery wood-ashes on the hearth. There was a stool, and table, and a straw bed. There were the four blackened walls, and a rusted iron ring in one of them.

"Pass that torch slowly along these walls, that I may see them," said Defarge to the turnkey.

"Stop!—Look here, Jacques!"

"A. M.!" croaked Jacques Three, as he read greedily.

"Alexandre Manette," said Defarge in his ear, following the letters with his swart forefinger, deeply engrained with gunpowder. "And here he wrote 'a poor physician.' And it was he, without doubt, who scratched a calendar on this stone. What is that in your hand? A crowbar? Give it me!"

He had still the linstock of his gun in his own hand. He made a sudden exchange of the two instruments, and turning on the worm-eaten stool and table, beat them to pieces in a few blows.

"Hold the light higher!" he said, wrathfully, to the turnkey. "Look among those fragments with care, Jacques. And see! Here is my knife," throwing it to him; "rip open that bed, and search the straw. Hold the light higher, you!"

With a menacing look at the turnkey he crawled upon the hearth, and, peering up the chimney, struck and prised at its sides with the crowbar, and worked at the iron grating across it. In a few minutes, some mortar and dust came dropping down, which he averted his face to avoid; and in it, and in the old wood-ashes, and in a crevice in the chimney into which his weapon had slipped or wrought itself, he groped with a cautious touch.

"Nothing in the wood, and nothing in the straw, Jacques?"

"Nothing."

"Let us collect them together, in the middle of the cell. So! Light them, you!"

The turnkey fired the little pile, which blazed high and hot. Stooping again to come out at the low-arched door, they left it burning, and retraced their way to the courtyard; seeming to recover their sense of hearing as they came down, until they were in the raging flood once more.

They found it surging and tossing, in quest of Defarge himself. Saint Antoine was clamorous to have its wine-shop keeper foremost in the guard upon the governor who had defended the Bastille and shot the people. Otherwise, the governor would not be marched to the Hôtel de Ville for judgment. Otherwise, the governor would escape, and the people's blood (suddenly of some value, after many years of worthlessness) be unavenged.

In the howling universe of passion and contention that seemed to encompass this grim old officer conspicuous in his grey coat and red decoration, there was but one quite steady figure, and that was a woman's. "See, there is my husband!" she cried, pointing him out. "See Defarge!" She stood immovable close to the grim old officer, and remained immovable close to him; remained immovable close to him through the streets, as Defarge and the rest bore him along; remained immovable close to him when he was got near his destination, and began to be struck at from behind; remained immovable close to him when the long-gathering rain of stabs and blows fell heavy; was so close to him when he dropped dead under it, that, suddenly animated, she put her foot upon his neck, and with her cruel knife—long ready—hewed off his head.

The hour was come when Saint Antoine was to execute his horrible idea of hoisting up men for lamps to show what he could be and do. Saint Antoine's blood was up, and the blood of tyranny and domination by the iron hand was down—down on the steps of the Hôtel de Ville where the governor's body lay—down on the sole of the shoe of Madame Defarge where she had trodden on the body to steady it for mutilation. "Lower the lamp yonder!" cried Saint Antoine, after glaring round for a new means of death; "here is one of his soldiers to be left on guard!" The swinging sentinel was posted, and the sea rushed on.

The sea of black and threatening waters, and of destructive upheaving of wave against wave, whose depths were yet unfathomed and whose forces were yet unknown. The remorseless sea of turbulently swaying shapes, voices of vengeance, and faces hardened in the furnaces of suffering until the touch of pity could make no mark on them.

But, in the ocean of faces where every fierce and furious expression was in vivid life, there were two groups of faces—each seven in number—so fixedly contrasting with the rest, that never did sea roll which bore more memorable wrecks with it. Seven faces of prisoners, suddenly released by the storm that had burst their tomb, were carried high overhead; all scared, all lost, all wandering and amazed, as if the Last Day were come, and those who rejoiced around them were lost spirits. Other seven faces there were, carried higher, seven dead faces, whose drooping eyelids and half-seen eyes awaited the Last Day. Impassive faces, yet with a suspended—not an abolished—expression on them; faces, rather, in a fearful pause, as having yet to raise the dropped lids of the eyes, and bear witness with the bloodless lips "THOU DIDST IT!"

Seven prisoners released, seven gory heads on pikes, the keys of the accursed fortress of the eight strong towers, some discovered letters and other memorials of prisoners of old time, long dead of broken hearts,—such, and such-like, the loudly echoing footsteps of Saint Antoine escort through the Paris streets in mid-July, one thousand seven hundred and eighty-nine. Now, Heaven, defeat the fancy of Lucie Darnay, and keep these feet far out of her life! For, they are headlong, mad, and dangerous; and in the years so long after the breaking of the cask at Defarge's wine-shop door, they are not easily purified when once stained red.

PART 4

Social Stress

Social Change

Since reality is a human construction it presents itself as a phenomenon that is constantly being added to and taken from. We must, therefore, assume that social change is a more or less potent force in any society at any time. This is especially true of modern society, where change, particularly technological change, is of the very essence of the period. Ogborn, for example, almost fifty years ago, posited the concept of "cultural lag." The thesis is that various parts of modern culture are not changing at the same rate, some parts are changing much more rapidly than others; and that, since there is a correlation and interdependence of parts, a rapid change requires readjustments through other changes in the various correlated parts of the culture. I would only reiterate that the marked and rapid changes of today should not blind us to the fact that change has always been, and will always be, with us; that is, man has always had to make readjustments.

Our primary concern, however, is with the effects of change on the individual. For if the "self system from its nature . . . tends to escape influence by experience which is incongruous with its current organization and functional activity," then a crucial fact about change is the point that the new order forces on the consciousness of the individual (whether he likes it or not) experiences that are indeed incongruous with an organization developed under the old order. The contrast is, of course, not as absolute as stated here, nor is it, by any means, as simple; the important point is that change inevitably engenders dissonance. And dissonance is not a comfortable psychological state.

Notice also that change need not necessarily lead to confusion. There are always those individuals, the adherents of the new, who are quite happy about social change.

Chapter 11

The first selection in this chapter is from Cervantes' *Don Quixote*. Here is an individual, a knight, who finds that his world is just no longer there. For the absolute state is now coming to the fore, and that state does not want to hear of the values associated with the world of knight errantry. Quixote is reduced to fighting windmills. We must not, though, lose sight of the fact that Quixote is also a universal figure of the first order. Is this the way that any society treats those individuals whose values are supposedly not relevant to the new order of things, and, more important, is this the way that any society treats *any* of its idealists?

The selection from Dostoyevsky is really unmatched in intensity. We find a confused and, as he himself tells us, a quite humiliated creature. The reason?

He does not believe in the old and he hates the new—symbolically, the Crystal Palace of the coming world of science. Again though, we should note that this confusion implies a value judgment on Dostoyevsky's part. For, as Donald Atwater writes, "the Russian word for underground is associated with the idea of vermin breeding in the darkness and preparing destruction." Change, of course, does not necessarily have to be destructive. Read what Marshall McLuhan has to say, for example.

The Balzac selection is much easier. The Revolution had come and it had drastically altered the status situation of the aristocracy. Esgrignon is completely unaware of this fact; tragedy and disappointment await him. For it is inevitable that he will not fit in.

Social Deviance

To say the least, human societies are not perfect. We must assume, therefore, that there are bound to be individuals who, in one way or another and for one reason or another, are dissatisfied with the existing reality (either personal or social or both). Now of course the individual does not have to register his dissatisfaction in an antisocial manner but, if he does—if, for example, he turns to crime or if, as in the case of the hippie, he just plain drops out of the "normal" society—we usually refer to him as a social deviant.

I would only add *"that social groups create deviance by making the rules whose infraction constitutes deviance,* and by applying those rules to particular people and labeling them as outsiders. From this point of view deviance is *not* a quality of the act that the person commits, but rather a consequence of the application by others of rules and sanctions to an offender. The deviant is one to whom that label has successfully been applied; deviant behavior is behavior that people so label."[1]

Chapter 12

The first selection in Chapter 12 is Jack Kerouac's presentation of what it meant to be a member of the "beat" generation. The reader might be interested in noting that the character of Dean Moriarity was based on a man called Neal Cassidy, who is also a leading figure in Tom Wolfe's *The Electric Kool Aid Acid Test.* Apparently, Cassidy went right on from the beat generation straight through to the innovations of the hippies. It is equally apparent, however, that there is a

[1] Howard Becker, *The Outsiders* (New York, 1963), p. 9.

400

decided *need,* on the part of a significant number of America's youth, for such groups. Was Woodstock the first major event in America's Cultural Revolution?

Maugham's book is supposedly based on the life of Paul Gauguin. It depicts an individual who could not and would not quell his desire to paint. For the "demon" which moved him was not to be held down. In the process of satisfying this desire, though, Strickland leaves his wife and children without any real consideration, to say the least. Moreover, he then conducts himself in what the society would probably deem an immoral manner. Is that really deviance? Should he not be allowed to satisfy the "demon" which would give him no rest? Does such an individual have to follow the same rules as you and I?

The final selection is from D. H. Lawrence's *The Fox.* It is a poignant expression of the dual loyalties which characterized March. Moreover, in contrast to the scornful manner in which the society at large usually regards homosexuality, Lawrence gives us a picture which penetrates the consciousness of the individual. He does not judge March; he "merely" calls attention to her conflicts.

Chapter 11

Social Change

CERVANTES

• *Don Quixote*

CHAPTER VIII. *Of the good fortune which the valorous Don Quixote had in the terrifying and never-before-imagined adventure of the windmills, along with other events that deserve to be suitably recorded.*

At this point they caught sight of thirty or forty windmills which were standing on the plain there, and no sooner had Don Quixote laid eyes upon them than he turned to his squire and said, "Fortune is guiding our affairs better than we could have wished; for you see there before you, friend Sancho Panza, some thirty or more lawless giants with whom I mean to do battle. I shall deprive them of their lives, and with the spoils from this encounter we shall begin to enrich ourselves; for this is righteous warfare, and it is a great service to God to remove so accursed a breed from the face of the earth."

"What giants?" said Sancho Panza.

"Those that you see there," replied his master, "those with the long arms some of which are as much as two leagues in length."

"But look, your Grace, those are not giants but windmills, and what appear to be arms are their wings which, when whirled in the breeze, cause the millstone to go."

"It is plain to be seen," said Don Quixote, "that you have had little experi-

SOURCE. From *The Portable Cervantes* translated by Samuel Putnam. Copyright 1949, reprinted by permission of the Viking Press.

ence in this matter of adventures. If you are afraid, go off to one side and say your prayers while I am engaging them in fierce, unequal combat."

Saying this, he gave spurs to his steed Rocinante, without paying any heed to Sancho's warning that these were truly windmills and not giants that he was riding forth to attack. Nor even when he was close upon them did he perceive what they really were, but shouted at the top of his lungs, "Do not seek to flee, cowards and vile creatures that you are, for it is but a single knight with whom you have to deal!"

At that moment a little wind came up and the big wings began turning.

"Though you flourish as many arms as did the giant Briareus," said Don Quixote when he perceived this, "you still shall have to answer to me."

He thereupon commended himself with all his heart to his lady Dulcinea, beseeching her to succor him in this peril; and, being well covered with his shield and with his lance at rest, he bore down upon them at a full gallop and fell upon the first mill that stood in his way, giving a thrust at the wing, which was whirling at such a speed that his lance was broken into bits and both horse and horseman went rolling over the plain, very much battered indeed. Sancho upon his donkey came hurrying to his master's assistance as fast as he could, but when he reached the spot, the knight was unable to move, so great was the shock with which he and Rocinante had hit the ground.

"God help us!" exclaimed Sancho, "did I not tell your Grace to look well, that those were nothing but windmills, a fact which no one could fail to see unless he had other mills of the same sort in his head?"

"Be quiet, friend Sancho," said Don Quixote. "Such are the fortunes of war, which more than any other are subject to constant change. What is more, when I come to think of it, I am sure that this must be the work of that magician Frestón, the one who robbed me of my study and my books, and who has thus changed the giants into windmills in order to deprive me of the glory of overcoming them, so great is the enmity that he bears me; but in the end his evil arts shall not prevail against this trusty sword of mine."

"May God's will be done," was Sancho Panza's response. And with the aid of his squire the knight was once more mounted on Rocinante, who stood there with one shoulder half out of joint. And so, speaking of the adventure that had just befallen them, they continued along the Puerto Lápice highway; for there, Don Quixote said, they could not fail to find many and varied adventures, this being a much traveled thoroughfare. The only thing was, the knight was exceedingly downcast over the loss of his lance.

"I remember," he said to his squire, "having read of a Spanish knight by the name of Diego Pérez de Vargas, who, having broken his sword in battle, tore from an oak a heavy bough or branch and with it did such feats of valor that day, and pounded so many Moors, that he came to be known as Machuca, and he and his descendants from that day forth have been called Vargas y Machuca. I tell you this because I too intend to provide myself with just such a bough as the one he wielded, and with it I propose to do such exploits that you shall deem yourself fortunate to have been found worthy to come with me and behold and witness things that are almost beyond belief."

"God's will be done," said Sancho. "I believe everything that your Grace says; but straighten yourself up in the saddle a little, for you seem to be slipping down on one side, owing, no doubt, to the shaking-up that you received in your fall."

"Ah, that is the truth," replied Don Quixote, "and if I do not speak of my sufferings, it is for the reason that it is not permitted knights-errant to complain of any wound whatsoever, even though their bowels may be dropping out."

"If that is the way it is," said Sancho, "I have nothing more to say; but, God knows, it would suit me better if your Grace did complain when something hurts him. I can assure you that I mean to do so, over the least little thing that ails me —that is, unless the same rule applies to squires as well."

Don Quixote laughed long and heartily over Sancho's simplicity, telling him that he might complain as much as he liked and where and when he liked, whether he had good cause or not; for he had read nothing to the contrary in the ordinances of chivalry. Sancho then called his master's attention to the fact that it was time to eat. The knight replied that he himself had no need of food at the moment, but his squire might eat whenever he chose. Having been granted this permission, Sancho seated himself as best he could upon his beast, and, taking out from his saddlebags the provisions that he had stored there, he rode along leisurely behind his master, munching his victuals and taking a good, hearty swig now and then at the leather flask in a manner that might well have caused the biggest-bellied tavernkeeper of Málaga to envy him. Between draughts he gave not so much as a thought to any promise that his master might have made him, nor did he look upon it as any hardship, but rather as good sport, to go in quest of adventures however hazardous they might be.

The short of the matter is, they spent the night under some trees, from one of which Don Quixote tore off a withered bough to serve him as a lance, placing it in the lance head from which he had removed the broken one. He did not sleep all night long for thinking of his lady Dulcinea; for this was in accordance with what he had read in his books, of men of arms in the forest or desert places who kept a wakeful vigil, sustained by the memory of their ladies fair. Not so with Sancho, whose stomach was full, and not with chicory water. He fell into a dreamless slumber, and had not his master called him, he would not have been awakened either by the rays of the sun in his face or by the many birds who greeted the coming of the new day with their merry song.

Upon arising, he had another go at the flask, finding it somewhat more flaccid than it had been the night before, a circumstance which grieved his heart, for he could not see that they were on the way to remedying the deficiency within any very short space of time. Don Quixote did not wish any breakfast; for, as has been said, he was in the habit of nourishing himself on savorous memories. They then set out once more along the road to Puerto Lápice, and around three in the afternoon they came in sight of the pass that bears that name.

"There," said Don Quixote as his eyes fell upon it, "we may plunge our arms up to the elbow in what are known as adventures. But I must warn you that even though you see me in the greatest peril in the world, you are not to lay hand upon your sword to defend me, unless it be that those who attack me are rabble and men of low degree, in which case you may very well come to my aid; but if they be gentlemen, it is in no wise permitted by the laws of chivalry that you should assist me until you yourself shall have been dubbed a knight."

"Most certainly, sir," replied Sancho, "your Grace shall be very well obeyed in this; all the more so for the reason that I myself am of a peaceful disposition and not fond of meddling in the quarrels and feuds of others. However, when it comes to protecting my own person, I shall not take account of those laws of which you speak, seeing that all laws, human and divine, permit each one to defend himself whenever he is attacked."

"I am willing to grant you that," assented Don Quixote, "but in this matter of defending me against gentlemen you must restrain your natural impulses."

"I promise you I shall do so," said Sancho. "I will observe this precept as I would the Sabbath day."

As they were conversing in this manner, there appeared in the road in front of them two friars of the Order of St. Benedict, mounted upon dromedaries— for the she-mules they rode were certainly no smaller than that. The friars wore travelers' spectacles and carried sunshades, and behind them came a coach accompanied by four or five men on horseback and a couple of muleteers on foot. In the coach, as was afterwards learned, was a lady of Biscay, on her way to Seville to bid farewell to her husband, who had been appointed to some high post in the Indies. The religious were not of her company although they were going by the same road.

The instant Don Quixote laid eyes upon them he turned to his squire. "Either I am mistaken or this is going to be the most famous adventure that ever was seen; for those black-clad figures that you behold must be, and without any doubt are, certain enchanters who are bearing with them a captive princess in that coach, and I must do all I can to right this wrong."

"It will be worse than the windmills," declared Sancho. "Look you, sir, those are Benedictine friars and the coach must be that of some travelers. Mark well what I say and what you do, lest the devil lead you astray."

"I have already told you, Sancho," replied Don Quixote, "that you know little where the subject of adventures is concerned. What I am saying to you is the truth, as you shall now see."

With this, he rode forward and took up a position in the middle of the road along which the friars were coming, and as soon as they appeared to be within earshot he cried out to them in a loud voice, "O devilish and monstrous beings, set free at once the highborn princesses whom you bear captive in that coach, or else prepare at once to meet your death as the just punishment of your evil deeds."

The friars drew rein and sat there in astonishment, marveling as much at Don Quixote's appearance as at the words he spoke. "Sir Knight," they answered him, "we are neither devilish nor monstrous but religious of the Order of St. Benedict who are merely going our way. We know nothing of those who are in that coach, nor of any captive princesses either."

"Soft words," said Don Quixote, "have no effect on me. I know you for what you are, lying rabble!" And without waiting for any further parley he gave spur to Rocinante and, with lowered lance, bore down upon the first friar with such fury and intrepidity that, had not the fellow tumbled from his mule of his own accord, he would have been hurled to the ground and either killed or badly wounded. The second religious, seeing how his companion had been treated, dug his legs into his she-mule's flanks and scurried away over the countryside faster than the wind.

Seeing the friar upon the ground, Sancho Panza slipped lightly from his mount and, falling upon him, began stripping him of his habit. The two mule drivers accompanying the religious thereupon came running up and asked Sancho why he was doing this. The latter replied that the friar's garments belonged to him as legitimate spoils of the battle that his master Don Quixote had just won. The muleteers, however, were lads with no sense of humor, nor did they know what all this talk of spoils and battles was about; but, perceiving that Don Quixote had ridden off to one side to converse with those inside the coach, they pounced upon Sancho, threw him to the ground, and proceeded to pull out the hair of his beard and kick him to a pulp, after which they went off and left him stretched out there, bereft at once of breath and sense.

Without losing any time, they then assisted the friar to remount. The good brother was trembling all over from fright, and there was not a speck of color in his face, but when he found himself in the saddle once more, he quickly spurred his beast to where his companion, at some little distance, sat watching and waiting to see what the result of the encounter would be. Having no curiosity as to the final outcome of the fray, the two of them now resumed their journey, making more signs of the cross than the devil would be able to carry upon his back.

Meanwhile Don Quixote, as we have said, was speaking to the lady in the coach.

"Your beauty, my lady, may now dispose of your person as best may please you, for the arrogance of your abductors lies upon the ground, overthrown by this good arm of mine; and in order that you may not pine to know the name of your liberator, I may inform you that I am Don Quixote de la Mancha, knight-errant and adventurer and captive of the peerless and beauteous Doña Dulcinea del Toboso. In payment of the favor which you have received from me, I ask nothing other than that you return to El Toboso and on my behalf pay your respects to this lady, telling her that it was I who set you free."

One of the squires accompanying those in the coach, a Biscayan, was listening to Don Quixote's words, and when he saw that the knight did not propose to let the coach proceed upon its way but was bent upon having it turn back to El Toboso, he promptly went up to him, seized his lance, and said to him in bad Castilian and worse Biscayan, "Go, *caballero,* and bad luck go with you; for by the God that created me, if you do not let this coach pass, me kill you or me no Biscayan."

Don Quixote heard him attentively enough and answered him very mildly, "If you were a *caballero,* which you are not, I should already have chastised you, wretched creature, for your foolhardiness and your impudence."

"Me no *caballero?*" cried the Biscayan. "Me swear to God, you lie like a Christian. If you will but lay aside your lance and unsheath your sword, you will soon see that you are carrying water to the cat! Biscayan on land, gentleman at sea, but a gentleman in spite of the devil, and you lie if you say otherwise."

" ' "You shall see as to that presently," said Agrajes,' " Don Quixote quoted. He cast his lance to the earth, drew his sword, and, taking his buckler on his arm, attacked the Biscayan with intent to slay him. The latter, when he saw his adversary approaching, would have liked to dismount from his mule, for she was one of the worthless sort that are let for hire and he had no confidence in her; but there was no time for this, and so he had no choice but to draw his own sword in turn and make the best of it. However, he was near enough to the coach to be able to snatch a cushion from it to serve him as a shield; and then they fell upon each other as though they were mortal enemies. The rest of those present sought to make peace between them but did not succeed, for the Biscayan with his disjointed phrases kept muttering that if they did not let him finish the battle then he himself would have to kill his mistress and anyone else who tried to stop him.

The lady inside the carriage, amazed by it all and trembling at what she saw, directed her coachman to drive on a little way; and there from a distance she watched the deadly combat, in the course of which the Biscayan came down with a great blow on Don Quixote's shoulder, over the top of the latter's shield, and had not the knight been clad in armor, it would have split him to the waist.

Feeling the weight of this blow, Don Quixote cried out, "O lady of my soul, Dulcinea, flower of beauty, succor this your champion who out of gratitude for your many favors finds himself in so perilous a plight!" To utter these words, lay hold of his sword, cover himself with his buckler, and attack the Biscayan was but the work of a moment; for he was now resolved to risk everything upon a single stroke.

As he saw Don Quixote approaching with so dauntless a bearing, the Biscayan was well aware of his adversary's courage and forthwith determined to imitate the example thus set him. He kept himself protected with his cushion, but he was unable to get his she-mule to budge to one side or the other, for the beast, out of sheer exhaustion and being, moreover, unused to such childish play, was incapable of taking a single step. And so, then, as has been stated, Don Quixote was approaching the wary Biscayan, his sword raised on high and with the firm resolve of cleaving his enemy in two; and the Biscayan was awaiting the knight in the same posture, cushion in front of him and with uplifted sword.

All the bystanders were trembling with suspense at what would happen as a result of the terrible blows that were threatened, and the lady in the coach and her maids were making a thousand vows and offerings to all the images and shrines in Spain, praying that God would save them all and the lady's squire from this great peril that confronted them.

But the unfortunate part of the matter is that at this very point the author of the history breaks off and leaves the battle pending, excusing himself upon the ground that he has been unable to find anything else in writing concerning the exploits of Don Quixote beyond those already set forth. It is true, on the other hand, that the second author of this work could not bring himself to believe that so unusual a chronicle would have been consigned to oblivion, nor that the learned ones of La Mancha were possessed of so little curiosity as not to be able to discover in their archives or registry offices certain papers that have to do with this famous knight. Being convinced of this, he did not despair of coming upon the end of this pleasing story, and Heaven favoring him, he did find it, as shall be related in the second part.

CHAPTER IX. *In which is concluded and brought to an end the stupendous battle between the gallant Biscayan and the valiant Knight of La Mancha.*

In the first part of the history we left the valorous Biscayan and the famous Don Quixote with swords unsheathed and raised aloft, about to let fall furious slashing blows which, had they been delivered fairly and squarely, would at the very least have split them in two and laid them wide open from top to bottom like a pomegranate; and it was at this doubtful point that the pleasing chronicle came to a halt and broke off, without the author's informing us as to where the rest of it might be found.

I was deeply grieved by such a circumstance, and the pleasure I had had in reading so slight a portion was turned into annoyance as I thought of how difficult it would be to come upon the greater part which it seemed to me must still be missing. It appeared impossible and contrary to all good precedent that so worthy a knight should not have had some scribe to take upon himself the task of writing an account of these unheard-of exploits; for that was something that had happened to none of the knights-errant who, as the saying has it, had gone forth in quest of adventures, seeing that each of them had one or two chroniclers, as if ready at hand, who not only had set down their deeds, but had depicted their most trivial thoughts and amiable weaknesses, however well concealed they might be. The good knight of La Mancha surely could not have been so unfortunate as to have lacked what Platir and others like him had in abundance. And so I could not bring myself to believe that this gallant history could have remained thus lopped off and mutilated, and I could not but lay the blame upon the malignity of time, that devourer and consumer of all things, which must either have consumed it or kept it hidden.

On the other hand, I reflected that inasmuch as among the knight's books had been found such modern works as *The Disenchantments of Jealousy* and *The Nymphs and Shepherds of Henares,* his story likewise must be modern, and that even though it might not have been written down, it must remain in the memory of the good folk of his village and the surrounding ones. This thought left me somewhat confused and more than ever desirous of knowing the real and true story, the whole story, of the life and wondrous deeds of our famous Spaniard, Don Quixote, light and mirror of the chivalry of La Mancha, the first in our age and in these calamitous times to devote himself to the hardships and exercises of knight-errantry and to go about righting wrongs, succoring widows, and protecting damsels—damsels such as those who, mounted upon their palfreys and with riding-whip in hand, in full possession of their virginity, were in the habit of going from mountain to mountain and from valley to valley; for unless there were some villain, some rustic with an ax and hood, or some monstrous giant to force them, there were in times past maiden ladies who at the end of eighty years, during all which time they had not slept for a single day beneath a roof, would go to their graves as virginal as when their mothers had borne them.

If I speak of these things, it is for the reason that in this and in all other respects our gallant Quixote is deserving of constant memory and praise, and even I am not to be denied my share of it for my diligence and the labor to which I put myself in searching out the conclusion of this agreeable narrative; although if heaven, luck, and circumstance had not aided me, the world would have had to do without the pleasure and the pastime which anyone may enjoy who will read this work attentively for an hour or two. The manner in which it came about was as follows:

I was standing one day in the Alcaná, or market place, of Toledo when a lad came up to sell some old notebooks and other papers to a silk weaver who was there. As I am extremely fond of reading anything, even though it be but the scraps of paper in the streets, I followed my natural inclination and took one of the books, whereupon I at once perceived that it was written in characters which I recognized as Arabic. I recognized them, but reading them was another thing; and so I began looking around to see if there was any Spanish-speaking Moor near by who would be able to read them for me. It was not very hard to find such an interpreter, nor would it have been even if the tongue in question had been an older and a better one. To make a long story short, chance brought a fellow my way; and when I told him what it was I wished and placed the book in his hands, he opened it in the middle and began reading and at once fell to laughing. When I asked him what the cause of his laughter was, he replied that it was a note which had been written in the margin.

I besought him to tell me the content of the note, and he, laughing still, went on, "As I told you, it is something in the margin here: 'This Dulcinea del Toboso, so often referred to, is said to have been the best hand at salting pigs of any woman in all La Mancha.'"

No sooner had I heard the name Dulcinea del Toboso than I was astonished and held in suspense, for at once the thought occurred to me that those notebooks must contain the history of Don Quixote. With this in mind I urged him to read me the title, and he proceeded to do so, turning the Arabic into Castilian upon the spot: *History of Don Quixote de la Mancha, Written by Cid Hamete Benengeli, Arabic Historian.* It was all I could do to conceal my satisfaction and, snatching them from the silk weaver, I bought from the lad all the papers and notebooks that he had for half a real; but if he had known or suspected how very much I wanted them, he might well have had more than six reales for them.

The Moor and I then betook ourselves to the cathedral cloister, where I requested him to translate for me into the Castilian tongue all the books that had to do with Don Quixote, adding nothing and subtracting nothing; and I offered him whatever payment he desired. He was content with two arrobas of raisins and two fanegas of wheat and promised to translate them well and faithfully and with all dispatch. However, in order to facilitate matters, and also because I did not wish to let such a find as this out of my hands, I took the fellow home with me, where in a little more than a month and a half he translated the whole of the work just as you will find it set down here.

In the first of the books there was a very lifelike picture of the battle between Don Quixote and the Biscayan, the two being in precisely the same posture as described in the history, their swords upraised, the one covered by his buckler, the other with his cushion. As for the Biscayan's mule, you could see at the distance of a crossbow shot that it was one for hire. Beneath the Biscayan there was a rubric which read: "Don Sancho de Azpeitia," which must undoubtedly have been his name; while beneath the feet of Rocinante was another inscription: "Don Quixote." Rocinante was marvelously portrayed: so long and lank, so lean and flabby, so extremely consumptive-looking that one could well understand the justness and propriety with which the name of "hack" had been bestowed upon him.

Alongside Rocinante stood Sancho Panza, holding the halter of his ass, and below was the legend: "Sancho Zancas." The picture showed him with a big belly, a short body, and long shanks, and that must have been where he got the names of Panza y Zancas by which he is a number of times called in the course of the history. There are other small details that might be mentioned, but they are of little importance and have nothing to do with the truth of the story—and no story is bad so long as it is true.

If there is any objection to be raised against the veracity of the present one, it can be only that the author was an Arab, and that nation is known for its lying propensities; but even though they be our enemies, it may readily be understood that they would more likely have detracted from, rather than added to, the chronicle. So it seems to me, at any rate; for whenever he might and should deploy the resources of his pen in praise of so worthy a knight, the author appears to take pains to pass over the matter in silence; all of which in my opinion is ill done and ill conceived, for it should be the duty of historians to be exact, truthful, and dispassionate, and neither interest nor fear nor rancor nor affection should swerve them from the path of truth, whose mother is history, rival of time, depository of deeds, witness of the past, exemplar and adviser to the present, and the future's counselor. In this work, I am sure, will be found all that could be desired in the way of pleasant reading; and if it is lacking in any way, I maintain that this is the fault of that hound of an author rather than of the subject.

But to come to the point, the second part, according to the translation, began as follows:

As the two valorous and enraged combatants stood there, swords upraised and poised on high, it seemed from their bold mien as if they must surely be theatening heaven, earth, and hell itself. The first to let fall a blow was the choleric Biscayan, and he came down with such force and fury that, had not his sword been deflected in mid-air, that single stroke would have sufficed to put an end to this fearful combat and to all our knight's adventures at the same time; but fortune, which was reserving him for greater things, turned aside his adversary's blade in such a manner that, even though it fell upon his left shoulder, it did him no other damage than to strip him completely of his armor on that side, carrying with it a good part of his helmet along with half an ear, the headpiece clattering to the ground with a dreadful din, leaving its wearer in a sorry state.

Heaven help me! Who could properly describe the rage that now entered the heart of our hero of La Mancha as he saw himself treated in this fashion? It may merely be said that he once more reared himself in the stirrups, laid hold of his sword with both hands, and dealt the Biscayan such a blow, over the cushion and upon the head, that, even so good a defense proving useless, it was as if a mountain had fallen upon his enemy. The latter now began bleeding through the mouth, nose, and ears; he seemed about to fall from his mule, and would have fallen, no doubt, if he had not grasped the beast about the neck, but at that moment his feet slipped from the stirrups and his arms let go, and the mule, frightened by the terrible blow, began running across the plain, hurling its rider to the earth with a few quick plunges.

Don Quixote stood watching all this very calmly. When he saw his enemy fall, he leaped from his horse, ran over very nimbly, and thrust the point of his sword into the Biscayan's eyes, calling upon him at the same time to surrender or otherwise he would cut off his head. The Biscayan was so bewildered that he was unable to utter a single word in reply, and things would have gone badly with him, so blind was Don Quixote in his rage, if the ladies of the coach, who up to then had watched the struggle in dismay, had not come up to him at this point and begged him with many blandishments to do them the very great favor of sparing their squire's life.

To which Don Quixote replied with much haughtiness and dignity, "Most certainly, lovely ladies, I shall be very happy to do that which you ask of me, but upon one condition and understanding, and that is that this knight promise me that he will go to El Toboso and present himself in my behalf before Doña Dulcinea, in order that she may do with him as she may see fit."

Trembling and disconsolate, the ladies did not pause to discuss Don Quixote's request, but without so much as inquiring who Dulcinea might be they promised him that the squire would fulfill that which was commanded of him.

"Very well, then, trusting in your word, I will do him no further harm, even though he has well deserved it."

FYODOR DOSTOYEVSKY

• *Notes from the Underground*

V

Come, can a man who attempts to find enjoyment in the very feeling of his own degradation possibly have a spark of respect for himself? I am not saying this now from any mawkish kind of remorse. And, indeed, I could never endure saying, "Forgive me, Papa, I won't do it again," not because I am incapable of saying that—on the contrary, perhaps just because I have been too capable of it, and in what a way, too! As though of design I used to get into trouble in cases when I was not to blame in any way. That was the nastiest part of it. At the same time I was genuinely touched and penitent, I used to shed tears and, of course, deceived myself, though I was not acting in the least and there was a sick feeling in my heart at the time. . . . For that one could not blame even the laws of nature, though the laws of nature have continually all my life offended me more than anything. It is loathsome to remember it all, but it was loathsome even then. Of course, a minute or so later I would realize wrathfully that it was all a lie, a revolting lie, an affected lie, that is, all this penitence, this emotion, these vows of reform. You will ask why did I worry myself with such antics: answer, because it was very dull to sit with one's hands folded, and so one began cutting capers. That is really it. Observe yourselves more carefully, gentlemen, then you will understand that it is so. I invented

SOURCE. From *Notes from the Underground* by Fyodor Dostoyevsky. Translated by Constance Garnett. Copyright 1960, reprinted by permission of the Dell Publishing Company.

adventures for myself and made up a life, so as at least to live in some way. How many times it has happened to me—well, for instance, to take offence simply on purpose, for nothing; and one knows oneself, of course, that one is offended at nothing, that one is putting it on, but yet one brings oneself, at last, to the point of being really offended. All my life I have had an impulse to play such pranks, so that in the end I could not control it in myself. Another time, twice, in fact, I tried hard to be in love. I suffered, too, gentlemen, I assure you. In the depth of my heart there was no faith in my suffering, only a faint stir of mockery, but yet I did suffer, and in the real, orthodox way; I was jealous, beside myself . . . and it was all from *ennui*, gentlemen, all from *ennui*; inertia overcame me. You know the direct, legitimate fruit of consciousness is inertia, that is, conscious sitting-with-the-hands-folded. I have referred to this already. I repeat, I repeat with emphasis: all "direct" persons and men of action are active just because they are stupid and limited. How explain that? I will tell you: in consequence of their limitation they take immediate and secondary causes for primary ones, and in that way persuade themselves more quickly and easily than other people do that they have found an infallible foundation for their activity, and their minds are at ease and you know that is the chief thing. To begin to act, you know, you must first have your mind completely at ease and no trace of doubt left in it. Why, how am I, for example, to set my mind at rest? Where are the primary causes on which I am to build? Where are my foundations? Where am I to get them from? I exercise myself in reflection, and consequently with me every primary cause at once draws after itself another still more primary, and so on to infinity. That is just the essence of every sort of consciousness and reflection. It must be a case of the laws of nature again. What is the result of it in the end? Why, just the same. Remember I spoke just now of vengeance. (I am sure you did not take it in.) I said that a man revenges himself because he sees justice in it. Therefore he has found a primary cause, that is, justice. And so he is at rest on all sides, and consequently he carries out his revenge calmly and successfully, being persuaded that he is doing a just and honest thing. But I see no justice in it, I find no sort of virtue in it either, and consequently if I attempt to revenge myself, it is only out of spite. Spite, of course, might overcome everything, all my doubts, and so might serve quite successfully in place of a primary cause, precisely because it is not a cause. But what is to be done if I have not even spite (I began with that just now, you know)? In consequence again of those accursed laws of consciousness, anger in me is subject to chemical disintegration. You look into it, the object flies off into air, your reasons evaporate, the criminal is not to be found, the wrong becomes not a wrong but a phantom, something like the toothache, for which no one is to blame, and consequently there is only the same outlet left again—that is, to beat the wall as hard as you can. So you give it up with a wave of the hand because you have not found a fundamental cause. And try letting yourself be carried away by your feelings, blindly, without reflection, without a primary cause, repelling consciousness at least for a time; hate or love, if only not to sit with your hands folded. The day after to-morrow, at the latest, you will begin despising yourself for having knowingly deceived yourself. Result: a soap-bubble and inertia. Oh, gentlemen, do you know, perhaps I consider myself an intelligent man only because all my life I have been able neither to begin nor to finish anything. Granted I am a babbler, a harmless vexatious babbler, like all of us. But what is to be done if the direct and sole vocation of every intelligent man is babble, that is, the intentional pouring of water through a sieve?

VI

Oh, if I had done nothing simply from laziness! Heavens, how I should have respected myself then. I should have respected myself because I should at least have been capable of being lazy; there would at least have been one quality, as it were, positive in me, in which I could have believed myself. Question: What is he? Answer: A sluggard; how very pleasant it would have been to hear that of oneself! It would mean that I was positively defined, it would mean that there was something to say about me. "Sluggard"—why, it is a calling and vocation, it is a career. Do not jest, it is so. I should then be a member of the best club by right, and should find my occupation in continually respecting myself. I knew a gentleman who prided himself all his life on being a connoisseur of Lafitte. He considered this as his positive virtue, and never doubted himself. He died, not simply with a tranquil, but with a triumphant, conscience, and he was quite right, too. Then I should have chosen a career for myself, I should have been a sluggard and a glutton, not a simple one, but, for instance, one with sympathies for everything good and beautiful. How do you like that? I have long had visions of it. That "good and beautiful" weighs heavily on my mind at forty. But that is at forty; then—oh, then it would have been different! I should have found for myself a form of activity in keeping with it, to be precise, drinking to the health of everything "good and beautiful." I should have snatched at every opportunity to drop a tear into my glass and then to drain it to all that is "good and beautiful." I should then have turned everything into the good and the beautiful; in the nastiest, unquestionable trash, I should have sought out the good and the beautiful. I should have exuded tears like a wet sponge. An artist, for instance, paints a picture worthy of Gay. At once I drink to the health of the artist who painted the picture worthy of Gay, because I love all that is "good and beautiful." An author has written *As you will:* at once I drink to the health of "any one you will" because I love all that is "good and beautiful."

I should claim respect for doing so. I should persecute any one who would not show me respect. I should live at ease, I should die with dignity, why, it is charming, perfectly charming! And what a good round belly I should have grown, what a treble chin I should have established, what a ruby nose I should have coloured for myself, so that every one would have said, looking at me: "Here is an asset! Here is something real and solid!" And, say what you like, it is very agreeable to hear such remarks about oneself in this negative age.

VII

But these are all golden dreams. Oh, tell me, who was it first announced, who was it first proclaimed, that man only does nasty things because he does not know his own interests; and that if he were enlightened, if his eyes were opened to his real normal interests, man would at once cease to do nasty things, would at once become good and noble because, being enlightened and understanding his real advantage, he would see his own advantage in the good and nothing else, and we all know that not one man can, consciously, act against his own interests, consequently, so to say, through necessity, he would begin doing good? Oh, the babe! Oh, the pure, innocent child! Why, in the first place, when in all these thousands of years has there been a time when man has acted only from his own interest? What is to be done with the millions of facts that bear witness that men, *consciously*, that is, fully understanding their real interests, have left them in the background and have rushed headlong on another path, to meet peril and danger, compelled to this course by nobody and by nothing, but, as it were, simply disliking the beaten track, and have obstinately, wilfully, struck out another difficult, absurd way, seeking it almost in the darkness. So, I suppose, this obstinacy and perversity were pleasanter to them than any advantage. . . . Advantage! What is advantage?

And will you take it upon yourself to define with perfect accuracy in what the advantage of man consists? And what if it so happens that a man's advantage, *sometimes,* not only may, but even must, consist in his desiring in certain cases what is harmful to himself and not advantageous. And if so, there can be such a case, the whole principle falls into dust. What do you think—are there such cases? You laugh; laugh away, gentlemen, but only answer me: have man's advantages been reckoned up with perfect certainty? Are there not some which not only have not been included but cannot possibly be included under any classification? You see, you gentlemen have, to the best of my knowledge, taken your whole register of human advantages from the averages of statistical figures and politico-economical formulas. Your advantages are prosperity, wealth, freedom, peace—and so on, and so on. So that the man who should, for instance, go openly and knowingly in opposition to all that list would, to your thinking, and indeed mine too, of course, be an obscurantist or an absolute madman: would not he? But, you know, this is what is surprising: why does it so happen that all these statisticians, sages and lovers of humanity, when they reckon up human advantages invariably leave out one? They don't even take it into their reckoning in the form in which it should be taken and the whole reckoning depends upon that. It would be no great matter, they would simply have to take it, this advantage, and add it to the list. But the trouble is, that this strange advantage does not fall under any classification and is not in place in any list. I have a friend for instance . . . Ech! gentlemen, but of course he is your friend, too; and indeed there is no one, no one, to whom he is not a friend!

When he prepares for any undertaking this gentleman immediately explains to you, elegantly and clearly, exactly how he must act in accordance with the laws of reason and truth. What is more, he will talk to you with excitement and passion of the true normal interests of man; with irony he will upbraid the short-sighted fools who do not understand their own interests, nor the true significance of virtue; and, within a quarter of an hour, without any sudden outside provocation, but simply through something inside him which is stronger than all his interests, he will go off on quite a different tack—that is, act in direct opposition to what he has just been saying about himself, in opposition to the laws of reason, in opposition to his own advantage—in fact, in opposition to everything. . . . I warn you that my friend is a compound personality, and therefore it is difficult to blame him as an individual. The fact is, gentlemen, it seems there must really exist something that is dearer to almost every man than his greatest advantages, or (not to be illogical) there is a most advantageous advantage (the very one omitted of which we spoke just now) which is more important and more advantageous than all other advantages, for the sake of which a man if necessary is ready to act in opposition to all laws; that is, in opposition to reason, honour, peace, prosperity—in fact, in opposition to all those excellent and useful things if only he can attain that fundamental, most advantageous advantage which is dearer to him than all. "Yes, but it's advantage all the same" you will retort. But excuse me, I'll make the point clear, and it is not a case of playing upon words. What matters is, that this advantage is remarkable from the very fact that it breaks down all our classifications, and continually shatters every system constructed by lovers of mankind for the benefit of mankind. In fact, it upsets everything. But before I mention this advantage to you, I want to compromise myself personally, and therefore I boldly declare that all these fine systems—all these theories for explaining to mankind their real normal interests, in order that inevitably striving to pursue these interests they may at once become good and noble—are, in my opinion, so far, mere logical exercises! Yes, logical exercises. Why, to maintain this theory of the regeneration of mankind by means of the pursuit of his own advantage is to my mind almost the same thing as . . . as to affirm, for instance, following Buckle, that through civilization mankind becomes softer, and consequently less bloodthirsty, and less fitted for warfare.

Logically it does seem to follow from his arguments. But man has such a predilection for systems and abstract deductions that he is ready to distort the truth intentionally, he is ready to deny the evidence of his senses only to justify his logic. I take this example because it is the most glaring instance of it. Only look about you: blood is being spilt in streams, and in the merriest way, as though it were champagne. Take the whole of the nineteenth century in which Buckle lived. Take Napoleon—the Great and also the present one. Take North America —the eternal union. Take the farce of Schleswig-Holstein. . . . And what is it that civilization softens in us? The only gain of civilization for mankind is the greater capacity for variety of sensations—and absolutely nothing more. And through the development of this many-sidedness man may come to finding enjoyment in bloodshed. In fact, this has already happened to him. Have you noticed that it is the most civilized gentlemen who have been the subtlest slaughterers, to whom the Attilas and Stenka Razins could not hold a candle, and if they are not so conspicuous as the Attilas and Stenka Razins it is simply because they are so often met with, are so ordinary and have become so familiar to us. In any case civilization has made mankind if not more bloodthirsty, at least more vilely, more loathsomely blood-thirsty. In old days he saw justice in bloodshed and with his conscience at peace exterminated those he thought proper. Now we do think bloodshed abominable and yet we engage in this abomination, and with more energy than ever. Which is worse? Decide that for yourselves.

They say that Cleopatra (excuse an instance from Roman history) was fond of sticking gold pins into her slave-girls' breasts and derived gratification from their screams and writhings. You will say that that was in the comparatively barbarous times; that these are barbarous times too, because also, comparatively speaking, pins are stuck in even now; that though man has now learned to see more clearly than in barbarous ages, he is still far from having learnt to act as reason and science would dictate. But yet you are fully convinced that he will be sure to learn when he gets rid of certain old bad habits, and when common sense and science have completely re-educated human nature and turned it in a normal direction. You are confident that then man will cease from *intentional* error and will, so to say, be compelled not to want to set his will against his normal interests. That is not all; then, you say, science itself will teach man (though to my mind it's a superfluous luxury) that he never has really had any caprice or will of his own, and that he himself is something of the nature of a piano-key or the stop of an organ, and that there are, besides, things called the laws of nature; so that everything he does is not done by his willing it, but is done of itself, by the laws of nature. Consequently we have only to discover these laws of nature, and man will no longer have to answer for his actions and life will become exceedingly easy for him. All human actions will then, of course, be tabulated according to these laws, mathematically, like tables of logarithms up to 108,000, and entered in an index; or, better still, there would be published certain edifying works of the nature of encyclopaedic lexicons, in which everything will be so clearly calculated and explained that there will be no more incidents or adventures in the world.

Then—this is all what you say—new economic relations will be established, all ready-made and worked out with mathematical exactitude, so that every possible question will vanish in the twinkling of an eye, simply because every possible answer to it will be provided. Then the "Palace of Crystal" will be built. Then . . . In fact, those will be halcyon days. Of course there is no guaranteeing (this is my comment) that it will not be, for instance, frightfully dull then (for what will one have to do when everything will be calculated and tabulated?), but on the other hand everything will be extraordinarily rational. Of course boredom may lead you to anything. It is boredom sets one sticking golden pins into people, but all that would not matter. What is bad (this is my comment again) is that I dare say people will be thankful for the gold pins then. Man is stupid, you know, phenomenally stupid; or rather he is not at all stupid, but he is so ungrateful that you could not find another like him in all creation. I, for instance, would not be in the least surprised if all of a sudden, apropos of nothing, in the midst of general prosperity a gentleman with an ignoble, or rather with a reactionary and ironical, countenance were to arise and putting his arms akimbo, say to us all: "I say, gentlemen, hadn't we better kick over the whole show and scatter rationalism to the winds, simply to send these logarithms to the devil, and to enable us to live once more at our own sweet foolish will!" That again would not matter; but what is annoying is that he would be sure to find followers—such is the nature of man. And all that for the most foolish reason, which, one would think, was hardly worth mentioning: that is, that man everywhere and at all times, whoever he may be, has preferred to act as he chose and not in the least as his reason and advantage dictated. And one may choose what is contrary to one's own interests, and sometimes one *positively ought* (that is my idea). One's own free unfettered choice, one's own caprice—however wild it may be, one's own fancy worked up at times to frenzy —is that very "most advantageous advantage" which we have overlooked, which comes under no classification and against which all systems and theories are continually being shattered to atoms. And how do these wiseacres know that man wants a normal, a virtuous choice? What has made them conceive that man must want a rationally advantageous choice? What man wants is simply *independent* choice, whatever that independence may cost and wherever it may lead. And choice, of course, the devil only knows what choice. . . .

VIII

"Ha! ha! ha! But you know there is no such thing as choice in reality, say what you like," you will interpose with a chuckle. "Science has succeeded in so far analyzing man that we know already that choice and what is called freedom of will is nothing else than—"

Stay, gentlemen, I meant to begin with that myself. I confess, I was rather frightened. I was just going to say that the devil only knows what choice depends on, and that perhaps that was a very good thing, but I remembered the teaching of science . . . and pulled myself up. And here you have begun upon it. Indeed, if there really is some day discovered a formula for all our desires and caprices—that is, an explanation of what they depend upon, by what laws they arise, how they develop, what they are aiming at in one case and in another and so on, that is, a real mathematical formula—then, most likely, man will at once cease to feel desire, indeed, he will be certain to. For who would want to choose by rule? Besides, he will at once be transformed from a human being into an organ-stop or something of the sort; for what is a man without desires, without free will and without choice, if not a stop in an organ? What do you think? Let us reckon the chances—can such a thing happen or not?

"H'm!" you decide. "Our choice is usually mistaken from a false view of our advantage. We sometimes choose absolute nonsense because in our foolishness we see in that nonsense the easiest means for attaining a supposed advantage. But when all that is explained and worked out on paper (which is perfectly possible, for it is contemptible and senseless to suppose that some laws of nature man will never understand), then certainly so-called desires will no longer exist. For if a desire should come into conflict with reason we shall then reason and not desire, because it will be impossible retaining our reason to be *senseless* in our desires, and in that way knowingly act against reason and desire to injure ourselves. And as all choice and reasoning can be really calculated—because there will some day be discovered the laws of our so-called free will—so, joking apart, there may one day be something like a table constructed of them, so that we really shall choose in accordance with it. If, for instance, some day they calculate and prove to me that I made a long nose at some one because I could not help making a long nose at him and that I had to do it in that particular way, what *freedom* is left me, especially if I am a learned man and have taken my degree somewhere? Then I should be able to calculate my whole life for thirty years beforehand. In short, if this could be arranged there would be nothing left for us to do; anyway, we should have to understand that. And, in fact, we ought unwearyingly to repeat to ourselves that at such and such a time and in such and such circumstances Nature does not ask our leave; that we have got to take her as she is and not fashion her to suit our fancy, and if we really aspire to formulas and tables of rules, and well, even . . . to the chemical retort, there's no help for it, we must accept the retort too, or else it will be accepted without our consent. . . ."

Yes, but here I come to a stop! Gentlemen, you must excuse me for being over-philosophical; it's the result of forty years underground! Allow me to indulge my fancy. You see, gentlemen, reason is an excellent thing, there's no disputing that, but reason is nothing but reason and satisfies only the rational side of man's nature, while will is a manifestation of the whole life, that is, of the whole human life including reason and all the impulses. And although our life, in this manifestation of it, is often worthless, yet it is life and not simply extracting square roots. Here I, for instance, quite naturally want to live, in order to satisfy all my capacities for life, and not simply my capacity for reasoning, that is, not simply one-twentieth of my capacity for life. What does reason know? Reason only knows what it has succeeded in learning (some things, perhaps, it will never learn; this is a poor comfort, but why not say so frankly?) and human nature acts as a whole, with everything that is in it, consciously or unconsciously, and, even if it goes wrong, it lives. I suspect, gentlemen, that you are looking at me with compassion; you tell me again that an enlightened and developed man, such, in short, as the future man will be, cannot consciously desire anything disadvantageous to himself, that that can be proved mathematically. I thoroughly agree, it can—by mathematics.

But I repeat for the hundredth time, there is one case, one only, when man may consciously, purposely, desire what is injurious to himself, what is stupid, very stupid—simply in order to have the right to desire for himself even what is very stupid and not to be bound by an obligation to desire only what is sensible. Of course, this very stupid thing, this caprice of ours, may be in reality, gentlemen, more advantageous for us than anything else on earth, especially in certain cases. And in particular it may be more advantageous than any advantage even when it does us obvious harm, and contradicts the soundest conclusions of our reason concerning our advantage—for in any circumstances it preserves for us what is most precious and most important—that is, our personality, our individuality. Some, you see, maintain that this really is the most precious thing for mankind; choice can, of course, if it chooses, be in agreement with reason; and especially if this be not abused but kept within bounds. It is profitable and sometimes even praiseworthy. But very often, and even most often, choice is utterly and stubbornly opposed to reason . . . and . . . and . . . do you know that that, too, is profitable, sometimes even praiseworthy? Gentlemen, let us suppose that man is not stupid. (Indeed one cannot refuse to suppose that, if only from the one consideration, that, if man is stupid, then who is wise?) But if he is not stupid, he is monstrously ungrateful! Phenomenally ungrateful. In fact, I believe that the best definition of man is the ungrateful biped. But that is not all, that is not his worst defect; his worst defect is his perpetual moral obliquity, perpetual—from the days of the Flood to the Schleswig-Holstein period.

Moral obliquity and consequently lack of good sense; for it has long been accepted that lack of good sense is due to no other cause than moral obliquity. Put it to the test and cast your eyes upon the history of mankind. What will you see? Is it a grand spectacle? Grand, if you like. Take the Colossus of Rhodes, for instance, that's worth something. With good reason Mr. Anaevsky testifies of it that some say that it is the work of man's hands, while others maintain that it has been created by Nature herself. Is it many-coloured? It may be it is many-coloured, too: if one takes the dress uniforms, military and civilian, of all peoples in all ages—that alone is worth something, and if you take the undress uniforms you will never get to the end of it; no historian would be equal to the job. Is it monotonous? It may be it's monotonous too: it's fighting and fighting; they are fighting now, they fought first and they fought last—you will admit that it is almost too monotonous. In short, one may say anything about the history of the world—anything that might enter the most disordered imagination.

The only thing one can't say is that it's rational. The very word sticks in one's throat. And, indeed, this is the odd thing that is continually happening: there are continually turning up in life moral and rational persons, sages and lovers of humanity, who make it their object to live all their lives as morally and rationally as possible, to be, so to speak, a light to their neighbours simply in order to show them that it is possible to live morally and rationally in this world. And yet we all know that those very people sooner or later have been false to themselves, playing some queer trick, often a most unseemly one. Now I ask you: what can be expected of man since he is a being endowed with such strange qualities? Shower upon him every earthly blessing, drown him in a sea of happiness, so that nothing but bubbles of bliss can be seen on the surface; give him economic prosperity, such that he should have nothing else to do but sleep, eat cakes and busy himself with the continuation of his species, and even then out of sheer ingratitude, sheer spite, man would play you some nasty trick. He would even risk his cakes and would deliberately desire the most fatal rubbish, the most uneconomical absurdity, simply to introduce into all this positive good sense his fatal fantastic element. It is just his fantastic dreams, his vulgar folly, that he will desire to retain, simply in order to prove to himself—as though that were so necessary—that men still are men and not the keys of a piano, which the laws of nature threaten to control so completely that soon one will be able to desire nothing but by the calendar. And that is not all: even if man really were nothing but a piano-key, even if this were proved to him by natural science and mathematics, even then he would not become reasonable, but would purposely do something perverse out of simple ingratitude, simply to gain his point. And if he does not find means he will contrive destruction and chaos, will contrive sufferings of all sorts, only to gain his point! He will launch a curse upon the world, and as only man can curse (it is his privilege, the primary distinction between him and other animals) it may be by his curse alone he will attain his object—that is, convince himself that he is a man and not a piano-key! If you say that all this, too, can be calculated and tabulated—chaos and darkness and curses, so that the mere possibility of calculating it all beforehand would stop it all, and reason would reassert itself—then man would purposely go mad in order to be rid of reason and gain his point! I believe in it, I answer for it, for the whole work of man really seems to consist in nothing but proving to himself every minute that he is a man and not a piano-key! It may be at the cost of his skin, it may be by cannibalism! And this being so, can one help being tempted to rejoice that it has not yet come off, and that desire still depends on something we don't know?

You will scream at me (that is, if you condescend to do so) that no one is touching my free will, that all they are concerned with is that my will should of itself, of its own free will, coincide with my own normal interests, with the laws of nature and arithmetic.

Good heavens, gentlemen, what sort of free will is left when we come to tabulation and arithmetic, when it will all be a case of twice two makes four? Twice two makes four without my will. As if free will meant that!

IX

Gentlemen, I am joking, and I know myself that my jokes are not brilliant, but you know one can't take everything as a joke. I am, perhaps, jesting against the grain. Gentlemen, I am tormented by questions; answer them for me. You, for instance, want to cure men of their old habits and reform their will in accordance with science and good sense. But how do you know, not only that it is possible, but also that it is *desirable*, to reform man in that way? And what leads you to the conclusion that man's inclinations *need* reforming? In short, how do you know that such a reformation will be a benefit to man? And to go to the root of the matter, why are you so positively convinced that not to act against his real normal interests guaranteed by the conclusions of reason and arithmetic is certainly always advantageous for man and must always be a law for mankind? So far, you know, this is only your supposition. It may be the law of logic, but not the law of humanity. You think, gentlemen, perhaps that I am mad? Allow me to defend myself. I agree that man is pre-eminently a creative animal, predestined to strive consciously for an object and to engage in engineering—that is, incessantly and eternally to make new roads, *wherever they may lead*. But the reason why he wants sometimes to go off at a tangent may just be that he is *predestined* to make the road, and perhaps, too, that however stupid the "direct" practical man may be, the thought sometimes will occur to him that the road almost always does lead *somewhere,* and that the destination it leads to is less important than the process of making it, and that the chief thing is to save the well-conducted child from despising engineering, and so giving way to the fatal idleness, which, as we all know, is the mother of all the vices. Man likes to make roads and to create, that is a fact beyond dispute. But why has he such a passionate love for destruction and chaos also? Tell me that! But on that point I want to say a couple of words myself. May it not be that he loves chaos and destruction (there can be no disputing that he does some-times love it) because he is instinctively afraid of attaining his object and com-pleting the edifice he is constructing? Who knows, perhaps he only loves that edifice from a distance, and is by no means in love with it at close quarters; perhaps he only loves building it and does not want to live in it, but will leave it, when completed, for the use of *les animaux domestiques*—such as the ants, the sheep, and so on. Now the ants have quite a different taste. They have a marvellous edifice of that pattern which endures for ever—the ant-heap.

With the ant-heap the respectable race of ants began and with the ant-heap they will probably end, which does the greatest credit to their perseverance and good sense. But man is a frivolous and incongruous creature, and perhaps, like a chess-player, loves the process of the game, not the end of it. And who knows (there is no saying with certainty), perhaps the only goal on earth to which mankind is striving lies in this incessant process of attaining, in other words, in life itself, and not in the thing to be attained, which must always be expressed as a formula, as positive as twice two makes four, and such positiveness is not life, gentlemen, but is the beginning of death. Anyway, man has always been afraid of this mathematical certainty, and I am afraid of it now. Granted that man does nothing but seek that mathematical certainty, he traverses oceans, sacrifices his life in the quest, but to succeed, really to find it, he dreads, I assure you. He feels that when he has found it there will be nothing for him to look for. When workmen have finished their work they do at least receive their pay, they go to the tavern, then they are taken to the police-station—and there is occupation for a week. But where can man go? Anyway, one can observe a cer-tain awkwardness about him when he has attained such objects. He loves the process of attaining, but does not quite like to have attained, and that, of course, is very absurd. In fact, man is a comical creature; there seems to be a kind of jest in it all. But yet mathematical certainty is, after all, something insufferable. Twice two makes four seems to me simply a piece of insolence. Twice two makes four is a pert coxcomb who stands with arms akimbo barring your path and spitting. I admit that twice two makes four is an excellent thing, but if we are to give everything its due, twice two makes five is sometimes a very charming thing too.

And why are you so firmly, so triumphantly, convinced that only the normal and the positive—in other words, only what is conducive to welfare—is for the advantage of man? Is not reason in error as regards advantage? Does not man, perhaps, love something besides well-being? Perhaps he is just as fond of suffering? Perhaps suffering is just as great a benefit to him as well-being? Man is sometimes extraordinarily, passionately, in love with suffering, and that is a fact. There is no need to appeal to universal history to prove that; only ask yourself, if you are a man and have lived at all. As far as my personal opinion is concerned, to care only for well-being seems to me positively ill-bred. Whether it's good or bad, it is sometimes very pleasant, too, to smash things. I hold no brief for suffering nor for well-being either. I am standing for . . . my caprice, and for its being guaranteed to me when necessary. Suffering would be out of place in vaudevilles, for instance; I know that. In the "Palace of Crystal" it is unthinkable; suffering means doubt, negation, and what would be the good of a "palace of crystal" if there could be any doubt about it? And yet I think man will never renounce real suffering, that is, destruction and chaos. Why, suffering is the sole origin of consciousness. Though I did lay it down at the beginning that consciousness is the greatest misfortune for man, yet I know man prizes it and would not give it up for any satisfaction. Consciousness, for instance, is infinitely superior to twice two makes four. Once you have mathematical certainty there is nothing left to do or to understand. There will be nothing left but to bottle up your five senses and plunge into contemplation. While if you stick to consciousness, even though the same result is attained, you can at least flog yourself at times, and that will, at any rate, liven you up. Reactionary as it is, corporal punishment is better than nothing.

X

You believe in a palace of crystal that can never be destroyed—a palace at which one will not be able to put out one's tongue or make a long nose on the sly. And perhaps that is just why I am afraid of this edifice that it is of crystal and can never be destroyed and that one cannot put one's tongue out at it even on the sly.

You see, if it were not a palace, but a hen-house, I might creep into it to avoid getting wet, and yet I would not call the hen-house a palace out of gratitude to it for keeping me dry. You laugh and say that in such circumstances a hen-house is as good as a mansion. Yes, I answer, if one had to live simply to keep out of the rain.

But what is to be done if I have taken it into my head that that is not the only object in life, and that if one must live one had better live in a mansion.

That is my choice, my desire. You will only eradicate it when you have changed my preference. Well, do change it, allure me with something else, give me another ideal. But meanwhile I will not take a hen-house for a mansion. The palace of crystal may be an idle dream, it may be that it is inconsistent with the laws of nature and that I have invented it only through my own stupidity, through the old-fashioned irrational habits of my generation. But what does it matter to me that it is inconsistent? That makes no difference since it exists in my desires, or rather exists as long as my desires exist. Perhaps you are laughing again? Laugh away; I will put up with any mockery rather than pretend that I am satisfied when I am hungry. I know, anyway, that I will not be put off with a compromise, with a recurring zero, simply because it is consistent with the laws of nature and actually exists. I will not accept as the crown of my desires a block of buildings with tenements for the poor on a lease of a thousand years, and perhaps with a sign-board of a dentist hanging out. Destroy my desires, eradicate my ideals, show me something better, and I will follow you. You will say, perhaps, that is not worth your trouble; but in that case I can give you the same answer. We are discussing things seriously; but if you won't deign to give me your attention, I will drop your acquaintance. I can retreat into my underground hole.

But while I am alive and have desires I would rather my hand were withered off than bring one brick to such a building! Don't remind me that I have just rejected the palace of crystal for the sole reason that one cannot put out one's tongue at it. I did not say that because I am so fond of putting my tongue out. Perhaps the thing I resented was, that of all your edifices there has not been one at which one could not put out one's tongue. On the contrary, I would let my tongue be cut off out of gratitude if things could be so arranged that I should lose all desire to put it out. It is not my fault that things cannot be so arranged, and that one must be satisfied with model flats. Then why am I made with such desires? Can I have been constructed simply in order to come to the conclusion that all my construction is a cheat? Can this be my whole purpose? I do not believe it.

But do you know what: I am convinced that we underground folk ought to be kept on a curb. Though we may sit forty years underground without speaking, when we do come out into the light of day and break out we talk and talk and talk. . . .

HONORE DE BALZAC

• *Gallery of Antiquities*

The disasters of 1813 and 1814, which brought about the downfall of Napoleon, gave new life to the Collection of Antiquities, and what was more than life, the hope of recovering their past importance; but the events of 1815, the troubles of the foreign occupation, and the vacillating policy of the Government until the fall of M. Decazes, all contributed to defer the fulfilment of the expectations of the personages so vividly described by Blondet. This story, therefore, only begins to shape itself in 1822.

In 1822 the Marquis d'Esgrignon's fortunes had not improved in spite of the changes worked by the Restoration in the condition of émigrés. Of all nobles hardly hit by Revolutionary legislation, his case was the hardest. Like other great families, the d'Esgrignons before 1789 derived the greater part of their income from their rights as lords of the manor in the shape of dues paid by those who held of them; and, naturally, the old *seigneurs* had reduced the size of the holdings in order to swell the amounts paid in quit-rents and heriots. Families in this position were hopelessly ruined. They were not affected by the ordinance by which Louis XVIII. put the émigrés into possession of such of their lands as had not been sold; and at a later date it was impossible that the law of indemnity should indemnify them. Their suppressed rights, as everybody knows, were revived in the shape of a land tax known by the very name of *domaines,* but the money went into the coffers of the State.

SOURCE. From *The Gallery of Antiquities* by Honore de Balzac. Volume 15. Copyright 1901, Avil Publishing Company.

The Marquis by his position belonged to that small section of the Royalist party which would hear of no kind of compromise with those whom they styled, not Revolutionaries, but revolted subjects, or, in more parliamentary language, they had no dealings with Liberals or Constitutionnels. Such Royalists, nicknamed *Ultras* by the opposition, took for leaders and heroes those courageous orators of the Right, who from the very beginning attempted, with M. de Polignac, to protest against the charter granted by Louis XVIII. This they regarded as an ill-advised edict extorted from the Crown by the necessity of the moment, only to be annulled later on. And, therefore, so far from co-operating with the King to bring about a new condition of things, the Marquis d'Esgrignon stood aloof, an upholder of the straitest sect of the Right in politics, until such time as his vast fortune should be restored to him. Nor did he so much as admit the thought of the indemnity which filled the minds of the Villèle ministry, and formed a part of a design of strengthening the Crown by putting an end to those fatal distinctions of ownership which still lingered on in spite of legislation.

The miracles of the Restoration of 1814, the still greater miracle of Napoleon's return in 1815, the portents of a second flight of the Bourbons, and a second reinstatement (that almost fabulous phase of contemporary history), all these things took the Marquis by surprise at the age of sixty-seven. At that time of life, the most high-spirited men of their age were not so much vanquished as worn out in the struggle with the Revolution; their activity, in their remote provincial retreats, had turned into a passionately held and immovable conviction; and almost all of them were shut in by the enervating, easy round of daily life in the country. Could worse luck befall a political party than this—to be represented by old men at a time when its ideas are already stigmatized as old-fashioned?

When the legitimate sovereign appeared to be firmly seated on the throne again in 1818, the Marquis asked himself what a man of seventy should do at court; and what duties, what office he could discharge there? The noble and high-minded d'Esgrignon was fain to be content with the triumph of the Monarchy and Religion, while he waited for the results of that unhoped-for, indecisive victory, which proved to be simply an armistice. He continued as before, lord-paramount of his salon, so felicitously named the Collection of Antiquities.

But when the victors of 1793 became the vanquished in their turn, the nickname given at first in jest began to be used in bitter earnest. The town was no more free than other country towns from the hatreds and jealousies bred of party spirit. Du Croisier, contrary to all expectations, married the rich old maid who had refused him at first; carrying her off from his rival, the darling of the aristocratic quarter, a certain Chevalier whose illustrious name will be sufficiently hidden by suppressing it altogether, in accordance with the usage formerly adopted in the place itself, where he was known by his title only. He was "the Chevalier" in the town, as the Comte d'Artois was "Monsieur" at court. Now, not only had that marriage produced a war after the provincial manner, in which all weapons are fair; it had hastened the separation of the great and little noblesses, of the aristocratic and bourgeois elements, which had been united for a little space by the heavy weight of Napoleonic rule. After the pressure was removed, there fol lowed that sudden revival of class divisions which did so much harm to the country.

The most national of all sentiments in France is vanity. The wounded vanity of the many induced a thirst for Equality; though, as the most ardent innovator will some day discover, Equality is an impossibility. The Royalists pricked the Liberals in the most sensitive spots, and this happened especially in the provinces, where either party accused the other of unspeakable atrocities. In those days the blackest deeds were done in politics, to secure public opinion on one side or another, to catch the votes of that public of fools which holds up hands for those that are clever enough to serve out weapons to them. Individuals are identified with their political opinions, and opponents in public life forthwith become private enemies. It is very difficult in a country town to avoid a man-to-man conflict of this kind over interests or questions which in Paris appear in a more general and theoretical form, with the result that political combatants also rise to a higher level; M. Laffitte, for example, or M. Casimir-Périer can respect M. de Villèle or M. de Peyronnet as a man. M. Laffitte, who drew the fire on the Ministry, would have given them an asylum in his house if they had fled thither on the 29th of July 1830. Benjamin Constant sent a copy of his work on Religion to the Vicomte de Chateaubriand, with a flattering letter acknowledging benefits received from the former Minister. At Paris men are systems, whereas in the provinces systems are identified with men; men, moreover, with restless passions, who must always confront one another, always spy upon each other in private life, and pull their opponents' speeches to pieces, and live generally like two duelists on the watch for a chance to thrust six inches of steel between an antagonist's ribs. Each must do his best to get under his enemy's guard, and a political hatred becomes as all-absorbing as a duel to the death. Epigram and slander are used against individuals to bring the party into discredit.

In such warfare as this, waged ceremoniously and without rancor on the side of the Antiquities, while du Croisier's faction went so far as to use the poisoned weapons of savages—in this warfare the advantages of wit and delicate irony lay on the side of the nobles. But it should never be forgotten that the wounds made by the tongue and the eyes, by gibe or slight, are the last of all to heal. When the Chevalier turned his back on mixed society and entrenched himself on the Mons Sacer of the aristocracy, his witticisms thenceforward were directed at du Croisier's salon; he stirred up the fires of war, not knowing how far the spirit of revenge was to urge the rival faction. None but purists and loyal gentlemen and women sure one of another entered the Hôtel d'Esgrignon; they committed no indiscretions of any kind; they had their ideas, true or false, good or bad, noble or trivial, but there was nothing to laugh at in all this. If the Liberals meant to make the nobles ridiculous, they were obliged to fasten on the political actions of their opponents; while the intermediate party, composed of officials and others who paid court to the higher powers, kept the nobles informed of all that was done and said in the Liberal camp, and much of it was abundantly laughable. Du Croisier's adherents smarted under a sense of inferiority, which increased their thirst for revenge.

In 1822, du Croisier put himself at the head of the manufacturing interest of the province, as the Marquis d'Esgrignon headed the noblesse. Each represented his party. But du Croisier, instead of giving himself out frankly for a man of the extreme Left, ostensibly adopted the opinions formulated at a later day by the 221 deputies.

By taking up this position, he could keep in touch with the magistrates and local officials and the capitalists of the department. Du Croisier's salon, a power at least equal to the salon d'Esgrignon, larger numerically, as well as younger and more energetic, made itself felt all over the countryside; the Collection of Antiquities, on the other hand, remained inert, a passive appendage, as it were, of a central authority which was often embarrassed by its own partisans; for not merely did they encourage the Government in a mistaken policy, but some of its most fatal blunders were made in consequence of the pressure brought to bear upon it by the Conservative party.

The Liberals, so far, had never contrived to carry their candidate. The department declined to obey their command, knowing that du Croisier, if elected, would take his place on the Left Centre benches, and as far as possible to the Left. Du Croisier was in correspondence with the Brothers Keller, the bankers, the oldest of whom shone conspicuous among "the nineteen deputies of the Left," that phalanx made famous by the efforts of the entire Liberal press. This same M. Keller, moreover, was related by marriage to the Comte de Gondreville, a Constitutional peer who remained in favor with Louis XVIII. For these reasons, the Constitutional Opposition (as distinct from the Liberal party) was always prepared to vote at the last moment, not for the candidate whom they professed to support, but for du Croisier, if that worthy could succeed in gaining a sufficient number of Royalist votes; but at every election du Croisier was regularly thrown out by the Royalists. The leaders of that party, taking their tone from the Marquis d'Esgrignon, had pretty thoroughly fathomed and gauged their man; and with each defeat, du Croisier and his party waxed more bitter. Nothing so effectually stirs up strife as the failure of some snare set with elaborate pains.

In 1822 there seemed to be a lull in hostilities which had been kept up with great spirit during the first four years of the Restoration. The salon du Croisier and the salon d'Esgrignon, having measured their strength and weakness, were in all probability waiting for opportunity, that Providence of party strife. Ordinary persons were content with the surface quiet which deceived the Government; but those who knew du Croisier better, were well aware that the passion of revenge in him, as in all men whose whole life consists in mental activity, is implacable, especially when political ambitions are involved. About this time du Croisier, who used to turn white and red at the bare mention of d'Esgrignon or the Chevalier, and shuddered at the name of the Collection of Antiquities, chose to wear the impassive countenance of a savage. He smiled upon his enemies, hating them but the more deeply, watching them the more narrowly from hour to hour. One of his own party, who seconded him in these calculations of cold wrath, was the President of the Tribunal, M. du Ronceret, a little country squire, who had vainly endeavored to gain admittance among the Antiquities.

The d'Esgrignons' little fortune, carefully administered by Maître Chesnel, was barely sufficient for the worthy Marquis' needs; for though he lived without the slightest ostentation, he also lived like a noble. The governor found by his Lordship the Bishop for the hope of the house, the young Comte Victurnien d'Esgrignon, was an elderly Oratorian who must be paid a certain salary, although he lived with the family. The wages of a cook, a waiting-woman for Mlle. Armande, an old valet for M. le Marquis, and a couple of other servants, together with the daily expenses of the household, and the cost of an education for which nothing was spared, absorbed the whole family income, in spite of Mlle. Armande's economies, in spite of Chesnel's careful management, and the servants' affection. As yet, Chesnel had not been able to set about repairs at the ruined castle; he was waiting till the leases fell in to raise the rent of the farms, for rents had been rising lately, partly on account of improved methods of agriculture, partly by the fall in the value of money, of which the landlord would get the benefit at the expiration of leases granted in 1809.

The Marquis himself knew nothing of the details of the management of the house or of his property. He would have been thunderstruck if he had been told of the excessive precautions needed "to make both ends of the year meet in December," to use the housewife's saying, and he was so near the end of his life, that every one shrank from opening his eyes. The Marquis and his adherents believed that a House, to which no one at Court or in the Government gave a thought, a House that was never heard of beyond the gates of the town, save here and there in the same department, was about to revive its ancient greatness, to shine forth in all its glory. The d'Esgrignons' line should appear with renewed lustre in the person of Victurnien, just as the despoiled nobles came into their own again, and the handsome heir to a great estate would be in a position to go to Court, enter the King's service, and marry (as other d'Esgrignons had done before him) a Navarreins, a Cadignan, a d'Uxelles, a Beauséant, a Blamont-Chauvry; a wife, in short, who should unite all the distinctions of birth and beauty, wit and wealth, and character.

The intimates who came to play their game of cards of an evening—the Troisvilles (pronounced Tréville), the La Roche-Guyons, the Castérans (pronounced Catéran), and the Duc de Verneuil—had all so long been accustomed to look up to the Marquis as a person of immense consequence, that they encouraged him in such notions as these. They were perfectly sincere in their belief; and indeed, it would have been well founded if they could have wiped out the history of the last forty years. But the most honorable and undoubted sanctions of right, such as Louis XVIII. had tried to set on record when he dated the Charter from the one-and-twentieth year of his reign, only exist when ratified by the general consent. The d'Esgrignons not only lacked the very rudiments of the language of latter-day politics, to wit, money, the great modern *relief,* or sufficient rehabilitation of nobility; but, in their case, too, "historical continuity" was lacking, and that is a kind of renown which tells quite as much at Court as on the battlefield, in diplomatic circles as in Parliament, with a book, or in connection with an adventure; it is, as it were, a sacred *ampulla* poured upon the heads of each successive generation. Whereas a noble family, inactive and forgotten, is very much in the position of a hard-featured, poverty-stricken, simple-minded, and virtuous maid, these qualifications being the four cardinal points of misfortune. The marriage of a daughter of the Troisvilles with General Montcornet, so far from opening the eyes of the Antiquities, very nearly brought about a rupture between the Troisvilles and the salon d'Esgrignon, the latter declaring that the Troisvilles were mixing themselves up with all sorts of people.

There was one, and one only, among all these folk who did not share their illusions. And that one, needless to say, was Chesnel the notary. Although his devotion, sufficiently proved already, was simply unbounded for the great house now reduced to three persons; although he accepted all their ideas, and thought them nothing less than right, he had too much common sense, he was too good a man of business to more than half the families in the department, to miss the significance of the great changes that were taking place in people's minds, or to be blind to the different conditions brought about by industrial development and modern manners. He had watched the Revolution pass through the violent phase of 1793, when men, women, and children wore arms, and heads fell on the scaffold, and victories were won in pitched battles with Europe; and now he saw the same forces quietly at work in men's minds, in the shape of ideas which sanctioned the issues. The soil had been cleared, the seed sown, and now came the harvest. To his thinking, the Revolution had formed the mind of the younger generation; he touched the hard facts, and knew that although there were countless unhealed wounds, what had been done was done past recall. The death of a king on the scaffold, the protracted agony of a queen, the division of the nobles' lands, in his eyes were so many binding contracts; and where so many vested interests were involved, it was not likely that those concerned would allow them to be attacked. Chesnel saw clearly. His fanatical attachment to the d'Esgrignons was whole-hearted, but it was not blind, and it was all the fairer for this. The young monk's faith that sees heaven laid open and beholds the angels, is something far below the power of the old monk who points them out to him. The ex-steward was like the old monk; he would have given his life to defend a worm-eaten shrine.

He tried to explain the "innovations" to his old master, using a thousand tactful precautions; sometimes speaking jestingly, sometimes affecting surprise or sorrow over this or that; but he always met the same prophetic smile on the Marquis' lips, the same fixed conviction in the Marquis' mind, that these follies would go by like others. Events contributed in a way which has escaped attention to assist such noble champions of forlorn hope to cling to their superstitions. What could Chesnel do when the old Marquis said, with a lordly gesture, "God swept away Bonaparte with his armies, his new great vassals, his crowned kings, and his vast conceptions! God will deliver us from the rest." And Chesnel hung his head sadly, and did not dare to answer, "It cannot be God's will to sweep away France." Yet both of them were grand figures; the one, standing out against the torrent of facts like an ancient block of lichen-covered granite, still upright in the depths of an Alpine gorge; the other, watching the course of the flood to turn it to account. Then the good gray-headed notary would groan over the irreparable havoc which the superstitions were sure to work in the mind, the habits, and ideas of the Comte Victurnien d'Esgrignon.

Idolized by his father, idolized by his aunt, the young heir was a spoilt child in every sense of the word; but still a spoilt child who justified paternal and maternal illusions. Maternal, be it said, for Victurnien's aunt was truly a mother to him; and yet, however careful and tender she may be that never bore a child, there is a something lacking in her motherhood. A mother's second sight cannot be acquired. An aunt, bound to her nursling by ties of such a pure affection as united Mlle. Armande to Victurnien, may love as much as a mother might; may be as careful, as kind, as tender, as indulgent, but she lacks the mother's instinctive knowledge when and how to be severe; she has no sudden warnings, none of the uneasy presentiments of the mother's heart; for a mother, bound to her child from the beginnings of life by all the fibres of her being, still is conscious of the communication, still vibrates with the shock of every trouble, and thrills with every joy in the child's life as if it were her own. If Nature has made of woman, physically speaking, a neutral ground, it has not been forbidden to her, under certain conditions, to identify herself completely with her offspring. When she has not merely given life, but given of her whole life, you behold that wonderful, unexplained, and inexplicable thing—the love of a woman for one of her children above the others. The outcome of this story is one more proof of a proven truth—a mother's place cannot be filled. A mother foresees danger long before a Mlle. Armande can admit the possibility of it, even if the mischief is done. The one prevents the evil, the other remedies it. And besides, in the maiden's motherhood there is an element of blind adoration, she cannot bring herself to scold a beautiful boy.

A practical knowledge of life, and the experience of business, had taught the old notary a habit of distrustful clear-sighted observation something akin to the mother's instinct. But Chesnel counted for so little in the house (especially since he had fallen into something like disgrace over that unlucky project of a marriage between a d'Esgrignon and a du Croisier), that he had made up his mind to adhere blindly in future to the family doctrines. He was a common soldier, faithful to his post, and ready to give his life; it was never likely that they would take his advice, even in the height of the storm; unless change should bring him, like the King's bedesman in *The Antiquary*, to the edge of the sea, when the old baronet and his daughter were caught by the high tide.

Du Croisier caught a glimpse of his revenge in the anomalous education given to the lad. He hoped, to quote the expressive words of the author quoted above, "to drown the lamb in its mother's milk." *This* was the hope which had produced his taciturn resignation and brought that savage smile on his lips.

The young Comte Victurnien was taught to believe in his own supremacy as soon as an idea could enter his head. All the great nobles of the realm were his peers, his one superior was the King, and the rest of mankind were his inferiors, people with whom he had nothing in common, towards whom he had no duties. They were defeated and conquered enemies, whom he need not take into account for a moment; their opinions could not affect a noble, and they all owed him respect. Unluckily, with the rigorous logic of youth, which leads children and young people to proceed to extremes whether good or bad, Victurnien pushed these conclusions to their utmost consequences. His own external advantages, moreover, confirmed him in his beliefs. He had been extraordinarily beautiful as a child; he became as accomplished a young man as any father could wish.

He was of average height, but well proportioned, slender, and almost delicate-looking, but muscular. He had the brilliant blue eyes of the d'Esgrignons, the finely-moulded aquiline nose, the perfect oval of the face, the auburn hair, the white skin, and the graceful gait of his family; he had their delicate extremities, their long taper fingers with the inward curve, and that peculiar distinction of shapeliness of the wrist and instep, that supple felicity of line, which is as sure a sign of race in men as in horses. Adroit and alert in all bodily exercises, and an excellent shot, he handled arms like a St. George, he was a paladin on horseback. In short, he gratified the pride which parents take in their children's appearance; a pride founded, for that matter, on a just idea of the enormous influence exercised by physical beauty. Personal beauty has this in common with noble birth; it cannot be acquired afterwards; it is everywhere recognized, and often is more valued than either brains or money; beauty has only to appear and triumph; nobody asks more of beauty than that it should simply exist.

Fate had endowed Victurnien, over and above the privileges of good looks and noble birth, with a high spirit, a wonderful aptitude of comprehension, and a good memory. His education, therefore, had been complete. He knew a good deal more than is usually known by young provincial nobles, who develop into highly-distinguished sportsmen, owners of land, and consumers of tobacco; and are apt to treat art, sciences, letters, poetry, or anything offensively above their intellects, cavalierly enough. Such gifts of nature and education surely would one day realize the Marquis d'Esgrignon's ambitions; he already saw his son a Marshal of France if Victurnien's tastes were for the army; an ambassador if diplomacy held any attractions for him; a cabinet minister if that career seemed good in his eyes; every place in the state belonged to Victurnien. And, most gratifying thought of all for a father, the young Count would have made his way in the world by his own merits even if he had not been a d'Esgrignon.

All through his happy childhood and golden youth, Victurnien had never met with opposition to his wishes. He had been the king of the house; no one curbed the little prince's will; and naturally he grew up insolent and audacious, selfish as a prince, self-willed as the most high-spirited cardinal of the Middle Ages,—defects of character which any one might guess from his qualities, essentially those of the noble.

The Chevalier was a man of the good old times when the Gray Musketeers were the terror of the Paris theatres, when they horsewhipped the watch and drubbed servers of writs, and played a host of page's pranks, at which Majesty was wont to smile so long as they were amusing. This charming deceiver and hero of the *ruelles* had no small share in bringing about the disasters which afterwards befell. The amiable old gentleman, with nobody to understand him, was not a little pleased to find a budding Faublas, who looked the part to admiration, and put him in mind of his own young days. So, making no allowance for the difference of the times, he sowed the maxims of a *roué* of the Encyclopædic period broadcast in the boy's mind. He told wicked anecdotes of the reign of His Majesty Louis XV.; he glorified the manners and customs of the year 1750; he told of the orgies in *petites maisons,* the follies of courtesans, the capital tricks played on creditors, the manners, in short, which furnished forth Dancourt's comedies and Beaumarchais' epigrams. And unfortunately, the corruption lurking beneath the utmost polish tricked itself out in Voltairean wit. If the Chevalier went rather too far at times, he always added as a corrective that a man must always behave himself like a gentleman.

Of all this discourse, Victurnien comprehended just so much as flattered his passions. From the first he saw his old father laughing with the Chevalier. The two elderly men considered that the pride of a d'Esgrignon was a sufficient safeguard against anything unbefitting; as for a dishonorable action, no one in the house imagined that a d'Esgrignon could be guilty of it. HONOR, the great principle of Monarchy, was planted firm like a beacon in the hearts of the family; it lighted up the least action, it kindled the least thought of a d'Esgrignon. "A d'Esgrignon ought not to permit himself to do such and such a thing; he bears a name which pledges him to make the future worthy of the past"—a noble teaching which should have been sufficient in itself to keep alive the tradition of noblesse—had been, as it were, the burden of Victurnien's cradle song. He heard them from the old Marquis, from Mlle. Armande, from Chesnel, from the intimates of the house. And so it came to pass that good and evil met, and in equal forces, in the boy's soul.

At the age of eighteen, Victurnien went into society. He noticed some slight discrepancies between the outer world of the town and the inner world of the Hôtel d'Esgrignon, but he in no wise tried to seek the causes of them. And, indeed, the causes were to be found in Paris. He had yet to learn that the men who spoke their minds out so boldly in evening talk with his father, were extremely careful of what they said in the presence of the hostile persons with whom their interests compelled them to mingle. His own father had won the right of freedom of speech. Nobody dreamed of contradicting an old man of seventy, and besides, every one was willing to overlook fidelity to the old order of things in a man who had been violently despoiled.

Victurnien was deceived by appearances, and his behavior set up the backs of the townspeople. In his impetuous way he tried to carry matters with too high a hand over some difficulties in the way of sport, which ended in formidable lawsuits, hushed up by Chesnel for money laid down. Nobody dared to tell the Marquis of these things. You may judge of his astonishment if he had heard that his son had been prosecuted for shooting over his.lands, his domains, his covers, under the reign of a son of St. Louis! People were too much afraid of the possible consequences to tell him about such trifles, Chesnel said.

The young Count indulged in other escapades in the town. These the Chevalier regarded as *"amourettes,"* but they cost Chesnel something considerable in portions for forsaken damsels seduced under imprudent promises of marriage: yet other cases there were which came under an article of the Code as to the abduction of minors; and but for Chesnel's timely intervention, the new law would have been allowed to take its brutal course, and it is hard to say where the Count might have ended. Victurnien grew the bolder for these victories over bourgeois justice. He was so accustomed to be pulled out of scrapes, that he never thought twice before any prank. Courts of law, in his opinion, were bugbears to frighten people who had no hold on him. Things which he would have blamed in common people were for him only pardonable amusements. His disposition to treat the new laws cavalierly while obeying the maxims of a Code for aristocrats, his behavior and character, were all pondered, analyzed, and tested by a few adroit persons in du Croisier's interests. These folk supported each other in the effort to make the people believe that Liberal slanders were revelations, and that the Ministerial policy at bottom meant a return to the old order of things.

What a bit of luck to find something by way of proof of their assertions! President du Ronceret, and the public prosecutor likewise, lent themselves admirably, so far as was compatible with their duty as magistrates, to the design of letting off the offender as easily as possible; indeed, they went deliberately out of their way to do this, well pleased to raise a Liberal clamor against their overlarge concessions. And so, while seeming to serve the interests of the d'Esgrignons, they stirred up ill feeling against them. The treacherous du Ronceret had it in his mind to pose as incorruptible at the right moment over some serious charge, with public opinion to back him up. The young Count's worst tendencies, moreover, were insidiously encouraged by two or three young men who followed in his train, paid court to him, won his favor, and flattered and obeyed him, with a view to confirming his belief in a noble's supremacy; and all this at a time when a noble's one chance of preserving his power lay in using it with the utmost discretion for half a century to come.

Du Croisier hoped to reduce the d'Esgrignons to the last extremity of poverty; he hoped to see their castle demolished, and their lands sold piecemeal by auction, through the follies which this harebrained boy was pretty certain to commit. This was as far as he went; he did not think, with President du Ronceret, that Victurnien was likely to give justice another kind of hold upon him. Both men found an ally for their schemes of revenge in Victurnien's overweening vanity and love of pleasure. President du Ronceret's son, a lad of seventeen, was admirably fitted for the part of instigator. He was one of the Count's companions, a new kind of spy in du Croisier's pay; du Croisier taught him his lesson, set him to track down the noble and beautiful boy through his better qualities, and sardonically prompted him to encourage his victim in his worst faults. Fabien du Ronceret was a sophisticated youth, to whom such a mystification was attractive: he had precisely the keen brain and envious nature which finds in such a pursuit as this the absorbing amusement which a man of an ingenious turn lacks in the provinces.

In three years, between the ages of eighteen and one-and-twenty, Victurnien cost poor Chesnel nearly eighty thousand francs! And this without the knowledge of Mlle. Armande or the Marquis. More than half of the money had been spent in buying off lawsuits; the lad's extravagance had squandered the rest. Of the Marquis' income of ten thousand livres, five thousand were necessary for the housekeeping; two thousand more represented Mlle. Armande's allowance (parsimonious though she was) and the Marquis' expenses. The handsome young heir-presumptive, therefore, had not a hundred louis to spend. And what sort of figure can a man make on two thousand livres? Victurnien's tailor's bills alone absorbed his whole allowance. He had his linen, his clothes, gloves, and perfumery from Paris. He wanted a good English saddle-horse, a tilbury, and a second horse. M. du Croisier had a tilbury and a thoroughbred. Was the bourgeoisie to cut out the noblesse? Then, the young Count must have a man in the d'Esgrignon livery. He prided himself on setting the fashion among young men in the town and the department; he entered that world of luxuries and fancies which suit youth and good looks and wit so well. Chesnel paid for it all, not without using, like ancient parliaments, the right of protest, albeit he spoke with angelic kindness.

"What a pity it is that so good a man should be so tiresome!" Victurnien would say to himself every time that the notary staunched some wound in his purse.

Chesnel had been left a widower, and childless; he had taken his old master's son to fill the void in his heart. It was a pleasure to him to watch the lad driving up the High Street, perched aloft on the box-seat of the tilbury, whip in hand, and a rose in his button-hole, handsome, well turned out, envied by every one.

Pressing need would bring Victurnien with uneasy eyes and coaxing manner, but steady voice, to the modest house in the Rue du Bercail; there had been losses at cards at the Troisvilles, or the Duc de Verneuil's, or the prefecture, or the receiver-general's, and the Count had come to his providence, the notary. He had only to show himself to carry the day.

"Well, what is it, M. le Comte? What has happened?" the old man would ask, with a tremor in his voice.

On great occasions Victurnien would sit down, assume a melancholy, pensive expression, and submit with little coquetries of voice and gesture to be questioned. Then when he had thoroughly roused the old man's fears (for Chesnel was beginning to fear how such a course of extravagance would end), he would own up to a peccadillo which a bill for a thousand francs would absolve. Chesnel possessed a private income of some twelve thousand livres, but the fund was not inexhaustible. The eighty thousand francs thus squandered represented his savings, accumulated for the day when the Marquis should send his son to Paris, or open negotiations for a wealthy marriage.

Chesnel was clear-sighted so long as Victurnien was not there before him. One by one he lost the illusions which the Marquis and his sister still fondly cherished. He saw that the young fellow could not be depended upon in the least, and wished to see him married to some modest, sensible girl of good birth, wondering within himself how a young man could mean so well and do so ill, for he made promises one day only to break them all on the next.

But there is never any good to be expected of young men who confess their sins and repent, and straightway fall into them again. A man of strong character only confesses his faults to himself, and punishes himself for them; as for the weak, they drop back into the old ruts when they find that the bank is too steep to climb. The springs of pride which lie in a great man's secret soul had been slackened in Victurnien. With such guardians as he had, such company as he kept, such a life as he had led, he had suddenly become an enervated voluptuary at that turning-point in his life when a man most stands in need of the harsh discipline of misfortune and poverty to bring out the strength that is in him, the pinch of adversity which formed a Prince Eugène, a Frederick II., a Napoleon. Chesnel saw that Victurnien possessed that uncontrollable appetite for enjoyments which should be the prerogative of men endowed with giant powers; the men who feel the need of counterbalancing their gigantic labors by pleasures which bring one-sided mortals to the pit.

At times the good man stood aghast; then, again, some profound sally, some sign of the lad's remarkable range of intellect, would reassure him. He would say, as the Marquis said at the rumor of some escapade, "Boys will be boys." Chesnel had spoken to the Chevalier, lamenting the young lord's propensity for getting into debt; but the Chevalier manipulated his pinch of snuff, and listened with a smile of amusement.

"My dear Chesnel, just explain to me what a national debt is," he answered. "If France has debts, egad! why should not Victurnien have debts? At this time and at all times princes have debts, every gentleman has debts. Perhaps you would rather that Victurnien should bring you his savings?—Do you know what our great Richelieu (not the Cardinal, a pitiful fellow that put nobles to death, but the Maréchal), do you know what he did once when his grandson the Prince de Chinon, the last of the line, let him see that he had not spent his pocket-money at the University?"

"No, M. le Chevalier."

"Oh, well; he flung the purse out of the window to a sweeper in the courtyard, and said to his grandson, 'Then they do not teach you to be a prince here?' "

Chesnel bent his head and made no answer. But that night, as he lay awake, he thought that such doctrines as these were fatal in times when there was one law for everybody, and foresaw the first beginnings of the ruin of the d'Esgrignons.

Chapter 12

Social Deviance

JACK KEROUAC

• *On the Road*

He came to the door stark naked and it might have been the President knocking for all he cared. He received the world in the raw. "Sal!" he said with genuine awe. "I didn't think you'd actually do it. You've finally come to *me*."

"Yep," I said. "Everything fell apart in me. How are things with you?"

"Not so good, not so good. But we've got a million things to talk about. Sal, the time has *fi-nally* come for us to talk and get with it." We agreed it was about time and went in. My arrival was somewhat like the coming of the strange most evil angel in the home of the snow-white fleece, as Dean and I began talking excitedly in the kitchen downstairs, which brought forth sobs from upstairs. Everything I said to Dean was answered with a wild, whispering, shuddering *"Yes!"* Camille knew what was going to happen. Apparently Dean had been quiet for a few months; now the angel had arrived and he was going mad again. "What's the matter with her?" I whispered.

He said, "She's getting worse and worse, man, she cries and makes tantrums, won't let me out to see Slim Gaillard, gets mad every time I'm late, then when I stay home she won't talk to me and says I'm an utter beast." He ran upstairs to soothe her. I heard Camille yell, *"You're a liar, you're a liar, you're a liar!"* I took the opportunity to examine the very wonderful house they had. It was a two-story crooked, rickety wooden cottage in the middle of tenements, right on top of Russian Hill with a view of the bay; it had four rooms, three upstairs and

SOURCE. From *On The Road* by Jack Kerouac. Copyright 1955, 1957 by Jack Kerouac, reprinted by permission of the Viking Press.

one immense sort of basement kitchen downstairs. The kitchen door opened onto a grassy court where washlines were. In back of the kitchen was a storage room where Dean's old shoes still were caked an inch thick with Texas mud from the night the Hudson got stuck on the Brazos River. Of course the Hudson was gone; Dean hadn't been able to make further payments on it. He had no car at all now. Their second baby was accidentally coming. It was horrible to hear Camille sobbing so. We couldn't stand it and went out to buy beer and brought it back to the kitchen. Camille finally went to sleep or spent the night staring blankly at the dark. I had no idea what was really wrong, except perhaps Dean had driven her mad after all.

After my last leaving of Frisco he had gone crazy over Marylou again and spent months haunting her apartment on Divisadero, where every night she had a different sailor in and he peeked down through her mail-slot and could see her bed. There he saw Marylou sprawled in the mornings with a boy. He trailed her around town. He wanted absolute proof that she was a whore. He loved her, he sweated over her. Finally he got hold of some bad green, as it's called in the trade—green, uncured marijuana—quite by mistake, and smoked too much of it.

"The first day," he said, "I lay rigid as a board in bed and couldn't move or say a word; I just looked straight up with my eyes open wide. I could hear buzzing in my head and saw all kinds of wonderful technicolor visions and felt wonderful. The second day everything came to me, EVERYTHING I'd ever done or known or read or heard of or conjectured came back to me and rearranged itself in my mind in a brand-new logical way and because I could think of nothing else in the interior concerns of holding and catering to the amazement and gratitude I felt, I kept saying, 'Yes, yes, yes, yes.' Not loud. Just 'Yes,' real quiet, and these green tea visions lasted until the third day. I had understood everything by then, my whole life was decided, I knew I loved Marylou, I knew I had to find my father wherever he is and save him, I knew you were by buddy et cetera, I knew how great Carlo is. I knew a thousand things about everybody everywhere. Then the third day I began having a terrible series of waking nightmares, and they were so absolutely horrible and grisly and green that I just lay there doubled up with my hands around my knees, saying, 'Oh, oh, oh, ah, oh . . .' The neighbors heard me and sent for a doctor. Camille was away with the baby, visiting her folks. The whole neighborhood was concerned. They came in and found me lying on the bed with my arms stretched out forever. Sal, I ran to Marylou with some of that tea. And do you know that the same thing happened to that dumb little box? —the same visions, the same logic, the same final decision about everything, the view of all truths in one painful lump leading to nightmares and pain—ack! Then I knew I loved her so much I wanted to kill her. I ran home and beat my head on the wall. I ran to Ed Dunkel; he's back in Frisco with Galatea; I asked him about a guy we know has a gun, I went to the guy, I got the gun, I ran to

Marylou, I looked down the mail-slot, she was sleeping with a guy, had to retreat and hesitate, came back in an hour, I barged in, she was alone—and I gave her the gun and told her to kill me. She held the gun in her hand the longest time. I asked her for a sweet dead pact. She didn't want. I said one of us had to die. She said no. I beat my head on the wall. Man, I was out of my mind. She'll tell you, she talked me out of it."

"Then what happened?"

"That was months ago—after you left. She finally married a used-car dealer, dumb bastit has promised to kill me if he finds me, if necessary I shall have to defend myself and kill him and I'll go to San Quentin, 'cause Sal, one more rap of *any* kind and I go to San Quentin for life—that's the end of me. Bad hand and all." He showed me his hand. I hadn't noticed in the excitement that he had suffered a terrible accident to his hand. "I hit Marylou on the brow on February twenty-sixth at six o'clock in the evening—in fact six-ten, because I remember I had to make my hotshot freight in an hour and twenty minutes—the last time we met and the last time we decided everything, and now listen to this: my thumb only deflected off her brow and she didn't even have a bruise and in fact laughed, but my thumb broke above the wrist and a horrible doctor made a setting of the bones that was difficult and took three separate castings, twenty-three combined hours of sitting on hard benches waiting, et cetera, and the final cast had a traction pin stuck through the tip of my thumb, so in April when they took off the cast the pin infected my bone and I developed osteomyelitis which has become chronic, and after an operation which failed and a month in a cast the result was the amputation of a wee bare piece off the tip-ass end."

He unwrapped the bandages and showed me. The flesh, about half an inch, was missing under the nail.

"It got from worse to worse. I had to support Camille and Amy and had to work as fast as I could at Firestone as mold man, curing recapped tires and later hauling big hunnerd-fifty-pound tires from the floor to the top of the cars—could only use my good hand and kept banging the bad—broke it again, had it reset again, and it's getting all infected and swoled again. So now I take care of baby while Camille works. You see? Heeby-jeebies, I'm classification three-A, jazz-hounded Moriarty has a sore butt, his wife gives him daily injections of penicillin for his thumb, which produces hives, for he's allergic. He must take sixty thousand units of Fleming's juice within a month. He must take one tablet every four hours for this month to combat allergy produced from his juice. He must take codeine aspirin to relieve the pain in his thumb. He must have surgery on his leg for an inflamed cyst. He must rise next Monday at six A.M. to get his teeth cleaned. He must see a foot doctor twice a week for treatment. He must take cough syrup each night. He must blow and snort constantly to clear his nose, which has collapsed just under the bridge where an operation some years ago weakened it. He lost his thumb on his throwing arm. Greatest seventy-yard passer in the history of New Mexico State Reformatory. And yet—and yet, I've never felt better and finer and happier with the world and to see little lovely children playing in the sun and I am so glad to see you, my fine gone wonderful Sal, and I know, I *know* everything will be all right. You'll see her tomorrow, my terrific darling beautiful daughter can now stand alone for thirty seconds at a time, she weighs twenty-two pounds, is twenty-nine inches long. I've just figured out she is thirty-one-and-a-quarter-per-cent English, twenty-seven-and-a-half-per-cent Irish, twenty-five-per-cent German, eight-and-three-quarters-per-cent Dutch, seven-and-a-half-per-cent Scotch, one-hundred-per-cent wonderful." He fondly congratulated me for the book I had finished, which was now accepted by the publishers. "We know life, Sal, we're growing older, each of us, little by little, and are coming to know things. What you tell me about your life I understand well, I've always dug your feelings, and now in fact you're ready to hook up with a real great girl if you can only find her and cultivate her and make her mind your soul as I have tried so hard with these damned women of mine. Shit! shit! shit!" he yelled.

And in the morning Camille threw both of us out, baggage and all. It began when we called Roy Johnson, old Denver Roy, and had him come over for beer, while Dean minded the baby and did the dishes and the wash in the backyard but did a sloppy job of it in his excitement. Johnson agreed to drive us to Mill City to look for Remi Boncoeur. Camille came in from work at the doctor's office and gave us all the sad look of a harassed woman's life. I tried to show this haunted woman that I had no mean intentions concerning her home life by saying hello to her and talking as warmly as I could, but she knew it was a con and maybe one I'd learned from Dean, and only gave a brief smile. In the morning there was a terrible scene: she lay on the bed sobbing, and in the midst of this I suddenly had the need to go to the bathroom, and the only way I could get there was through her room. "Dean, Dean," I cried, "where's the nearest bar?"

"Bar?" he said, surprised; he was washing his hands in the kitchen sink downstairs. He thought I wanted to get drunk. I told him my dilemma and he said, "Go right ahead, she does that all the time." No, I couldn't do that. I rushed out to look for a bar; I walked uphill and downhill in a vicinity of four blocks on Russian Hill and found nothing but laundromats, cleaners, soda fountains, beauty parlors. I came back to the crooked little house. They were yelling at each other as I slipped through with a feeble smile and locked myself in the bathroom. A few moments later Camille was throwing Dean's things on the living-room floor and telling him to pack. To my amazement I saw a full-length oil painting of Galatea Dunkel over the sofa. I suddenly realized that all these women were spending months of loneliness and womanliness together, chatting about the madness of the men. I heard Dean's maniacal giggle across the house, together with the wails of his baby. The next thing I knew he was gliding around the house like

Groucho Marx, with his broken thumb wrapped in a huge white bandage sticking up like a beacon that stands motionless above the frenzy of the waves. Once again I saw his pitiful huge battered trunk with socks and dirty underwear sticking out; he bent over it, throwing in everything he could find. Then he got his suitcase, the beatest suitcase in the USA. It was made of paper with designs on it to make it look like leather, and hinges of some kind pasted on. A great rip ran down the top; Dean lashed on a rope. Then he grabbed his seabag and threw things into that. I got my bag, stuffed it, and as Camille lay in bed saying, "Liar! Liar! Liar!" we leaped out of the house and struggled down the street to the nearest cable car —a mass of men and suitcases with that enormous bandaged thumb sticking up in the air.

That thumb became the symbol of Dean's final development. He no longer cared about anything (as before) but now he also *cared about everything in principle;* that is to say, it was all the same to him and he belonged to the world and there was nothing he could do about it. He stopped me in the middle of the street.

"Now, man, I know you're probably real bugged; you just got to town and we get thrown out the first day and you're wondering what I've done to deserve this and so on—together with all horrible appurtenances—hee-hee-hee!—but look at me. Please, Sal, look at me."

I looked at him. He was wearing a T-shirt, torn pants hanging down his belly, tattered shoes; he had not shaved, his hair was wild and bushy, his eyes bloodshot, and that tremendous bandaged thumb stood supported in midair at heart-level (he had to hold it up that way), and on his face was the goofiest grin I ever saw. He stumbled around in a circle and looked everywhere.

"What do my eyeballs see? Ah—the blue sky. Long-fellow!" He swayed and blinked. He rubbed his eyes. "Together with windows—have you ever dug windows? Now let's talk about windows. I have seen some really crazy windows that made faces at me, and some of them had shades drawn and so they winked." Out of his seabag he fished a copy of Eugene Sue's *Mysteries of Paris* and, adjusting the front of his T-shirt, began reading on the street corner with a pedantic air. "Now really, Sal, let's dig everything as we go along . . ." He forgot about that in an instant and looked around blankly. I was glad I had come, he needed me now.

"Why did Camille throw you out? What are you going to do?"

"Eh?" he said. "Eh? Eh?" We racked our brains for where to go and what to do. I realized it was up to me. Poor, poor Dean—the devil himself had never fallen farther; in idiocy, with infected thumb, surrounded by the battered suitcases of his motherless feverish life across America and back numberless times, an undone bird. "Let's walk to New York," he said, "and as we do so let's take stock of everything along the way—yass." I took out my money and counted it; I showed it to him.

"I have here," I said, "the sum of eighty-three dollars and change, and if you come with me let's go to New York—and after that let's go to Italy."

"Italy?" he said. His eyes lit up. "Italy, yass—how shall we get there, dear Sal?"

I pondered this. "I'll make some money, I'll get a thousand dollars from the publishers. We'll go dig all the crazy women in Rome, Paris, all those places; we'll sit at sidewalk cafés; we'll live in whorehouses. Why not go to Italy?"

"Why yass," said Dean, and then realized I was serious and looked at me out of the corner of his eye for the first time, for I'd never committed myself before with regard to his burdensome existence, and that look was the look of a man weighing his chances at the last moment before the bet. There were triumph and insolence in his eyes, a devilish look, and he never took his eyes off mine for a long time. I looked back at him and blushed.

I said, "What's the matter?" I felt wretched when I asked it. He made no answer but continued looking at me with the same wary insolent side-eye.

I tried to remember everything he'd done in his life and if there wasn't something back there to make him suspicious of something now. Resolutely and firmly I repeated what I said—"Come to New York with me; I've got the money." I looked at him; my eyes were watering with embarrassment and tears. Still he stared at me. Now his eyes were blank and looking through me. It was probably the pivotal point of our friendship when he realized I had actually spent some hours thinking about him and his troubles, and he was trying to place that in his tremendously involved and tormented mental categories. Something clicked in both of us. In me it was suddenly concern for a man who was years younger than I, five years, and whose fate was wound with mine across the passage of the recent years; in him it was a matter that I can ascertain only from what he did afterward. He became extremely joyful and said everything was settled. "What was that look?" I asked. He was pained to hear me say that. He frowned. It was rarely that Dean frowned. We both felt perplexed and uncertain of something. We were standing on top of a hill on a beautiful sunny day in San Francisco; our shadows fell across the sidewalk. Out of the tenement next to Camille's house filed eleven Greek men and women who instantly lined themselves up on the sunny pavement while another backed up across the narrow street and smiled at them over a camera. We gaped at these ancient people who were having a wedding party for one of their daughters, probably the thousandth in an unbroken dark generation of smiling in the sun. They were well dressed, and they were strange. Dean and I might have been in Cyprus for all of that. Gulls flew overhead in the sparkling air.

"Well," said Dean in a very shy and sweet voice, "shall we go?"

"Yes," I said, "let's go to Italy." And so we picked up our bags, he the trunk with his one good arm and I the rest, and staggered to the cable-car stop;

in a moment rolled down the hill with our legs dangling to the sidewalk from the jiggling shelf, two broken-down heroes of the Western night.

3

First thing, we went to a bar down on Market Street and decided everything—that we would stick together and be buddies till we died. Dean was very quiet and preoccupied, looking at the old bums in the saloon that reminded him of his father. "I think he's in Denver—this time we must absolutely find him, he may be in County Jail, he may be around Larimer Street again, but he's to be found. Agreed?"

Yes, it was agreed; we were going to do everything we'd never done and had been too silly to do in the past. Then we promised ourselves two days of kicks in San Francisco before starting off, and of course the agreement was to go by travel bureau in share-the-gas cars and save as much money as possible. Dean claimed he no longer needed Marylou though he still loved her. We both agreed he would make out in New York.

Dean put on his pin-stripe suit with a sports shirt, we stashed our gear in a Greyhound bus locker for ten cents, and we took off to meet Roy Johnson who was going to be our chauffeur for two-day Frisco kicks. Roy agreed over the phone to do so. He arrived at the corner of Market and Third shortly thereafter and picked us up. Roy was now living in Frisco, working as a clerk and married to a pretty little blonde called Dorothy. Dean confided that her nose was too long—this was his big point of contention about her, for some strange reason—but her nose wasn't too long at all. Roy Johnson is a thin, dark, handsome kid with a pin-sharp face and combed hair that he keeps shoving back from the sides of his head. He had an extremely earnest approach and a big smile. Evidently his wife, Dorothy, had wrangled with him over the chauffeuring idea—and, determined to make a stand as the man of the house (they lived in a little room), he nevertheless stuck by his promise to us, but with consequences; his mental dilemma resolved itself in a bitter silence. He drove Dean and me all over Frisco at all hours of day and night and never said a word; all he did was go through red lights and make sharp turns on two wheels, and this was telling us the shifts to which we'd put him. He was midway between the challenge of his new wife and the challenge of his old Denver poolhall gang leader. Dean was pleased, and of course unperturbed by the driving. We paid absolutely no attention to Roy and sat in the back and yakked.

The next thing was to go to Mill City to see if we could find Remi Boncoeur. I noticed with some wonder that the old ship *Admiral Freebee* was no longer in the bay; and then of course Remi was no longer in the second-to-last compartment of the shack in the canyon. A beautiful colored girl opened the door instead; Dean and I talked to her a great deal. Roy Johnson waited in the car, reading Eugene Sue's *Mysteries of Paris*. I took one last look at Mill City and knew there was no sense trying to dig up the involved past; instead we decided to go see Galatea Dunkel about sleeping accommodations. Ed had left her again, was in Denver, and damned if she still didn't plot to get him back. We found her sitting cross-legged on the Oriental-type rug of her four-room tenement flat on upper Mission with a deck of fortune cards. Good girl. I saw sad signs that Ed Dunkel had lived here awhile and then left out of stupors and disinclinations only.

"He'll come back," said Galatea. "That guy can't take care of himself without me." She gave a furious look at Dean and Roy Johnson. "It was Tommy Snark who did it this time. All the time before he came Ed was perfectly happy and worked and we went out and had wonderful times. Dean, you know that. Then they'd sit in the bathroom for hours, Ed in the bathtub and Snarky on the seat, and talk and talk and talk—such silly things."

Dean laughed. For years he had been chief prophet of that gang and now they were learning his technique. Tommy Snark had grown a beard and his big sorrowful blue eyes had come looking for Ed Dunkel in Frisco; what happened (actually and no lie), Tommy had his small finger amputated in a Denver mishap and collected a good sum of money. For no reason under the sun they decided to give Galatea the slip and go to Portland, Maine, where apparently Snark had an aunt. So they were now either in Denver, going through, or already in Portland.

"When Tom's money runs out Ed'll be back," said Galatea, looking at her cards. "Damn fool—he doesn't know anything and never did. All he has to do is know that I love him."

Galatea looked like the daughter of the Greeks with the sunny camera as she sat there on the rug, her long hair streaming to the floor, plying the fortune-telling cards. I got to like her. We even decided to go out that night and hear jazz, and Dean would take a six-foot blonde who lived down the street, Marie.

That night Galatea, Dean, and I went to get Marie. This girl had a basement apartment, a little daughter, and an old car that barely ran and which Dean and I had to push down the street as the girls jammed at the starter. We went to Galatea's, and there everybody sat around—Marie, her daughter, Galatea, Roy Johnson, Dorothy his wife—all sullen in the overstuffed furniture as I stood in a corner, neutral in Frisco problems, and Dean stood in the middle of the room with his balloon-thumb in the air breast-high, giggling. "Gawd damn," he said, "we're all losing our fingers—hawr-hawr-hawr."

"Dean, why do you act so foolish?" said Galatea. "Camille called and said you left her. Don't you realize you have a daughter?"

"He didn't leave her, she kicked him out!" I said, breaking my neutrality.

They all gave me dirty looks; Dean grinned. "And with that thumb, what do your expect the poor guy to do?" I added. They all looked at me; particularly Dorothy Johnson lowered a mean gaze on me. It wasn't anything but a sewing circle, and the center of it was the culprit, Dean—responsible, perhaps, for everything that was wrong. I looked out the window at the buzzing night-street of Mission; I wanted to get going and hear the great jazz of Frisco—and remember, this was only my second night in town.

"I think Marylou was very, very wise leaving you, Dean," said Galatea. "For years now you haven't had any sense of responsibility for anyone. You've done so many awful things I don't know what to say to you."

And in fact that was the point, and they all sat around looking at Dean with lowered and hating eyes, and he stood on the carpet in the middle of them and giggled—he just giggled. He made a little dance. His bandage was getting dirtier all the time; it began to flop and unroll. I suddenly realized that Dean, by virtue of his enormous series of sins, was becoming the Idiot, the Imbecile, the Saint of the lot.

"You have absolutely no regard for anybody but yourself and your damned kicks. All you think about is what's hanging between your legs and how much money or fun you can get out of people and then you just throw them aside. Not only that but you're silly about it. It never occurs to you that life is serious and there are people trying to make something decent out of it instead of just goofing all the time."

That's what Dean was, the HOLY GOOF.

"Camille is crying her heart out tonight, but don't think for a minute she wants you back, she said she never wanted to see you again and she said it was to be final this time. Yet you stand here and make silly faces, and I don't think there's a care in your heart."

This was not true; I knew better and I could have told them all. I didn't see any sense in trying it. I longed to go and put my arm around Dean and say, Now look here, all of you, remember just one thing: this guy has his troubles too, and another thing, he never complains and he's given all of you a damned good time just being himself, and if that isn't enough for you then send him to the firing squad, that's apparently what you're itching to do anyway . . .

Nevertheless Galatea Dunkel was the only one in the gang who wasn't afraid of Dean and could sit there calmly, with her face hanging out, telling him off in front of everybody. There were earlier days in Denver when Dean had everybody sit in the dark with the girls and just talked, and talked, and talked, with a voice that was once hypnotic and strange and was said to make the girls come across by sheer force of persuasion and the content of what he said. This was when he was fifteen, sixteen. Now his disciples were married and the wives of his disciples had him on the carpet for the sexuality and the life he had helped bring into being. I listened further.

"Now you're going East with Sal," Galatea said, "and what do you think you're going to accomplish by that? Camille has to stay home and mind the baby now you're gone—how can she keep her job?—and she never wants to see you again and I don't blame her. If you see Ed along the road you tell him to come back to me or I'll kill him."

Just as flat as that. It was the saddest night. I felt as if I was with strange brothers and sisters in a pitiful dream. Then a complete silence fell over everybody; where once Dean would have talked his way out, he now fell silent himself, but standing in front of everybody, ragged and broken and idiotic, right under the lightbulbs, his bony mad face covered with sweat and throbbing veins, saying, "Yes, yes, yes," as though tremendous revelations were pouring into him all the time now, and I am convinced they were, and the others suspected as much and were frightened. He was BEAT—the root, the soul of Beatific. What was he knowing? He tried all in his power to tell me what he was knowing, and they envied that about me, my position at his side, defending him and drinking him in as they once tried to do. Then they looked at me. What was I, a stranger, doing on the West Coast this fair night? I recoiled from the thought.

"We're going to Italy," I said, I washed my hands of the whole matter. Then, too, there was a strange sense of maternal satisfaction in the air, for the girls were really looking at Dean the way a mother looks at the dearest and most errant child, and he with his sad thumb and all his revelations knew it well, and that was why he was able, in tick-tocking silence, to walk out of the apartment without a word, to wait for us downstairs as soon as we'd made up our minds about *time*. This was what we sensed about the ghost on the sidewalk. I looked out the window. He was alone in the doorway, digging the street. Bitterness, recriminations, advice, morality, sadness—everything was behind him, and ahead of him was the ragged and ecstatic joy of pure being.

"Come on, Galatea, Marie, let's go hit the jazz joints and forget it. Dean will be dead someday. Then what can you say to him?"

"The sooner he's dead the better," said Galatea, and she spoke officially for almost everyone in the room.

"Very well, then," I said, "but now he's alive and I'll bet you want to know what he does next and that's because he's got the secret that we're all busting to find and it's splitting his head wide open and if he goes mad don't worry, it won't be your fault but the fault of God."

They objected to this; they said I really didn't know Dean; they said he was the worst scoundrel that ever lived and I'd find out someday to my regret. I was amused to hear them protest so much. Roy Johnson rose to the defense of the ladies and said he knew Dean better than anybody, and all Dean was, was just a very interesting and even amusing con-man. I went out to find Dean and we had a brief talk about it.

"Ah, man, don't worry, everything is perfect and fine." He was rubbing his belly and licking his lips.

W. SOMERSET MAUGHAM

• *The Moon and Sixpence*

The Avenue de Clichy was crowded at that hour, and a lively fancy might see in the passers-by the personages of many a sordid romance. There were clerks and shop-girls; old fellows who might have stepped out of the pages of Honoré de Balzac; members, male and female, of the professions which make their profit of the frailties of mankind. There is in the streets of the poorer quarters of Paris a thronging vitality which excites the blood and prepares the soul for the unexpected.

"Do you know Paris well?" I asked.

"No. We came on our honeymoon. I haven't been since."

"How on earth did you find out your hotel?"

"It was recommended to me. I wanted something cheap.".

The absinthe came, and with due solemnity we dropped water over the melting sugar.

"I thought I'd better tell you at once why I had come to see you," I said, not without embarrassment.

His eyes twinkled.

"I thought somebody would come along sooner or later. I've had a lot of letters from Amy."

"Then you know pretty well what I've got to say."

"I've not read them."

SOURCE. From *The Moon and Sixpence* by W. Somerset Maugham. Copyright 1919 by W. Somerset Maugham, reprinted with the permission of Doubleday Books.

I lit a cigarette to give myself a moment's time. I did not quite know now how to set about my mission. The eloquent phrases I had arranged, pathetic or indignant, seemed out of place on the Avenue de Clichy. Suddenly he gave a chuckle.

"Beastly job for you this, isn't it?"

"Oh, I don't know," I answered.

"Well, look here, you get it over, and then we'll have a jolly evening."

I hesitated.

"Has it occurred to you that your wife is frightfully unhappy?"

"She'll get over it."

I cannot describe the extraordinary callousness with which he made this reply. It disconcerted me, but I did my best not to show it. I adopted the tone used by my Uncle Henry, a clergyman, when he was asking one of his relatives for a subscription to the Additional Curates Society.

"You don't mind my talking to you frankly?"

He shook his head, smiling.

"Has she deserved that you should treat her like this?"

"No."

"Have you any complaint to make against her?"

"None."

"Then, isn't it monstrous to leave her in this fashion, after seventeen years of married life, without a fault to find with her?"

"Monstrous."

I glanced at him with surprise. His cordial agreement with all I said cut the ground from under my feet. It made my position complicated, not to say ludicrous. I was prepared to be persuasive, touching, and hortatory, admonitory and expostulating, if need be vituperative even, indignant and sarcastic; but what the devil does a mentor do when the sinner makes no bones about confessing his sin? I had no experience, since my own practice has always been to deny everything.

"What, then?" asked Strickland.

I tried to curl my lip.

"Well, if you acknowledge that, there doesn't seem much more to be said."

"I don't think there is."

I felt that I was not carrying out my embassy with any great skill. I was distinctly nettled.

"Hang it all, one can't leave a woman without a bob."

"Why not?"

"How is she going to live?"

"I've supported her for seventeen years. Why shouldn't she support herself for a change?"

"She can't."

"Let her try."

Of course there were many things I might have answered to this. I might have spoken of the economic position of woman, of the contract, tacit and overt, which a man accepts by his marriage, and of much else; but I felt that there was only one point which really signified.

"Don't you care for her any more?"

"Not a bit," he replied.

The matter was immensely serious for all the parties concerned, but there was in the manner of his answers such a cheerful effrontery that I had to bite my lips in order not to laugh. I reminded myself that his behaviour was abominable. I worked myself up into a state of moral indignation.

"Damn it all, there are your children to think of. They've never done you any harm. They didn't ask to be brought into the world. If you chuck everything like this, they'll be thrown on the streets."

"They've had a good many years of comfort. It's much more than the majority of children have. Besides, somebody will look after them. When it comes to the point, the MacAndrews will pay for their schooling."

"But aren't you fond of them? They're such awfully nice kids. Do you mean to say you don't want to have anything more to do with them?"

"I liked them all right when they were kids, but now they're growing up I haven't got any particular feeling for them."

"It's just inhuman."

"I dare say."

"You don't seem in the least ashamed."

"I'm not."

I tried another tack.

"Everyone will think you a perfect swine."

"Let them."

"Won't it mean anything to you to know that people loathe and despise you?"

"No."

His brief answer was so scornful that it made my question, natural though it was, seem absurd. I reflected for a minute or two.

"I wonder if one can live quite comfortably when one's conscious of the disapproval of one's fellows? Are you sure it won't begin to worry you? Everyone has some sort of a conscience, and sooner or later it will find you out. Supposing your wife died, wouldn't you be tortured by remorse?"

He did not answer, and I waited for some time for him to speak. At last I had to break the silence myself.

"What have you to say to that?"

"Only that you're a damned fool."

"At all events, you can be forced to support your wife and children," I retorted, somewhat piqued. "I suppose the law has some protection to offer them."

"Can the law get blood out of a stone? I haven't any money. I've got about a hundred pounds."

I began to be more puzzled than before. It was true that his hotel pointed to the most straitened circumstances.

"What are you going to do when you've spent that?"

"Earn some."

He was perfectly cool, and his eyes kept that mocking smile which made all I said seem rather foolish. I paused for a little while to consider what I had better say next. But it was he who spoke first.

"Why doesn't Amy marry again? She's comparatively young, and she's not unattractive. I can recommend her as an excellent wife. If she wants to divorce me I don't mind giving her the necessary grounds."

Now it was my turn to smile. He was very cunning, but it was evidently this that he was aiming at. He had some reason to conceal the fact that he had run away with a woman, and he was using every precaution to hide her whereabouts. I answered with decision.

"Your wife says that nothing you can do will ever induce her to divorce you. She's quite made up her mind. You can put any possibility of that definitely out of your head."

He looked at me with an astonishment that was certainly not feigned. The smile abandoned his lips, and he spoke quite seriously.

"But, my dear fellow, I don't care. It doesn't matter a twopenny damn to me one way or the other."

I laughed.

"Oh, come now; you musn't think us such fools as all that. We happen to know that you came away with a woman."

He gave a little start, and then suddenly burst into a shout of laughter. He laughed so uproariously that people sitting near us looked round, and some of them began to laugh too.

"I don't see anything very amusing in that."

"Poor Amy," he grinned.

Then his face grew bitterly scornful.

"What poor minds women have got! Love. It's always love. They think a man leaves only because he wants others. Do you think I should be such a fool as to do what I've done for a woman?"

"Do you mean to say you didn't leave your wife for another woman?"

"Of course not."

"On your word of honour?"

I don't know why I asked for that. It was very ingenuous of me.

"On my word of honour."

"Then, what in God's name have you left her for?"

"I want to paint."

I looked at him for quite a long time. I did not understand. I thought he was mad. It must be remembered that I was very young, and I looked upon him as a middle-aged man. I forgot everything but my own amazement.

"But you're forty."

"That's what made me think it was high time to begin."

"Have you ever painted?"

"I rather wanted to be a painter when I was a boy, but my father made me go into business because he said there was no money in art. I began to paint a bit a year ago. For the last year I've been going to some classes at night."

"Was that where you went when Mrs. Strickland thought you were playing bridge at your club?"

"That's it."

"Why didn't you tell her?"

"I preferred to keep it to myself."

"Can you paint?"

"Not yet. But I shall. That's why I've come over here. I couldn't get what I wanted in London. Perhaps I can here."

"Do you think it's likely that a man will do any good when he starts at your age? Most men begin painting at eighteen."

"I can learn quicker than I could when I was eighteen."

"What makes you think you have any talent?"

He did not answer for a minute. His gaze rested on the passing throng, but I do not think he saw it. His answer was no answer.

"I've got to paint."

"Aren't you taking an awful chance?"

He looked at me. His eyes had something strange in them, so that I felt rather uncomfortable.

"How old are you? Twenty-three?"

It seemed to me that the question was beside the point. It was natural that I should take chances; but he was a man whose youth was past, a stockbroker with a position of respectability, a wife and two children. A course that would have been natural for me was absurd for him. I wished to be quite fair.

"Of course a miracle may happen, and you may be a great painter, but you must confess the chances are a million to one against it. It'll be an awful sell if at the end you have to acknowledge you've made a hash of it."

"I've got to paint," he repeated.

"Supposing you're never anything more than third-rate, do you think it will have been worth while to give up everything? After all, in any other walk in life it doesn't matter if you're not very good; you can get along quite comfortably if you're just adequate; but it's different with an artist."

"You blasted fool," he said.

"I don't see why, unless it's folly to say the obvious."

"I tell you I've got to paint. I can't help myself. When a man falls into the water it doesn't matter how he swims, well or badly: he's got to get out or else he'll drown."

There was real passion in his voice, and in spite of myself I was impressed. I seemed to feel in him some vehement power that was struggling within him; it gave me the sensation of something very strong, overmastering, that held him, as it were, against his will. I could not understand. He seemed really to be possessed of a devil, and I felt that it might suddenly turn and rend him. Yet he looked ordinary enough. My eyes, resting on him curiously, caused him no embarrassment. I wondered what a stranger would have taken him to be, sitting there in his old Norfolk jacket and his unbrushed bowler; his trousers were baggy, his hands were not clean; and his face, with the red stubble of the unshaved chin, the little eyes, and the large, aggressive nose, was uncouth and coarse. His mouth was large, his lips were heavy and sensual. No; I could not have placed him.

"You won't go back to your wife?" I said at last.

"Never."

"She's willing to forget everything that's happened and start afresh. She'll never make you a single reproach."

"She can go to hell."

"You don't care if people think you an utter blackguard? You don't care if she and your children have to beg their bread?"

"Not a damn."

I was silent for a moment in order to give greater force to my next remark. I spoke as deliberately as I could.

"You are a most unmitigated cad."

"Now that you've got that off your chest, let's go and have dinner."

13

I dare say it would have been more seemly to decline this proposal. I think perhaps I should have made a show of the indignation I really felt, and I am sure that Colonel MacAndrew at least would have thought well of me if I had been able to report my stout refusal to sit at the same table with a man of such character. But the fear of not being able to carry it through effectively has always made me shy of assuming the moral attitude; and in this case the certainty that my sentiments would be lost on Strickland made it peculiarly embarrassing to utter them. Only the poet or the saint can water an asphalt pavement in the confident anticipation that lilies will reward his labour.

I paid for what we had drunk, and we made our way to a cheap restaurant, crowded and gay, where we dined with pleasure. I had the appetite of youth and he of a hardened conscience. Then we went to a tavern to have coffee and liqueurs.

I had said all I had to say on the subject that had brought me to Paris, and though I felt it in a manner treacherous to Mrs. Strickland not to pursue it, I could not struggle against his indifference. It requires the feminine temperament to repeat the same thing three times with unabated zest. I solaced myself by thinking that it would be useful for me to find out what I could about Strickland's state of mind. It also interested me much more. But this was not an easy thing to do, for Strickland was not a fluent talker. He seemed to express himself with difficulty, as though words were not the medium with which his mind worked; and you had to guess the intentions of his soul by hackneyed phrases, slang, and vague, unfinished gestures. But though he said nothing of any consequence, there was something in his personality which prevented him from being dull. Perhaps it was sincerity. He did not seem to care much about the Paris he was now seeing for the first time (I did not count the visit with his wife), and he accepted sights which must have been strange to him without any sense of astonishment. I have been to Paris a hundred times, and it never fails to give me a thrill of excitement; I can never walk its streets without feeling myself on the verge of adventure. Strickland remained placid. Looking back, I think now that he was blind to everything but to some disturbing vision in his soul.

One rather absurd incident took place. There were a number of harlots in the tavern: some were sitting with men, others by themselves; and presently I noticed that one of these was looking at us. When she caught Strickland's eye she smiled. I do not think he saw her. In a little while she went out, but in a minute returned and, passing our table, very politely asked us to buy her something to drink. She sat down and I began to chat with her; but it was plain that her interest was in Strickland. I explained that he knew no more than two words of French. She tried to talk to him, partly by signs, partly in pidgin French, which, for some reason, she thought would be more comprehensible to him, and she had half a dozen phrases of English. She made me translate what she could only express in her own tongue, and eagerly asked for the meaning of his replies. He was quite good-tempered, a little amused, but his indifference was obvious.

"I think you've made a conquest," I laughed.

"I'm not flattered."

In his place I should have been more embarrassed and less calm. She had laughing eyes and a most charming mouth. She was young. I wondered what she found so attractive in Strickland. She made no secret of her desires, and I was bidden to translate.

"She wants you to go home with her."

"I'm not taking any," he replied.

I put his answer as pleasantly as I could. It seemed to me a little ungracious to decline an invitation of that sort, and I ascribed his refusal to lack of money.

"But I like him," she said. "Tell him it's for love."

When I translated this, Strickland shrugged his shoulders impatiently.

"Tell her to go to hell," he said.

His manner made his answer quite plain, and the girl threw back her head with a sudden gesture. Perhaps she reddened under her paint. She rose to her feet.

"*Monsieur n'est pas poli,*" she said.

She walked out of the inn. I was slightly vexed.

"There wasn't any need to insult her that I can see," I said. "After all, it was rather a compliment she was paying you."

"That sort of thing makes me sick," he said roughly.

I looked at him curiously. There was a real distaste in his face, and yet it was the face of a coarse and sensual man. I suppose the girl had been attracted by a certain brutality in it.

"I could have got all the women I wanted in London. I didn't come here for that."

14

During the journey back to England I thought much of Strickland. I tried to set in order what I had to tell his wife. It was unsatisfactory, and I could not imagine that she would be content with me; I was not content with myself. Strickland perplexed me. I could not understand his motives. When I had asked him what first gave him the idea of being a painter, he was unable or unwilling to tell me. I could make nothing of it. I tried to persuade myself that an obscure feeling of revolt had been gradually coming to a head in his slow mind, but to challenge this was the undoubted fact that he had never shown any impatience with the monotony of his life. If, seized by an intolerable boredom, he had determined to be a painter merely to break with irksome ties, it would have been comprehensible, and commonplace; but commonplace is precisely what I felt he was not. At last, because I was romantic, I devised an explanation which I acknowledged to be far-fetched, but which was the only one that in any way satisfied me. It was this: I asked myself whether there was not in his soul some deep-rooted instinct of creation, which the circumstances of his life had obscured, but which grew relentlessly, as a cancer may grow in the living tissues, till at last it took possession of his whole being and forced him irresistibly to action.

The cuckoo lays its egg in the strange bird's nest, and when the young one is hatched it shoulders its foster-brothers out and breaks at last the nest that has sheltered it.

But how strange it was that the creative instinct should seize upon this dull stockbroker, to his own ruin, perhaps, and to the misfortune of such as were dependent on him; and yet no stranger than the way in which the spirit of God has seized men, powerful and rich, pursuing them with stubborn vigilance till at last, conquered, they have abandoned the joy of the world and the love of women for the painful austerities of the cloister. Conversion may come under many shapes, and it may be brought about in many ways. With some men it needs a cataclysm, as a stone may be broken to fragments by the fury of a torrent; but with some it comes gradually, as a stone may be worn away by the ceaseless fall of a drop of water. Strickland had the directness of the fanatic and the ferocity of the apostle.

But to my practical mind it remained to be seen whether the passion which obsessed him would be justified of its works. When I asked him what his brother-students at the night classes he had attended in London thought of his painting, he answered with a grin:

"They thought it a joke."

"Have you begun to go to a studio here?"

"Yes. The blighter came round this morning—the master, you know; when he saw my drawing he just raised his eyebrows and walked on."

Strickland chuckled. He did not seem discouraged. He was independent of the opinion of his fellows.

And it was just that which had most disconcerted me in my dealings with him. When people say they do not care what others think of them, for the most part they deceive themselves. Generally they mean only that they will do as they choose, in the confidence that no one will know their vagaries; and at the utmost only that they are willing to act contrary to the opinion of the majority because they are supported by the approval of their neighbours. It is not difficult to be unconventional in the eyes of the world when your unconventionality is but the convention of your set. It affords you then an inordinate amount of self-esteem. You have the self-satisfaction of courage without the inconvenience of danger. But the desire for approbation is perhaps the most deeply seated instinct of civilised man. No one runs so hurriedly to the cover of respectability as the un-conventional woman who has exposed herself to the slings and arrows of out-raged propriety. I do not believe the people who tell me they do not care a row of pins for the opinion of their fellows. It is the bravado of ignorance. They mean only that they do not fear reproaches for peccadillos which they are convinced none will discover.

But here was a man who sincerely did not mind what people thought of him, and so convention had no hold on him; he was like a wrestler whose body is oiled; you could not get a grip on him; it gave him a freedom which was an outrage. I remember saying to him:

"Look here, if everyone acted like you, the world couldn't go on."

"That's a damned silly thing to say. Everyone doesn't want to act like me. The great majority are perfectly content to do the ordinary thing."

And once I sought to be satirical.

"You evidently don't believe in the maxim: Act so that every one of your actions is capable of being made into a universal rule."

"I never heard it before, but it's rotten nonsense."

"Well, it was Kant who said it."

"I don't care; it's rotten nonsense."

Nor with such a man could you expect the appeal to conscience to be effective. You might as well ask for a reflection without a mirror. I take it that conscience is the guardian in the individual of the rules which the community has evolved for its own preservation. It is the policeman in all our hearts, set there to watch that we do not break its laws. It is the spy seated in the central stronghold of the ego. Man's desire for the approval of his fellows is so strong, his dread of their censure so violent, that he himself has brought his enemy within his gates; and it keeps watch over him, vigilant always in the interests of its master to crush any half-formed desire to break away from the herd. It will force him to place the good of society before his own. It is the very strong link that attaches the individual to the whole. And man, subservient to interests he has persuaded himself are greater than his own, makes himself a slave to his taskmaster. He sits him in a seat of honour. At last, like a courtier fawning on the royal stick that is laid about his shoulders, he prides himself on the sensitiveness of his conscience. Then he has no words hard enough for the man who does not recognise its sway; for, a member of society now, he realises accurately enough that against him he is powerless. When I saw that Strickland was really indifferent to the blame his conduct must excite, I could only draw back in horror as from a monster of hardly human shape.

The last words he said to me when I bade him goodnight were:

"Tell Amy it's no good coming after me. Anyhow, I shall change my hotel, so she wouldn't be able to find me."

"My own impression is that she's well rid of you," I said.

"My dear fellow, I only hope you'll be able to make her see it. But women are very unintelligent."

D. H. LAWRENCE

• *The Fox*

"Dear Henry,

"I have been over it all again in my mind, this business of me and you,
and it seems to me impossible. When you aren't there I see what a fool I am.
When you are there you seem to blind me to things as they actually are. You
make me see things all unreal, and I don't know what. Then when I am alone
again with Jill I seem to come to my own senses and realise what a fool I am
making of myself, and how I am treating you unfairly. Because it must be unfair
to you for me to go on with this affair when I can't feel in my heart that I really
love you. I know people talk a lot of stuff and nonsense about love, and I don't
want to do that. I want to keep to plain facts and act in a sensible way. And
that seems to me what I'm not doing. I don't see on what grounds I am going
to marry you. I know I am not head over heels in love with you, as I have
fancied myself to be with fellows when I was a young fool of a girl. You are an
absolute stranger to me, and it seems to me you will always be one. So on what
grounds am I going to marry you? When I think of Jill, she is ten times more
real to me. I know her and I'm awfully fond of her, and I hate myself for a
beast if I ever hurt her little finger. We have a life together. And even if it can't
last for ever, it is a life while it does last. And it might last as long as either of
us lives. Who knows how long we've got to live? She is a delicate little thing,
perhaps nobody but me knows how delicate. And as for me, I feel I might fall

SOURCE. From *The Fox* by D. H. Lawrence. Copyright 1923 by Thomas B. Seltzer; renewed 1951 by Frieda Lawrence, reprinted with the permission of The Viking Press.

down the well any day. What I don't seem to see at all is you. When I think of what I've been and what I've done with you, I'm afraid I am a few screws loose. I should be sorry to think that softening of the brain is setting in so soon, but that is what it seems like. You are such an absolute stranger, and so different from what I'm used to, and we don't seem to have a thing in common. As for love, the very word seems impossible. I know what love means even in Jill's case, and I know that in this affair with you it's an absolute impossibility. And then going to Canada. I'm sure I must have been clean off my chump when I promised such a thing. It makes me feel fairly frightened of myself. I feel I might do something really silly that I wasn't responsible for—and end my days in a lunatic asylum. You may think that's all I'm fit for after the way I've gone on, but it isn't a very nice thought for me. Thank goodness Jill is here, and her being here makes me feel sane again, else I don't know what I might do; I might have an accident with the gun one evening. I love Jill, and she makes me feel safe and sane, with her loving anger against me for being such a fool. Well, what I want to say is, won't you let us cry the whole thing off? I can't marry you, and really, I won't do such a thing if it seems to me wrong. It is all a great mistake. I've made a complete fool of myself, and all I can do is to apologise to you and ask you please to forget it, and please to take no further notice of me. Your fox-skin is nearly ready, and seems all right. I will post it to you if you will let me know if this address is still right, and if you will accept my apology for the awful and lunatic way I have behaved with you, and then let the matter rest.

"Jill sends her kindest regards. Her mother and father are staying with us over Christmas.

"Yours very sincerely,

"ELLEN MARCH"

The boy read this letter in camp as he was cleaning his kit. He set his teeth, and for a moment went almost pale, yellow round the eyes with fury. He said nothing and saw nothing and felt nothing but a livid rage that was quite unreasoning. Balked! Balked again! Balked! He wanted the woman, he had fixed like doom upon having her. He felt that was his doom, his destiny, and his reward, to have this woman. She was his heaven and hell on earth, and he would have none elsewhere. Sightless with rage and thwarted madness he got through the morning. Save that in his mind he was lurking and scheming towards an issue, he would have committed some insane act. Deep in himself he felt like roaring and howling and gnashing his teeth and breaking things. But he was too intelligent. He knew society was on top of him, and he must scheme. So with his teeth bitten together, and his nose curiously slightly lifted, like some creature that is vicious, and his eyes fixed and staring, he went through the morning's affairs drunk with anger and suppression. In his mind was one thing—Banford.

He took no heed of all March's outpouring: none. One thorn rankled, stuck in his mind. Banford. In his mind, in his soul, in his whole being, one thorn rankling to insanity. And he would have to get it out. He would have to get the thorn of Banford out of his life, if he died for it.

With this one fixed idea in his mind, he went to ask for twenty-four hours' leave of absence. He knew it was not due to him. His consciousness was supernaturally keen. He knew where he must go—he must go to the captain. But how could he get at the captain? In that great camp of wooden huts and tents he had no idea where his captain was.

But he went to the officers' canteen. There was his captain standing talking with three other officers. Henry stood in the doorway at attention.

"May I speak to Captain Berryman?" The captain was Cornish like himself.

"What do you want?" called the captain.

"May I speak to you, Captain?"

"What do you want?" replied the captain, not stirring from among his group of fellow officers.

Henry watched his superior for a minute without speaking.

"You won't refuse me, sir, will you?" he asked gravely.

"It depends what it is."

"Can I have twenty-four hours' leave?"

"No, you've no business to ask."

"I know I haven't. But I must ask you."

"You've had your answer."

"Don't send me away, Captain."

There was something strange about the boy as he stood there so everlasting in the doorway. The Cornish captain felt the strangeness at once, and eyed him shrewdly.

"Why, what's afoot?" he said, curious.

"I'm in trouble about something. I must go to Blewbury," said the boy.

"Blewbury, eh? After the girls?"

"Yes, it is a woman, Captain." And the boy, as he stood there with his head reaching forward a little, went suddenly terribly pale, or yellow, and his lips seemed to give off pain. The captain saw and paled a little also. He turned aside.

"Go on, then," he said. "But for God's sake don't cause any trouble of any sort."

"I won't, Captain, thank you."

He was gone. The captain, upset, took a gin and bitters. Henry managed to hire a bicycle. It was twelve o'clock when he left the camp. He had sixty miles of wet and muddy crossroads to ride. But he was in the saddle and down the road without a thought of food.

At the farm, March was busy with a work she had had some time in hand. A bunch of Scotch fir trees stood at the end of the open shed, on a little bank where ran the fence between two of the gorse-shaggy meadows. The farthest of these trees was dead—it had died in the summer, and stood with all its needles brown and sere in the air. It was not a very big tree. And it was absolutely dead. So March determined to have it, although they were not allowed to cut any of the timber. But it would make such splendid firing, in these days of scarce fuel.

She had been giving a few stealthy chops at the trunk for a week or more, every now and then hacking away for five minutes, low down, near the ground, so no one should notice. She had not tried the saw, it was such hard work, alone. Now the tree stood with a great yawning gap in his base, perched, as it were, on one sinew, and ready to fall. But he did not fall.

It was late in the damp December afternoon, with cold mists creeping out of the woods and up the hollows, and darkness waiting to sink in from above. There was a bit of yellowness where the sun was fading away beyond the low woods of the distance. March took her axe and went to the tree. The small thud-thud of her blows resounded rather ineffectually about the wintry homestead. Banford came out wearing her thick coat, but with no hat on her head, so that her thin, bobbed hair blew on the uneasy wind that sounded in the pines and in the wood.

"What I'm afraid of," said Banford, "is that it will fall on the shed and we shall have another job repairing that."

"Oh, I don't think so," said March, straightening herself and wiping her arm over her hot brow. She was flushed red, her eyes were very wide open and queer, her upper lip lifted away from her two white, front teeth with a curious, almost rabbit look.

A little stout man in a black overcoat and a bowler hat came pottering across the yard. He had a pink face and a white beard and smallish, pale-blue eyes. He was not very old, but nervy, and he walked with little short steps.

"What do you think, father?" said Banford. "Don't you think it might hit the shed in falling?"

"Shed, no!" said the old man. "Can't hit the shed. Might as well say the fence."

"The fence doesn't matter," said March, in her high voice.

"Wrong as usual, am I!" said Banford, wiping her straying hair from her eyes.

The tree stood as it were on one spelch of itself, leaning, and creaking in the wind. It grew on the bank of a little dry ditch between the two meadows. On the top of the bank straggled one fence, running to the bushes up-hill. Several trees clustered there in the corner of the field near the shed and near the gate which led into the yard. Towards this gate, horizontal across the weary meadows, came the grassy, rutted approach from the high road. There trailed another rickety fence, long split poles joining the short, thick, wide-apart uprights. The three people stood at the back of the tree, in the corner of the shed meadow, just above the yard gate. The house, with its two gables and its porch, stood tidy in a little grassed garden across the yard. A little, stout, rosy-faced woman in a little red woollen shoulder shawl had come and taken her stand in the porch.

"Isn't it down yet?" she cried, in a high little voice.

"Just thinking about it," called her husband. His tone towards the two girls was always rather mocking and satirical. March did not want to go on with her hitting while he was there. As for him, he wouldn't lift a stick from the ground if he could help it, complaining, like his daughter, of rheumatics in his shoulder. So the three stood there a moment silent in the cold afternoon, in the bottom corner near the yard.

They hear the far-off taps of a gate, and craned to look. Away across, on the green horizontal approach, a figure was just swinging on to a bicycle again, and lurching up and down over the grass, approaching.

"Why, it's one of our boys—it's Jack," said the old man.

"Can't be," said Banford.

March craned her head to look. She alone recognised the khaki figure. She flushed, but said nothing.

"No, it isn't Jack, I don't think," said the old man, staring with little round blue eyes under his white lashes.

In another moment the bicycle lurched into sight, and the rider dropped off at the gate. It was Henry, his face wet and red and spotted with mud. He was altogether a muddy sight.

"Oh!" cried Banford, as if afraid. "Why, it's Henry!"

"What!" muttered the old man. He had a thick, rapid, muttering way of speaking, and was slightly deaf. "What? What? Who is it? Who is it, do you say? That young fellow? That young fellow of Nellie's? Oh! Oh!" And the satiric smile came on his pink face and white eyelashes.

Henry, pushing the wet hair off his steaming brow, had caught sight of them and heard what the old man said. His hot, young face seemed to flame in the cold light.

"Oh, are you all there!" he said, giving his sudden, puppy's little laugh. He was so hot and dazed with cycling he hardly knew where he was. He leaned the bicycle against the fence and climbed over into the corner on to the bank, without going into the yard.

"Well, I must say, we weren't expecting *you*," said Banford laconically.

"No, I suppose not," said he, looking at March.

She stood aside, slack, with one knee drooped and the axe resting its head loosely on the ground. Her eyes were wide and vacant, and her upper lip lifted from her teeth in that helpless, fascinated rabbit look. The moment she saw his glowing, red face it was all over with her. She was as helpless as if she had been bound. The moment she saw the way his head seemed to reach forward.

"Well, who is it? Who is it, anyway?" asked the smiling, satiric old man in his muttering voice.

"Why, Mr. Grenfel, whom you've heard us tell about, father," said Banford coldly.

"Heard you tell about, I should think so. Heard of nothing else practically," muttered the elderly man, with his queer little jeering smile on his face. "How do you do," he added, suddenly reaching out his hand to Henry.

The boy shook hands just as startled. Then the two men fell apart.

"Cycled over from Salisbury Plain, have you?" asked the old man.

"Yes."

"Hm! Longish ride. How long d'it take you, eh? Some time, eh? Several hours, I suppose."

"About four."

"Eh? Four! Yes, I should have thought so. When are you going back, then?"

"I've got till to-morrow evening."

"Till to-morrow evening, eh! Yes. Hm! Girls weren't expecting you, were they?"

And the old man turned his pale-blue, round little eyes under their white lashes mockingly towards the girls. Henry also looked around. He had become a little awkward. He looked at March, who was still staring away into the distance as if to see where the cattle were. Her hand was on the pommel of the axe, whose head rested loosely on the ground.

"What were you doing there?" he asked in his soft, courteous voice. "Cutting a tree down?"

March seemed not to hear, as if in a trance.

"Yes," said Banford. "We've been at it for over a week."

"Oh! And have you done it all by yourselves then?"

"Nellie's done it all, I've done nothing," said Banford.

"Really! You must have worked quite hard," he said, addressing himself in a curious gentle tone direct to March. She did not answer, but remained half averted staring away towards the woods above as if in a trance.

"*Nellie!*" cried Banford sharply. "Can't you answer?"

"What—me?" cried March, starting round and looking from one to the other. "Did anyone speak to me?"

"Dreaming!" muttered the old man, turning aside to smile. "Must be in love, eh, dreaming in the day-time!"

"Did you say anything to me?" said March, looking at the boy as from a strange distance, her eyes wide and doubtful, her face delicately flushed.

"I said you must have worked hard at the tree," he replied courteously.

"Oh, that! Bit by bit. I thought it would have come down by now."

"I'm thankful it hasn't come down in the night, to frighten us to death," said Banford.

"Let me just finish it for you, shall I?" said the boy.

March slanted the axe-shaft in his direction.

"Would you like to?" she said.

"Yes, if you wish it," he said.

"Oh, I'm thankful when the thing's down, that's all," she replied, non-chalant.

"Which way is it going to fall?" said Banford. "Will it hit the shed?"

"No, it won't hit the shed," he said. "I should think it will fall there—quite clear. Though it might give a twist and catch the fence."

"Catch the fence!" cried the old man. "What, catch the fence! When it's leaning at that angle? Why, it's farther off than the shed. It won't catch the fence."

"No," said Henry, "I don't suppose it will. It has plenty of room to fall quite clear, and I suppose it will fall clear."

"Won't tumble backwards on top of *us*, will it?" asked the old man, sarcastic.

"No, it won't do that," said Henry, taking off his short overcoat and his tunic. "Ducks! Ducks! Go back!"

A line of four brown-speckled ducks led by a brown-and-green drake were stemming away downhill from the upper meadow, coming like boats running on a ruffled sea, cockling their way top speed downwards towards the fence and towards the little group of people, and cackling as excitedly as if they brought news of the Spanish Armada.

"Silly things! Silly things!" cried Banford, going forward to turn them off. But they came eagerly towards her, opening their yellow-green beaks and quacking as if they were so excited to say something.

"There's no food. There's nothing here. You must wait a bit," said Banford to them. "Go away. Go away. Go round to the yard."

They didn't go, so she climbed the fence to swerve them round under the gate and into the yard. So off they waggled in an excited string once more, wagging their rumps like the stems of little gondolas, ducking under the bar of the gate. Banford stood on the top of the bank, just over the fence, looking down on the other three.

Henry looked up at her, and met her queer, round-pupilled, weak eyes staring behind her spectacles. He was perfectly still. He looked away, up at the weak, leaning tree. And as he looked into the sky, like a huntsman who is watching a flying bird, he thought to himself: "If the tree falls in just such a way, and spins just so much as it falls, then the branch there will strike her exactly as she stands on top of that bank."

He looked at her again. She was wiping the hair from her brow again, with that perpetual gesture. In his heart he had decided her death. A terrible still force seemed in him, and a power that was just his. If he turned even a hair's breath in the wrong direction, he would lose the power.

"Mind yourself, Miss Banford," he said. And his heart held perfectly still, in the terrible pure will that she should not move.

"Who, me, mind myself?" she cried, her father's jeering tone in her voice. "Why, do you think you might hit me with the axe?"

"No, it's just possible the tree might, though," he answered soberly. But the tone of his voice seemed to her to imply that he was only being falsely solicitous, and trying to make her move because it was his will to move her.

"Absolutely impossible," she said.

He heard her. But he held himself icy still, lest he should lose his power.

"No, it's just possible. You'd better come down this way."

"Oh, all right. Let us see some crack Canadian tree-felling," she retorted.

"Ready, then," he said, taking the axe, looking round to see he was clear.

There was a moment of pure, motionless suspense, when the world seemed to stand still. Then suddenly his form seemed to flash up enormously tall and fearful, he gave two swift, flashing blows, in immediate succession, the tree was severed, turning slowly, spinning strangely in the air and coming down like a sudden darkness on the earth. No one saw what was happening except himself. No one heard the strange little cry which the Banford gave as the dark end of the bough swooped down, down on her. No one saw her crouch a little and receive the blow on the back of the neck. No one saw her flung outwards and laid, a little twitching heap, at the foot of the fence. No one except the boy. And he watched with intense bright eyes, as he would watch a wild goose he had shot. Was it winged or dead? Dead!

Immediately he gave a loud cry. Immediately March gave a wild shriek that went far, far down the afternoon. And the father started a strange bellowing sound.

The boy leapt the fence and ran to the fringe. The back of the neck and head was a mass of blood, of horror. He turned it over. The body was quivering with little convulsions. But she was dead really. He knew it, that it was so. He knew it in his soul and his blood. The inner necessity of his life was fulfilling itself, it was he who was to live. The thorn was drawn out of his bowels. So he put her down gently. She was dead.

He stood up. March was standing there petrified and absolutely motionless. Her face was dead white, her eyes big black pools. The old man was scrambling horribly over the fence.

"I'm afraid it's killed her," said the boy.

The old man was making curious, blubbering noises as he huddled over the fence. "What!" cried March, starting electric.

"Yes, I'm afraid," repeated the boy.

March was coming forward. The boy was over the fence before she reached it.

"What do you say, killed her?" she asked in a sharp voice.

"I'm afraid so," he answered softly.

She went still whiter, fearful. The two stood facing one another. Her black eyes gazed on him with the last look of resistance. And then in a last agonised failure she began to grizzle, to cry in a shivery little fashion of a child that doesn't want to cry, but which is beaten from within, and gives that little first shudder of sobbing which is not yet weeping, dry and fearful.

He had won. She stood there absolutely helpless, shuddering her dry sobs and her mouth trembling rapidly. And then, as in a child, with a little crash came the tears and the blind agony of sightless weeping. She sank down on the grass, and sat there with her hands on her breast and her face lifted in sightless, convulsed weeping. He stood above her, looking down on her, mute, pale, and everlasting seeming. He never moved, but looked down on her. And among all the torture of the scene, the torture of his own heart and bowels, he was glad, he had won.

After a long time he stooped to her and took her hands.

"Don't cry," he said softly. "Don't cry."

She looked up at him with tears running from her eyes, a senseless look of helplessness and submission. So she gazed on him as if sightless, yet looking up to him. She would never leave him again. He had won her. And he knew it and was glad, because he wanted her for his life. His life must have her. And now he had won her. It was what his life must have.

But if he had won her, he had not yet got her. They were married at Christmas as he had planned, and he got again ten days' leave. They went to Cornwall, to his own village, on the sea. He realised that it was awful for her to be at the farm any more.

But though she belonged to him, though she lived in his shadow, as if she could not be away from him, she was not happy. She did not want to leave him: and yet she did not feel free with him. Everything round her seemed to watch her, seemed to press on her. He had won her, he had her with him, she was his wife. And she—she belonged to him, she knew it. But she was not glad and he was still foiled. He realised that though he was married to her and possessed her in every possible way, apparently, and though she *wanted* him to possess her, she wanted it, she wanted nothing else, now, still he did not quite succeed.

Something was missing. Instead of her soul swaying with new life, it seemed to droop, to bleed, as if it were wounded. She would sit for a long time with her hand in his, looking away at the sea. And in her dark, vacant eyes was a sort of wound, and her face looked a little peaked. If he spoke to her, she would turn to him with a faint new smile, the strange, quivering little smile of a woman who has died in the old way of love, and can't quite rise to the new way. She still felt she ought to *do* something to strain herself in some direction. And there was nothing to do, and no direction in which to strain herself. And she could not quite accept the submergence which his new love put upon her. If she was in love, she ought to *exert* herself, in some way, loving. She felt the weary need of our day to *exert* herself in love. But she knew that in fact she must no more exert herself in love. He would not have the love which exerted itself towards him. It made his brow go black. No, he wouldn't let her exert her love towards him. No, she had to be passive, to acquiesce, and to be submerged under the surface of love. She had to be like the seaweeds she saw as she peered down from the boat, swaying forever delicately under water, with all their delicate fibrils put tenderly out upon the flood, sensitive, utterly sensitive and receptive within the shadowy sea, and never, never rising and looking forth above water while they lived. Never. Never looking forth from the water until they died, only then washing, corpses, upon the surface. But while they lived, always submerged, always beneath the wave. Beneath the wave they might have powerful roots, stronger than iron; they might be tenacious and dangerous in their soft waving within the flood. Beneath the water they might be stronger, more indestructible than resistant oak trees are on land. But it was always underwater, always under-water. And she, being a woman, must be like that.

And she had been so used to the very opposite. She had had to take all the thought for love and for life, and all the responsibility. Day after day she had been responsible for the coming day, for the coming year: for her dear Jill's health and happiness and well-being. Verily, in her own small way, she had felt herself responsible for the well-being of the world. And this had been her great stimulant, this grand feeling that, in her own small sphere, she was responsible for the well-being of the world.

And she had failed. She knew that, even in her small way, she had failed. She had failed to satisfy her own feeling of responsibility. It was so difficult. It seemed so grand and easy at first. And the more you tried, the more difficult it became. It had seemed so easy to make one beloved creature happy. And the more you tried, the worse the failure. It was terrible. She had been all her life reaching, reaching, and what she reached for seemed so near, until she had stretched to her utmost limit. And then it was always beyond her.

Always beyond her, vaguely, unrealisably beyond her, and she was left with nothingness at last. The life she reached for, the happiness she reached for, the well-being she reached for all slipped back, became unreal, the farther she stretched her hand. She wanted some goal, some finality—and there was none. Always this ghastly reaching, reaching, striving for something that might be just beyond. Even to make Jill happy. She was glad Jill was dead for she had realised that she could never make her happy. Jill would always be fretting herself thinner and thinner, weaker and weaker. Her pains grew worse instead of less. It would be so forever. She was glad she was dead.

And if Jill had married a man it would have been just the same. The woman striving, striving to make the man happy, striving within her own limits for the well-being of her world. And always achieving failure. Little, foolish successes in money or in ambition. But at the very point where she most wanted success, in the anguished effort to make some one beloved human being happy and perfect, there the failure was almost catastrophic. You wanted to make your beloved happy, and his happiness seemed always achievable. If only you did just this, that and the other. And you did this, that, and the other, in all good faith, and every time the failure became a little more ghastly. You could love yourself to ribbons and strive and strain yourself to the bone, and things would go from bad to worse, bad to worse, as far as happiness went. The awful mistake of happiness.

Poor March, in her good-will and her responsibility, she had strained herself till it seemed to her that the whole of life and everything was only a horrible abyss of nothingness. The more you reach after the fatal flower of happiness, which trembles so blue and lovely in a crevice just beyond your grasp, the more fearfully you become aware of the ghastly and awful gulf of the precipice below you, into which you will inevitably plunge, as into the bottomless pit, if you reach any further. You pluck flower after flower—it is never *the* flower. The flower itself—its calyx is a horrible gulf, it is the bottomless pit.

That is the whole history of the search for happiness, whether it be your own or somebody else's that you want to win. It ends, and it always ends, in the ghastly sense of the bottomless nothingness into which you will inevitably fall if you strain any farther.

And women?—what goal can any woman conceive, except happiness? Just happiness for herself and the whole world. That, and nothing else. And so, she assumes the responsibility and sets off towards her goal. She can see it there, at the foot of the rainbow. Or she can see it a little way beyond, in the blue distance. Not far, not far.

But the end of the rainbow is a bottomless gulf down which you can fall forever without arriving, and the blue distance is a void pit which can swallow you and all your efforts into its emptiness, and still be no emptier. You and all your efforts. So, the illusion of attainable happiness!

Poor March, she had set off so wonderfully towards the blue goal. And the farther and farther she had gone, the more fearful had become the realisation of emptiness. An agony, an insanity at last.

She was glad it was over. She was glad to sit on the shore and look westwards over the sea, and know the great strain had ended. She would never strain for love and happiness any more. And Jill was safely dead. Poor Jill, poor Jill. It must be sweet to be dead.

For her own part, death was not her destiny. She would have to leave her destiny to the boy. But then, the boy. He wanted more than that. He wanted her to give herself without defences, to sink and become submerged in him. And she—she wanted to sit still, like a woman on the last milestone, and watch. She wanted to see, to know, to understand. She wanted to be alone: with him at her side.

And he! He did not want her to watch any more, to see any more, to understand any more. He wanted to veil her woman's spirit, as Orientals veil the woman's face. He wanted her to commit herself to him, and to put her independent spirit to sleep. He wanted to take away from her all her effort, all that seemed her very *raison d'être*. He wanted to make her submit, yield, blindly pass away out of all her strenuous consciousness. He wanted to take away her consciousness, and make her just his woman. Just his woman.

And she was so tired, so tired, like a child that wants to go to sleep, but which fights against sleep as if sleep were death. She seemed to stretch her eyes wider in the obstinate effort and tension of keeping awake. She *would* keep awake. She *would* know. She *would* consider and judge and decide. She *would* have the reins of her own life between her own hands. She *would* be an independent woman to the last. But she was so tired, so tired of everything. And sleep seemed near. And there was such rest in the boy.

Yet there, sitting in a niche of the high, wild cliffs of West Cornwall, looking over the westward sea, she stretched her eyes wider and wider. Away to the West, Canada, America. She *would* know and she *would* see what was ahead. And the boy, sitting beside her, staring down at the gulls, had a cloud between his brows and the strain of discontent in his eyes. He wanted her asleep, at peace in him. He wanted her at peace, asleep in him. And *there* she was, dying with the strain of her own wakefulness. Yet she would not sleep: no, never. Sometimes he thought bitterly that he ought to have left her. He ought never to have killed Banford. He should have left Banford and March to kill one another.

But that was only impatience: and he knew it. He was waiting, waiting to go West. He was aching almost in torment to leave England, to go West, to take March away. To leave this shore! He believed that as they crossed the seas, as they left this England which he so hated, because in some way it seemed to have stung him with poison, she would go to sleep. She would close her eyes at last and give in to him.

And then he would have her, and he would have his own life at last. He chafed, feeling he hadn't got his own life. He would never have it till she yielded and slept in him. Then he would have all his own life as a young man and a male, and she would have all her own life as a woman and a female. There would be no more of this awful straining. She would not be a man any more, an independent woman with a man's responsibility. Nay, even the responsibility for her own soul she would have to commit to him. He knew it was so, and obstinately held out against her, waiting for the surrender.

"You'll feel better when once we get over the seas to Canada over there," he said to her as they sat among the rocks on the cliff.

She looked away to the sea's horizon, as if it were not real. Then she looked round at him, with the strained, strange look of a child that is struggling against sleep.

"Shall I?" she said.

"Yes," he answered quietly.

And her eyelids dropped with the slow motion, sleep weighing them unconscious. But she pulled them open again to say:

"Yes, I may. I can't tell. I can't tell what it will be like over there."

"If only we could go soon!" he said, with pain in his voice.

Acknowledgment, Ch. 3, Identity and Anxiety, pp. 101-116

SOURCE: From *The Thibaults* by Roger Martin du Gard, translated by Stuart Gilbert, Copyright, 1939 by the Viking Press, Inc., and renewed, 1967. Copyright, 1922, 1923, 1928, 1929, by the Librarie Gallimard, France. Reprinted by permission of the Viking Press and Bantam Books, Inc.

Acknowledgment, Ch. 6, Reference Group, pp. 244-252

SOURCE: From *Summer 1914* by Roger Martin du Gard, translated by Stuart Gilbert, Copyright, 1939 by the Viking Press, Inc., and renewed, 1967. Copyright, 1922, 1923, 1928, 1929, by the Librarie Gallimard, France. Reprinted by permission of the Viking Press, Inc.